DAVID NORTH

GUARDIAN OF ASTER FALL

Book Two

ASTER
FALL

High Peak Publishing.

Cover illustration by MiblArt.

Interior logo design by E.L. Geron.

CONTENTS

AUTHOR'S NOTE

If you would like a summary of the events in earlier books or to reach out to me, you can follow the link below to the Guardian of Aster Fall Discord server.

https://discord.gg/HH2KZPxH5a

There is a "recap" channel for each book there.

There is also a general channel for discussion of the latest events, frequently asked questions, and some art for the books. We even have Aster Fall emojis.

Remember to be careful of spoilers and to only look at the channel for a book if you want a summary of what happened. The channels are labeled to help.

For Patreons who are following the early release chapters of the next book, there are additional discussion channels, more art, and other features.

You can find the Patreon link here:

https://www.patreon.com/riverfate

Enjoy!

~David North

CHAPTER ONE

LEAVING THE VILLAGE

It probably wasn't a good idea to incinerate the villagers, but it was tempting.

Currently, a pack of idiots was blocking their path out of Cliff's End. They were led by Nelgen, the village's main landlord who was more than a little shady.

This conflict had been building up over the last three days, ever since the crook had come to bother them and his father had tossed him out onto the street.

"Move aside," Jeric's voice rang out in the air as he frowned at Nelgen, who was standing in front of them. His voice was a low growl filled with warning. "You don't have the right to block our way, nor do you have the ability. You should have recognized this already."

Sam was fairly sure his father's thoughts were leaning in the same direction as his, except that Jeric didn't want to cause trouble while his wife and daughter were right next to him. Only that and some old familiarity with these people was keeping him from moving them out of the way.

They'd been home for three days. Most of that time had been taken up by packing. They had enough dimensional bags that they'd been able to take everything important. They'd never had that much.

Now, they were leaving, or at least they were trying to.

Since returning, he'd learned quite a bit about the village that he'd never known, including how deeply Cliff's End was connected to bandits in the area. Finding that out hadn't made him happy. People only moved here when they were desperate, like his parents had been.

Cliff's End was one of the few independent villages in the kingdom. Something about the location meant monsters didn't come here very often, which allowed it to exist where other villages couldn't. It was distant enough from the major trade routes that the cities weren't interested in it, but it had become a popular resupply point for bandits.

It wasn't entirely bad. The village council did a good job of maintaining peace in the village, under the theory that a neat house was better for business than a messy one.

Nelgen was one of the main contacts between the council and the bandits. He sold illicit goods through the village to make them look more legitimate and provided the bandits with supplies. The rest of his money came from owning a significant chunk of the village and charging rent.

He was a weakling, but he was good with money, which gave him some leverage.

Now, Nelgen had set his sights on Sam's mother, which was the main reason Sam wanted to send him to an early grave. The possessive gleam in his eye made everything clear, especially to someone with a Wisdom as high as Sam's.

It didn't help that Jeric and Sam were hiding their identities. As far as Nelgen knew, they were an adventuring party who'd come to pick up Aemilia. Jeric was pretending to be his own cousin and Sam was a reclusive Wizard who was part of the group.

"Aemilia, please...a Seer is so important to the village." Nelgen looked stubborn as he tried to fold his arms across his flabby stomach. His lanky hair and goatee were combed flat, making him look like a drowned rat that had tried to give itself a bath. "Won't you stay? How can you be sure these adventurers can guarantee your safety? Isn't it better to stay here and let the village protect you?"

For all of his fake concern, the men blocking the road made it clear that he'd come to stop them by force if they didn't agree to stay. Specifically, if Sam's mother didn't agree to stay.

Jeric was at the front of the group, leading a horse that Aemilia was riding. Sam was doing the same for his sister. Next to him, Krana was riding on her pony. Lesat was on his horse at the back, still dressed in his usual full plate, except that his helmet was hanging from his saddle.

They hadn't brought extra horses with them when they arrived in the village, but these were more than strong enough to carry double.

He could feel pulses of mana fading away from his amulet as it made the villagers' gazes slide away from him. When he'd made the new chain to hang it from, he'd enchanted that with a pattern to blur the sight of anyone looking. It helped to keep some of the mana expenditure down if people kept trying to see him.

It made him look like a blurred, cloaked figure with indistinct edges.

"Aemilia," Nelgen continued, directing his quavering voice to Sam's mother, "can't you see that these adventurers are no good? They have no respect for laws or authority! They'll probably abandon you to bandits as soon as you leave. You don't know how many are out there. Stay here where I can keep you safe."

Sam listened to the man's nonsense with one ear as Crystal Focus spread out more widely around him, but nothing else was moving so far.

Perhaps he should have expected something to happen. Life in the village had always been full of problems.

Sam glanced toward his mother and hid a smile. From the way her eyes were narrowing, it looked like she might beat Jeric to the punch. Literally.

Objectively, it was easy to see why Nelgen was interested in her. His mother was a statuesque beauty with classic features, high cheekbones, and blond hair that ran down her back like a waterfall. Her eyes were the blue of a summer sky, and just as likely to be filled with sunlight as a storm.

Even if he'd been honest about his interest and everything else had fallen into place...the rat in front of them was in no way suitable for her. He had money, but in every other way, Nelgen was reaching above his station.

Not that Sam was biased, of course.

Since they'd arrived home, they'd been left mostly alone by the other villagers, except for a few friends of his mother's, who had come by to say their farewells and share their regrets that Jeric and Sam had never been found. That had been strange to listen to when he was standing right there.

They needed to find a better place to live, somewhere secure where they could grow in peace, developing their skills and new classes. Somewhere that had access to the wild areas to hunt monsters and was close enough to a large city that they could take advantage of the resources there.

They needed to establish a real home.

That was why they were leaving the village. It wasn't a suitable place for them any longer. It lacked the resources that a larger city would have and the people here knew too much about Sam and Jeric's old difficulties in unlocking their class.

News was slow to reach the village, but a way to change a primary class or the appearance of a demon would still draw attention.

They weren't sure where they were going to settle down, but they could discuss it while moving toward one of the larger cities. They needed one with a school for Altey, so that she could be prepared for her Class Day. She was at the right age now to start that. They also needed some shops where Sam could acquire materials for enchanting and where his father could sell what he made.

Perhaps they would go to Ebonfar, a medium-sized town that they'd passed on the way here from Osera, or to Highfold, which was near the mountains to the east. That one was a bit farther away, but it offered better access to wild areas for hunting monsters.

Sam pulled his attention back to the conversation in front of him. Growing up here, Sam had seen a lot of village nonsense, but he'd still expected better of Nelgen. Apparently, he'd been wrong.

"But Aemilia, think of the village and all the good you could do here." Nelgen wrung his hands together as he looked between Jeric and Aemilia. "The village will be so desolate without you. A Seer is such an important class here!"

This time, a weak red aura was beginning to radiate out from Nelgen as he spoke. The energy in the ability was familiar, marking it out as some form of Persuade. Sam shook his head as he saw it, as well as the rising red-gold aura around his father that reached out to block it. His father's face was hard.

Nelgen was still pretending to be polite, but in reality, he just wanted a Seer to assist with his illegal business, as well as Aemilia herself. His ability wasn't very powerful compared to Jeric's, probably still in the Basic tier, so the attempt ended there, but it did mark out Nelgen's personality.

The thugs behind Nelgen were moving closer. There were five of them, none with a very good reputation. Surtek, the Smith, was one of the strongest and rudest individuals in the entire village.

The others were part of the semi-official village guard force, a sort of militia that helped to protect the wall in normal times, but the worst of the bunch. They were the ones you'd find drunk or harassing someone in the tavern rather than doing their real job.

Over the months of travel back to the village, Krana had helped him to acquire the Analyze skill, which came in handy now. It was still at Basic, but it was extremely useful. His attention swept across all of the guards. He already knew their names, so the prompts came up with those as well.

Nelgen. Human. Level 34 Merchant/Messenger.
Surtek. Human. Level 32 Smith/Warrior.
Tuni. Human. Level 21 Guard/Carpenter.
Hatlis. Human. Level 24 Warrior/Mason.
Yuro. Human. Level 25 Hunter/Farmer.
Berek. Human. Level 20 Guard/Smith.

It was nothing very impressive. Sam had been at Level 42 when they left the tunnels and he'd jumped up to 45 on the way home. The points from those had gone into Intelligence and Aura, bringing him up to 88 in each, and to Wisdom, bringing it to 46.

For two and a half months, it wasn't a lot of experience, but there had only been a few monsters on the way. His father had reached Level 38, and Krana and Lesat were Level 37. Altogether, it placed their group well above whatever Nelgen thought he could accomplish here.

His mother's experience was growing as well, now that she was using her Seer abilities every day. She'd reached General Level 18, but her Historian class was still stuck at Level 1 until she wrote down what she saw. They'd brought some blank books from Ebonfar, but she hadn't had a chance to write in them yet.

The magical abilities that came with Seer meant his mother could deal with some of these thugs on her own, if needed. The person Sam had to worry about the most was Altey. She was only ten, almost eleven now, and she didn't have any magic or Stamina to protect herself. He would need to create a protection amulet of some type for her.

As soon as the thought occurred to him, he began to design what it would look like. A three-dimensional image of an amulet began to spin in his mind's eye as runes surrounded it. He let the idea float to one side as he focused his attention back on Nelgen.

Once they were settled down, the whole family could focus on growing stronger together and on paving a better way for Altey in the future. He had a job to do when it came to sealing Flaws and fixing the Seal, but he needed to grow as much as possible first.

"Nelgen, this is not your business," Aemilia spoke up from next to Jeric, her voice firm. "You do not even know what you are talking about. I have no reason to stay in the village. Now, move aside before you cause any more trouble."

The reins pulled in Sam's hand as the gelding tossed his head and stamped. He saw Altey reach out to pat the horse on his neck, which made him smile before his attention was drawn back to the front.

"Move, Nelgen," Aemilia ordered, her voice hardening. "You may think that you have the authority in the village, but you do not. The village has a council and you are only one member. You should remember that. But even if the entire council were standing here, we would still be leaving. This is no longer a place for Altey and me to live."

"I'm sorry, but I can't let you go." Nelgen's jaw wobbled as he tried to harden his approach. "You're too important to risk. You've already been able to send messages for us that would take days normally, without the risk of traveling! You could do so much good here."

"By good, you mean the messages you want me to send to your trading partners." Aemilia frowned at Nelgen. Her temper was legendary and it was starting to come out now. "I've told you before that I won't help you with that. I know how you got the money you have and I'll have nothing to do with it. Are you really trying to trick a Seer?"

"My connections protect this village! How do you think we can live here without cooperating!" Nelgen's thready voice was rising as well now. "Giving them a few messages and supplies is the least I can do! I thought you would know what was best for you. When you settled here twenty years ago, I was the one who gave you a place to stay! I didn't even charge you rent the first month!"

"You only owned the house, Nelgen!" Aemilia was getting angrier. "The rent was paid then and it's more than paid now. Now get out of the way!"

Nelgen started to say something else, his arms rising into the air as he began to gesticulate, but Jeric cut him off.

"Enough!" Jeric ordered, his voice booming as his own anger at Nelgen began to overflow. "Last chance to move aside and make this polite, or I'll be moving all of you together. We have places to be and the daylight is burning. Your connections are your business as long as they don't come to trouble us."

Nelgen's mouth hung open like a fish gasping for air as he tried to find new words. He wasn't used to being defied in the village.

"Are you threatening me?" Nelgen's pitch rose higher, like a goose being strangled, as he began to fumble in his pockets. A moment later, he pulled out a short metal rod with a translucent crystal affixed to one end. He held up the wand, pointing it at Jeric. His posture changed, becoming more confident now. "I knew you were a criminal!"

His attention turned to Aemilia. "You have to stay here for your safety! I won't allow you to risk yourself!"

Nelgen turned toward the thugs with him as he ordered, "Stop them! Throw the adventurers out of the village and take Aemilia back to her house."

The thugs started to walk forward, their muscles flexing, at the same time as shielding abilities flared to light around Jeric, Aemilia, and the others. It seemed they wouldn't be leaving here without some trouble after all.

Sam shook his head as crystal flame began to condense in the air. To onlookers, it looked like the silent wizard in the group had suddenly erupted into flame. A growing spiral of cerulean blue flames was rising up all around him.

He'd seen enough bandits on the way home to create a special category in his mind for people who would rather prey on others than fight monsters for resources. If someone wanted to act like a monster, he didn't mind treating them like one.

Behavior was what defined the difference between what was human and not. These thugs were overconfident and willing to do whatever Nelgen told them to, whether it hurt someone or not, which put them on the same level as monsters.

They were making the wrong choice in bothering his family.

The thugs came closer, with Surtek leading the way. The Smith was renowned for his drunken behavior, but even Sam was surprised when he pulled a club from his belt. Behind him, the others did the same, pulling out short truncheons and blackjacks.

With a wave of Sam's hand, the crystalline geometry of an Essence Shield formed in a half sphere in front of their group. A moment later, a wave of crystal flame flowed forward and sealed the area around the thugs and Nelgen, locking down everything around them in a Crystal Field. Nelgen and the thugs froze in place, their movements halted.

The only thing stopping him from going further was that Surtek's son, Kilien, had once been a friend of his. A half dozen points of his essence flowed away into the spell as he felt them struggling against him, but it wasn't difficult to hold it. None of them had significant abilities to fight against the Crystal Field.

Sam's palm straightened and he swept his hand to the side, sending the entire pack tumbling away as he cleared the road. It was a bit of a strain to move that much weight at once and ten points of essence drained away, but the effect was satisfying. The thugs went flying, rolling across the ground until they slammed to a halt against the wall of a nearby house.

As for Nelgen, Sam sent him rolling a bit farther, making sure that he landed a good forty feet away. By the time he got there, he was covered in a thick mixture of dirt, mud, and horse manure.

The Crystal Field around them disappeared, letting the thugs shake themselves out as they tried to stand back up. They'd landed fairly hard, so they were a bit slow. Nelgen was even worse, shaking in anger as he tried to straighten his clothes. When he managed to stand back up, his face was a mask of frustrated rage.

He'd lost his wand in the impromptu flight. Now, it was lying on the ground to one side of the road. Sam picked it up with a flicker of crystal flame, bringing it to his hand as he analyzed it.

Wand of Ice Bolt (Basic)
[Ice Bolt: Fires a directed bolt of ice at a specific target. Damage is related to the amount of mana infused.]

It wasn't anything special, but it could be a good toy for Altey, to help her protect herself in the wild. Sam wiped away the traces of Nelgen's energy from it with a flicker of crystal flame. Then he tucked it into one of his belt pouches. He'd alter it for her later.

"Let's go," Sam suggested. He continued to maintain the Essence Shield around them, turning it into a full sphere in case anything else happened. His parents looked back at him and then toward Nelgen.

"He deserves that and more," Aemilia said with a sigh, "but it's good that you didn't hurt him. Let's go. Hopefully that's the end of it."

His father gave him a short nod of approval. Then he turned back to the front as he led Aemilia's horse toward the village gate. Sam tugged on the gelding's reins as well, pulling Altey along. Behind him, the rest of the party moved as well.

Lesat brought up the rear, turning his head to glare at the villagers who looked in their direction. The guard had promised to follow Sam and he wasn't pleased with the way this was going.

He was a solid fellow, unruffled by most things and loyal to whomever he chose. At the moment, that was Sam.

Some of his story had come out over the journey to Cliff's End, including that he'd grown up homeless in Osera as the illegitimate child of a town guard, but he hadn't shared too much yet.

Krana's eyes shaded to silver as she rode next to Sam, looking around. Slowly, she shook her head. It was becoming difficult to see small events around Sam with her Foresight, since they were just ripples in the ocean that surrounded him, but she had a feeling that this wouldn't end so simply.

As if reinforcing that, Nelgen's thready voice shouted out from behind them as they left the village.

"I'll show you who has the power in this village!"

Sam ignored him as they passed out of the gate, which opened onto the cliffs around the village. Once they were in the open, the full beauty of Aster Fall's wilderness reached out to greet them. It was an unending ripple of rolling hills and plains that stretched into the distance, a purple and golden landscape streaked with a thousand colors of flowering vines and the rippling light of a mid-morning sun.

In front of them, the road cut down in tight switchbacks, slicing through the hard stone that made up the base of the mountain under Cliff's End. Sam swung up into the saddle behind Altey, laughing as he brushed her hair out of his face. He was already putting Nelgen's threats behind him.

His father did the same with Aemilia, wrapping his arms around his wife. His smile widened as he looked into the distance.

The ringing beat of horse hooves sounded on the stones as they left the village, heading down the mountain. They weren't sure where they were going yet, but they were heading for a better future. Sam's eyes softened as he looked down to his sister in front of him and he made himself a promise.

He was going to build a home for his family where they would all be safe.

CHAPTER TWO

BENEATH THE TRIPLE MOONS

The world of Aster Fall stretched out in front of the Hasterns and their allies as they rode across the plains that surrounded Cliff's End. The village was to the far southwest in the Kingdom of Aethra, bordering an area known as the Broken Lands.

That was a range of shattered mountains that had somehow been crushed down into the earth. The land there was a chaos of ravines, sharp peaks, and twisted cliffs that suddenly ended. Travel through the area was nearly impossible by foot, at least for humans. If you wanted to cross the area, you needed to fly.

The Broken Lands stretched in a long line for nearly three thousand miles to the north and south, creating the western border of the kingdom. Cliff's End was nestled near the middle of that range, about a hundred miles to the east and a little to the south.

Twelve hundred miles farther south, there was the Inner Sea, an enormous body of salt water that took up the southern portion of the kingdom. That area was filled with seafolk, sirens, and shipping.

To the east of the village, where they were riding, there were the Storm Plains, a broad area of rolling hills and scattered elemental forests that densely covered a large portion of the western provinces of Aethra. Cities dotted the area here and there, but none was closer than a few hundred miles.

The location of Cliff's End was remote and not favored by merchants, but there was one main road that led across the western Storm Plains toward Ebonfar, the first city on the way. If they proceeded in that direction, it would take them about two weeks to reach it.

There was a branch in the road halfway there that led toward Highfold instead, which was in a high mountain range a little over a thousand miles to the east. That road would take them nearly a month. Even those cities were considered to be the western edge of the kingdom. The world was vast and Aethra was only one of the middle-sized kingdoms in it.

Starting from the Broken Lands and the Inner Sea, the kingdom stretched thousands of miles to the east and north. All around, it was bordered by kingdoms and empires that were even larger.

According to what Sam had heard, the world of Aster Fall was theoretically about a hundred and fifty thousand miles in diameter, but there were strange effects when you tried to cross over it. Travelers routinely went missing in dimensional gaps that could spring up closer to the edges of the world.

For that reason, most of the stable kingdoms were located on a vast continent near the center of the world. Aethra was to the southwest of that cluster.

They'd been riding out from Cliff's End for several hours now and the sun was moving toward noon, radiating down through the sky. He could feel the complex energy from it sinking into the earth all around him. It was fire, life, space, and more distant things.

The sky was an intense blue, like an ocean that became deeper toward the horizon. All across it, light pink and silver clouds were drifting, marking out the flow of Aster Fall's mana through the air.

"What's that?" Altey was riding in front of him, happily asking questions about everything that she saw. At the moment, she was pointing to a grove of trees to their right, which they were about to pass.

"Lightning oaks," Sam replied with a smile. "You see the little elemental sparks running along their leaves? The white and blue ones? They're difficult to cut, but I hear they make good timber."

"Can we build a house out of them?" Altey was bouncing in the saddle between his arms and he had to adjust his grip on the reins. Her excitement at leaving the village was overflowing.

"Maybe," he replied as he reached out and mussed up her hair, which got him a discontented pout. That made him laugh again. "But we have to reach our destination first. If there aren't lightning oaks there, I'm sure there will be something else interesting. We'll have to hire a good builder."

Just in front of him, his parents were riding. Krana was to his side and Lesat was behind them, as usual. As Sam spoke, Jeric turned his head to look back at his son and daughter, his eyes shining. He had never been happier to be back with his family, especially when life was looking up.

"We'll stop tonight and discuss it, sunshine," he grinned. "We have some ideas, but we need to decide together. Now that we're out of the village and no one's listening in, we can figure it out."

Krana turned her head to look at the exchange between the family and Sam caught her quick grin before she hid it again. She liked Sam's family. They were honest and forthright, and they knew where their priorities were. When she'd told them about her vision, they'd only been afraid for Sam, not for themselves. Now, they just needed to work together to figure out how to get strong enough to make a difference.

She'd been helping Aemilia with her Seer subclass, teaching her how to use her abilities, and she'd also been teaching Sam what she knew about smithing and enchanting, from a dwarven perspective. She was going to do her best to get them into shape for what was to come.

Behind them, Lesat's eyes were also sparkling. He'd grown up alone for the most part, and being surrounded by the Hastern family was making him sentimental. They were a good family, something worthy of being protected. He was glad he'd decided to come.

"Aemilia," Krana spoke up with a smile. "Why don't we practice with Far Sight on the road? We can probably find a good place to stop for the night. It's one of the reasons that caravans always ask a Seer or Visionary to come along."

"That sounds wonderful," Aemilia replied, turning from where she was riding behind Jeric to look back at the dwarven Seer. She and Krana were quickly becoming friends. Their ages were similar, which wasn't what she'd expected when they met.

Aemilia's eyes turned a light golden color as she turned back to the front, her arms wrapping around her husband as she began to search the distance.

In the middle of it all, Sam looked around him with a sense of satisfaction. This was how it was supposed to be.

***

The rest of the day passed in a combination of rolling hills and Altey's questions, each of which Sam tried to answer. He was enjoying himself. All of them were slowly relaxing as they put more distance between themselves and Cliff's End, even as they kept an eye out for wandering monsters.

Most monsters on the Storm Plains were under Level 40, and more often around 20 to 30. They usually hunted alone or in pairs. There was a chance of stronger monsters, but most of those had their own territory and wouldn't come too near the road.

If they wanted to find them, they'd have to go looking.

There were also beasts, which were generally more cautious than monsters. They were less likely to attack a party of travelers, so they didn't need to worry about them too much. A single traveler alone might have looked appetizing, but their party was large enough to scare away the normal ones looking for a meal.

So far, no monsters had appeared either, but Sam kept Crystal Focus flowing around him as they rode. Altey stayed with him at the center of the group, where their defense was the strongest.

As evening approached, the triple moons of Aster Fall became visible. They were light green, soft blue, and dusky purple, the colors accenting the heavens in their separate orbits. He'd never noticed the colors too much while he was growing up, but now they radiated unique energy signatures to his eyes, making him aware of exactly where they were.

All around them, the Storm Plains were full of energy if you knew where to look. Mana gathered like rivers in open areas, flowing across the plains in streams of mist. Most of the elemental groves around them, like the lightning oaks that Altey had pointed out, grew within those streams.

The mana rivers were best visible from above. After they rode down onto the plains and into the midst of them, they became more transparent, but Sam could still see where they were. He'd only been able to see energy like this since his transformation into an Outsider.

As evening approached, Aemilia and Krana located a campsite that was inside an elemental grove and they headed off the road toward it. It was about a mile away, close enough to the road to reach easily, but distant enough that they could set up camp and keep watch without being bothered by other travelers. Not that there was anyone else on the road right now.

They were too close to the Broken Lands for travel to be popular. There was a chance they'd see a rare traveler or merchant, but for the most part, it would be a week or so before traffic picked up, once they got closer to the road that led to Highfold.

The campsite that Aemilia and Krana had located was in a grove of wildthorn trees, a type of tree with a long, narrow trunk that rose up into a canopy of slender green leaves and light blue flowers. Long vines with thorns that were three inches long wrapped around the trunk and draped down from the branches, swaying in the air.

They settled down in a clearing between the trees, using them to block the view from the road. Making camp was a familiar matter for most of them, with Altey tumbling from one area to the next as she explored the camp. Her voice sparked answering calls from the birds in the branches.

Before long, stray branches were gathered for firewood, a few small tents were erected, and Sam ignited the fire with a wave of his hand, encouraging it to settle into a cheerful blaze. The sky above was just starting to darken as the light from the moons became brighter. The conversation turned toward their destination.

"Ebonfar or Highfold, do you think?" Sam asked them, as his attention flowed around the campsite. Even now, Crystal Focus was still active, tracking anything that came too close to them.

There was a half-completed set of warding stones in his bag, which he intended to finish soon. He'd settled on using some of the horns from the Horned Water Lizards for it, the ones they'd killed in the tunnels under the Abyssinian Plains. When it was done, it would create a defensive Water barrier around their camp that could be activated.

Over the last couple of months, he'd been working on that and other projects, from his amulet chain, to improving Lesat's armor, to making new spell scrolls. With Krana's help and some examples he'd acquired in Osera and Ebonfar, he'd managed to improve his Enchanting to Level 23, his Smithing to Level 14, and his Essence Scribe profession to 21.

Among other things, he'd finally managed to create some healing scrolls, which were carefully tucked away in everyone's dimensional bags in case they were needed. They were a standard adventuring item, and one that was absolutely essential.

Right now, the main problem was the lack of resources to advance his professions. He still had some materials, but he would need a lot more, including some rarer ones as the professions continued to increase. A better workshop would help too, but for now he was able to make do with the tools he'd acquired so far. Krana had helped with that, giving him a connection to a dwarven smith in Osera. Most of his gains from up to that point had gone into them.

Now, he had a compact forge that was similar to the one Krana had let him use, a good range of small and medium tools, and a dimensional vest full of pockets to store it, with its own runes for durability and self-repair. It was a good purchase, especially since he could study how it was made.

The runes from it had given him a number of ideas that he'd applied to Lesat's armor on the way home, enhancing the durability and repair of the Guard's full plate. He'd also taken the opportunity to extend the enchantment on that across the entire set of armor. Now, using the enchantment wouldn't stress the metal so much and it had the ability to repair itself if it wasn't damaged too badly.

He had a large list of other projects in mind, including making new armor and weapons for his father, weapons for himself, and other things, but he needed better materials first. He also wanted to alter the wand from Nelgen into something Altey could use without a mana skill and to create a defensive amulet for her. They would both need to have stored mana, since she didn't have much of her own.

"Do you think Nelgen will be a problem?" Lesat's question brought Sam's attention back to the present as everyone gathered around the campfire.

"It's possible," Jeric replied, a brief frown flickering across his face. "He does have some connections with the local bandits. I'm not sure how deep they run or if he has any influence with them."

"I'd like to think better of him, but he's very petty when he's angry," Aemilia said as she joined in, sitting down next to her husband. A smile flitted across her face as she looked at Altey.

Sam's sister was playing with a translucent, blue horn that looked like crystal. It was one of the remaining horns from the Horned Water Lizards, and Sam had given it to her to study on the road. The ripple of Water energy around it was still there, flowing over the surface in a spiral as she tilted it one way and then another.

"He's someone who doesn't have much of a conscience," Aemilia added, her expression becoming more serious again. "He'll easily do something to harm others for the sake of his pride, or because he wants to get back at us for a perceived slight."

"The fault was always his own," Jeric shook his head. "He's a small-minded sort. I wouldn't be surprised if he tries something. "The group he's connected to is called the Silver Vipers. They've been in the area for a long time, since before we moved here. I'm not sure how strong they are, but they have to be at a higher level than most in the village.

"Let's keep an eye out behind us. Hopefully, we won't see anything more of them, but there's only one main road that leads away from Cliff's End. Going through the wilderness directly isn't an option."

Jeric looked back toward the road and then shook his head as he continued to think about which way they should travel. "The world is very large. It shouldn't take us too long to put some distance between us and then it will be a moot point. For now, however, we need to decide which way to head."

"Between the two options, Highfold would be better," Krana suggested as she looked toward Jeric. "Have you ever heard of the Festival of Three Crowns?"

"What's that?" Sam asked, turning toward her with a puzzled look. The name caught his attention, but he didn't know what it was.

"Something useful to us and to many crafters," Krana replied with a grin as she pointed to the sky above them, where the light of the three moons was growing stronger. "Do you see how close the moons are now to one another? In a little over two months, the triple moons will align for the first time in seven years. That alignment will last for a week, and it will be celebrated heavily by the sylphs and mountain dwarves who live in Highfold."

Krana's grin grew bigger as she looked around the group, taking in the confused expressions. She'd been thinking about this for a while and it was the best plan she could come up with based on their current needs.

"A few thousand years ago, the citizens of Highfold discovered a set of ruins with some enchantments that awaken during the triple alignment. In particular, there are three giant peaks called the Three Crowns. Each one of them aligns with a moon.

"No one ever figured out how to use those enchantments, but a thriving population of crafters has grown up around them. They study those old ruins and trade ideas. During the festival, there will be a large influx of visitors. The guilds there invite everyone to come and see the ruins and to contribute their theories.

"As a result, Highfold itself has become a popular area for merchants who want to buy interesting enchantments." Krana smiled as she looked toward Sam. "Your class is unique and the description is connected to ancient enchantments. Between those ruins and the monsters in the mountains nearby, I can't think of a better place for you. Hiding your features will be a problem, but privacy is valued by the crafters there. We'll just have to keep you away from the crowds."

Chapter Three

On the High Road

The road stretched ahead of them across the Storm Plains. It wasn't much more than a beaten cart track that somehow resisted the encroachment of time and grass. Whatever had gone into its construction, there was something about it that endured, like the western provinces themselves.

His gaze pierced back through the miles toward Cliff's End. The low mountain that marked the village was just barely visible across the plains. The rolling hills were covered in a mist of purple mana that ran with storm sparks, little lights like embers from a fire that danced along the top of the grasses.

An elemental storm would soon roll through the plains, marking out the event that gave them their name. These sparks were purple-white, which meant it would be a lightning storm. If the mana flow was too intense, it would be dangerous.

The best thing to do was to find a lightning oak grove and settle down in it for a while, to wait for the storm to pass. Sheltering among trees of the same element created a sort of shield, where the storm's energy either flowed into them or skipped past. Earth or Wood-variant trees would work almost as well.

It was a little past noon, but from the density of mana in the air, it was hard to tell. It was like being inside a cloud. He didn't have any trouble seeing through it, but it did make everything seem a bit darker.

Even regular humans were able to see the mana at this point, since it was condensing so much. He'd watched many similar storms form from the walls of the village when he was growing up. They looked almost like rain clouds, but they followed different paths across the terrain, the same ones as the mana rivers. Those he hadn't been able to see before.

The position of Cliff's End up on its mountain meant that it avoided most of these storms. They tended to split around it, even though the mountain wasn't that high. It made him curious about what that mountain was made from. He shook his head as he turned back to the front, keeping Altey balanced in front of him. It was fortunate that his mother and sister didn't mind his new appearance too much. They were just happy that he'd returned.

It was a small price to pay.

He glanced at his status sheet, which summarized the changes over the last couple of months.

Sam Hastern
Level: 45
General Experience: 3,163,070 / 3,437,500
Class Experience: 3,139,540 / 3,437,500
Class: Battlefield Reclaimer
Subclass: The Scion of the Crystal Flame
Race: Outsider (Aster Fall)
Health: 400
Aura: 88
Mana: 88
STR: 20 (21 with Spear of Umbral Flame)
CON: 40 (41 with Spear of Umbral Flame)
AGI: 20 (21 with Spear of Umbral Flame)
WIS: 46 (52 with Staff of Withering Stasis)
INT: 88 (94 with Staff of Withering Stasis)
AUR: 88
CHA: 30
Professions:

- **Enchanter, Level 23.**

- **Smith, Level 14.**

- **Essence Scribe, Level 21.**

With his Charisma at 30, he was better looking than when he left, and many of his original human features were obvious. The low attribute had been hampering that at first, when it had only been at 4.

He was still Sam and his family recognized him. His features were more devilish now, but angular and handsome. His slit-pupiled eyes were sharp and intelligent, often flaring with crystal blue light. The horns that curled up on either side of his temples were more regular as well and about six inches high. They were thick and gnarled at the base, and then rose gradually to a sharp point. His increased Constitution had the effect of strengthening them along with the rest of his bones and skin.

Constitution had enhanced the talons on his hands as well, making them even sharper and harder, but he seemed to have an innate awareness of how to keep them out of the way, so that they didn't scratch Altey or anything he was working on.

The enhanced Charisma had made his long ears a bit sharper and his hair had grown darker, more of a midnight black. It was still strange to look in a mirror, but it didn't shock him as much as it had before. From the feel of it, he'd reached a sort of natural plateau in Charisma now. Adding more didn't feel like it would dramatically change his features again, not unless it was an extreme amount. What it did instead was add an increasing force of personality to his actions and his essence.

Overall, he looked like an intellectual, scholarly demon, rather than the frightening and skeletal version of himself from when he first transformed. The improved attributes had smoothed everything out.

As for his professions, he'd just entered the Advanced stage for Enchanter and Essence Scribe. The skills weren't strictly limited to the tiers, since he'd been able to make Advanced items a few times before reaching Level 20 in each, but it was an overall marker of his progress.

"It looks like a storm is approaching," he called out to his father. "Should we find a grove to camp in early today?"

"Already looking," Jeric laughed as he called back over his shoulder. His mood was good.

"There's a lightning grove about half an hour from here," Aemilia said after a few minutes, her eyes shaded with mana as she searched the distance. "We can head there."

Krana, who was riding behind Sam, just smiled. She was watching all around them as much as possible, as well as helping Aemilia with practice. She was pleased with how quickly the new Seer was progressing.

At the moment, her main challenge was mana. She didn't have a lot, since her primary class hadn't leveled up yet. Once they found a good campsite, she was going to have to start writing down some of the things she saw.

Every level, a Historian got +1 Wisdom and +1 Intelligence, which happened to be the same as a Seer. That was one reason the classes were such a good combination. It shouldn't take her too long to get through the first ten or so levels. Then she'd be much more effective in a fight too, if something came up.

"What class do you think I'll get?" Altey spoke up with a grin, tilting her head back to look into Sam's hood. Even now, he was riding with it up and with his amulet active. It was a brief effort of will to drop the effect for her, as he reached out to control the flow of mana through the amulet, but it let her see his face.

She grinned as she saw his horns.

"You'll be a wonderful spell caster of some type," Sam told her with a grin. "But if not, we'll just get you a good subclass and everything will work out. When we get to Highfold, we'll have to find you a school that can help."

"I'd rather stay with you," Altey frowned at him, reaching up to poke at one of his horns. It felt odd, like someone tapping his knuckles. "You can teach me how to be an Enchanter."

"The world is very big and maybe you'll be something even better than an Enchanter," Sam laughed back at her. "How do you know until you try? A school will help teach you all sorts of things that I don't know, to give you the best chance to succeed no matter what class you get."

"Those things can't be that important," Altey pouted. "What if someone bullies me?"

Sam looked down at Altey and gave her a quick flash of his fangs as he grinned again.

"Who would be able to bully you?! Tell them your big brother will come and punch them."

Inwardly, however, the question made him turn his mind back to the wand that he'd taken from Nelgen. When they stopped in a bit, he'd work on converting it for her. That way, she'd always have a weapon on hand.

His thoughts on bullies were similar to his view of beasts. If they didn't bother you, ignore them. If they did, then crush them.

He'd need to make her that defensive amulet too, and the message amulet to call him if there were any trouble...and to get strong enough to destroy anything in the city that bothered her. Sam's eyes flared with cerulean crystal light as he looked down at her and grinned.

She'd be the best protected student in the entire city by the time he was done. Maybe Lesat could go with her. That should keep most of the trouble away.

Runes flowed through his mind as he turned his attention back to the models that were always present there. He continued to add touches to them, working to incorporate each new insight that he had.

***

The lightning oak grove that Aemilia had chosen was much larger than the one they'd stayed in the night before, practically a forest of its own. As they settled down into their campsite, the trees around them swayed in the wind, violet-white sparks flickering wildly from the tips of the leaves.

The approaching elemental storm was charging the area with mana, and the trees here soaked it up, creating a null space that was safe to camp in. The Storm Plains were a difficult area to live in, but if you knew the patterns, it was possible to survive.

Outside the grove, lightning began to rain down onto the plains, exploding across the grasses and stones as the mana clouds grew darker. The wind whipped through the trees, blowing against Sam's face as he looked out at it.

The plain was a black and violet cloud of churning mana as the ground was torn apart. If they'd been out in it, it was possible to survive, but it wouldn't have been pleasant. They would have needed to dig a quick cave into a hill, one with some large stones farther up the slope to attract the lightning.

Staying in the grove was easier.

He'd grown up on the Storm Plains. He knew the weather and the feel of the mana here. The lands were desolate, but in their own way they were full of life thriving on the edge. He reached out to where lightning sparks were fluttering around a branch and touched it, letting them flow across his hand. Ripples of crystal flame rose up from his palm, dancing around the sparks.

He shook his head. His body was filled with his own essence and if he held his concentration in the right way, the lightning here flowed over the surface of his skin. He hadn't been able to do that before. Out in the storm, he could hear the faint song of natural runes, like a particular pitch of mana that vibrated in his bones and along his meridians. His eyes traced the pattern of the winds, feeling for it, before he slowly shook his head.

Time.

Perhaps if he had a dozen years, he could meditate on the meaning of the Storm Plains and make the runes here his own.

He gave the storm a last look before he turned away, heading back to the campfire. When the chores were done and everyone was studying, he settled down and began pulling items from the dimensional pockets in his vest. He was wearing it like a tunic over his shirt, which made it easy to access.

In a couple of minutes, he set up a quick workshop with his materials, including the ice bolt wand from Nelgen. On one side of the table, there were two Level 25 monster cores, some water lizard horns, and some rough chunks of silver. He'd purchased the silver in Ebonfar, for less than it would have cost as coins, but the quality was lower. In a pack to one side, he also had more than two dozen crystal spheres filled with Earth mana. He'd barely used his supply of those.

Near the campfire, Altey was sitting between her parents, talking animatedly about the storm out past the trees. She'd never been outside in one before, so it was new to her.

His talons tapped on the table as he looked at everything, and then he picked up the ice wand, turning it over in his hands as he let his essence flow into it. The wand turned translucent and the runes of the enchantment began to gleam in his eyes.

His sister hadn't had her Class Day yet, so she didn't have active skills, but that didn't mean she couldn't use the wand. It just wouldn't be as easy for her. If he had to guess, his sister's attributes at the moment were somewhere between 4 and 10, except perhaps for Charisma. She was cute, so that was at least a 12.

He chuckled to himself as he turned the wand over, examining it. She probably only had about four or five mana, which wasn't much. Even if she concentrated as hard as possible, it was unlikely she would be able to use more than a point or two of it. He would need to change the enchantment on this so that it didn't require her to do more than activate it with a thread of mana. The easiest thing to do would be to imbed a core, which could be used to store mana.

A higher-quality core might have been able to even regenerate mana over time, but the ones he had right now were not that good. He'd have to charge it for her, or perhaps she could learn how to do it herself, at a point or so an hour. If she did, then when she received her class, she was likely to get a few meditation and mana control skills as soon as the World Law assessed her abilities. That would be good for her.

Right now, the wand had a basic enchantment. There was quite a bit of unused space on it. He just needed to surround it in a more advanced rune pattern and imbed the core. He'd figured out the basics of imbedding cores from some items he'd seen in Ebonfar, but this would be the first time he did it himself. If it worked, he'd use the other core as the base material for a shielding amulet.

Crystal flames flowed out of his hand, swirling around the wand as he poured his aura into it, searching through it for flaws as he began to purify it further. Whoever had done it the first time had low standards. He needed to overwrite the signature of their enchantment and make it his own, purify it a bit more, and then he could get started.

Sam began to hum. Crystal flames swirled around him and the wand, twisting into curling patterns as he tested out concepts. A moment later, a stick of chalk appeared in his free hand and he began to sketch on the table, holding the wand with the other as he glanced at it.

***

As day turned into night, the elemental storm continued to lash against the plains with no sign of stopping. The lightning sparks on the trees grew brighter as the canopy started to glow, brightening as it absorbed more energy. After several hours had passed, there were violet, blue, and white arcs leaping from leaf to leaf, playing between the branches. It was eerie and mystical, like a swarm of faeries were waging war in the forest.

It was well past sunset, but it was almost as bright as day.

The wand in front of Sam bore little resemblance to the artifact that it had once been. It had been a white metal wand with a crystal on one end, the sort of bland artifact that apprentices made in large quantities. Now, it was something different.

The monster core was fused into the material a few inches from the end, giving it a spherical bulge. The color had changed from white to light blue and there was a runic pattern in a double spiral around it that looked similar to lightning bolts. The new runes gleamed with icy light, especially three prominent symbols for *ice, slow,* and *mana.*

The *ice* and *slow* runes dictated the effects that Sam had intensified in the wand, but the *mana* rune was the most important. If she concentrated and poured her mana into that point, it would help her connect to the wand. She could then turn her mana into an attack.

At the base of the wand above the monster core, there was a *charge* rune, which would allow Altey to infuse her mana into it, if she had any to spare. More likely, Sam or one of their parents would end up doing that.

The binding pattern that held it together was the same Expert-level one that he'd borrowed from the original illusion amulet Krana had drawn for him, but a slightly reduced version. It would help to bind the core to the wand and improve the overall efficiency. He had ended up erasing most of the original enchantment and redoing it, altering it to fit his personal standards. Once upon a time, that sort of thing would have been difficult, but after so many months of intensive enchanting, it had become almost second nature.

The lines of the new enchantment were gleaming with crystal blue essence, which roiled inside them like an ocean of flames trying to burn away the material, but it was well contained. Sam tapped the activation rune, watching as the lines of mana began to surge. The first rune began to gleam with energy as it absorbed the essence he'd poured into it. Unlike the temporary enchantments he'd made, this time he felt the aura he'd poured into the runes swirling faster, heading through the pattern to the monster core.

The runes came to life one after the other, etching themselves more deeply into the material until the entire wand was covered in a web of light. Then the enchantment intensified, rising off the surface until it floated above the wand. Mana and aura flared through the wand, spreading out evenly across the entire pattern, and then the enchantment collapsed inward. The core was the eye of a whirlwind at the base. It absorbed all of the energy and then spun it back out, redistributing it evenly through the runes.

The wand gleamed on the table, the tiny runes on it etched in an icy blue light. A moment later, a notification appeared, along with a sparkling surge of experience that danced along his nerves.

Wand of Slow Freeze (Advanced)

[Enchantment of Slow Freeze: Creates an ice bolt that does initial impact damage and then covers the target in a layer of ice, slowing its movements. Charges: 20. Duration: Permanent.]

Congratulations, Enchanter. You have crafted an Advanced Enchantment.

You gain 2,500 Class experience. (100% contribution from Enchanter)

Class Experience: 3,142,040 / 3,437,500

Sam waved away the notification with a shake of his head, focusing his attention on the wand as he tilted it from side to side. It would take something like 120 similar items if he wanted to reach the next level through enchanting, so he'd started ignoring the experience numbers. It was better to just focus on the sense of progress from crafting and the surge of experience itself. Each point was more than he had before.

A small smile played across his features as he turned toward the campfire, searching for Altey. He was looking forward to her reaction. Unfortunately, she was asleep already, tucked away in the blankets of her tent. Sam sighed as he tucked the wand away in his pouch. He'd been so focused that he'd forgotten about that. He'd give it to her when she woke up.

He didn't need a lot of sleep anymore, another side effect of Constitution. Four hours was usually enough. Currently, Lesat was the only other one awake. Sam gave him a nod. It was almost time for his own watch, so he might as well stay awake.

Lightning sparks danced through the canopy as the storm roared across the plains.

CHAPTER FOUR

NIGHT OF LIGHTNING

Everyone else was sleeping as Sam kept watch. It was near the middle of the night now, and except for the lightning, everything else was silent. The elemental storm was showing no sign of its force decreasing, which meant they might be here for a while, perhaps for a day or two.

The storms were the main reason that the plains saw few visitors and had almost no settlers. They had been part of the plains for as long as anyone knew. There were ones for most elements, although some were rarer than others. They came from the intense elemental mana that accumulated here, part of the rivers of mana that he'd seen pouring down from the mountains and across the land.

They could be avoided if you found the right type of shelter, and if you knew the signs that they were approaching. Most were diffuse and not too dangerous, but if you were caught in them unprepared, they could be deadly.

An Earth storm could create boulders the size of a man, and a Fire storm could create a true inferno if the mana was intense enough, but it was rare. They were usually just a rain of pebbles or of hot sparks that scorched things, leaving behind blackened grasses that recovered in a few days.

The Storm Plains did not burn easily. Everything here was saturated with mana, which gave it a natural resistance.

The most dangerous type of storm was Wood, since even the minor ones caused the grasses to grow and whip around. Grass was everywhere on the plains and it could strangle a traveler caught outside, like a thousand arms reaching up to grab at you, particularly since the storms were most intense right above the ground.

To survive, you needed a cave in the earth, to be on top of a stone mountain, or to be in a forest. Any type of forest would help, since the trees absorbed most of the mana, but you still wanted to find a clearing without too many grasses. Failing that, you could try to climb a tree and hope that it was strong enough to absorb the excess mana around it...and that there weren't any vines nearby.

There were also mixed elemental storms, but they were infrequent. Lightning and Ice, or Fire and Wind, for example. Those were particularly deadly. Those could form into whirling blades of Fire that cut across the ground. Sometimes, not even the forests survived that.

The night passed on until the middle of Sam's watch, when a distant roar echoed through the trees. His attention turned toward it, his ears tilting. After a moment it came again. It didn't sound like a roar this time, but clashing steel. There was a strange wave of mana with it that shook the lightning in the canopy, making it dance.

The sound of clashing blades came again. Then there was a wailing howl and the sound of a voice shouting indistinctly. There was something demanding in it.

He was the only one awake, so he couldn't leave to investigate, but it sounded like it was coming closer. He walked to the edge of the clearing and looked into the distance, trying to see between the trees.

Violet sparks of lightning were dancing all across the forest floor and throughout the canopy. The trees were tall with wide gaps between, which let him see a good distance. With all of the lightning, there were only a few shadows, strange ones squiggling here and there as they crawled between the trunks and hid beneath stones.

All he could make out was a swirling mass of sparks and the shadows. It was an eerie sight, one transposing over the other in alternating light and dark, like something from a dream. The canopy above his head rustled in the breeze and the leaves parted, revealing the light of the three moons. As with the sun, there was a strange energy to the moonlight that gleamed in his eyes, which fell through leaves to mix with the lightning sparks.

Everything was still.

There was energy in nearly everything he saw now, particularly in sunlight and the clouds, but also the trees and elements. It was everywhere. He'd tried to reclaim some types of it already, but it didn't respond, so he'd started to ignore it. He still couldn't help wondering if it was what his class description spoke about.

The Battlefield Reclaimer is an ancient enchanter and smith who uses aura and essences from the elements, including rare ones like the sunset, aurora, or ocean light, to imbue items with rare and inexplicable properties.

Perhaps he wasn't skilled enough to gather it, or perhaps he was missing something. If he could pull an aura from the moonlight, and weave that into an enchantment, he wondered what the result would be. Maybe he should try something simpler first, and figure it out from there.

When monsters came through a Flaw, they consumed part of the world, which turned into an aura that he could reclaim. That damaged Aster Fall in some way. Even if he could do it himself, he was sure the World Law wouldn't tolerate it. They were already on ambiguous terms. Pushing it like that would be foolish.

Since he had the class, however, which was approved by the World Law, there had to be some other way to do what it said in the description, another way to harness "aura and essences" for enchantments.

Krana's words about the ruins at Highfold were on his mind, including the enchantments there. He'd never heard of them before, but he wanted to know what they were. Hopefully, they would help him understand his class better and advance his skills. Essence Control might give him an advantage since it allowed him to look into enchantments and to see their structure.

It was something he didn't plan to tell the guilds about, since it would only cause trouble. Regular Enchanters had to study the runes from the outside and estimate the enchantment patterns from that. Perhaps the enchantments there would be too strange or incomplete, but he wouldn't know until he saw them.

His talons tapped along the trunk of a tree as he watched the sparks flow through the forest. He wasn't sure where the sound had come from, but it seemed like this direction. Echoes were warped inside the storm, so it was hard to tell. After a few minutes, a swirl of movement beneath the trees caught his attention as the storm sparks there intensified, outlining two forms flickering in and out of view. They were hard to see at first, just indistinct blurs of light and shadow, but they became clearer as he looked.

Crystal Focus spread out as far as he could, trying to see better, but the images were beyond his range. The first thing he noticed was that neither of them was human and that they were fighting. The clang of metal came again, the mana in it shaking the lightning sparks all around like a swirl of snow.

One figure was a brutish, humanoid figure with bulging muscles and bony ridges covering its skull and arms, almost like innate armor. It had two long horns on its head, much bigger than Sam's. Its eyes were red slit-pupils. Almost as if it felt him watching, the figure turned toward him and a snarl ripped out of its mouth, with long fangs flashing as a pointed tongue flickered into the air.

There was a weight of power in its eyes that trapped his gaze. He felt a pressure against his mind, like an echo that reached for his soul. Then it was gone, thrown backwards as the other figure advanced on it.

This one was something tall and thin that looked like a blur of liquid silver, as if it were made of metal. Its body was as narrow as a sapling, with six limbs like spider legs that lashed out at its enemy. Its eyes were violet slashes, and the light throughout the forest reflected from its surface. Whatever it was, it looked dangerous, like an array of swords had come to life. He could feel a similar pressure from it, something that felt like the storm here.

There was a clash of metal against bone as the figures met, their blow landing on each other. The silver figure advanced as the demon retreated, its limbs stabbing forward. As it crossed in front of Sam, its thin head turned to look at him. He felt a pressure scraping against his soul again, but this time it was like the storm, a wild chaos of power that felt like Aster Fall. For just a moment, he glimpsed the lightning runes, their forms striking like bolts of thunder.

Then both of the figures shattered into sparks and floated away, blurring back into the forest like ghosts without leaving anything behind. The runes dissipated as well, flowing away like smoke before he could comprehend them. Silence returned to the forest, followed a moment later by the crash of lightning. Sam frowned as he looked after the figures, searching for anything remaining, but there was only the storm. Slowly, he shook his head.

There were legends about the Storm Plains. Some said they had been formed by a battle between gods, the same one that created the Broken Lands, but nothing he'd heard explained what he'd just seen. Perhaps those two figures had been foot soldiers. An echo of long ago.

The rest of his watch passed without interest, accompanied only by the storm. When he fell asleep that night, streaks of multicolored elemental lightning flickered through his mind.

He'd felt a dangerous pressure from the two gazes that had touched his soul. Now that feeling returned, like daggers held against his stomach, as a cold wind began to swirl around him. The Guardian Star on his hand flickered softly, a bright white light coming from it as it pulsed in time with his heart.

The stars in the sky above moved closer, hanging low over his head as the dimensional space of the world warped. Sam tossed on his bedroll as vivid, cataclysmic dreams flowed through his mind. Flickers of the world appeared in his mind.

A vast expanse of stone and mountains, stretching beyond sight. Above it, a wind with no warmth blew and darkness stretched out beyond the horizon, speckled with the distant light of stars.

Then a shattering *krrraaAAack* echoed across the stone as a great rift appeared in it. The earth heaved, rolling beneath the distant stars, as it fractured into pieces.

A second great crack echoed through the stone, throwing him out of the dream as the stone began to fall apart, revealing a glowing, rainbow cloud of brilliant energy that had been lying beneath it. Space around the crack warped, pulled toward that cloud of energy. A tug on Sam's soul pulled him toward it as well, irresistibly drawn toward the energy that was swirling there, both in this realm and in another.

The sound of another great crack suddenly threw him back to consciousness. When he woke, his body was covered in cold sweat.

Nexus.

The word whispered across his consciousness, a harbinger of the past and the future.

***

It took more than two days for the storm to end. The lightning hadn't formed any other images after that first one, at least not that Sam had seen, but the dream that he'd had was still hanging on his mind. It was somehow connected to the elemental storms, as if they'd triggered it. Or perhaps it had been the gazes of those things in the vision, the demon and the elemental.

Nexus. It was part of the world, perhaps its history. He could feel it. He felt a slow pulse of energy from the Guardian Star on his hand as he muttered the word to himself, like a confirmation. The images of the dream were vivid in his mind, and he turned them over again, frowning.

If it was connected to the world, to the Guardian Star, and to him somehow...then the only thing that made sense was that it was part of his job. That glowing cloud of energy had felt a lot like a Flaw.

The first Flaw...or the first Breaking? He wasn't sure, but it felt like he was on the right track. The Nexus had something to do with the origin of Outsiders and of Aster Fall. He looked down at himself and at his hands that ended in sharp talons. He curled them into fists and relaxed them again.

He needed to know what was going on and more about the world itself. Perhaps something else would come in a dream, but the only thing he could do right now was to keep training and improving his class. That meant becoming better as an Enchanter and Smith, the two main focus points of it, and preparing for his eventual Evolution at 100.

If he wanted the best Evolution possible, he needed to maximize all of his current skills, and to try to get them to the Epic tier by the time he hit 100. He nodded slowly as he looked at his hands again, uncurling them. It was time to train his skills and to work on understanding his Class better.

Whatever the Nexus really was, he was nowhere close to understanding it yet, much less being capable of dealing with it. The Guardian Star on his hand was a reminder that he needed to become better. Fortunately, he knew exactly where to start to improve himself.

They were heading to Highfold, which was a higher level area than Cliff's End or the Storm Plains. It was also cold and high up in the mountains. This journey would take a month and they would need a lot of enchantments to help them survive there. There should also be some opponents on the way to hone his class abilities.

With the goal in mind, he set out a training plan for himself, reviewing his abilities as he searched for the most effective way to increase his strength and live up to his responsibilities. Whatever happened, he had to make sure that his family was safe in the world.

He couldn't allow another Breaking.

He spent the rest of the time during the storm studying. He also started to work on a shielding amulet for Altey based on the other monster core he had.

At the same time, Aemilia started to write in the books that she had, gaining experience in her Historian class. When Sam asked what she was writing, she told him it was an account of her life, since that was the easiest thing to start with.

She also continued working with Krana to advance her Seer abilities, and she started a second book to record what she could see on their journey. It would be an account of their travels, although she didn't plan to include any information about Sam's transformation or the specifics of his class.

The main focus of the Historian class was recording and transferring information. She'd tried writing on stone and clay before, but it had never worked for her, perhaps because she hadn't seen it the right way. Class requirements were sometimes in the mind as much as in reality. It was possible that she'd never seen those materials with the right perspective to make them work. The books were already designed to be read and transferred to others.

When the storm passed, they continued along the road toward Highfold and when night arrived, he returned to working on the amulet for Altey.

He'd been struck by some inspiration from the storm, so after he crafted the base from silver, he inscribed it with lightning runes. The result was a small, palm-sized disk of silver with a bulge in the center where the monster core was embedded.

The front of the amulet was engraved with two concentric circles that surrounded double runes for *lightning* and *shield*. The supporting pattern around it was filled with smaller lightning runes as a way of distributing the energy, as well as storage runes.

Amulet of Lightning Shield (Advanced).
[Enchantment: Lightning Absorption.
Effect: Creates an absorptive shield of variable size and duration, depending on the number of charges used. Effect can be activated

**passively by an incoming attack. Charges: 25. Duration: Perma-
nent.]**

The pattern would help to absorb incoming attacks, surrounding her in
a crackle of lightning if anything tried to bother her. It should have a visual
effect as well, to intimidate the enemy. On the back, there were *charge* and
mana runes, so that Altey could infuse her mana into it. Originally, he'd
planned to make an Earth shield for her, but the lightning sparks in the
forest had given him the idea when he watched them gather and spread
apart.

They also gave him an idea on how to train Crystal Focus, to get it past
the Basic tier. He could already feel that the ability was starting to advance.
Aura of Crystal Flame was at the Expert tier and part of everything he
did. Raising it ahead of the others helped to lay the foundation for their
advancement.

The camp was broken down and packed away into dimensional bags by
the time he was finished. Altey was running around by the horses, trying
to feed them bits of grass that she'd pulled up, and laughing as they stole it
from her hands.

The sky had cleared, but the storm had left the forest glowing. The
lightning oaks were covered in a silver mist that sent zipping bolts through
your skin if you touched it, and the leaves were covered in sparks that were
three times more intense than usual. It was harmless, but it made the forest
look like the domain of gods and elementals. Every branch was outlined
with shimmering light.

"You need to wear this all the time," he said as he hung the amulet
around Altey's neck and showed her how to activate it. Then he handed her
the wand as well, showing her where the runes were to use it. "With these,
you'll be able to defend yourself a bit. Make sure to practice with them
while we're traveling. I'll recharge them for you if they get too low." As he
looked at her, his mood turned more optimistic again, and he grinned as
he ruffled her hair.

It was the first thing he could really do for his sister, besides spending
time with her. Everything else was just a part of life, but enchanting...that
was his. It was something he could do better than anyone else. "If you
practice really hard, maybe you'll get a special class or subclass."

"I'll be the best battle Wizard ever!" Altey declared as she looked at the
wand with wide eyes. Then she hugged him, wrapping her arms around

his neck. "I'll never let anyone find out that you look like a demon. If they try, I'll beat them up."

"Don't use that on anyone that you don't want to kill," Jeric warned sternly, as he came over and crouched down next to Altey. "That's a weapon, not a toy." He didn't take the wand away. Instead, he curled her hand around it and looked into her eyes.

"Your brother made these for you, and I want you to make me a promise now," he said, "that you will use these if your life is in danger, or if you're really afraid of someone and they're about to attack you. Spells are like swords and arrows. They're to be used against enemies."

"I know," Altey promised, with a seriousness that was wiser than her years. "I'll use it if it's important." Then a glint came into her eyes. "Like on Nelgen."

"Maybe on him," Jeric said with a laugh. "He's a snake, but only use that on him if he's attacking you or one of us. Or a monster. Those, you can attack.

"The World Law will give you a prompt to tell you if it's a monster." Jeric continued. "With bandits, it's harder to tell. They're civilized races, so you have to judge by their actions instead."

"All right," Altey promised slowly, but she didn't let go of the wand. Her hand was gripped around it as if she would never let it go. "I'll use it on monsters and enemies."

"Good," Jeric approved as he ruffled her hair. "Now, let's get back on the road. Highfold is a long way from here."

Sam picked Altey up and set her on the saddle, and then he swung up behind her. When they were ready to go, he reached down and took her hand, showing her how to activate the amulet. With a *tap*, a shimmer of lightning covered her body, spreading outward into a shield that faded away in the air. To Sam's eyes, faint tendrils of energy crackled back toward the amulet and then circulated out again, creating a passive sphere around her.

Since he was next to her, the shield also spread out around him. He interlaced it with a second layer of Essence Shield, a passive form that was ready to spring to life. He raised his eyes again, looking out at the world around them, and then toward the road to Highfold.

The last three days had been peaceful enough, but most of that was thanks to the storm. Before long, Altey might need to rely on the amulet to survive.

Nothing in Aster Fall stayed peaceful for long.

CHAPTER FIVE

THE ROAD TO HIGHFOLD

"No." The answer was said without any particular emphasis.

"What do you mean *no*?" Nelgen was staring at a whipcord thin, vicious-looking man in front of him. There was a prominently-placed tattoo of a silver viper curling around his forearms, which shone with some type of totemic magic.

"I mean no. They're poor villagers, which means they have no money, and they have an adventuring party with them," the man replied blandly. "So, *no*. There's no value in it."

"But that wizard has to have good things on him!" Nelgen pressed. "And the dwarf will have gems or metals, for sure."

"They have a Seer," the man replied, shaking his head. "They'll see us coming. Your idea to keep her here was fine, but now she's gone. The Silver Vipers didn't survive in the Storm Plains for this long by being stupid."

Nelgen's mind raced as he tried to think of a way to convince the man in front of him to do what he wanted.

"But that little girl..." he finally said, slowly, since it was crossing a line even for him. "She's the great-great granddaughter of the Tower Reach Hasterns. If you let her grandparents know that she and her mother have been abducted by a mercenary party...."

"Lie to the Hasterns?" the man laughed, as the corner of his mouth crooked up. "They aren't a nice family, so also *no*. They could have found the girl before now if they cared. I can send a message about what happened, and tell them their granddaughter is running around unsupervised, but that's it. Whether or not they believe it, it's up to them."

"But at least you'll keep an eye on them and see which way they go?" Nelgen insisted. He didn't want to lose Aemilia, not if there was a chance he could get her back.

"Fine," the man agreed, gazing upward. "We have some hawks that can keep an eye on them from above, and a Beastcaller to direct them and see through their eyes. Maybe the Hasterns will pay for the information, since you aren't. But add ten percent to the next shipment."

"Good." Nelgen clenched his fists on the table as he thought about Aemilia, even as the price pained him. That additional ten percent was several gold, and it would cut into his profits for months.

If the Hasterns showed up, they'd take the girl away, but what would they care about a useless Historian, even if she was a Seer? They had plenty of those. That idiot Jeric might be descended from them, but she wasn't. Those old families were insular, and he doubted they'd care about her much.

If they didn't want her, he'd find a way to bring her back to the village. If they did want her...well, he doubted life as a servant of the Hasterns would be a good one. He couldn't imagine that they would see her as anything else. They didn't have that kind of reputation.

That would work too.

***

The three moons were hanging brightly on the western horizon as they continued along the road toward the fork that led to Highfold. It was mid-morning now and a low golden haze filled the air to the east as the sun continued to rise behind a bank of mist. At this rate, they would reach the turn in the road in another day or two.

When they did, he would have to be more careful about hiding his features.

The road between Ebonfar and Highfold was the main route on the western side of the Storm Plains. It had branches in various areas, some of which led to abandoned villages and old ruins. It was frequently traveled by merchants, mercenary groups, and adventurers.

Every once in a while, the Church of the World Law sent a band of Paladins and Priests down it as well, looking for monsters and to keep the peace. They cleared out bandits where they could find them. The Guardian Star on his hand should be proof enough of his shared purpose to keep them from attacking him, but showing it to them before that happened was a problem. He didn't feel like meeting any of them.

The last couple of days had passed without much difficulty, except for a pack of Darkfrost Wolves that tried to ambush Lesat's horse. They'd run away when Sam threw a few crystal flame arrows at them. It wasn't worth it to chase them. For the Storm Plains, it was fairly quiet.

Right now, Sam was keeping an eye out for more things, while practicing with Crystal Focus. He could feel the ability bubbling quietly, like it was under pressure and trying to advance. He just needed to find the right key. Krana was riding next to him and talking to Altey.

"Do you know the ancient names of the moons?" the Seer asked, pointing up to where they were on the horizon. They were shining with a soft halo of energy that drew Sam's attention to them now and then. "It might help at the Festival, so you know what people are talking about. They are gathered together right now, preparing for the Festival of Three Crowns, but they are not always so close together."

Altey shook her head, looking between Krana and the sky.

"The green moon is Silvas, the Moon of Forests, and the kindest of the moons, because forests provide shelter and food. She is the Wanderer, but she can always be found if you look to the west at dawn on the first day of the year." Krana smiled as she pointed to the green moon on the left.

"In the middle and a bit higher up, the blue moon is Caelus, the Moon of the Heavens." Krana's hand traced an arc across the sky to point to it above the other two. "He is the oldest of the moons, the Watcher, and the one who saw the world formed. Time and space are part of his realm, and he sees all things pass. Look for him to be high in the sky at both noon and midnight.

"The third moon, the purple one," Krana's voice dropped lower as her voice became solemn. Her hand moved to point to the last moon on the right, which was a bit lower than the other two and set off at an oblique angle.

"That is Amaris, the Moon of Passion and Madness. She is the youngest of the moons, and her path is erratic. She crosses in front of the others, disturbing their journeys. Sometimes they follow her and sometimes she walks alone. She is also the moon of monsters and beasts, and the darker side of the heart, where vengeance lies. She is part of who we are, but we have to be careful with her."

Altey's eyes widened as she looked up at the moons, their reflection filling her pupils. "Are the other two moons good then?"

"Amaris is not an evil moon," Krana shook her head. "Although some things that are evil may happen under her influence. The other two moons are also not just good. Silvas is helpful, but she oversees ancient forests that cover many bones, and Caelus observes everything from on high without comment or aid."

Altey's eyes were growing wider, but at that same moment, Krana's attention was pulled away. Her eyes shaded to silver as she looked off to the left of the road ahead of them.

"Hold!" she called out a moment later. Her words drew the horses together around her. She glanced ahead of them to where a small grove of trees was on the left of the road. It was about a mile and a half away. Then she turned to Aemilia. "Do you see it?"

Aemilia's eyes were also covered by her mana, a bit more brightly than they had been a few days ago, thanks to her deepening mana pool. After a moment, she nodded.

"Ten Flamecaller Devils and two Storm Striders," she said with a frown. "Those might be difficult. The devils are Flame Jaw Asarets, specifically, Level 29-33. They must be bound to the Striders. Those are Level 44 and 46."

Sam frowned as he heard the report. Those were not the easiest monsters. They could deal with them, but it would be best to plan first.

Devils was a generic term for any sort of vaguely humanoid monster, usually with fangs and claws. The World Law sometimes gave them more unique names, but adventurers defaulted back to the general term, since calling them "devils" was easier.

The Storm Striders were more of a problem. They were a unique existence in the Storm Plains, one of the monsters you didn't want to run into if you could help it. They were basically ten-foot-tall storm wraiths with skeletal bodies and claws like knives. More importantly, they had magic that could summon up miniature storms or wind blades, and sometimes other things.

When his mother finished explaining what she saw, Krana nodded in agreement.

"You want to keep a low-mana scan going at most times, especially while traveling," she advised. "It's one of the main tasks a Seer always has in a party." The Seer turned toward Jeric, announcing the rest of the information. "It doesn't look like we can avoid them. They're watching the road ahead and we'll have to pass by them. Going around would also get their attention and the plains here are difficult to move on quickly. The road would be a better place to meet them.

"The Flamecaller Devils are devourers. These are about half the size of a human and have elongated heads with large jaws. They'll eat anything. We'll have to be careful of their bites, which can go through steel." Krana's voice paused as her attention turned toward the road ahead of them. "Wait, there's something else."

A moment later, she spoke up again, her voice holding a new note that wasn't common for her. One of exasperation.

"A group of adventurers is on the road ahead of us. They have a Visionary with them who's spotted the devils as well, and they're moving toward them."

"Good, they can deal with it then," Sam interjected, as he looked from his mother to his sister. He would pick up any experience they ran across, but he'd rather get his family away from anything dangerous first.

"Let them have them," Jeric agreed. He also looked relieved. "It's better to avoid trouble. Can we go around them?"

"Not without attracting attention from both of them." Krana shook her head. "Waiting here to see what happens is better. We can move on after."

"Mhmm," Jeric nodded, with a sound of agreement. "Keep an eye on them for us?"

"I can go help if it looks like they're in too much danger," Sam added as he glanced down at Altey in front of him. "No reason to let humans die to monsters. Hopefully, they know what they're facing."

He would just have to keep his hood up and it shouldn't be a problem. They'd passed a lot of people on the way home from Osera and none of them had caused him any trouble yet. It had boosted his confidence in the illusion amulet. Intervening probably wouldn't be necessary anyway. If that group was attacking so quickly, they had to be prepared for what they were facing.

"I want to help too," Altey declared, raising the wand in her hand.

"When you're bigger," Sam replied, shaking his head. Then he picked Altey up and passed her over to Krana, who swung the girl up in front of her. She gave him a nod. Altey didn't weigh that much, and Krana had good shielding and Foresight abilities. It would let him maneuver more, if needed.

Lesat scanned the area behind them and then moved up next to Krana.

"I'll keep an eye on you and your mother," he said, giving Altey a brief smile. "If something comes this way, it'll have to deal with me first."

A few minutes passed as Krana reported what the other party of adventurers was doing. She summoned an illusory image in front of them, which showed the party heading closer to the monsters.

The devils and Storm Striders were hiding in a small fireleaf grove. The bark of the trees resembled jagged scales and their leaves had wisps of flame running along them. The trees almost looked like devils themselves. That similarity was probably why the monsters had chosen it, hoping it would hide their energy. Storm Striders were one of the smarter monsters on the plains.

There were seven people in the adventurers' party. One was a Visionary, and as Krana pointed them out, the rest of the classes became clear as well. They were all around Level 40 with combat main classes, which was probably where they got their confidence. They were also subclassed in combat specialities, rather than the more common crafting backups. It was one of the things that marked them out as adventurers.

They had three melee classes: a Warrior-Barbarian, a Guard-Battlecaller, and a Warrior-Knight. Battlecaller was some type of bard subclass, perhaps. Or maybe a shaman one. He wasn't familiar with it.

They also had an Archer-Scout, a Wizard-Mage, and a Mage-Arcane Healer. The seventh was the Visionary, who was subclassed as an Arcane Healer too. It was a pretty well-balanced party.

Arcane Healers were a necessary class if you didn't have a Priest around and you didn't want to spend the money on healing pills or scrolls. They could learn spells for healing and were very popular among adventurers. It was an expensive class to unlock and train, since the spells were mana intensive and sometimes required reagents, but it was worthwhile.

The healers made Sam wonder about Ayala. What was the church princess up to in Osera and had her father returned yet? With her Earth-walker Mage-Priestess classes, it would have been useful to have her around. He shook his head as he turned his attention back to the illusion. The Warrior-Barbarian seemed to be the leader.

He was the highest level of them all at 43. He was also the roughest-looking of the whole group, with a leather jerkin sewn with metal rings that had seen better days.

At his directions, all of them except the Warrior-Knight dismounted. The group split into two parts, leaving the Visionary holding the horses. The archer and three casters stayed in the back, forming a rough half circle as they spread out. There was a brief flash of shielding spells from the Mages and then the two melee and the mounted Knight moved forward, heading for the grove.

Krana's spell was extremely lifelike, and it was possible to see the activation of abilities all around the adventurers. The only thing the spell didn't do was sound. They didn't even know they were being spied on. The Battlecaller chanted something that surrounded the melee in a purple aura and stamina abilities glowed around the other two. The Barbarian's skin turned red as a mist rose off of it.

When the group was halfway to the forest, the monsters burst out of it, rushing at them.

The Flamecaller Devils came first, darting forward in blurs like red streaks of flame. They were short and squat, about four feet tall and more than half that wide, with scarab-like mandibles. They looked a lot like a goblin had been squashed together with a scarab, but despite the weird appearance, they were dangerous.

They had four muscular lizard legs that let them race along the ground and two arms with sharp talons at the ends. Their mandibles were lined with dark scarlet flames that ran along the wickedly curved edge. From their mouth, black saliva sizzled as it flew to the sides.

Behind them, the Storm Striders came, gliding silently out of the trees like ghosts. They were about ten feet tall and extremely thin, with waists perhaps only eight inches across. Their chest and hips were broader, giving them an angular, hour-glass appearance. Their skin was dusky ivory with mottled patches of grey and their hair was long, white-grey strands that ran down their backs and spread across the ground.

Their arms dangled near their knees, and their fingers were bony blades. Their knees were double-jointed, like an insect, making it look like they were about to leap at any moment. Their faces were triangular wedges, blank except for two indentations for the nose and diamond-shaped eyes that held a stormy white-grey light.

Tendrils of snow, ice, flame, and lightning swirled out around them as their gazes locked on the adventurers, creating a chaos of elemental mana that erupted into sparks as it collided with trees and the grass.

They were dangerous, but the adventurers didn't hesitate. Sam had to commend them for bravery, even if he wasn't sure they knew what they were getting into. From the looks of it, that group was composed of mostly common and uncommon classes and subclasses. Their abilities might be enhanced by their levels, if they'd made the right choices, but only half of them were Level 40. At most, they probably had one or two abilities at the Expert level, and they weren't likely to be the most flexible ones.

The melee fighters might have an attack ability at Expert, but their defense was unlikely to be as good. The casters would need to try and shield them. If they'd trained as a team and made choices with that in mind, it could work, but that was something a military would do. Adventurers were not usually so unified.

A chaotic storm was building up around the Storm Striders as the Flamecaller Devils reached the melee. Right before they clashed, more abilities glowed around the humans, particularly from the Battlecaller. It looked like he was shouting as he raised a long-handled maul into the air. The Barbarian in the front had a large, double-bladed battle axe. His skin was covered in a glowing red energy as he swung toward the first devil.

At the same moment, the archer and the casters behind them began to move. Spell energies and arrows rose up around them and flew forward, heading for the devils. There was an array of magic bolts that gleamed with a twisting violet light from the Wizard-Mage and a dozen spheres of red flame from the other mage. The Visionary was the only one who didn't attack, apparently waiting as a healer as he held the horses.

The Barbarian cut an arm off the devil that was attacking him as the spells arrived, but it was only the beginning. Unfortunately for the adventurers, the Storm Striders were not a stupid enemy. Before the spells could land and destroy their troops, a wave of mixed elemental energy collided with them, turning both sets of spells into a wild eruption of sparks and explosions in the air above the battle.

Sam frowned as he summoned a wave of crystal flame around him, condensing it into a battle spiral. His horse stamped at the ground beneath his feet, but that was all. It was very accustomed to spell effects.

The casters on the other side attacked again, with a new wave of spells that flew forward, and the melee pressed into the devils. The Storm Striders blocked with a wave of twisting air blades that shot forward toward the melee. The blades were like spinning scythes with different elements sparking away from them.

The attack made the Barbarian dodge to the side, and the Battlecaller shouted something as the blades approached him. A purple shield appeared, but it fractured as the air blades hit it. He was picked up by the impact and tossed ten feet away, sent rolling across the ground.

The Wizard-Mage stepped forward right then and raised a crystal sphere in his hands as he chanted something. The sphere ignited, turning a burning white that resembled the blessing spells Ayala had used once. Then he tossed it into the air above the monsters.

"Damn it," Krana muttered, "Those idiots! That's a Holy Sun sphere. It's going to make the monsters go crazy. It should only be used in larger battles to cause a rout. He must have panicked...or was that their trump card because he thought they were being overwhelmed?"

Sam didn't understand what she was talking about at first, so he kept his eyes on the image. An inferno of white light exploded into the air above the devils and Storm Striders, like a miniature sun being born. Their skin began to crisp, turning darker from the energy in it, and they screamed.

It was audible even across the mile or more that separated them from Sam.

The Flamecaller Devils and Storm Striders both went insane, their actions turning to a wild chaos of flailing limbs as they tried to run away from the light. They spun in place, heading away from the party that they'd just been fighting, tearing up the ground at their feet as they tried to put distance between them and the sun sphere.

Unfortunately, now they were heading right for Sam and the others, and it didn't look like they were going to stop until they ran right through them.

Chapter Six

Worthless Adventurers

"Damned adventurers," Sam muttered, agreeing with Krana as he jumped off his horse and walked forward in front of the others. If the adventurers had planned better, they wouldn't have made the monsters go crazy.

Now they'd made them his problem. The Storm Striders and all ten of the Flamecaller Devils were heading straight for them. They were only mildly injured and they were far more enraged than they had been before, which meant their attacks would be suicidal. He gave his sister and mother a look as he passed them, a feeling of worry passing over him. This wasn't how he'd wanted to have this fight.

They had a minute or two before they arrived, but not long. The monsters were fleeing straight down the road, since it was the clearest path, and they would arrive in a moment. Crystal flame began to spiral all around him as he prepared an Essence Shield to block them. A flight of a dozen crystal flame arrows also formed, hanging in the air around him, but he was going to need something bigger than that. Those were just for anything that strayed.

His Aura of Crystal Flame and Flame Strike were both at the Expert tier, which let him create a significant amount of damage, but his Essence Shield was only at Advanced. He needed to boost that before the monsters arrived.

The Storm Striders and Flamecaller Devils looked crazy now. Even on a normal day, they would attack anything in their way. Now, he wasn't sure what they would do. He couldn't divert them to the sides, since that would just send them toward his family. He either had to create a bubble to keep them all safe until the monsters passed or to try and kill them here.

Killing them first was better.

A bubble probably wouldn't work, since the monsters would stop and attack it. There was enough distance from the sun sphere that their natures would revert to bloodthirst. Then it would just turn into a battle to the death anyway.

There was one thing he could do to strengthen his shield, but he hadn't practiced with it too much yet. Plans flickered like crystal lightning through his mind as he decided what to do. He frowned as he extended his senses into his aura storage and sorted through what was available.

Of the auras he'd collected so far, including on the entire trip from Osera, he had six types. There was one Aura of Rebellious Flame, 12 Auras of Reclusive Tide, and 22 Auras of Shifting Shadow left over from the battle with the Bloodweaver. He had added 5 Auras of Thorny Pine, 4 Auras of Verdant Leaf, and 7 Auras of Frozen Lightning on the way home, from various monsters that had attacked them.

It was a good supply, and he'd been frugal in using them. All of them were fully charged to 20 essence. After a moment, he pulled out one of the Auras of Frozen Lightning and held it between his hands. It was a swirling, misty sphere of blue-white light. Miniature bolts of electricity crackled across the surface and through the interior.

It came from a group of Thunderfreeze Bats that had attacked them in a mountain pass halfway to Osera. They were large monsters that hunted in packs, so he'd been able to identify the aura and claim several of them.

The Essence Shield in front of him was a construct of energy and he glanced down at the aura again before he raised it up. His hands slowly pressed into it, flowing into the interior as the lightning and ice crackled around his skin. He hadn't done this much before because it was wasteful of his auras, but this was the right time. He reached out to the newest ability he had, the one he'd gained after reaching Level 40.

Assume Aura.

The aura flowed into his hands and then through them, moving outward to pour all of its stored essence and energy into the shield's structure. The Essence Shield was normally a geometric grid of interlocking hexagons that glowed with the translucent, cerulean light of his crystal flame.

As the Aura of Frozen Lightning flowed into it, a layer of ice began to spread across the surface, along with crackling bolts of electricity. The shield became lighter in color as the energies mixed, more of a white-blue, although it kept the darker blue in the center.

Assume Aura could be used in a couple of different ways, but this one let him pour the energy from an aura into his spells, charging them with unique attributes if he had enough time. It also gave him a way to use the essence he'd stored without having to combust it directly.

The other version of Assume Aura let him temporarily change his body into those attributes, but that was something he hadn't touched yet. He didn't like the idea of it, although it might be useful for something like Shifting Shadow if he needed to hide.

Behind his shield, Krana was raising earthen spikes into a low barrier wall. The spikes were jagged spears of stone that slanted outward at a diagonal angle, pointing down the road. Everyone else dismounted, handing her the reins to the horses so they could fight on foot. She staked the reins to the ground with more earthen spikes, so the horses wouldn't run around when they saw the monsters.

She didn't have as much control over Earth as Ayala had, but she was an Earth Seer and could manipulate it to an extent. Aemilia and Altey stayed near her and a shimmer of mana covered both of them as they made sure their shielding abilities were active. Aemilia had a shielding spell as part of her Seer class and Altey had the amulet. Hopefully, they didn't have to use them.

"What's a Holy Sun sphere?" Aemilia asked as she pulled Altey closer to her. The girl had her fingers wrapped tightly around the new wand in her hand as she stared toward the monsters. They were just visible in the distance now as they raced closer. Her expression was wide-eyed and determined at the same time. She'd never seen monsters charging at her before.

"It's something the Church sells to adventurers," Krana replied, her words choppy as she focused on extending the spike barrier and reinforcing it. "There's Light magic inside it. Expensive, but useful. A good backup if you're overwhelmed, since it scares monsters off. Weaker ones, at least. They don't like Light for some reason. Maybe they were trying to break up the group with it, but they messed it up."

Sam's attention was focused on the approaching monsters. His blood began to hum, the stars of essence scattered through it resonating as his battle intent built. His face was hard as his hands rose into the air again, followed by an intensifying spiral of crystal blue light.

Between his hands, an Essence Blade began to form, the triangular blade of the spell compressing onto itself again and again as the edges hardened and began to shine like diamond. Twenty six points of essence flowed into it.

He had 88 essence total, and he was already down to 46. Nearly all of the energy for the Essence Shield had come from the aura, but he'd infused four points to create the basic structure. He grabbed two of the Auras of Shifting Shadow and combusted them, taking him back to full.

The infused Essence Shield spread in front of the party in a semi-circular wall of electric blue ice. It was twenty four feet across, enough to cover the road and a bit more as it flowed back to either side.

Behind it, Krana's spikes created a semi-circle and she was continuing to add more to make a full circle around the party. His father and Lesat had their weapons drawn and were waiting to either side, near the edge of Sam's shield and inside the spikes, for any monsters that made it through.

As the monsters came closer, Sam stood at the front with the Essence Blade and the flight of crystal flame arrows flaring around him. Behind them, he could see the adventurers gathering together now and starting to chase the pack. They were more than a half mile behind, however, and they weren't going to arrive in time to do anything useful.

The idiots, Sam muttered to himself again. This type of thing was why adventurers had a bad reputation. They caused chaos everywhere they went, broke things in town, intimidated the locals, and generally acted like criminals until they were caught by a military and pressed into forced service.

As the monsters closed the distance, he pushed a last bit of energy into Essence Blade and raised his hands. When they were a hundred yards away, he released it. The spell cut through the Essence Shield with a rippling *hiss* of crackling energy as it shot forward, blurring through the air. It ripped up a trail of dust along the road as shearing winds blasted away from it.

There were nine Flamecaller Devils at the front, their mandibles *clacking* with flames and droplets of black saliva as their four lizard-like legs propelled them across the ground faster than a man could run.

Behind them, the two Storm Striders were following. Their gangly legs looked awkward, but it was an illusion. They had a drifting, ethereal quality to their movements. Their pace was smooth and remarkably fast as they glided forward, their shoulders rolling up and down. It looked like their limbs were rotating around their wasp-like waists.

Behind them, the last Flamecaller Devil followed, howling as it tried to keep up. Its balance was off from the missing arm, and it was stumbling here and there. As Sam's spell approached, the Storm Striders raised their hands in unison, combining their efforts. A whirling wind of fire and lightning sparks formed into a giant blade of spiraling winds in front of them. It was almost as wide as the road. It didn't take them long.

Almost instantly, it shot forward over the heads of the devils. They were trying to block the Essence Blade before it reached the devils, like they'd done against the adventurers. The two spells collided in a twisting hurricane of force thirty feet in front of them. Winds whipped out in every direction, tearing at the road and the dirt.

Four of the devils were too close to it as they continued to run forward, and they were picked up by the blast and thrown off to the sides of the road. A moment later, Essence Blade tore through the windstorm and continued into the ranks of the devils just behind that, where it exploded into an arc of crystal flame.

The explosion had been from the wind blade breaking around it. Its speed had slowed down a little, but the Storm Striders hadn't been able to destroy Sam's spell. The next rank of Flamecallers Devils exploded apart, four of them splitting into chunks that went flying in every direction, and then the remaining energy of the Essence Blade washed over the others.

The crystalline flame slashed across the area as it scattered the remaining devils on the road. When it dissipated, six of them were still alive, as well as the two Striders, but their advance had slowed down.

Most of the devils were sliced or burnt in some way by the flames, but it was minor damage. The Striders were unharmed behind a swirling barrier of elements. Their fangs were bared in a snarl as they focused their attention on Sam, their claws rising to begin another spell.

The monsters were only twenty feet away now, and the Flamecaller Devils ripped up dirt from the road as they caught their balance and raced forward again. Ripples of oily flames poured across their skin as they slammed into the Essence Shield with bone-cracking impacts that caused it to shudder. The flames around them spread forward, *hissing* against the ice and lightning coating the shield as it tried to corrode the barrier.

Here and there, the devils seemed to stick to the barrier, their bodies crackling with icy steam and lightning as their flames and the energy in the shield collided. In one spot, a devil's arm turned whitish, crackling with lightning before it exploded into chunks.

The shield had about twenty four points of essence in it to start, but it was dropping swiftly. The remaining six devils crashed into it one by one, their claws and mandibles tearing at it. Their spit was corrosive as well, and the shield crackled with icy electric bursts as it destroyed the droplets.

An Earthen spear summoned by Krana shot up from the ground in front of the shield, piercing through the leg of one of the devils, but the devil ripped itself free and ignored the wound as it threw itself against the shield again. Cracking thuds echoed along the length of the shield as Sam poured more essence into it, devoting his attention to defense even as he worked with half his attention to condense more crystal flame arrows around him.

Every hit on the shield was draining another point of essence, and his pool was quickly down to 60 again.

If it had just been the Flamecaller Devils, it wouldn't have been a huge danger. They weren't very smart and he could have just picked them off. But with a group of them and with the Storm Striders behind them, it was a different matter.

Jeric and Lesat were already running around the edge of the shield, their defensive spells flaring around them. They could see what was happening as well. They had to relieve some of the pressure on the shield, so Sam could switch back to offense.

If they let the Storm Striders build up a bigger spell, they could be in trouble.

The adventurers were about a half-mile away now and racing closer. Spells surrounded them, but Sam didn't have time to watch what they were doing in detail.

His father was surrounded in a golden-red Earthen Shield as he slammed into one of the devils from the side, his hammers singing through the air. They were still the same weapons that Sam had made for him back in the Abyssinian Plains, but Sam had enhanced the enchantments a bit, adding another layer to make them stronger.

Golden stamina flared as Jeric used a Reverberating Blow, sending his hammer down with a wave of sonic force that crushed the skull of the devil in front of him. Claws scraped along his shield and mandibles snapped on his skin, but glanced off.

On the other side, Lesat hit the devil in front of him with an Enhanced Shield Charge, throwing it back from Sam's barrier, and then he waded forward, his sword slicing out. The enchantments on his armor gleamed as he kept his back to the shield.

The Storm Striders had paused in place now, twenty feet away, and whistling winds were gathering around them as they worked together. Sparks in green, red, blue, white, and yellow began to spiral around them, creating a slowly growing disk. Tearing forces spun above it as the elements collided with each other.

A new wave of crystal flame arrows was forming around Sam, but he could only devote a bit of attention to them as he continued to brace the shield. He couldn't afford to let anything through. Krana's spikes were there, but they were just a backup.

His father and Lesat grabbed the attention of the devils a moment later and pushed them back from the shield a bit, which gave him a chance to turn his efforts toward the Storm Striders. The wave of crystal flame arrows shot toward them, releasing crackling sounds as they shot past the shield.

The elemental storm around the Storm Striders was already nearly forty feet wide and growing larger. It obscured the area all around him and their forms were already starting to blur away inside it, making it clear where they got their name. Five elements were mixed together in their spell, turning it into a chaotic hurricane that flared with fire one moment and caused shards of ice to spray outward a moment later.

If there was any monster that was symbolic of the Storm Plains, it had to be these things. They were immune to all but the most severe storms here. They used them to hunt, looking for travelers pinned down in them. They were one of the reasons no one should travel the plains alone.

The crystal flame arrows shot into the storm with a crackle of essence, tearing their own paths through the wind, but they disappeared as they flew toward the center. There were several explosions that echoed out with dull sounds, but he couldn't tell if they'd hit the striders or not.

He frowned as he began to gather an Essence Blade in front of him, pouring his energy into it. By the time it was formed, his father and Lesat had finished off four of the devils and were pinning down the last two between them, leaving him a clear line of sight. There were another few broken Earth spears from where Krana had joined in on the battle.

He thought his mother had also attacked once or twice, but it was hard to tell. Her only attack spell was illusory.

A moment later, a crackling bolt of icy blue light shot past him, exploding against the inside of his shield. A point of essence flared away, and he glanced back to where his sister was holding the wand he'd given her. His own spells were the only ones that could go through his shield, unless he deliberately opened them.

"Save that in case they get through!" he shouted as he gave her a nod of approval. It had cost him a point of essence to stabilize the shield, but that was fine. He was glad that she was learning to fight.

That was all he had time for, since the Essence Blade came together at that moment. He saw his mother pulling her back before he turned his attention to the Storm Striders.

Ahead of him, the storm began to shake, wisps of the energy burning away as flares of violet light and red streaks slashed through it. He frowned. The only thing that would cause that....

His father and Lesat were working on the last two devils as he released the Essence Blade. It tore through the air and blasted inward, burning away the winds that made up the storm as it headed toward the Storm Striders at the center. He wasn't sure exactly where they were, but it should be close enough.

A moment later, the spell exploded in the center of the storm with a roiling crackle of crystal flame that tore outward, disrupting the other energies as it revealed the gangly forms of the striders. The center of the storm turned blue-white as it became a giant conflagration. The elemental essence the monsters had summoned was reacting with the crystal flame that was burning at it.

The spell caused the storm to become unstable and the disk shape of it began to warp, turning oblong and thinning in areas as the energy in it collapsed.

A new flight of crystal flame arrows followed, heading for the revealed forms of the monsters as they were still trying to deal with the explosion. At the same moment, arcs of twisting violet light flared through the storm from the other side, followed by arcing spheres of red flame.

Unfortunately, those spells missed the striders completely, soaring through the air as they headed for Sam's shield. Sam snarled as the rest of his essence poured out from him, infusing the barrier in front of him. In front of it, Jeric and Lesat saw the approaching spells and tried to dive to the sides.

They managed to get out of most of the blast range, but a couple of the violet arrows exploded against their barriers anyway as they flung themselves away. They hit the ground and rolled, putting some distance between them and the spells before they jumped back to their feet. The rest of the ill-considered spells collided against Sam's shield, shaking it in an explosion of violet steam and arcs of bubbling red flame.

The violet streaks seared Sam's eyes as they impacted the shield, shattering into shards of light that disintegrated as ice lightning lashed back out at them. The red spheres stuck to the shield instead, burning away at it as their energies slowly faded, until they turned ice blue and cracked, exploding away with arcs of lightning.

Cracks tried to appear in his shield, but they sealed themselves over again a moment later as the essence he was pouring into it reinforced it.

The Striders in front of them were half-wounded, and rage boiled through Sam's veins. The song that was always in his blood grew louder, intensifying. Three auras flowed out of his storage and he combusted them, the essence merging into his body as he snarled, his fangs flashing.

Crystal flame exploded upward away from him in a gigantic pillar that roared into the sky. Crystal Focus flowed through every part of it as his mind locked onto the structure of the flames and condensed it, his will forcing it to his design. The pillar condensed as it broke into three dozen crystal flame arrows, which ripped forward through the air, heading for the Storm Striders.

They were injured, and he wasn't going to give them the time to recover. With their storm disrupted, he had to take advantage of the opening. He'd deal with the adventurers after. A moment later, the wave of arrows struck the Storm Striders, exploding through their bodies like streaking meteors.

Even so, they were durable. As the arrows struck them, they didn't shatter to pieces. Their Constitution or innate abilities were too durable for that. Their bodies spun to the left and right, and then back again, twisting like wild, spinning tops in the air as the arrows ripped through them, leaving holes behind. They were flung in one direction and then back in the other, their bodies slowly disintegrating as chunks were ripped away.

By the time all three dozen arrows had passed, there wasn't much left. Their tattered forms wavered in the breeze, their gangly limbs only half attached. Then, like a leaf drifting in the wind, they slowly collapsed to the ground.

All around them, the storm began to clear. The energy in it dissipated into the plains. When it passed, it revealed a group of adventurers standing on the other side, their weapons raised. There were six of them, and their expressions were dark. The Barbarian was at the front and as he saw them, his eyes widened. His face went pale for a moment and then turned red, his expression turning into a snarl as he yelled through the air.

"What the hell are you doing in the way, you damned scum?!" he roared, his words revealing that whatever was inside his skull, it was barely functioning. "Are you trying to steal our monsters?! Hand over the corpses and get out of here, or I'll show you what happens to thieves!"

Sam stared back at him through the Essence Shield, his eyes narrowing into thin lines of disbelief.

Did this idiot think his group had killed all the monsters?

The adventurers had been stupid enough to attack the monsters from the start without planning, scared the monsters into running directly into a group of other travelers, chased them and then attacked without consideration of what was on the other side, and still dared to think they were in the right?

His father and Lesat moved in front of the shield, facing off against the adventurers. Their weapons were in their hands. Jeric's face was much darker than that of the Barbarian. He was also projecting a much more threatening aura, despite the five levels the Barbarian had on him.

Sam glanced back to where his mother and sister were still safe, standing behind his shield. They'd been directly in the line of attack from these adventurers. If the shield hadn't been there....

"Stop there," Jeric growled at the Barbarian. His voice was cutting ice that was growing colder by the word. "You send a wave of monsters at us, attack us, *endanger* my family, and now...*now* you want to come here and threaten us?"

The hammers in his hands hummed as his grip on them tightened, his muscles bulging. The fight had left him with a series of cuts down his arms and legs, and there was a scorched and mottled bruise across his left abdomen where a mandible had tried to take a bite out of him before it was deflected from his skin.

"Twist your head back on straight or I'll do it for you!" Jeric roared, more furious than Sam had ever seen him before. Even Nelgen hadn't made him this angry. It was clear that he wasn't going to give any ground.

The Essence Shield behind Jeric crackled with icy lightning and emphasized his words as Sam pushed a couple more points of essence into it, reinforcing it in case it was needed. At the same time, he pulled another two auras from his storage, combusting them as he stared across the twenty feet to the adventurers. After what he'd just seen, he felt a burning desire in his blood to leave their corpses here on the plains.

No one would miss them.

CHAPTER SEVEN

THE TASTE OF ASHES

The Barbarian stared at Jeric as the threat to twist his head back on straight registered. Then he barked out a rough laugh. Unfortunately for him, Jeric's anger wasn't dissipating, and he took a step back as he assessed the situation.

"For thieves, you have balls." He looked around, taking in Sam and Lesat. His gaze slid away and he frowned as he tried to look at Sam again.

It happened again and he forced it back, trying to focus on him. It was like staring through a hailstorm. His eyes wanted to close and look somewhere else. His gaze drifted away before he could stop it. It gave him an unsettling feeling to not be able to tell who the caster was.

From the giant spell barrier across the road, it was obvious the caster wasn't a pushover. It was a huge barrier and it was crackling with ice and lightning, which meant the caster was strong and specialized in either double elements or a merged one. That was rare.

The guard in full plate was a bit intimidating, since he reminded him of town guards. He couldn't tell his exact class, but it had to be something like that. It was also clear that his armor was heavily enchanted, which wasn't good news. It meant wealth or strong connections. Things that could cause him trouble.

The guard was nowhere near as powerful-looking as the Barbarian-type in front of him though. He didn't know what to make of the angry, bearded man who was standing in his way.

He finally saw the women behind them as he kept looking. His eyes skipped over Krana and settled on Aemilia and Altey, who were clearly being protected, his expression turning to one of disbelief. He shook his head, looking back toward Jeric.

"Who are you people and what the hell are you doing bringing a weak woman and a girl to the Storm Plains? Are you an escort team? What company are you with?" He looked at the monster corpses and at the wounds they had, frowning as he realized that none of those wounds looked like they'd been delivered by his party.

He'd rushed after the monsters to try and get them while they were distracted. His casters had been attacking and he'd thought they'd gotten lucky in killing the Storm Striders when the cloud broke up. He'd expected to find the devils still alive, only to see these people instead. He wasn't one to admit that he was wrong though, even when he saw the truth of it. Instead, he blustered ahead as he focused on Jeric's words.

"You want to play with me? All right, you and me, we'll see who's the real man. Let's settle this. Winner takes all of the corpses and the cores."

Sam shook his head as he analyzed the man.

Human. Warrior-Barbarian. Level 43.

It was clear that he had no idea what he was facing.

Jeric walked forward, golden energy radiating from him. He was about to take the adventurer up on his offer and show him why he should have looked before attacking. If that happened, Sam had no doubt his father would win, but he didn't trust the adventurers enough to let it happen. They would try something.

"Leave now. The corpses are not yours," Sam interrupted coldly, his voice cutting through the air. "All that is yours is the blame for this. You sent a wave of monsters at us and then attacked."

There was a desire for battle singing between the essence stars in his blood that made him want to leap forward and rip the adventurers to pieces with his talons. He pushed the feeling down. Perhaps it would be better for the world if these adventurers were buried here, but the fact that they were human and that it *might* have been an accident was keeping him from attacking them.

His amulet pinged as the Barbarian looked toward him and then away again. He'd combusted five auras now, which was getting close to what he could handle without damaging his meridians. One more would be his limit for the next couple of hours. If he hadn't used so many, this would have gone in an entirely different direction.

The wild attacks from these adventurers had come straight for them, as if they didn't care about attacking other people at all. He wasn't planning to drop his shield until he was sure his mother and sister were safe.

Unfortunately, the Barbarian had to push his luck.

"Who the hell are you to talk to me like that?" His skin turned red as a mist started to form around him again, and he glared toward Sam. His vision kept sliding away, and Sam's amulet *pinged* with the departing charges each time.

"He's my son," Jeric growled, as he looked back to Sam and then Aemilia and Altey. He nodded as he let out a breath. Then he pulled himself back together, firming his stance but not going any farther forward. "You're lucky your attacks didn't harm my wife or daughter. Now get out of here."

"You think you can kill my monsters and take what's *mine*?" The Barbarian growled as he raised his axe into the air. "I don't care if you're the Onyx Hand itself."

As he spoke, the rest of the Barbarian's team moved up behind their leader, presenting a more threatening front as they stared at Sam's group. Of the six, there were two women, the Archer-Scout and the Wizard/Mage, but they glared at Sam along with the rest.

The exchange was interrupted a moment later by the Visionary who was bringing up the rear. He rode up on one of the horses, leading the rest of them behind him. When he saw what was going on, his eyes skipped over their party. His eyes widened as he caught sight of them, and his attention settled especially on Sam. He jumped off his horse next to the Barbarian and leaned over to whisper something in his ear, unaware that his voice carried to Sam's ears.

"Jaser, slow down," the man hissed. "That caster has double unique classes and is an *Outsider*. I don't know why he's working with humans, but don't push him. You know what they're like. He'll use your skull as a wine cup. As for the others, the leader is a rare melee and unique subclass, although it's just a merchant one. The guard is nothing special, but the two women in the back are Seers. That's too much to handle."

The Barbarian paused as he listened. A trace of nervousness flashed through Jaser's expression, but it wasn't the terror Sam would have expected the name Outsider to create. The red mist around him fluctuated and then died down as he turned back to them, staring at them silently. His gaze moved across each of them as his frown deepened, but he focused mostly on Sam. The amulet *pinged* again several times.

The two groups stared at one another across the distance. The corpses of the Storm Striders and the Flamecaller Devils were scattered across the ground and Sam's Essence Shield crackled with lightning, adding an implicit threat.

"Fine." Jaser pulled himself back together and glared at them, but he lowered his axe. "We're not ones to cause trouble, but we have you out-numbered here, two to one with real fighters. Hand over the cores and you can keep the rest."

"No," Sam spoke before anyone else could say anything. His voice res-onated with contained anger. To the adventurers, he was an enigma. The only sign of his power was the giant barrier across the road, which crackled threateningly with his words. "You will leave."

Jaser tried to stare at Sam again. Then he gave the Visionary a glare as if it were his fault. His hands clenched as he tightened them around his axe, the knuckles whitening.

"Fine," he snarled after a moment. "We'll keep you in mind in the future." He turned to the others, waving his hand as he yanked the reins of his horse away from the Visionary. "Let's go."

The party slowly rode away, growing more distant as Sam watched. His frown deepened as he watched them go, a flare of crystal flame surging around him. Jaser's reaction to him being an Outsider was less than he'd expected.

That was strange.

He wasn't sure what the result of this encounter would be, but it wasn't good news. Unfortunately, he couldn't do anything about them knowing. Not unless he wanted to kill them all. The thought crossed his mind, but it wasn't who he was. It left the taste of ashes in his mouth.

A lot depended on what they did with the information, and if anyone was able to find him and his family and act on it. The information was going to get out eventually anyway, as soon as a Seer saw him, but he'd have to hope the Guardian Star kept the bigger players from acting.

No one else had heard what the Visionary had said, not unless Krana or his mother had somehow, but he'd have to tell them in a minute. He pushed the thought aside as he focused on what was more immediate. He looked back at his mother and Altey again. Aemilia looked angry as she stared after the adventurers. His sister just looked confused. Her wand was still gripped tightly in her hand. Both of them were fine.

His father's injuries were minor and would fade shortly, since his Constitution was over 80 now. That was also why the devils hadn't been able to really harm him. He would be fine. Lesat was a bit more banged up. His left arm was torn up, with scorched blood and mangled steel wrapped around it, and his armor had seen better days. The devils had broken through the enchanted barrier and torn gouges in it, destroying sections of the metal.

His shield was barely recognizable. The once smooth edges of the kite shield had bites taken out of it and there were large chunks missing. It was covered in scorch marks and acid-etched trails from the devils' saliva. The repair enchantments might be able to handle it, but it would take a week or so. The guard would have to add some new metal and keep infusing the repair enchantment with mana.

Despite that, their hasty defense had worked. Partly because he'd used up so many auras. Lesat's arm was the only thing that needed real attention. Sam shook his head as he reached into his belt pouch and pulled out a healing scroll, passing it to Lesat. The guard had his own, but Sam had more of them.

Lesat nodded his thanks and unfurled the scroll in his hands, activating it. A moment later, a surging aura of white light rose out of the scroll, flowing around his body as his wounds began to heal.

"Let's collect the experience," Sam said finally, his mood improving as he looked toward the corpses. He'd used up more auras than he'd wanted to, but at least everyone was fine.

He leaned over and touched a devil corpse that was near him, searching for the aura in it. He'd seen it while he was fighting, a bright orange-red energy that ran through their bodies. It didn't take long. A sense of liquid flame filled his mind, with a flavor like a volcano mixed with tar. It was magma mixed with pockets of dark oil compressed beneath the earth. An explosive pressure accompanied it, waiting for a breeze to ignite it into an inferno.

You have encountered an unknown aura.

Do you wish to Reclaim it (35% chance) or to Identify it?

His Wisdom was up to 46 now, and 52 with the Staff of Withering Stasis, but the chance to reclaim an unknown aura had maxed at 35%. The increased Wisdom did make it easier to identify things, however. The aura burned away in his grasp, consuming itself in a self-contained explosion that left behind the taste of scorched earth and boiling coal.

The aura has been consumed.

Your Fire Affinity has boosted your chance to Identify this aura (10%).

You have Identified the aura.

Aura of Compressed Flame.

The aura dissipated, turning to strands of energy as the remaining part of it flowed away into the world. A moment later, a new notification appeared, one that he wasn't expecting. It was accompanied by silver chimes that resonated with joyous abandon in his mind.

Congratulations, Battlefield Reclaimer.

For Identifying an Aura in a single attempt, your Identify Aura ability has reached the Advanced Tier.

Advanced: You gain a +10% chance to Identify new auras in a single attempt.

Sam glanced at the notification before nodding in appreciation. He'd been wondering what it took to get that ability, and his others, to Advanced. It looked like the Advanced tier added a 10% chance to instantly Identify an aura. It should also improve his ability to Identify higher-level auras, although he hadn't seen anything except a Basic one so far. He needed to get Reclaim Aura up first.

There were nine more of the devils, and he went around to each of them, reaching down to collect their auras.

Reclaiming Basic auras that he'd identified was easier than it had been in the past. His success had maximized at an 85% chance once he hit 45 Wisdom. With his Fire Affinity adding another 10% on these, it was almost guaranteed. In short order, he collected the remaining nine auras and he felt a bit better about his expenditures.

Then he turned to the Storm Striders, leaning down over their corpses. As he did, he couldn't help studying their strange bodies and the mottled grey patterns on their pale skin. They were strange things. *What had created monsters like this?*

He touched the corpse of one, searching for the thread of aura, and it came to him in a whirlwind of clashing elements filled with streaks of shattered light and shadow. Lightning, wind, earth, ice, fire, and wood swirled through the world, colliding and separating in a hurricane force as they were all pulled around a dark center. It was a void that reached out to consume the elements, pulling them toward itself.

Do you wish to Reclaim this aura (35% chance) or to Identify it?

It was tempting to try and reclaim it, but he chose to identify it. There would probably be more Storm Striders in the future. The whirlwind swirled through his mind. He could sense the different elements swirling around the darkness at the center, each of them held apart and made to cooperate under its influence. The energy at the center dwarfed everything around it, easily ten times stronger than any element by itself. Then it was gone, as the aura burned itself away to nothing in his grasp.

Identification is 60% complete.

Your chance to reclaim this aura has risen to 55%.

Sam frowned as he reached down and touched the other Storm Strider, or what was left of it. His spells had ripped this one apart more than the other and it was in several pieces. Fortunately, that didn't affect the aura or experience it had.

The whirlwind filled his mind again and his impression of the mixed elements became even stronger, and for just a moment he had a flash of understanding for how they could all cooperate, their principles balanced in cooperation. Before he could remember it, it was gone, the aura dissipating in his hands.

You have Identified an aura.

Aura of Elemental Void (Basic).

Your chance to reclaim this aura has risen to 85% percent.

He frowned as he looked down at the Storm Strider and shook his head. He needed to get Reclaim Aura to Advanced, and then maybe he could get an Advanced aura out of monsters. After that, he went around collecting experience from the corpses, joining everyone else.

Threads of bubbling energy flowed into his body, sparkling like effervescent stars of merriment. It helped him to relax a bit, as the energy boosted his mood and filled his spirit. All around, everyone was doing the same thing, touching each corpse as they walked past it.

One thing he'd come to understand more about over the past few months was how party experience worked. There was a part of his status sheet where he could request that the World Law divide experience equally with his party. Ever since he'd found it, it had been set that way. He just needed to go around and collect his part from each monster. That was what everyone else was doing at the moment. Before long, more threads of bubbling energy were soaring through his blood, which made him feel a bit more cheerful.

You have used your Class abilities to slay your enemies.
You gain 210,500 Class experience.
Total Class Experience: 3,355,040 / 3,437,500

It wasn't enough to raise his level, but it did put him with less than 100,000 to go until Level 46. It was getting close. There was no notification about reaching the experience maximum. That had increased significantly after passing Level 40, and it continued to go up with each level. It would take a larger fight than this to hit it.

Experience was an extremely potent energy, and his body could only handle so much of it at once. He shook his head as he started to search for the cores in the Storm Striders. The two he'd used for his sister's wand and amulet had been the last ones he had.

These and the Flamecaller Devils should both have decent cores, which meant that he could get started on some of the other projects he had in mind. His thoughts were focused on the future as he tried to put the adventurers out of his mind, debating how to tell his family that the news was out.

***

Unnoticed, a hawk floated in the sky above them. It was more than a mile away and its eyes were fixed on remains of the battle below. The Beastcaller behind it felt a sense of astonishment after what had just happened and he shook his head.

He was Level 40, but he would not have wanted to be in front of that horde of monsters. He was impressed, and also happy that Nijama, the head bandit, had decided not to attack them. Watching them had proved it wouldn't be an easy fight.

If they'd shown everything they could do, he had confidence that the Silver Vipers could win, but they might have to call out the totem to deal with that strange caster. The thought made him shiver. The Silver Viper required a large price to make an appearance, one that was paid in blood and mana. It wasn't something to do lightly.

He ordered the hawk to continue to follow them, but he planned to keep as far away as possible. He just needed to see which way they were going.

CHAPTER EIGHT

A THOUSAND RUNIC LEAVES

"So, that Barbarian knows you're an Outsider," Jeric frowned as he took in Sam's words. The fork toward Highfold was just ahead of them and the afternoon sun was bright in the western sky, radiating out a liquid gold energy across the horizon.

"What I don't understand is why he had so little of a reaction to it." Sam frowned. "The Visionary with him made it sound like they were familiar with Outsiders...and not just as enemies. It doesn't make sense."

The Visionary's words echoed in his mind. *"I don't know why he's working with humans, but don't push him. You know what they're like."*

"That means they've talked to one before, or they work with them." Aemilia spoke up, her voice calm, as she turned in the saddle to look toward her son. As always, her words were insightful. "Even if it's hard to believe, we have to consider that."

It had taken his mother a couple of days to adjust to being a Seer on the road, but she was on top of it now. Krana had helped to show her what to do and she was constantly scanning the area around them, pushing the boundaries of her abilities. His mother had gained a lot of general experience from the battle, taking her up to General Level 27. Her class hadn't leveled from that, but it had already reached Level 8 from her efforts during the journey.

Most of her attribute points had gone into Wisdom and Intelligence, as well as a bit of Constitution, and her mind was sharper than ever. Sam had no doubt that leveling up to higher tiers would come naturally to her.

"That's what I don't understand," Sam grumbled. He understood the logic, but he still found it strange. "How could he know about other Outsiders, or have met them? Wouldn't the World Law disapprove?"

"Maybe, and maybe not," his father shook his head as he glanced over. "The World Law has troubles, which show up as Flaws and more, like our old class. It may not be able to keep track of everything. If some weaker Outsiders came in, or had a way to hide themselves, or the church didn't find the Flaw in time...." Jeric's words led in the same direction as Sam's thoughts.

"So, there might be more Outsiders around," Sam concluded with a sigh. "The question is what they're doing here."

"Whatever they want, most likely," Aemilia said, shaking her head. "We can't assume they have a concerted plan or that they're even working together. Every myth says that Outsiders are chaotic and destructive."

"And clever," Sam agreed. "They may be hiding from the church or even working with mercenary bands or merchants from behind the scenes, which would explain Jaser's group knowing about them. It would help them gather resources...or whatever else they want."

"More importantly, what does that mean for us?" Jeric brought up the next point as he looked toward Sam, his gaze concerned. "Is it going to be easier for you or harder, if people are on the lookout?"

"Remember that city walls have wards against illusions," Krana was riding nearby and looked over, shaking her head. "That's one reason Sam never entered the major cities before this. His amulet isn't good enough to block them yet. Highfold is a smaller city, but it will likely be the same."

"So, this problem may be well known to the forces in power..." Aemilia concluded, as she gave Krana a long look. "There has to be a reason the cities have wards for that. It also suggests the Outsiders might have found a way around them."

It was both good news and bad, and Sam was being forced to adjust his perspective of the world again. For a while now, he'd thought he was the only Outsider in the world. Growing up, myths of Outsiders had always been of great monsters and demons that destroyed cities and terrorized the world, but perhaps those were only the most famous ones.

On the positive side, it meant that the higher forces of the world might ignore him more than he thought, as long as he didn't cause trouble and tried to stay away from them. On the other side, it meant that there might be organized efforts by the church or cities to find Outsiders that they *knew* were around, so they could eliminate them. He didn't feel like being caught up in some general purge.

"I'll create a place outside of the city to stay until I can get around the wards," he added, thinking about it. Staying in Highfold would be best for his family, but not for him.

There were probably some areas outside the city where he could find an inn. That was what he'd done near Osera and Ebonfar. Cities were usually surrounded by smaller villages and markets that wanted to avoid the taxes inside, as well as the city guard.

"Are you going to be in trouble?" Altey asked, joining in on the conversation from where she was riding in front of him.

"No, it will be fine," Sam said immediately, shaking his head. "I'll just stay out of the way of anyone looking for Outsiders." He didn't say that it might be hard to do.

"I'll protect you from anyone who wants to bother you," Altey declared, tilting her head up to look back at him.

"I'm the big brother," Sam laughed, ruffling her hair. "I'm supposed to take care of you."

"I can help," she insisted, giving him a determined look as she tried to be fierce. At that moment, she looked very protective. Her eyes were sharp and there was a serious frown on her face.

"One day, you will be Altey the Magnificent, Archmage of the Seven Winds." Sam grinned as he ruffled her hair again. "Then no one will dare to contradict you."

"I will be," Altey agreed immediately, nodding at him. The wand he'd given her was tucked into her belt within easy reach, and the defensive amulet was hanging around her neck.

To the side, Krana's eyes suddenly flared with a bright silver gleam as she turned her attention to Altey. She let out a thoughtful *hmm* as she rubbed at her chin, giving the girl a long, meditative look. She didn't say what she'd seen.

Sam just grinned down at his sister.

***

One day rolled into the next as they encountered the fork in the road that led toward Highfold. Other travelers were rare, but two or three appeared in a day now, usually a merchant wagon or a small party of adventurers. Most kept to themselves, nearly as wary of other travelers as they were of monsters. Bandits were always a problem on the road. Adventurers and small mercenary groups could also cause unwanted trouble.

Since the encounter with Jaser's group, Sam had been thinking through what he could do to improve himself and gain more strength. That event had raised several key issues in his mind.

The first was that he needed to figure out a way to upgrade his amulet, to see if he could make it block Analyze. The original model from Krana had that capability, so even without the complete pattern, there had to be something he could do. There were quite a few runes on the original amulet that he wasn't familiar with. Dozens of them, in fact. There were also more patterns connecting them that he needed to figure out.

He was an Advanced Enchanter, but he still felt like his understanding of the basics was a bit haphazard. In terms of upgrading the amulet, he didn't have the ability yet, but he could plan for the future. He had plenty of Earth mana, but he would need some rare materials, ones that could augment the enchantment.

Embradium, perhaps. It was a well-known metal that augmented magical effects. He'd have to talk to Krana about what could work. Her knowledge of materials was much larger than his still.

The second thing he needed to do was to improve his spells, especially his understanding of Crystal Flame. He needed to study it at a deeper level and create more spell versions that he could use for Flame Strike and Essence Shield.

As for whether or not there were Outsiders around in the world, he set that thought to work at the back of his mind as he focused on the training that he could accomplish now.

The pattern of the illusion amulet appeared in his mind, outlined in crystal blue flames as it spun in three dimensions. The gaps on the interior where he didn't have the pattern were more clear to him than ever. He kept just a thread of attention on the world around him, enough to keep Altey balanced and the reins in his hands, as he turned his attention inward.

One by one, he began to isolate the runes that he didn't know, sorting them out as he copied them into columns to the side. He had quite a few python hides and other assorted skins in his dimensional bags that could be used as a base material. To experiment with these, he didn't need to create a full spell scroll. Instead, he would inscribe each one onto a small piece of hide, perhaps a rectangle that was a few inches long and an inch or two wide.

The hide would absorb his essence better than regular wood or stone. The wood or leaves from the elemental trees on the plains might also work, since they were infused with mana. He could gather some leaves from the trees when they stopped.

All he needed to do was inscribe a rune and a simple activation pattern, and maybe a storage rune for extra power if the rune was complex. The result would be something like a talisman, but a reduced version. Then he could practice activating them and see what they did. With each new rune he learned, he would add more to his capabilities.

With the outline of an idea in place, he continued sorting through the field of crystalline runes, organizing them into columns by how simple or complex they were. Then he further arranged the columns by difficulty, dividing them into ones that seemed related to runes he already knew and ones that were completely unfamiliar.

By the time he was done, there were 48 runes in the simple column, 32 in the advanced column, 71 in the expert column, and 178 that were completely unknown and even more difficult.

He had his work cut out for him.

***

That night, they stopped near a grove of nimbus willows. It was a type of Wind elemental tree that had long, swaying branches that dropped in elegant arcs until they brushed across the top of the grass below. Misty clouds spiraled along the branches and wound between the long, spear-shaped leaves, leaving silver streamers in the air.

As he walked through the grove, he gathered hundreds of leaves and even some pieces of stray wood, taking a bit from each branch that he walked past. He added it all to a swiftly accumulating collection of materials in his dimensional bags. He'd gathered some along the road from other elements as well, and he would continue to do so. They were free crafting materials now.

He'd also given a large python hide to Lesat and had him cut it into perfectly rectangular slips. Each of them was three inches long by one and a half inches wide. The guard's subclass as a Leatherworker meant he had some abilities to manipulate skins quickly, including *Model Pattern, Mend, Fuse Material,* and *Prepare Leather.*

His main focus was on mending materials, which let him repair things more easily, and he'd upgraded that ability to Advanced when he hit twenty. It hadn't taken him long to reduce the python hide to a pile of slips for Sam to use.

With all of his materials gathered, Sam returned to the clearing where his family was and set up his worktable. Of the options on the Storm Plains, Wind leaves were probably the best elemental material to use for unknown runes. Wind had the habit of augmenting other elements, rather than conflicting with it.

Wind and Water turned into rain...Wind and Fire into an inferno, and so on for the other elements. The Storm Plains themselves were proof enough of that. Wind was behind all of the storms here. Not every rune would have a primary element, since some of them were far more abstract, but it was a good place to start.

As he got comfortable, his mind turned to the first column of runes, the simple ones that were probably Basic or Advanced. Runes didn't perfectly follow the tiers, so he'd been guessing when he sorted them. Included in the column were also symbols that might be part of binding, support, or storage patterns. He wasn't sure what everything was yet.

48 simple runes.... He'd have to try out each one in a few different ways. The python hide would be his default material and then he'd test each one out on the nimbus willow and other leaves after that, to see if it had a different effect. He would also only use his own mana and aura for this, to minimize unintended effects.

His stylus and a slip of python hide appeared in his hand as he started to draw the first rune in the column. At the same time, he was examining it from every side as he turned a model of it around in his mind, working to understand it more deeply. This one looked a lot like the rune for "sight," but it was a version he wasn't familiar with. It might be something else entirely.

It didn't take long for him to draw out the rune. It was just a few curves of his stylus and a small infusion of essence, about a point. He kept the expenditure low so the rune wouldn't be too dangerous. It was from an illusion amulet and not a weapon, but that didn't mean it was harmless. A rune for darkness or light could turn into a nice explosion if there was enough mana behind it.

When he was done, the leather slip had the single unknown rune at the center and an activation rune connected to it that was charged with a single point of essence. He walked a little bit away from the clearing and surrounded himself with an Essence Shield. Then he touched the activation point as he tossed the slip away from him.

A moment later, the hide slip exploded into a flare of energy. A small twist of white-blue energy appeared, twining around itself. Then the mana in it burned out, the energy dissipating into the air. As it did, the resonating *hum* of a concept was in the air, and Sam's ears tilted toward it as he concentrated on the fading energy. It was a song particular to this rune. Flickers of meaning flowed away from the explosion, but they were too quick to grasp.

When the energy was gone, he studied where it had been, his gaze considering. It was as if he'd heard one note in a song, just a fraction of the whole.

"Well, let's do it again," he muttered as he headed back to make another slip. Perhaps if he heard it enough, more of the song would become clear to him.

For the rest of the evening, one small, brilliant explosion after the other flared through the clearing. Sam's shield blocked the sound from traveling, and as everyone started to go to sleep, he strengthened it so it blocked the light as well. Each time a slip exploded, a strange, ethereal note rippled through the air.

***

As they stayed on the main road to Highfold, travel became easier and the quality of the road continued to improve. It wasn't up to the standards of the central kingdom yet, but it had turned from a barren track to a more established road made from large paving stones. Hundreds of years of carts and travelers passing over it had left wide ruts, which made him glad they were riding horses and not on a cart. It would have been a bumpy trip.

Altey was riding with Krana today as he continued to practice with runes. His stylus was in his hand as he pulled a nimbus willow leaf out of his pouch. A quick sketch of a rune and an activation symbol turned it into a hasty talisman, and he tossed it to the side of the road as he activated it. A moment later, there was a flare of bright green light as a wind surged away from the twist of mana, leaving the haunting sound of a harp in the air.

"Hmm, something to do with *voice*, maybe," Sam muttered, as he listened to the sound of it. "Perhaps to enhance it?"

Or it could have been related to music. Maybe the real illusion amulet could hide sounds as well, or create them.

The first rune was related to *color*, as it turned out. He'd had to combine it with a different rune for *vision*, and then it had worked to change the color of things. After a bit of practice, he'd shown it to Altey, who had thought it was an excellent game. Now, her clothes looked like a rainbow.

He'd just given his mother a grin when she asked him what he was doing, and told her it would wear off in a few days. It was the most harmless version of magic he'd ever used, and it was fun. With more of a combat focus, the rune could be used to make a camouflage spell, if he worked with a few other things to enhance it, but it was nice to have something to play around with that wasn't so serious.

A couple of minutes later, another hasty talisman exploded off to the side of the road, releasing the same sound of a harp. It was a bit lower in pitch and had less force than before. He'd used the python hide for this one, so the Wind element wasn't augmenting it.

He moved the rune over to a new "sound" category in his mind as he started to make a new slip. Even if a rune didn't have an immediate use, it was still important. Great things couldn't be built without smaller parts. The illusion amulet had all of these runes for a reason. Perhaps if he understood enough of them, he could figure out how to walk invisible through a crowd, conceal his voice behind a barrier, or completely change his appearance.

All of those would be a step in the right direction.

In order not to bother the others with the explosions, he continued to surround them in an Essence Shield, which gave him the advantage of practicing with that ability too. He was working to block out the exact qualities of the light and sound generated by each explosion, which forced him to focus his attention and sped up his comprehension of the rune.

Slowly, as hour after hour passed and one day flowed into the next, the number of leaves and hide slips that he went through grew. One turned into a dozen, and a dozen into a hundred. Each rune gave off a unique note as its energies flared to life.

From a hundred, it became more, until a thousand runic leaves swirled through the world around him in a river of enchantment. The current carried away the ones that had sung their song, and more continued to replace them in an endless stream. The echoes built into a melody in his mind, one that advanced slowly toward greater understanding.

CHAPTER NINE

REDFROST PINE ENCHANTMENTS

A couple of days later, they stopped for the night near a grove of scattered redfrost pines. A lone merchant wagon was the only other traveler on the road here, heading in the opposite direction. They waited for it to pass before they cut off into the grove, which was far enough away to give them some privacy.

After everyone was settled in, Sam set up his work table and returned to his enchanting practice. Caelus, the distant blue moon, was a quarter of the way up in the sky, marking that it was halfway between dusk and midnight. To the side, he flicked a talisman that he'd been working on, listening to the note it made as it burned away in the air.

It was a new rune, the eighteenth from the simple column. Of the ones so far, he'd identified runes for *color, voice, sound, image, sight, harp, flute, shout, music, shape, obscure, vibration, silence, soft, loud, heat,* and *air.* The last two were probably some form of self-heating enchantment that was bound into the original, which was designed to keep the wearer comfortable.

Several of the runes were variants of runes that he already knew, which had sped up the process of learning them. He wasn't sure why there were variant runes, but he had the feeling that if he understood the song that went to them, it would all make sense. It probably had something to do with tilting them toward one affinity or another, like projecting *sound* compared to hearing it.

At any rate, his knowledge was expanding. The notes he could hear that were unique to each rune were still hanging in his mind, like stars in a galaxy. He wasn't sure if it was really a sound or some part of the rune's innate magic that he was interpreting as that.

Its inherent concept.

It was something that he was starting to understand in a broader way, even after just a few days of working with the new runes. The more he understood the concept of a rune, its path of magic and truth, the better he would be able to use it. It was the essential truth of it that underlay its existence in the world.

At the moment, as a way of understanding each of the runes, he'd come up with a new game for Altey, which let him practice at the same time as keeping her busy. He'd taken a collection of different elemental woods, each of them a rectangle about two inches long and less than an inch wide. Then, he'd inscribed all the runes related to sound that he knew on them, a distinct one to each, and strung them together into a necklace.

When she touched a rune with a bit of her mana, it created a note. It was a sort of musical necklace. Based on the amount of aura he'd infused and its harmless nature, it would last for a week or so before the wooden slips crumbled.

Altogether, it had runes for *sound, shout, whisper, music, harp, flute, soft, loud, silence,* and *voice,* with differing elemental affinities from the woods they were made from that changed the quality of the sound they produced. It was perfectly noisy and awful, which meant that Altey loved it.

She spent all day playing with it, infusing tiny pulses of mana to see what sort of sounds she could make. The road around her echoed with ghostly whispers, booming shouts, airy harps, shrill flutes, and other random things. His mother was already exasperated.

He grinned as he turned back to his work, his job as older brother complete for the day. In his defense, it was good magical training. She got to practice infusing her mana in a way that had a realistic effect, reinforcing the basic concepts that would be useful to her in the future. With a bit more practice, she would probably unlock Mana Control as soon as she had her Class Day.

He started to inscribe the eighteenth rune onto another nimbus willow leaf, studying its structure as he let the echoes from it resonate in his mind. It slightly resembled the rune for *shield,* but it was a bit different. It took three deft movements of his stylus to finish inscribing it again, and then a few more to surround it with a simple support structure. When it was ready, he infused it with a point of essence and tossed it away from his work table, watching more closely for the flow of energy.

This time, as the rune ignited, the energy in it flowed outward, forming into a sort of silver-white bubble, and then it shattered, popping like a soap bubble with a soft *tiiiingg* as it faded away into the air. He rubbed his chin as he looked at where it had been, recalling the form it held as he let the sense of it flow through his awareness.

Time began to pass around him, and he felt the two traits that he'd gained months ago nudging at him, accelerating his thoughts and helping him to fall into the flow of the rune's meaning. *Craftsman* helped him fall into a working trance where time felt like it didn't matter, letting him concentrate for long periods without getting distracted. The words of the World Law echoed in his mind as he called the trait up again.

"You will find it easier in the future to fall into a working trance and to endure long hours of labor. You will also find it easier to relate to other Craftsmen, gaining a natural Charisma bonus when speaking with them."

The second trait, *Mystical*, was more enigmatic and perhaps even more valuable. *"You will find that it is easier to understand natural forces in the future."* He wasn't sure how the trait was helping him, but it was true that understanding the runes was moving quickly, at least for the simple ones.

He switched to python hide for the next talisman, and then to a sliver of redfrost pine wood, watching how the energy changed as it moved through affinities. The results left him a bit puzzled. Unlike the other runes so far, this one wasn't changing when he used different materials for it.

He leaned forward, his elbows on his work table, as he observed the flow of energy in the air through all of his senses. The meaning of it was just...there. He poured his attention toward it, reaching out with his essence to touch the concept behind the rune. Then, like lightning striking as he crossed over some unnamed barrier, the name and meaning of the rune rumbled through his mind.

Barrier. The rune formed in his mind, outlined in crystal flame as it shimmered there, demanding his attention. He held himself still, breathing in time with the flow of the rune's meaning as he touched it, turning it this way and that.

It was more abstract than *shield*, focused on other concepts. Shield was for blocking damage. This one was for blocking other things. It was the first of the runes he'd seen that might lead him in the direction of how to block *Analyze*, a fragmented gift arriving in the midst of the night. It wasn't enough by itself, but it was a step in the right direction.

His hand flashed out, carving the rune in the air as crystal flame trailed after his fingers, as he tried to inscribe it into the wind on a sudden surge of inspiration. The crystal flame crackled, holding its shape for just a moment, as he felt the beginning of a translucent barrier forming, and then it flowed away.

His depth of understanding still wasn't quite enough to hold the meaning of the rune in its entirety with just his will. A new nimbus willow leaf appeared in his hand as he took advantage of the moment of enlightenment and began to inscribe it again. This time, his rune had more depth to it, a quality that seemed to pervade the symbol and make it more than just a series of lines and swirls.

The meaning resonated, like the work of a sculptor whose touch was ineffable and inspiring, adding just that extra *something* to the work that made it a masterpiece. He had touched upon the concept behind it and the rune was starting to come to life.

As he inscribed the rune, he spent longer meditating on it, feeling for the meaning that was unique in it. It wasn't just a note in a melody now. There were other layers past that. The runes were representations of natural power, truth in a condensed form. That was how they channeled mana to create an effect.

As he focused on studying the rune, the air around him occasionally rippled with ethereal currents of energy as his aura and the world interacted, forming translucent barriers that faded away again a moment later.

***

With the rune fresh in his mind, he fiddled with a piece of redfrost pine, turning it over in his hands as he poured crystal flame into it. It was a couple of times larger than the usual slips, and he'd selected it from the best quality wood he could find around the clearing.

Redfrost pine had a blue-red hue, as if blood had frozen inside a deep blue glacier and then given rise to a tree. In the depth of the wood, there was a rich sanguine hue, which turned sky blue as you looked over the grain. It changed with the weather, and the wind turned cold enough, the edges of it would fade to a translucent white, like arctic ice.

There was something ineffable about it that made it hard to comprehend, similar to a rune. He was coming to realize that just like a rune, the world itself existed in layers of understanding. Perhaps that was what ability tiers helped you to access, putting you in touch with deeper and more real forms of power that could be molded to your will, if you had the capability.

His talons tapped along the wood as he continued to turn it around in his hands and purify it with his aura. The blood and ice colors of the wood were intensifying as he did, and the grain was becoming smoother, less visible. When it was ready, he chose not to use his stylus to inscribe it. Instead, he used his talons directly, slowly carving the *barrier* rune into the center of the wood. His talons were as sharp as blades, and the work proceeded quickly.

His stylus felt like an extension of his body when he used it, but it was still a tool. His talons were truly part of him and infused with the purest form of his aura.

CraaaAAack. A moment later, the rune rippled on the surface of the wood, and then the entire chunk of wood exploded into fragments, sending chunks whistling away until they crashed into a hasty Essence Shield. For just a moment, a translucent barrier gleamed where the wood had been, its presence more clear than before.

He let out a deep breath as he picked up the next piece of wood, a smaller one this time, and pulled his aura in tighter. Then he began to purify the new material. In the end, his stylus was a tool. A useful one, but it was still a layer of separation between him and the meaning of the runes, isolating his aura from them. He needed a more direct experience, even if it resulted in explosions.

For a while after that, the evening peace of the forest glade was lit by the cerulean glow of his crystal flame as he purified and inadvertently destroyed one piece of redfrost pine after another. But with each section, he came a little bit closer to fusing his aura with the meaning of the *barrier* rune. If he could get it exactly right, it would be a sign that he understood the rune well enough to balance the energy with his own. Perhaps that could actually be called the first level of mastery.

He didn't know if any other Enchanter used this type of system to understand their work, but it felt like the right path to him. If he could learn how to engrave a rune with just his aura, he could hold the concept of it in his crystal flame. Where he could go with it was unknown, but it would be one step closer to the level of a natural rune, like the lightning runes that existed across the Storm Plains or the Song of the Earth from when his father gained his subclass.

Another explosion *crackled* through the area as the piece of wood he was working on shattered, turning to dust in his hands. Splinters flew away from his skin in a glowing, sanguine cloud. Fortunately, there was a lot of wood in the grove.

***

Sam's work to understand the runes continued as they traveled for that day and the next. He'd collected hundreds of pieces of redfrost pine to use. Something about its colors appealed to him, especially how it changed to a translucent white. It reminded him of his crystal flame, so it had become his new favorite base for testing ideas.

Fortunately, there were nearly endless forests to discover on the Storm Plains, and the proportion of it to other types of trees was increasing as they continued down the road toward Highfold. It was a popular tree in the mountains, and that was where the city got its name.

The elevation of the land was slowly increasing as they followed the road, cutting up gradual switchbacks in the rolling hills that went up more than they went down. Behind him, when he turned to look, the Storm Plains were visible for dozens of miles.

The rivers of mana, swathes of grass, and dense forest groves were scattered across the land, as haphazard as a child's set of toys as they followed a rhythm that was entirely their own. They weren't that high up in the mountains yet, but the view was even better from here than it had been from the walls of Cliff's End. The sight of the land stretching away in front of him made something in his spirit relax, as if the world had suddenly become a little lighter. Above, the clouds drifted in a spiral of purple-white, silver, and rose gold, backlit by the midmorning sun.

Ahead of them, the mountains rose ever higher, climbing in a series of jagged white and blue peaks like a dragon's teeth as they formed the Western Reaches, the tallest mountain range in the interior of the kingdom. Up there, all sorts of monsters and beasts were common, from griffins and wyverns to frost titans and icescale wyrms. Those were the monsters that embodied the ice and wind and the sere frost of the sky. There were also other elements, but the Western Reaches were known for their cold.

He glanced down at his belt, where his dimensional bags were, and nodded slowly as he considered what else his family might need to be comfortable there. Heating stones, perhaps even self-contained enchantments on their clothing, more defensive amulets.... Maybe other things.

Along with his work on the simple runes, he'd also been starting to work on message amulets for all of them, an idea he'd had for a long time now. With his growing understanding of enchantments, he thought he'd finally figured out a way to transfer the enchantment from a message scroll onto an amulet and to make it permanent, with a monster core as the base.

With the right inscription, he might even be able to link them together, to create a sort of communication web between all of them, and a way to signal if the amulet lost contact with its owner. That way, if Altey or anyone were in trouble, they would all know it. He didn't think Highfold would be a directly hostile location, but that didn't mean he trusted it completely.

Once they arrived, perhaps he could open a business selling similar enchantments to the people there. Offering solutions to common problems was a popular service. It would be better than selling weapons or enchanted armor. That would get a lot of attention he didn't want and there was something in him that rebelled against the idea of providing his enchantments to someone who might use them against him.

Selling things to help people survive in the wilderness and that might improve their lives was better. Maybe he could also sell some smaller, more casual things, like the toys he'd made for Altey, if people were interested in enchantments to change the color of their clothes or an amulet to project their voice over a crowd.

Ideas flickered through his mind as he took in the stark peaks of the mountains that pierced the sky.

***

The effort to engrave the *barrier* rune with solely his talons was gaining traction, but he ended up setting it aside for a bit the following day to work on something that wouldn't explode on him. He wanted to test the functionality of the rune against different spells and abilities.

When he was finished with the base material, it was an elegant rectangle of redfrost pine that he'd purified until it glowed with rich hues from deep inside. On the surface of the pine, there was a *barrier* rune surrounded by an intricate support structure and storage runes. This was a proper enchantment, unlike the talismans he'd been fashioning from leaves. He'd used the best of his abilities to create something that would bring out the concept at the heart of it. He gave the enchantment a nod as he reached out and tapped the activation point at the corner of the pine slip, holding his breath as he waited to see what would happen.

A translucent, shimmering dome appeared around him, rotating slowly through the air. Unlike a *shield* spell, it felt thin and nearly invisible, as if it were barely there. There was a hint of frosted blue to it, which came from the redfrost pine's Ice affinity. Without that, it would have been completely transparent. He stood up from his work table and walked toward the others, heading for the circle where they were gathered around the campfire.

"Krana, could you try and Analyze me?"

He doubted it would be so simple, but every success has to begin somewhere. This test would generate more ideas.

CHAPTER TEN

ASCENDING THE WESTERN REACHES

Highfold was still two weeks away on their travels, but the Western Reaches were already looming large above them, their towering forms stretching higher into the sky ahead. The city was nestled on the shoulder of a high peak above one of the rare passes through the mountains.

For the human inhabitants, it was a difficult place to reach without a strong Constitution, since the wind and the cold were fierce. It was said that on a clear night, the wind there could cut through your skin like a blade, leaving only a skeleton beneath the morning sun. It was not a place to visit unprotected.

Humans were not the primary races that inhabited Highfold. It was predominantly settled by mountain dwarves and elemental races, like Wind Sylphs and Ice Sylphs, who delighted in the environment. It was particularly pleasant for the Ice Sylphs, who were the most at home in such a place.

"The dwarves who live there are a particular sort," Krana added, as they continued to ride up through the switchbacks that cut across the foothills. "They've lived there for so long that some folks call them Ice Dwarves, and their classes and natures are certainly more attuned to that element than to others, although they still have a strong connection to the Earth." She paused, raising a hand to shield her eyes as she scanned the peaks rising above them. There was a distant look in her eyes as she thought of their future plans and how she could help.

"I have a couple of connections there that we might be able to meet with for advice," she added. "Friends of my family."

"Ice Sylphs..." Aemilia murmured, as she listened to Krana's suggestion. An old memory occurred to her as she heard the name, one she hadn't thought about in many years. It brought with it a faint memory. "You know, I haven't thought of it in ages, but an old friend of my family used to live here, I think. I wonder if she still does. It's been so long that I barely remember, but she used to come and visit me as a child."

"She was an Ice Sylph?" Altey asked immediately, looking over at her mother. "What are they like? Are they blue?"

Sam was riding along, runes flickering across his talons and through his aura as he continued to practice shaping the ones from the simple column. He gave his sister a grin, shaking his head.

"No, they're not blue," Aemilia laughed as she answered. "Ice Sylphs are an elemental race. They look somewhat like humans, but they are thinner, more magical, and live much longer. She did have blue eyes though, and long white-blue hair that looked like ice." Aemilia's gaze turned inward through the years as she tried to recall the figure she remembered.

"My side of the family lived in Ten Rivers," she added slowly, bringing up a topic that she usually avoided, given the way her family had treated her and cast her aside as a teenager. "Her name was Siwaha...and even then, she seemed ancient. She was kind to me. She was an Herbalist and there was always something about her that was magical.

"She came there to gather herbs from the river valleys, and my family was one of the merchants she dealt with. She used to tell me stories as a child of ice drakes and the wind that lives in caves, high up in the mountains." She gave Altey and Sam both a smile. "I told you both some of those stories when you were small. Do you remember them?"

Sam *hummed* thoughtfully to himself as he thought back to the legends he'd heard as a child, and slowly nodded. It was true that many of them were stories of ice and high mountain peaks. His mother had loved those stories, but he'd never heard where they'd come from before.

There were only a handful of large cities in the Western Province, so it wasn't strange that she had a connection of some type to Highfold. It was just a surprise that she hadn't remembered it until now. It must have been a very distant childhood memory.

Aemilia looked ahead toward the sharp peaks again, her eyes thoughtful. "I hadn't thought of her in years...but Krana's words reminded me. I wonder if she is still here."

"Ice Sylphs live for hundreds of years," Krana reassured her. "It's very likely that she still does, unless she's encountered some calamity since then. When we arrive, we can ask for Siwaha the Herbalist and see if anyone knows of her. If she was powerful enough to travel to the Ten Rivers to gather herbs, she is probably well known."

"It would be wonderful to see her again," Aemilia said with a smile, before something darker passed across her eyes. "Even if I don't speak to my family any longer, I don't think she would hold that against me. She was like a grandmother to me, and always full of stories. I think she liked children."

"Will she tell me stories? What are the Ice Sylphs and the Ice Dwarves like?" Altey asked at that moment, demanding more details. Her eagerness made the rest of the party laugh.

"You'll see when we get there, soon enough," Jeric said with a grin as he teased her. "Why so eager? It'll just spoil the surprise."

"Daaaad!" Altey complained, starting to pout. "Tell me...."

"Haha," Jeric laughed again as he looked over at her.

Then, giving in, everyone began to tell her what they knew about both races.

"Ice Dwarves are a lot like other dwarves," Krana said helpfully. "Their skin color is a bit lighter and their eyes tend toward blue as well. Some of the most interesting craftsmen have abilities to mold ice and stone together into intricate sculptures, and they specialize in enchantments for the same type of thing.

"I understand that Highfold's city walls and all of the major buildings are built with their skills. I've heard that it's an impressive sight and I'm looking forward to it. I haven't been there before either."

"Ice Sylphs..." Aemilia added, "they're hard to describe. I can only tell you a little bit about them. Think of a tall, willowy human with bright blue eyes and ice-white hair. Their complexion tends toward ivory with a light shade of blue. They have an innate grasp of Ice magic, and like all Sylphs, they are in tune with the elements."

"They love the cold and the heights," Krana added. "They're most comfortable there. Their magics are what make the city habitable for humans, too, keeping the worst of the storms at bay, but it's still cold there. You'll need to wear warm clothes."

As the explanation continued, Sam began to nod as plans flickered through his mind. He was perhaps even more interested in the information than Altey, but for a different reason. He wanted to know what he could sell to the people there, and what enchantments he could make for the visitors to the city.

The Festival of Three Crowns was coming up, and they would have about a month to set up shop. Travelers would arrive before that, and he wanted to have some things prepared already. They would need money and a place to stay, and he felt the weight of that responsibility on his shoulders.

He would also need to fashion some type of heating enchantment for his mother and sister, whose Constitutions were not high enough yet to endure the cold. Fortunately, the simple runes from the amulet were already pointing him in the right direction.

***

As they traveled up through the foothills, Sam continued to work on understanding the runes. The first layer of the amulet was designed for ease of life, with runes related to sound, appearance, vision, and personal comfort, including ones for temperature control, like the *air* and *heat* runes he'd learned already.

So far, *barrier* was the only rune that pertained to blocking Analyze, but he could tell that it wasn't the rune's main purpose here. Instead, it was necessary to give the wearer a way to moderate body temperature and block out the sound of voices for privacy. The varied, complex use of the amulet was a window into what was expected of high-level enchantments. It was also a useful discovery, even if it didn't help with Analyze, since it gave him access to a number of runes he could use immediately and fashion into enchantments to sell.

Sound barriers for private conversations, temperature barriers to keep the cold or heat away, illusions to change the color of your clothes or eyes...and a lot more. His mother and sister needed a warming enchantment, and the Ice Sylphs in the city might be just as interested in a cooling enchantment.

For practice, he started to create a number of small and useful enchantments as the initial concept pieces. Since they were for his family, as well as for Krana and Lesat, he put far more work into them than he intended to for the ones he sold.

He started with the python hide and asked Lesat to make him a selection of sturdy belts. Each was able to function as either a weapon belt or just a belt for pouches and dimensional bags. The ones for his sister and mother were a bit thinner than the others, which suited them better. Then, he had Lesat inlay them with silver, making them look more elaborate. Across the silver and leather, he engraved a series of runes to block the cold, cool and heat the wearer, to add durability, and to give the belt the capacity for self-repair.

For the last step, he embedded a small beast core near the buckle, where it wouldn't be in the way. When he was finished, the pleasant chime of a notification rang in his mind, along with a surge of bubbling experience. An elegant leather belt worked with a silver inlay rested in his hands.

Belt of Gentle Climes.

[Enchantment: Gentle Breezes. The wearer of this enchantment will find a comfortable breeze flowing over their body, keeping them at a constant, pleasant temperature. The enchantment can be set for hotter or colder preferences.

Adds +2 Constitution to the wearer.

Duration: Permanent.]

When it was finished, he gave it a satisfied nod. The belt would be useful. The added Constitution was a bonus that came from the durability runes on the belt, which lent some of their strength to the wearer.

Over the next couple of days, he made a belt for everyone. The sizes and the styles of the silver inlays varied, but the enchantment was the same. By the time he was done, he felt more comfortable with the idea of his family living in Highfold. The added Constitution even applied to Altey, despite the fact that she hadn't had her Class Day, which gave him some ideas for how to help protect her more.

"Is there a limit to how many attribute-boosting enchantments someone can wear?" he asked suddenly, turning to Krana, who was riding alongside him again.

"Usually about 40% of their base attribute," the Seer replied, shaking her head. She could already see where he was heading with the idea. "Altey will need to grow up a bit more before she can make the most of them. The belt should be about right for her Constitution, but you could make other ones for her. A bit of extra mana wouldn't hurt her, if you can figure out how to make her a mana storage enchantment, but those are notoriously unstable."

Sam rubbed his chin thoughtfully as he turned the idea around in his mind. That might be possible if he used the right sort of storage rune...but it would be safer to make her something else like the wand, which just had charged mana for her to use. He didn't want anything blowing up on her.

The beast cores for the belts came from a series of small fights they had along the way, particularly from a herd of Pinefrost Beetles that decided to attack them as they camped in a redfrost pine grove. He'd worried that his supply of cores would run out soon, but as it turned out, the local wildlife was quick to volunteer to be enchanting materials. The result was more than a dozen cores for Sam to use, and by the time he finished making the belts he still had half of them left over, which would be enough for a second project.

The differences between beasts and monsters was on his mind as he turned one of the small, bluish-green cores over in his hands, examining it. Beast cores and monster cores were basically identical, as far as he could tell. He pulled out a Flamecaller Devil core and held it up in his hand, comparing the feeling of the reddish-orange core with the bluish-green one. Besides the elemental differences, there wasn't much else to distinguish them.

The core from the Pinefrost Beetles was an Aura of Frosted Pine. In the same way, the core from the Flamecaller Devils had the Aura of Compressed Flame inside. Both of them were fragments and not complete enough to reclaim.

Many people used the terms beasts and monsters interchangeably, but based on everything he'd seen so far, beasts were natural to Aster Fall, the true wild inhabitants of the world. They generated a core as they grew and became more in tune with the world, and so the aura in their core had an affinity for a natural element.

Monsters were different. They came into the world as Outsiders and as they arrived through a Flaw, they consumed part of Aster Fall, usually the part closest to their own natures, as if it called to them. That bit became the aura they carried, which he could reclaim.

When the Outsiders were killed, the World Core recreated them as monsters, which transformed their essence into experience. They were born into the world with the stolen aura still a part of them, and it helped them to form a core in the same way as a beast. When they were killed, the aura was released back into the world, completing the process that the World Core had created to deal with the invasions.

At that point, equilibrium returned to the world. The core was all that was left behind, which functioned in the same way as any other beast core.

Monsters could be reborn sometimes, and he was pretty sure that was because their auras were too difficult for the World Core to reclaim in a single attempt. They would be reborn in a new form, die, and then be reborn again, with each cycle grinding away a bit of the Outsider influence until the aura in them could be reclaimed.

The only thing that interrupted that process was him, since his class let him reclaim the aura before it returned to the world and gave him the ability to use it for his enchantments. When he used it up, it also returned to the world, completing the process in a different way. He shook his head as he turned his thoughts back to studying the runes in his mind. He still had a lot of other things he needed to make before they reached Highfold.

***

Over the next week, more beasts and monsters attacked them on the road as they continued to climb through the foothills, but there was nothing that was significant enough to threaten them. The danger would increase as they got higher in the Western Reaches, where it was more likely that a stray wyvern or ice drake would become hungry and fly down from the heights.

Wyverns were monsters and had a very unpleasant disposition. Even young ones were around Level 40 or 50, and the older they got, the meaner they were. By the time they were fully grown, they could reach their First Evolution.

Ice drakes were natural beasts, but no less dangerous for that. They were extremely fierce and territorial. Wyverns were sheep in comparison. An ice drake could fly, blend in with the snow and ice to become nearly invisible, and use both magical and physical attacks. They started out around Level

80 and they were not something you wanted to deal with until at least your First Evolution.

For now, both of those threats were distant, and they were only harassed by things in their 30s and low 40s. Things lower than that ran away when they sensed their auras. The attacks began to come with an increasing frequency as the elevation rose, making it clear why there were few lone travelers on the road. The only other people they saw now were in heavily guarded merchant wagons and small bands of adventurers.

Those groups were happy enough to keep their distance.

As a result of the attacks, Sam's collection of cores continued to grow and he was able to gather a few auras as well, which boded well for their settlement in Highfold. It looked like the hunting here would be exactly what he needed to grow stronger. The more materials he could acquire now, the better. If nothing else, he could sell some of them and the other materials they'd gathered for an initial starting sum to set up a shop.

The monsters rarely came in groups larger than three or four, but experience from the fights trickled in. Over the course of a week, everyone gained nearly 400,000 experience. It brought Sam to Level 47. He glanced at his status sheet to see the results.

Class Experience: 3,755,040 / 3,912,500

His father, Lesat, and Krana all reached Level 40 and broke into the Expert tier, which significantly boosted their fighting strength. They'd been on the edge for a while.

As for his mother, she had reached General Level 32 due to helping in the battles. Now, she was working on getting past the First Cliff. Her Class Level wasn't as quick to level, but it rose to 14 as a result of her constant work in writing down their travels and the story of her life.

In many ways, this trip to Highfold was a forging experience for them all. It let them experiment with their abilities, fight, and grow. Over that time, and with the help of some spare ore, Lesat's armor and shield also slowly repaired themselves, and Sam paid careful attention to how the self-repair runes functioned, looking for ways to optimize the process.

The chunks that were missing from where the devils had bitten it slowly fused back together as the runic lines gleamed with light. It was like watching water flow into the cracks where the holes had been, and the chunk of ore that Lesat held to it slowly dwindled away.

The main function of a repair rune was to remember the structure of the enchantment around it and the material it was affixed to. It was a type of memory rune. The result looked exactly the same as the original, even down to the hammer blows that had forged it and the inscriptions that Sam had engraved into the steel. At the same time, Sam's work on the message amulets and the other small enchantments he'd come up with continued to progress.

Near the end of that week, he was focused on infusing a blank disk of gem silver when Crystal Focus began to surge around him with a feeling like it was boiling outward. He'd just finished forging the disk and was working to purify it when he felt it happen, and he looked up instantly, his senses sweeping outward in alarm.

He'd never felt anything like it before. It felt like his perception of the world, which had become so much a part of his unconscious awareness, was suddenly warping and flowing outward, as if it couldn't contain the pressure inside of it. Flickers of intense sensory input ran through his mind, colors and auras of the dirt, earth, flowers, redfrost pines, beetles sleeping in the bark of the trees, and the current of the winds slipping through the grove.

It was an intense, incredible overload of his senses. Then it suddenly stopped as he felt Crystal Focus surge outward on a wave, its usual 40-foot distance doubling as it reached 80 feet and halted. The pressure began to fade away. The intense feeling of the world was still there, but he could feel his mind and senses adjusting, bringing it back down to a manageable level. A shimmering silver chime rang out brightly in his mind as the pine and ice-flavored world around him slowly returned to calm.

Crystal Focus has reached the Advanced tier.

Sam let out a long breath as he looked around, taking in the world around him with a new level of clarity.

***

As he slept that night, flickers of intense color and imagery passed through his mind, an impression from the world that was seeping into his consciousness. It was spurred on by the development in Crystal Focus. His senses were chaotic from the sudden advancement.

Sparks of elemental energy that were floating in the air beneath the redfrost pines gathered around him, drifting motes of sanguine red, chilly blue, and starry white. The images settled into his mind as the Guardian Star flickered. Its slow, white light pulsed in time with his heart and the flicker of his eyes as he jerked his head from side to side.

The vast expanse of stone filled his mind, shattered now into pieces as it stretched out beyond sight into an airless dark void. Above, starry light shimmered in a thousand colors, their unique mana signatures flooding the void with life and energy. The glowing cloud that was born in the heart of the shattered stone began to move, swirling like a whirlpool, as a brilliant point of energy was born at the center. It was like the heart of a star, burning endlessly in the void.

Uncountable time passed as the light grew brighter.

Then it split apart at the center, like a slit-pupiled eye opening, revealing a dark black portal that was filled with a different type of energy, one that was like and unlike the stars in the void. Even dreaming, Sam could feel the draw of essence in the flaw, calling to him to enter it.

The flaw ripped open at the center, becoming wider as it was pulled toward the sides of the swirling energy that made up the Nexus. From within the void, three demons walked out of the darkness, their slit-pupiled eyes blazing like the flaw itself. Their auras blazed around them, matching their eyes.

Prominent horns curled back from their foreheads like marks of honor. One was shrouded in an aura that was brilliant orange, like a sunset on fire burning on the edge of the world. Another was glowing with a red light so dark it was nearly black, the shade of ancient blood with hidden depths. The third's energy was crystal blue, as piercing as the heart of a sapphire star burning in the dark.

Their figures were handsome, beautiful, and elegant, but they radiated with a presence that warped the world around them, making such terms useless. They drew the eye like moths to a flame.

From all around, the stars pulled closer to the void, streaks of energy forming in the dark as other forms appeared, taking on the shapes of a welcoming party. The first to arrive was a youthful human with grave and noble features, followed by a long, curling dragon with diamond-shaped scales of a thousand colors. Next was a fey-like woman with beautiful, glittering wings whose aura was like silver smoke, flowing all around her.

Last was a muscular titan as tall as the sky, whose skin shone like a golden sun.

Familiar, silvery energy burned through all of them, the same as the stars above.

First Contact. The word whispered in his mind, its tone as desolate as the wind blowing across the stone that had once been in this place.

As the three demons and the four astrals looked at each other, one of the demons stepped forward, the one with a dark red aura. He looked toward the stars throughout the void and then down to the four people in front of him. A slow smile spread across his face.

Then the image shattered into fragments of a thousand swirling hues as the dream faded. The motes of elemental energy pulled away from Sam, leaving him thrashing from side to side and drenched in sweat.

CHAPTER ELEVEN

THE TOUCH OF ICE

As the elevation increased, so did the cold and wind until they were a constant, cutting force against Sam's skin. His Constitution and the Belt of Gentle Climes kept him from being uncomfortable, but there was an implicit threat in the touch of the ice. The dream from the night before was on his mind as he thought over the scene he'd seen, and the words "*First Contact.*"

He glanced down at the Guardian Star on his hand, a slight frown forming on his face. *Was it sending him these dreams?*

It wasn't a constant thing, but he could feel the slow flow of energy through the star like a small fire burning comfortably on the back of his hand. He could also feel that the dreams were true, a record held within the world itself. The other thing he could feel was that the world around him was the same place as where that glowing cloud of energy had once been.

The Nexus. It felt like Aster Fall.

Even the memory of it called to him, burning with the impression of *home*. He shook his head slowly as he pushed the thoughts to the back of his mind, focusing on the world around him.

He didn't know why the dreams were coming to him, but perhaps it was the Astral Guardian sending him information that would help. Or perhaps it was some unique feature of his class as he touched the aura of Aster Fall and stirred up some memory of history. Either way, he could tell it wouldn't be the last dream he had.

There was a lot of information in those two dreams already that was filling his mind, impressions from the energy all around him, as if he'd seen the forces of nature herself. After seeing them, he felt like he understood the world a bit better, as if he'd pulled back the curtain and seen the truth of reality.

He was already at work thinking of how to apply that knowledge to his spells, imagining new forms of Flame Strike and Essence Shield, as well as new ways to apply runes to his enchantments. Since these dreams weren't harming him, he would just have to take them as they came. Perhaps they would be helpful.

Snow began to drift through the air as they climbed higher, a light swirl in the air that was always present. It slowly floated down onto his skin and face, covering the reins and his horse's mane until a movement shook it free. It never seemed to build up to more than a dusting, as if some strange force prevented it from accumulating, but it became a steady presence. It melted away as it touched the ground, which was still green from grass and moss.

Day by day, whether the sky was clear or dark, snowflakes danced through the air. The horse beneath him stamped its feet and tossed its head, shaking the flakes free from its mane. The flakes were strange, perfect even as they slowly melted, as if something beyond nature held them together. His Fire Affinity was not comfortable here.

Flames flared around him constantly as if spiteful of the snow. Flickers of crystal flame snapped like hissing dragons from his skin, flowing around his clothing and sparking against the air as it kept snowflakes from landing on him. It wasn't just because of the cold, however. His eyes narrowed in consideration as he let Crystal Focus flow through the snow.

When he found it, his jaw clenched into a deep frown. There was a very faint presence of something else in the snow, something that sent shivers of cold along his skin and gave him the desire to rip it away for himself.

Essence.

He froze in place as he gripped the reins. Stars flickered in his blood with a resonance like a battlefield, each of them calling to the others in expectation of destruction. A desire to conquer rolled through him like a wave. He let it subside before he pushed it back down.

It was not what he had expected to find here. He'd thought that Highfold would just be a high mountain city, a place to grow and practice with his abilities. One that was normal.

He looked around him at the redfrost pine forests that were growing thicker on the foothills, and the rising slopes that led up into the Western Reaches ahead. The mountains were streaked with white, ice blue, stone grey, and patches of brilliant purple and green where forests and mana-infused ore gleamed from the slopes.

He let out a light sigh as he adjusted his view of the future. It seemed like it wasn't going to be as simple as he'd hoped. Part of his deal with the Astral Guardian was to defend the world and try to fix the seal, and he was sure that when he got closer to the source of this, the Guardian Star on his hand would notify him about it.

The World Law might push him to do it as well. He and his father both needed to close four more flaws to remove the Defiant trait. His senses reached out again as he studied the essence in the wind. The advancement of Crystal Focus brought the world into stark relief with a level of detail that was much greater than the Basic tier.

He used it to study the snow as they rode, examining its crystalline structure as he searched for the essence in it. He could feel the slow flow of mana through the wind and the stone, and how ice crystals formed in the sky between the tumbling wind and cold. The structure was similar in some ways to his Essence Shield and Crystal Field.

As he examined it, he compared those two abilities to it, looking for ways to improve them as he separated out the essence from the rest. It was less than one percent of the energy in the snow, perhaps just one ten thousandth of it, a thin thread of sparkling energy like nothing else on Aster Fall.

It was unmistakable.

Hours flickered past as they rode, with Sam's attention fixed on the snow. Whatever had caused the essence in it, it was old. That was one of the few things he could identify from it. There was a flavor to the essence that said that, something that echoed with age.

Strangely, it wasn't the only power in the snow.

Beyond the essence, there was some great force of Ice here that gave life to this snow, making it more real than it otherwise would have been, more enduring of the heat and the lower hills. That was why it was constantly in the air, never melting until it touched the ground. When it did land on the grass or the road, it didn't melt in a normal way. Instead, it evaporated completely, returning to the power that had created it.

Perhaps there was some truth to the legend that the Western Reaches were the back of a great ice dragon who was only sleeping here for a time.

The essence was something he would have to investigate. It raised the question of where it had come from. One that he needed to answer. It was also a warning that sent a constant prickle of alarm through him. Jaser's mercenary group had spoken like they were familiar with Outsiders. It hadn't seemed like they were from Highfold, but it had never come up either. *Did they know what was here?*

The other possibility was that there were more Outsiders in the world than he'd thought. He shook his head. If there were an Outsider aligned with Ice here somewhere, it would be drawn to him in the same way as he was drawn to it. He would have to set up his family in the city and live outside it himself, where it would be safer if it found him.

***

They paused for the evening in a grove of rare starleaf maples that were growing in the foothills. The trees had a reddish-gold bark streaked with silver flecks like tiny stars. Their leaves were a bright red with five angular lobes, which looked like delicate starbursts.

When everything was settled, Sam set up his work table and pulled out materials for the blank disks that he was planning to turn into message amulets, setting the ore and other parts around the table in front of him as he rubbed his chin thoughtfully. His progress with the simple runes was speeding along, giving him more options for devices that could be added to these amulets. He was at 34 of 48 runes now, and several of them were related to *voice* and sending messages.

The original amulet had the capability for messages and privacy barriers, things a diplomat would need. He didn't know exactly how those enchantments had functioned, but the runes were enough for him to make something intricate of his own. These amulets would be more complicated than anything he intended to sell in Highfold, and as a result he was going to forge gem silver disks for the base material and soak them in the Earth mana to give them an initial charge, the same as he'd done for his avoidance amulet.

The Earth mana would help to stabilize the enchantment and to add a sense of protection and defense to the enchantment. He was also planning to add defensive shields, so that they would protect his mother and Altey, as well as a last line of defense for everyone else.

He sorted through his available materials as he looked at what he had available, before an idea occurred to him. He had to make six of them, which was going to take a while. That meant he needed some focused time without distractions. He left his work table where it was and headed for the campfire.

"If the enchantments go well, we'll be able to communicate and have better protection when we reach Highfold," he explained. "It will be worth a short delay."

"We don't have any reason to get there immediately," Jeric agreed, nodding at Sam's words. "The festival is coming up, and we'll want to set up a shop for it, but a few days won't make much of a difference."

"If you need the time, we'll stay," Aemilia added with a smile. She reached out and tucked a strand of Altey's hair back behind her ear. "And if the amulet you're describing will be as helpful as it sounds, then we should definitely wait for it. I don't want to be separated with no way to communicate again."

Their family had been separated enough, and none of them had any desire for it to happen again. Even with his mother's new Seer abilities, it would be difficult to have a conversation from both sides.

"There's plenty of time left until the festival," Krana agreed. "Getting there early is best, but we can do this first. Do you need help with the forging?"

"I do want to ask you about a few materials to try out." Sam grinned. There were still some ores and other things he wanted to experiment with, but he wasn't sure exactly how they would act.

Lesat didn't have any objections either. He was content to follow along as a guard and friend of the family, which was what he was slowly becoming. Months ago, Sam had agreed to pay him a salary, but by this point, he was with them because he wanted to be, rather than as a hired guard, and he had an equal share in everything.

When they reached Highfold, Sam was hoping that he would take up the task of protecting Altey if she went to attend a school. Wealthy families often sent guards or retainers for their children, to keep an eye on them and to keep them on task, so it wouldn't be out of place. It would make him more comfortable if Altey had someone with her.

Sam gave the group a grin before he turned back to his work table. He settled in again as he looked at the materials in front of him and sorted through the auras in his specialized pocket dimension.

Aura of Swirling Wind, he decided. It was one of the few Wind-focused auras he had, which would work well for messages and shields, and he had a dozen of them. That should be enough to enchant the amulets, as long as he added some of his own essence and the Earth mana.

The auras had come from a flock of Bonewind Vultures that attacked them a week before, when they passed through a particularly barren area in the foothills. Unlike normal vultures, they were monsters with fangs, pointed tails, and the ability to whip bone spikes at their prey, accelerating the projectiles with a strong Wind element. The auras that had come from them were a good payment for the delay.

Krana walked over to the side of his table and pulled up a camp stool to sit on as she looked over what he had available. To one side of the table, there was the dimensional bag of rare ores and crystals that he'd taken from the Dark Chryso Bloodweaver months ago.

He hadn't used many of them yet. He knew the names of what was inside, thanks to his Analyze ability, but he didn't have a full grasp of all their properties yet. They weren't necessary for regular enchantments. Krana picked up the bag, poking through it as she looked toward the silver ore and gems that Sam planned to use.

"Is there anything in there that would help augment messages, privacy barriers, defensive shields, or connect the amulets together so we can all communicate at once?" Sam asked, looking over at her with interest. "I know there's one small piece of embradium in there, but I don't know if it's useful for this."

"Embradium is a good metal for augmenting spells and defensive barriers," she agreed, rubbing at her chin as she continued to poke through the bag. "Unfortunately, there's not enough embradium here to use for these. Ebonstone would help with anything related to obscuring something.

"You have several pieces of argentscale quartz, which could help augment a defensive shield, and also some small blood-ore diamonds. Those could be used to create a blood bond with the wearer, so that no one else can use the amulet."

Krana picked several small crystals and gems out of the bag, setting them in front of Sam as she indicated them. The ebonstone was a soft, dark chunk of ore that looked like compressed shadows. There was barely a line on it and it seemed slightly larger than it was when he touched it. It was absorbing the light around it.

The argentscale quartz was a translucent silver-white chunk of crystal that had tiny, angular silver flecks in it that looked like scales. The light twisted around the scales as it passed through the stone, making the silver lines gleam.

The blood-ore diamonds were embedded in a larger chunk of dusky red stone, like blood-red stars appearing in a twilight sky. Each of them was tiny and barely visible, but they flickered intensely in the light of the sun.

"For privacy..." she mused to herself as she sorted through the bag again, before finally pulling out a chunk of light green ore that held ripples of other colors in it, like a subtle rainbow that was constantly changing as the light struck it. "Wild moonstone should work. It may seem odd, but if you blend it into the mix, it will help the energy in the amulet be in tune with nature. It will be harder for anyone to sense what's happening within the amulet, and that will apply to privacy barriers and the words said behind them.

"Even if a Seer pushes on the barrier, all they'll sense is the wild chaos of the world. They would have to be very skilled and powerful to get through it. The more mana is flowing in the amulet, the more that quality will be enhanced, as well. When it's combined with the Earth mana..." Krana paused as she looked toward the crystal sphere of mana that Sam had set to one side of the table. She was still surprised that he'd managed to take so much of it.

Sam followed her gaze and smiled slightly, laughing at himself. He'd hidden that mana from her for a long time, only revealing it to her after they left Cliff's End. It had been for no particular reason except a desire for secrecy, and she'd proven herself trustworthy long ago.

"That should be enough, I think," Krana concluded, as she pushed the four materials across the table toward him. "I'll show you how to melt them in the best way as we make the gem silver."

Sam gave her a grateful nod. He'd known for a long time that she was a skilled crafter, but he hadn't realized at first that it was her subclass.

She was an Earth Seer and a Dwarven Crafter, which apparently was a special racial subclass for Dwarves. Unlike the better-known ones, it didn't specialize in a particular type of material. Instead, it helped her to gain skills in many areas and was a platform for several future Evolutions. It was the first time he'd heard of an initial subclass being just a foundation, and it made him shake his head. His understanding of the world was continually expanding.

"Let's get started then," he said as he pulled out the portable forge from his dimensional vest. He was looking forward to having some dedicated time to craft. If he were lucky, his Smithing profession might also break through to 20 from this. At the moment, it was only 14, so it had a ways to go.

***

The dusk faded into night as Sam worked on the amulets with Krana's help. He started with the base materials, dividing the ores and added crystals into six separate groups. Each of these amulets was Advanced in their own right, and probably on the higher end of Advanced, since he was combining multiple enchantments into them.

To forge the initial base material, he first used his crystal flame to extract the silver from the ore, letting it pool into the crucible below his hands. At the same time, he purified it, filtering it for impurities as he burned them away. The result was a molten pool of shimmering silver that was already imbued with some of his essence and the natural mana of the world. To that, he added a small emerald to turn it into gem silver. The gemstone melted away into the silver as he mixed them together, giving it a soft emerald green tint as it hardened the metal and enhanced its magical properties.

Emeralds combined well with both Wind and Earth, and he was trying to keep the elemental affinities in balance. The Wind would come from the aura, while the Earth would come from the Earth mana. The runes on the amulet would be primarily Wind focused as well. The Earth mana would enhance it with a bit of extra stability. To that mixture, he then took a Wind-aligned monster core from the same Bonewind Vultures that he'd purified and added it. It was filled with enough energy that it wouldn't melt in the silver.

He was planning to do the amulets in stages, to make it simpler, and so as the first pool of molten silver was ready, he set it aside in a mold. The core floated in it, a nearly invisible lump that would become the center of the enchantments. On top, he placed thirty drops of Earth mana, letting them fall one by one onto the cooling pool of liquid. Unlike water, they were hot to the touch, like lava.

As they struck the surface, they sizzled as they melted into it, the energy flowing outward to merge with the silver. After the first ten drops, the rest began to gather on the surface, creating a silver-white layer that slowly sank lower as its energy infused into the material. It wasn't much compared to what he'd used in the past to forge his amulet, which had absorbed 500 drops, but Krana was already wincing by the time he went past five.

"One or two drops is enough to bless a normal item and increase its stability," she offered, explaining some of the techniques the dwarven craftsmen used for this type of mana. It was so rare that it was almost never seen and the excess pained her. "Past that, you're better off just using regular mana. The only reason to use more is if it's a very large item or it's incredibly difficult to stabilize the forces in it."

Sam nodded at her as he placed the mold to the side and began to melt another pool of silver for the second amulet blank. He'd used a lot of Earth mana in the past, when he'd been right next to the pool that was filled with it, so he didn't think of it with quite the same rarity, but it was true.

He still didn't feel bad about using thirty drops on each amulet. Even if it only helped a little bit, they were for his family. He started to hum as he worked, turning the silver ore around in his hands as crystal flames surged. Threads of molten silver ran down from the ore, flowing over his hands and reflecting the light of the rising moons as they fell into the crucible below.

CHAPTER TWELVE

ICY PEAKS LIKE DRAGON FANGS

Tower Reach

On the western edge of Tower Reach, the city retreated in the face of rich mansions and manicured lawns. Magical fountains bubbled through elegant wooded glades and fields of flowers, scattered amongst edifices of marble and gold. No peasant stepped foot in this area to disturb the serenity of wealth. They were kept away by guards who were quick to kick at a passing beggar.

In the center of that wild opulence, a broad marble tower rose into the air. It was more a palace than a tower, but given the family that lived there, no one would dare to tell them such a thing. They were well known throughout the city and beyond, one of the foundations of its magical research and famous for past achievements. A strong magical bloodline ran through the family that made them highly attuned to mana, and their classes usually reflected it. Most of them were powerful wizards or mages.

"One of our couriers has received a letter." The voice was smooth and held more than a touch of arrogance. The speaker was a tall, elegant man who looked young, but the lines at the edges of his eyes revealed the passing of many years.

It wasn't clear how old he was, since a high Constitution from his youth had locked in a youthful appearance. He could have been 40 or 400, with little to show the difference. The room around him was near the top of the tower, and he was standing near the window that looked out onto the gardens below. The sunlight framed his golden-brown hair, making him look like a spirit from the sky.

"What is it about?" The reply came from an equally elegant woman who was draped over a couch halfway across the room, her head reclined as she looked up toward a pattern of constellations on the ceiling. A crystal wine glass was dangling from her hand. Like the man, she had nothing to worry about when it came to appearance or Constitution. She was intensely beautiful and her clothing was fashionable, but her gaze was distant.

"It can't be about the dimensional studies," she added, her tone distracted as she continued to study the ceiling. "Those have barely progressed over the last five years. The Flaws are still increasing. Is it about that?"

"No, it is not about your pet project." The man dismissed the idea with a snort. "The dimensions around Aster Fall are unstable, as they have always been, and research into them is doomed to failure. There are too many variables to control. You have always been interested in foolish things."

His words were harsh, as was her indifferent reaction to them. After a very long marriage, it wasn't clear if the two loved or hated one another more.

"The Flaws are linked to them," the woman replied without bothering to turn her head. The wine glass in her hand bubbled as the level of liquid in it rose, and she took another sip from it. "The kingdom has also asked us to study them. There is a 7% increase in their frequency and intensity this year compared to last year. Last year, it was a 5% increase. They are becoming worse."

"Slowly, over decades," the man replied dismissively as he flicked his hand toward the ceiling where the star patterns were engraved. They gleamed with a soft blue and silver. "It's happened before, which means it's a natural cycle, like the waxing and waning of the moons. It will stabilize. It is not worthy of our attention."

"And if you're wrong and it's the prelude to a Breaking?" the woman asked as her eyes traced another curve of the stars. Her attention was far away, but her voice was sharper than before. "The increase in the strength of the Flaws has never shown a definable pattern. It cannot be called a cycle. More than that, this time is different. The increase is far greater than anything that we've recorded and much too quick. Something is happening in the Seal."

"It's irrelevant," the man replied, shaking his head as he ignored her words. "It's more important to focus on what's in front of us. Don't you want to know what the message was about?"

"No," the woman replied, before she took another drink from her glass.

"You should be. You remember that useless grandson of ours, Alister, the one with the unique class he could never unlock?" The man answered anyway, a slight smirk on his face. "It seems he had a son and a grandchild, and the grandchild is still alive. A girl. What do you think of that?"

"What about her?" The woman's attention finally turned toward the man as a flicker of warning appeared in her eyes.

"Apparently," the man paused dramatically as a small, victorious grin appeared on his face, "she and her mother have been kidnapped by some mercenaries running around the Storm Plains."

"And?" The woman sighed, turning her attention back to the ceiling. "That's all you have to say?"

"I knew you would be interested, despite your effort to seem other-wise," the man continued to grin, "you always cared about our descendants more than you should have. Based on our old agreement, the girls are yours. So, what do you think we should do about this?"

"Let her live her life," the woman replied, her voice fading back to indifference. "It's not our business."

"Isn't it?" The man smirked, continuing his latest game to see how much he could anger his wife. They hadn't had a good fight in a while and he had the feeling she was hiding her strength. "It seems they're heading to Highfold. What if I send someone to get her and bring her back here for you?"

"Do as you like." The woman's voice was faint now, almost tired, even as a spark of something that was hidden very deeply flickered in her eyes, out of her husband's sight. "The Flaws are more important."

She returned to looking at the ceiling, but the wine in her glass bubbled as it began to refill itself again, the level rising. On the surface of the liquid where the man couldn't see, an image appeared. As she took a sip, she breathed out a simple message that was transmitted to the person on the other side of her portal.

"*Find her.*" A sense of what she wanted was compressed into those two simple words.

"I think I'll retrieve her," the man continued as he looked out the window again. "It will be interesting to see how far Alister fell and what influence he left on his descendants."

***

The Western Reaches

It took Sam the better part of a day to make the six amulet blanks, but eventually six shimmering disks of silver rested on the table in front of him. Their surfaces gleamed with an emerald-green tint that was similar to the light of Silvas in the sky, making it look like the Forest Moon had blessed them.

Sam looked up at the moon and gave her a respectful nod. They were in one of her forests. If she was a divine force of Aster Fall as the legends said, then there was no reason to be impolite. He didn't have any real belief in gods, but he had met the Astral Guardian and a powerful Outsider ruin, and their abilities were incomprehensible.

There were forces out there far greater than him. *Who was to say the moon wasn't one of them?*

The four rare materials that Krana had helped him select had been alloyed into the amulets, giving only a slightly denser feel to them when he picked them up. The process was complex, since each material had a different melting point and needed to be strictly controlled so it didn't disturb the final result, but it worked.

The next step in making the message amulets was to enchant them. Then, he would imbue them with the Aura of Swirling Winds and his own personal essence before activating them. He picked up the first of the blanks as he began to pour his aura into it, letting it fill the material as he searched for any impurities or flaws. When he was satisfied, he set the disk back down again and moved on to the next, double checking each of them before he moved on. His stylus appeared in his hand, the silver tool surrounded by a nearly invisible halo of crystal flame, as he picked up the first amulet and looked toward the pattern he'd created for it.

The chalk design on the work table was a complex pattern of three interlinked circles that spiraled in and out of each other, with the outer edge of each circle forming the point of a triangle. The core that was at the heart of the formation was embedded precisely where all three circles met, at the very center of the amulet. It would regulate the flow of energy, charge the circles, and store both mana and aura.

This pattern was different from anything he'd tried before. It wasn't going to be engraved just on the surface of the amulet, but on the interior as well. He would have to engrave that part with a projection of his essence through his stylus, carefully marking it into the center. When it was complete, it would be more stable than anything he'd created so far as well.

Runes for *wind, message, mana, charge, voice, barrier, shield, distance, receive, send*, and more were placed throughout the three circles, creating an internal formation for each one that crossed over with the others. There was also a special durability and charging pattern that surrounded the core and linked it to each of the circles. The binding pattern to join the enchantment to the base material looped around the amulet in a spiral of stately runes, connecting everything together. It was the same Expert-level one that he'd used for his avoidance amulet.

Now, he just needed to inscribe each amulet and pour as much of his own essence as possible into it as he worked, letting the core and the gem silver absorb the initial charge. The stylus in his hand flickered with crystal flame as he brought it forward for the first swirling line.

Silvas rose through the heavens and set again, followed by Caelus, who watched it all. Eventually, the sun rose again as well, the light of dawn falling down through the grove to illuminate the table where Sam was working. Beneath that light, his hands were surrounded by crystal flame, moving like the wind and flowing water as the amulets took shape.

***

Two days later, Sam was pulled out of his work by the absence of anything left to do. Time around him felt like a compressed ocean, flowing softly away on the waves, and he blinked as he brought his attention back to the present. On the work table in front of him, there were six completed amulets. He'd been woken up while trying to reach for a seventh.

A series of chiming, bright notifications was waiting for him, along with a river of experience that was rushing through his veins, roaring like a waterfall. Each of the amulets lying in front of him was identical.

Amulet of Swirling Winds (Advanced, Special).

[Enchantments: Swirling Winds, Wall of Swirling Wind, Voice of the Wind, Winds of One Storm, Blood Bond. This amulet holds multiple enchantments that mutually reinforce one another.

Swirling Winds: *Creates a barrier of wind that surrounds the bearer and creates a private area, preventing others from eavesdropping on them. Attempts to pierce this barrier will alert the bearer and result in a backlash of wild mana.*

Wall of Swirling Wind: *Creates a defensive barrier of hardened Wind to protect the bearer from attacks. The barrier will absorb and deflect blows.*

Voice of the Wind: *Allows the bearer to communicate with others by sending their voice along the wind. The messages are shrouded in wild moonlight and shadow, keeping them from being observed.*

Winds of One Storm: *Allows the bearer to locate others who are wearing amulets of the same type and to sense their general health. Distance: 100 miles.*

Blood Bond: *Attunes the amulet to the first bearer, so that it cannot be used by another.*

Charges: 150/150.

Duration: Permanent.]

The number of enchantments was more than he'd seen on anything except the original illusion amulet, which had dozens at least. It was more than he'd ever added to a single artifact before.

He'd poured over 200 points of essence into each amulet as he was working, but the charge at 150 was better than he'd expected, about five times what the core was originally able to hold. The Earth mana and the other materials had increased the amulet's strength. The notification from the amulets faded away, replaced by the ones from the World Law that had accumulated while he was working.

Congratulations, Enchanter. You have created an Advanced Item with multiple enchantments, marking it as a Special Artifact.

You gain 5,000 Class experience per item, as well as bonus experience for making a Special item.

You gain 45,000 Class experience.

You are now a Level 21 Smith.

You are now a Level 29 Enchanter.

You are now General Level 48.

General Experience: 3,945,470 / 4,154,500
You are now a Level 48 Battlefield Reclaimer.
Class Experience: 3,921,940 / 4,154,500
You gain +1 Aura, +1 Intelligence, and have three free attribute points to distribute.

The roiling, silvery torrent of the experience continued for a little while, flowing throughout his body until it finally settled down.

When his mind was clear again, he added one free point to Constitution, bringing it to 45, and then one each to Aura and Intelligence, taking them to 93. With the Belt of Gentle Climes, his Constitution was up to 47 overall, which would have to be enough for now. He planned to keep increasing it slowly, since he wanted to keep it close to his overall level in order to give himself a solid defense.

It wouldn't be enough on its own to completely resist like-level attacks, but it would be enough to deal with glancing blows and to reduce what might kill him to something that just injured him. The resistance to temperatures, healing ability, and lifespan that came with Constitution also made it an incredibly important attribute.

He looked down at the six amulets in front of him and slowly reached out to pick up the first one, holding it up in the light of the three moons that were all in the sky above.

It was the third night since he'd started. Now, it was near midnight and the triple light of the moons shone on the amulet, setting off subtle rainbows from the ores and crystals that were alloyed in it. It was an emerald silver overall, but as the moonlight struck it, the edge of that shade was tinted with a vibrant light green.

He looked over toward the others, but everyone except his father was asleep now. Jeric was keeping watch and keeping an eye on Sam at the same time, making sure that he was fine. Sam gave him a smile as he stood up and stretched, looking out over the campsite and his other sleeping family members.

His gaze settled on Krana and Lesat, turning over what they meant to him as he debated whether to include them in that small group as well. They were already friends, but they hadn't been with him for that long yet, and he hesitated to take the last step. A family is many things, but time is one thing that makes it the most meaningful.

He glanced down at the amulet in his hand, and then back toward the people for whom it was intended, as he asked himself what the difference was between a friend and family. With essence in the snow, the area around Highfold was going to be more dangerous than he'd expected, and that meant making sure that everyone was safe. The amulets were one part of that.

He'd spent a long time hiding secrets from them, like the Earth mana, that he'd only recently started to reveal. Now, he was questioning the reason for it. He sighed as he closed his fingers around the amulet in his hand, feeling it press into his palm. Krana had long ago proved herself a good friend, and Lesat had done the same in his own silent way.

At some point, you have to trust people.

***

The lofty peaks stretched higher in front of them as they climbed higher into the Western Reaches, until they were so tall that they obscured the sky ahead, towering into the distance.

The snow around them began to slowly accumulate as they moved closer to Highfold, the flakes that hit the ground refusing to melt as they built into thin layers, until one morning when he woke, the world around him was covered in crystalline white. Ice stretched out across the world as it hung from branches and glazed the rocks and earth around him, a shining, crystal cold that was laden with just a hint of impending trouble.

As they rode, the mountains around them continued to rise, each peak a separate tooth, as if they were riding into a dragon's maw filled with danger on every side. At the same time, the snow also increased, the level slowly rising until with each step of the horses' hooves, a flurry of white blew away, and their hoofprints sank four inches deep into the surface of the road.

Either through an enchantment or some skill of its construction, the road was more clear than the surroundings, where the snow was already knee-high. To Altey, it was a wonderland of things to build and jump through, but to Sam it was a mark of increasing danger.

He hadn't shared the unsettled feeling with the others immediately, since he wasn't able to pinpoint where it was coming from, but as they continued toward Highfold, the amount of essence in the snow continued to intensify. The only reason he hadn't mentioned it yet was that there was a good chance that the origin of the essence wasn't located in Highfold itself, which meant the city would still be safe for his family.

He didn't want to ruin their hopes.

It was possible that the Outsider lived on one of the peaks around here or in a cave in the mountains, somewhere that the snow passed as it formed. He wasn't sure why its essence was slowly leaking out into the elements, but he'd hoped it would fade as they headed toward the city.

Unfortunately, it didn't.

Now that they were getting closer to Highfold, it meant he had to bring it up. Even if the city wards kept it from entering the city, there was an Outsider somewhere around, and it was not a weak one. He reached down and touched the amulet on his chest, feeling the thread of energy that told him the others around him were fine and close by.

He'd moved his illusion amulet to his belt, hanging it there instead. It would have the same effect no matter where he wore it, and it kept the two amulets from becoming twisted together. Everyone was wearing the new amulets now, and he'd shown them how to use them. They'd all dripped a bit of blood on the amulets to bind them to themselves.

He would give it the rest of the day, to see if he could pinpoint where it was. If the level of essence was still increasing by then, he would bring it up with them tonight.

Over the last week, after finishing the amulets, he'd spent the evenings working on smaller enchantments, more weather-resistant belts, simpler amulets that just had privacy barriers, some mana manipulation tools like Altey's necklace, and more. His dimensional bags were full of things to sell. He also had a collection of monster cores and other rare materials if needed to finance the shop and house that they wanted to buy. The small attacks were still frequent on the road, which meant that his supply continued to increase. In that regard, at least, this was an ideal location to live.

He touched the amulet on his chest again as he looked at the sky above him and the encircling mountain peaks that were capped with silver and blue ice. Hopefully, the Outsider minded its own business.

Sam's eyes flashed with a flare of crystal blue light as his hand clenched around the amulet, feeling its edge cut into his palm again. A surge of anger flared through his blood, demanding that he find it and eliminate it before it could become a threat.

Otherwise, it was going to have a problem.

CHAPTER THIRTEEN

AT THE GATES OF HIGHFOLD

The road to Highfold was covered in snow. There was only a day left in their journey and it was nearly up to the horses' knees. Even the sturdy beasts were having trouble breaking through it now. The level of essence was not decreasing, but fortunately, it was no longer increasing either. It seemed like they'd reached a point where it saturated the area. That made it difficult to pinpoint where it was coming from.

Its presence was a strange and unsettling feeling, as if an enemy were constantly breathing down his neck. It made him uncomfortable, but more than that it raised his anger, as if there were a challenge constantly pressing in around him. Sam frowned as he looked at the ice-laden peaks around them, searching in each direction for the origin. It had to be up there, somewhere on the higher slopes.

He tried to place himself in the position of an Outsider who loved the snow and ice, and he couldn't see himself settling into a valley. No, an Outsider's innate arrogance would demand that he be at the top. Up on a mountain peak that he'd made his own.

The night before, he'd told his family about the Outsider around, and it had drawn deep concern but it hadn't been enough to change their plans. They'd already known from Jaser's group that Outsiders were in the world. Without more information, they couldn't change their plans. Highfold was still a good place to live, especially with the ruins around it for Sam to study. It was doing business as normal, which meant it should be safe enough for them.

They just needed to make a home here.

The amulets he'd made would help to protect them and keep them all connected. Now that those were done, some of his worry for their safety had lessened. It would take a concerted effort to break the shields. They would hopefully see anything like that coming.

Still, as he looked at the snow around him and he felt the presence on his skin, his frown couldn't help but deepen. His crystal flame lashed out, burning away another drift of snowflakes that tried to land on him. It was a good place to settle, and his family might be able to live with this presence around them, since they were oblivious to it, but for him...his eyes couldn't stop tracking along the slopes of the mountains, searching the peaks for signs of the Outsider's presence.

It was dangerous, a threat that he could constantly feel, and it left him unable to calm down. He could feel the urge from the essence stars in his blood, pushing him toward battle, and it was possible that was influencing him, but he couldn't pull his mind away from the idea that this area was...

His.

A satisfied anger rumbled through his veins with that word. This world and this city were his territory. He needed to Evolve and to become capable of holding the world together, and of living up to his duty. That meant there was only one option. There was a roaring, star-like call in his blood pushing him toward the decision. His knuckles clenched on the reins as the demand rippled through him.

It wasn't rational to seek out a strong monster immediately, but it didn't matter. Whatever it was, and no matter how strong it was...

He was going to kill it.

A flare of crystal flame burned around him like a battle halo as his eyes turned toward another peak.

***

The road to Highfold narrowed as it cut up along the final cliff that led to the valley around the city, hugging tight to the shoulder of the mountain that was called Sky Guard, one of the main defenses of Highfold. It gave way on the open side to a sheer cliff that dropped away like a knife toward the slopes below. They were so high up that the bottom of the cliff was invisible, covered over by blowing snow and wind. This cliff was also part of the city's defenses, making sure that no large force could arrive here by foot.

The open sky ahead of him was pierced by the peaks of the neighboring mountains. Between them, he could see the forms of griffins in the air. Their wide wings and eagle-like heads arced like blades as they flew from peak to peak and down into the valleys below. They were how the city communicated and moved goods quickly from place to place.

Griffins were a strange race, one of several that were halfway between being beasts and civilized. They were intelligent, clever, and powerful. Sometimes, they even deigned to speak. As they leveled up, they gained the ability for mental speech, usually by the time they were adults. They didn't give experience if you killed them, which made them allies of a sort, and the Ice Sylphs here had an agreement with them to support the city. They were a proud race, but some of them found it profitable to fly things up and down the mountains, something for which they were well rewarded.

He turned his attention back to the road, his eyes moved across a few travelers around them who were also heading to the city. As usual, they kept their distance.

When they rounded the final curve, there was a tall stone wall ahead of them that sealed the road, stretching from the slope of Sky Guard on the left to the cliff on the right. The gate in it was open, allowing traffic to flow through freely. There were no guards stationed here, but Sam's eyes could see the faint pattern of enchantments laid into the stone.

They outlined stone golems resting in hidden alcoves along the front of the wall and in the two towers above the gate. He could also see enchantments covering the face of Sky Guard, ones that were so old they were almost invisible. The mana in them had long ago begun to merge with the natural patterns of the world.

Each of the golems in the wall was around ten feet tall and half that wide. Their bulky forms were humanoid, but their heads were only a wedge-like protrusion above their torsos, with no neck to be seen. The valley was open to visitors, but it was not undefended. These golems could spring to life and close the gate at a command, and then take up guard here until a stronger force arrived.

Instead of frightening him, the sight made him want to study the en-chantments. Whatever runes were in them, they would be useful. He forced himself to push aside the desire as they rode through the gates, pulling his hood closer over his face as he felt the *ping* of his amulet resounding. There weren't many travelers on the road, but there were some. Here at the gate, everyone was being pushed together, and gazes were unavoidable.

Beyond the golems, he didn't see any alarm or Analysis enchantments on the gate as they rode through. If those existed, they were farther in. As soon as they were on the other side of the wall, the cliff to the right disappeared, changing to solid ground, and the slope of Sky Guard retreated to the left, giving way to a vast, open valley.

The first impression that struck him was the intensity of the sky. The clear brilliance of golden sunlight and the reflection of ice brightened the air here, all of which was tinted with emerald from the valley below. Stretching in front of him for dozens of miles was a verdant, green valley that was sprinkled with interlaced patches of fields and forests. Drifts of alabaster snow hugged the edges of the valley, and a light breeze of swirling flakes brushed his face as they danced through the air, but the valley was otherwise absent of snow.

In the distance, three mountains that were even taller than Sky Guard soared into the sky, like three kings holding court over the valley in front of him. The city of Highfold was nestled at the base of those three moun-tains in a sprawling expanse of buildings, domineering walls, and ice-white towers. It was perhaps twenty miles away from where he was standing, but its enormous size was enough to draw the eye no matter where you stood in the valley.

There was a shining, ice-blue palace at the highest point of the city like a sapphire gem set at the base of a crown. The light reflecting from its walls shone out over the rest of the city and the valley all around.

"Those are the Three Crowns," Krana said softly, from her position near his shoulder. She was also impressed by the view, but she'd been more prepared for it. "The city is large enough that it covers the base of all three mountains in the valley. It holds nearly a million people."

From his feet, the slope of the mountain leveled out, running down through a series of interconnected roads and then up again in a gentle curve toward the city itself. All across the valley, there was a sprawling connection of villages, fields, farms, and tiny houses like wild alpine flowers springing up from the ground. The weather here was warmer than outside, the cutting force of the ice absent. The fields that stretched across the plain were vibrant with green stalks and fruits. It was like walking from a winter storm into a spring cavern.

Now, he understood how Highfold could exist here. It wasn't just a city perched on a solitary mountainside. It was a powerful existence in its own right that soared over this valley, protecting its population and producing its own food and culture. He couldn't help but feel amazed. He'd seen Osera and Ebonfar, but Highfold's position in the Western Reaches was unique. None of this would have been possible without the Ice Sylphs and other races who'd created it. It was their magic that kept the valley green.

"In about a month, the Festival will take place and the moons will align above the three peaks. Then they will truly look like crowns," Krana continued with a slight smile on her face as she looked up toward the mountains. "The ruins you want to study are above the city, on those slopes. They are extremely large, even bigger than the city of Highfold itself."

Sam's eyes widened further as he took in her words. He'd thought the ruins would be small. Apparently, he was wrong.

"They are also filled with the local monsters and beasts," Krana continued, as she looked toward the others, pulling them into her explanation as well.

"Ice wraiths, mountain trolls, wyverns, cave goblins, monsters and devils of various sorts...sometimes even an ice drake is seen there, since it covers so much of the higher slopes. They prefer the peaks and claim them as their own.

"The ruins are frequently visited by adventurers looking for ancient treasures as well as enchanters who want to research it," she concluded. "We should be able to find some maps inside the city to help."

Aemilia looked forward with a happy smile, and Jeric at her shoulder started to laugh. It was a long, rolling sound as he looked toward the area that would be their new home. After a moment, Altey joined in, her higher tones sparkling through the air of the valley that was as warm as a new summer day.

They were a group of six tiny figures set against a vast mountainscape, their forms infinitesimal compared to the Western Reaches rising above them. Hope spread like wildfire in their hearts as they looked forward.

Only Sam felt the threat that was still hanging in the air, pressing down on the enormous valley ahead of them. All around him on the slopes of the mountains, he could feel the drumbeat of essence burning in his blood. It was more clear than it had ever been before. At the same time, a flickering pulse of warning from the back of his hand caught his attention as the Guardian Star began to burn with a faint, half light. It had been silent before, but now that they'd entered the valley, something had caught its attention.

He waited for the World Law to announce a Flaw in the area, but nothing happened. He looked around, sensing the pull from the star as it tugged his attention toward the slopes around the valley again, the same place he felt the essence.

***

"I'll stay out here in this village," Sam suggested, as he looked at Krana and then toward the small village where they'd just stopped. It was about halfway through the valley and still a dozen miles from Highfold's walls. His voice was quiet, even though no one was close enough to overhear, and his hood was pulled around his face again. Even so, from time to time he felt the *ping* of his amulet warning him of a passing gaze.

This halfway point was where shops and taverns were starting to appear, ones catering to farmers and merchants who bought grain or other simple goods and sold cloth and necessities to the villages. Up to now, they'd mostly been riding through scattered fields and forests, sometimes with a few farms around, but now that they were deeper into the valley proper, the villages around them had begun to increase in frequency.

The valley here was as verdant as the rest, holding the taste of magic that was everywhere in the air. He could feel some faint enchantment covering it all. He wasn't sure if it was one ancient spell or many, but the echo of power was old and vast, changing the weather here into something pleasant for people.

On the slopes just a few hundred feet above the valley, there were clouds of white-blue mana gathering around the peaks, coating them in snow and ice, but down here the weather was warm and calm. The breeze that blew through the valley was a strange mix of greenery, pine, and frost. It felt as if it had two sides, one warm and one cold. The threat of frost hung in it with a promise to return.

Whatever the Ice Sylphs had done here, it was impressive. Perhaps they found this constant reminder of the cold refreshing.

"That inn looks promising," he added, nodding toward one on the edge of the village in front of them. There was a simple sturdiness to its construction that he liked, as if it had no pretensions. "That way, I won't have to deal with the city guards or the wards trying to Analyze me."

Staying out here in the middle of the valley was best, where it would be hard for him to be noticed. The village here was a little battered by time, but it would work. He didn't want to get too close to the city. Out here, where patrols might not appear very often was the best. This area was in the middle of it all, just a little ways off the main road, but beyond the sturdy buildings of the village, there wasn't much remarkable about it.

It was perfect.

He didn't want a famous shop where he would be well known. He just wanted a quiet place to work. He could set up a workshop here, as well as a place to live, and then his father could take the items into the city to sell. It required buying two places to live, but it was the best plan he'd come up with.

The sound of faint, icy bells rang through the air, making the party turn toward the city in the distance. They were at different pitches, chiming as if to mark the arrival of winter, and somehow the sound carried out across the miles, ringing even here in the distant villages.

"The Frost Bells," Krana spoke up as they listened to them. "They mark out the hours of the city and the changing of the guard. They're one of the better-known magical artifacts in the city. It's said that they can also aid in its defense."

"If you're staying out here, then so are we," Jeric said as the sound of the bells faded away, turning toward Sam. "I don't want you to be out here alone."

"Altey would be safer in the city," Sam protested. "Monsters might still attack here, outside those wards, even with the enchantments on the weather."

It had been known to happen, although not too frequently. Only the city of Highfold itself had wards against them. The city guard was supposed to patrol the valley, but rumors said they focused more on the city and that the monsters in the surrounding peaks were always hungry.

"There should be some schools or academies inside for her as well," he added.

"We'll stay together," Aemilia agreed with her husband, looking over to their son as she shook her head. "Once we have a place to stay and perhaps a workshop out here, we can look into a school. A month or two makes no difference. A future is built brick by brick, and not by jumping to sudden decisions."

"I agree. This seems like a good place to settle," Krana added, as she nodded in agreement. "I'll need to go into the city to meet my relatives and to see what permits are needed for shops and homes here, if there are any. I can do that alone though."

"I'll go with you," Lesat offered after a moment, as he glanced toward Sam and then Krana. He felt a tug in both directions. When Sam had given him the Amulet of Swirling Winds, he'd had to hold back hot tears, and it wasn't because it was a powerful artifact. The amulet was part of a family set, one made to connect people together so they could never be lost.

Giving it to him made him feel like part of this family. From his childhood, he'd been alone on the streets of Osera. He'd only had a few friends, including Yeres who had died in the Abyssinian Plains. When he'd chosen to follow Sam, at first it had just been a convenient job, but now.... He looked down toward the amulet on his neck that was the same as everyone else's. Now, perhaps it was becoming something more.

He wasn't sure of everything yet, but he didn't want to let any of them go into danger if he could help it.

"It'd be best if at least two of us traveled together," he added slowly to Krana, testing out the new idea. "I wouldn't like anyone to be alone in a new place. You never know what'll happen." Krana gave him a quick grin in return, before she nodded in agreement.

"Let's settle in first," Sam suggested, pulling everyone's attention back to the present. His head turned toward the inn that was still a couple hundred yards away, where he could see a couple of merchants and some people on foot milling around. "We can look into all of that once we have a place to stay."

With a tap of the reins, he sent his horse forward toward the inn. The gelding's hooves *clopped* on the stones of the road, ringing out the sound of their arrival. The inn was just a little distance off the road. There was a large building beside it that was acting as both stables and warehouse. The doors were open and a couple of merchant wagons and some horses could be seen inside.

"Leave me be!"

As they rode toward the front of the inn, a shout pulled Sam's attention toward one of the merchant wagons that was being loaded near the stables. It was loaded with copper-ringed barrels of different sizes. A boy was sitting on the bench, holding the reins, and an older man was trying to climb on, apparently to ride away, but three burly humanoids had stepped forward to block him.

The largest of them was nearly ten feet tall. His arms and legs bulged with muscle and his face was slightly misshapen, his forehead and skull meeting with an indented ridge. His nose was flat and broad.

Human-Ice Giant. Warrior. Level 49.

He was a mix between a human and a giant, which was something Sam would have said was impossible if he hadn't seen it. The giant's huge, pale hand fell on the older man's shoulder, pulling him back from the wagon. The hand was large enough that it covered the man's shoulder and neck, making him gasp with pain as his body locked up.

Human. Merchant-Brewer. Level 32.

The merchant was a late middle-aged man with a short, white beard. He was wearing a faded, brown leather jerkin. The rest of his clothes were plain and had seen better days. The boy on the wagon was dressed similarly, his level a sign of his young age.

Human. Merchant-Brewer. Level 12.

The other two thugs accosting the merchant looked disreputable and had strange classes. One of them was clearly a melee type, but Sam had never seen his class or subclass before. He looked mostly like a normal, muscled warrior, but his joints seemed to meet at slightly odd angles and there was something snake-like about him. His race was also...strange.

Human (?). Brawler-Body Transmuter. Level 41.

The last individual was a scruffy-looking, whipcord man with a thin, brown goatee that instantly reminded Sam of Nelgen.

Human. Merchant-Sorcerer. Level 48.

"I've told you," the merchant forced out, his voice rising in strained panic as he looked between them, "I'm not paying your fees. The city guard will take care of you soon enough. This is a peaceful valley and you have no right to interfere with my business."

"Well, if you don't want to pay the fee," the Sorcerer said with a flat smile as a sphere of swirling blue-white frost appeared in his hand, "why don't you let your boy there come and work for us? We'll waive all of your taxes in the future. I'm sure he'll do wonderfully as a new initiate for the Iceblood Guild. We could always use a Brewer."

The Ice Giant hybrid stomped forward, dragging the merchant with one hand as his other reached toward the boy who was sitting on the seat of the wagon.

"No! He's my grandson!" The merchant tried to struggle against the giant's grasp, but he was dragged along unwillingly as the giant squeezed tighter around his neck and he let out a sharp gasp of pain. "Leave us alone! Rusel, go...*run!*"

The boy's face was paler than the snow as he trembled in place, his hands gripping the horse's reins, but he was too terrified to flee.

"*Help!*" the merchant's half-strangled voice rang out in the air with a note of desperation as he called out for anyone nearby to save him.

Chapter Fourteen

THE ICEBLOOD GUILD

The half-giant's hand landed on the boy's neck, scooping him off of the wagon seat like a strangled chicken.

"*Ucgghk...!*" As he was swept into the air, a choked-off scream echoed from the boy's throat. He dangled there, held up only by the giant's hand as his face turned red and he struggled to breathe.

"Of course, if he doesn't want to work for us, we can always freeze off some extra bits until he agrees. A Brewer only needs his hands." The sorcerer laughed as he raised the frost orb higher. A cold wind spiraled around him, hardening into a frosty edge like a blade.

His magic was strange in Sam's senses, somehow part of him and not at the same time. The force of the ice did not fit the sorcerer. It felt like it belonged to something else, a more powerful concept or being than the thug should have been in contact with. Before Sam could create a plan, he'd taken in what was happening and a wave of anger swept through his body.

The boy, Rusel, had to be 18 to have his class, but he was small and looked three years younger. He reminded Sam of himself when he was younger and weaker. He didn't know the merchant or his grandson, but everything about this encounter reminded him of Nelgen and the thugs in Cliff's End, as well as Nelgen's threats.

The constant irritation of the essence in the air was also making him short tempered. He decided to do something about it.

A sudden, warning sense of danger caused the giant to look around as he felt something approaching him, only to see a flight of crystal blue arrows heading his way. The giant was large, but clumsy, and before he could react, the arrows slammed into his shoulder, legs, and arms, ripping narrow holes through his body as they exploded out the other side.

Frost-tinged blood ran out of the wounds, pouring down the giant's body as he shuddered. The boy fell out of his numb grip, tumbling to the ground like a wet sack of potatoes. He lay there, shaking as he tried to catch his breath. His chest was heaving in quick jerks and starts, and his face was purple-red.

The giant was frozen in place for a moment as blood poured out of the half-dozen wounds on his body. Then, he gathered himself together as he slowly turned toward Sam, his mouth dropping open in a roar.

GGRaAAAGGh!!

A thunderous, rolling echo burst out through the area, like a wave of sonic force. It sent Sam's cloak flaring into the wind and the horse beneath him shook, an instinctive fear rising up in it as it tried to buck. Sam's knees clamped down on it, holding it in place for a moment before he jumped off the saddle and pulled out his staff.

He slammed the butt into the ground in front of him, his left hand pushing outward as an Essence Shield formed in the air between his group and the three thugs, blocking the rest of the roar. The wounds on the giant were already sealing over. The frost in the blood was hardening into an icy white layer as it stopped the bleeding. He hadn't been trying to kill the giant, but the hybrid's durability was higher than he'd expected. He'd thought it would at least fall down. By that point, the advantage of surprise was gone as the other two thugs spun toward Sam.

At the same time, his father and Lesat jumped off their horses and came to stand beside him. Behind them, Krana was with his mother and sister, a bright yellow Earth shield surrounding them all. The weight of the new amulet on Sam's chest gave him the reassurance to push for what was right. Without that, he might have chosen to protect his family first and ignore this conflict. It seemed his father was of the same mind.

"Leave these two alone and go," Jeric ordered as he glared at the thugs. His hands were on his hips as his face hardened into sharp lines. "Otherwise, it won't be just a wake-up call."

His words framed Sam's attack as something minor, a warning tap rather than a dangerous assault, but he wasn't bothering to use Persuade on them. Perhaps he also wanted to fight.

A spiral of crystal flame flared out around Sam as he compressed his aura. An even larger flight of a dozen arrows formed above him. In his left hand, a roiling sphere of crystal flame appeared at the same time, far more intense than the frost sphere that the sorcerer was playing with. Flickers of crystal blue light radiated out across the area, glinting on the green of the grass and the stones of the road.

The sorcerer and the brawler turned toward them then, their faces turning to snarls of anger. The giant *roared* again, but the sound waves shattered against the Essence Shield in front of Sam, barely creating a ripple.

"Be careful!" the merchant shouted as he scrambled forward, grabbing at his grandson under the shoulders as he dragged him to the side. "They're from the Iceblood Guild! They're dangerous!"

It looked like the merchant wanted to go even farther away, but once he got Rusel to his wagon, he hesitated, looking back toward Sam and the others and then toward the Iceblood Guild. He pulled Rusel up into the back of the wagon and stopped, turning around again with a look of conflicted desperation on his face.

He couldn't run away right now.

Sam's attack had placed him in an even worse position in some ways. Before, he might have been able to bribe his way out, but now he had to hope that the newcomers won this conflict. If Sam lost, the Iceblood Guild would take out their anger on him and his grandson. He was forced into being a supporter by default.

"They're stronger than they look!" he shouted, adding what bit of help he could.

"I don't know who you are," the sorcerer sneered as he raised the sphere of frost up in the air, "but you'll pay for interrupting my business and attacking us."

Despite his words, he hesitated as he looked toward Sam and the Essence Shield that was covering the area between them. He glanced at the wounds on the giant and then shot a glare at the merchant that promised pain. The amulet at Sam's belt *pinged* repeatedly as it deflected the gazes that were turned toward him.

"These are criminals, right?" Sam growled, glancing over his shoulder toward the merchant as he took advantage of the sorcerer's delay to ask the most important question. He just wanted to confirm something before he killed them all. He didn't feel like getting in trouble with the city guard right now, not when they wanted to live here peacefully, but he hadn't been able to stop himself from jumping in.

"Uh...yes," the merchant mumbled, his eyes widening as he stared back and forth between Sam and the sorcerer. He couldn't make out Sam's features beneath the grey hood. The strange caster was an enigma, his form blurry.

There was a threatening spiral of strange, crystalline flame surging around him in a bright, burning halo of rippling light. The frost that often touched the air was boiling away from him as the entire area heated up. He wavered for a moment, before he decided to throw the rest of his chips in on the only bet he had left.

"They're a band of thugs who have been harassing people throughout the villages around here for the last year. They have some strange and powerful Ice magic behind them...nothing I've ever seen before. They're dangerous."

"Good enough." Sam nodded as he turned his attention back to the sorcerer. A weight of self-restraint lifted off of his chest. The sphere in his hand burned brighter as he poured more essence into it. "That's all I needed to know."

"I'm going to kill all of you," the sorcerer snarled as he looked toward the merchant and then back at Sam. His expression was ugly and dark. "First you, Henar, and then these idiots. Those women will be my serving maids, licking my feet as I crush their will day by day."

Before Sam or his father could attack, an Earthen spike exploded up from the ground between the sorcerer's legs, heading straight up. A strangled shriek broke off in the sorcerer's throat as he tried to throw himself out of the way, but he was a bit too slow. The stony spear shredded his thigh as he tumbled to the side.

"That's enough of that," Krana rumbled from behind Sam.

At that point, there was no need for more discussion. Jeric and Lesat shot forward to the sides, angling around Sam's shield as they headed for the enemies.

At the same time, the flight of arrows above Sam *hissed* forward in burning trails of crystal flame, separating into three groups of four as they headed toward each of the enemies. This time, he was targeting their heads and hearts.

The sorcerer reacted, his frost sphere expanding into a swirling, icy barrier in front of him that was covered in streaks of white and blue. The four arrows heading his way slammed into it with shattering explosions, tearing gaps in the ice before they burned away.

To the side, the brawler dodged, his body flowing like a serpent as he tried to weave out of the way of the oncoming barrage. He was fast, but two of the arrows still hit him, tearing a hole through his right bicep and abdomen. He let out a sharp hiss of pain as he completed his spin and kicked off the ground, shooting toward Lesat, who was approaching him at a run.

The half giant was slower, and all four arrows *slammed* into his body, tearing holes in him. One exploded directly against his forehead and three others across his chest in a scintillating burst of crystal flame, but it wasn't enough to take him down. His bones had to be as hard as magical steel, or perhaps he was using some defensive ability now, since the arrows burned out before penetrating all the way through.

The levels of these thugs were all in the 40s, which meant it was a fairly even fight, but Sam's side still had the advantage. The tier upgrade at Level 40 had significantly advanced his father and Lesat's skills as well, and with the enchantments from Sam, they had the advantage as they crashed against the two thug melee fighters. Jeric was surrounded by a swirling yellow-gold Earthen Shield as his hammers appeared in his hands.

He'd upgraded the shield to Expert as his 40th tier choice, giving him an immensely strong defense against spells and other abilities. His hammers resonated with a soul-stirring clash of deep, bass notes as he raised them in the air and activated both Reverberating Blow and his new tier ability.

Rain of Hammers.

His attacks slammed down toward the giant like meteors falling to earth, crashing into the giant's arms that slowly rose to block, and then into his undefended legs. Six attacks hit at once as Jeric's hammers *blurred* through the air, slamming into him again and again.

The giant was immensely durable, but a bit slow, and against Jeric's assault he was like an unrefined block of stone waiting for the sculptor to break it down. Ringing *thuds* and *cracks* echoed from the impacts as Jeric pressed forward. His face was a mask of seething anger. These three had threatened his wife and daughter. The giant's body shook with each blow as he stepped back, his feet slamming against the ground with heavy *thuds* as he tried to defend. Even with Jeric's massive strength, the giant wasn't being knocked down, but he wasn't able to respond either.

On the other side, Lesat was having a harder time of it against the Brawler-Body Transmuter. The man was a bit shorter than Lesat and he slid around his attacks as if he didn't have bones, his fists, palms, and feet lashing out. *Thuds* and *cracks* rang out as the attacks slammed against Lesat's shield and barriers. The guard was forced to shift to a more defensive posture as he was pushed back. He wasn't taking any damage yet, since he had several defensive barriers to take up the slack, but it wasn't clear how long the charges in them would last. The brawler's attacks were coming hard and fast.

Crystal Focus extended across the area as Sam took in everything that was happening. Behind him, he could sense Krana and his mother starting new spells. Altey also had her wand in her hand, looking for an opening. Her little face was frozen in concentration, her eyes tracking the battle. She looked a bit scared, but more than that she was determined.

At that moment, Sam's crystal flame sphere exploded against the sorcerer's ice barrier, shattering it and revealing a furious, dark expression. A circle of white frost formed on the dirt around the sorcerer as he raised his hands, chanting something under his breath. He gripped at the air as he released his spell. Two icy blue claws formed in front of him, each about six feet across, resembling the talons of some giant beast, including bony, spiked knuckles and crescent-shaped scales along the sides.

"Die!" the sorcerer snarled as he lashed forward with his hands again, controlling the claws. The tips were sharp wedges nearly a foot long that glinted like frozen blades as they shot toward Sam.

His Essence Shield shuddered as the spell slammed into it, but held. The area where the claws touched the barrier began to crystallize, the sorcerer's mana pouring away as it was locked down by the ability. The thug clawed at the air again, trying to slash forward through the barrier, but Sam had already had enough of him.

The energies of the world resonated around him with a bright *hum*, like a memory of the dreams he'd had of the Nexus. The images from the dreams gave him some more ideas on how to use his Aura of Crystal Flame, especially when he'd seen those three demons walk out of the Nexus and the four Astrals who met them.

Now, he decided to try something new.

Eighteen points of essence poured out of his body in an instant, condensing into a star-like sphere. Instead of the simple, condensed flame that made up his usual fireball spell, which exploded outward on impact, this one had layers. At the center, there was a bright, translucent spark of crystal flame, surrounded by four rotating spheres of cerulean blue that shaded darker toward the edges. Each layer was made up of a few points of essence, and the bright heart at the center of the spell was a half dozen points on its own.

It looked like a star gleaming in the air, surrounded by layers of crystalline light. As it hung there, echoes of the energy condensing in it pulsed out into the world, carrying a deep warning of the threat inside.

Starflame. The spark at the center was a nascent rune for *star*, although it wasn't fully formed yet. He felt a sense of mental strain that tugged at his mind and soul as he held the complicated spell form together.

With a flick of his will, the starflame sphere shot forward, heading straight for the sorcerer as it flew through the gaps in the claws. As soon as he released it, Sam stepped forward, his hands outstretched to the sides as he slammed them together. The Essence Shield in front of him responded, its sides curving toward the sorcerer as it surged ahead, following behind the starflame sphere as it formed a bubble around the sorcerer. The claws were swept up by it, forced backward as Sam poured more essence into reinforcing the shield.

The sphere tumbled through the air toward the sorcerer, the layers in it spinning around one another as flares of energy flickered from the sides. It struck him on the chest as it shattered. The rune at the center flared, igniting the four layers surrounding it. One by one, each of them ruptured, burning outward like a miniature nova. Then the entire five-meter-wide area inside Sam's Essence Shield disappeared in a wash of brilliant crystal light. A giant, ear-rattling explosion ripped through the air, accompanied by a flare of light so bright it was probably visible from Highfold.

For a moment, a miniature sun was born where his spell had hit. Then it was gone, the energy flowing upward as the shield channeled it toward the sky. The Essence Shield was made from the same energy, so it was fairly efficient for him to block it. Most of the direct force from the explosions had rolled off it. Only the sonic force and the exploding dirt and stones had drained his energy to contain them. Sam pulled the shield back toward him, revealing what was left of the area.

The first thing he saw was a scorched black area, and then there was a huddled, charred form at the center that slowly, trembling, stood up. The sorcerer's clothes were nothing but rags and a large part of his body was burnt. His features were barely recognizable, but he was still alive. There was the shattered flavor of ash and broken ice in the air around him. The taste of it drifted in Sam's senses, evidence of some enchantment or artifact having exploded and saved his life.

Pity. But it was something that he could fix. Sam raised his hand as he summoned another flight of crystal flame arrows to finish him off.

"I will...kill you..." the sorcerer gasped out as he haltingly reached into a pouch at his waist and pulled out a small, icy blue pill that he threw into his mouth. The sorcerer's earlier hesitation was gone as he let out a groan, grabbing toward his stomach and throat.

As soon as he swallowed the pill, Sam felt a weird surge of energy that echoed with a trace of essence. At the same moment, a layer of white-blue frost began to flow out of the sorcerer's skin and cover his body. A moment later, he was encased in the frost, like an elemental that had come to life, and he tilted his head back as he let out a pained roar. Spikes of ice burst out of his skin, forming a layer of frozen armor around him. Whatever he'd taken, it looked like it was causing him a great deal of pain.

It was also healing him.

"The Iceblood Guild will not allow you to live after attacking us," the sorcerer hissed. His voice was a strange, uneven warble of frozen vowels and cracked vocal cords. "I don't know who you are, but your days have ended.

The sorcerer glanced toward his allies. At that moment, the giant was being beaten back by the repeated blows of Jeric's attacks, staggering as he kept his arms raised to protect his face. It didn't look like he was going to fall down anytime soon. On the other side, the brawler was beating on Lesat like a child kicking a tin can, leaving repeated ringing sounds hanging in the air, but he was unable to break through his defense, leaving their match as a stalemate.

"Retreat," the sorcerer hissed again, his words crackling as he spoke to the other two. At the same time, he slammed his hands together in front of his face and a huge wave of white-blue ice burst out from the ground at his feet, like a tide heading for Sam, Lesat, and Jeric. The front edge of it was a wall of jagged ice like tumbled spears, their tips bright and dangerous.

It forced Lesat and Jeric to take a step back, their shields hardening around them as they braced themselves against it, and a moment later it was surging over them with a sound like shattering glass. It crashed against Sam's Essence Shield with a force that was three times stronger than before, and the trace of essence in the ability was even more obvious.

It was the same as he'd felt in the snow, just vastly weaker, and it was pouring out of the sorcerer with a stunning lack of control, making it clear that the thug had no idea how to use it. Perhaps he didn't even have the ability to channel it properly. It wasn't his own power. His abilities had been augmented somehow.

It raised several important questions in Sam's mind, including how this Iceblood Guild was related to the force he'd felt in the snow. *Why were these thugs working with it...and why was it allowing that?* An Outsider's arrogance would only ever see humans as servants or slaves.

What did it want? His questions were distracted as the icy tide faded away.

It gave the three thugs enough time to disengage and they grouped together, turning as they ran off together into the distance. Except for the brawler, their steps were limping, but they covered the ground easily. After a moment, the giant picked up the sorcerer and carried him in one arm, his legs stretching out as he ran faster. After a moment, they were gone, fading away into the distance.

The only thing left behind was the shattered ice on the ground and the echoes of the fight that were still fading away. Heads and frightened eyes began to pop out of the inn and stables as they looked toward what had just caused all of the commotion.

To the side, the merchant wiped frozen sweat off his forehead with a trembling hand as he looked toward Sam and then after the Iceblood Guild. His lips shook as he mumbled something to himself. He looked down at his grandson, who was still safe in the back of the wagon, and then he turned toward Sam and the others, staring at them.

"I have to thank you," he mumbled slowly, shaking his head in confusion as he looked after the Iceblood Guild and then back to them. "I thought we were dead there after you attacked. But you don't know the trouble you've gotten yourselves into or the trouble you've brought on me for sure now."

He sighed as he looked down at his grandson and shook his head again. Then he turned toward Sam and stomped over on half-numbed legs, examining them from head to toe with wary eyes.

"I'm Henar," he said bluntly, as he started to grimace. "That's my grandson Rusel. I thank you for your help." He looked around again at the heads sticking out windows and two large guards from the inn who were stomping toward them.

"You've saved our lives," he added, the grimace deepening, "or close enough. But you've also taken some options away and made some things harder. I can't buy them off now." He looked after the thugs again, as if thinking about something. Then he finally came to a decision as he looked back at Sam and Jeric, as well as the others who were gathering together in front of him now.

"Unfortunately, without you around in the future, we'll just be dead again unless we want to flee from Highfold. And right now, I'd rather not do that. I still have family here." He looked between the group, his gaze sliding away from Sam several times. His aged eyes took in Aemilia and Altey and softened slightly as he let out some of the breath he'd been holding. His gaze moved on to the others, finally settling on Jeric as he singled him out as the oldest and the most likely to be the leader here.

"Instead, it looks like I'll have to throw my lot in with you," he said with a sigh, "whoever you are. But at least you can't be worse than them. The woman and the kid with you prove that." He stuck his hand out toward Jeric.

"So, now you've got yourself a brewer. Pleased to meet you, I suppose." He glanced back toward the wagon as Jeric took his hand, and then he looked back, his eyes meeting Jeric's in a direct, honest gaze. "I hope you like ale."

Over his shoulder, Sam stared into the distance as he tracked the direction that the Iceblood Guild had run, wondering where they were going, and when they would be back. He had no doubt that they would be. The ice on the ground was shattering, turning into drifts of snow that began to blow through the air, as his hands curled into fists.

Crystal flame crackled around him, burning away the essence in the snow as it tried to land on his shoulders.

Chapter Fifteen

TIME TO KILL

"What is this Iceblood Guild?" Jeric asked Henar as the party and the two new additions settled into a private meeting room in the inn. His voice was concerned. It had taken them a half hour or so to calm down the innkeeper and the guards, but the Iceblood Guild was already known for causing trouble. In the end, all they'd had to do was blame it on them.

It was also true. The innkeeper had looked suspicious at first, but at the sight of a gold coin, he'd promised to alert the city guard about what happened and told them they were welcome to stay here.

According to Henar, the Iceblood Guild was competent enough that they'd be able to find them wherever they went in the valley, so staying here was no different from anywhere else. At least here, there were beds. From the bit he'd said already, it seemed like even if they hadn't intervened, the Iceblood Guild would have caused them trouble. The thugs had been terrorizing the villages in the valley for the past year, but they'd focused their attention on the lesser known merchants and farmers, since the city guard cared less about them. They would have been a target as soon as the Iceblood Guild noticed them. At least this way, they'd warned them off.

If he were able to make it happen, the next meeting would not end well for the Iceblood Guild. He was angry that they'd threatened his mother. He was also curious about the talisman or artifact that the sorcerer had used to survive his new spell, and the strange pill he'd taken before running away. Those did not seem like things the sorcerer should have had, so the question was where they had come from, and what they had to do with the essence in the snow.

He felt the *ping* of his amulet as Henar and Rusel looked at him, but he was standing on one side of the room, working on a temporary enchantment for the walls. He'd started as soon as they arrived, adding runes for privacy and a basic shield. It was a variant of a warding spell he'd developed after studying the illusion amulet, and it should create a safe area for them to converse here. It wouldn't hold up to much, but if it broke, it would give them a bit of warning. It was also good practice in applying the runes he was learning and kept him out of Henar's direct eyesight.

So far, it sounded like the Iceblood Guild had left the important areas in the valley alone, including the inns, even as they'd stolen supplies and wealth from many of the villages in the area. They'd especially avoided foreign merchants and any traders with backing. That was the main reason the city guard hadn't pursued them very hard.

The second reason was that they'd been stealing instead of killing and they were difficult to find. It wasn't clear if they had a scrying ward or if the city just hadn't found it worthwhile to assign Seers to tracking them yet. Sam shook his head as he drew another runic line on the wall of the room. When it was complete, he poured his essence into it and then moved on to the next part of the pattern.

He was using a combination of *privacy*, *shield*, *mana*, and *barrier* runes to create a quick shielding formation, as well as a *wood* elemental rune to attune the pattern to the wood of the walls. Hopefully, it would last a little while.

This was a common room connecting a handful of chambers, making a sort of suite for traveling merchants and guards that took up half of the top floor. The gold coin that Jeric had given the innkeeper was enough for them to stay here for a month, if they wanted to, although it didn't include food. Once this ward was done, he planned to reinforce the other rooms as well, making sure that there was at least one layer of defensive shielding around them all. It shouldn't take him more than a few hours.

The enchantment would last the whole month if he stabilized it now and then, but the walls weren't strong enough to hold too much mana. It was more of a warning system than anything else. If he wanted a stronger defense, he'd have to spend a lot longer on it, building the enchantment into the walls itself and changing out the materials. That wasn't a commitment he planned to make for a temporary inn room.

The shielding amulets he'd made his family were their real protection. While he worked, his parents slowly got Henar to open up, explaining more about what was going on around Highfold.

"It all started about a year ago," Henar explained slowly, his eyes distant as he looked around the room, causing Sam's amulet to *ping* again. "They didn't call themselves the Iceblood Guild back then." He paused as he gave Sam a long gaze, trying to focus on him before his attention slid away, but it was no use and after a moment, he gave up on it. Instead, he looked toward his grandson, who was sitting next to him.

"Some of them have been around for a while...born here, or close enough." He let out a deep breath as he continued. "That half-giant, for example, he's been around this area for at least twenty years. He's not the brightest and has been kicked out of most villages for causing trouble and breaking things, attacking people...but the other two are new. The short version is that a bunch of local thieves and ne'er-do-wells joined together about a year ago and started causing more organized trouble, taking hostages for ransom...for small things at first, like a barrel of ale...and then holding up local merchant wagons, and so on.

"It was always isolated folks, unlikely to go for help," he said as he let out a bitter laugh. "Like me just now, I suppose, though I didn't think they'd dare to come so close to an inn. They must be getting bolder."

Sam listened in as he let his father do the talking, focusing on the key parts as he continued his enchanting work.

"They've been doing some pretty bad things, but what they said just now was worse than I've heard before. I don't know why they wanted to kidnap Rusel here, but I'm pretty sure they were after that more than my ale."

"They wanted a Brewer for something?" Krana asked, frowning as she listened to the story. "That's strange."

"I suppose so, miss," Henar replied, nodding toward Krana politely. It seemed like he was starting to relax a bit, now that the guild was gone. "That's about all I know of them. All I can say is that something's happened to make them stronger than they should be. I saw that pill the sorcerer used. I've never seen something like that before. They must have found a backer recently, so they've become more violent."

"We just wanted a peaceful stay here," Jeric rumbled with a frown as he exchanged a glance with his wife. The concern in his eyes was clear. Aemilia looked back at him with a steady gaze, just nodding in reassurance. Then he looked toward Sam then, debating how all of this would play out for their secrets.

"It seems we've already made some enemies," he said. "That's unfortunate. Do you think they'll be back soon to find revenge? If so, we can try going to the city guard."

Henar hesitated as he looked at Jeric and then around the room before he shook his head slowly. "That's been tried, but it hasn't worked so far. It looks like you can defend yourselves though, which is why I decided to take your side just now. I don't know if you want to seek them out, but at least they might avoid you, and me by association."

"So, it's our problem to deal with then?" Sam spoke up from the side of the room, turning his attention away from the runes for a moment. "The city guard won't help at all?"

"Well," Henar hesitated as he looked toward Sam. He looked a bit nervous, probably because Sam's face was still hidden. "You're not from Highfold proper, and the city guard has a bit of a bias about that. There's a pretty big divide in how they see the villages compared to themselves. You're not foreign officials or a big merchant group."

"I see," Sam said simply, turning away again as he looked at the half-completed enchantment on the wall. "Then they won't interfere if we take care of the problem either?"

"No, they'd probably happily overlook it," Henar agreed, his eyes lighting up a bit. "You'd be getting rid of an irritation for them. Do you think you can do it? You'd be doing a service to all the villages around here."

"Hold on a bit now," Jeric said, raising his hand as he looked around. He was feeling frustrated, since he'd only wanted to find a calm place for them all. "I don't want to get into a battle as soon as we've arrived, but it's true we might not be able to avoid it." His eyes narrowed as he looked at Henar, trying to assess the quality of the man in front of him. "Before that, I'd like some more information from you."

Henar nodded and turned to Rusel. "Run on down and grab one of the small blue barrels, the Highsun Copper Ale," he told him. "It sounds like we may be here for a bit." A moment later, the boy ran out of the room and Henar turned back to look at Sam and then at Jeric.

"It'll take him a minute to find that and unbury it," he said slowly as a frown appeared on his face. "Go ahead and ask."

"What's your story?" Jeric asked immediately. "Why is the Iceblood Guild bothering you? You're local here."

"My wife passed away years ago and my children ran away to be adventurers." Henar shook his head, his hands rising in the air helplessly. "I suspect they've passed away as well by now. All I have left for family is Rusel here...and that makes me an easy target." Henar shrugged, the motion somehow fatalistic as if he'd long ago accepted whatever life had in store for him.

"There's not much else to say besides that. They target whoever looks good. I'm not sure why they wanted a Brewer either. Maybe they were thirsty. The only abilities for the class are mixing liquids, infusing herbs or other plants, and adding mana or other properties. A good Brewer can make a nice, restorative ale, I suppose. Maybe that's what they're after." He looked around the room, his gaze trying to settle on Sam, before he turned back to Jeric.

"I'd like the answer to a few questions of my own, if you don't mind," he added. "I've thrown my lot in with you, it seems, and I'd like to know who I'm working with, to make it blunt."

"Ask," Sam said, his voice resonating around the room before the others could respond. In his opinion, it was only fair. The merchant should know what he'd signed up for. The only question was whether or not he'd give him all the details.

Henar turned around in his seat as he stared at Sam, or tried to, his voice sharpening. "You seem like a good family, but your caster there is strange. What's going on with that hood and illusion?"

Sam smiled under his hood as he looked back at Henar, wondering if the man really wanted the truth.

"He's our son," Jeric said immediately, reaching out for Aemilia's hand. "That's all that's important. The illusion is more to protect him than to worry you."

"What do you mean?" Henar grumbled in irritation as he tried to look toward Sam again. There was curiosity in his eyes, but no trace of trouble that Sam could see.

"A curse," Sam said simply, as he looked toward Henar and made a decision. "I'll show you what I look like, but don't react badly. I'm still human."

According to the World Law, that wasn't true, but Sam felt like he could make up his own mind about that sort of thing. He wasn't going to let the World Law take his humanity away from him just by changing a word on his status page. It would also be a good test of the man's character. If he reacted badly, it would mean he wasn't as trustworthy as he seemed.

"A curse?" Henar grumbled again. He looked like he wanted to spit when he heard the word, but there was no bucket around, so he was forced to swallow it. At the same time, his interest was piqued. "What could possibly be so weird that you're hesitating to show it off? Do you have three noses?" He tried to look under Sam's hood, but his gaze slid away again.

"I tried Assessing you, but all I can tell is that you're over Level 40. My ability is too low to give me information about the Expert tier."

Sam shrugged as he deactivated his amulet and reached up to his hood, pushing it back around his neck as he looked toward Henar. The man froze, his face paling to an odd shade that was a mix of tanned skin and fear, as his hand on the table trembled. He stared at Sam as the joints in his body locked into place.

"A demon!" he forced out, his voice shaking as he tried to hold himself together. Only the idea that it was a curse and that he'd just been speaking normally to Sam kept him from jumping out of his seat and running away. "You're a demon?!"

"No. A curse made me look like this," Sam replied calmly as he pulled his hood back up and reactivated his amulet. As soon as he did, Henar relaxed and took a deep breath as he looked toward Jeric and Aemilia. It took him a moment to pull himself back together, but since no one else in the room was reacting, he was forced to accept that it wasn't as strange as he thought.

"He's really your son?" he asked hesitantly, searching for confirmation.

"Yes," Aemilia said firmly, nodding at him. "There's also a Guardian Star symbol on his hand to show that he's on the side of the church. You can be at ease." There was a flicker of maternal warning in her eyes to not push the matter any further or she'd become upset with him, which Henar recognized from his own wife, years ago. It made his heart seize up a bit before it relaxed again.

"Well then," Henar let out another long breath. "Right, I'll just blame my own curiosity for asking. That was a surprise...but a curse is a curse, I suppose." He shook his head. "Now I see why you're not showing everyone. I apologize for asking."

His reaction was less dramatic than Sam had feared, which made him like the man a little bit. He was also interested in the abilities Henar had just mentioned, the brewing of liquids and mana. He rubbed his chin thoughtfully as he thought about the pill the sorcerer had eaten and why they might want a Brewer. He didn't know a lot about alchemy or herbalism, but he wouldn't put it past the Iceblood Guild to be experimenting with something like that.

"We should focus on what we can deal with now," he offered eventually, "like how to get rid of that guild and whatever is behind them."

"We won't have any rest here until we do, it looks like," Jeric agreed slowly, nodding his head. "We'll also need a good place to stay long term, once we move out of this inn."

"Well, that's a bit of a problem actually," Henar interrupted as he caught his breath and looked around the room again, trying to calm himself.

"What do you mean?" Jeric asked, feeling puzzled as he looked toward the brewer.

In response, however, Henar just held up a hand for calm as he looked off toward the ceiling, apparently focusing his thoughts. A minute or two passed as Henar thought, and before long Rusel returned carrying a small keg with copper rings and a blue swab of paint on the side.

"You're not from around here," Henar answered once ales were poured around the room, "so you don't know this, but Highfold is a bit particular when it comes to dwellings. You're welcome to stay in any of the inns, or even as a guest in a particular home for a little while, but since you're planning to stay here for a longer time, the Ice Sylphs have a rule for the area."

"What's that?" Sam asked, as his curiosity rose.

"Well, it's pretty simple really. To settle here, you're going to need the permission of an Ice Sylph. Anyone will do, but finding them is harder than you think. They're a very reclusive people. It's customary to take some gifts as well."

"That's a strange tradition," Jeric spoke up, rubbing his beard as he thought. "Seems straightforward, but what happens if you don't get their permission?"

"Then you can't stay, except in an inn," Henar replied, raising his hands in the air helplessly. "The Ice Sylphs are the original founders of the valley and this is still their tribe's land. They're very hands-off about it all, but that's one rule that's stuck around, and it's tied into the magic that keeps this valley warm. The problem is, they don't much like visitors and they often ignore people asking. Finding one to ask is just the first part. If you're born here, it's a different matter, but for folks from outside, it's harder.

"If you try to settle here without their permission, well, you'll find the land itself working against you to expel you. There's usually pleasant weather here, but only if you're invited. Snow will bury your home, ice will freeze your fires, cold will seep into your bedrooms, your plants won't grow, your livestock will die of exposure...." Henar's voice trailed off.

"I get the idea." Jeric made a rumbling sound of displeasure, turning his thoughts over as he looked toward his wife. He hesitated for a moment, debating whether to bring it up, since her past was always a delicate subject, but he remembered something that she'd said on the ride here.

"Didn't you say you knew an Ice Sylph as a child?" he asked at last. "Do you think she'd approve of us staying here if we can find her?"

Aemilia was silent for a moment as she looked inward and then she spoke, turning to Henar. "Have you ever heard of an Ice Sylph called Siwaha...an Herbalist? I knew her a long time ago and she used to live here."

Henar thought for a moment and then shook his head. "I wish I could help, but the Ice Sylphs are reclusive and often don't even share their names. I've never heard of her, but she could still live here. If you have a connection to her, it'd be easier to ask her than anyone else. If you can find her."

Sam nodded as he heard the brewer's answer. It would have been too much to expect that he'd know about Siwaha, especially if the sylphs were as private as he'd said. They would have to spend some time looking for her. He was also interested in learning more about his mother's past. She'd never spoken much about it.

"I'll ask my relatives in the city," Krana spoke up, looking optimistic. "If she's around, they might know something about her."

"Well then, it looks like our path is clear." Jeric said as he pounded his fist lightly on the table. It was a sturdy table, but it still shuddered under the force of the blow. "We just need to get a few things in motion and figure out how to deal with that Iceblood Guild."

The idea of a battle didn't bother him, once he'd accepted the need for it. He'd wanted to avoid the trouble, but since there was no other way, he was fine with cleaning up the area before they settled down. The guild had already crossed his bottom line when they'd threatened his family.

"How many more people do they have?" Sam asked, as he turned the conversation toward their preparations. He wanted to know how many of them he was going to have to track down.

Henar's answer was only a shake of his head, indicating that he didn't know.

Sam frowned as he turned back to the enchantment on the wall, his plans forming in his mind as he continued to add runes, pouring his essence into them to stabilize them. As he did, he sorted the new information into a series of tasks he needed to accomplish.

There were three major issues in front of them before they could settle here. First, he needed to eliminate the threat from the Iceblood Guild, as well as whatever was creating the essence in the snow. Second, they had to set up a safe home and protect it. To do that, they needed the permission of an Ice Sylph, which meant getting in touch with Siwaha, if they could find her, and then building or reinforcing a home.

Third, he needed to set up a workshop and produce more items to sell before the Festival of Three Crowns started in a month.

It was a short list, but it didn't look like he'd be able to skip any of the steps. If he wanted this area to be safe for them, he was going to need to make it that way, and the first thing on that list was making sure the Iceblood Guild didn't cause them any more trouble.

His left hand curled into a fist as he stared at the rune on the wall. A surge of expectation ran through his veins, resonating through his body as the essence stars in his blood sang out with battle lust.

Chapter Sixteen

Hunting Bandits

"Can you see their trail?" Sam asked as he turned toward Krana. "How far did they run?"

The party was gathered in the inn, looking out the window toward the distance where the Iceblood Guild had gone. The essence stars in Sam's blood were singing, pushing his senses to alertness, making his mind and movements accelerate. He didn't want to wait for them to come back, not if he could find them while they were injured and take care of the problem.

It would be best to cut down any trouble before it could start.

"Those three, yes," Krana agreed as she looked out the window too, her eyes shading to silver. "I've been keeping an eye on them since they fled. They're about a dozen miles away, in a cave at the edge of the valley, on the lower slopes." She raised her hand as if waving away fog in front of her eyes, frowning slightly.

"They seem to be alone so far, but I get the feeling that they're waiting for someone. There has to be more of the group around somewhere, but I haven't found them yet."

"It would be best to get them before they can meet up," Sam agreed. "Then we can prepare a greeting for their backers." He paused as an idea occurred to him. "Can you see much about the cave? Have they been living there?" The answer would help to explain the guild's infrastructure.

"There are a few barrels and supplies in it, but not much else," Krana replied, shaking her head. "Some type of temporary area, which means it's not where they've been living."

"So it's a hideout or a supply point," Sam mused, rubbing his chin as he looked out the window. "How injured is the sorcerer? Did that ice effect fade?" More importantly, he was interested in whether the essence was still there. At the rate the sorcerer had been wasting it, it was probably gone by now.

That one pill had held at least twenty points of essence, if he compared it to his own spells. Ten or so for the ice wave and another ten for the transformation into a sort of ice golem.

"The ice is gone, but he's not dead," Krana replied as she continued to look at the bandits with *Far Sight*. "It's hard to tell the extent of his injuries, but he's still burned at least. It didn't heal him all the way."

"Good. Let's go take care of them before their friends show up," Sam suggested, flexing his hands as he looked back around the room. He didn't like the idea of splitting up, but it made more sense for his mother and sister to stay here. That meant at least one or two others needed to stay too.

Jeric looked at his wife and daughter, and then toward his son, a frown forming.

"I'll stay with Aemilia and Altey," Krana offered, as she saw the problem. "With the defensive amulets you made, and our spells and other artifacts, we'll be fine. It's unlikely they'll dare to attack the inn anyway."

Jeric gave his wife a long look and it wasn't until Aemilia nodded in agreement that he gave a sharp nod of his own.

"All right," Jeric replied, "then it's Sam, me, and Lesat. We should be enough to take care of those three."

"We won't let them get away this time," Sam agreed as he thought about the last fight. He wanted to finish what he'd started with that sorcerer. The thug was vile and the world would be a better place without him. He'd used frost magic, like in the pill, so he was some type of frost-aligned sorcerer.

"*Iceblood*...." Sam muttered, thinking through the connections he could see.

Sorcerer was an uncommon class and it usually ran in families. It was also nearly always a primary class, tied into that family's bloodline and whatever mystical nature they had. To acquire it as a subclass meant something interesting had happened, like a blood transfusion, something to transfer the magical nature from a source to the new sorcerer.

He rubbed his chin again, wishing for a moment that he had a beard to tug. Unfortunately, there was no sign of stubble on his face. The transformation into an Outsider had removed that. It was just a hypothesis, but he'd give it better than even odds that the sorcerer's class had come from the Iceblood guild's backer.

Somehow.

Why else would a small-time thug be running around with a class like that? It must have also come with a significant cost, if not to the sorcerer himself then to the backer. As for the pill, even if he had more of them, that sort of thing had to come at a cost too, which was why he'd only used it when he was close to death.

If it hadn't been Sam's first time using Starfire, he probably could have killed him with that one hit, even through the defensive artifact, but the rune he was using to hold the spell together wasn't complete yet. It was the beginning of a new path for his crystal flame, one that had come to him as a mix of studying natural runes and his practice with forming them from his aura.

The dream he'd had of the stars had shown him the missing piece, although it had taken him a few days to realize it. A rune wasn't just a symbol, it was a concept, and in almost all ways, the concept was more important than the rune itself. The lines of the rune just gave it structure. That was what he'd been missing when he'd been trying to draw the runes before. He'd been trying to copy the lines first, without trying to replicate the more important concept behind them.

As soon as he switched his effort around, it started to work better.

Even at the Expert stage of both Aura of Crystal Flame and Flame Strike, he was stretching the limit of what he was capable of right now just to form the most basic concept of a rune with his aura, but that meant it was good practice. The *star* concept came from his dreams, where he'd seen them hanging in the void. They had a primal force that had embedded itself in his mind. It wasn't complete in Starfire yet, but it still helped him to channel his crystal flame.

"Let's head out then," he suggested, nodding toward his dad and Lesat. "We should be able to catch up to them in an hour or so."

"We'll leave the horses here and go on foot," Jeric agreed with a rumble, his arms folded over his chest as he looked out the window toward the cave that was in the distance, too far away to see. "Less chance they'll spot us that way."

A moment later, everyone exchanged a few last words and then Sam, Jeric, and Lesat were off, heading out of the building.

**

The cave that Krana had seen was about an hour away on foot. Their steps were light and quick as they jogged toward it. Their Constitution was high enough that running for that distance was no trouble at all. Emerald-green grass and flowering alpine meadows flickered past them as they moved, leaving the road behind as they headed cross country.

On the way, Sam's mind was filled with patterns of crystal flame as he considered how to improve Starfire. From what Henar had said, the Iceblood Guild was going to give him plenty of targets to practice on. The brewer hadn't been sure how many people were involved with the guild, but he did know that there were more than just these three. From the sound of the attacks over the last year, Sam figured there had to be at least a dozen of them, and perhaps twice that.

Krana's directions were easy enough to follow as they continued to run, their boots thudding nearly silently on the grass and dirt. Before long, a sharp spur of stone came into sight as they neared the edge of the valley. It was about a hundred feet above the valley floor, part of a prominent shoulder of the mountain that loomed above them.

The cave was located at the bottom of that mountain, concealed behind a snow-streaked pine grove, just beyond the edge of the valley proper. Above it, the wild slopes of the surrounding mountains held dominance over the area. Unlike the valley behind them, snow covered this area in constant drifts and flurries. The ground all around was coated in a layer nearly a foot deep. It was a sharp contrast from the gentle, early summer weather of the valley. No one lived this far out, not unless they'd been exiled. This was the domain of the monsters and beasts that lived in the cold.

The opening to the cave was hard to spot, even with Krana's guidance. The entrance was hidden in a patch of shadow below an overhanging rock, making it look like nothing more than another part of the mountain. The blowing snow here had already covered over any tracks that the bandits had made on their way in. The three of them didn't speak. They just looked at one another and nodded. They'd already discussed their plan.

Lesat and Jeric spread out to the sides, taking up positions on either side of the cave mouth. Jeric's eyes went distant for a moment as his Earth Sense extended into the cave, and then he looked back at Sam and gave him a single, firm nod.

The bandits were still inside.

A spiral of crystal flame poured out of Sam's body, rising into a spiral all around him as he poured essence into his spell. A dozen crystal flame arrows separated out from it and then he started to condense a sphere with a flickering rune at the center. He was planning to throw another Starfire into the cave, to finish this quickly.

SKREEEE!

At that moment, the piercing screech of something large and angry sounded from the slope above the cave as a ten-foot-long, green and white-scaled lizard with two bat-like wings and only rear legs swooped down. It had a long, bony head with prominent fangs jutting out from its mouth that gave it a cruel smile. Its wings were nearly twenty feet wide, twice its length. Its tail stretched out behind it with a sharp bone spur on the end, which could be used both for clubbing and impaling.

The monster reared back, its jaws splitting open to reveal foot-long fangs and a long grey-white tongue that lashed around like a whip before it released another high-pitched shriek.

Ice Wyvern. Level 46. (Alpine)

Sam stared at it for a moment, even as he started to pour even more essence out into his spell, redirecting it toward the new threat. It was a far more dangerous opponent than the bandits inside the cave.

How had an ice wyvern suddenly appeared? Had it followed the bandits here, waiting to attack them and make a meal out of them...and now that it had seen Sam and the others, it wasn't willing to let them steal its prey? He wasn't sure, but that was the only thing that made sense.

Based on its size and level, it was a juvenile wyvern, but it was no less dangerous for that. Even a young wyvern was strong enough to kill almost everything at its own level. Their scales were as hard as mountain stone and their claws sharper than most swords. At this age, it shouldn't have many abilities besides its physical body, but that wasn't much consolation. It was a monster that was built for killing everything around it.

Their simple hunting mission had just become a lot more complicated. His father and Lesat jumped backwards, their weapons in their hands as shielding spells surrounded them. Without hesitating, they took in what was happening and attacked the wyvern from both sides.

Unfortunately, the thing was *fast*. It spun in place as its tail whipped around. The bone spur on the end cut through the air as fast as a striking viper, heading for Jeric. At the same time, its wing lashed out to the other side, whistling like a saw cutting the air as it headed for Lesat. The wing was edged with bony spurs that could tear through unprotected flesh as easily as a saber.

His father and Lesat dove out of the way, hurling themselves out of range of the attacks in ungainly somersaults as they sacrificed finesse for speed. They went rolling across the ground when they hit, twisting themselves into another roll as they tried to put more distance between them and the monster.

At the same time, the screech that the thing let out was more than loud enough to alert the bandits inside. A moment later, the three thugs came rushing out from the entrance, surrounded in a blur of energy from their abilities. The three of them stared around the area, taking in what was happening.

The brawler and the half-giant looked none the worse for the battle a couple of hours before, but the sorcerer was still burnt across most of his body. Whatever else that ice pill had done to him, he hadn't been able to heal much yet. The sorcerer's eyes were wide with surprise as he saw who they were.

"Kill them!" he shouted.

For a moment, Sam thought they hadn't noticed the wyvern. He was surprised it didn't take advantage of that opportunity to seize one of them and take off with its prey. Then he saw the wyvern responding to the command, ignoring the bandits as it headed after his father, chasing him across the snowy grove in a flurry of lunging steps. At that point, everything clicked into place.

This thing wasn't hunting for food. It was a guard. He'd never heard of a monster working for humans before, and he had no idea how it was possible. *Had they tamed it somehow or seized control of its mind?*

He didn't know of a class that could do that with monsters. There were Beastcallers in the world, but beasts and monsters were different. Humans were only food to monsters. The wyvern's instincts should have rebelled as soon as it saw them. He didn't have any longer to think about it, since at that moment, the wyvern lunged again, snapping at his father.

Its fangs were half a foot long, with easily a dozen of them along its top and bottom jaws. Its attack splintered off of a golden-yellow shield as Jeric rolled wildly out of the way, but the shield wavered. The wyvern's attacks were incredibly powerful, the strength behind them like a mountain collapsing.

At that moment, the bandits joined in on the attack, charging forward behind the wyvern. The brawler headed for Lesat again as the half-giant raced after the wyvern, heading for Jeric. The sorcerer raised his arms as a swirling, icy-blue wind gathered around him, forming into a gale. A surge of intense alarm shot through Sam like a lightning bolt.

This was not good.

His hand dropped with a flick as he released all twelve of the crystal flame arrows that he'd prepared, hurling them toward the sorcerer. They *hissed* through the air with crackling trails behind them. An instant later, they slammed into the ice storm that he was summoning, tearing holes through it as they headed inward.

Seven of them broke apart as they shattered the storm wind, but the remaining five flew through, crashing against a shield that surrounded the sorcerer at the last moment. The bandit staggered, his hands flailing in the air as he tried to control the backlash from his spell. Sam didn't have any more time to watch him as his Crystal Focus spread through the area, tracking the movement of everything around him.

Just then, the starfire spell that he'd been condensing finally came together, with four layers of crystal flame surrounding the intense, white rune at the center that was still only partially complete. He raised it as he turned toward where the wyvern was chasing his father, holding the concept of the spell tightly with his soul. At that moment, his hood fell back from his face, revealing long, curving horns that stretched back from his forehead and brilliant, crystal blue eyes with vertical pupils.

All around him, the snow burned away as his crystal blue aura flared higher, leaving him standing alone in the center of a swirling sphere of power.

CHAPTER SEVENTEEN
ICE WYVERN

Crystal flame burned around Sam in a raging torrent as he released the Starfire spell in his hand, targeting the sorcerer in front of him.

It was an instant decision between the wyvern and the bandits, and he doubted that the wyvern would go down quickly. It was better to eliminate the trash and then deal with the wyvern with their complete focus. He also wanted to take care of any other surprises the sorcerer might have, before he could pull them out.

The sphere of starfire headed toward the bandit like a meteor. The layers of crystal flame surrounding the central rune rotated, each of them turning in a different direction. It gave the sphere a blurred, starlike effect as it flew.

The brawler and half-giant were already a dozen steps away from the sorcerer by the time the spell arrived. The sorcerer saw it coming and the icy blue shield that had blocked the crystal flame arrows sprang up in front of him, growing brighter as he channeled more energy into it.

The sphere collided with that shield almost gently, like a burning star falling into an arctic lake. Crystal Focus tracked the exact moment it hit. At first, the outer layers of the sphere bent, pressing up flat against the shield as they spread slightly outward. Then the *star* rune struck the barrier as the crystal flame layers compacted back toward it, like a white spark landing on ice.

The rune at the center exploded outward, igniting the layers of crystal flame around it one after the other in a cascade of power. Each layer fed into the blast, magnifying the effect as it rippled outward.

The sorcerer's shield was at the center of that explosion, taking the brunt of it as the first expanding ring slammed into it. He was Level 48, but he was already wounded and the shield crumbled away half an instant later. The sorcerer braced himself, trying to reach into his dimensional pouch for something, but he was much too slow. The second, third, and then fourth expanding rings washed over him, disintegrating his body in a flare of crystal flame and burning starlight. A series of metal objects on the sorcerer's body warped, turning to slag with ringing explosions as the intense heat shattered them.

A moment later, his dimensional bag fell to the ground, its edges smoking. Spatial objects were protected by the folded space inside, like an inner bubble, making them difficult to destroy without crushing the entire space. The explosion expanded, covering close to thirty feet in diameter within a tightly contained radius. The snow in the area evaporated, as did the grass beneath it and the few tree branches. A moment later, the spell evaporated, leaving a charred circle in the stony ground that sizzled with residual heat.

Sam spun toward his father, tracking the movement of the half-giant and the wyvern. Lesat had fought the brawler before, and he would have to hold out for a moment on his own.

Jeric was rolling away from another attack as the wyvern snapped forward, chasing after him. He jumped to his feet and continued to evade, trying to put as much distance as possible between him and its fangs. The wyvern was much larger than him, which made it easier for it to cross the ground. Its movements were quick and darting.

It was a predator of the high peaks, one of the deadliest things a person could encounter here. Its natural abilities gave it nearly perfect camouflage, speed, crushing force, and flight. Unfortunately, Jeric was a moment too slow and the monster's fangs sheared through his Earthen Shield, ripping a deep, bloody gash down his calf and nearly tearing off his boot as he tumbled away.

His father's shield could handle some physical attacks, but it was designed for magical ones. It wasn't able to block more than a glancing blow from the wyvern. A new, swirling white shield appeared around Jeric, blocking the following bite and claw slash as the wyvern chased him, knocking him forward like a toy.

The Amulet of Swirling Winds. Under the wyvern's attacks, even that shield was unlikely to last for more than three or four hits.

A moment later, Sam's attention was pulled toward the half-giant. The bandit was outside of the blast radius, and he spun in place as he let out an enormous *roar*, his voice swelling with infused mana. A sharp wave of sound tore out from him, flattening the tree branches and grasses nearby as he hammered his fists together and changed his target, turning to charge toward Sam instead of Jeric.

The half-giant's body began to glow with a blue light that swirled into a pattern of natural runes. The air around him sparkled as the vapor in it froze and shattered, covering him in a swirl of snow and ice. Another racial ability, probably one that enhanced his strength or durability.

As the giant raced toward Sam, the wyvern continued to chase Jeric, its fangs swooping down like icy daggers. Its claws tore forward just as Jeric sprang to his feet again and turned to face it head-on, bracing himself for the impact. He must have been tired of running. His face was set in hard lines as he glanced toward where Sam was and then at the giant running toward him.

His golden-yellow Earthen Shield surrounded him as his hammers rose in the air, the enchantments on them pulsing with multi-toned vibrations. The wyvern's claws crashed against Jeric's shield, shredding it apart. Jeric's hammers landed, shattering scales on the wyvern's head, but then they hit the bone beneath and glanced off, sliding to the side as they rebounded.

The force of it spun him around. Then the wyvern's fangs tore through the unprotected air and into his left shoulder and arm. In that moment, Jeric's Constitution was the only thing holding him together as the wyvern seized him in his jaws and reared upward, flinging its head left and then right, shaking him like a rag doll as it tried to tear him apart.

His Enhanced Physique made his bones and skin harder, but all it could do was hold him together. The wyvern's fangs drove deeper, piercing toward his bones as they tore muscle and veins. The shield from the Amulet of Swirling Winds tried to form, flickering in shards of white light, but it shattered against the wyvern's scales. It couldn't create a solid barrier with something interrupting it.

Blood flew across the snow as the wyvern tossed Jeric back and forth. As he saw it happen, Sam's mind flashed back to being the boy in the tunnels. He'd changed an incredible amount since then, but it was less than half a year ago. The memory of his old panic rushed through him, when he worried that his father would die from the gnome marauder. Back then, he'd been helpless to save his father. This time he could do something about it.

Sam's mind went blank as the anger he'd been bottling up surged out of him. It came from the constant irritation of the essence in the snow, from the bandits threatening his family, and now from this wyvern attacking. He'd wanted to come to Highfold to live a simple life, enchanting and studying as they grew stronger. Then, one day, they would go out and find the Flaws in the Seal and fix them, ensuring a stable future.

Peaceful, calm...the result of planning and progress.

Unfortunately, the slow and steady route wasn't one that was open to him. Just like when the World Law had pushed him into a conflict, the situation in Highfold was doing the same. Even if they hadn't come chasing these bandits, something like this would have happened soon enough. He'd accelerated this meeting by a handful of days or a few weeks at most.

They would never have been left in peace. Rage boiled through him. It was directed at himself for not being strong enough and at the world for not making it easy. The essence stars in his blood intensified, acting like miniature furnaces as they took that anger and burned it, converting it into a source of energy. Crystal Focus grew stronger as time slowed down.

A flight of crystal flame arrows formed and ripped toward the giant in front of him, but he didn't wait to see them land. He tracked the wyvern's movements as the crystal flame around him built to a peak. As soon as it did, he compressed it, forming it into an Essence Blade.

The diamond-shaped spell blasted forward from his hands, flying toward the wyvern that was still trying to toss his father into the air. It hit the wyvern low on the abdomen, just in front of its rear legs, as it was about to jerk its head up into the air again. The crystal blade *sizzled* as it blasted into the monster's stony hide, melting through the tough scales.

Then it exploded. The wyvern's side tore apart in an explosion of scales, blood, and muscle. At the same time, a storm of crystal flame surged outward, blasting away into the air. The force sent the monster's rear legs tumbling, throwing it into a roll. At the same time, its jaws opened in a bloodcurdling shriek that tore at Sam's ears. Jeric fell out of its jaws, rolling across the ground away from the wyvern. His shoulder and left side were covered in a waterfall of blood, but he was moving.

A moment later, the wyvern's claws dug into the ground as it caught its balance. It spun in place, its right leg dragging. Its hips were crooked now and there was a hole the size of a cart wheel in its side. A river of whitish-green blood was pouring out, staining the snow around it. It let out another rattling *shrieeeek* in the air as its wings flapped, stirring up the snow. Then it lowered its head and charged toward Sam in a stumbling half run, half glide.

At the same moment, the looming figure of the half-giant staggered into view, bleeding from half a dozen points as it closed in on Sam, raising its arms to grab at him.

Sam's staff appeared in his hands as more crystal flame poured out of him, and then he sidestepped, swinging the staff toward the giant. Essence poured down his hands into the runes on the staff. The end of the staff thudded into the giant's side at the same time as an oversized hand swept through the air where his head had been.

The staff flickered and struck as a swirling yellow light rose out of the runes and poured their energy into the giant's body. An illusory web of essence that was like drifting yellow spider silk appeared, sinking into the giant's muscles and bones as it froze him in place.

Sam used the force of the rebound to throw himself backward again, trying to avoid the giant's reach. He spun around, ducking behind the giant's frozen form to put it between him and the wyvern as he compressed another Essence Blade in front of him. The paralytic effect of the Staff of Withering Stasis would hopefully last for a moment.

The wyvern was already there, however, barreling into the giant as its clawed wings ripped through the air. The force of its charge threw the half-giant to the side, tearing through him with no regard for friend or foe. If it was working with the bandits, it definitely didn't care about this one. Then it slipped on the snow, bracing itself on its good leg as its wings flapped in the air for balance. A flurry of snow swept out around it, making eyesight useless. Only Crystal Focus kept track of its location as Sam released his spell.

The second Essence Blade sliced through the air at point-blank range as Sam's essence dropped to almost nothing. A warning pulse of emptiness spread through his body with a sharp ache. The snow evaporated around the spell as it cut a path toward the wyvern's sternum, where huge, corded muscles joined together that led back to its wings.

The wyvern shrieked again, the sound choking off a moment later as its wings flared. It reared up, trying too late to avoid the blast. The spell exploded against its chest, flaring with brilliant cerulean light as the energy ripped through the outer scales and exploded against its breastbone. Blood and viscera erupted outward as the monster stumbled back half a dozen paces, its wings beating frantically at the air like an ungainly bat as it tried to stabilize itself. Its movements were uncoordinated, its wings moving out of sync with one another, and the left wing started to droop down as the muscles controlling it snapped, but that wasn't enough to stop it.

The wyvern's head shot down, barreling toward Sam as its fangs flashed. Rows of them like icy knives gaped wide, driving toward his head. The crystal barrier of an Essence Shield appeared between them and the wyvern's head *slammed* into it, its fangs crashing against the shield.

Like porcelain shattering, the shield broke apart under the force, splintering into crystal blue shards. He didn't have enough essence to sustain it. The wyvern's head crashed through, slamming into his shoulder as its fangs ripped their way through his skin. Points of burning, cold pain tore across his side.

Then he was released, the fangs tearing free as the wyvern's wing claw crashed into his left leg, tearing across it as it sent him flying through the air in a tumble of limbs. The Amulet of Swirling Winds activated, surrounding him in another shield as he crashed into the snow a dozen feet away. It cushioned his impact, but he felt the shattering force of bones breaking in his ribs and arm.

The wyvern staggered after him, blood running down its chest and rear leg as it tried to move forward in an ungainly, sliding hop. Then it seemed to freeze, rearing up into the air as it released another piercing *shrieeeek*.

At that moment, two forms appeared on the other side of the wyvern, a sword and a spear glowing with enchantments as they drove the weapons into the wyvern's abdomen, tearing at the wound there to make it larger. The wyvern's wings flapped, its long neck stretching out as it whipped around. Its tail spun through the air, slamming down toward Jeric and Lesat.

Lesat took the blow directly on his shield. The enchanted metal caved in with an enormous dent as the bone spur at the end of the tail struck it. The guard was thrown backwards, tumbling head over heels. At the same moment, Jeric moved in, his hands wrapped around an old, familiar spear. The edge of the Spear of Umbral Flames was covered in black fire that sizzled as Jeric raised it and stabbed it into the wyvern's side again, jamming it deeper into the wound.

The world around Sam spun as he tried to force himself to his feet. His left leg collapsed under him as he tried to put weight on it, forcing him to shift his balance to his right as he wobbled. He could feel blood running down his shoulder and side in hot pulses. Flickering blue flames accompanied it, burning across his skin. His right arm hung limp. He was still able to reach into his aura storage as he pulled out three auras, the dimensional pocket responding to his will more than his movements. His veins felt like they were on fire as he staggered, combusting the auras one after the other.

Each one took him about a second, and in that time, the wyvern reared up again, its wings trying to beat at the air as its tail swung around a second time toward Jeric. This time, the bone point on the end shone with a glaring white aura as shards of ice hurtled through the air next to it.

Jeric grunted as he stabbed the spear deeper, the swirling white barrier of his amulet surrounding him. The wyvern's tail hammered into the shield as he spun, his hands switching positions on the shaft. He was trying to redirect the force of the blow down the spear and back into the wyvern, to make it drive the spear home for him. Unfortunately, the angle wasn't quite right.

The spear tore free as the shield around Jeric shattered. The icy shards all around the tail slammed home, stabbing into his arms, legs, and chest like knives as he was thrown backwards. The spear ripped out of his hands, tearing a long gash along the wyvern's side.

At that moment, Sam finished combusting the last aura. He tried to step forward, but he staggered as his left leg collapsed. The crystal flame in the air condensed around him as a flight of crystal flame arrows *hissed* as they shot forward and headed for the wyvern's open wounds. The dozen arrows were bolts of sizzling cerulean light as they struck, burning their way inward as they tore new paths through the opening. Now that the wyvern's scales were broken, the arrows were much more effective than they'd been in the past. The monster reared again and let out another sharp scream, staggering backward as the arrows seared through its intestines.

Crystal Focus flowed through the air, locating his father where he was lying on the ground. Sam let out a quick hiss of air as he saw the damage, but his dad was still breathing. The only thing he could do right now was

to try and kill the wyvern as fast as possible. His aura burned around him as
the rest of the essence he'd just absorbed flared upward, billowing outward
around him.

Another quick Essence Blade formed in front of Sam and he sent it
hurtling forward. It ripped through the air as it exploded into the open
wound in the wyvern's abdomen, crystal flame burning in blazing streaks
all around it as it incinerated the wyvern's flesh and cut deeper into its
body.

The explosion this time came from deeper in the wyvern's stomach, as its
body bulged outward from the inside. The scales were working against it
now as the force of the spell was contained by its own scaly hide. The shriek
died in the thing's throat as it staggered, its wings flailing as it thrashed
around, half-falling on the ground. As the spell shredded its abdomen, it
slumped over, its wings trying to beat at the air as its fangs bit wildly at
nothing.

Then whitish-green blood erupted from the wounds on its body and its
throat, gushing out like a river. It was durable enough that the explosion
didn't kill it, but it fell to the side, thrashing weakly as it tried to recover. An
icy light began to radiate from its scales, starting to seal the wounds closed.

Another Essence Blade formed in front of Sam as he took stock of the
battlefield, looking for the other enemies. The half-giant was lying dead
on the ground now, its body torn in multiple places. Claw marks from
the wyvern were mixed with wounds from sword and hammer that had
finished it off. Clearly, his father and Lesat had killed the bandit before they
attacked the wyvern.

The brawler was lying dead off to the side as well. He was a broken figure,
half-twisted around his own body, tossed to the ground a few dozen feet
away. His skin had transformed to something like scales in many places.
The bandits were all dead, which meant the wyvern was the only enemy
left now.

At that moment, Lesat stood back up, forcing himself to his feet. His
shield was concave with a massive dent in the center, and it looked like his
left arm behind it was broken. It was twisted and hanging at his side. His
sword was in his hand as he started to walk forward.

"Heal my father!" Sam shouted at him, his voice hoarse. His left hand
pointed toward where Jeric was lying, dragging Lesat's attention toward
it.

Lesat took in what was happening and then nodded, changing his target as he ran toward Jeric. He sheathed his sword and reached to his belt for a healing scroll.

The wyvern was still thrashing around weakly, and Sam kept an eye on it as he reached into his belt pouch, pulling out a healing scroll of his own. He activated the scroll, which dissolved into a swirl of brilliant white light that settled into his body. He felt the energy surge through his veins, sealing his wounds closed as the bleeding slowed. Some strength returned to his left leg too, but testing revealed that it still wouldn't take his weight.

He grabbed his staff in his good hand as he limped in a circle around the wyvern, finding the best angle as a new Essence Blade began to condense in front of him. The spell tore through the air with shredding force, ripping through the wyvern's torn abdomen as it headed upward toward its heart. A moment later, it struck the rib cage from the inside and the force contained in it exploded outward.

The wyvern shuddered, its body swelling in the center as its chest inflated, but its scales contained the full force of the explosion. Its ribs cracked, rupturing under the pressure. Its fangs glinted in the frost as it let out a final weak roar and then it toppled over to the side, its head and neck crashing to the ground, followed a moment later by its wings.

Snow exploded outward, covering everything in a veil of white flakes that were tinted red. The entire area was covered in blood.

CHAPTER EIGHTEEN

ARCTIC WIND

Sam limped as fast as he could, circling around the dead wyvern as he raced toward his father. He pulled out all the healing scrolls he had from his pouch, which ended up as half a dozen sheets in his hand. When he got there, his left leg gave out and he collapsed on the ground next to his father. He dropped his staff to the side as he activated the first scroll and pressed it to his father's chest.

Jeric was covered in blood, with gashes across his shoulder, left arm, chest, abdomen, and both legs. Shards of ice were still embedded in some of the wounds, preventing them from bleeding as much as they would have, which was a small mercy. His eyes were half-open and he was barely conscious as Sam shoved another scroll into his good hand. He'd have to wait for the first one to do its work, but it would be better if he could activate it himself. It would be more effective that way.

As the white light of the first spell surrounded his father, Sam's left hand radiated soft crystal flame as he began to pull out the ice shards, slowly, one after the other. The edges of them melted, but he gripped them with both essence and flame as he pulled them out.

His right arm was still broken, probably in more than one place, and hanging at his side. His breath was also coming in sharp, short gasps as he felt his cracked ribs on that side. He didn't pay any attention to his own wounds. He was just staring down at his father as he used his good hand to remove more of the ice shards. As he touched them, the mana in them conflicted with the crystal flame, and they melted away. Steam rose from them as the white light of the healing spell ran across the wounds where they had been.

Jeric gave out a short, sharp cough as he turned his head and spat clotted blood to the side, clearing his lungs as they started to reinflate. When that light faded, Jeric activated the scroll in his hand and the process continued. On the other side of Jeric, Lesat was also helping, adjusting Jeric's position and pulling out ice shards as well.

All around them, the snowy grove echoed with new silence, the flurries of snow whistling against the rocks above. Red and white-green blood stains covered everything nearby, but now the snow started to fall, gently. Single, solitary flakes drifting down through the air came to rest on top of the blood. Then they melted away and were replaced by another, a moment later. Slowly, inexorably, the snow continued to fall...flake after flake settling around them as they continued to heal Jeric.

It took half an hour and five healing scrolls to remove all of the ice shards and to seal over most of his wounds, and by then he still wasn't fully healed. As Sam tried to activate the last scroll, Jeric shook his head.

"That's enough," he growled, stubbornly. "You need that more than I do now."

Sam tried to refuse, but Jeric had enough strength back that he pushed the scroll toward his chest, plastering it to his son as the white light poured out of it. Sam felt the healing spell running through his bones as his ribs, left leg, and the bones in his arm started to fuse back together. The gashes down his shoulder and side from the wyvern's bite also closed more, but one scroll wasn't enough to finish the job.

Sam searched through his bags, but all he had left were a few healing pills. He pulled them out, passing two to his father as he ate the last one himself. The pills weren't as effective as the scrolls, but at least they should help regenerate their blood and seal over the wounds.

He'd been confident that half a dozen healing scrolls would be enough for most things, but he'd been wrong. It was barely enough to stabilize their injuries. He shook his head as he gave his father a long look, making sure that his wounds were sealed. At Level 40, his father's base Constitution was 84, plus two more for the Belt of Gentle Climes and an additional four if he held his hammers. Sam let out a slow breath.

It would be enough. His dad could heal the rest on his own.

As for him, his Constitution was up to 47 with his belt. The broken bones would finish healing back together in a day or two, even if he didn't use any more healing spells. Something loosened in his chest as he realized that it would be all right. A wave of exhaustion rolled over him, bringing a leaden weight to his arms and legs that felt as heavy as the wyvern's corpse.

He looked around the clearing at the slowly falling snow. The blood was gone, buried under soft, silent drifts that continued to settle on it, returning the area to a nearly pristine white. Even the broken branches on the trees were invisible now, covered over by the snow. The remains of their battle just a few minutes before had nearly completely disappeared. The only interruptions to the peace of the grove were the oddly shaped hills of the bandit corpses and the huge corpse of the wyvern.

It looked smaller now, lying flat against the ground. Its wings were outstretched, covered in snow and visible only at the tips of its claws that still protruded above the drifts. Its body was still visible, but there was a swiftly accumulating layer on top of it. At this rate, it would be buried within an hour. Sam slowly stood, putting his weight on his left leg as he tested how well it had healed. It held, but it threatened to buckle when he put too much pressure on it.

He dug down into the snow, pulling out his staff from where it was buried, and Crystal Focus swept out around him, searching beneath the drifts as he identified the location of everything in the clearing.

"Can you walk?" he asked, as he reached down to pull his father to his feet. They needed to collect what they could and leave here as soon as possible. He still had auras to combust if he needed more essence, but they weren't in a good shape to fight another battle right now. They had to get back to the inn and rest.

"I'll manage," Jeric growled softly as he took Sam's hand and pulled himself to his feet. Lesat also helped, stabilizing his shoulders as he stood.

"*We're on the way.*" At that moment, Krana's voice whispered in Sam's ears, a distant calling and a reminder of the others. "*We're bringing our healing scrolls and the horses. We'll be there soon.*" She must have seen them in Far Sight.

"*We're all coming,*" Aemilia's voice whispered in after that, resonating through the Amulet of Swirling Winds. "*We'll be there soon.*" She didn't say anything else, but the worry in her voice was clear. The only thing keeping it from exploding was probably that she could sense they were alive through the amulet.

A flash of guilt ran through him as he took in their state and what his mother would say, and then he let out another breath as he pushed it away.

There hadn't been a good way to avoid this, not without just being better than he was now. If they'd ignored the bandits, they would have returned at some point, perhaps with the wyvern, and then it would have been an even more dangerous fight when they were surprised.

The problem now was that his mother and sister were coming this way, and he wasn't sure the area was safe. He could feel the pulse of their presence growing incrementally closer as he sank his senses into the amulet. He knew why they were coming, since it was better to travel all as a group than to leave just Aemilia and Altey behind, but he still wished there was a better solution. He didn't want them out here in the wilderness, where more bandits or wyverns could be hiding.

"Nothing for it," Jeric said aloud. He sent his reassurances back along the amulet to his wife, and then he reached out to pat Sam's shoulder. "We're alive, and that's what counts. We'll head back together as soon as the horses arrive."

There were a dozen questions swirling in Sam's mind, all of them focused on the wyvern and the bandits, but he pushed them away as he nodded at his father.

"Let's clean up here and meet them," Sam said, a frown tugging at his features as he looked around, "and then we can talk it over back at the inn."

"Aye, let's collect the bandits' equipment and go," Jeric agreed. "The wyvern too...that might be some materials for you."

"I can use the hide and scales to make some decent armor, if Sam enchants it," Lesat offered slowly, as he looked around too. "It's a very high-quality leather, with quite a bit of mana in it."

Sam just nodded, his mind skipping ahead to the next steps in what they needed to do, as he headed toward the sorcerer's body and the dimensional bag that was lying beneath the snow. He didn't know how the bandits were controlling the wyvern or where the sorcerer had gotten that pill earlier, but there was clearly more to what was going on here than he'd thought. Hopefully, that bag held some answers.

As he went for that, his father and Lesat headed for the equipment and dimensional bags from the other two bandits. When he reached the sorcerer's corpse, or what was left of it, he stuck his hand into the snowdrift, searching through it for the bag that he could sense there.

After a moment, he found it and he held it up, examining the damage from Starfire. It was blackened from the flames, the enchantment on it cracked and starting to unravel, but for now still intact. It wouldn't last long. Maybe another day or two at most, but that was enough for him to see what was inside. He opened the bag, his hand pressing on the opening as he flooded it with mana and poured it into an empty dimensional bag of his own. The items inside slid from one dimensional storage to the other, barely causing a ripple in the air.

It was mana intensive, but the easiest way to empty a bag. When he was done, he glanced inside at what was there. There was one more of those white pills, radiating the unsettling feeling of foreign essence. There was also a number of typical things, including random pills and some vials that he wasn't familiar with, assorted weapons, food, and some coins, but nothing that stood out. It was generic, useful equipment. Only the pill was strange.

If the sorcerer had anything else of interest, it had exploded under the effects of Starfire. There were lumps of unrecognizable metal in the snow from the things he'd been wearing.

As he looked over the area, Sam reached out and grabbed the ones that looked salvageable, including a scorched mithril bracer, a couple of rings, and an amulet. The rings were also made from mithril, which was why they had survived. The amulet was an alloy that he couldn't identify in its current state. He frowned as he turned away, shoving the ruined items into his bag. The metal might be useful if he could reforge it, but whatever else they had once been was lost, including if there had been some control spell for the wyvern or an identifying mark.

The enchantments on them had been weaker than the base materials, which was why the runic patterns had burned away and left the metal behind. They had probably been Basic or Advanced at most. He headed for the wyvern's corpse, joining the others as they gathered around it. Lesat had located a couple of healing scrolls in the brawler's dimensional bag and he passed them over to Jeric silently, with no need to speak.

Jeric gave him a nod and took one of them, handing the other to Sam. When Sam tried to push it back, he glared at him until he accepted it. Sam sighed, glancing at the scroll to make sure it was safe. Then he activated it, letting the swirl of white light settle into his bones and fuse them back together a bit more. When it was done, he turned his attention to the wyvern, studying its corpse. The others were waiting for him and his father gave him a nod.

Sam reached out, searching for the silver thread of experience in the beast as he pulled it toward himself. It was a huge strand, far more than any of them could absorb at once, and as he pulled it free, he felt it separate into three parts. The experience flowed toward him, his father, and Lesat, even as he felt the remaining portion of it dissipate into the world, claimed by the World Law to repair the Seal.

A moment later, he heard the silvery chime of experience as energy shimmered through his blood, burning and freezing at the same time. Effervescent bubbles of positivity flowed through him, surging into his mind as he felt his muscles relax. It was like a good beer at the end of the day, or a specially-brewed wine, softening out the rough edges of the battle as it left him feeling more energetic.

You have used your Class abilities to slay your enemies.
You gain 210,000 Class experience.
Congratulations. You are now a Level 49 Battlefield Reclaimer.
Class Experience: 4,161,940 / 4,400,000
You are now General Level 49.
General Experience: 4,185,470 / 4,400,000
You gain +1 Aura, +1 Intelligence, and have three free attribute points to distribute.

The area here was apparently far enough from Highfold that the experience reduction of being near a city didn't apply. It meant that it was a good area to hunt.

The boosts to Aura and Intelligence brought both of them to 94. He glanced at the free points, hesitating for only a moment before he assigned all three to Constitution, bringing it up to 48. The new points there would help to accelerate the healing of his current wounds and it kept him on his plan to keep his Constitution equal to his level. The reason why was obvious. If he'd taken the same injuries that his father had, it was unlikely that he would have survived.

He needed to work on a new weapon and a better defense, and to upgrade his aura abilities so he had more essence at hand, as soon as he could.

When that was done, he placed his hand on the corpse, searching for the thread of aura in it. After a moment, he found it, a surging green-white aura that exploded in his senses like an angry, piercing shriek. It was snow and ice settling into ancient grooves in the stone of a mountain and forming into layers that grew heavier with time. A high mountain wind screamed across the surface of the ice, tearing away at the layers of snow with a touch like steel talons, even as it chilled them more, packing them harder and denser.

It ripped the weakness from them, the moisture and the softness, leaving only the barren, icy cold behind.

You have encountered an unknown aura.

Do you wish to Identify it or to Reclaim it (35%)?

He chose to identify it and the aura ignited, combusting itself in his hand as the threads of energy burned away. He felt the taste of snow that settled on the land like ash, covering everything in a quiet blanket of death, an eternal stillness of ice and cold. Then the taste was gone, as knowledge suddenly erupted in his mind, his Advanced ability to instantly identify the aura activating.

You have Identified the aura.

Aura of Arctic Wind (Basic).

This time, unlike every other time he'd reclaimed an aura, he could feel something behind the basic aura that was evaporating into the world. That energy in the air hovered there for a moment, with the sense of something greater than what he'd just claimed, pressing into his senses as he reached out toward it. Then it was gone, disappearing as he tried to touch it, but it left an impression behind of an aura that was greater and far more complex than anything he'd just gained.

An Advanced aura. It had layers and depth to it, and the promise of a greater concept behind it. If the Basic aura was Arctic Wind, then this was something more, something primal, a higher concept of ice that explained what the wyverns were at a deeper level. He let out a deep breath as he felt the remains of the Basic aura crumble away in his hand, leaving only the taste of frozen air behind.

He pulled his attention away from the aura, looking over to where his father and Lesat were starting to work. They'd absorbed their share of the experience, and Lesat was already getting started on one side, his sword out as he struggled to cut through the wyvern's hide, reducing it into large, rectangular strips. After a moment, Jeric joined him, his steps slow as he limped over, pulling out the Spear of Umbral Flame again.

Sam reached down, picking up a wyvern scale, and scraped it with his talon. A gouge lifted up from the scale, the stony hide curling back like wood, and he nodded. His talons were even sharper than the wyvern scales. Too bad they were so small, or he could have used them on it. He shrugged, bending down to grab more loose scales as he started to transfer the materials to his dimensional bags. Where his father and Lesat were using their weapons, crystal flame surrounded his talons instead, cutting through the wyvern's hide with a sharp *hisss*.

When it had been alive, its mana had infused its body, making it even harder and interfering with spells targeting it. Now that it was dead, it was little trouble for him to cut it apart. Material of this quality still held quite a bit of its natural mana and affinity, but it didn't hold up to his talons or flame. Long strips of wyvern hide, scales, and then bones and meat went into his bags. The meat of a high-level beast like this was also dense in mana, and it could be eaten or sold. Eating it could help with some forms of stamina and mana regeneration, and also speed healing, but its real value would be in selling it to a high-level cook who could do even more with it.

Some wyverns were known for their venom, but this one had an ice affinity, which meant that it should be safe to consume. As he worked, he studied the monster, considering where it had come from. Krana hadn't seen it hiding here, but Far Sight wasn't perfect. She would have needed to look in the right area, and even then it was only like seeing that area with your eyes. Wyverns were notorious for stealth in the mountains. It had probably been hidden in a crevice of the stone or beneath a snow drift.

When it came to Foresight, that ability was too random to count on in regular battles. If it had activated, she would have warned them, but expecting that it would was too much.

It took about half an hour for them to reduce the wyvern to little more than a smear of blood and guts on the snow. All the hide, scales, and even its bones were stored away in their dimensional bags. As for the wings, Sam took them. The leathery expanses would make excellent spell parchments, especially for anything related to ice or wind. He needed to make quite a few more healing scrolls, as soon as he could.

Sam bottled up as much of the blood as he could gather, collecting it into a rare dimensional bottle that he had that was fashioned from a type of enchanted crystal. Perhaps it could be sold to an alchemist or maybe Krana would help him find some use for it in smithing. Of all the wyvern's materials, the talons, fangs, and blood had the strongest Ice affinity in them. The last thing from the wyvern was a Level 46 core, which glowed softly with swirling green and white mana. Sam tucked it away in his dimensional bag, as a material for some later enchantment.

When that was done, he checked his amulet to see where Krana and his mother were, but they were still a quarter of an hour away.

"Let's check the bandits' cave," he suggested, as he turned toward it. "Krana said they had supplies in there."

All around him, the snow continued to fall, drifting silently down through the air as it landed on top of the blood and the remains of the wyvern. It was a slow and relentless advance, covering over the efforts of man and monster as it replaced it with the simple, eternal stillness of the snow. A cold wind whistled through the mountain peaks above, sending the snow spiraling all around.

CHAPTER NINETEEN

A WARNING PREMONITION

"Let's see what those bandits thought was good enough to steal," Jeric agreed, cracking his knuckles as he looked toward the cave. It was hidden behind the trees and snow now, the entrance invisible, but it was within the range of both Crystal Focus and Earth Sense. He wiped the wyvern blood that was still on his hands away on the snow, rubbing off the last of it, and then he gave Sam a nod.

Together, the three of them wrapped up their collection of the wyvern materials and headed for the cave where the bandits had been hiding, with Sam leading the way. They were in good enough condition to fight if they had to, but they weren't at full strength. Hopefully, there wasn't another monster inside.

The entrance was narrow, barely wide enough to fit the half-giant, which was reassuring in a certain way. It meant that a wyvern wouldn't fit. As they moved through the narrow tunnel, Sam debated what he was going to tell his mother. She was definitely not going to be happy. They were partly healed now, but their clothing was a mess of blood and gashes. The self-repair enchantments would take some time to work, at least a couple of days.

We're supposed to be living a peaceful life here, he grumbled to himself as he tried out different explanations. Perhaps they'd been overeager in chasing down the bandits. He pushed the thought away, shaking his head. If he'd known about the wyvern, he would have just prepared more for it. The Iceblood Guild was causing trouble and something needed to be done.

As for the essence pill and the wyvern…they had clearly stumbled into a bigger problem with those. It just wasn't clear what it was yet. The narrow tunnel opened onto a low cave that was about twenty feet wide and twice that deep. The ceiling was slanted, angling down toward the back in rough ripples of stone.

There were scratches and debris along the sides and the back, signs that someone had tried to expand it, but they hadn't gotten very far. Scattered across the floor in the center, there was a rough campfire with an iron cooking rack around it, three bedrolls, and some scattered bones and logs. The bandits had been living here for a while. There were old smoke stains along the ceiling and some of the bones were shattered by passing feet.

The most interesting thing was that along the sides and the back of the cave, there were dozens of stacked barrels of all shapes and sizes, as well as some bolts of cloth, bundles of hide and leather, and even some ingots of different metals. Those stacks took up nearly half of the available space in the cave. Sam frowned as he looked around, taking it all in.

It was a little too normal. *Where was the connection to the pill and the wyvern?*

"That is a lot of supplies." Jeric frowned, his arms folded over his chest as he looked around.

"Too many for just three bandits," Lesat agreed, nodding at Jeric. "Either they were habitual thieves and stole far more than they needed, or…"

"Or there's a much bigger organization that they're a part of," Sam concluded, as his view of the supplies changed. "The question is what that organization is, how many of them there are, and where they are."

The sheer amount of the supplies was troubling. They would need to open the barrels to confirm it, but it looked like enough to supply a small bandit group for months. *Had all of this been stolen from merchants in the valley?*

Sam frowned, looking around as he identified some marks burned into the barrels. He walked over to them, searching the stacks as he located one type of mark after another. After a moment, his father and Lesat saw what he was doing and joined him.

"Osera, Highfold, Ebonfar, Hisal's Peak, Norset…" Jeric identified one mark after another as he started to assess the barrels and the materials inside. "These have come from all over the province, but mostly from the Western Reaches and the Storm Plains. That's to be expected of merchants coming to Highfold, I suppose."

"So, these could have been stolen from local merchants or small foreign traders." Sam nodded, rubbing his chin as he thought.

"There's also another question," Lesat declared as he looked around. "Are we going to give it back or keep it?"

Sam paused, looking around the room again as he counted up the barrels. There were well over a hundred of them, of different types. Had the bandits really gathered all of this in the last year?

"If we can identify who it belongs to, then I suppose we could give it back," Sam said with a shrug. "But I doubt we can find most of the owners, and there's no good way to verify whose it was besides asking them, and then relying on them to tell the truth."

It was tempting to keep it all as spoils, since it would make a good collection of supplies to start off their stay here.

"We can ask Henar about it," Jeric said after a minute. He frowned as he looked around the room. "I'm not sure all of this would be useful to us anyway."

"The foreign traders are long gone, most likely, which means this is abandoned," Lesat suggested. "We should take what we can. If there are other bandits around, they may take it before we return."

"Either way, we shouldn't leave it here," Sam said as he looked around, counting the barrels. "That's just helping the bandits."

"Aye, let's clean it up," Jeric agreed, his frown deepening. "We can take whatever looks useful or more valuable, and then we can report the rest to Henar and the guards. He can contact any merchant friends he has to come and get the other part, whatever's too much for us to carry."

With that, the three of them began to pull open barrels and to rummage around in the stacks, looking for useful things as they began to fill their dimensional bags. They had quite a few dimensional bags by this point, but a lot of them were already filled with items from their home. At best, they might be able to take half of what was here.

Crystal Focus poured through the barrels as Sam sensed what was inside. The supplies were mostly common things, like flour, ale, various grains, and some smaller barrels of whiskey and spirits. As many of the barrels as he could manage went into his dimensional bags. He focused on the better grains and more expensive things as he sorted through them. It would be a good supply to keep his family fed this year, if everything else fell apart.

When he was done with that, he turned his attention to the crafting materials. The ingots and stacks of metal bars caught his eye and all of the ones in the room went into his bags. They would be useful for making enchanted items and for practicing smithing. He ended up with a decent collection of ingots made of common and uncommon ore, including dozens of iron, copper, tin, and others, but those were only a window dressing to the main prize.

At the end of the cave, there was a small, locked chest sitting on top of a barrel. It was about the size of his two hands together and reinforced with steel and mithril bands. On the lock, there was a small enchantment with runes for *lock*, *durability*, and *repair*. There was no keyhole visible, which was perhaps why the bandits hadn't opened it. Crystal Focus told him what was inside.

Inside, there was a small collection of tools, including three small bars of mithril, a few bars of gold and silver, and some assorted gems. The bandits must have robbed a gemsmith at some point. Sam flooded the lock with crystal flame, melting the enchantment and the points holding it together until it sprang open. Then, he pulled out the mithril bars. They looked like blued silver with a rainbow of other shades inside, but the real sign of mithril was that they weighed almost nothing. Each of them was about six inches long and an inch square.

If he were frugal and combined this mithril with the remains of the bracer that the sorcerer had been wearing, he might be able to forge something useful for himself. A new bracer wasn't a bad idea, since it would leave his hands free to cast. Ideas for enchantments that he could make began to flit through his mind, including ways to focus his spells and avoid damage.

A few minutes later, the sound of muffled hoofbeats echoed through the cave as riders approached. He looked toward the entrance with a conflicted expression, thinking about what his mother was going to say.

***

"We can't keep doing this." Aemilia said firmly with worry in her eyes as she looked at the healing wounds on Sam and Jeric. "That was a wyvern!"

She was not pleased as she looked between her husband and son. Her Far Sight had given her a clear picture of what had happened.

"If the bandits are somehow working with a wyvern, it's much too dangerous," she continued as she examined Jeric's wounds, rubbing the dried blood off to see what was underneath. "Let the town guards handle it."

"They've been ignoring it, love," Jeric replied helplessly as he raised his hands in the air, letting her continue her examination. "Henar said they've been bothering the village for a while. They would have come to find us next."

"But I doubt they would have brought the wyvern with them!" Aemilia frowned back at him, her words sharp. "This is not just a bandit group, and it's not something we need to be involved in."

"We'll do what we have to, to keep our family safe," Jeric said as he pulled Aemilia into a hug, wrapping his arms around her. "We won't go out of our way looking for trouble, I promise."

Aemilia relaxed slightly as she heard his reassurance, but she was still unhappy with the danger here. Monsters and Outsiders were a fact of life, but that didn't mean you had to go looking for them.

"The wyvern is the strange part," Krana spoke up. "The monster shouldn't have been here, and there was that pill too." Her hands were on her hips as she turned in a circle, examining all of the barrels and supplies. "This doesn't make sense for a group of three bandits. There are too many supplies here, and there's no sign that they were planning to sell it."

"What do you think it's for then?" Lesat replied from where he was working on his gear. He was trying to remove some of the dents and nicks from it, so that the self-repair runes would work faster. A lump of steel was in his free hand.

"It looks like a supply depot, or a collection point." Krana frowned. "There has to be a bigger group behind them, and if they somehow have control of a wyvern...and an alchemist, then there's only a couple of possibilities that come to mind."

"How could they control a wyvern?" Sam asked. The question bothered him, since he'd never heard of anything like it. "That shouldn't be possible."

"That might be the worst news, if it's what I think it is," Krana replied as she looked toward him. "You're right that the bandits couldn't do it, since monsters can't be controlled with beast-taming skills." Krana paused as she got everyone's attention, and then she announced what she'd been thinking. "The only possibility is an Outsider."

Everyone's head turned toward her.

"What do you mean?" Jeric asked immediately, glancing at Sam and then back at Krana. "How could an Outsider control monsters?"

"When Outsiders come through a Flaw..." Krana said slowly, as she sorted through the explanation in her mind, trying to simplify it. "If they stay too long, something about them attracts monsters, especially if they share an elemental affinity, like ice for the wyverns and the Outsider that Sam felt here.

"It's one of the reasons the Church tries to hunt down Flaws and close them, as well as kill everything that's come through. Flaws attract monsters to them. At the same time, those monsters start to obey the Outsiders that have come through, and before long..." Krana looked around the room as she caught everyone's attention. "You have an army of monsters on your hands, led by something even worse."

"So, this wyvern..." Sam said as he put the new information together. "You think it was under the command of an Outsider? The one I sensed here?" If Krana's suggestion was right, they'd just found the connection between the wyvern and that Outsider.

"It's the only thing that makes sense," Krana agreed, nodding at him. "I can't think of any other way that a wyvern would be working with bandits. Something must have commanded it to guard them or this cave."

"It didn't care much about that half-giant," Jeric pointed out as he frowned, rubbing his hand over his beard in thought. He was trying to find a flaw in the idea, but it was a thin one. "It went right through it."

"It was still a monster," Krana replied with a shrug. "You said it obeyed the sorcerer, but we don't really know more than that. Maybe it was only told to protect the sorcerer, or to protect the cave and these supplies."

"Are wyverns smart enough for that?" Lesat asked. "It's just a big lizard with wings."

"Wyverns are extremely clever, like most higher-level monsters," Krana answered. "When they're past their First Evolution, they sometimes even speak. They're also known for being voracious, cunning, and destructive. You shouldn't underestimate them."

"So, it might have attacked that giant just because it didn't care about him," Jeric said. "It sounds like we've got a big problem on our hands then, and more than that Highfold has a problem on its hands."

"Do you think the city guard will be interested in this now?" Sam asked, an idea springing up in his mind. "The Festival of Three Crowns is coming up. They're not going to be happy that there's an Outsider in the area gathering monsters around it."

"Hopefully," Krana agreed with him. "The Flaw might still be somewhere in the mountains here as well." She frowned again as she looked around at the roof of the cave, her gaze seeming to pierce through the stone above. "It's rare for one to be close to a city, but this area is a special case. The energy here is extremely well contained within the confines of the valley, and the mountains around it are a different thing entirely."

"Wouldn't the World Law sense it?" Sam asked, frowning as he looked down at the Guardian Star on his hand. "And then send people to deal with it?" He hadn't received a command to go and find a Flaw here.

"It may have been reported a while ago and no one came to deal with it," Krana replied, shaking her head. "It depends on where they are and how many others are opening at the same time, as well as what else is happening. Flaws can be concealed sometimes, if the Outsider has enough time. "On top of that, these ruins have strange enchantments and it's possible that they're hiding it here."

"What type of Outsider do you think it is?" Aemilia asked, frowning herself as she thought of what to do and how to keep her family away from it. "Surely, the guards won't ignore it now?"

"It has to be at least somewhat intelligent, since it's working in the shadows and has managed to recruit these bandits," Krana said. "I can try to search for it, but I doubt I will be able to find it. Outsiders are very good at hiding themselves from Seers." Krana looked toward Sam, before she added another thought.

"We can't tell the city guard what you sensed about the Outsider, since that would raise too many questions about you...but with the wyvern as proof, it might be enough, and that it was here with the bandits."

"Bandits working for an Outsider," Jeric muttered as he looked around. His arms were crossed on his chest and his fingers tightened as he considered the ramifications, pressing into his biceps.

"Traitors to Aster Fall," Lesat finished, scowling, as he brought his whet-stone down on the edge of his sword.

"The question is what they were doing," Krana agreed, nodding slowly.

The group looked around at each other, taking in the dark expressions, but no one had a good answer.

"Let's finish packing this up and then we'll let the guards know," Jeric said slowly, before he nodded. He turned away, looking at the rest of the barrels in the cave. "I doubt Highfold wants anything interrupting the festival."

"I'll ask my relatives there about Siwaha and warn them," Krana said. "They can help get the word to the city council."

"I'm sure Highfold can handle it," Aemilia said, trying to be reassuring as she held Altey's hand, keeping her away from the barrels and other things in the cave. It was a dangerous situation, but she still let out a sigh of relief as she realized her husband and son weren't going to run off after monsters and bandits right now.

Sam gave the cave around him a long look as doubt brushed against his mind. Everything told him this was the edge of a much larger problem.

"*A year ago...*" he muttered to himself. Finally, he shook his head. Their plans hadn't changed, but the magnitude of the problem had. While Krana and his father headed to the city, he'd have to see what he could do about fortifying their position.

Whether Highfold knew it or not, the valley was under siege by an Outsider, and perhaps by a Flaw that was hidden in the ruins. What was worse, it was an enemy that was smart enough to stay out of sight, to recruit bandits, and to stockpile supplies, all while threading its presence through the snow. The timing was more than suspicious.

Whatever the thing was up to, he had the distinct feeling that it had something to do with the Festival of Three Crowns. Over the next month, the number of travelers and enchanters in the valley would accumulate, and then they would go into the mountains...searching for enlightenment as they poured into the ruins. Ruins that were very far from the wards and defenses of Highfold. In other words, there would be thousands of targets full of experience for the Outsider to consume.

The festival was going to be a bloodbath.

***

As they rode away from the cave, high on the peaks and out of sight, there was a slender, blue and white figure watching them. In appearance, he was humanoid, but his skin was white with swirling blue patterns across it. His long hair ran down his back in jagged, frozen blue waves and it was tangled with ice crystals as the wind blew through it.

His eyes were a piercing blue like cut crystal sapphires. His body was thin, with evidence of lean muscles, and he had delicate, refined features with high cheekbones and long, diamond-pointed ears. More than anything, he resembled a spirit of the ice. He was thin enough that from the right angle, he looked like an icicle that had come to life.

He was swathed in a long white and blue-swirled cloak that blended into the stones behind him, making it look like he'd walked out from the stone of the mountains. His hands were on his hips as he studied the party below. The ice sylph's eyes narrowed in puzzlement as he saw the woman, the dwarf, and the child arrive, joining the three who were already in the cave.

When they came out a little later and remounted their horses, Siwasir continued to watch. He kept his eyes carefully off the caster who looked like a demon, making sure that his attention wasn't noticed. He could feel the ward around him that was blocking sight, like a cloak radiating outward into the snow, but Siwasir's attention was like the snow itself, diffused everywhere through the land, and he was able to keep track of them all.

He'd felt the disturbance in the local area caused by the wyvern and had come to investigate. He'd arrived in time to see the end of the fight, as well as the caster's demonic features. At first, he'd been ready to attack. Only the fact that the caster was with the humans and fighting against one of the old enemies of his tribe had stayed his hand.

The wyverns and the ice sylphs had vied against each other for dominance over the icy peaks here for thousands of years. To see one die was satisfying, even if it was only a young one. One less wyvern to attack their tribe and those who lived on their lands. It should not have been down here on the edge of the valley at all. He frowned as he looked toward where the corpse had been, easily sensing the remains of the monster under the snow.

To him, the snow was welcoming, revealing its secrets with a touch. His people stayed far away from most of those who lived in their lands. In their minds, it was a silent partnership. The icy sylphs were content to let the guests bring prosperity to the land and grow their crops, while the tribe kept watch over the snow and ice. Each supported the other, but that didn't require conversation, as long as the old customs were maintained.

His people appreciated the trade in crops, since growing them had never been their greatest strength. Over the millenia, the small farming community they'd allowed here had become much larger.

With a fluid gesture, the sylph's form blurred away, fading into the drifting snow as he departed, carrying the news of what he'd seen back to his tribe.

CHAPTER TWENTY

GUARDIAN OF ASTER FALL

When they returned to the inn, they spoke to Henar briefly about the supplies in the cave, so he could send his merchant friends after them. His eyes widened when he heard the amount.

"I'll round up a few to go and look," he said, his voice gruff. "You've done a good thing here." With that, Henar turned away, calling to Rusel. "Grab the cart, lad! Then go tell Old Eapar, Jinel, and the others."

"We'll head for Highfold," Jeric said a moment later, after Henar stomped out. Krana was standing beside him and his expression was worried as he looked between his wife and children. "We'll try to be back tonight, but tomorrow is more likely. Make sure to stay safe here."

It would take them an hour or two to get there, and then they needed to find the right people. Hopefully, the guards would listen about the wyverns and the Outsider that was targeting the festival.

"I'll add more enchantments to the rooms," Sam told him, sharing a solemn gaze with his father. "We'll be prepared if anything comes by."

"Hurry back," Aemilia said as she hugged her husband. There was worry in her eyes, but also determination. "I'll keep an eye on you from a distance, and at least we can talk to each other now."

Jeric gave her a nod and then, with a final look around the room, he and Krana headed out. Lesat took up a guard position by the door, where he sat down and continued to repair his armor. Even while he worked, his attention was fixed on the entrance.

At the table in the center of the room, Aemilia sighed as she looked
around, and then she sorted out some work to keep herself occupied. She
started to write in her journals for class experience, while Altey studied a
handful of runes that Sam had taught her, drawing them out in a pile of
sand.

When that was settled, Sam spent about an hour adding a more intensive
shield enchantment to the runes on the wall. For this one, he took one of
the weaker cores in his collection and embedded it directly in the center
of the pattern, so that it bulged out of the wall. Then he revised the
enchantment lines to fit, circling around the core as a central focus to the
defense. It was a quick and brutal enchantment, but it would hold for a
little while.

With the core, it could be recharged easily, even if it wasn't very efficient.
It made sure that if anything attacked the room, the core would shatter
before it broke through the enchantment.

After that, he set up his work table just below where he'd inscribed the
enchantment and pulled out several items, arranging them in front of him.
From the sorcerer, there was the white pill, the scorched mithril bracer, two
rings, and an amulet. Next to that, he set the mithril bars and tools from
the gem smith box.

On another section of the table, there were materials from the wyvern,
including some scales, a chunk of bone, the ice-aligned blood, and its core.
Past that, he arranged some other crafting materials and cores that he had.
Then he looked down at the collection, his talons tapping on the edge of
the table as thoughts began to race through his mind.

There was a lot that he needed to do.

The defenses he'd just worked on would hold for now, but he needed a
better weapon and defensive artifacts, to master more of the amulet runes,
to figure out this essence pill, to study the ruins that were probably a
death trap.... The number of things on his list of essential work was only
increasing the more he learned.

They could leave Highfold and let the people here deal with the Outsider
and the festival, but it didn't feel right. It would be abandoning everyone
else who lived here, people like Henar and Rusel, who had no good defense.
The idea of the ruins teaching him something about his class was still the
best path he had, and now that an Outsider was involved, this was also part
of his mission from the Guardian.

He just needed to make sure that his family would be safe here, so that he could take care of things. He felt the weight of responsibility pressing down on him as he looked at the key items on the table. These would be the beginning of his response. Plans formed like stars in his mind as he began to arrange his ideas into a constellation, from the quickest and most practical, to the ones that were a long path. When he had it all in place, he nodded.

First things first.

He reached out to pick up the essence pill, turning it from side to side. More than anything, he needed to know more about the Outsider. It was his natural enemy. As soon as the two of them got close enough to one another, the essence in them would resonate, pulling them toward battle. He had no idea how intelligent the thing was, but the bandits had been protected by its wyvern. That implied some level of communication.

There might be other elements in play that he hadn't discovered, but he would have to wait until they appeared. All he could do was prepare and make sure that if they faced each other, the Outsider would be the one to die. His senses surrounded the pill, crystal flame tracing every part of the surface.

"Now, what are you..." he muttered to himself as he examined it. His aura poured through the pill gently, like a flicker of passing heat, as he analyzed the layers that made it up. There was a core of essence in it, almost like a drop of blood, and he carefully skirted around the edges of that. He could sense the freezing volatility inside.

If he touched that, it would probably explode on him. The make-up of the pill was interesting, condensed layers of herbs with high levels of mana and an affinity for ice, and he memorized the ingredients as he went. When he didn't know the name for something, he remembered its flavor instead. It was different from a healing pill, but not that different. The major thing was just the essence at the center.

Two ideas came to him as he finished his analysis.

One was to consume it himself. Not by swallowing it the way the sorcerer had, but more directly, the way he'd ripped the essence from the Outsider spiders before. He could feel the energy there, and he might be able to claim it for his own. The other idea....

"*Wake up,*" he muttered as he glared at the Guardian Seal on the back of his right hand, which was also holding the pill. "*If you're going to be useful at all, now would be the time.*"

He felt a bit like an idiot as he tried talking to it, but the Guardian had told him once that it would give him information. He was hoping that the presence of essence in the pill would alert it somehow, and that it would give him more information about what he was facing. There was no response from the star, but he could feel the energy burning inside.

His left hand brushed across the back of it and the recorded conversation that he'd had with the Guardian rushed into his mind again, filling his thoughts with every detail of what had happened. He ignored that part, since there was nothing new there. He'd read it many times.

If the star was going to be useful, he needed it to do more than that. The Astral Guardian had given it to him as a communication tool, but it hadn't done much since then. He'd said it was for information, and for...what? There had been things he hadn't had time to say. It had to be able to do something more than alert him when Flaws were around. The World Law already did that.

When it had spoken to him once before, it had almost sounded intelligent, like a miniature version of the World Law, but ever since then it had been quiet. He wasn't even sure what it really was. If he pushed it in the right way, maybe it could help him find the Flaw here and figure out what the Outsider was doing.

"*Study this!*" he tried, as he touched the essence pill to the back of the star. At the same time, he poured his will into it. "*Tell me what it's from. What type of Outsider?*"

When nothing happened, he reached out to it again, pushing his aura of crystal flame into it. He'd tried examining the star many times before, every way he could think of, so he wasn't surprised when there was still no response.

"*How about this?*" he directed his thoughts to it as he began explaining exactly what was going on. "*There's an Outsider invasion somewhere in the mountains here, a breakthrough point in the Seal. There's a Flaw that hasn't been identified and some humans and monsters are working for it. I need you to tell me where it is.*"

He muttered the words under his breath as he spoke to the star. As he did, he felt something, a little bit of a response. On certain words, it felt like the star was flickering, just like when he got a warning from it: *Outsider, invasion, breakthrough, Flaw, monsters...*

He repeated them over to it again, getting the same response, but beyond that, nothing happened. That was all, until he finally became irritated with it and decided that he was wasting his time. If the Guardian had wanted the star to work for him, he would have made it easy.

"Guardian," he finally growled at it. His mind flickered through everything that the Guardian had told him. *"Stop being useless. You said you'd give me information."*

The Guardian had given him a lot of information in a very short time, but there was one thing that he'd told Sam repeatedly. In fact, it was the entire reason Sam had gotten in trouble in the first place. Finally, he shouted that at the star.

"There's a threat to the Seal!" As he shouted at it, he poured all of his awareness of the outsider and the essence in the snow into the star.

This time, a flare of energy poured through his hand as the Guardian Star began to glow, growing warmer on his skin. At the same time, he felt a drawing sensation as the star pulled a bit of energy from him.

It grew brighter, until it was a sparkling, nine-pointed star shining in the air above his hand. It looked white usually, but as the energy in it intensified, it began to gather other colors to it, from a bright silver to a rainbow swirl. A voice echoed in his mind. It was similar to the all-pervasive voice of the World Law, but not as deep. There was a bright vibration to it that *thrummed* through his bones.

Scanning for threats to the Seal.

He felt a pulse of energy flare outward from the star, sweeping through the area around him and then out farther in every direction, past where he could sense. After a moment, the pulse of energy returned and the energy in the star dimmed slightly. The voice spoke again.

No active threats detected within a five-mile sphere.

The star hung there, waiting expectantly as if it wanted him to do something. He could feel the energy in it fading away slowly, like a fragile bubble. Whatever power the Guardian Star had, it was not unlimited. The search had taken a lot of energy from it. Perhaps that was why it didn't interact with him much.

Sam wasn't sure what to do, so he repeated everything he'd told it before, when it hadn't been listening. He didn't know if the star was a miniature version of the World Law or just a communication channel to the Astral Guardian, but at least he'd gotten a reaction from it. The star flickered, the energy in it pulsing outward again as it began to build to a higher level. After a moment, it stopped and the voice spoke again.

Infuse more energy to support an advanced search.

Sam didn't hesitate as he poured his essence into the star, one point after another. A stream of crystal flame flowed along his arm, feeding directly into the heart of the star, which turned a brighter blue shade as it absorbed it. Five points, ten...twenty....

Point by point, he sent more essence into the star. Fifty points later, it flickered, brightening again as it burned above his hand with a bright silver-blue flame. Its light was steadier now, pulsing strongly.

Advanced search commencing.

The nine points brightened, energy from each of them blasting outward into the surrounding area in a pulse that was many times stronger than the previous one. A wave of information flowed into Sam's mind, as he felt his consciousness traveling along with the energy from the star.

The land blurred past him, faster than he could see, as the valley stretched out all around. He could see it from every direction, as if his mind had expanded to encompass it in a sphere, but it moved by so quickly that he couldn't gather many details. He saw crops, trees, grass, mountainsides, the walls of the city, and then the scan was carrying him farther, up into the mountains as he felt the valley receding.

Shards of information came, bringing back the impression of broken walls, fragments of unfamiliar runes carved on stone, and shattered veins of metal and crystal. Those had to be the ruins above the city. Somewhere in that area, he felt a ripple of a response, like a saw grating across metal with a grinding sound. It echoed unpleasantly in his bones, a vibrating irritation that was out of place.

Then he was moving back, his mind flashing across the valley as his awareness slammed back into the room where he was sitting. His vision doubled and wavered as a feeling of exhaustion hit him. The star dimmed and then it brightened slowly, pulsing nine times as the energy from its scan seemed to return to it.

Dimensional ripples are present thirty four miles from this point. Evidence suggests a concealed Flaw in that location.

Age of Flaw: Estimated at 1.3 local years.

Guardian of Aster Fall, your duty is to protect the Seal. Eliminate the threat.

A warning flare pulsed through the star, tugging his attention in that direction as the star dimmed again, fading as it returned to his hand. The light from it died down, as if it had never been there. The only thing left behind was the awareness of the Flaw, as the star continued to point him toward it. It was like a thread in his mind that was tugging him in that direction.

He focused on it, and the feeling grew stronger. He could feel a resonating danger and the sense of the world crumbling away. Other than that, the star was silent again. Sam frowned at it, puzzling over what it had just done as he put it all together. The Guardian Star hadn't given him all the information he wanted, but it seemed like it *had* detected the Flaw.

It wasn't entirely useless. He'd just had to activate it on his own.

The location was key information, since he doubted the Outsider would go very far from that point. At the same time, the World Law had not spoken up when the Flaw was detected, which meant that the Guardian Star wasn't sharing information with it, at least not as far as he could tell. They were two separate things.

It looked like he'd figured out a way to use the Guardian Star. It was a type of scanning artifact, one that was unique to him. If he could use it to find Flaws, it had just become an excellent hunting tool.

It had also called him *"Guardian of Aster Fall."*

Sam's eyes turned toward the horizon as he followed the thread of warning in the star that was pulling his attention in that direction, his gaze passing across the distance as he looked toward the Flaw. After a moment, he looked back to where his mother and Altey were studying. Their attention was still fixed on their work, which meant that only he had seen the star activate.

The meaning of the title the star had given him resonated in his mind, echoing as he looked at his family, but he had a long way to go if he wanted to live up to the meaning in it.

His gaze moved back to the table in front of him and the items that were laid across it, especially the mithril and the wyvern's core. Then he held up the white essence pill as he studied it. The essence in it felt like it was boiling, trying to escape from his grasp. He held it in place with a sphere of crystal flame as he felt the essence stars in his blood singing.

It was time to see what he could do with this.

Without hesitating any longer, he reached into the center of the pill with his will and *ripped* at the essence inside.

CHAPTER TWENTY-ONE

A NEW WEAPON

The essence from the pill was a small, icy star. It struggled in his grasp, but it was a single point compared to the seventeen that were already in his blood. It had no chance against the force he exerted against it. The essence rose up into the air as the pill around it crumbled, turning to dust that blew away.

With a jerk of will, he pulled it toward himself. It flew toward him, its color changing from ice to crystal blue as it hit his body and sank into his blood. A moment later, it fused into the network of essence stars that were already there.

Instead of immediately turning into an 18th star, the essence diffused outward through the ones that he already had, strengthening them. The network became a little stronger, the resonance between the stars a little louder. After a moment, he felt a new 18th star starting to form on its own. It was different from the other times, and not instant.

The feeling of strength stabilized as the star rested there, half-formed. It gave him the sense of something just born that was able to grow if he fed it more essence. As the dust of the pill blew away, he looked down at where the pill had been, rubbing his chin.

It was strange, but he was pretty sure he knew what was going on. Each time he'd gained a new star, it had been because he'd just killed an Outsider and then pulled their essence from them. That was one path, what he might call the path of *life essence*.

This pill was something else. The essence in it had been touched by the Outsider, converted to whatever form this was, but underneath that it was some type of distilled energy. When he'd absorbed it, he'd converted it to his own type of essence, which was why it had turned the color of his crystal flame. The new star that was starting to form in his blood was interesting, evidence of a path he hadn't considered.

This was the second path, something like *natural essence*. Maybe it was the essence of the herbs from the pill, or of the ice attribute elements that made it up. Whatever it was, it was supporting his growth, rather than adding to it directly. Perhaps this was how Outsiders grew in power without killing one another. He studied the difference in his essence stars, deciding after a moment that it had strengthened him by five percent or so.

It wasn't as good as killing an Outsider and taking their essence directly, but if he could find enough of these pills, or figure out how to make them, then perhaps he could advance his essence base that way. The information was more useful than the strength from the pill.

He'd thought it might be life essence at first, but he supposed it would have been strange for the Outsider to put its life essence in a pill, if it were even possible. It would have required sacrificing part of itself and giving it to a minion. That wasn't likely.

Outsiders were selfish.

The more he thought about it, the more interested he was in how these pills were made and how much he could strengthen his essence by eating them. The alchemical pills he'd heard about before were different. They focused on healing, restoring mana or stamina, boosting Strength and Constitution, and so on. High-tier Alchemists could supposedly create pills and elixirs that permanently increased your attributes, but he hadn't seen them yet. He would have to look more into alchemy if he had time.

However the Outsider was making these pills, it seemed like he was handing them out to his followers. That implied a level of intelligence, but it wasn't clear what the goal was. It was also hard to believe the Outsider was giving out these pills to save its minions. That showed a level of concern that went against everything he knew about Outsiders.

Greed, power, vindictiveness, certainly, but not concern for others.

The most critical question was what level the Outsider was and what abilities it had. All he could say right now was that it was probably stronger than the wyvern. He brushed the remains of the pill away from his table as he turned his attention to the array of crafting materials in front of him.

He picked up the scorched mithril bracer, turning it from side to side as he examined it. The sorcerer had been wearing it, but it wasn't possible to tell what the enchantment had been. It could have been offensive, defensive, or something stranger, like a training aid that attuned his energy more easily to ice. Whoever had placed the original enchantment hadn't bound it well to the material. Now, it was just a blank piece of mithril.

The question was what *he* needed it to be. He needed something that was made for him. A bracer was a good idea, since it would leave his hands free to cast. The Staff of Withering Stasis was powerful, but it always felt like it was getting in the way when he held it. Perhaps something that would help him channel Starfire more quickly, or that held a spell he couldn't create directly, like Altey's ice wand.

A battle artifact. Something to help him kill wyverns. Ideas began to flicker through his mind, combining into runic patterns and then swirling away again, as his eyes went distant.

The last weeks of practice had significantly bolstered his enchanting skills, especially as he worked his way through the simple runes and made them his own. There were only five of those left that he didn't understand. All of them were focused on illusions, appearance, sound, temperature, and other things for daily life. Learning them had pushed him well along the path to being a basic Illusionist, at least when it came to crafting items.

They had taught him a lot about combining runes as well.

Everything he'd learned from the amulet poured through his mind as he considered the best way to bind an enchantment and to bolster it, as well as how to design something more complex than he ever had before. After a while, a piece of chalk appeared in his hand and he began to sketch on the work table, creating a runic diagram.

***

Sam's hands flickered as he pulled the portable forge from his dimensional vest and placed it in front of him. To his right, the wyvern core, mithril bars, and some other items were gathered. The runic pattern he'd created for the bracer was laid out on the table in front of him. He'd spent hours working on it, refashioning it into distinct parts, considering what he needed it to do, and then ripping it apart and rebuilding it again.

Each time, he considered how the enchantment was built from its smaller parts, unified together to a greater purpose. That was the single most useful concept he'd learned from the illusion amulet. As best he could tell, the difference between an Advanced enchantment and an Expert one wasn't in the quality of the individual runes. It was that an Expert enchantment was a complex network, binding together multiple patterns to a more powerful effect.

There were some other details, including the level of the Binding pattern and the support structure for the runes, but he was fairly sure that he was on the right track. An Expert enchantment wasn't just powerful...it was artful, blending concepts and building on them. That was also why he needed to use a better method to engrave it than he ever had before. The plan for how to do that was hanging in his mind.

In the beginning, he wanted the bracer to do many different things, but as he continued to work on it, he realized that he was only diluting the potential of the enchantment. It would be better for it to do one thing well. He had the mithril rings and the blank amulet to use for other effects, once he was done with this.

In the end, he'd boiled the concept of the bracer down to a single concept.

Star.

The pattern that was laid out on the table was complex, but the intent was simple. At the heart of it, there was the single rune for *star* that he was using to focus Starfire. All around that, there were buffering, stabilizing, clarity, storage, and enhancement patterns, as well as an ornate rune pattern with five key runes: *crystal, flame, focus, construct,* and *projection.*

Those runes surrounded the central *star* rune in five gleaming points, marking out its arms. Prominent sections of the pattern were dedicated to focusing his crystal flame and to conceptualizing runic constructs, but they all fell under that single concept.

The illusion amulet had come in handy there, giving him the necessary runes for attuning energy, projecting images, and constructing models. If the bracer worked as he hoped, it would be attuned to his crystal flame and to that single concept of *star*. It would also be able to store some of his essence as charges, giving him an offensive artifact if he were out of energy, one that was better than a simple wand.

On top of that, by channeling his essence through the pattern, he would empower the *star* rune at the center. The rune would then coalesce, allowing him to manipulate it quickly. He'd designed it as both a weapon and a training aid, one that would help him to reinforce his knowledge of *star*.

It would reflect his understanding of the rune back at him as he shaped it again and again, engraving its meaning in his mind. He'd left a bit of space at the center of the pattern so that he could add to the *star* rune if he learned a more advanced form of it. The more he used it, the better his understanding of *star* would become, and the more powerful the artifact would be.

The *flame* pattern around the outside would let him use the charges directly too, like a miniature version of his Starfire spell.

He'd debated adding a defensive shield, but he already had one of those in the Amulet of Swirling Winds and it would have altered the purpose of the bracer too much. He was planning to use the mithril rings to make lifesaving artifacts after this, similar to what the sorcerer had. They would trigger when an overwhelming force threatened the life of the wearer. He needed a bit of the mithril from the bars for his bracer, but he could melt down the rest to make more rings, so that everyone had one.

He reached out and picked up the wyvern core, examining it before he placed it next to the mithril bracer. Then he picked up the bracer itself, holding it steady between his hands. Crystal flame poured through his arms as it began flowing into the material. His awareness sank into the metal, flowing through its structure as he searched for impurities and burned them away. The metal began to glow, brightening to a silver-cerulean glow.

Mithril was a complex and extremely durable metal. The damage from the battle had added some flaws to its structure, but they weren't significant. The structure reformed itself as he worked. It would take him a little while to purify it for his purposes and to erase all traces of what had been here before.

***

Hours passed as the sun outside set over the valley. The sunset was visible through the window, which faced to the west, toward Highfold. In the distance, the mountains towered, bringing an early evening to the valley as the sun sank behind them. Aemilia and Altey had moved the table over near the window, watching the road that led away from the inn as they kept an eye out for Jeric and Krana.

Aemilia's eyes turned distant, gleaming with golden light from time to time as she looked for where her husband had gone. On the other side of the room, the corner of the room around Sam burned with flickers of crystal flame and heat that washed outward, crashing against a translucent ward that he'd erected.

If it hadn't been there, it was likely he would have burned down the inn. He'd moved all of the wooden items out of the area around him and collapsed the portable table, bringing it down to knee height as he sat on the floor behind it. As for the floor, he'd had to take a few extra minutes to engrave a ward on that as well, so he didn't burn it.

The area around him was filled with crystal flame, swirling in a vast spiral around the inside of the ward. In his hands, there was the bracer and his stylus. The bracer gleamed a bright silver-blue as it absorbed the energy from his aura, which was constantly pouring into it.

Carefully, Sam inscribed a line on the bracer. Then he turned it gently to reach the inside and did the same again. The stylus glowed with a brilliant flare of crystal light as his aura poured through it, the cutting force reaching into the center of the mithril as he engraved the rune into the internal layers of the material as well. The runic pattern was nearly complete. It wrapped around the bracer from every angle, flowing through its inner and outer layers.

The material was better than anything he'd ever used before, and the amount of effort he was putting into the creation reflected that. The bracer absorbed his aura like a desert, its structure continuing to change as the essence in it increased. The wyvern core was embedded on the surface, near the back part of the bracer that would be closer to his elbow. He'd also mixed in a number of materials to enhance the mithril, including sacred Earth mana and several types of gems.

Normally, an Ice and Wind-element core would have conflicted with Fire, but Crystal Flame wasn't really a Fire enchantment. The rune for Flame was not the same as the element of Fire. You could have an Ice Flame, or a Star Flame, or an Earth Flame. It was a matter of projected energy. Instead of conflicting, the core added stability, acting as a cooling force that brought extra clarity and crystallization to the focus enchantment.

Wind wasn't a problem either, thanks to its typical habit of increasing the energy of other things. It was past the middle of the night and nearing the small hours of the morning when he finally added the last lines to the enchantment, finishing the durability and self-repair runes, as well as the binding pattern that pulled it all together.

Without hesitating, as he completed the last line and set down his stylus, he reached out with an expectant hand and touched the activation sigil that brought it all together. A liquid wave of crystal flame surged through the runes and raced around the bracer. Instead of filling the lines with mana, he'd attuned the bracer to himself and every line of the enchantment was filled with condensed crystal flame and his essence.

The enchantment pattern burned outward from the bracer, forming a three-dimensional sphere in the air that was made from crystal blue flames. All across the surface, the runes from the bracer began to appear, lighting up one by one. Lines of burning essence shot across the space inside the sphere, connecting the runes to the ones on the opposite side.

Then a line of energy shot out from that side, connecting back to another part of the sphere. Before long, an intricate network of crystal flame was burning in the sphere, the connections between the runes forming hundreds of lines inside. At the heart of the sphere, surrounded by all of those lines, the *star* rune floated in space. Around it, the other five key runes formed the tips of a star, giving it a frame.

The sphere spun around the runes, feeding energy into them. Sam's eyes traced the connections, one to another, as he made sure that there were no flaws in the pattern. Then his will swept into the sphere, flowing through it as he poured even more crystal flame and essence into the pattern.

The sphere began to burn brighter, flickers of flame pouring out of it, and then it shrank, reducing swiftly as it collapsed back down into the bracer. The runic lines etched themselves more deeply into the surface as his essence filled them, finishing the final step in the process. The bracer glowed as bright as a star as the pattern finished etching itself into it. Then the pattern faded away, invisibly embedded into the surface of the bracer, which glowed with a bright cerulean crystal light that rippled over the silvery mithril.

A chime rang out in Sam's mind as a thousand small bubbles of experience flooded into his body, floating through his meridians as they sank into him. An ornate, silver-bordered notification appeared, its style archaic and authoritative.

Congratulations, Scion. You have created your first Expert enchantment.

You receive bonus Experience for your Enchanter profession.

You gain 50,000 Class Experience.

You are now a Level 30 Enchanter.

For creating an Expert enchantment before reaching the Expert tier, you have demonstrated significant ability.

Your Skill: Essence Control is upgraded to become the Ability: Essence Control, granting you increased effectiveness.

It is now assigned to your Innate Abilities.

Your Ability: Essence Control has reached the Expert tier.

A whirlwind of energy from the World Law poured into his body as he felt the spark of the ability flaring to life in his mind, resonating through his meridians and bones. At the same time, a new awareness poured into his mind and raced along his nerves, deepening his ability to control essence directly.

In many ways, it was a confirmation of what he'd already been doing, but he could feel an added depth to the ability that hadn't been there before, making it easier than ever to manipulate essence. It took a little while for the whirlwind of energy to fade away, and when it did, peace returned to his small corner of the room.

The bracer he'd just created floated up from his hand, hanging in the air in front of him as he examined it.

Starflame Bracer (Expert, Unique)

[Enchantments: Focus of Crystal Flame, Runic Construction, Starflame.

Focus of Crystal Flame*: The enchantments inlaid into this bracer focus the unique energy of crystal flame, assisting the wearer in channeling it into a runic construct.*

Runic Construction*: Assists the wearer in training their energy to form runic constructs, clearing the mind to focus on the forces of nature.*

Starflame*: Releases a focused spell of Starflame. The drain on the bracer's charge is variable, from 1 point to 20.*

Material: Purified Mithril.

Attributes: +6 Aura, +6 Intelligence.

Charges: 200/200.
Duration: Permanent. Attuned.]

Sam looked over the information and nodded, satisfied with the result. Now, he had a weapon of his own, rather than just relying on combusting auras. He reached out and slid it onto his left arm, where it *clicked* with a resonance that he felt in his soul as it secured itself, shrinking slightly to fit.

He looked up, glancing around the room, but his father and Krana hadn't returned yet. When he touched the amulet on his chest, he sensed their presence, still distant in Highfold. His mother and Altey were asleep, but from the unlined look on Aemilia's features, she wasn't worried yet. She'd been watching them all day. There was just enough time left for him to catch some sleep before dawn. In the morning, he could work on the rings and some healing scrolls.

There was still a month before the festival, but that wasn't much in the grand scheme of things. If he wanted to survive the festival and explore the ruins, and clear out the Outsider that was living there, he was going to need some more levels. The same was true for his family. They all needed to be stronger to ensure their safety in the world.

That meant some hunting expeditions would be necessary, up into the peaks surrounding the valley where there were monsters to fight. Perhaps even more wyverns. The Guardian Star flickered on his hand as it sensed the Flaw, pulling him toward it like a void in the night sky.

CHAPTER TWENTY-TWO

A LOST PALADIN

When evening fell, Sam headed outside the inn to a semi-secluded area behind the stables. Few people came out here, especially at night, which meant that it was an excellent area to train. It didn't take him long to set up a privacy ward to conceal sound and light from the surroundings. The Amulet of Swirling Winds was useful for it, acting as a focus. Normally, the amulet could only create a small barrier about ten feet across, but he needed something larger for what he had in mind.

He walked around the empty field as he marked out a runic circle, burning sigils into the ground at specific points. When he was done, a line of crystal flame connected the runic sigils on the ground to the amulet on his neck. The runes began to gleam as the amulet linked into the temporary enchantment and its energy poured out, empowering the new circle.

A few minutes later, a swirling barrier of wind surrounded Sam in a circle that was nearly a hundred feet across. With the increased size of the barrier, the amulet's charge would only last for an hour or two, but that should be enough for his practice. He looked down at the new bracer on his arm, studying the item he'd made. It was a bright, silvery mithril that hugged his skin.

It was too thin to look like proper armor and light enough that he barely felt its presence. It was a comfortable fit, resting just on top of his skin. A few runes spiraled across the surface, marking out an elegant curve of crystalline blue energy as they gleamed softly in the night. No one would mistake the bracer for anything other than what it was—a powerful enchanted item.

Unlike his earlier work, the runic pattern on this one was almost invisible. Most of the bracer looked blank, concealing the hundreds of runes hidden inside. Perhaps that was a sign of Expert work, where the runes were incorporated more deeply into the material itself. It was also why the illusion amulet was so hard to copy. If the outer runes were all he'd seen of this bracer, he would barely have any idea how it functioned.

As it was, he'd come here so that he could test it. He'd built it to be a focus, but he wasn't sure exactly how it would work. The warded area around him was silent as he looked around, his aura pouring through the wards as he checked the barrier one last time. When he was sure that it was silent, crystal flame poured out around him, flowing through the artifact.

As soon as he started, he felt a resonance from the bracer, a sensation of fluidity that enhanced his speed at summoning and condensing his crystal flame. That had to be an effect of Focus of Crystal Flame, the first enchantment he'd laid into it. Flame spiraled around him as he shaped his essence into a crystal flame arrow, starting with the simplest spell he used.

The single arrow turned into a dozen as he poured more essence into it, and then they all merged together into a larger one as he manipulated the flames. He kept the majority of his attention on the bracer as he studied how it reacted. With the six points of Aura and Intelligence that the artifact added, his essence pool was at exactly 100 right now, which meant he had plenty of essence to test things with.

He broke the spell back into a dozen smaller arrows and hurled them into the field in front of him, targeting the dirt. Crackling explosions of crystal flame rose up from the dirt as the grass above it burned away. The spell felt more stable and sharper than ever, although it was hard to tell if it had done more damage to the dirt. He could feel a *hum* from the bracer on his arm as he used his crystal flame, like an echo that was supporting it.

May as well clear that grass out, he decided, as he condensed more flame into a sphere, his attention still on the bracer. An Essence Shield formed in front of him, marking out a target circle, and he hurled the sphere at the center of it.

A moment later, there was a barren, scorched circle of earth in front of him. The Essence Shield had contained the spell within the limits of the target area. Someone might come down in the morning and wonder why there was a ten-foot scorched circle on the ground, but it shouldn't cause any real trouble. It would just be seen as a fight between spell casters or a spell getting out of control.

The spell forms so far were too easy for a real test, but it felt like it was supporting his efforts.

Perhaps a 10 or 20% boost in summoning speed and focus? It certainly felt like it was faster than ever to condense the flames into a spell form. It might boost his damage as well, since the spells would be sharper, but even if it didn't, the effect was extremely useful.

The bracer's primary purpose, however, was to assist with runic construction, so that was what he moved on to next. A sphere of Starfire began to form above his hand as he concentrated, starting from the rune at the center as layers of crystal flame began to condense on the outside.

The *star* rune was always clear in his mind, but it sprang into existence more easily than ever before, outlined in brilliant white lines as it took shape from his aura. This was the point where he'd failed before, in creating a perfect form of it. This time, the bracer resonated with a bright, silvery *hum* as he felt the model of the rune brightening in his mind. The rune at the heart of the spell followed suit, resonating with the energy from the bracer as the lines became outlined in stark relief, more detailed than he'd ever managed before.

The last few times he'd summoned this spell, it had been a struggle to get the rune to form inside his aura, since he wasn't controlling it with a stylus or carefully drawing each line. Now, it almost sprang into existence by itself, the lines forming easily as they copied the rune that was etched into the bracer. At the same time, he could feel a resonance from the rune feeding back into his mind, pulling at his essence as it helped him to shape it.

It only took him a couple of seconds before the Starfire spell was complete.

The brilliant rune hung at the center of it like a white heart, surrounded by the four layers of crystal flame that were compressed so much they looked like liquid. Perhaps one day, he would be able to create an even more advanced form of this spell that was condensed until it looked like hardened crystal. He studied the sphere, especially the rune at the center, as he felt how it was constructed and how his aura wrapped through it and around it, holding it together.

The bracer gave him a pattern to follow, helping him to hold his aura in place, but the concept still came from him. The rune hung there like a silent threat, the energy in it ready to be released as it ignited the outer layers. With the fully-formed rune, the spell felt much stronger than before. It was also faster to summon.

He wasn't sure what that would do when it hit, but he was looking forward to finding out.

The bracer wasn't limited to just boosting Starfire either. If he practiced with it, he might be able to embed star runes into his arrows or even Essence Blade. With a gesture, he raised an Essence Shield around the target circle. Then he hurled the Starfire spell at the center. The spell felt different now that the rune was complete and it flew toward the target like a streaking, crystal blue meteor.

The bright *star* rune at the center left an after image in his eyes like a celestial tail.

KraaTTOOOmmMMM!

The target circle shuddered as an explosion like a volcano rocked it. The Essence Shield contained the explosion as the top layer of soil melted away, fragments of earth turning to glass and molten stone as a cloud of particles boiled upward.

At least 40% stronger.

The complete rune was doing more than just adding power to the spell. He could feel a difference in the energy that was released across the area. The quality of his crystal flame had changed a bit, incorporating something of the rune's concept. There was more heat and intensity to the spell, as well as a particular, brilliant energy like a star shining in the night.

It was similar to when he identified an aura or a natural rune, an impression of something transcending the ordinary.

A concept.

He wasn't sure what would happen when the spell hit an enemy, but it was unlikely to end well for them. Stars held the domineering, explosive force of heat and life, at the same time as they were distant and cold. It was a good concept to use with his crystal flame, which held similar qualities.

As he summoned another Starfire, slowly this time so he could examine how the bracer was augmenting his efforts, he couldn't help but wonder what the future held. *Was it possible to string together many runes like this, forming all of them from their unique concepts, and to create a spell that worked like an enchantment?*

If so, the future of his spell work and his enchanting would walk hand in hand. The vision of a spell made up of hundreds of runes and stretching out over an entire battlefield sprang into his mind...but after a moment, he shook his head and pulled his attention back to the present.

Right now, he needed to work on the *star* rune and to improve his innate understanding of it. He had to walk before he could run. He would also need to comprehend the innate concept of all the runes he wanted to use that way, and that was going to be a long road. He released the energy from the spell, trying to reclaim as much of it as he could, as he tested his control over it, and then he created another one, pushing it as fast as possible.

He released that as well and then built up another one slowly. Bit by bit, he tested how quickly he could summon them and whether he could add more layers.

Right now, each Starfire took 18 essence, and he knew that if he understood the *star* concept better, the bracer would augment his ability even further. Until then, he would just have to practice. Another explosion rang out inside his shield, reheating the shards of glass and stone that were just starting to cool off. Heat like a blast furnace roared away from the circle, washing comfortably against his skin.

The night stretched out around him, his privacy barrier creating an island of peace and quiet.

***

Lenei was feeling very annoyed as she rode into the small village near the center of the valley around Highfold, heading for the single inn that she'd seen from the road. Caelus was rising toward the center of the sky, marking out that it was almost midnight, and Hero stamped his hooves in displeasure at the hour. They'd been riding since before dawn and he was ready for a stable and a bucket of oats. Lenei patted him on the neck in silent agreement.

Well, oats for him and a soft bed for her. It looked like it was too late to expect a meal. She'd have to make due with her travel rations until the morning. She'd been a fully-fledged Paladin of Law for a few months now, but it wasn't going the way she'd thought.

There should have been some Outsider to kill or an invasion to put down, which was what Paladins were supposed to do with their time, but so far her Calling had told her to wander across nearly the entire Storm Plains.

First, it had sent her to the west until she was almost in the Broken Lands, near some random village called Cliff's End that was infested with bandits, and then northward into the Abyssinian Plains, and then back toward Osera. Most recently, it had demanded that she wander along the *entire* Law-be-damned high road between Ebonfar and Highfold.

It was infuriating.

How was that what she was supposed to be doing?!

It was the first time she'd felt the Paladin's Call, since she'd only received the ability at Level 60, but from everything she'd heard, it felt like it was supposed to. It was a strong pull toward a distant place, like a string tugging at her.

The problem was...what other Paladin had their Calling move along the road from spot to spot, changing every day?

A Call was an alert from the World Law to come to a specific location. *They weren't supposed to move!* She didn't know what it was trying to make her find, but it was extremely aggravating. She was supposed to be hunting down Outsiders and solving problems for the World Law, not wandering all over the place.

The Guardian Star amulet on her chest flickered, a symbol of the Call, as she felt it tug her onward. She could feel a sense of connection to something, the target she was supposed to find. It was difficult to tell distance with a Call. All it did was pull you onward until you found it. According to the senior Paladins, it was a continual lesson in patience and humility.

Our duty is endless, and the journey is the reward. She was supposed to be grateful for the constant task in front of her, never worrying about time or tiredness.

Just move forward, always forward. That was part of the Paladins' creed. Never doubt, never stop, be relentless and enduring. She was tempted to give in to doubt as she wondered if the false legend about the World Law failing was true.

The Call was supposed to lead her to something the World Law needed her to fix, but hers had just dragged her around the entire Western Province. It was sacrilegious to doubt the all-encompassing power of the Law, but she had no idea what was going on.

Her armor shifted fluidly around her as she swung out of the saddle and pulled Hero along by his reins, heading across the inn's yard. He was a good horse, a strong fellow who'd carried her across a lot of miles. Hopefully those stables were better than they looked, since he deserved it. As she crossed the yard, she suddenly felt the position of the Call shift, swinging back in the other direction.

She froze in an instant, glancing down at the amulet. She stepped back, retracing her steps as her heart quickened. Her hand rose, settling on the spear that was in the stirrup by her saddle.

The Call was coming from right behind the stables.

She hooked Hero's reins to a free post. Then, she slung her shield up around her arm and tightened her grip on her spear. A glowing white light sprang out of her body as she called upon one of her main abilities, Holy Armor, the only Paladin ability that she had at Elite. A moment later, her spear and shield also started to gleam as she activated Spiritual Infusion, pouring her mana into them to enhance their damage.

Then she stalked around the edge of the stables, tracking the movement of the Call as she headed straight for it. She pressed herself up against the wall and then ducked her head out for an instant to look before pulling it back. There was nothing back there except a blank field and the soft whistle of the wind, but she could feel the Call drawing her to it. All of her senses were fixed on the open area as her heart raced.

It looked empty, but Outsiders were often dangerous mages...there could be a hidden Flaw there!

This had to be why she had been Called to this place. She hadn't expected that she would find it so suddenly, but a Paladin had to move with the will of the World Law.

She ducked around the corner again, and this time she could feel that there was something strange about the yard there...it was *too* quiet and peaceful, and where was that breeze coming from that was flowing away from it? It had to be a barrier of some type, but how were the people in the inn ignorant of it?

The Outsider must have just arrived here, somehow. She pushed her doubts out of her mind as she readied her spear, infusing even more mana into it as she raised it into the air.

"For Aster Fall!" She charged around the corner with a hair-raising shout, activating an infused Shield Charge as she hurtled toward the open air in front of her. She felt a layer of resistance made of whipping winds that shoved her backward, and then the sense of a spell cracking as she crashed into it with her shield.

The scene in front of her changed, revealing a hooded caster in a grey cloak who was raising his hands as a glowing sphere of some evil blue spell flared like a star in the sky. Lenei's Spiritual Awareness swept out around her, analyzing everything in the air as the figure started to turn toward her. As he did, his hood slipped back from his head, falling away to reveal two stark black horns curling back from his forehead and slit-pupiled, crystal blue eyes that flared with the same light as the spell.

"Demon!" she shouted, her eyes widening as she poured more energy into her Holy Armor. It wasn't just a simple Outsider, a wolf or something that had escaped from a Flaw!

It was a demon...one of the Lords of Destruction, an Unholy Ruler of the Abyss, the Walkers in the Dark, the Plaguebringers, the World Breakers!

The list of names went on, but Lenei forcibly stopped her mind as she whispered a blessing in her heart and consigned herself to death. She didn't know what she'd stumbled upon, but she knew she wasn't a match for a demon. All she could do was die and hope that the World Law sent an army to kill the demon and let her rest in peace.

As she raised her spear and rushed forward toward the demon, she could feel the twisted aura of a *"Defiant"* radiating outward from him, making her lips curl in displeasure. She didn't have time to be confused or to wonder why that trait was on a demon. Her spear was closing in on him as she surged across the ground, its point shining like a diamond as her mana infused it.

The last thing she saw was the caster swearing, something that sounded a lot like a very annoyed young human saying, *"Damn it."*

KRaaaTTOOOOOMmmm!

A sphere of burning white and crystal blue light exploded all around her as it hurled her backward.

CHAPTER TWENTY-THREE

WITH A STAR ABOVE

The Starfire spell exploded against the intruder as Sam's curse echoed in the air. The explosion hurled her backward even as she raised her shield to block it, picking her up like a rag doll and throwing her across the ground. Half of the practice area between him and the stables was consumed in a fiery, blue-white conflagration as the spell erupted in a sphere of burning energy, scorching the earth as the top layer began to melt.

The Starfire spell was nearly 50% stronger than it had been against the wyvern. His practice had resulted in some improvements over the course of the night. A thunderous echo roared out around the impact, and Sam reflexively blocked in the spell with an Essence Shield, keeping it from expanding past the privacy barrier. He also reached out with the same shield and *swatted* at the paladin who was tumbling across the ground, knocking her back toward the center of the circle and away from the center of the blast.

He didn't know who she was, but it was obvious *what* she was.
Human. Paladin of Law-Healer. Level 60.
Someone from the church. He didn't want her to escape from the privacy barrier, but he also didn't want to kill her. He'd only had time to glance at her, but she radiated a sort of pure honesty that appealed to him.

Even if she had been trying to kill him.

Over the past months, he'd decided that in his dealings with the church going forward, he was going to have to be tolerant of their initial impression of him. Otherwise, it was just going to turn into a war and they had a lot more troops than he did.

As the paladin rolled across the ground and tried to get back to her feet, he reached out and strengthened the barrier around them, draining most of the charge from his amulet as he pushed more mana into the swirling winds. He didn't need everyone in the inn running out here to see what was going on.

Then, he reactivated his illusion amulet, obscuring his features as he pulled the hood back up over his head. A spiral of crystal flame condensed around him, wavering on the verge of condensing into another Starfire spell. He had been practicing for a while and he was low on essence. He only had one large spell he could cast without combusting an aura.

Fortunately, the Starflame Bracer was still at a nearly full charge. There were almost 200 starflame arrows in there waiting to be used.

Through the amulet, he could feel his mother and Altey starting to move. They'd probably sensed his alarm when he was attacked. Hopefully, they would stay inside until he figured out what to do about this paladin.

He studied her as she staggered to her feet, trying to find her balance. The majority of the spell had struck her kite shield, which was half-melted from the heat, but she'd avoided most of the damage. She was in full plate armor that was even more ornate than the version he'd enchanted for Lesat. She also had long, dark hair pulled back behind her head, which she probably wore under a helm when she was better prepared for battle, but she wasn't wearing that at the moment.

In her hands, there was the mangled kite shield and a wicked-looking spear as tall as she was, both of which she'd managed to keep in her grip despite her flight across the circle.

Her body and equipment glowed with a subtle white light, similar to the healing magic that Ayala had used with her Priestess class, and the familiar pressure of the World Law radiated from her.

Perhaps if he'd been an evil Outsider, it would have bothered him, but as it was, it was a semi-comfortable presence. The only reason to dislike it was that it reminded him of the World Law's inflexibility. He didn't know how a paladin had suddenly shown up here, but she had definitely attacked him, and his mind raced as he looked for a way to make her stop.

Given everything he knew about paladins, she was unlikely to back down unless something shocked her.

That was basically the entire legend of paladins. They were relentless. On top of that, she'd seen his face and there was no reason for her to doubt that he was a demon. So, as she gathered herself and prepared to charge at him again, he did the only thing he could think of that might convince her they were on the same side.

He poured essence into the Guardian Star on his hand and held it up in front of him, willing it to become as large as possible.

"HOLD!"

A flare of brilliant, rainbow-tinted white light blasted out of the Guardian Star on his hand, rising into the air like the sun dawning. It was so bright that the area inside his practice circle flared into blinding relief. He blinked back tears as his eyes stung at the intensity.

"Ahh!" Across from him, a young woman's surprised shout rose into the air, and his senses tracked the paladin's movements as she staggered backwards, her melted shield rising to block her eyes.

"I don't need my eyes to see, demon!" Her shout rang out an instant later, as she gathered herself and rushed forward, her spear raised.

"*Gods damn it,*" Sam muttered to himself again, as he studied her. More than just her connection to the church, something was telling him that he shouldn't hurt her, even if he didn't know why.

Maybe she reminded him of Ayala, or perhaps it was that aura of innocence around her. He just had the impression that she was a good person. Or maybe it was the fact that she was stunning, even rolling across the ground and half burned. Paladins focused on Charisma and Wisdom, and hers was obviously very high.

"That's the Guardian Star!" he shouted as he used a flare of Essence Shield to shove himself to the side. It wasn't a tactic he'd used before, but it came to him on the spur of the moment. He'd moved other people with it, so why not himself?

The pulse of energy flung him halfway across the circle and out of the range of her lunge, where he caught himself and slid to a halt, wobbling slightly. Before he could recover his balance all the way, the paladin pivoted in place and lunged at him again, her figure blurring across the distance. He threw up an Essence Shield in front of her at an angle, using it to deflect her blow as he threw himself in the other direction.

"Stop attacking!" he shouted, trying to convince her they were on the same side. "We're allies!"

"False demon! Lord of Chaos!" the paladin shouted back, her voice hoarse. "Even if I have to die, I'll take you with me!"

Sam narrowly evaded another lunge, using Essence Shield again to throw him backward and out of the way. The paladin was fast, nearly as fast as that wyvern had been. Her level was also higher than his, although it didn't matter so much as long as he didn't let her hit him.

"*For Aster Fall!*" A shining, white spear *blurred* across the area as it headed toward his heart, and Sam barely got an Essence Shield up in time to divert it as he threw himself to the side again.

Evading wasn't taking as much essence as attacking her would have, but if this kept up, he'd have to waste some auras. The paladin wasn't paying any attention to the enormous Guardian Star that was still shining in the center of the practice area. She was probably too stunned by his appearance to notice.

There had to be a way to make her see it.

***

As she lunged toward the demon again, Lenei was surprised that she was still alive. The demon's initial attack had been powerful enough to kill her, but it felt like something had knocked her away from it at the last moment. Perhaps the World Law was looking out for her. The impact had rattled her and she could feel the hot pain of burns across her body, but almost all of the attack had been absorbed by her shield and Holy Armor.

Her shield was twisted unrecognizably, but it had done its job and was still attached to her arm. The blessed light of her Holy Armor had also collapsed and was trying to reform, which was why she hadn't been injured more. It was ablative, shattering outward as it tried to redirect damage away from her.

Unfortunately, the blessing from the armor was also what gave her most of her physical power, adding half of her Wisdom and Charisma attributes to her Strength and Constitution. It hadn't reformed yet, so she was weaker than normal.

The demon was head and shoulders taller than her, and as she tried to pin him down again, he was using some form of crystal blue flames to throw himself from place to place, almost like a pulse. It was a strange evasion ability and he didn't look coordinated with it at all, which was odd, but perhaps she'd been able to surprise him.

Maybe the World Law was limiting his abilities and helping her?

As she lunged at him again, he caught his balance and pushed himself away with a pulse of crystalline flames as he dodged again.

"Damn it. Stop that!" the demon shouted at her, his voice sounding deceptively young and human. He was even mimicking an affronted indignation that would have made her hesitate if it had come from a human. Fortunately, she was a Paladin of Law and well prepared for demon tricks. She turned her attention away from her hearing, focusing on her sight instead.

Her mana was already down to half, thanks to the damage she'd taken in the first exchange, and she didn't have time to heal herself. She pushed the burns out of her mind as she called on Aura of Law, an area ability that created a field of energy in front of her to burn demons and monsters.

A large arc of golden-white light blasted out of her shield and across the area in front of her, bringing with it a relaxing warmth that washed back against her burns, soothing them. The light covered half of the demon's circle, searing outward across his body as she caught him on the edge of it.

The demon blinked, his eyes watering with crystalline tears as he held up a hand to block the light, but a moment later, his demonic energy flared around him and he dodged off to the side again. Lenei tracked him, pivoting in place as she held her shield high and prepared for another lunge. Hopefully, that ability would burn him and give her an opening.

Oddly, however, the demon didn't seem to be harmed at all by the Aura of Law, except that he was cursing and holding his hand in front of his eyes again as she brought the arc of light back toward him. A surge of fear rushed through her as she saw that.

He was immune to her best attacks? She didn't understand what was going on. Even if he was a powerful demon, how could he resist the power of the World Law itself? He should have looked uncomfortable, at least.

She was preparing to lunge forward again, her mana flowing into her spear, but at that moment, a golden-haired woman and girl burst through the demon's wind barrier.

Human. Historian-Seer. Level 32.
Human. Child.

"STOP!" The woman's hand was raised in a command to hold and her eyes shone with golden light as she shouted across the field. Her expression was stern and the authority in her voice was unmistakable. Her undone hair flew behind her like a golden banner of war, floating in the wind from the barrier.

She looked like a veteran Paladin or Priestess, a holy mother commanding the hearts of the faithful. Her command resonated outward with a palpable force, carrying a crushing force of emotion that hit Lenei like a storm wave, making her freeze in place.

Love, anger, care...

Without meaning to, Lenei leaned backward to get away from her. For some reason, she felt a thread of guilt. The little girl next to the woman didn't hesitate at all, however.

Chiingg!

The next thing Lenei knew, a tiny bolt of magical ice slammed into her breastplate. It wasn't even enough to make her step backwards, but the sound was a crisp, bright note that resonated in the air as the bolt shattered on the enchanted steel.

"Stop attacking my brother! Bandit!" The girl's voice rang out in the air, her tone almost as stern as the woman's, except that it had the bright resonance of youth.

Lenei glanced down to where the ice bolt had hit. Her brow furrowed in confusion. She raised her shield, easily blocking another ice bolt that struck and shattered, the shards ricocheting.

This little girl was apparently very fierce, but why was she attacking her and not the demon?

She had to protect these humans from the demon, but she was so surprised by their arrival and the woman's command to stop that she momentarily forgot to move. She didn't know why they were yelling at her, but any moment now, the demon was going to kill them or take them as hostages. She brought her spear back around, readying her shield and blocking another small bolt of ice as she turned to see where the demon was.

The crystal-eyed invader was standing on the other side of the circle now, in front of the woman and the girl. His hand was raised and a bright blue shield hung in front of him like a wall of geometric crystals, but he was doing nothing else. The woman and girl looked strangely calm next to him.

"Look up." The woman's command rang out in the night air as she raised her hand to point toward the sky.

Lenei couldn't help but follow the gesture, her eyes rising until she saw what was shining in the air above the demon's circle. It was a brilliant, nine-pointed, silver and white Guardian Star, flaring in the air like the mandate of the World Law itself. A rainbow of other hues ran through it, sparkling with all the light of the distant stars.

The thread of the Call was pulling her directly toward it, making her feel like she could walk into the air and straight into the star. The fight went out of her when she saw it.

Her legs were unsteady as she sank backward, and she drove her spear into the ground beside her, holding onto it as she fell onto her butt, still looking upward at the star. She didn't know why it was there, but the Guardian Star's presence was as clear as day, driving home the message that whatever she thought was going on, it was something completely different.

The feeling of the Call echoed around her, filling the area now with a satisfied hum of energy as she felt the thread move from the star down to the demon who was standing there. Her eyes settled on him, and then on the woman and girl behind him. From his posture, it was clear as day that he was protecting them...from her.

A feeling of vertigo hit her. The world spun as her expectations and reality clashed, and she had trouble putting the two back together.

She had no idea why the demon would be protecting those two humans, or why they were so clearly trying to protect him.... A moment later, a man in armor arrived, his sword drawn as he rushed into the area and put himself in front of the woman and girl.

"What...is going on?" she asked, weakly, holding onto her spear as if it were the last bastion of steadiness in the world. The pain of her burns rushed into her awareness as the area inside the demon's circle became calm and tranquil. "Who are you people?"

Chapter Twenty-Four

LENEI

Sam pulled a healing scroll out of his belt pouch, one of the limited few that he'd made in between working on his bracer, and handed it to Altey. His sister was holding onto her Wand of Ice Bolt with a fierce determination, even as she was hiding behind him and looking across the circle with wide eyes. Aemilia's hand on her shoulder kept her from moving any farther forward.

"Go heal her," he suggested, nodding toward the paladin. From everything he could tell, there was no way that the paladin would harm Altey, but he was still planning to keep an Essence Shield around her.

Behind him, he felt the force of his mother's illusion spell fade, but it was still projecting the force of her emotions outward. That had been what got the paladin's attention. The paladin had a subclass as a healer, but he figured the offer to heal her was more important than pointing that out.

"Why should we heal her?" Altey frowned up at him, not taking the scroll. She peeked out from behind him as she examined the paladin. "She was attacking you."

"She didn't mean it," Sam said as he tried to maintain his calm. He held out the scroll. "She thought I was evil. Go on."

"No." Altey refused to take the scroll again, shaking her head adamantly. "She doesn't deserve it."

His mother took the scroll from his hand instead, and then walked forward to the paladin who was still staring at them in shock. Lesat stayed next to her, his hand on his sword as he gave the paladin a guarded look. It was clear that he recognized her class, and it made him uneasy. Sam shifted his Essence Shield, keeping it around his mother as Aemilia knelt down next to the woman.

"Not everything in the world is what you think," Aemilia said simply, answering the question the paladin had asked a moment before. Her voice was firm, but her anger had faded a bit now that Sam was unharmed. "Hold still," she commanded as she reached out with the scroll.

"No!" The paladin's hand shot out, grabbing for Aemilia's wrist. The only result was a flare of crystal blue as the Essence Shield knocked her hand away.

"Stop fussing," Aemilia replied sternly. "It's just a healing scroll." She held it up where the paladin could see, the standard healing runes on it clearly visible.

"My son made it, and there aren't very many of them," she continued. "If he's polite enough to give it to you, the least you could do is say thank you and hold still so I can use it."

"But he's a demon!" The paladin protested, her voice wavering as she looked between Aemilia, Lesat, Altey, and Sam. Her voice trailed off, before she tried again. "How could a demon be...?"

"My name is Sam," he answered, his voice echoing across the field as he turned the topic to something more useful. "What's yours?"

Behind him, he checked to make sure the privacy barrier was still intact. It was on its last legs now. Three people breaking through had disrupted it. He infused a few more points of essence into it to stabilize it, leaving himself almost out of essence. An aura floated on the edge of his storage, ready to appear in his hand if he needed more.

"My name is Lenei," the paladin answered, slowly, as she studied the scroll in Aemilia's hand. She wasn't an Arcane Scribe, but she'd seen enough healing scrolls that it was easy to tell it was real. A moment later, she let Aemilia activate it.

Sam looked around the circle, including at all of the torn up dirt and seared grass, and shook his head. Perhaps he should have chosen a different place to practice. The innkeeper wasn't going to be happy that half of his back field was scorched, but another gold coin would probably make him look the other way.

"Well, Lenei," Aemilia suggested as the paladin's burns began to disappear, "why don't we all go upstairs and have a chat together? You'll have to promise not to attack until you hear the full story."

"I'm not a demon," Sam added as he raised his hand and showed her the mark on the back of it. "Trust in the Guardian Star."

He considered using the story that his appearance was a curse, but he decided not to this time. There was a legend that paladins could tell a lie when they heard it. His appearance was a problem, but it was also what made him who he was. Lenei hesitated, but as she looked at Aemilia and then at Altey, and then at Sam who was standing there calmly, she slowly nodded.

"All right," she said, letting out a sigh as the healing scroll finished its work. "Can someone explain what by the Law is going on?"

***

A little while later, the five of them were seated around the table in their room, with Sam and Lenei at opposite ends of the table.

"That doesn't make any sense," Lenei said, frowning as she listened to the full story. "How could you transform into that? And have your race changed? I've never heard anything like it."

"I can't explain it, but that's what happened," Sam offered as he wrapped up his explanation. After hearing her story, it was clear that Lenei had been following him since he and his father activated the ruins by Cliff's End, at the beginning of this all. The World Law had announced back then that it had summoned an authority to investigate.

Apparently, that was Lenei. He hadn't expected that it would be a Level 60 paladin. At the time, it would've been enough to crush them. Even now, she was 11 levels higher than him, although his bracer and class abilities were making up the difference. With everything taken into consideration, it didn't seem like that strong of a response for an Outsider ruin.

Perhaps the World Law had other troubles.

"You said your Call brought you here, right?" he asked as he decided to turn the conversation in the most important direction. "And it's still calling you toward me? Well, we need your help. Perhaps that's why you're really here. Maybe the World Law sent you to help us."

"What do you mean?" Lenei frowned. "A Paladin has to follow the Call, yes, but...you don't look like someone I'm supposed to be helping."

"Try to get past that," Sam answered drily. "There's an unknown Outsider and a concealed Flaw in the mountains here, near the ancient ruins above Highfold. I could use your help to kill it and close the Flaw."

Lenei frowned as she heard the request. It was true that it was the sort of thing she was supposed to be doing, but she was still having a hard time putting it all together and changing her mind so quickly. The feeling of the Call that was tugging her toward Sam was still there, though, which lent his words extra force.

"Haven't you told the church and local forces here?" she asked, her frown deepening. "They should be taking care of this area."

"We're trying that too," Aemilia spoke up. "That's where my husband and another friend are now. She's a Seer. They're in Highfold trying to convince them to listen, and explaining how a wyvern was acting under something's orders."

"The church can be difficult," Lesat added, shaking his head. He was watching Lenei with guarded suspicion. "We can't have them chasing after Sam just because he has horns, so we're being careful about it."

It didn't take too long to explain the rest of the details to Lenei, and as they did, her frown continued to deepen. The dark-haired young woman leaned forward intensely, her elbows on the table, as a sense of determination radiated from her. It was a pose that showed off her character as strongly as a masterful sculptor could have captured it in stone.

Her lean muscles in her arms and the strong line of her jaw demanded attention. Her almond-shaped, green eyes tilted upward slightly at the corner, and her skin was a rich olive that was bathed in the light from the fireplace at the side of the room.

More than that, there was a feeling of heightened emotion constantly swirling around her, filling the area and making it impossible to mistake what she meant. Her every action demanded attention. It was the effect of her Charisma.

For the first time, Sam began to realize what the attribute could really do. She was impressing her will on the world around her just by existing, almost like a powerfully enchanted artifact.

To an extent, he could feel that he was doing the same, just not as strongly, and it helped to bring the importance of the attribute into focus for him. Perhaps he should add more to it, when he had the points. It would help in situations like this, if he had to explain himself to people. His Charisma was still 30, the same as it had been for months.

"You're right that the Call is still pulling me toward you," she said, returning to study Sam intently. She'd been doing that for most of the time they'd been in the room. "I don't feel a threat from you, and the Guardian Star is on your hand...but even with that it's hard to accept what you're saying without more proof. You are just too strange."

"The World Law itself has authorized my existence," Sam said as he stuck to the facts that he thought might convince her. "It considers me a full citizen of Aster Fall and someone who is working in its interests. Otherwise, your attacks might have injured me."

Lenei frowned as she thought back to the Aura of Law that she'd tried to use against him, as well as the meaning of the star. As a Paladin, that star was the symbol of her entire Order, and to see it on the hand of a demon was deeply unsettling, but if what he said was true.... She would have to meet with the other seer in their party and talk to her, to see if she was telling the truth about the Breaking that was coming.

Paladins didn't have the exact ability to discern truth from lies, but her Spiritual Awareness was highly attuned to emotions and changes in character. It let her read expressions and some emotions, giving her insight into whether people believed what they were saying. These three all believed what they were telling her and the story was consistent.

"I don't have another explanation yet," she said at last, "but I'm also not going to leave until my Call changes. If what you're saying is true...then show me where the Outsider is and I'll do my best to kill it. As a Paladin of Law, it's my duty to Aster Fall. If you're right about it, maybe I'll be able to trust you."

"Good enough," Sam agreed, nodding at her. "It's still several hours to dawn, so let's call this a truce? We can all get some sleep and wait for my father and Krana to return. Then we can decide what to do about the Outsider."

Lenei looked around the room, and then she gave him a firm nod, her movement still somehow more graceful and forceful than he expected, even when he knew about her Charisma. "We'll speak again in the morning," she agreed as she pushed up from the table. She paused, looking toward the door and around the room as she realized that the innkeeper was probably already fast asleep. She'd have to wake him up to get a room.

"You can borrow Krana's room," Aemilia offered, nodding toward one of the doors that opened onto the common area.

Lenei hesitated for a moment, with one last long look at Sam.

"Thank you." Her voice was softer, kinder than it had been before. She didn't trust them yet, but she had to admit that there were a lot of things in their story that rang true. The thing that really made her accept their story was the Call and the Guardian Star. If she doubted those, she would be doubting her entire life that had led her to this point.

The star on Sam's hand was still shining with a version of the World Law's aura in her senses, letting off a gentle, reassuring presence, as she shook her head and walked toward the room Aemilia had indicated. She would put up a blessing around the room before she fell asleep, which would give her some warning if anyone attacked, but from the looks of it, they wouldn't.

Except for the little girl, she added as she glanced back. Altey looked like she still wanted to shoot her with that ice wand. Lenei hid a smile. This family was strangely fierce. Perhaps that was what came from forging their own way in the world.

For a first Calling, this was nothing at all like she'd expected.

***

After Lenei left, Lesat went to keep watch outside in case anyone else came by, and Aemilia and Altey went to sleep again, leaving Sam alone in the room. He returned to his work table, his chin on his hand as he leaned forward, studying the enchantment on the wall. He was debating whether to strengthen it before he went to sleep, and also whether to divide Krana's room off from the others, but after a moment, he shook his head.

His mother and sister had their amulets, which would trigger defensive shields if Lenei tried anything. That was enough reassurance. From what he'd seen of the paladin, it wasn't in her to attack his mother and sister, and he doubted that she would break her word and attack him either. It should be safe enough.

He looked out the window to where Caelus was moving toward dawn and shook his head, considering the work that he still needed to do. He'd get a few hours of sleep, but after that there were a few things he needed to finish before going after the Outsider. Healing scrolls were on the top of the list, along with an idea he was working on to protect his family.

Avoiding Lenei's attacks had also given him an idea for how to use Essence Shield for evasion. He would need to put some effort into studying that. Just standing there and absorbing blows on his shield wasn't a very good tactic, especially if there were more wyverns, since it drained his essence too quickly. It would be better to evade and save his energy for attacks. Thoughts spun through his mind as he leaned back against the wall behind him, his eyes drifting closed. With everything on his mind, he forgot about his bed.

His work table felt more familiar anyway.

***

"I need to get my shield repaired, which means I have to stop by a church armory," Lenei announced, as she looked down at her shield the following morning. The shield was still mangled, its enchantment damaged. "I tried to repair it, but it's beyond my skills. There should be an armory in Highfold."

"Let me see it," Sam offered, yawning as he stood up from his work table. He tucked the healing scroll he'd just finished away in his belt pouch. It joined a swiftly growing stack of others there, which was what he had spent most of the morning working on. It took him about an hour to make one, these days.

"You..." Lenei hesitated, looking at Sam with some doubt. His illusion amulet wasn't active, so his demonic features were on full display. She'd agreed last night to work with him, but it was still a bit difficult to wrap her mind around it.

"If I wanted to harm you, I would have tried already," Sam said bluntly as he held out his hand. "I'm an Enchanter. Maybe I can fix it." He also wanted to study the enchantment and see how the church did things.

Lenei hesitated, studying him, and then a bright white light began to radiate out from her, concentrating on her hand. She could still sense the unpleasant aura of a Defiant around him, but based on his story, she understood why it was there.

"I believe your story, but...if you can take my hand," she said slowly, as she held it out to him, "I'll trust you with my shield. It's already broken."

Sam shrugged as he wrapped his hand around her wrist and shook her hand. The energy around her flowed across his skin harmlessly. He snagged the shield from her and wandered over to his work table, where he set it down and began examining it. Behind him, Lenei's expression shifted to confusion, and she let out a sigh as she followed him, pulling up a stool to sit down on the other side of the table.

"So you're really not a demon," she muttered, half to herself. "It's just hard to accept, especially when your race shows up as Outsider."

"Outsider of Aster Fall, not a demon," Sam muttered back as he turned the shield around, infusing it with a thread of his aura as he began to study the enchantment. "And that's only because the World Law didn't know what else to call me."

Essence-Infused Human or something would have been better, in his opinion, even if he did look like a demon.

"Do you know much about the history of the church?" Lenei asked with a frown, as she looked at the star on the back of his hand.

"Which part?" Sam spoke, half-distracted as most of his attention was on the shield.

"The legend of the last Breaking and how the church was formed, and the role that the demons played in it."

Sam shook his head, since he had no idea what she was talking about.

"Where's a bard when you need one..." Lenei looked around the room hopefully, as if a bard might jump into the area now that they'd been invited. When nothing happened, she continued. "There's a song about it...a very long one called the Cycle of Ages. It's nearly four thousand years old, if you trust the bards who sing it."

"About a demon?" Sam asked, with some curiosity.

"About three of them," Lenei agreed slowly. "You reminded me of it, since they are known by the color of their auras. Did you know, supposedly there have only ever been three real demons in the legends? Every sighting of them has been attributed to one of those three, although there have been some lesser versions reported as well, avatars or lieutenants perhaps."

"What?" Sam asked, turning to look at her with more attention as he processed what she was saying, and why she was bringing it up. "What do you mean? Surely there's been more than three?"

He wasn't sure what she was talking about, but the idea brought back the three demons he'd seen in his dream, from the First Contact.

"No, just three, at least for those who fought the gods. Red, orange, and blue," Lenei shook her head. "The Demon of Sundered Blood, the Demon of Demented Passion, and the Demon of Shattered Skies." She looked up, as if looking into her memory. "I'll paraphrase the songs, since I'm not much of a singer.

"The Demon of Blood commanded blood to flow. He ripped it from peoples' veins while their hearts were still beating until it turned to a rushing tide across the ground, drowning city walls.

"The Demon of Passion drove the world to madness and despair, until no one could see the difference between family and foe, and murder was more common than breathing.

"The Demon of Shattered Skies ripped heaven and sea asunder, pouring one into the other until the earth shattered, the stars fell, and the elements failed. She drowned the world in tears and storms, turned the air to fire and the earth to wind."

Lenei was watching him closely as she spoke, as if she wanted a reaction. When she didn't get any, she just nodded.

"Those are the Three Demons of Aster Fall," she added. "Blue was the Demon of Shattered Skies. That's the one whose color you have. It's said she was the last to retreat from the world, fighting even as the gods descended to repair it." With that, she sat down across from him, looking pointedly at him and then at the shield in his hands.

"So, can you fix it?"

CHAPTER TWENTY-FIVE

LEGEND OF THREE MOONS

Lenei's words echoed in Sam's ears as he looked down at the shield. He'd never heard the Cycle of Ages, and no bard had ever come to Cliff's End, but the names of the demons resonated. The three demons he'd seen in his dream had auras that fit that story. He was pretty sure what he'd seen in that dream had been the very first time the demons and the Astrals met, not the most recent Breaking.

First Contact.

Had those same three demons returned, like harbingers of destruction, for every Breaking of the world after that? *How many had there been?* He shook his head as he continued examining the shield's enchantment. He didn't have that answer. He'd had some other dreams since that one about First Contact, most of them in fragments of images from the past.

"The moons are said to be the guardians against those three demons," Lenei added. She was watching him from across the table as she spoke, as if she were still testing his reaction. "Silvas to guard life, Caelus to guard the elements, and Amaris to guard our hearts."

"Wait, what?" Sam said suddenly, looking up in surprise as Lenei's words rang out, distracting him from his study of the shield.

"Supposedly, the moons were not always here," Lenei said after she looked at him for a moment. When it was clear that he didn't know what she was talking about, she continued. "They were added by the gods as the three guardians of the world. Each of them is designed to block the influence of one of the demons and to stabilize the World Seal."

Sam let the shield fall back to the table. Without saying anything, he stood up and walked to the window, looking out across the distance toward Highfold. Beyond that, his gaze traveled to the ruins above the city. He knew Lenei was bringing up this story for a reason. There was an idea she was suggesting, or some connection.

"The Festival of Three Crowns is in less than a month," he said slowly. "The moons will align with the ruins there, waking up the enchantments on them."

Lenei turned to watch him, saying nothing else as she waited for him to put it together.

"You're suggesting that it's no coincidence an Outsider and a Flaw would be located near those ruins, aren't you?" His thoughts raced as he put the ideas together, as he looked upward to where Caelus was beginning his climb across the sky. It wasn't long past dawn right now.

"The church has wondered for a long time if there's a connection between Highfold's ruins and the Seal," Lenei agreed. "It's a topic that comes up every time the festival nears, so...every seven years."

"What would happen if an Outsider managed to disrupt the ruins then?" Sam asked. "You think it will affect the Seal?"

"One of the theories is that the ruins are part of an ancient formation laid down by the gods, which aligns with the triple moons. That's why no one can understand the symbols on them." Lenei's voice was hesitant as she added another idea. "Some even suggest that the moons' alignment is a power source for the ruins or a balancing of the energy within the Seal."

Sam's expression turned harder as he listened.

"The problem is, although everyone knows about it, only a few people really believe that theory. There are a lot of legends about the Seal, and this is just one of them.

"If you listened to all of the stories, every rock and abandoned pillar in the world would be part of the Seal. Most people just think they're old ruins and that anything else is the result of an overactive imagination."

"Do you believe it?" Sam asked, turning around suddenly to look at Lenei.

"I think that if your story is true, and there's an Outsider in those ruins," Lenei said slowly, holding his gaze, "then we can't take the risk of letting it stay there. We have to close that Flaw before the moons align."

Sam frowned again as he recalled the strange feeling of essence in the snow, the bandits' excessive number of supplies, the controlled wyvern, and the way the Flaw was concealed. The supplies suggested a bigger force was expected, somewhere, and that was not good news. It also had to be difficult to conceal a Flaw, which meant resources and intelligence had been devoted to it.

What would an Outsider be capable of with time to plan? This one had already been here for over a year, keeping a low profile as they took control of the area.

"The ruins are connected to the moons," he said slowly, as he put it all together. "If they're also connected to the Seal, then that Flaw is much more dangerous than we thought, and much more strategic."

"It may not be true," Lenei replied, her words hesitant. "I could be jumping to conclusions by suggesting it. All of this is just legends from a song and theories."

"Is that what your heart tells you?" he asked, shaking his head. "You brought it up for a reason. Even if it's not true, we can't take that risk, now that we know about the possibility."

He looked down at the Guardian Star on his hand and thought about how Lenei had arrived here, following her Call. The Guardian had said the star would provide information. Perhaps this time, Lenei was the information he'd sent. He didn't know how easy it was for the Guardian to contact him, or if he had to work through the World Law, but if anyone could alter a paladin's Call and send them at the right time, it would be the Guardian.

He turned back to the window as he looked toward the ruins and then to Caelus in the sky above. He'd been planning on slowly working his way up through more levels before heading to the ruins, but it looked like they weren't going to have that luxury. They needed to know what was going on.

"I think you need to head into Highfold and warn the church," he said at last. "I've been trying to avoid them, but this isn't the type of problem to keep to ourselves. Even if they don't listen, at least give them a warning about the Flaw and request reinforcements."

"We have no evidence to show them," Lenei warned, although she didn't disagree. "They may just say I'm an idealistic young paladin, with my heart in the right place and my mind in the clouds, dreaming of being a hero. It wouldn't be the first time I've heard that."

Sam's eyes pierced the distance as he looked toward the ruins, searching for the Flaw that he knew was there. Streams of silver-purple mana hung densely around the peaks of the Three Crowns, the energy in them highlighted by the rising sun in a wash of pink and orange. Stimulated by the sunlight, a river of mana poured down the slopes of the largest mountain, running straight through the ruins to the valley below.

Why had the ruins been built here, near where mana gathered at the top of the world? And why were they connected to the moons?

If Lenei's suggestion was true, then the ruins here were not just a remnant of an old civilization. He didn't know what would happen when the moons aligned during the Festival, but there was no way that he would allow an Outsider to take control of them.

Even with his concern, Lenei's warning of being ignored rang heavily in his mind. He had the feeling that she was right. The problem with any large institution like the church was that they couldn't afford flights of fancy, and without evidence, they wouldn't move. He would contact his father and Krana, to see what sort of success they'd had so far in warning the city guard. Perhaps if they tried from every angle, it would get the right reaction.

"Even if they don't listen, then we will at least have tried," he said finally.

***

A couple of hours later, Lenei headed toward Highfold while Sam returned to his crafting. Her shield had some unfamiliar runes on it that he'd memorized, which were related to Agility and Constitution, but beyond those, it had been relatively simple to repair. The core runes on it hadn't been damaged, so he'd reinscribed the support structure and infused it with a bit of mana to restart the repair process.

Lenei had been able to take over from there.

He'd also taken the opportunity to study the runes on the rest of her armor, which had given him some new options for attributes. Her armor was enchanted with +5 to Strength and Constitution and her shield was +5 to Agility and Constitution. She had other pieces as well: her bracers had +5 to Charisma, her leg greaves were +5 to Wisdom, and her belt was +5 to Intelligence. The only attribute she didn't have boosted by her equipment was Aura.

It reinforced the idea that Aura was rare, and apparently not part of the standard equipment issued to Paladins.

Hopefully, she would be able to contact the church and get some support for investigating the ruins, but if not, they were no worse off than they were now. At the same time, his father and Krana were delayed in Highfold, and it might be another day or longer until they returned. From the sound of their messages, they were getting the run-around from the city guard. They were too used to ignoring the valley, and showed no interest in what a wyvern was doing here.

"*They said it's the Ice Sylphs' job to protect the valley, not theirs,*" his father's words rang out in his mind as he recalled their brief conversation. "*We're still looking for word on Siwaha. We might have a lead. I'll fill you in when we return.*"

That gave him a day or so to prepare as many healing scrolls as possible and to work on his other project. Once everyone was back, they would head for the ruins. The only problem was where his mother and sister should stay, since it wasn't advisable for them to go along. If it came down to it, the city was on the way to the ruins and they could rent a room at an inn there. They would be safe enough behind the city walls.

With another look out the window toward the Three Crowns, where liquid clouds of mana were gathering like an ocean in the sky, Sam turned his attention back to his work.

***

It took Jeric and Krana almost three days to return from Highfold, and it was close to evening by the time they got back. Meanwhile, Lenei had not returned yet. Whatever she was doing, it was taking her a while. Hopefully, she would be able to convince the church to send some support.

The only advantage to the delay was that Sam had filled it with crafting and had a pile of scrolls ready. Most of them were for healing, but he'd made some battle scrolls and a few message scrolls. If Lenei didn't show up in another day or so, he'd use one to contact her.

After hugging his wife and daughter, Jeric grumbled as he dropped into a chair beside the table where everyone was seated. The guards had not been cooperative, and he was still irritated by it. They'd already explained about Lenei over the amulets, so as soon as they arrived, Sam turned the topic to their mission.

"Did you have any success with the guards?" Sam asked as he looked between his father and Krana.

"Stubborn bugg…" Jeric cut himself off as he looked toward Altey and changed what he was going to say. "I mean, there's good news and bad news."

Lesat poured a mug of golden ale from the keg Henar had left and slid it across the table to him. Jeric took it with a grateful nod and took a sip, letting himself relax. A moment later, his expression turned into a smile as he looked toward Aemilia and Altey. He'd only been away for a few days, but he hadn't liked it. He was already starting to relax now that he was back with his family.

"We tried to tell them," Krana said with a frown, taking over the account. "After the initial failure, we pushed a bit and met with one of their captains, but he wasn't interested. In the end, the best we could get was a promise to pass it on. Hopefully the word reaches the right person. The guards seem to be more interested in the flow of travelers for the festival. All of their attention is on security within the city." She looked around the table for a moment, gathering everyone's attention before she continued.

"We did manage to meet my relatives, however, and that's the good news. They've promised to pass the word about the wyvern and the Outsider on to their contact on the city council. It doesn't look like we can expect any help from that direction right now, but maybe they'll come through later, if things get serious. In other good news, we managed to get this." Krana reached into her dimensional vest and pulled out a folded parchment, smoothing it out as she placed it on the table.

When it was open, it was clear that the parchment was a detailed map of the valley. The peaks were outlined in white and blue and the valley itself was a diamond-shaped wedge in the center that took up most of the space. The detail was much denser on the valley itself, with various villages and farms labeled, and more sparse on the peaks, which only had a few names and landmarks. Curling names in an old-fashioned script labeled each notable point.

Whoever had made the map, they hadn't left the valley much.

"This is a fairly standard valley map, although one of the more expensive ones," Krana announced as she traced her finger across the valley, landing on a point to the northwest. "My uncle knows the location of a few Ice Sylphs, or at least where they sometimes are, and he suggested that we head here to look for one."

Sam leaned forward as he looked over the map, turning his attention to what they had managed to get.

"We asked about Siwaha," Jeric added, his finger coming down to touch near Krana's on the map. He was indicating a spot slightly closer to the edge of the valley, at the base of the mountains where there was no village marked. "This was the best location they could give us. They don't know anyone by that name, but there's supposed to be an Herbalist around here, if we can find them, living in the wilderness.

"We've acquired some of the traditional gifts for the Ice Sylphs: fruits and grains, ice wine...but it's hard to say what we'll find there or if they'll be willing to let us stay."

"We can head there tomorrow morning," Aemilia said, looking up with determination in her eyes. "We need to ask for permission to stay and, if we're lucky, perhaps we'll find Siwaha. It's been a very long time since I've seen her. It would be lovely to know how she's doing." Her gaze turned toward the window as she looked out into the approaching dusk.

Sam looked at his parents and his sister as he thought about the Outsider and the monsters around the valley. He couldn't avoid going after the Flaw, but the same wasn't true for them. It felt like a mountain was pressing down on his shoulders at the idea of putting them in danger.

"Once we find the Ice Sylphs, if we get their permission to stay," he suggested slowly, "why don't I go look for the Outsider alone? Lenei and maybe Lesat can come with me. That should be enough."

It would set his mind more at ease if his family stayed out of it completely. How could he explain it to his mother if his father ended up hurt again? That wyvern had been a wake-up call. If they'd had a few less healing scrolls....

"Absolutely not!" his father responded immediately, his expression tightening as he looked toward Sam. His hands balled into fists as he sat up at the table.

"No!" Aemilia chimed in at the same time, shaking her head emphatically as her eyes widened. "We are not letting you go by yourself!"

"I promised that I wouldn't let you do this job alone," Jeric growled, speaking before Sam could say anything else. He pounded his fist on the table, creating a loud *thump* that shook the legs. "You may be an adult now, but you're still my son. Your problems are my problems. I'm not going to let you go into a battle without me. If that means finding a Flaw and getting rid of it, and of any Outsiders in the way, then that's what we'll do."

His mother and father both looked across the table at him. Their eyes were blazing as they held him in their sight, as if he would run off at any moment if they didn't keep an eye on him. Sam looked around the table, including at Krana and Lesat, but the seer only shook her head at him.

"Definitely not," she said. "I'll be going with you." She'd promised to keep him company and make sure he fulfilled her prophecy, preventing the Flaws from destroying the world. She wasn't going to change her mind now.

As for Lesat, he was also silent as he raised one eyebrow and took a drink from his mug. As far as he was concerned, that was the end of the matter.

"We're all in it together, and all we can do is face what's in front of us," Jeric said, his tone suggesting the discussion was over. "Right now, that's making sure we're all safe, and that includes keeping you safe, even if you're fighting."

"Altey and I will stay behind," Aemilia suggested. "We're no use in a fight, but we can watch over you. If you get into trouble, I'll call for the city guard. Hopefully, they'll help."

A troubled expression drew lines across Jeric's forehead at that and he frowned, but he said nothing else. It was clear he didn't plan to rely on the guards.

"All right. I have something for everyone," Sam said, changing the topic as he pulled out the items he'd finished crafting over the last couple of days and set them on the table.

There were several stacks of healing scrolls, as many as he'd been able to make in the time available. Next to the scrolls, there were six small mithril rings, each of them shining with a crystal blue light as the small cores embedded in them swirled with energy. His family deserved a simple, easy life where they could just be happy, one where no bandits or monsters were going to attack them. He couldn't make that happen, so these six rings were the next best thing.

After he'd completed his bracer, they had been the major focus of his attention.

He pushed the rings and the stacks of scrolls across the table. There were six healing scrolls for everyone, even Altey, plus a few extra. Making all of them had used up an entire wing from the wyvern. The rings had used up the rest of the mithril he'd gained from the bandits and half a dozen ice-aligned cores, along with some more of the Earth mana. Making all of it had brought him up to Level 25 as an Essence Scribe and Level 32 as an Enchanter.

"These are..." Jeric looked down at the ring with puzzlement as he picked one up and examined it.

"Protective artifacts," Sam said. "It should be enough to block any strike at the Expert tier, at least." He looked around the room as he caught everyone's gaze, and then down at the rings.

Ring of Crystal Shield (Advanced)
[Enchantments: Lifelink, Crystal Shield.

This enchantment is designed to activate when the bearer's life is in danger, if no other shielding spell is available. It creates a one-time shield of crystalline energy surrounding the wearer that will apply its full charge to resisting the attack.

It has been created with a small amount of sacred Earth mana, an Ice-aligned core, and purified mithril, ensuring that the charge does not degrade over time.

Once activated, the core in the ring will crumble to dust. The mithril is durable enough that there is a chance it could be reused.

Material: Purified Mithril.
Charge: 200/200.
Duration: Single Use.]

"I hope they're never needed, but please, put them on."

One by one, everyone slid their ring onto a finger and dripped a bit of blood on it to bind it, including him. A moment later, the light in the rings dimmed, fading away until they looked like unremarkable mithril jewelry, or at least as unremarkable as mithril ever looked. The metal still had that unique rainbow reflection on top of the blue-silver base.

Sam looked around, taking in the matching rings and amulets that everyone was wearing, and he let out a slow breath. He might not have the resources of the church, but with every passing day, he was a better Enchanter than he'd been before. He couldn't keep his family out of danger, but he would make sure they survived it.

Chapter Twenty-Six

An Unexpected Battle

"It should be somewhere around here," Jeric said as he glanced at the forest ahead of them, which was filled with silverbark pines. Ice crystals glinted on the bark of the trees, created by the Ice-aligned mana that infused the air as it touched them, freezing the wind into a second layer of bark.

"Legend says silverbark pines were formed when a god threw a spear of ice at the world," Lenei spoke up from where she was riding beside Sam. "Sometime during the last Breaking. The spear stuck, and when the war was over, the mana infused the forest around it, turning all of the trees into silverbark pines. It's said they still radiate with the cold ice of his attack."

She'd returned from Highfold earlier that day, but she'd had no luck in warning the church. As far as she could tell, they were ignoring her. A young paladin telling them about an invasion that was coming, but without any proof, was just too fanciful for the old priests and warriors of the church. The church was extended in a thousand directions, and even with their size, they could barely manage them all.

They'd told her to come back with a dead Outsider or the World Law's command, if she wanted them to believe her. If she had that, they would redirect some of their current forces to deal with it. It was possible for the World Law to grant one of its followers an aura, of sorts, to make their message believable. At the moment, she didn't have that aura.

She had known not to say anything about Sam's appearance, and Paladins were routinely independent as they followed their Call to Law, so she'd simply left again, without trouble. She had taken the opportunity to pick up a few standard supplies, which gave the trip some value. Now, the group was near the edge of the valley, a couple of hours' ride from the inn. They were looking for the village where the Ice Sylphs supposedly lived.

"According to the map, these are the foothills of Winter's Peak." Krana spoke up as she shaded her hand and looked at the peak that was towering into the sky above them. They were just below the most southern of the Three Crowns, the one farthest to the left if you were looking straight at Highfold.

"Winter's Peak, Sun's Rest, and Sky's Descent," she added, pointing at the other two giant peaks that stretched to the north. She'd just learned their traditional names from the map that morning. The humans tended to call them the Southern Crown, Middle Crown, and Northern Crown, but the Ice Sylphs had more respectful names for them.

In reality, the Three Crowns were so large that only their shoulders curved together here at the valley. Their peaks were a dozen miles distant and perhaps eight or ten thousand feet higher in the sky. Stretching outward from there, their bases stretched for fifty or sixty miles farther, falling slowly away until they merged with the Storm Plains. The peak of Sun's Rest was more distant than the other two mountains, creating a rough triangle between the three of them, but it was also the largest, so it looked like it was just as close.

That morning, they had managed to acquire another horse from the innkeeper, so Aemilia and Altey were riding together, looking around at the valley as it turned from green fields to snow here at the edge. Sam's attention was on the foothills above, looking from one area to the next as he searched the expanses of silverbark pines for signs of Ice Sylphs.

At that moment, Krana looked up from the map she was studying, a frown flashing across her face. Her eyes turned a bright silver as she looked up at the base of Winter's Peak. A pulse of warning ran through Sam's heart as he saw her expression change.

"There's something happening up there," she muttered as her frown deepened, "but it's behind a veil of some type. Be careful. It came so suddenly that some magic is involved here."

"Is it the Ice Sylphs?" Sam asked, looking over at her. "Can you see their village?"

"I can't tell what it is," she replied, her expression turning troubled, "but I have a bad feeling about it. It feels like...there's blood in the snow."

She looked around at the others, all of them riding on horseback against the blowing white snow. They looked idyllic, like travelers on the first days of the world where the land was untouched and pristine. If the warning she'd just felt was right, it was a scene of peace that was about to be abruptly broken.

Sam's senses swept ahead as well, reaching outward as far as he could with Crystal Focus, but his range was very short compared to Krana's. Even with Crystal Focus at Advanced, his aura only stretched for eighty feet. His eyesight and the mana signatures he could see were much more reliable at a distance. He looked around, trying to see what had disturbed her.

The snow around them flurried with particles of ice as it drifted on the light breeze, carrying a gentle but deadly bite. Without the weather-resistant belts he'd made, it would have been difficult for Aemilia and Altey to travel any higher. The sun was clear and bright, promising a day of ice-edged brilliance that pierced his eyes. In the sky all around and above him on the slopes of Winter's Peak, he could see the mana gathering in the air, ready to pour down to the lower slopes.

All he could feel out of place was the essence tainting the snow, filling it with a sense of twisted energy, like blood on porcelain. It felt stronger here than it had down in the valley. Perhaps that was what Krana had felt as well?

At that moment, the Guardian Star on his hand began to flicker, a pulse of energy sweeping outward from it as it scanned the local area. Then its voice rang in his mind, bringing with it a heavy warning that struck his heart and made his blood run faster, like the beat of a drum calling him to war.

Guardian, a second concealed Flaw has been detected two miles from your location.

At least two dozen Outsiders are present near it.

Two Flaws so close to each other indicate a Grand Flaw may be present.

A moment later, the World Law's voice resonated with cold authority in his mind and everyone's in the party.

All Nearby Authorities of Law are Summoned to Defend Aster Fall from Outsider Invasion.

An Outsider breakthrough has been detected near your location. As the closest combatants, you are required to assist. Refusing to do so will mark you as Defiant.

You are currently Defiant. Assist in the sealing of four Flaws to remove this Trait.

Failure to assist will result in Greater Defiance.

Estimated Outsider Threat Level: Moderate.

Time Until the Flaw is Sealed: Unknown.

A sense of horror hit Sam as he looked toward his mother and sister, and then a building fury. They were much too close to the battlefield, far too close to send them back and protect them. This was not what he'd expected to have happen while looking for Ice Sylphs. All of them with combat classes would have heard that same command.

His sister was too young to be involved, and he could only hope that his mother had been left out of it as well, since she didn't have a combat class. He didn't want her to fight here. He wasn't sure how the Flaw was being concealed, but even if Highfold received the same message and was able to send forces, there was no guarantee they would arrive anytime soon.

"Rally behind me!" Lenei's voice echoed out with calm clarity as she spurred her horse forward, moving to take the lead at the head of their group. A brilliant white glow radiated out around her, carrying a sense of spiritual connection and a bright force that touched each of them.

It was like a gossamer thread as it touched Sam, bringing with it a sense of connection to everyone else around him, one that was even stronger than the Amulet of Swirling Winds. As soon as it touched him, he could feel everyone's location, their presence and thoughts swirling at the edge of his mind. He instantly knew their position, general health, and general emotional state.

"This is a Battle Formation, a skill common to Paladins that is part of Spiritual Awareness," Lenei's voice echoed in their minds, faster than the words could have been said. The information came with pulses of emotion and intent that gave it depth and made the meaning clear. *"It will help us to keep track of each other and to communicate, as well as to coordinate our attacks.*

"This Call is unexpected, but I doubt that the timing is a coincidence. The wyvern you killed and our attempts to warn the city may have been noticed, accelerating our enemies' timeline. The Ice Sylphs are key figures in the valley

and one of the allies we need. If they are under attack ahead of us, we
have to help them or the balance of power here will fall apart."

Frustration and anger surged through Sam's veins, waking up the
essence stars that slumbered there. He couldn't leave his mother and
sister here, but he also couldn't refuse to help. The stars surged to life,
creating an internal web of energy that began to sing as it called him
forward to battle.

Ahead of him, he felt a thin barrier shatter like dust in the wind,
and suddenly he could feel the distant pull of essence, like bloody stars
burning in the dark.

"We can't leave you, so move to the center!" he called to his mother,
waving his hand toward the center of the party as he tried to sound
reassuring. "Focus on defending yourself and Altey. Use the defensive
amulets. We'll take care of the rest."

His mother had a Spell Shield ability as a Seer, which would last for
as long as she had mana. They also had the defensive amulets and the
rings he'd made. Sam pulled a handful of scrolls from his belt, mostly
Earth and Fire, and pushed them into his mother's hands.

"Take these and use them as needed."

Ahead of him, his father's face was pale as he looked back toward his
wife and daughter. His strong hands clenched on the reins, the sign
of an internal struggle that passed through his mind in an instant. An
instant later, he gave his wife a reassuring nod as a golden-yellow shield
flared up from his skin, burning with a furious light.

"We'll take care of it. Keep Altey safe." He cared more about defending his family than he did about closing the Flaw, but there was no way
to run from this battle. Not in the long run. If the Ice Sylphs died here,
their hope of staying in the valley would go with them. More than that,
the politics in the valley would fall apart, and perhaps the magics that
sustained it as well.

Whatever the enemy hoped to achieve here, they couldn't let them
have it.

Only a handful of moments had passed since the World Law's command echoed in their mind, and an instant later, they were moving.

"Let's go!" Lenei called as she spurred her horse forward, heading in
the direction of the World Law's summons.

Straight ahead of them were the icy slopes of Winter's Peak, where some shroud hid the Flaw among the wind and snow.

***

A shimmering veil that was felt instead of seen burst apart as Sam and Lenei led the way, riding through the field of snow toward the call of the World Law. There was a sense of displacement as they broke through it, as if the veil were trying to redirect their attention, but Sam ignored it as he followed the summoning that was pulling him forward. Ahead of them, the view of the mountain changed.

It had looked like a clear, snow-covered slope that rose gradually upward toward the peak. Now, it was a sprawling village, filled with small, circular houses with pointed, thatched roofs in vibrant shades of sharp violet, icy blue, and summer green. Swirling designs like billowing clouds and wind marked out the walls and doors. The area around the village was clear of snow, except for a dusting that seemed to float in the air like a reminder of the ice outside.

At the edge of Winter's Peak, far past the houses, the real slope of the mountain rose upward. It was a hidden valley on the shoulder of the mountain's slope, surrounded by the barrier they'd just ridden through. The houses looked as if they'd grown from the grass here and then been painted and decorated. From the look of it, they were moveable with a bit of effort. The Ice Sylphs had a semi-nomadic lifestyle as they moved around the slopes of Winter's Peak, the mountain that was their traditional home.

The summon from the World Law and the sizzling power of the stars in his blood pulled Sam's attention instantly away from the village to the far side, where a group of a dozen Ice Sylphs was facing off against a much larger horde of Outsiders and monsters. The Ice Sylphs were recognizable in an instant, even without Analyzing them. They were dressed in white cloaks with swirling blue patterns, with blue-white hair, bright eyes, and thin builds. A wave of information came to Sam as he looked at them.

Ice Sylph. Hunter-Smith. Level 56.
Ice Sylph. Sky Mage-Healer. Level 87.
Ice Sylph. Ice Weaver-Ranger. Level 61.
Ice Sylph. Cook-Ranger. Level 72.

Ice Sylph. Ice Spirit-Trader. Level 64.

Their classes were a mix of crafts and combat, but they all had at least one crafting or support class. Despite their levels, they didn't look like they were warriors. They looked like villagers who were defending their home. Behind them, Sam's eyes skipped back to a point near the center of the village, where a group of younger and smaller Ice Sylphs were gathered around an older Ice Sylph woman. Most of their levels were in the teens and 20s, except for her.

Ice Sylph. ?

When he tried to Analyze her, the skill failed, returning no information. It was the first time that had happened to him, which meant her level was higher than anything he'd seen so far.

He only had time to Analyze a handful of the sylphs before his attention was pulled back to the battle and the enemies they were facing. Splatters of blue, green, and red blood, as well as other stains, covered the ground between the Ice Sylphs and the monsters attacking them. The pulsing of the Guardian Star in his mind marked them out as enemies, along with the feeling of burning essence that radiated from some of them.

There was a mix of monsters and Outsiders, but that wasn't the only problem.

Icesoul Wraith. Level 47.

Arctic Cave Troll. Level 52.

Greenscale Abyssal Serpent. Level 58.

Ice Wyvern. Level 48. (Alpine)

He only had time to scan one of each type, and even as he did, he was jumping off of his horse and running forward. There was a hundred yards to the nearest edge of the village, and the battle was even more distant. If they wanted to help, they had to hurry.

He kept pace with Lenei and the others followed, all of them heading toward the group of young Ice Sylphs in the center of the village. From there, they could move forward and join the battle. Even as he watched, the dozen Ice Sylphs were being pushed back by the forces arrayed against them.

Ice walls and arrows, bolts of venom, and shrieks of battle cries filled the air.

The only good news was that the enemies only had a single wyvern. It wasn't the highest level of them, but it was large enough to hold down the center of the battlefield by itself. Around the wyvern, there were half a dozen or more of each type of monster, from the ice wraiths to the trolls and serpents.

The sylphs were outnumbered three to one.

Essence radiated from the wraiths and serpents, proving that they'd come through a flaw, but the wyvern and the troll were regular monsters from the mountains here. The wyvern looked very similar to the other one they'd fought, except that the pattern of its scales was a slightly darker green and it was a couple of levels higher.

The trolls were large, blocky humanoids that looked like a walking boulder with arms. Their bellies were so large and round that their legs were nearly invisible beneath them, like short, squat pillars holding up a globe. Their bodies were pale white with patches of a mottled greenish-grey that resembled camouflage. Against the background of a snowy cliff, they would probably blend right in. Their bodies bulged with muscles and raw strength. Their arms were nearly as big as Sam's entire body, and their heads were broad wedges with small eyes, with tusked mouths that looked large enough to eat a human in two or three bites.

The Icesoul Wraiths were nearly invisible, like frosted blue glass hanging in the air. They didn't have humanoid forms. Instead, they were like tangled, nearly invisible sheets that floated in the wind, only visible because their bodies were a different shade than the snow and sky behind them. Claws and fangs were visible at the edge of their forms, more substantial than the rest of their bodies.

The Greenscale Abyssal Serpents were much as their name described, greenish-black serpents that resembled enormous vipers, perhaps twelve to fifteen feet long and more than a foot wide. Their heads were triangular wedges with black-striped cheeks that marked out their venom glands and hooked fangs nearly a foot long were visible as their jaws opened. Behind that terrifying horde, three solitary figures stood like commanders behind their troops.

Iceblood Warrior. Level 54.
Iceblood Hunter. Level 52.
Iceblood Shaman. Level 65.

Their equipment differed, but they were angular, thin humanoids between eight and nine feet tall with skin that was a pale, unearthly blue. Mottled white streaks ran across their skin like veins, and their eyes were opaque, white gashes hidden under thick brows, making them look almost blind. Their hair was a yellowish-white, close to stained ivory in color, and it tumbled down their backs in a snarled waterfall past their knees. Their hands and feet were oddly outsized, two or three times larger than a human's.

Behind them, a rainbow gash was torn in the world, one almost large enough to allow the wyvern through it. The Flaw scintillated with a raw fluctuation of power that pulled at Sam's senses, calling to him like a distant home that promised blood and satisfaction. The names of the three Outsiders and the feeling of the essence radiating from them drove home what was happening.

It also answered some of the questions that had been stirring in Sam's mind. The connection between these Iceblood Outsiders and the so-called "Iceblood Guild" was clear now, with the wyvern as the proof of the connection. He felt a sense of dawning horror as he looked across the battlefield at them. Whatever they had just stumbled upon, this wasn't a problem of a single Outsider. This was an entire tribe.

They hadn't just stumbled into a battle, they'd run straight into a war.

CHAPTER TWENTY-SEVEN
WAR AT THE VILLAGE

The Ice Sylphs on the far side of the village were holding against their attackers for now, but they were badly outnumbered. Even their higher levels weren't enough to fix that. Sam and the others came to a stop in the center of the village, a couple of dozen feet from the unidentifiable old woman who was guarding the children. He would have run straight into the battle, but something about the old Ice Sylph made him halt.

She turned to look at them, her eyes a brilliant, piercing blue like the sky above the mountains. A sense of crushing pressure washed over him. There was a brilliant, icy threat in it like a blade pressed against his skin, clearly warning him not to move any closer. The pressure faded slightly as her gaze continued on, but the threat remained.

As the Ice Sylph's gaze fell on Aemilia, her eyes suddenly widened, some of the chill in them disappearing as her mood shifted.

"Sun Child, is that you?" The woman gasped in surprise, her hand rising to touch her heart. She had met this little golden-haired girl many years before in a distant place, but she recognized her in an instant.

"Siwaha!" Aemilia called in shock, as she slid from her horse and pulled Altey into her arms. "What is happening?!"

"Come over here at once, girl!" Siwaha ordered, pointing to the group behind her. "Bring the child with you!"

Her gaze traveled back to Sam and the others, her attitude toward them shifting as she suddenly decided that they were allies instead of enemies. Now that she'd seen Aemilia, the threat in her aura disappeared as the feeling of ice turned to a refreshing breeze. As she looked at them and then to the Flaw that had appeared by her village just a few minutes before, she understood why they had arrived so suddenly.

When a Flaw appeared, the World Law assessed the danger in it and then summoned nearby forces to deal with it. If the available forces in the local area were too weak, it sent the Call farther out. If Aemilia and her group were here at the World Law's command, then they had come to help.

"All of you, if you are able to fight, you may assist in the battle," she announced as a sparkle of icy blue light sprang from her hand, striking them all in the chest. "The Ice Sylphs formally request your aid."

A feeling of warmth spread through Sam's body, sinking into his veins like a winter's kiss. He could feel some of his attributes rising, especially his Constitution. It was similar to when Ayala had blessed them before a battle.

"You are marked as allies. The Valley will support you. Go and aid my kin!" Siwaha waved her hand forward, pointing them toward the battle. "The warriors are away right now fighting a larger force. Only the villagers are left to protect our home. I will defend the children here, but you must help them. If the village falls, the magics tied to the valley will be damaged. The Blessing of the Ancients is fragile and tied to the hearthstone here. Go!"

Sam shoved his questions to the back of his mind as he pushed his horse's reins into the hands of one of the young Ice Sylphs, and then he turned toward the battle. He ran forward as a torrent of crystal flame surged out of his body and condensed into a spiral around him.

Beside him, Lenei, his father, Krana, and Lesat kept pace with him. All of them were surrounded by radiant energy in brilliant white, gold, yellow, and silver as their abilities activated.

"*Flank to the right!*" Lenei's voice carried to his mind as she shared the plan that was on her mind.

Crystal Focus and his high Intellect both enhanced Sam's mind enough that he had time to think during the battle, but the events still moved quickly. Their group sprinted to the right of the Ice Sylphs, running up a short incline as they curved around and came back toward the enemies from the side. The Ice Sylphs were fighting a mad battle, erecting ice walls that shattered as the trolls crashed into them.

Whistling arrows, flaring blue and white ice bolts that crackled like lightning as they shattered the air, and a growing hurricane force of icy winds and shredding hail blasted outward from the defenders, heading toward their enemies as they pushed them back again. The Ice Sylph Sky Mage was summoning the storm, his hands raised as he poured more mana into it, and in front of him, the leading edge of the monsters were being frozen in a wave of ice.

Beside him, the Ice Spirit disappeared, turning into a blur of blue-white mana that flickered across the distance, twin blades in his hand stabbing outward to tear apart one of the serpents before he flickered back to his position. The Rangers and Hunter fired arrows imbued with flickering mana, which split in the air into a hail of deadly points, slamming home into the serpents and trolls as they tore sizzling paths through their bodies.

Their efforts were filling the battlefield with magic, but it wasn't enough to keep down the larger and more numerous monsters. There were several enemy bodies scattered across the ground, but they weren't killing them quickly enough. One on one, the sylphs' skills could have worn their enemies down, but right now it looked like they would be overwhelmed unless something changed.

Even as he watched, the sylvan Ice Weaver raised his hands and ice flowed up around one of the troll's legs, tearing its leg off with an edge like a blade, but the troll beside it continued to charge forward, slamming into the defensive ice wall. The Sky Mage shuddered backward as an Icesoul Wraith dove from the sky toward him, its fangs and claws splintering off of a swirling shield that surrounded him.

A moment later, the wraith exploded into a crackle of icy lightning, its form disintegrating as the Sky Mage tore it apart. Then the sylph turned his attention back to the other mobs, pouring more mana out into the storm. Lightning crackled along the ice wall, stabbing outward in splintering arcs to blow holes in the enemy lines.

The Greenscale Abyssal Serpents spit streams of venom that eroded the ice defenses and their scales left sizzling burns as they passed, slowly winding their way over the wall. The three Iceblood Outsiders behind it watched it all with cold detachment, a cruel smile on their faces. The shaman's oversized hands rose as he sent a web of energy outward, which sank into the serpents' scales and enhanced their speed.

As he took it all in, Sam's hands rose and he concentrated on his bracer, pouring his essence through it as a Starfire spell took shape in his hands. They needed something big to throw the enemies backward, to give the Ice

Sylphs time to wear down the enemy forces with their higher levels. That job fell to him.

Sizzling energy from the essence stars in his blood surged through his veins, bringing with it clarity, battle lust, and a killing intent that demanded blood for satisfaction. He wanted to rip the Outsiders apart, tear their limbs from their bodies, and hurl their broken corpses into the sky in a shower of gore.

Two seconds later, the Starfire spell shot ahead of him, exploding between a pack of trolls and serpents in a roaring, blue-white fury as the rune erupted into an expanding sphere of blinding flames.

KraaAAATTOOOOOMMMmm!

Screams rose up from the trolls as they stumbled backward, the flames eating away at their skin that was accustomed to the cold. The serpents writhed, their scales turning charred and dark as they were tossed backward through the air, their spines cracking like whips. They weren't all dead, but Sam didn't pay attention to the rest of that group as he formed another spell as fast as he could.

In an instant decision, he channeled his energy into the bracer, summoning out a hundred charges of Starflame at once. The largest flight of arrows that he'd ever formed sprang into existence. They were similar to his crystal flame arrows, but they had a gleaming sapphire light and their tips glinted with the white fire of the *star* rune.

With a flick of his hand, the arrows blasted forward, tearing through the sky toward the horde of Icesoul Wraiths that were hovering over the battlefield. They struck the translucent forms like a storm of meteors striking an ocean, tearing holes through the wraiths' bodies as they exploded outward. Then he did it again, pouring out the last remaining hundred charges of essence from his bracer into a second flight of Starflame arrows.

The *star* runes on their tips tore through the enemies as they exploded across the battlefield, shredding trolls, serpents, and wraiths all at once. Some of the arrows exploded against ice or stone, but most struck home in the enemy. He needed the biggest offense he could summon, and he poured everything he'd prepared into the battle, trying to swing it back in favor of the Ice Sylphs.

Beside him, Krana took up her own position, as stone spears rose out of the earth, stabbing upward through the trolls' legs and the serpents' scales.

His father, Lenei, and Lesat raced forward, heading into the battle with their weapons drawn.

Lenei was surrounded by a brilliant white aura that flared out from her like a sun, her Holy Armor gleaming as it infused her spear and shield. Jeric was surrounded by his golden-yellow Earthen Shield and his hammers reverberated in the air, singing with a deep-throated hum as the land around him echoed with the force of the runes.

Lesat's sword, shield, and armor were heavily enchanted as well, gleaming with power as he Shield Charged a serpent, throwing it backwards in a twisting coil, before he brought his sword around to slice at it.

The three of them stuck together in a tight triangle with Lenei at the point, her aura washing backward over all of them. Slowly, they cut their way through the edge of the enemy and across the field as they headed for the Ice Sylphs' right flank. Once they got there, Lenei's plan was to take over the close-range defense, to give the sylvan archers and mages the space they needed to make full use of their abilities.

Sam finished forming a second Starfire and threw it into the enemy, aiming for where a group of trolls was trying to force their way past the sylphs' ice wall.

With the addition of the five of them, the enemies still outnumbered the defenders by two to one, but the Ice Sylphs had the advantage of levels on their side. They were also defending their home. They fought with a cold, brilliant savagery as they increased their offense and tore into the serpents and trolls that were closest to them. If that had been the only force attacking them, it would have ended there as they slowly ground them down.

Unfortunately, the ice wyvern, the wraiths, and the three Iceblood Outsiders were still free to attack. Sam's Starflame arrows had torn apart half of the wraiths and injured the other monsters, but the remaining half were still flying above the battle. Wisps of misty vital energy rose up from the blood and gore on the ground as it was devoured by the wraiths, and the holes in their forms began to close over again.

Sam's vision narrowed as he focused on the remaining problems, another Starfire forming in his hands.

At that moment, the wyvern charged forward, throwing aside a troll and serpent that got in its way as it crashed toward the ice wall in front of the sylphs. It was unable to fly with the lightning and ice storm that was covering the area, so instead it targeted the defenses the Sky Mage was controlling. The ground all around echoed with a resounding crack of shattering ice as the monster slammed into the ice barrier.

The Sky Mage was the strongest of the defenders and almost forty levels higher than the wyvern, but his attention was split in many directions. Size had a power all its own. The wyvern's momentum caused the ice wall to buckle inwards, the lightning and ice along its length exploding outward. Some of the trolls and serpents near it were killed in an instant from the backlash, but the wall began to crumble. Sam hurled the Starfire spell at the wyvern's abdomen, just in front of its rear legs.

KraaAAATOOOOMmmm!

The rune sphere exploded with a roaring, blue-white fury that picked the wyvern's rear legs up from the ground and flung it away from the wall, sending it rolling across the ground. Scales and a rain of green blood erupted outward, charring black in an instant as the heat of the blast washed over them.

A moment later, the wyvern thrashed around as it forced itself back to its feet, its abdomen dragging in the snow as it left a trail of blood behind. It wasn't enough to kill the monster, but it had definitely distracted it. There was a six-foot-long gash in its abdomen now where its scales and flesh had been torn apart.

He was down to 46 essence as he reached into his storage, grabbed the first two auras he found, and combusted them, bringing him back up to 86. He had plenty of auras at the moment, nearly 65 of them, but he was limited by the number that he could combust without damaging his meridians.

An idea occurred to him as he seized an Aura of Compressed Flame, one from the Flamecaller Devils that they'd fought on the way to Highfold. He glanced up at the five remaining wraiths that were hovering in the sky. With a gesture, a rolling line of crystal flame formed between his hands, the Crystal Wave he'd used a few times before.

The Aura of Compressed Flame was in his right hand as he infused its aura into the spell, calling on Assume Aura as he forced the divergent energies to merge together. The aura crumbled to ash in his hand and he replaced it with another, infusing that aura into the spell as well. He looked upward as he unleashed the Crystal Wave. The spell was a thin line of condensed crystal flame as it flew across the sky, extending in either direction like a rope as it became larger and larger.

As soon as it hit the edge of his aura, he ignited it.

The line exploded outward into a roaring wall of compressed red and crystal blue flames that was twenty feet high and sixty feet long, searing the sky with light as it tore across the remaining distance toward the wraiths. The floating forms of the wraiths screamed as the opposing energy of the flames tore at their translucent bodies, disintegrating them in chunks that burned like parchment before they turned to ash.

The spell wasn't wide enough to encompass all of the wraiths, but he got three of them, leaving only two still alive.

A wave of his hand summoned two dozen crystal flame arrows and he infused another Aura of Compressed Flame into each set of twelve. A dozen arrows burned with hellish red light and flaring crystal as they surged toward each of the remaining wraiths. The wraiths tried to evade, but the lightning storm in the sky above limited how high they could go. All they could do was swoop into angled dives that carried them toward the ground.

Their screams echoed out, piercing through the air with a high-pitched sonic vibration that tore at Sam's ears.

A dozen arrows ripped through each of them, tearing their cloak-like forms into burning strips that still echoed with their death screams. An ecstatic satisfaction surged through Sam's veins as he heard his enemies' death cries and his mouth parted, his fangs bared as he roared into the air. He wanted their blood and deaths.

This was *his* world.

They had dared to attack near his family, to disrupt the valley he'd chosen as a home. Their lives threatened everything that was important to him. He would not allow them to continue to exist. He turned his attention to the wyvern and the serpents as crystal flames poured out of him, rising higher into the air. There, in all of the dead Outsiders, the wraiths and the serpents that had been slain, he could feel the burning flickers of essence.

The stars in his blood roared with him, an echoing, deep-throated command tearing across the battlefield in a wave that was half sound and all emotion.

"Stars of Aster Fall, RISE!"

His aura surged outward as he commanded it and his hand clawed through the air, ripping it from their corpses as he called it to him.

Burning stars in greenish black and translucent blue separated from the corpses of the dead Outsider serpents and wraiths, floating like sparkling souls against the snow as they obeyed Sam's command and flew toward him.

Across from him, the Iceblood Outsiders shouted, their voices turning ugly as their expressions changed for the first time. The Iceblood Outsider's eyes turned to lock on Sam and he felt the *ping* of his amulet sounding like a vibrating gong played by a madman as they tried to pierce his illusion. The Iceblood Shaman's arms rose, and Sam felt a tug against his aura as the Outsider tried to interfere.

The essence stars flickered, but they were already in his control. They spun through the air like dancing ghosts, flying toward his chest as their colors began to turn to a bright crystal blue.

"*Come!*" he roared out, his hand rising as his talons reached out to them across the battlefield. "*Come to me!*"

CHAPTER TWENTY-EIGHT

CALL ESSENCE

As the essence stars flew toward Sam, the Icebloods glared across the distance at him. There was a cloud of confusion in the shaman's eyes. His expression turned ugly and then to something else.

Unease.

The shaman couldn't see beneath Sam's hood, but now that he was commanding the essence, it was clear that he was also an Outsider. The Iceblood didn't understand how that could be, unless one of their enemies from home was taking advantage of the battle to attack them. As for *how* Sam was gathering the essence, that was what worried the shaman the most.

If it had been him, he would have had to eat the hearts of his enemies. Even that wasn't a perfect absorption of essence, just the most concentrated part. To get the rest, he would have had to consume their muscles and blood. All three of the Icebloods forgot about the battle against the Ice Sylphs as they turned their full attention to Sam.

A howling roar tore out of the Iceblood Shaman's throat. The hunter and the warrior echoed him a moment later. The shaman's hands rose to shape a spell and the Hunter summoned a spear of jagged ice in his hand as he raised it to throw across the distance. At the same time, the Iceblood Warrior launched himself forward, his oversized feet slamming into the ground as he sprinted toward Sam.

To the side, the wyvern and the remaining nine serpents and five trolls were trying to assail the ice wall again, holding the Ice Sylphs and their allies down. It gave the Icebloods a clear line of approach to Sam.

Before they could cross a quarter of the distance, the essence stars that Sam had called out of the corpses arrived. Their colors changed to bright crystal blue and sank into Sam's body, fusing through his skin and muscle. There were already seventeen essence stars and a nascent eighteenth in his blood. Now, dozens of new stars joined them from the fifteen Outsider corpses that he'd called upon.

The essence stars had fallen in his world. In death, they would serve him.

They merged into his blood in a constellation of new stars like a celestial storm was being born in the distant reaches of the universe, its fires giving life to new suns. Each of the Outsiders was around level 50. They had far more essence in them than the Red-Striped Hell Spiders he'd faced before. The size of Sam's essence network expanded in an instant, snapping into place according to some enigmatic pattern as each of the original stars became a hub in the new pattern, which spread outward at lightning speed.

Racial Essence: 347 / 1,000

Each of the Outsiders gave him about 20 essence stars as their energy converted into his. Resonant strength and a sense of increased durability rushed into Sam's limbs and meridians, flowing through every muscle and vein. Unexpectedly, other notifications sounded in his mind, flaring with silver light and archaic, star-edged borders.

Racial Ability Identified: Call Essence.

New Attribute Gain Quantified by Aster Fall Standard.

Strength increased by 3.

Constitution increased by 5.

Agility increased by 2.

Intellect increased by 6.

Aura increased by 6.

The talons on his fingers grew sharper, surrounded by a cutting force, and the horns on his forehead grew darker and larger, gaining an inch in height. The stars grew brighter, locking into place as energy burned outward from them. His meridians expanded and grew tougher, their durability improving. The unique sense he gained from essence expanded as well, rushing outward around him as he felt the Outsiders' presence more keenly than ever.

As the three Icebloods rushed toward him, he felt the essence that flowed through them, the strength of their vitality, and the weight of danger they radiated. It was similar to Analyzing their levels and classes, but the information was far more visceral, like a blade in his intestines. Three of them at once was going to be difficult, even with the increased attributes. Even the Hunter was a few levels higher than him.

A snarl burst out of his mouth as the battle lust that was resonating between the stars strengthened, flaring through his muscles with the relentless demand that he rip his enemies apart with his bare hands. His essence was at 58 and he had time to grab two more auras from his storage and combust them before the Icebloods arrived, bringing him back up to 98.

Then they were on him, as the hunter's ice spear flew toward his chest and exploded against a crystalline, geometric Essence Shield that flared with a brilliant blue light. Sapphire crystalline flames blazed around him as he flexed the talons on his hands and shot toward them, taking the battle to them. His blood was boiling. His mind was searing heat and glacial ice.

A flight of two dozen crystal flame arrows blasted away from him, targeting the Iceblood Warrior, which was the closest. Then he infused as much essence as he could, hardening his aura. The spiral of crystal flame around him condensed, its edge turning into a cutting blade that ripped through the air. Cerulean flames surrounded his hands and lined the edge of his talons. All around him an Essence Shield hardened his skin.

It was a natural body strengthening spell that came from his essence flowing through the starry constellation in his blood. It also drained his essence even more than a Starfire spell. Activating it took 20 essence, and it felt like it would take the same with each passing minute. At best, he had about three minutes. Less, if he used his essence for spells. The World Law's cold, analytical voice echoed in his mind.

Racial Ability Identified: Battle Aura (Basic).

He ignored it as the crystal flame arrows slammed home against the warrior. At the moment they struck, however, the Outsider's pale blue skin radiated with icy light. At the same time, his movements sped up, turning to a blur as he crashed toward Sam. He wasn't holding a weapon. Instead, icy blades extended from his hands like curving scimitars and slashed through where Sam was standing.

Krrii'Tttiiiinkshh.

The blades crashed against his spiraling aura with a shattering sound and a hiss as ice met crystal flame. The warrior specialized in melee combat and Sam didn't. A moment later, the ice scimitars whipped around again, returning along the same path. Sam's Agility was higher than before, but not enough to dodge in time.

The double blades crashed against a hastily erected Essence Shield and he was sent tumbling to the side, where he hit the ground and rolled. He sprang to his feet, putting some distance between him and the warrior as he dodged again to evade an ice spear that the hunter hurled toward him. The spear exploded against the ground where he'd been standing, creating a foot-deep divot in the earth as dirt and stone erupted outward. The flying chunks were coated in ice and shattered into frozen dust as they flew through the air.

At that moment, the shaman completed the spell he'd been preparing and an icy blue-green serpent of essence shot through the air toward Sam. It was half ghostly, about a dozen feet long and a foot wide. Its scales were patterned like a viper in layers of overlapping pale blue and white triangles. Its fangs were bared, shining with crystalline droplets of frozen venom.

Sam saw it coming with Crystal Focus and threw himself to the side, rolling again, but he wasn't able to escape the oncoming spear from the hunter, which struck where he landed. An explosion of pale ice erupted against his right side, digging into his abdomen and ribs with burning pain. The force of the attack hurled him across the ground, throwing him nearly ten feet.

His enhanced body helped to hold him together as he tucked himself into a roll and tried to use the force of the blow to get farther away, but he was still spinning out of control as he landed again. He crashed to the ground with an echoing crunch of cartilage and bones shifting. The shaman's ghostly viper whipped toward him as he landed, speeding through the air like a crossbow bolt.

In a flash, it coiled around his body and drove its fangs toward his neck.

The Essence Shield around Sam's skin flared outward, ripping the serpent off him as he shoved it away. Whatever was on its fangs, he didn't want to be bitten by it. An instant blast of focused crystal flame followed as he poured essence through his bracer and formed a hasty fire sphere. The *star* rune flickered quietly at the center, an instant version of it that was not much bigger than the one in the starflame arrows.

The fiery blast picked up the serpent and hurled it a dozen feet away, the speed making its body crack in the middle like a whip. The sound echoed out through the area. Sam realized his mistake in closing into melee range with the Outsiders at the same time. His new aura made him stronger in melee, but going up against three at once wasn't a good idea, and definitely not against the warrior, which was specialized in it.

He focused on Essence Shield as he pushed away to evade. The focused blast threw him back from the trio, giving him some space. It was the same tactic he used to evade Lenei, but more practiced now. He was able to mostly stay upright as the ground passed beneath his feet. He used the moment of separation to change his tactics, focusing his essence into a new Starfire spell between his hands. He hit the ground, spinning in place as his feet swept around for balance.

The shaman's serpent was returning, covered in a pale blue aura as ice crystals shattered in the air around it, and another jagged spear of ice from the hunter was also closing in. Sam dove to the side, rolling out of range as he came back up to his feet. The spell blasted out of his hands as soon as he was stable, heading for the hunter.

It was the most tactical choice, given that the hunter was Level 52 and likely had the weakest defense. Going for the warrior or the shaman would turn into a longer fight, and he needed to take out one of them quickly to get the initiative back. The Iceblood Hunter tried to dodge, as a pale blue and white-streaked aura surrounded him, accelerating his movements.

Unfortunately for him, it wasn't enough to evade the blast radius of Starfire. The spell erupted five feet from the hunter, exploding outward to envelop him in the expanding rings as the *star* rune at the center blazed like the white heart of a sun. Shimmering white streaks floated through the dark blue flames, searing the Iceblood Outsider.

The hunter's skin darkened, the pale blue color turning black as his skin cracked and began to disintegrate. He was picked up by the blast and flung away with the flames adhering to him like living things.

KrisshSSshhHh.

A flight of a dozen crystal flame arrows tore through the air after him, chasing him before he could land and dodge. The arrows tore through him in explosions of sapphire light, blowing holes in his arms, chest, legs, head, and heart. Light blue blood boiled away, searing in the air as a cloud of disintegrating Outsider flew in every direction.

The success didn't come without a cost.

The momentary pause to cast both spells gave the warrior enough time to close the distance to Sam, his icy scimitars tearing downward. Slashing lines of pain ripped across his right leg and abdomen as he tried to evade, but he was a bit too late. The warrior's strength was incredible and the ice blades had an edge sharper than steel. Sam's Essence Shield cracked beneath the blows.

The blades dug deep wounds before he could get out of range. The only advantage was that the attack also threw him out of the way of the shaman's serpent, which was returning again, as well as a pale blue-white web of searing energy that shot past his head. The shaman was adding new spells now.

He went rolling across the ground, hurling crystal flame behind him as he pushed the wounds out of his mind. His Constitution was kicking in, sealing the bleeding and stabilizing his muscles, but the cuts were deep. Siwaha's blessing burned in his chest like a cooling bath, flowing toward the wounds.

As he rolled, another Starfire formed between his hands. As he forced himself to his feet again, he hurled it at the oncoming warrior. The Ice-blood was chasing him, closing the distance in an instant, and took the Starfire spell directly in the face. An enormous, point-blank blast hurled Sam and the warrior apart, picking them both up and tossing them both across the ground.

For Sam, the force of the blast was absorbed by the Essence Shield on his skin, and he redirected the force into his evasion, sending out a couple of other pulses of crystal flame to push himself toward the shaman.

The warrior was not so lucky. His body was covered in a pale blue shell like ice as he tried to absorb the force of the blast, but he was only Level 54. Sam's offensive abilities were both at Expert, even before the boost from the bracer was added into it. In pure offense, he could probably give a Level 80 Wizard a run for his money.

The blast ripped through the warrior's spell defense, driving a wedge of burning crystal flame deep into his skin as it tossed him through the air. The brilliant white of the *star* rune seared him like a trout over a campfire, leaving sizzling lines burned inches deep through his body. Only his enhanced bones and durability kept him from being torn apart. It wasn't enough to kill him, but it threw him backwards dozens of feet

On the other side, the blast sent Sam hurtling toward the shaman and he pushed more energy into the battle aura all around him. As soon as he landed, he spun on his feet and launched himself at the shaman, as lines of brilliant crystal flame exploded from his talons. The aura around him spiraled faster, like a cutting blade. Something in him demanded that he bathe in his enemies' blood, and there was no reason to suppress it.

The shaman's spells struck home in a burning impact of ice shards that stabbed fierce spear points deep into his chest and arms. His Essence Shield absorbed what it could, but cracking sounds resonated across his body like frozen drum beats as the shards broke through. At the same time, his spiraling aura slashed through the shaman's defensive shield, shattering it into shards as his talons ripped toward him.

In gouts of icy-hot, pale blue blood, he ripped the shaman's abdomen open from groin to throat.

KRruukGgGshhh. A deep, guttural howl rose from the shaman's throat, choked off a moment later as his lungs filled with blood. Sam's hand drove farther into his chest and wrapped around a lump of still beating flesh. Sapphire blue crystal flames burned around his hand, searing into the shaman's body as he looked into the shaman's fading eyes. With an explosive jerk, he ripped the heart out of the Outsider's ribcage, crushing it in his grip.

"Don't threaten my family." Sam's voice was a guttural, growling thing, half whispered and half shouted from a tightly locked throat. *"Aster Fall is mine."*

His hand clenched down around the heart, his fingers tearing lines through it, ripping it into chunks that slowly blackened and turned to char. He could sense the warrior approaching, and he only had time to turn part of the way around before icy scimitars struck across his side, hurling him away from the shaman's corpse.

A snarl ripped out of his throat as the last of his essence poured into his Essence Shield and shattered, failing to absorb the blow. The spiraling blade of his aura disintegrated. The cutting flames on his talons faded into dying sparks. He tumbled through the air, flying a dozen feet from the warrior as he felt bones breaking in his ribs and arm.

He landed heavily on the earth, falling into a tumbling, uncoordinated roll. As he landed, he could feel people rushing toward him, the approach of his father and Lesat as they came to his defense.

As he rolled, he reached into the aura storage over his shoulder, tearing out two more auras. He combusted them as he came to a halt, feeling the dull pain in his meridians that told him he was starting to near his limit. Six auras was one more than he'd been able to use easily before, so the essence absorption had definitely strengthened them. He tried to push himself to his feet, but his limbs weren't responding well.

Instead, he pushed himself upward on a flare of crystal flame as he turned toward the oncoming warrior, channeling his energy into a Starfire spell. He supercharged it, feeling an echo of resistance in his meridians as he forced a quarter more essence than normal into the spell.

As the warrior crashed into him, he felt a blade stabbing through the left side of his abdomen, but at the same time, crystal flame surged around his talons as his aura came to life again. He tore a path through the warrior's chest with his left hand, creating a gap between the ribs.

Then he drove the Starfire spell straight into the warrior's lung. He shoved the Outsider away, kicking him backward at the same time as he used the last of his essence to evade, hurling himself across the ground. A brilliant explosion of crystal flame filled the air, filled with searing chunks of pale blue skin that flew in every direction. Burning chunks struck him in the air, disintegrating into ash against his skin.

He hit the ground with a resounding, dull thud. His bones creaked as the earth reached up to embrace him, creating a divot around him. His senses spread outward, spinning slowly with the rotation of the heavens as he searched for remaining enemies.

He hadn't tracked what the Ice Sylphs were doing while he fought, but now it was clear they had won their battle as well. The echoing silence of dead Outsiders filled the air.

Chapter Twenty-Nine

ICE SYLPHS

"Hold still, son," Jeric's voice rumbled as he loomed in Sam's vision. "You're a bit of a mess, but you'll be fine."

Sam and Jeric's view of wounds had changed a bit over the last year, since they had more access to magical healing than they'd ever had before. As soon as Jeric saw that Sam was still breathing, he relaxed. The rest was fixable.

He felt his father pulling at his limbs to straighten them. The energy of a healing scroll flooded across his chest. His meridians were itching with a sizzling pain, but the increased durability was enough that it was only annoying.

He sat up slowly. Broken ribs cracked as he moved, sliding back into place as his Constitution and the healing scroll worked. The blessing from Siwaha was there as well, adding a layer of cool, icy energy that sped things along.

Killing the Icebloods hadn't come without a cost.

His right arm and right leg were both broken, sending jagged points of pain up his nerves, and a deep, curving wound pierced through his abdomen low on the left side. He also had wounds slicing across his right arm, right side, and hip, cutting two to three inches deep. Most of them had hit the bone, where they'd rebounded after taking out a chip or breaking it. There were other, smaller wounds and cuts. Bruises covered most of his body, but those weren't important.

He reached into his belt pouch and pulled out a few more healing scrolls, activating another as the first one faded. He pressed it on top of the wound on his abdomen. If his Constitution were lower, it would have been worse.

He had enough in that attribute to endure the wounds. It would take him a little while to get fixed up, but he wasn't going to die. The major problem was the hole from the warrior's scimitar and the deeper slashes that tore through his muscles and right lung.

He blocked out the sensations of healing as he looked around, examining the aftermath. His father was in front of him, holding another healing scroll as he looked for larger wounds. Beside him, Krana, Lesat, and Lenei were just running up. Echoes of the last few moments came to him as he examined his memory.

At the same time as he'd killed the Iceblood Warrior, the sylphs and his family had brought down the wyvern and the last couple of serpents and trolls.

In the village a couple of hundred yards away, his mother and sister started to run toward him now that it was safer, but Siwaha held them back with a patient hand. She shook her head, and he saw her tell them something. He wasn't sure what she said, but they relaxed and waited near her. Lenei's hands gleamed white with healing light as she laid them on his shoulders.

"*Healing Touch*," she said quietly, as he felt the energy pouring in, adding to what was already there. "My main healing ability."

For a moment, he'd forgotten she was both a Paladin and a Healer. Lenei ignored the crowd as she continued pouring her mana into healing spells. From the look of it, he was the only one of their group who needed much healing. The Ice Sylphs' defensive tactics had kept everyone in good shape, even against the wyvern's speed and the serpents' acidic venom.

The arctic trolls had been the easiest to kill, despite their strength and dense hides. They were not very bright.

"Nice kick," Lesat said as he looked at Sam. A slight grin lurked at the edges of his mouth. "I've never seen an Outsider explode quite like that before."

Past Lenei, the Ice Sylphs who'd defended the village were gathering, forming a loose circle as they studied the newcomers, especially him. Their eyes were intense, piercing blue like glacial ice. Their gazes never left his face. Right then, he realized that his hood had fallen off during the battle.

He felt a bolt of panic that almost made him jump. His illusion amulet had run out of charges. The Icebloods and even the villagers must have been looking at him constantly while he was fighting. The crowd gathered closer, peering inquisitively at him.

"You have helped us," one of the Ice Sylphs said as he examined Sam. He had a stoic expression that hid his thoughts, but his tone was kind. "And Elder Siwaha has blessed you, marking you as a defender of the valley." He turned slightly toward the other sylphs, making it clear that his words were a speech to those around him as much as they were addressed to Sam.

He examined Sam from head to toe, nodding slowly in time with his words.

"Therefore, you are not an evil Outsider, and not a demon," he concluded, passing judgment on Sam's appearance. "You are a civilized race, one who is blessed by the World Law and who was summoned to aid us in battle." He was shaping the narrative, his voice rising so that all of the villagers could hear him. "And so, our hearts are at ease. But for our curiosity...could you tell us about yourself? Where did you come from?"

As soon as he spoke, more of the Ice Sylphs jumped in, asking questions of their own.

"You fought with brilliant savagery," one of the younger Ice Sylphs added with a positive uptilt in his words that made it into a compliment. "You have a natural gift for killing."

"That's not a bad thing," the first Ice Sylph added as he glanced at his companion and back to Sam. "I understand other races may think of things different, but here, we are more in tune with nature."

"What do you mean?" Sam asked as his forehead furrowed. He had been worried that they would find his appearance and tactics to be demonic. He'd ripped the shaman and warrior apart with his bare hands.

Instead of being disgusted, they seemed to like it?

"Your violence was worthy of a true warrior," another sylph spoke up, adding his opinion with a nod. "I'd just like to know why you look like a demon. Your Race is an Outsider as well, but you're from Aster Fall?"

More voices joined in, a chorus of questions and compliments that became overwhelming in an instant.

"An excellent end to those enemies of nature."

"How satisfying to see them ripped to shreds."

He wasn't sure how to respond. For the last half year, he'd mostly been alone except for his family. Even before that, he'd only had a couple of close friends. He wasn't used to so much attention. All around the buzz of Ice

Sylphs asking question after question resonated in Sam's ears, surrounding him in a peaceful buzz of vibrant village life. Not a single one of them mentioned the battle in a negative light.

Fortunately, Krana came to his rescue.

"Before we answer that, let's gather up everything and loot the monsters," she advised. "It looks like we're going to need everything we can gain from here. These definitely weren't working alone. There has to be a lot more where they came from. That Flaw is strange, and from what I've heard of such things, this looks like a Grand Flaw network."

"A Grand Flaw?" he asked, turning toward her. The Guardian Star had mentioned the same thing.

"It's a type of bigger Flaw that can develop if a Flaw is left alone for a while." Krana nodded. "It can create copies of itself, which the Outsiders start to use as portals around the local area."

"A Grand Flaw is one of the signs that there's a major problem in the area," Lenei added. "We need to alert the authorities again and then try to find the origin point. You can see the difference in the Flaw here. It's less vibrant than a regular one." Her hands were still glowing with healing magic as she poured the remainder of her mana into *Healing Touch*. "If we don't find it and seal it, we might have an even bigger problem on our hands soon. The entire valley could be lost, becoming a hub for a terrible invasion."

By the time she was done, his major wounds had finished sealing over and he could feel threads of mana reinforcing his cracked bones, holding them in place. Tentatively, he got to his feet, wincing slightly as he felt things shifting. Cracks of flaring pain ran along his bones where they'd been broken. There was a splintering stab from the wound in his abdomen.

The damage was sealed, but it would take a day or so to be fully healed, even with more magic. Even if it were complete now, he'd still feel it for a while. Magical healing could fix you up, but it was difficult to remove the echo of the damage. That took a little while to fade.

"All right, let's gather up what's here," he said as he pressed his left hand to his side.

His dad gave him a long look and nodded. Then they all turned toward the remains of the monsters. It took a little while to clean up the battlefield, but between their group and the Ice Sylphs, it was efficient. For the second time in his life, the silver shimmer of experience built up around Sam's skin as they looted the corpses.

Slowly, the rainbow gash of the Flaw where the Icebloods had been standing grew smaller, as the flow of energy in the world moved toward it. It was different from the last Flaw he'd faced, and he studied it as he thought about Krana and Lenei's words.

In some strange way, he could feel that it wasn't as complex and it didn't extend as far. The Flaw that had led toward the Hell Spiders had been raw, with a sort of primal energy flowing through it that attracted him. This one had some of that energy, but not as much. He was able to look at it without feeling much interest. Part of the experience that was gained from the Outsiders was diverted to closing it, and eventually the Flaw sealed shut as the elemental energies and auras of the world flowed over it.

The notification came in a shimmer of silver chimes and a cascading border with flaring, nine-pointed stars at the corners.

You have used your Class abilities to defend Aster Fall from an Outsider Threat.

You are *Acknowledged*, Battlefield Reclaimer.

You need to assist in the sealing of three more Flaws to remove *Defiant*.

As a reward for your efforts, the remaining experience after sealing the Flaw is diverted to you and your allies.

Experience is allocated according to your contribution in the battle. The World Core will assist you with absorbing it.

You gain 2,340,000 experience.

Congratulations. You have gained seven Class Levels. You are now a Level 56 Battlefield Reclaimer.

Class Experience: 6,621,940 / 6,770,000.

You have gained seven Levels. You are now General Level 56.

Total Experience: 6,645,470 / 6,770,000.

You gain +7 Intelligence, +7 Aura, and have 21 free attribute points to distribute.

The silver bubble of experience began to pour into him, rushing through his veins in dancing explosions of starry light that were streaked in a thousand rainbow hues. It was the first time in a while that he'd had such a large boost of strength. He felt the World Core keeping control of the energy as it flowed into his veins, but the massive amount of experience didn't overwhelm him in the same way it had before in the tunnels.

Perhaps it was because he was a higher level, or maybe his higher attributes were moderating the impact. All around him, he could see the others covered in the same light, absorbing their share of the experience. He felt his mind expanding and becoming sharper as his Intelligence rose to 107, and then his Aura followed as the strength of his spirit grew stronger.

One of his main deficits was still essence, so without thinking about it any longer, he added ten each of the free points to Intelligence and Aura, bringing them both to 117. His mind sharpened, but it wasn't as dramatic a change as it had been when he'd been at a much lower level. Instead of completely remodeling his awareness, it felt like it was enhancing the vibrancy of his memory recall and increasing the number of things he could focus on at once.

As for the one free point, he added it to Wisdom. It would do more good there than in other places, especially if he needed to reclaim new auras.

After a few minutes, the flow of energy stabilized and he turned his attention to the rest of the loot, going around the battlefield to search all of the enemies. He needed to restore some of the auras he'd used and there were 36 monsters and Outsiders here. The extra point of Wisdom didn't change his 35% chance to identify or 85% chance to reclaim a Basic aura, but he was looking toward the future. Once he was able to work with Advanced auras, it would be important.

It took him two or three lost auras to identify each type, but by the time he was done, he had several new gains in his storage. It was good progress, even with a few of the corpses that he wasn't able to reach, since they'd died before he arrived. If the idea of the Grand Flaw was true, then he was going to need all of them.

There were eight Auras of Dark Acid from the Greenscale Abyssal Serpents, which tasted like ashen stone that was eroded by venom, dripping from holes in endless caves.

Four Auras of Enduring Stone from the Arctic Cave Trolls: those were like silent cliffs, high in the mountains, where the wind constantly howled and the ice built up over long years, layer after timeless layer, until from deep within its heart, glacial elementals were born with slow, rippling thoughts.

Five Auras of Desolate Life from the Icesoul Wraiths: those were the taste of death fleeting in the air after battle, the tinge of blood on the wind, and the feeling of endless grass blowing away across a field.

Of all of the auras he'd ever gathered, those were the ones that troubled him the most. Auras came from Aster Fall, which meant that these were part of the world. They reminded him of the desire for blood that he'd felt during the battle, and the way that he'd ripped the Icebloods apart.

Nature was not always peaceful.

He was content with that idea in his heart, but it still troubled him in his mind. He'd been raised to be kind and civilized. He pushed the thought away as he turned toward the Icebloods, looking down at the remains of their corpses. He hadn't been able to gather the auras from them, but he had identified what the aura was, and it was both troubling and fascinating.

The Aura of Blood Winter.

It was the sudden edge of a wintry gale, its winds so sharp that they cut exposed skin like a knife, drawing blood that froze before it reached the open air. It was a cold that sank into the bones, freezing the veins and vessels before it eroded the nerves and shattered the marrow. It was skeletons drifting on the snow, their skulls rolling over like foam on a wave as they flowed down from the peaks to a village below.

He shook himself, shaking free from the feeling as he felt the last of the Icebloods' aura crumble away in his hand. Then he turned to the battlefield, spreading out his aura as he *called* to the essence stars that were scattered everywhere here. With a slash of his talons, he tore them free from the corpses.

Some of the enemies were little more than discolored smears on the snow, but the stars rose from that all the same. There were twelve Outsider corpses left, including the three Icebloods. This time, even the ones the Ice Sylphs had killed counted. Dozens of essence stars ripped free, flying toward him in a river of energy that resembled a sparkling galaxy spinning on end in the night.

Images from his dreams came to him as he saw it, an echo of the distant stars in the void. The essence stars changed from their original shade to a bright sapphire crystal, scintillating as they sank into his veins. 290 new stars joined the ones already present, adding to the growing constellation like new leaves on a branch.

Racial Essence: 637 / 1,000.

A pulse of increased strength ran through him as he felt his attributes rising. The echo of the same archaic notification sounded in his mind.

Attribute Gain Quantified by Aster Fall Standard.
Strength increased by 2.
Constitution increased by 4.
Agility increased by 1.
Intelligence increased by 4.
Aura increased by 4.

The Iceblood Shaman had more essence stars than the others, probably due to his level, around thirty instead of twenty.

STR: 25
CON: 57 (59 with belt)
AGI: 23
WIS: 47 (53 with staff)
INT: 121 (127 with bracer, +133 with bracer and staff)
AUR: 121 (127 with bracer)
CHA: 30

He felt the attributes strengthening him as he examined the essence web in his blood. It was starting to form a diagram, but it wasn't clear what the full version would be yet. Each star was a node, connected to the others by a strand of essence that was similar to a meridian. Whatever it was creating, when it reached 1,000 stars, something was going to happen. It resembled a formation, but it was too complex for him to fully understand, especially when it wasn't complete.

All around, the others were finishing up their own experience gains and harvesting the corpses. The Ice Sylphs, in particular, were stripping the enemies of anything valuable. Troll skin, bones, the serpents' scales, fangs, and organs, the wyvern's blood and scales, everything was being collected. Without needing to ask, he joined in, helping to strip the skin from the serpents and the wings, blood, and scales from the wyvern.

His crystal flame was useful in breaking through the wyvern's bones, although the Ice Sylphs were also able to form sharp daggers from ice that did the job. It didn't take too long for the village to gather everything of use. They also weren't stingy with their new allies, pushing many of the gains toward them. They were very appreciative of them coming to their aid.

Sam ended up with another wing from the wyvern, some serpent skins, and other items that would be useful for spell scrolls. He also got all the items that were on the Iceblood trio, although they didn't have much. There was a bone amulet and bone dagger from the shaman, a few pieces of clothing made from a strange hide, and, most importantly, a couple of dimensional bags.

Inside the bags, there was a strange collection of objects, mostly herbs and bone shards covered in swirling runes, a few mana crystals, and several of the white essence pills. It wasn't clear if the bone shards were some type of talisman or perhaps coins, but there was a trace of essence swirling through them. When they were done, the Ice Sylphs gathered around again, asking him the same questions as before about his appearance and origin.

This time, Siwaha came to find him, thankfully interrupting all of it.

"Shoo...shoo.... Leave the young man alone," she grumbled, waving off the other Ice Sylphs as she walked through the crowd. She didn't have a cane, but it felt like her glance was as strong as one. She prodded people away with a look and a tilt of her head. When she arrived, she looked down at him and gave him a single, serene nod.

Beside her, his mother and sister were following. His mother looked worried. If Siwaha hadn't stopped her, she would have run up to him before. The old Ice Sylph had assured her that he was fine.

"Come along, young man," Siwaha said peacefully as she examined his wounds. Then she nodded and turned around. "We need to talk." She began to walk back toward the village, without looking behind her.

"Follow me to my house."

CHAPTER THIRTY

SIWAHA

Siwaha's house was a small, elegant cabin with walls made from some thick hide that was tightly stretched between wooden supports. The frame arched to form a square enclosure about twenty feet across. The thatch of the roof above was a verdant blue-green grass that smelled like snow and winter flowers, with a faint hint of wintergreen. On the floor, a mat of woven grasses was warm from the fire that sat to one side of the house, which was banked to a low, red heat.

Overall, it was a refreshing, gentle place that complemented and contrasted the elder's commanding nature. He wasn't sure what to expect from his mother's old friend, but the first impression was her strength. From the weight of her aura, she was the strongest person he'd met so far and probably past her First Evolution. He wasn't sure why she had held back in the battle.

Perhaps she had been guarding the village or its hearthstone, acting as a last line of defense. Or perhaps she wasn't very good at attacking, depending on her class. Her blessing had been useful, so perhaps that was her focus. He still wasn't able to analyze her for more information. As they entered, she showed them to low seats, which were cushions that rested on the grass mat.

Siwaha turned to the fireplace on the far side, filled a kettle with water, and placed it over the coals, which she began to stir to a higher heat. So far she hadn't spoken. Echoes of the injuries flickered through his bones like a ghost, so he took the time while she was busy to clear his mind. He also sorted through the items he'd gained, putting everything away.

The Outsiders' dimensional bags were from this world and nothing special, but the items inside were strange. When he had some time, he'd have to investigate what the shaman's dagger, amulet, and the bone shards were. Perhaps he could break down the shards to figure out their purpose.

A spellbook, talismans made from essence, some version of a scroll...weapons, money? There were a lot of possibilities. It didn't take him long to finish. While he sorted things, no one felt the need to speak.

The silence in the cabin was peaceful, a quiet rest like deep snow on mountain peaks. It pressed down on his shoulders with a gentle weight and he found himself relaxing, like there was a heavy blanket calming his mind. The fire was built from some strange, thick grass that was similar to the thatch in the roof. As it burned, it let out threads of smoke that drifted through the room like winter wisps, idly twisting through the air in cloudy spheres and curls.

The smoke tickled his nose and eyes with a scent like silverleaf pine and green apples.

Siwaha pulled out a few small bags from a chest and took some herbs from them, which she started to prepare for tea. Her hands flickered as she combined items, and there was a swirl of subtle, shifting magic in her gestures. Gentle, icy mana streamed around her, especially her hands, and poured into the herbs. At the same time, it was also wild and intense, like a hawk soaring above the mountains that chose to calm down and rest on Siwaha's arm.

He wasn't sure if it was her control over the Ice mana that made it gentle or something else, but her gestures carried a natural harmony that brought it all together. When she was done, she turned around, which outlined her features in the firelight. She had elegant, high cheekbones and features that were too thin for a human, with eyes that were slightly larger. Her hair was pure white, flowing down her back like a white-topped river of the ages.

Her gaze moved to Jeric, Altey, and Sam, and then the others, resting gently on each of them in turn as her crystal blue eyes took in who and what they were, before she returned her attention to Aemilia with a smile.

"Sun Child, it has been such a short time," she said softly, "but filled with changes. I remember you as a small, golden-haired girl with a perpetual smile. And now you are grown and have children of your own. Time passes so quickly in my eyes. When I visited the Ten Rivers many years ago, and found that you were no longer there, I spoke with your parents."

She frowned, a quick twist of her lips that passed over her features and was gone like a cloud in front of the sun.

"Their answer about where you were was not acceptable, so I pushed harder. When I found out what they had done, I confronted them with it. Years had already passed and they didn't know where you were by then. After that, I severed my connection with them, much to their disappointment."

"It was a long time ago," Aemilia sighed, shaking her head. Siwaha's words made her relax, easing an old pain in her heart. "I'm so glad you tried, and that you don't share their views."

"Tell me of your life," Siwaha smiled, looking from Aemilia to the others, and then back again. "Help me to understand what has passed since then."

For a while, the cabin was filled with Aemilia's story, her life in leaving the Ten Rivers at 18 and going to Tower Reach, where she met Jeric at a laborers' pool, looking for daily jobs. From there, years passed as they were married and moved to Cliff's End, traveling with a merchant caravan for safety, and then of Sam and Altey's younger years, until she brought them up to the present and the journey to Highfold.

"I am glad that you have chosen your own path," Siwaha said at last, smiling again as Aemilia finished her story. "It cannot have been easy for you to do, but you have achieved wonderful things. Now, unfortunately, we must turn our attention to the matters that press us from the outside and that currently threaten this ancestral valley."

Siwaha turned her attention to Sam, nodding at him. "When it comes to your path, young man, are you content with what has happened? What is your goal in life now?"

Sam hesitated for a moment, but something about the cabin and the fire, and the scent of the wild ice in the air made it easy for him to speak.

"I'll take care of any Outsider who threatens the world," he said, speaking his mind, as he thought about the future ahead of him. "They're a problem to us, and not one that I can ignore. I'll do my duty."

"Yes, they are a problem," Siwaha agreed. "They have been for a very long time, since the very origins of my people. But why are you doing it? Is it for wealth, or power, or something else? What drives you forward?"

"No, not for those things," he said as he turned the question around in his mind, examining it from different angles until he found an answer that felt right. "Or at least, not directly. It's not that complicated. I just want the world to be a better place for my family. If wealth or power helps with that, then it's necessary on the way."

He knew it wasn't the answer that most young men would have given. Others his age were driven by the need for self-respect, or a desire for authority and power, or just for girls to pay attention to them. He was simpler. He'd grown up with his family constantly under pressure from the outside, making their lives difficult. All he wanted was for them to be free of that.

He knew it wasn't a complicated desire, but he hadn't had a lot of other experiences in his life yet. Perhaps in a few years, he would be able to come up with a better answer.

"I want to make sure the future is different from the past," he added, holding nothing back. "I didn't want to become Aster Fall's guardian, but it's necessary."

"And once your family is safe, what then?" Siwaha asked as the blue-green smoke in the room grew thicker, its curls dancing like wild sprites in the air. "What will you do with yourself?" The weight of the world hung close around him, like a familiar, trusted touch.

"I'll..." Sam hesitated. It wasn't something he'd thought much about, since it was too far in the future. "I suppose I'll create new enchantments and try to understand the meaning of Aster Fall, and the stars, and things like the ruins here. I want to understand the natural powers of the world, the runes that come from Aster Fall, and to create magic that resonates with them."

Siwaha listened to his answer and then nodded slowly. There was a smile on her face as she came to some decision. Her hand rose as she reached out and touched his forehead. A cool, pleasant burst of energy passed through her touch to his skin, like the blessing she'd given him before.

"Study," she said slowly. Her hand stroked across his forehead, like a cool compress, bringing clarity of mind and thought.

"Family." She paused, and her hand brushed across his forehead again.

"Strength." She pulled back her touch, but the sense of her energy remained, like a comfortable breeze.

"Make those three your touchstone, and you will find your balance in life, no matter where you go next." The smoke in the room cleared, along with Sam's mind, but the presence of her touch was still there. The other questions on Sam's mind rushed back in and he looked at her curiously.

He wasn't sure what had just happened, but it was relaxing to speak his mind. Something about the icy smoke here, or her words, and helped him to focus on what was important.

"You're not worried that I'm a demon?" Sam asked, puzzled, as he remembered how the sylphs had all seen his appearance.

"Should I be?" Siwaha asked calmly as she turned her attention to the kettle for tea, pulling it from the coals.

Sam frowned, thinking about it. He knew he must have looked brutal fighting the Outsiders. The memory of the battle lust and the desire to rip his enemies apart with his bare hands was sharp in his mind. Strangely, none of the Ice Sylphs seemed to be disturbed by it. If it had been him watching, he wasn't sure he'd be so accepting.

"I don't know," he said at last. "Why doesn't it bother you?" During the battle, and even now if he were being honest with himself, the desire to kill his enemies in the most effective and violent way was simple in his mind.

The rules of civilized life dictated that enemies be dealt with cleanly, offered the chance to surrender, and so on, but in his mind they were his enemies. Why would he be gentle with them? He wasn't planning to torture them, since it was a waste of time, but he was all for the quick and brutal approach to killing them. Talking it over first was not required.

The problem was that his innate desire to kill them without mercy was causing a conflict with some of the beliefs that he'd been raised to hold true, especially in regards to civilized races and intelligent life. When he'd been fighting monsters before, the question of intelligence had never come up. Having his family around him, especially his mother and sister, who had seen him like that, was making him critical of himself.

"Appearance is one form of truth, but not the only one, and often not the most important one." Siwaha shook her head slowly as she mixed more of the herbs into the kettle. "It's just the first thing that is seen. Some of the Outsiders think and speak, but they are not your allies, nor would they spare you. The fate of anyone who falls into their hands is miserable. There is no reason to spare them. This is a war for survival. Either they die or the world will die, and all of us who live on it.

"Does a hawk regret the death of the mouse it eats? Does an ice drake regret the death of a wyvern who invades its nest and tries to steal its hatchlings? You are who and what you are. They are the same. That is all. Nature is violent at times. What matters the most is that you direct your efforts in the proper way. Protect your family and deal with your enemies. That is all. There is only a need to worry if you confuse the two.

"Now, have some tea," she said as she passed small cups around. There was a solemn gravitas in her eyes as she handed it to each of them. It was a pale blue-green tea that steamed with a light layer of white mist, which hovered just above the surface, forming into patterns like snow crystals and frost.

The brew smelled like wintergreen leaves and snow, with a faint touch of something icy and ancient that drifted past his nose, like oaks that had grown for a thousand years.

He wasn't sure he knew what *ancient* smelled like, but somehow this tea did. It made him think of tumbled ruins and passing time, and cliffs high up in the peaks that were always assailed by the wind. Without thinking about it anymore, he took a drink. The others around him did as well. The world spun away into a mist of blue-green sky and frozen clouds, of icy peaks piercing through the heavens.

When it stabilized again, the room was the same, but different. All around him, there was a swirling mist of icy energy floating in the air. It resonated with the *hum* of natural energy, similar to the runes of the Storm Plains, and it shared a certain quality with redfrost and silverbark pines that he'd seen before, making it familiar to him.

It felt like it had always been there, perhaps most intensely here in this cabin and in the valley all around them, but he'd never paid enough attention to it before. He wasn't just seeing it now, but feeling it. He could follow the flow of that mist all around him. It extended from here and out through the walls, into the wider world. Somehow, his senses had been opened.

Congratulations, Battlefield Reclaimer.
You have gained the Trait: *Initiate of Ice*.

The others all blinked, their expressions changing to shock and surprise, as questions began to rise. Siwaha held up her hand, bringing calm silence back to the room.

"Welcome to my valley, young ones," Siwaha said with a smile as she looked around at their reactions. There was approval in her voice. "And to the first step in your Initiation of Ice. This is something that all young Ice

Sylphs receive, and I give it to you as a blessing. You will need it to help with the dangers of your journey, and it will aid you in your time in my home. It is not a reward for your aid, since friends do not weigh such things, but rather a gift as we look to the future together."

As she spoke, her presence became more clear in his mind.

Siwaha. Ice Sylph. Alchemist-The Speaker of the Snow. Level 135.

"The more you can attune yourself to the world here, the more the valley and the snow will aid you. Even now, having just opened your senses, you should find it easier to walk on snow and ice, and the weather here will be more comfortable. You may also find this is a new path for you to follow, if you wish to learn more of Ice and make it part of your future, but that is up to you."

"Can you tell us more about this Initiate of Ice?" Krana asked as she looked at the room around her with shock. It looked like she could see the Ice mist as well. "What is the best way to use it?"

"It is the path of Ice that is most familiar to my people," Siwaha said with a smile. "Ice Sylphs are a young race, born from Winter's Peak here when the Goddess of Life wept on top of the mountain after her son was lost in the First War between the gods and the Outsiders.

"Her grief formed the snow and her tears formed us, the people of Ice, giving life to the memory of her son. For the 60,000 years since then, we have lived here, remembering her words and tears, which are carved into our hearts.

"The tea that I gave you was mixed from the snow of Winter's Peak and some of the herbs that grew here as the goddess wept. They share an origin with us, the Ice Sylphs, and they carry some of that element of Ice in them, as well as the force of creation. You will find that the heart of Ice is open to you. If you continue to meditate on Ice, paths will appear for you to continue on your journey.

"Now, I formally welcome you to this valley as the Speaker of the Snow. You are welcome to stay here for as long as you like and to settle on an area of your choosing that is not already taken. I know that is what you came here to ask. Unfortunately, now we must turn our attention to more immediate matters, and make a plan to deal with our enemies."

***

After that overwhelming introduction, the rest of the conversation in Siwaha's cabin turned to more practical matters.

"A Grand Flaw is incredibly dangerous, and it has to be dealt with," Lenei's words carried across the room, "but it also offers great opportunity. The World Law heavily rewards those who deal with them, particularly with experience, but sometimes also with other things. It's rare to find someone at their First Evolution who hasn't dealt with at least one, and sometimes more. You can consider it a rite of passage. What we need to do now is contact the church in Highfold and then begin a more concerted, and fortified, effort to find the original Flaw. It's essential that we stop it from spreading any further."

"It should be somewhere in the ruins," Sam spoke up, "but the question is where." His vision from the Guardian Star hadn't been very specific, but it had given him the general direction. Once he got closer, he should be able to locate it.

"The ruins are nearly a hundred miles across," Siwaha said gently, nodding her head. "And they rise for nearly twenty miles from the base to the shoulder of the peaks, across all three of Great Mountains, but they are most concentrated on the slopes of Sun's Rest, and the least on Winter's Peak."

"That's a lot of square miles to cover," Jeric said with a frown. "That'll take a while."

"If we can get within five miles or so, I should be able to find it," Sam offered. "I'll be able to feel it when we're close enough."

"All right." Lenei nodded. "That means we still need to create a path through the ruins that covers everything within five miles, or perhaps more if there's any interference with your ability. So that's...." She frowned as she began to sketch a path in the air in front of her, white light following her finger to create a map. "At least four points from top to bottom and then another twenty points across...so we're looking at something like eighty points to check on this side of the mountain.

"That'll make it simpler, but from what I've heard of the ruins, they're not just a flat plain, nor always easy to cross."

"They are not," Siwaha nodded in agreement. "With the blessing of Ice, you will find it somewhat easier to travel through them, since some of the obstruction is due to the weather. The other part is due to monsters and uneven terrain, and that the ruins are broken in many places. I estimate it will take you at least a week to check all of those areas, but more likely two. I will speak with the warriors of our people, who travel much more quickly. They are currently fighting another group near the ruins and should return soon. Perhaps they have seen something."

"Will the church help with this?" Lesat spoke up, looking toward Lenei. "Now that you have proof?"

"I'll take them the heads of the Icebloods and some of the serpent fangs," Lenei agreed. "They won't be able to deny it then. The only question is how fast they can act and move more troops here. A Grand Flaw will be enough to summon their attention, but it will be at least a week to gather a large force, and even then they will need a target."

"So our mission is to scout the ruins, gather information, and eliminate any small bands of Outsiders or monsters we find as we assess the threat," Sam concluded, looking around the group to see if anyone disagreed. "If possible, we'll close the Flaw ourselves. If it's too large, we'll wait for reinforcements."

"We'll need to keep in touch with the church periodically," Lenei agreed. Then she turned to Siwaha. "And with you, elder, or your warriors?"

"Yes, they will aid you if you can find the target," Siwaha agreed. "They will also be searching on their own. I will arrange a way for you to contact them, so that whoever finds the original Flaw first can reach out to the others for support. "Make sure to prepare well for the hunt."

Chapter Thirty-One

THE HUNT BEGINS

"Let's head back to Highfold to warn the church, and from there up into the ruins," Lenei suggested as they left the Ice Sylph village.

Except for her, they were on foot now, since the horses wouldn't do as well once they climbed up into the slopes. Hopefully, the Initiate of Ice trait would help them to move a bit more swiftly than before. Behind them, Aemilia and Altey were standing next to Siwaha as they watched them go. The elder had agreed to watch over them. It wasn't just a place for them to stay. She'd also offered to help them train their magic and to come to a greater understanding of Ice.

It was a very important offer for both of them, but perhaps especially for Altey, who was young enough that it might shape her entire life. Now that the Path of Ice was open to her, Sam's sister already looked like a young ice spirit. There were flickers of tiny blue and white sparks dancing in the air around her as she moved. She didn't have any control of her magic yet, but Siwaha's tea had awoken a deep elemental affinity and Aster Fall was responding.

Her mana and affinity were reacting with the elements of the world, especially when her emotions flared. Siwaha planned to help her with meditation and control, teaching her the same way she would a young Ice Sylph. Sam turned back to Lenei as he looked away from his mother and sister, toward the battle in front of them, as he held their images at the back of his mind.

"We might need the church's help, but it means splitting up again," he replied, trying to focus on what was ahead. "We can start looking around the foothills and you can come to find us after."

"That will work." Lenei nodded in agreement. "I'm sure I can convince them this time. My Call is still pulling me to you, so I'll have no trouble finding you afterward."

"We're not sure where the Outsiders are, or where they've holed up," Jeric agreed, as he held up a glowing blue crystal that Siwaha had given them. "Once we've found them, we'll let everyone know." He also looked back, also distracted by the sight of his wife and daughter, before he turned toward Highfold.

They would be safe here, even more than they had been at the inn. With Siwaha's permission, they could settle in the valley. It was the beginning of a promising future. Before they could do that, they had to take care of the Outsider invasion. Otherwise, there wouldn't be a valley to live in. He exchanged a long look with his son that held a fierce determination, the fire that was burning in both of them to make the future a better place.

"Let's head out."

***

The road from the Ice Sylph village to Highfold was a dozen miles in a straight line, but perhaps twice that as it wound through the foothills of Winter's Peak. The land here had more rises and falls than it had coming from the other direction, since they were closer to the mountains. As they reached the fork in the path toward Highfold, Lenei turned in that direction alone. The rest of them turned toward the slopes of Sun's Rest that loomed in the distance.

"We should reach the outer edge of the ruins in an hour or two," Krana announced as she shaded her eyes with her hand. She was scanning the road ahead with Far Sight, looking for signs of enemies and their destination. "It depends on how well we handle the slopes. We'll also need to keep an eye out for other travelers, since they've already started to gather for the festival. Even in a normal year, the ruins would have a few adventurers in them."

"I'll keep my hood up," Sam agreed as he checked to make sure that his amulet was on. The Ice Sylphs hadn't cared much about his appearance, but he'd also been killing their enemies at the time, so they'd given him the benefit of the doubt.

He looked up to the peak of Sun's Rest, his eyes following the clouds of blue-white mana gathering there. Soon, it would pour down the slopes and into the valley below. The new sense of ice he'd gained drifted around him as he looked toward it. The flows of mana looked almost the same as they had before, but some of the currents of energy had gained more depth, or perhaps a more brilliant color.

There was a sparkling icy blue light spiraling through those clouds that seemed more welcoming than before. It called to him like an old friend, letting him know it was there. To a lesser extent, that same energy was in the air all around him right now, but more diffuse. It floated in crystalline strands and flecks through the air, swirling through the valley as it touched the top of the grass and was repelled again.

That had to have something to do with the Ice Sylph's magic. He could sense a current of energy along the ground now that was subtly pushing the ice away. Before, he'd sensed Ice as just one variety of mana, and it hadn't called to him like it was now. Now, it had come to life, flowing with layers of emotion and subtle, shifting hues that gave it a sense of personality. He reached out to touch one of those strands with a flicker of essence, gathering some of the flecks together.

A thin layer of ice formed on his hand, crackling with his energy as it coated his skin. It was a translucent, light blue and it shone with the reflected light of the sun like a faceted diamond, sending flickers across his vision. After a moment, more wisps of ice mana gathered above it, forming into dancing spheres and curls like the ones that were following his sister around. They were a thousand shades of blue and white, each of them changing from instant to instant.

Then ice shattered into snow, breaking away from his skin as he released the essence holding it together. As the snow fell toward the ground, it evaporated before it could touch the grass, returning to mana that flowed back into the air. His Essence Control applied to Ice, giving him some ability to manage it directly, even if he wasn't very good at it yet. Otherwise, he might have gained an Ice Manipulation skill with enough practice.

He didn't have any spells for Ice yet, but if he created the right one, he could use it. Unfortunately, that would take a little while, so the best he could do right now was straight up manipulation, which was going to be more limited and energy intensive. It would take some practice to find the best way, and it wasn't as responsive as his crystal flame, but it might be important here where the element was so common.

More than that, ice naturally had a crystalline structure. Without that, he wasn't sure his innate Fire Affinity and this Ice trait would have got along. Of all the thoughts he'd had since acquiring the trait, that was the most important, as well as whether or not he could combine the two. If he meditated on Ice, perhaps he could come to a deeper understanding of the crystal aspect of his flames and strengthen Essence Shield and Crystal Field, or invent new spells.

Heat and cold were two sides of the same coin. He would have to meditate on Ice in the mountains, once they took care of the Flaw. For now, however, there were too many enemies ahead of them.

He pulled his thoughts back to the present, examining the valley around him as they walked. The weather here felt more comfortable now, as if the ice had become warmer. He poured out a wave of crystal flame in front of him. The flames twisted into a rough map of the ruins. With a shift of his intention, eighty points appeared on the map, detailing the areas they needed to reach.

"As long as we can get to each of those points, it should be possible to sense the Flaw," he said, calling the others' attention to the map. "With the Outsiders, monsters, and travelers around it, along with any adventurers, it could get pretty chaotic."

"We can start at the closest and work our way outward," Jeric said with a frown as he pointed toward the nearest point, one that was just to the southwest of Highfold on the lower slopes of Sun's Rest.

Sam nodded as he looked up at the mountain ahead of them. He wasn't sure how many Outsiders had come through the Flaw, but he had the feeling that exploring the ruins wasn't going to be easy. There was a looming threat to the valley, and a glint of battlelight flickered in his eyes as his gaze traversed the peaks.

***

The first glimpse Sam had of the ruins was a pillar of fallen stone. It lay half-buried in a layer of snow, fallen sideways across the path in front of them. Half-buried wasn't saying much for this pillar, since there was nearly a dozen feet exposed above the snow. When it was standing, it must have been enormous. To his left and right, stretching out into the distance, there were a few similar pillars, marking out what must have been an enormous wall or a pillared gallery that had stretched for over a mile.

Above, an early evening was descending on the slopes of Sun's Rest as the sun moved down behind the peak. The slope here was rippled, as if the ground had rolled with a sudden fury at some point and scattered the ruins across the surface. Behind the first pillar, there were other chunks of stone, big ones as tall as a horse and others that were two or three times that size. They lay scattered across the ground, mostly hidden by the layer of snow, but their visible surfaces were engraved with swirling patterns that resembled flowing clouds.

Or perhaps they resembled the rivers of mana that descended from the peak of the mountain.

All of them were made of a dense grey stone with a nearly invisible grain, similar in some ways to basalt, but it shimmered with a silver-green gleam in the depths, marking it out as anything but normal. It was either a strange ore, an alloy, or imbued with magical properties, or perhaps all three. It gave off a low-level hum that resonated in his senses, the pitch matching the fluctuation of the energy inside.

There were no discernable runes on the stones that he could make out, but the patterns gleamed with a subtle force in his mind. Even broken, they seemed more real than the rest of the world around them, holding the remains of the power that had once flowed there. That power drew him toward it like a will-o-the-wisp in the night, echoing with a force like the natural runes of the world that made it difficult to pull his gaze away.

"Impressive, isn't it?" Krana asked as she joined him next to the pillar that he was studying. "Siwaha said they were broken more than 12,000 years ago, during a massive Outsider invasion. That was 6,000 years before the last Breaking. Except for the Ice Sylphs, I've never heard of anyone having a record of them. Even the church only has theories."

Sam nodded as he pulled his eyes from the patterns and looked to the sky, searching for the moons. He knew Caelus was up, but it was hidden behind the mountain to the west. Silvas and Amaris had not yet risen. Despite that, he could feel a strange force in the air, as if there were something waiting, and there was that shimmering, silver-green light that was building up around the runes. It was subtle and barely visible against the stone, but it was there, and it was part of what was calling him toward the pillar.

It felt...*expectant*.

"What sort of enchantment requires the power of three moons to align?" he muttered to himself, thinking out loud without realizing it. "And what are these patterns?"

"Something big," Krana answered, unable to hold back her own feeling of awe. "Even if the legends are wrong and it doesn't have anything to do with the Seal, it's definitely something on the world level. This type of enchantment has to affect a huge area."

Sam rubbed his chin thoughtfully and looked at the stone pillar, and then up to the sky again, where the moons were absent. His thoughts were pulled back to the present when his father spoke.

"It looks like some adventurers are making their way up the slope behind us," Jeric announced, his tone displeased as he looked behind them. "Let's try to keep ahead of them. We don't need the distraction."

With that, the four of them began to move again, walking easily across the snow. Either the snow was packed firmly here or their Initiate of Ice trait was making things easier, since the snow was firm beneath their steps, offering a secure footing.

Once they'd passed by, a wind brushed away their footprints. Sam glanced back at their trail and watched it for a moment. It was already disappearing. All around him, his Crystal Focus was pouring through the snow, telling him how deep it was and what was underneath it, but even without it, he felt like the world here was comfortable, almost permeable, as if he could move freely in it.

The snow was friendly, offering up its aid. Whatever Siwaha had given them, and no matter how much she had described it as a simple gift, he had the feeling it wasn't a simple thing at all.

"The force of Creation," he muttered, as his thoughts began to turn in an ever-increasing spiral, focusing on the ruins, the mountains, the moons, and the legend that he'd heard from Siwaha.

He wasn't sure if the ruins had really been built by the gods to balance the energy in the Seal, or if they were the work of an ancient civilization whose secrets had been forgotten. It was even possible they had something to do with the history of the Ice Sylphs and the Goddess of Life who had created their race, since this was their ancestral home, although Siwaha hadn't suggested that.

She had said there were other tribes of Ice Sylphs in the world, branches that had left to explore the world, but that they had all started here, from that same origin.

Perhaps the Sylphs had built these ruins once and forgotten them, similar to the hearthstone they had to manage the weather in the valley, which had been made by their ancestors. Whatever was true, he had the feeling that somehow everything was connected.

In the sky above, the faint light of three moons was beginning to rise, their multi-colored rays stretching out across the growing dusk. On the slopes, the snow glimmered as the moonlight descended, giving rise to icy wisps that danced above the surface in slowly shifting patterns, their natural blue-white turning to hues of green, purple, and blue.

***

The four of them pushed on, heading farther up Sun's Rest as they moved toward the first point on their map. So far, the Guardian Star was silent. It was faster to move across the snow than before, but the ruins didn't make it easy. They had been built directly into the slope, in what must have been terraces or a series of stacked buildings.

Once upon a time, there had been staircases or perhaps magical transportation from level to level, but now it was a tumbled mountain of broken stone, shattered pillars, and fallen walls. All of it was built from the same grey stone with silver-green energy in the depths. They located one staircase up to a higher level, but it was almost completely obscured by a rockfall, which meant they had to make a longer detour up and around the edge of the ruin, on the untouched portion of the slope.

As a result, progress to the next level was slow. For every mile they gained in a straight line, it was twenty or thirty times that winding through the ruins as they searched for a viable path. Even detouring completely onto the snowy slopes outside the ruins wasn't possible. It was like trying to get around the edge of a city. The ruins were too large for it to be practical. If they constantly had to leave the city and come back in from a different angle, and then leave and try again when that road was blocked, it made for delays.

It took them half a day to reach the first point, which was nothing more than a tumbled pile of stone in the snow. When they got there, Sam activated the Guardian Star directly, letting it scan the local area, which absorbed eighteen essence. Its response came almost immediately as a multi-colored rainbow star with nine points rose out of his hand and spun in the air, flickering as its scanned the area.

No Flaw detected within five miles.

Concealed Flaw detected within the vicinity. Unable to pinpoint with greater precision.

The star's voice was flat and then it fell silent again, as if the effort had exhausted it, even with Sam providing the energy. Now that they were closer to the Flaw, it wasn't able to help as much. He had to find the origin point on his own.

"Nothing's here," he announced as he looked around the area, recalling the map of the ruins in his mind as he plotted out the best path to get to the next star.

This one was almost directly above Highfold, and it would be easiest to go sideways for now, staying on the same level of the ruins. Perhaps they could cut horizontally around the mountain and only climb up to a new level once for each terrace.

The others nodded, and another half a day passed as they headed toward the next point. From time to time, they noticed other travelers, but they did their best to avoid them. There was no need to get entangled with local issues.

"Hold on a moment," Lesat called, pulling Sam's attention away from the path. The guard was bringing up the rear defense and had stopped now to study the road behind them. "We have a problem heading this way. It looks like that same group of adventurers we saw yesterday."

Sam turned around, following Lesat's gaze to see what he was talking about. It didn't take long to find it. About a quarter of a mile below them, on a lower level of the ruins, there was a small band of what had to be adventurers running wildly through the ruins.

They were easy enough to spot from this height, especially since they were outlined against the snow as spells and shields of various colors flared around them. Behind them, there was a pack of Outsiders chasing them. Sam's eyesight picked out the details without trouble.

The Outsiders were a strange mix of things, with a long lower body that resembled an obscenely-muscled wolf and an upper body that looked vaguely human, almost like a wolf centaur. Their four feet were broad and tufted with fur, allowing them to run quickly on top of the snow. The forward part of their body was humanoid, but there were two long, curved blades of ice in place of their arms. Their jaws were a wide-gaping horror of fangs that glistened with shiny blue saliva.

Coldfang Beheader. Level 45.

The one at the head of the group was half again larger than the others.

Coldfang Beheader Pack Leader. Level 58.

"Looks like they're in trouble down there," Jeric grumbled as his hands flexed, reaching for the hammers at his belt. "They're only in their 40s and there's four of them. They're outnumbered two to one, plus the pack leader to make nine."

Sam turned his attention to the adventurers, scanning over them as he debated whether or not to get involved. Closing the Flaw was more important than dealing with random adventurers and he had a distaste for them in general. Every time he encountered them, they lived up to their reputation for causing trouble. Maybe the world would be better if he just left them to their own devices.

Human. Barbarian-Tundra Walker. Level 47.

Lykaris. Ranger-Shaman. Level 44.

Human. Wizard-Ice Mage. Level 45.

Human-Water Spirit. Arcane Scribe-Priestess. Level 42.

He almost turned around again, but it was the Half-Spirit who got his attention. She was the weakest of the group and her Scribe class made him curious. Spirits were an elemental race, often friendly with others, but it was the first time he'd ever encountered one of them, or at least a human half-blood. Before now, he'd only heard of them in stories. She reminded him both of himself and of Ayala, which made him wonder how the young priestess was doing in Osera.

Also, they were being chased by Outsiders, so he'd have to deal with those at some point anyway. Even though he wanted to avoid trouble, it wasn't a difficult decision to help.

"We'll have to intercept their opponents," he said as he scanned the distance between the adventurers and the Coldfangs that were swiftly approaching.

"Down there," Krana pointed toward a point that was lower in the ruins, where a tumbled wall fell down toward the lower level. "If we jump down from here, we'll land safely enough. Then we can head between them."

At that moment, a drifting scream carried up from the group below as the priestess stumbled, falling to one knee. The other three paused, sliding in the snow as they spun around to see what had happened. Behind her, the Coldfang Beheaders sprinted closer, their bladed arms rising as clouds of snow flew up explosively from around their feet.

CHAPTER THIRTY-TWO

COLDFANG BEHEADERS

Sam sprinted forward, pushing himself ahead with a burst of crystal flame as he launched himself off the upper wall. Another flare of flame beneath his feet slowed his landing as he hit the snow below. It felt like the snow compacted, shifting to support him and absorb the impact, but he didn't have time to pay too much attention to it.

The ruins were uneven here, with many stones hidden beneath the snow, which was probably what the priestess had stumbled over. Now that they were closer, he could see the adventurers were all wearing some type of snowshoe. Since he'd decided to help, there was no reason to hesitate. The adventurers were about two hundred yards away now and he was heading for them at full speed.

Even so, the Coldfang Beheaders were closer to them than he was. The adventurers turned to fight them, forming a tight group around the priestess who was just starting to climb back to her feet. It made him like them just a bit more than before, since they hadn't abandoned her to save themselves.

The Coldfang Pack Leader was at the head of the Outsiders and it slammed into the Barbarian-Tundra Walker, who had moved to the front of the group. The man was holding a huge spear and tried to brace himself against the assault as a shield of golden Stamina flared around his body, but it wasn't enough to stop the charge.

The crunch of the impact was audible even from where Sam was running, and the barbarian doubled over, sliding backwards as the Pack Leader's bladed arms swept toward his head.

The Lykaris had a bow in her hand and a series of flaming arrows blasted away from her, sizzling through the air toward the Coldfang to intercept the blow. The arrows were enough to halt its movements as it raised its arms into the air to cover its face. The icy blades on its arms grew outward, transforming into a broader shield as they struck. They bored into the ice with sizzling explosions of steam.

From behind the Pack Leader, the howls of the other Coldfangs rose into the air as they closed the gap.

The Lykari were a strange race, tall and thin humanoids with an affinity for Fire and a penchant for fits of rage. Legends said they were descended from fire spirits, or perhaps cousins to the sylphs, but their personalities were very different.

He'd never met one before, but this one was identifiable on sight. She was nearly nine feet tall, and incredibly thin, less than a foot across at the hips, like a tall, angular blade. Her limbs were also longer than a human's, with joints that looked more flexible. He'd heard they made excellent blademasters and scouts.

This one proved the truth about her race's inclination for anger as she let out a howling scream and threw herself forward at the Coldfang. A sphere of fire burned around her like she was an orange fireball as twin khopeshes appeared in her hands. Her attacks were broad, slashing cuts as she darted toward the Coldfang and back out again. She spun back from another angle a moment later, demonstrating a lithe grace.

Her blades struck together, curved back along their paths, and struck again, slicing chunks out of the Pack Leader's shield, but she was unable to break through it.

A howl rose up from the rest of the Coldfangs as they closed in.

The Wizard-Mage summoned up a violet defensive shield around the group, but it didn't look like it would last long. He was hurriedly pulling objects from his pouches, activating them in a blur of movement.

Behind Sam, his father, Krana, and Lesat sprinted across the snow, surrounded by the glow of their mana and enchantments as they headed on a slightly different path to intercept the Outsiders, curving around to the left.

A Starfire spell formed in Sam's hands as he got close enough to help. He targeted the rear of the Coldfang pack as he released it, sending it hurtling forward with a whistling sound as it tore through the air. The spell exploded among the back rank of the Outsiders, tossing four of the Coldfangs away in a tumble of wolfen limbs and flailing ice blades.

A loud *skrreewckk* rose up from them with a sound more like an angry spider than the misshapen wolves they resembled. The Coldfangs' mouths gaped a foot wide as their fangs flashed and blue spittle flew from their jaws. He had no interest in drawing out the fight, nor in getting into a melee battle with the things.

A wave of 200 Starflame arrows ripped through the air in front of him as he unloaded every single charge in his bracer. At the same time, another rippling blue-white sphere of Starfire appeared in his hand as he slid to a halt a few dozen feet from the adventurers. The arrows hit before the Coldfangs could advance any faster and tore through the Outsiders like a storm of lightning going through a spider's web.

Explosions of sizzling blue-black blood erupted from their bodies as limbs went flying into the air, some of them even heading in his direction to crash against an Essence Shield that he hastily raised. A moment later, a wave of earthen spikes from Krana tore through their ranks and then his father and Lesat were there, slamming into the remaining Coldfangs from the side.

It was more than enough to kill them.

The Lykaris and other adventurers didn't refuse the help. They simply poured on their attacks as they focused on the Pack Leader, which Sam's group left for them to handle.

The Ranger-Shaman continued her flaming dance with the twin khopeshes, and the barbarian joined in, now that he had a chance to regain his feet, stabbing forward with his spear as he tried to break through the Outsider's defense.

Whirling icy shards broke free from the Pack Leader's shield as it split back into blades and intercepted the attacks. It was far stronger than the other Coldfangs behind it and proved it as it forced the adventurers back step by step. The wizard's shield flared a brilliant violet as it shuddered under the creature's blows and then stabilized as the priestess joined in on the defense, her hands glowing with white mana as she poured her support into the spell.

By then, the last of the eight regular Coldfangs had been crushed under Jeric and Lesat's assault and the battle was already decided, but it took a little while to bring it to a conclusion.

Only the Pack Leader presented a real obstacle. Sam kept his eye on it as the Starfire spell floated in his hand, waiting to see if it would be necessary. As it turned out, it wasn't. The addition of their force was enough to take the pressure off the adventurers and gave them the chance to slowly wear down the Pack Leader. The Barbarian and Lykaris took some injuries from being in melee range, but the priestess's healing magic was already at work on them.

As the battle settled down, Sam took control of the essence in his Starfire spell, slowly stripping it away layer by layer. He couldn't reclaim it for his essence pool, since it didn't seem to work like that, but he could send it into his bracer to recharge it.

It would take a little while to refill the artifact, but it was too important of a weapon to ignore. He could have held some of it back, but he had a preference for keeping his essence in reserve instead, especially when he didn't know the adventurers' intentions. Plus, it had been too tempting to annihilate the Coldfangs with overwhelming force.

When everything was settled, he pulled back farther, letting his father take the main stage as the focus of the adventurers' attention. He had no desire to let them see his features. If he'd had his preference, they'd leave again at once, but that would probably come across as strange and memorable. It was also tempting to see if they had any information about the ruins.

"Thank you for your help," the barbarian said with a frown as he looked between Jeric and Lesat, and then toward Krana and Sam. "Without you, we'd be dead by now, I'm sure."

Now that the Pack Leader was dealt with, the adventurers pulled themselves together and stood shoulder to shoulder, looking across the dozen or so feet that separated them from Jeric and Lesat.

Farther away, Krana had come up by Sam's side and was keeping him company, making him look less suspicious. There were a few *pings* against his amulet, but as far as the adventurers could tell, he was just a reclusive caster keeping his distance.

"Who are you? Are you adventurers?" The Lykaris was looking around the area and at them with quick, darting glances, her hands on her

khopeshes. Her long limbs twitched with restless energy, as if it was difficult for her to not move, which gave her every action an unsettling
nervousness.

She looked uncertain, turning from one of them to the next as she
wondered if these newcomers were dangerous, or even planning to kill
them themselves, now that they were worn down. They'd saved them, but
that didn't mean they were friends.

The barbarian was a tall, muscular man with dark hair who looked to be
in his early thirties. His main distinguishing feature was a dark, mottled
scar that cut down the side of his neck and shoulder, eventually moving
under the fur he had wrapped around him like a cloak. Whatever healing
he'd had for that, it hadn't been enough. Perhaps he was keeping it as a
souvenir.

He was only wearing the fur cloak and a tunic, plus breeches and the
snowshoes tied below his boots, making it clear that his Constitution was
high enough for him to not worry much about the snow here.

As for the Lykaris, she was wearing a ranger's leathers, a tight-fitting suit
of mottled browns with some embroidered leaves edged in fire. It looked
like her race's penchant for flames extended to their clothing as well. Her
features were angular with sharp planes that marked out her cheeks and
eyes. Like her limbs, her face was longer than a human's, resembling a
stretched-out blade.

The Wizard-Mage was a middle-aged man with sandy brown hair whose
face was streaked with sweat. He was slightly overweight and bundled up
in layers of furs, on top of a warming artifact that was gleaming around one
wrist. From the look of it, he was the worst off of the lot in this weather.

The half-Water Spirit Priestess was a slender woman with bright blue
eyes and ivory skin that gleamed with a subtle inner light, almost as if there
were water mana shining outward from her skin. It was hard to tell her
age, but from her posture, he'd put her closer to thirty than to twenty, or
perhaps older. Her features were delicate and composed, despite the brush
with disaster. Her gaze moved past Jeric and Lesat to settle on Sam, and he
saw her frown as his amulet pinged again.

"We're not adventurers," Jeric replied, shaking his head to deny that. He
barely held back an expression of distaste. "We're here looking for Outsiders, to make sure they die. That's what you just fought, so we helped.
There's a Flaw here, somewhere, and we need to find it and close it."

His words were direct and blunt. He'd hooked his hammers back on his belt to be less threatening. His hands were on his hips as he looked from one of them to the next. There was no reason to hold back their mission, especially since it was one that would put them in the good graces of most people in the world.

"You're with the church?" The Water Soul's expression perked up as surprise and doubt flitted across her face. "You don't look...quite like a church team."

"No, although we do have a Paladin with us," Jeric replied, shaking his head. "The information about the Flaw is new, and she's off in Highfold gathering more troops. We're here scouting the ruins for the exact location."

"I see," the barbarian said, relaxing a bit as he heard their purpose. He looked between them and then the Water Soul, gauging her reaction, and then nodded. "Let's split up the experience here and then we can talk. We've seen a couple of things that might be useful to you. "These aren't the only Outsiders we've seen here and we were wondering what was going on. If there's a Flaw, things are going to get worse. Even without the church or the World Law conscripting people to help, it'll be hard to avoid that."

The barbarian's tone suggested he'd prefer to stay far away from the Flaw and any Outsiders. He looked at Jeric's forthright expression and then toward the others, his gaze stopping on Sam for a moment with a trace of puzzlement, but his worries were fading now that he'd heard their purpose. He just wanted to leave as quickly as possible, so he didn't get wrapped up in it.

"We'll tell you where we saw those Outsiders, and then maybe you can help us with our goal," he said, now that he was fairly sure they weren't bandits. "We're looking for a specific formation here in the ruins, which is useful to Selis and Arene. It's supposed to have the ability to enhance elemental affinity." He nodded toward the Lykaris and the priestess.

"There's no reason to keep that secret, since it's where the rest of the Outsiders are that we saw." He grimaced as he considered the opposition they were facing in getting to it, as well as that he'd have to get close to a Flaw. "Maybe your Flaw is nearby and we can all help each other out. You deal with your target and we'll deal with ours."

With that, the two sides relaxed a bit and turned toward the corpses, gathering the experience from them together. There was no silver bubble of experience from them this time, perhaps because they weren't near a Flaw, and the World Law was silent, but there was a typical party split of experience between everyone there. As far as the World Law was concerned, all eight of them were a group for this battle.

You have used your Class abilities to slay enemies of Aster Fall. You gain 542,720 Class experience.

Congratulations. You have gained two Class Levels. You are now a Level 58 Battlefield Reclaimer.

Class Experience: 7,164,940 / 7,540,000

You have gained two General Levels. You are now General Level 58.

Total Experience: 7,188,190 / 7,540,000

You gain +2 Aura, +2 Intelligence, and have six free attribute points to distribute.

When the shimmering chime of the experience notification faded away and the energy settled into his body, he divided the free points between Intelligence and Aura, which left him with 126 in each attribute. With the Starflame Bracer, he was up to 132. He kept finding himself in larger battles that lasted for a while, which meant that he needed to increase his essence pool.

When that was done, he turned to the monsters and tore the essence stars out of their corpses. According to his father, the stars pulling free from the corpses and flying to him were visible to others, but the flaring light and auras that he saw weren't as intense for them. They just looked like small flickering stars.

Racial Essence: 832 / 1,000

Attribute Gain Quantified By Aster Fall Standard.

Strength increased by 2.

Constitution increased by 3.

Agility increased by 1.

Intelligence increased by 4.

Aura increased by 4.

The essence stars locked into place, expanding the essence constellation in his blood, expanding the network further, but when it was done it still wasn't clear what the final form would be. One more big fight and....

"What are you doing?" the Water Spirit interrupted with a frown, walking closer to him as she watched. The enemies were dead, but she'd never seen anything like it before.

"My class is unique, Battlefield Reclaimer," Sam replied, trying to hold back his irritation at the disruption as he gave the excuse he'd come up with. He didn't bother turning around. "I'm reclaiming part of their energy to use in battle."

It had the advantage of even being true in case someone was trying to detect that, like Lenei, although what he was actually doing was far more important.

Unique classes were a well-known topic in the world, although rare, and he was offering up the information easily enough. If she kept pushing, it would be impolite, like prying into his secrets and asking exactly how much mana or Constitution he had. Asking that sort of thing wasn't appropriate, not unless you were someone's student or a very good ally.

"I see," she said slowly, before her words turned in a direction he hadn't expected, her voice sharpening as she tried to stare beneath his hood. "Are you really working with the church...Outsider?"

A sharp feeling like a drawn blade surged in his awareness as the priestess's hand slashed out toward him. Sam turned toward her as a wave of anger ran through his chest, his hand slamming up against hers as he gripped her wrist, halting the descent of a silver dagger in her hand. Crystal Focus had outlined the movement in sharp detail, and she was far weaker than he was, but she didn't stop there.

Her other hand came out with another knife and slashed toward him again, which he knocked away with his bracer. He spun in place, twisting her arm around and down as he threw her away from him. She landed half a dozen feet away, upside down in the snow.

"Traitor!" The Lykaris's shout echoed through the air as her bow came out. Before he could say anything, three flaming arrows headed in his direction.

The arrows crashed against a hasty Essence Shield as Sam's hands rose into the air, the heat from them creating weird purple-orange sparks as the energy from the Lykaris's flames hit the shield.

The anger in his chest reverberated with the essence stars in his blood, intensifying as it flowed from star to star like an echo, cycling through his blood and returning again, growing stronger with each beat of his heart. A surge of overwhelming pride, the desire to conquer everything before him, and volcanic wrath came with it.

How dare this weak thing challenge me.

Before he could think about what he was doing, a pulse of crystal flame flared around him and he shot toward the Lykaris as his battle aura rose from his skin.

She was drawing the bow back for another shot as his talons stretched out around her neck, seizing her in a death grip. She was too tall for him to raise from the ground, but his arm was locked in place as she rose onto her toes, trying to back away from his grasp.

KrgghhkkK. A choked sound issued from her throat.

When she wasn't able to escape, a halo of orange flames surged up around her skin as she tried to fight back. The flames washed against his hand like questing fingers, filled with her unique mana signature and some element of jittery, frenetic energy. They tried to stab at him like little daggers, digging at him, but they failed to even touch his skin as the flames washed over him, flowing away with no effect.

Another choked sound came from the Lykaris. Sam's grip was tight as he held her at arm's length, stretching her out as high as he could reach, but the wrath that was flowing through him was so intense that he couldn't form his thoughts into speech. All that came out of his throat was a low, reverberating growl.

CHAPTER THIRTY-THREE

FOUR ADVENTURERS

The only thing that held Sam back from breaking the Lykaris's neck was that she wasn't an Outsider. He also remembered the last civilized person he'd killed, that wizardess who had attacked him in the tunnels. He still didn't feel guilty about that, but it wasn't something he was going to repeat when he knew what was going on. Perhaps it was a sign that he wasn't as young and foolish as he'd been back then.

As soon as the other two adventurers saw what was happening, the barbarian started to charge his way, but Jeric intercepted him, throwing him backward with a double-handed shove to the chest. The blow was hard enough that the barbarian went tumbling head over heels in the snow.

"Stop!" Jeric shouted angrily, as the golden-red aura of Persuade began to radiate outward from him through the area. "You don't know what you're doing!"

Persuade wasn't enough to stop these adventurers in the middle of a fight, but it was enough to get their attention. The barbarian hit the ground and sank half a foot into the snow before he flailed his way back to the surface, roaring as a red aura began to shine out of his skin. The wizard was the slowest of the group, his expression befuddled, but when he saw the barbarian thrown back, he started to pull a wand from his belt.

Krana intercepted him, knocking him away with a bright yellow shield as her warhammer came around and swept the wand out of his hand, twisting his wrist to the side.

"Stop!" she shouted, pressing close as she grabbed at his collar and pulled him down to her face. "This is all a misunderstanding! Sam is not your enemy!" Her voice was an angry rumble as silver energy from her Seer class began to cascade around her.

The Lykaris twisted in Sam's grip, which he tightened as his talons dug in. He had to force back his aura, otherwise he would have cut through her neck. Despite his restraint, a surging, volcanic anger was flowing through his veins, swirling from one essence star to the next as it traced out the mostly-complete formation.

The stars resonated in time with his heart. He could almost feel the formation stretching, as if it wanted to be complete so it could show the world what it could do.

The priestess, the source of the trouble, was just now climbing to her feet near Sam. He'd felt sympathetic for her earlier, but that had flown out the window. He needed to do something before she got to her feet and made things worse. With his anger, the answer was clear.

Overwhelming force.

Crystal flame surged up in a rush as he poured it outward, extending it in a field around the priestess and the Lykaris. Then he clamped down on it, freezing everything nearby in a Crystal Field. Both of them froze in place as a geometric pattern of interlocking crystal blue patterns appeared all around them, binding their limbs and the area nearby. It was a faint sapphire blue at the edges, and a deeper blue where the patterns met up.

It took thirty points of Essence to get the field into place, and he felt the two adventurers struggling, but he had the strength to keep them locked down. When they were frozen, he still held the Lykaris in his hand as he turned toward the priestess, glaring at her.

"You think that you, a novice priestess, can see more clearly than the Seer I am traveling with? You were able to Identify my race, but you missed everything else." His voice was a rough snarl as he pushed the words out past the desire to tear them apart. "You couldn't put two thoughts together to realize that I just saved you from Outsiders and that our plan is to kill more of them! "

With that, he threw the Lykaris to the ground next to the priestess, holding onto the Crystal Field as he turned away. As much as he wanted to pay them back for the attack, he wasn't a monster. He wasn't going to kill everyone who made him angry.

The barbarian and wizard were being held back by his father and Krana. They stared in his direction as he pushed his hood off, glaring at them. He shook the folds of the cloak free until his features and horns were on full display, and he watched their faces pale as they caught sight of him.

"Pay better attention," he growled with disgust. "It's just a transformation spell to make me look like this. We'll take you up on the offer to show us where the Outsiders are. If you have any more doubts about what I've told you, then you can watch as all of them die. But if you attack me again, you won't live to make it there." With that threat hanging in the air, he turned away, heading toward the Coldfang corpses as he went to gather the auras.

Behind him, his father and Krana kept an eye on the four adventurers as they started to come to terms with reality. He understood why they were shocked, but he didn't have it in him to care.

Blasted adventurers, he muttered to himself, his old disgust for them returning in a wave. *They must be born with half a brain. Not only do they attack without thinking, but they're wasting the opportunity to have a normal life.*

***

The auras from the Coldfangs were as sharp as the winter ice that formed along the edge of a cliff in layer after cutting layer that waited for an unwary traveler to grip them. It was a cold that cut to the bone and froze the blood in its path, severing nerves and life in a silent brush with death.

You have identified a new Aura.
Aura of Frozen Blades.

It took three tries to fully identify the aura, and then he gathered four more of them from the other Outsiders. After that, he turned toward the last one and searched for the thread of energy there. It was a frozen, cutting smoke that drifted around the thing, weaving through its wolfen fur and the ice blades that made its arms, which now lay dully on top of the snow. Whatever energy had once enlivened them, it had fled with the thing's death.

As he pulled the aura toward himself, there was a sudden feeling of depth, as if the aura in his hand had suddenly become heavier, and he was able to feel it more intensely than any of the others. Not just cutting ice, but an ice that hungered for life, that wanted nothing more than to freeze it in place and bring it to a sharp, bitter stillness.

It was still the Aura of Frozen Blades, but there was *more* to it, a sense of life and emotion that hadn't been there before.

At that moment, a chiming golden notification appeared in his mind, accompanied by the clarion call of trumpets unfurling in the dawn. It was one that he'd been waiting for a very long time.

Congratulations, Battlefield Reclaimer. You have touched on a deeper layer of existence.

Your Class Ability *Reclaim Aura* has reached the Advanced Tier. You may now gather Advanced Auras.

The aura separated from the Coldfang like coiling blue smoke, swirling into a sphere in Sam's hand. It came with the taste of cold that cut to the bone, leaving an aching pain in his lungs.

Aura of Frozen Blades (Advanced).

The sphere looked very similar to one of the Basic auras on the outside, but inside he could sense the cold, brutal intent that had been part of the Coldfang Beheaders. This was the distilled element of a frozen blade itself. It was like a higher-tier rune, something much more complex and dangerous than the Basic versions he'd collected just before this.

What would happen if this were added to an Ice-enchanted blade? The thought spun through his mind in a torrent of expectation as he looked at the aura in his hand.

As he put it into his storage, a strange thing happened, and the new aura disappeared as it was pulled away, blending into the space of the storage. A pulling and twisting sensation followed, as he felt the dimensional pocket *warp* under the force of the aura that had just entered it. The energy from the aura pressed against the constraints of the space there, forcing the dimension to become wider.

From the outside, another force that he didn't understand pushed back, and for the first time he felt the edges of the dimensional pocket as if it were a unique existence on its own. As that force pushed against them, they became somehow denser, until the pressure from the Advanced aura and the external pressure reached an equilibrium. A moment later, a second notification came on the tails of the first.

Aura Storage has reached the Advanced Tier.

Spatial density enhanced to contain more complex forces. Dimensional capacity increased from 500 to 1,000 auras.

He wasn't entirely sure what the notification about spatial density meant, but it was obvious that the ability had been upgraded. As for holding 1,000 auras, he'd never reached the 500 limit and hadn't even been aware there was one. The possibilities of what he could do with Advanced auras danced in his mind as he turned away from the Coldfangs, feeling pleased.

Behind him, the adventurers had just started to calm down, although from the arguments he'd heard, it had been a rocky conversation.

Krana had explained her vision of the Breaking, and Jeric's steady assurance that Sam was his son had swayed their opinions. Most of their reaction had been due to the stress of nearly dying, and now that they were no longer in danger, they were thinking more clearly. Without the help, they knew they would have died here.

"The place we're trying to reach is about twenty miles to the west and up a level," the barbarian announced as he gave Sam a guarded look. He didn't fully trust this strange wizard, but so far he had done nothing but help them. "We were heading there when these Coldfangs caught sight of us. They were gathering around another point, one that's pretty close to it, and they caught us by surprise as we passed."

"There were at least a dozen more Outsiders or monsters there too," the priestess added with a grimace as she looked between Sam and Jeric. "If you're really not an Outsider...I'm sorry I attacked you."

Sam just shook his head and pushed all of the nonsense away, focusing on what was more important. He didn't need these adventurers to be his friends. He just needed them to show him where the Flaw was.

"Don't focus on it," he replied, waving the comment away. "Just help us deal with the problem. It sounds like your goal is on the other side of our enemies anyway, so we may as well work together. We'll clear out the areas together and then you can find your elemental pillar."

The elemental pillar they were talking about was something he wanted to see. If it was part of the ruins, it might be important, whether or not it enhanced elemental affinities. If these four joined forces with them, even though they were a bit lower level, it would help to reinforce their side of the battle. Then, they might actually do some good for the world.

The battle at the sylph village and now this one with the Coldfangs had been enough to get his father up to Level 52. Krana was Level 51 and Lesat was Level 53. Their forces were slowly but surely improving. If they had more battles like this, then the ruins would be an excellent proving ground. He looked around at the remains of the Coldfangs and at the new Advanced aura in his storage, his thoughts running ahead to the future.

The real test would be when they found the Flaw, along with whatever was guarding it. He had no doubt that the forces there would be worse than anything they'd seen so far.

***

The adventurers sorted themselves out and healed up, and Sam took the opportunity to recharge his bracer. A couple of hours later, they led Sam and the others back in the direction that they had come, sticking to the same level of the ruins. From time to time, Sam paused and checked the area with the Guardian Star, but so far there was no sign of the Flaw. All he could do was record their progress on a rough map, marking out the areas he'd already checked.

About an hour into their journey, a message formation appeared in the air near him, its double-circled construction spinning in place. It was one of his. He reached out and tapped it, activating the stored voice.

"I've alerted the church," Lenei's voice echoed out from the message runes. "The heads from the Icebloods were enough to get their attention, so they're gathering a force. There will be a group of about twenty church warriors, knights, paladins, and priests ready within a day.

"They'll need a target, or else they plan to break down into teams and start searching the area on their own. They don't trust that the Flaw is in the ruins, so they want to look for it themselves. It would be time-consuming and scatter the group. If you have any new intelligence, please send it to me. I'll stay here for another day or two as an intermediary and then come join you."

The runes inside the message formation faded, bringing an end to the spell. The formation spun in the air a few more times and then crumbled away to dust.

"So you do have a Paladin," the barbarian grumbled as he looked back, half-turned toward the message scroll. The other three adventurers were with him at the head of the party, while Sam's group was following. It didn't make the adventurers comfortable, but so far Sam had been more trustworthy than them.

"We need a target to give them," Sam replied, ignoring the question as he focused on the more important matters. "Let's hope that we find something useful ahead of us. How long until we get there?"

"Another two hours or so," the barbarian growled back, but his posture relaxed a bit more when he saw that Sam was planning to work with the church.

Sam pulled out a message scroll of his own, recorded a short message to tell Lenei about the Coldfangs and their plans, and sent it off. Perhaps it would be enough for the church to send their main force here. After that, he focused on studying the enchantments on the stones as they passed, recording the shapes in his memory, where they swirled like clouds in the sky.

The lines on the grey stones were only abstract swirls and jagged lines, but he had the feeling that there was something deeper there, something that gave rise to that silver-green energy that was still slowly building. Above, Caelus was high in the sky as the day headed toward noon.

***

About twenty feet ahead of them, there was a bank of snow resting on top of an overhanging stone. As the Lykaris passed under it, it slid off, falling directly on top of her. It was deep enough to bury her to the waist and it left her covered in snow that sat heavily on her fur cap and shoulders. A muffled exclamation of anger erupted from her as she struggled to escape, tossing snow in every direction.

Little flickers of flame ran along her skin, melting some of it, but it wasn't enough to remove all of it. It just left her half wet and miserable.

"I hate snow," the Lykaris grumbled from ahead as she tugged her foot out of the snowbank, her movements jittery. As it turned out, her name was Selis. She was covered in the stuff, which was stuck to her in wet clumps.

"The feeling is mutual, I imagine," Arene replied drily. The priestess tried to help as she dusted the Lykaris off, sweeping off piles of the stuff. "It clearly hates you back."

Serves them right for causing trouble.

By comparison, Sam was feeling very comfortable. The snow was pleasantly brisk and as soon as it touched his skin, it brushed along and then fluttered away again, almost as if it were greeting him. There wasn't a trace of it melting or making him uncomfortable, even when it met his crystal flame. Somehow, the two elements danced around each other, each in their own place.

Even the flurry that had been kicked up from the falling snowbank simply blew past, leaving him untouched.

His father and the others were the same. All of them were relaxed in the snow, supported by the Ice trait that Siwaha had given them. So far, the adventurers hadn't really caught on, although they did send them a dirty look from time to time when the snow seemed to glide around them. Sam didn't feel obliged to tell them the reason. Even if he'd wanted to, it was more the Ice Sylphs' secret to tell than his.

Instead, he just took it as a small bit of justice that the adventurers were having a worse time than he was.

"The point we're heading for is just around that bend," the barbarian announced, whose name was Cesten. "There's still a little way to go, but we should be able to see it clearly from there. It's time to keep quiet."

From what Cesten had said, the Coldfangs were gathered around a broken stone building just up ahead. Past that, on the next layer up, was the pillar they were looking for. The two locations were visible to each other, but if they were careful, they might be able to draw out the rest of the Coldfangs without alerting anything above. Beside him, the wizard-mage, Obel, frowned and reached into his sleeves, pulling out a wand that he had there.

"Aren't a dozen too many to handle?" he asked nervously, with quick darting glances at the snow ahead and then to the side. "What if there's another Pack Leader, or two...or something worse?"

The wizard was a bumbling, frightened sort, not at all what Sam had expected of an adventurer, but he seemed to have the right instincts in a fight, even if it was mostly to hold the defense.

"We'll see what's there and work together," Jeric replied. "If it's too much, or if there's a Flaw there, we'll call for reinforcements first."

At that reminder, Sam woke up the Guardian Star again, letting it search the area. When it finished, its words were simple and blunt.

No Flaw detected within five miles.

"Let's take a few minutes to get ready, before we go looking for trouble," Cesten suggested, looking at Selis and then at the others. The Lykaris was still disgustedly trying to scrape snow out of her clothing. "Whatever you fellows can do, we're probably going to need it."

Sam reached into his belt and pulled free a couple of the scrolls he'd made back at the inn, studying them. After a moment, he looked up. All around him, there was blue-white snow drifting through the air and he could feel the currents of mana flowing past him from the peak as they headed to the valley below.

Thoughts about Advanced auras, spell patterns, and the resonance of natural runes flickered in his mind as he considered how to cause the most destruction possible.

CHAPTER THIRTY-FOUR

A RUINED BUILDING

The building in front of them was a tumbled-down circular ruin, more intact in some parts than in others. What had once been the front wall and entrance was a shattered mess, but the back and sides were still standing and had most of a roof attached. The snow was piled up half a dozen feet deep around the sides of the building, like a silent blanket cradling the structure.

Above, the sky was just starting to fade to dusk as Caelus moved across the horizon. From their position now, the blue moon was almost directly above Sun Rest, waiting to fall below the horizon on the opposite side.

As the moonlight touched the mountain, the silver-green energy in the ruins hummed more loudly, its pitch increasing until it was impossible for Sam to ignore. It wasn't exactly a sound, but instead the vibration of the mana here rising until it was as distracting as a river rushing through a stone valley.

As the moonlight fell, the ruins started to glow in the dusk, the silver-green energy rising up out of the stones to illuminate them. All around, tumbled stones and broken buildings came to life, their forms shining beneath the snow.

It was an ethereal sight, a ghostly, silver-green city sleeping beneath the snow.

"Now," his father whispered, his hand resting on Sam's shoulder as the two of them moved forward. To the left and right, the others moved forward as well, with everyone divided into pairs.

Krana was with Lesat to the left, heading up around the corner of a broken wall as they moved forward toward the target. The adventurers were off to the right, divided into two teams with the wizard and ranger together in one and the barbarian and priestess together in the other.

Selis and Obel, and Cesten and Arene, he muttered to himself, reminding himself of their names. If they were going to work together, he should at least try to remember that.

If he wanted to get along with people in the world, he was going to have to make allowances for their initial reaction to his appearance. Maybe his standard greeting in the future would be a death threat. It had worked pretty well on these four.

Get over it or die.

He smiled for an instant before he pushed the thought aside and headed around the corner, keeping pace with his father.

They'd spent a little while spying on this building, and as far as he could tell, there were at least ten more Coldfang Beheaders here, including one Pack Leader. It looked like half of their force had gone off to chase the adventurers before.

Hopefully, there would be some evidence here that led them to the Grand Flaw.

There were four guards visible on the outside of the building, keeping watch with their long, furred bodies lying in the snow while their heads turned from side to side. Their eyes were a bright blue-green and reflected the light of the moon above. For now, they were calm. They almost looked half asleep as they kept watch.

On the slope above, the pillar that Cesten's team wanted to reach was just out of sight around a curve in the stone. It was likely that anything they did down here would draw attention, so he had to make sure to be ready for whatever came.

He could sense the essence in the guards like a beacon, one that was singing with a threat. It was a sizzling presence. He did his best to keep his own essence calm, trying to hide his presence. So far, it seemed like it was working.

Now.

The signal passed in a wave from Jeric to Cesten. The amulet on Sam's chest pulsed a moment later with Krana and Lesat's acknowledgement. All four teams attacked at the same time, each of them targeting a guard with their swiftest spells and abilities.

A row of earthen spikes formed from the ground beneath the Cold-fang on the left, followed by a violet bolt of energy, a sphere of white flame, and a trio of flaming arrows that came in from the right. A Starfire flew out from Sam's hand, heading for one of the two middle guards.

The spells hurtled through the air, closing the distance in an instant, but before they could get too close, the four guards let out a roar as they surged to their feet. A dusky blue shield formed around them as they raised their bladed arms into the air, crossing them in front of their chests.

Their eyes swiveled toward Sam and a pulse of awareness echoed through the essence stars in his blood. An answering pulse came back from him, as he felt their presences pushing up against his senses. An emotion that was a lot like mockery pressed against his senses as their eyes settled on him.

Damn it. They were waiting for us.

Either his efforts to conceal his presence hadn't worked or they'd already known they were there. Their passivity had been a ruse.

KraaAATOOOOmmm!

At that point, the attacks collided with the Coldfangs' barriers, re-sulting in an explosive impact that ripped through the area. The force washed over their defense, eroding patches of their shield and tearing holes, but it was nowhere near as effective as he'd hoped it would be.

Most of the sound came from the explosion of Starfire, but the other attacks added their own reverberating notes that turned the area around the building into a beacon for anything within a mile or more. He cursed, wishing he could have raised a privacy barrier, but it hadn't been possible with the distance.

The attacks killed two of the four, including one of those hit by Starfire, but the other two survived. The Outsiders' heads tilted back to the sky as they let out another roar, further ruining any attempt at stealth as they alerted everything inside the building.

A surge of more Coldfangs poured out of the ruined wall that made up the face of the building, their blade arms raised. The wall was broken enough that they were outside in an instant, eight of them joining the two still alive.

He was expecting the ten Outsiders to charge forward and attack, but strangely, they didn't. Their eyes glittered with a cold malice and a sheen of threatening blue energy ran up and down their ice blades, but they held their position.

Thud.

The ruins trembled as something inside the building began to move, sending out a deep, muffled echo. Strangely, the stones beneath the blanket of the snow didn't shift at all, and neither did the mountain beneath his feet. The sound was unnatural, felt more in his blood and essence sense than in reality. His father frowned, turning toward the sound as well, which meant that Sam wasn't the only one to hear it.

ThuuUUdd.

It came again, even louder, as something large forced its way out of the ruined building. The first glimpse of it was of something with scales. It was green, with striations of white and grey mixed in, like lichen that was growing where the scales met.

A large, bumpy head forced its way out of the ruined building, letting out a roar as its mouth dropped open to reveal a set of fangs twice as large as the wyverns he'd seen before. Its head swiveled toward them as large grey eyes swirled, hidden deeply within hardened ridges of green scales. They held a deadly, shining light.

Greystone Basilisk. Outsider. Level 68.

The Outsider forced its way out of the ruins, shouldering aside slabs of stone and snowdrifts. The building was barely able to hold it. Every moment or two, another *thud* echoed out in the area. Its eyes were the size of dinner plates, dominating its bumpy, scaled head that resembled a lizard's. A series of rough, stubby spikes rose out of the back of its skull like a mane and continued down its spine.

When it was fully revealed, it was nearly forty feet long and almost fifteen feet wide at the shoulders. It had four legs, similar to a lizard. The bumpy green scales with grey and white growths along them covered it from head to tail, with darker scales on its back and sides and a pale, white-green underbelly.

Its tail was long with a bone club and spike at the end, and it lashed at the ground as it walked. As it struck the ground, the *thud* rang out again.

There was a dense glow of essence around the thing's head and tail, and from the pressure it was giving off, it was clear the basilisk was the strongest enemy he'd ever faced.

If it had to fight a wyvern, unless the wyvern managed to fly away, this thing would pulverize it. Its scales looked at least twice as thick as a wyvern's, along with whatever abilities it had as an Outsider.

Now that it was free of the building, its gaze lashed around the area, taking in everything that was happening. A long, rolling *hisss* came out of its mouth as it saw them, followed by a wave of pressure.

It hit their senses like a tidal wave, rolling over them with a crushing intent that tried to lock them in place.

The essence stars in Sam's blood and his crystal flame both surged in response, pushing outward as his battle aura surrounded him instinctively, along with a massive wave of crystal flame that spiraled around his body.

He could feel the aura trying to sink into him, weighing down on his limbs and lungs, but his defenses pushed it back with a competing pressure, burning it away.

Essence-Based Attack Detected.

Ability Analyzed: *Aura of Paralysis*.

World Core Alerted to Outsider Presence....

The Guardian Star suddenly spoke up, followed a moment later by the cold voice of the World Law that resonated in his mind.

Non-Authorized Essence-Based Entity Detected.

Analysis received from Guardian Star of Sam Hastern.

Outsider Identified: Escaped Prisoner from Aster Fall World Seal.

As the closest Authority of Law, you are tasked to eliminate it.

Time Limit: One day before other authorities are summoned.

Elite Tier Reward Available.

"This isn't good." Beside him, his father's face was strained, but he was still moving and able to speak. His Constitution and Earth class were enough to withstand the basilisk's Aura of Paralysis, but past him, it looked like the others were in more serious trouble.

"Nearly everyone is frozen in place."

The basilisk outleveled most of them by fifteen to twenty levels, and its aura was wreaking havoc.

Sam didn't have much time to analyze what the World Law was telling him, but it was clear that this Outsider was different from the Coldfangs. It was the first thing he'd ever encountered that made the Guardian Star react like this.

Because it had escaped from the Seal.

That meant every other Outsider so far had come in from somewhere else.

Memories of the void stretching out into the distance came to him from his dreams, and the Outsiders' desire for the stars. They weren't just in the prison of the World Seal. They were still out there somewhere among the stars, wherever they had first come from.

The other side of the Nexus.

He didn't know what they were doing here or how they were all working together. They could be trying to free the prisoners or the basilisk might have escaped due to the presence of the Flaw.

Whatever it was, he had to stop it.

He couldn't imagine this thing stomping its way through the Ice Sylph village, heading for his mother and sister.

That was all he had time to consider as the basilisk turned its head from side to side, studying them as its jaw gaped wide, revealing teeth the size of Sam's arm and a pointed, grey and pink tongue.

Its tail rose into the air and slammed to the ground with another great, resounding *thud* that shook through his bones. It let out a roar as spit flew from its jaws, making the Coldfangs in front of it shake as the force passed over them.

The roar mixed with the Aura of Paralysis and became an attack all its own. When it hit him, he felt the sonic vibration of it trying to shake him apart, as well as that heavy, deadening pressure from the aura trying to sink into his limbs.

The basilisk's abilities were a powerful combination for fighting crowds, paralyzing them and then shaking them apart, and that was before its size and strength came into play.

Whatever place this beast came from, it was beyond dangerous.

The essence stars in his blood formed an internal network that was resisting part of the pressure, but it wasn't enough by itself. The formation there wasn't complete and it wasn't able to operate efficiently.

However the ranks of essence worked, this beast was much stronger than him.

His Aura of Crystal Flame and essence pool took up the slack, pouring out of his body and pushing aside the attack as they gave him the space to move.

Beside him, his father was surrounded in the golden gleam of stamina and his Earthen Shield. His veins stood out in stark lines against his muscles as he pushed forward, his hammers in his hands.

His Constitution was still enough to resist, but it wasn't clear how long he could endure it.

"We have to stop that thing," Jeric growled, looking to both sides as he pushed forward. "Or we're all going to die. Sam, you figure out a way to shut it up and get rid of this pressure, if you can. The others aren't handling it well. I'll work on the Coldfangs and try to lead it in a circle. It can't be that fast in all this snow."

With that, Jeric let out a roar of his own as he burst into movement, racing bravely across the top of the snow toward the basilisk.

He was a tiny figure compared to its bulk, but the weight of his presence in Sam's mind was much more important.

A spike of true panic passed through Sam for the first time in months as he saw his father running into danger. Even against the first wyvern, as bloody as that had been, he'd been confident in fixing things.

Now, he wasn't so sure.

Ahead of him, the Coldfangs split into a wave that charged forward, their clawed feet carrying them on top of the snow. The basilisk was the main force, but these were the scouts, light and quick, to harass the foe.

If he didn't deal with them, they would end up pinning his father down.

He unleashed every charge he had in the Starflame bracer at them, sending a wave of 200 star-tipped blue arrows hurtling across the snow like a field of sparkling meteors.

Their bladed arms rose and blue shields surrounded them again. At the same time as he attacked, he saw other attacks coming in from the left and right.

The Coldfangs were in a loose half-circle and explosive impacts rippled across their shields, tearing through the gaps.

Starflame arrows exploded around their legs, backs, under their feet, and shattered chunks of their barriers, tearing holes for other arrows to rip through.

Shattering eruptions of blue and white light, star-like bursts as each arrow exploded, and then flares of Earthen spikes and other spells all arrived at once.

A flare of yellow Earth magic sprang up from his left as Krana's spells struck, letting him know that she'd managed to resist the aura and was still there.

Next to her, Lesat was having a much harder job of it, straining to move as the enchantments on his armor and shield buffered him from the attack. There was blood leaking from the corner of his mouth.

The adventurers to his right were less successful, but there was a shaky violet bolt that came in from Obel, who was doing better than Selis. The Lykaris seemed to be frozen in place, her skin turning grey.

Past them, Arene was slumped forward, her hand outward as she tried to ward off the basilisk's aura, but she hadn't managed it completely. Half of her arm was also turning grey. Cesten was next to her, his legs braced as he raised a spear into the air to throw.

Useless, he growled as he pushed them out of his mind. His father was the only one he needed to worry about.

The snow flickered under his feet as he raced forward, his battle aura springing out from the partially-completed essence formation.

CHAPTER THIRTY-FIVE

GREYSTONE BASILISK

His father raced through the scattered Coldfangs, following the path that the starflame arrows had cleared. A moment later, he sprang into the air, leaping twenty feet as he aimed for the top of the basilisk's head.

The basilisk reared upward, its head tilting back like a lizard's as its mouth opened, preparing to swallow him. A yellow Earthen Shield appeared below Jeric's feet as the monster's fangs tried to close around him, giving him enough of a platform that he launched off again, jumping onto the back of its head.

His hammers swung down, resonating with their enchantments as he slammed them into the basilisk's eye ridges. The Outsider reared up again, tossing its head backward, but Jeric hooked an arm around one of its spines and attacked again.

He wasn't doing much damage, but he was definitely getting its attention. The Outsider's aura wobbled, weakening for an instance before coming back even stronger than before as it let out another roar.

Going head-on with a Level 68 Outsider the size of a building was not a good idea. They had to find a weakness.

Sam grabbed two auras from his storage as he followed his father, combusting them to top his essence off.

Two dozen crystal flame arrows blasted away from him, dividing into groups as they flashed toward the remaining Coldfangs. Four of the ten had survived his first bombardment and their shields were in tatters. They were scattered across the snowy field in front of the building.

The arrows impacted in sizzling streaks, tearing holes through the injured creatures. Their blade arms blocked a few, but they were too slow to get most of them. Chunks of Coldfang exploded outward from the impacts.

Another flight of arrows followed, targeting the two that were still moving as he cleared the path. As he continued forward, a row of earthen spikes rose up from beneath the basilisk's feet, stabbing into its claws. It was enough to make it shift its position, pulling up that foot as it moved to the side.

To his left, Krana was a shimmering silver and yellow figure as her mana poured out into the world. She was trying to help where she could, earthen spikes and shields forming to assist Jeric.

His father took advantage of the beast's movement to hook his arm more securely around the spikes at the back of its head. His free hand came down again, hammering into the beast's scales with a resonant tattoo as he worked to break through its scales.

Whatever else it was, the basilisk was not a normal Level 68 monster. Its scales began to gleam with a grey-green light as the essence in it surged, flooding upward toward the human who was bothering it.

A flare of warning passed through Sam. He couldn't let that ability land. It would probably turn his father into a stone statue.

A Starfire formed in his hand as he threw it toward the basilisk, aiming for the area directly under its chest. The spell exploded under the basilisk at the same time as Jeric abandoned his position and leapt away, jumping off before the grey-green light could reach him.

The Starfire's eruption sent the basilisk rearing upward, its neck and head flexing like a whip as it absorbed the brunt of the impact. Its front feet went ten feet into the air and a series of explosive cracks sounded from the giant armor scales on its chest.

A wave of rocky spikes stabbed up from below, filling the space below it as the basilisk crashed down on top of them. Shards of rock went flying in every direction as Krana's spears exploded from its weight.

Streaks of green blood poured out from its chest, and for a moment, Sam thought the attack might have worked, or at least broken the basilisk's armor. Then, the Outsider's grey-green essence rippled over its chest, sealing the wounds as a layer of stone appeared on top of them.

Small injuries weren't going to be enough to stop it.

Jeric landed on the ground to the far side of the basilisk, turning his jump into a roll as he hit. He sprang to his feet and pulled a scroll from his belt as he turned, activating it with one hand.

A storm of icy shards flew outward from him, slamming into the basilisk's face and making it turn toward him. He spun away, another scroll appearing in his hand as he ran toward the ruined building, trying to lure it after him.

Thud.

The basilisk's tail slammed into the ground as it spun around, shattering more of the stone spikes beneath it. It took several quick steps after Jeric, its movements faster now that it was angry. He'd managed to get its attention.

The Aura of Paralysis around the area was still strong. If he could get it far enough away, perhaps the others would be able to recover, but it would be better to deal with it directly.

Sam's mind raced as he thought of the possible options, and how his crystal flame would damage the basilisk. If he poured in enough energy, he was able to cut through stone, but the basilisk had a huge body.

Relying on his own energy and combusting auras would only give him a dozen or so Starfires. He wasn't sure that would be enough. He needed to get through the scales.

Fortunately, he had some other options.

His hands flickered as he pulled a series of auras out of his storage, tracking the basilisk's movements as it started to pursue his father. After that, he pulled a scroll from his belt. He used tendrils of crystal flame to float it all in front of him, giving him extra hands.

It was an Advanced-tier Wind scroll and it dissolved in a spiral of whipping, silver light that turned into a tornado of force in his hand. He held it there, wrapping the spell structure in his essence to stabilize it as he pulled an aura toward him.

Aura of Spiraling Wind.

With his essence as a guide and the practice from creating a layered spell with Starfire, he infused the aura into the spell, using Assume Aura to pour it into the spell structure.

They were both Wind-aligned and the spell soaked up the aura in the same way that an enchantment would. The whirlwind spun faster, its energy taking on a green tinge. It was good that his Essence Control was at the Expert Tier, or what he was doing now might not have been possible.

He grabbed another aura, this one of Verdant Leaf, and poured that into the spell as well. He didn't try to infuse this one into the heart of the spell. Instead, he created a layer of energy around it that glowed with a healthy green light.

Following that, he added another layer from an Aura of Compressed Flame, and then he took an aura from the Icesoul Wraiths, the Aura of Desolate Life, and poured it into a third layer. For the final layer, he used an Aura of Shifting Shadow, covering the spell in a dark grey, swirling barrier that concealed much of the energy inside.

The scroll had started out with about thirty points of essence. When he was done, it was strengthened with twenty from the Wind aura and then covered in four layers of enhancive energy that had another twenty each, for a total of 130.

He looked up, tracking the basilisk. It was chasing his father, stomping back toward the ruined building. Jeric was taunting it, darting in and out as he attacked its face to keep its attention.

Sam held the layered scroll in his left hand as he ran forward. An Essence Blade began to form in his right, its focused cutting edge more useful right now than the all-encompassing blast of Starfire.

As best he could, he focused on the *star* rune in his bracer, using it to help construct the Essence Blade. He'd experimented with the bracer on forming spells besides Starfire, but he wasn't as practiced with them.

The result was slightly unstable and not really an Essence Blade at all. The structure had changed to something halfway between it and Starfire, warping into a triangular wedge with a rippling white core. The *star* rune was at the point, just behind a single layer of crystal flame.

He was going to have to recreate all of his spells to use the *star* rune as a central concept.

The basilisk roared as it chased Jeric, stomping through the deep snow and hurling it in every direction. Its tail swept across the ground, sending up a wave of snow and rocks that crashed toward Sam as he got closer.

An Essence Shield flowed around him, tearing through the snow as stones rang off the edges and flew away. Then he was through, closing in on the ruins and the backside of the basilisk.

The monster's tail swept backward again, the spiked club on it hurtling toward him in a deadly blur. He sensed it with Crystal Focus as he threw himself to the ground, cradling the spells in front of his chest as he landed on his shoulder and rolled.

Then he was up and running again. His Constitution made the fall irrelevant. Ahead of him, the basilisk's rear leg was like an armored pillar, and he sprinted around it, his attention focused on its movements.

His father was back on top of the thing, hammering at its right eye with one hand while hanging on with the other. The basilisk reared up as it flung its head into the air, trying to dislodge him. The grey-green energy of its essence began to ripple through its scales.

"Look over here!" Sam shouted at it, trying to get its attention as he sprinted toward its head. A half dozen crystal flame arrows surged ahead of him, striking like fireflies just behind its right shoulder, where its scales were thinner.

The basilisk let out an angry hiss, annoyed more by the essence in the arrows than the damage. Its legs shifted sideways as it stomped around, spinning in place toward the new threat. Its head was the size of a carriage, horses included, and its eyes were swirling disks as big as a door, far larger than they should have been for its size.

He felt the attack before he saw it as a web of essence flared out of those eyes and headed straight for him. It was a sticky spiderweb of grey-green lines and as wide across as the basilisk's head.

The attack collided with his Essence Shield in front of him, which flared to life with a brilliant sapphire flame. The basilisk's essence was a cold, grasping hand that pulled at his energy, trying to drain it away and convert it to something else as it worked to petrify his flames.

The crystalline structure of his shield worked in his favor, slowing down the effect and holding it off as he burned away the strands one by one, but it slowed him down.

An enormous, scaled foot slammed into his shield before he could move as the basilisk's right foreleg came around, its claws as long as his arm.

The impact lifted him off the ground and sent him flying two dozen feet away as another dozen points of essence went into his shield. Its jaws gaped wide as it swung its head back toward him and surged forward, ignoring Jeric on its back as it tried to bite the enemy in front of it.

Sam rolled across the ground as he absorbed the impact of the blow and sprang to his feet just in time to see the head swinging in his direction. The basilisk's gaping maw loomed over him. Since it was giving him such a large target, he couldn't help but oblige it.

Both of the spells in his hands flew forward, first the Essence Blade and then the layered Wind spell. They headed straight for the basilisk's open mouth.

He had time to see them fly into its throat, but that was all. The basilisk bit down on the spells and suddenly bent in a half-circle, its tail flying toward him, and he threw a burst of crystal flame in front of him as he flung himself backward.

The explosions were a muffled, distant echo as the tail swept toward him. It undulated in the air, surrounded by the basilisk's essence, as it soared toward him. His evasion wasn't taking him out of range fast enough. It felt like the air around him was trying to turn to stone, making it hard to move.

A moment later, the tail slammed into his Essence Shield with the force of a mountain erupting, like a boulder breaking through a castle wall. It wasn't just a normal weapon. It had some strange effect of extra weight to it. Shards of crystal flame flew in every direction and turned to wisps as the bone club on the end slammed into Sam's chest.

His battle aura buffered some of the impact in a giant flare of energy as his essence exploded outward, but he felt his ribs shattering and the left side of his torso collapse as he was picked up and hurled away.

The weight of the strike stayed with him, pressing into his bones as he felt the energy in it trying to twist him out of shape. It wanted to break every part of him, to crush him and grind him to dust.

The partially-complete essence formation in his blood resisted the pressure as the stars flared to life, burning outward as they tried to absorb it, but they had limited success. He flew through the air for fifty feet before he slammed into a snowbank that had built up against a stone pillar.

The weight of the strike followed him, crushing down on top of him again with what felt like the basilisk's entire body. It was like a mountain landing on him. The essence formation flared to brilliance as tiny crystal blue stars appeared across his body, burning so brightly that they were visible through his skin.

The Amulet of Swirling Winds also came to life, pouring its mana out as it tried to block the strike, but its barrier shattered a moment later as it ran dry, leaving only the formation and what remained of his essence pool to resist.

The attack wasn't dissipating like it should have. Whatever strange ability the basilisk had used, it was sticking to him like the strike still wanted to wipe him from existence. He felt his skin cracking as lines of blood emerged, bursting to the surface. Flickers of crystal blue flame escaped.

He had about sixty essence left and he poured nearly all of it into an Essence Shield. The crystalline dome flared with scintillating light as he tried to push himself away from the strike.

The power of the attack slammed down on him and he felt his shield shattering as a heavy, twisting force ripped it apart from opposing angles.

The Ring of Crystal Shield shattered next, the core in it exploding as it released all of its energy. 200 points of essence flared, surrounding him in a shield like a crystal egg.

He used the last of his strength for evasion, pushing off from the ground as he shoved the energy to the side and rolled away. It was like levering off a boulder, but he managed it with a mangled growl, his remaining lung barely working.

The crystal shell from the ring parted, releasing him as it stayed behind, and a moment later it shattered as the basilisk's attack drove through it and into the rock behind.

His bones and muscles were mangled, many of them broken in multiple places by the twisting force, but the essence formation in his blood flowed into the broken areas, spreading farther than ever before as it stretched outward, filling the areas that had just been drained of energy.

For that moment, it supported him, an internal web that held his bones and muscles together and forced his lungs to work, but it wasn't free. It was enough to let him move, but he felt his essence draining away moment by moment, as well as a building need for more.

He rose shakily to his feet, staggering, as a burning emptiness spread through him, demanding that he fill it. It was an all-consuming hunger, like a devouring void that stretched into the darkness.

Looking down, he saw tendrils of dark energy running across his body, connecting the essence stars.

The stars and their connections were usually a crystalline blue, lighter or darker sometimes, but always blue. Now, that dark hunger had joined it, forming its own type of energy.

Somehow, he'd reached a critical moment.

Using the formation to block some of the attack had triggered it, as if the threat of death were a dangerous catalyst. Now, he either had to finish the essence formation and fill it with energy, or this hunger would tear it apart and kill him.

Across the field, the basilisk hadn't escaped unscathed from his attack. It was hunched close to the ground and thrashing, its eyes closed in pain as its mouth hung open. Chunks of internal organs and shattered teeth had been vomited across the ground, and there was a growing pool of blood all around it.

His father was on its head again, hammering down as the enchantments on his hammers built higher. There was a reverberating cascade of notes humming as natural runes began to form around him, the echoes coming to life.

Sam turned toward the corpses of the Coldfangs they'd just killed, the demand for essence sweeping outward. It felt like the world was falling in on him, the veins of mana and the auras of the world crumbling away to nothingness.

His eyesight blanked out as he stumbled, falling to the side. When he opened them again, an empty void stretched out in front of him, speckled with stars that were going dark.

To anyone watching, streamers of the same dark energy from the essence formation were now flowing through his eyes. The hunger twisted inwards as the dark threads grew thicker, taking over more of the blue.

A wordless roar ripped out of his mouth, his fangs bared as he slashed outward around him, his talons cutting toward the corpses of the Coldfangs.

A storm of essence sparks rose out of the dozen corpses all across the snowy field and filled the air with hundreds of flickering lights, like an army of spirits had been born from the ice.

At that moment, the basilisk let out a vicious roar as well. Its half-glazed eyes opened as its attention turned to the essence storm that was filling the air. A sense of palpable hunger poured out from it.

The basilisk's Aura of Paralysis flared all around the area. The sparks that were starting to flow toward Sam hesitated for a moment, slowing down as if they were suddenly surrounded by sand.

The Outsider's mouth opened as it lunged toward the essence, even as Jeric's hammers crashed into its skull again. Its eyes went unfocused for a moment, but it ignored the blows as it pushed itself to its feet. Its gait was unsteady, but it was moving, pulled by a deep-seated need.

If it got ahold of all of that essence, it wasn't clear what would happen.

Sam snarled, the dark lines devouring his energy growing thicker by the instant, as he *called* out to the essence all around him. There were no words in his call, just a command.

It was a matter of life and death. Either he absorbed that essence, or in the next few instants, everything that made up who he was would be consumed by the void that was expanding through his blood.

The essence was *his*. He would not abide a challenger.

The basilisk's attempt to gain control of the essence was stronger than the Iceblood Shaman's had been, but it wasn't enough to interfere with Sam's call for long. As if sensing that, the basilisk began to move more quickly, its feet scrabbling at the snow and stones as it pushed toward the feast in front of it.

It paid no attention to Jeric's continued attacks, even as the scales around its eyes and forehead started to shatter, or to the adventurers all around who were starting to recover from the Aura of Paralysis now that its attention was distracted.

The parts of their bodies that had turned to stone were not recovering, which left Selis and Arene half-crippled, but those with a higher Constitution were starting to move. Lesat was on the border and as the aura faded from him, his strength returned. He and Krana began to rush forward, chasing after the basilisk.

Sam ignored all of it as he focused on the essence in front of him. It felt like his body was tearing apart as the void between the essence stars expanded again.

Come to me!

He called to the essence again, commanding it, and it jerked free of the
basilisk's distraction, flowing across the snow toward him faster as its color
began to change to a deep crystal blue. When the first sparks hit his body,
it was like cool water on a parched desert, soaking into his skin with an
instant sense of relief.

The void stretched before his eyes as the flicker of new stars appeared in
the distance. Tiny, blue stars that gleamed with life. They began to spiral
around, flowing through the void as they moved toward the darkness.

It wasn't enough and the strength of his call intensified, pulling more
toward him. All around him, the storm of essence surged, turning to a
brilliant blue as it flew into him in a swirling cloud.

The dark lines edging his eyes turned bright sapphire as he felt something
in his body cracking and expanding. His meridians burned and the lines of
the constellation that was the essence formation shifted, carving new lines.

A second system.

The new essence flowed into his blood, filling the darkness with life. Star
after star was born as strands of essence connected them together, and they
flew into place in the constellation, completing it.

It was a swirling, multi-layered formation that spiraled through his body
and soul, its lines gleaming bright blue.

Racial Essence: 1,147 / 1,000.

There was a silence that pervaded everything as the world around him
paused. The attention of the World Law pressed down on him with the
all-encompassing weight of a mountain.

**Congratulations, Essence Bearer. You have formed your initial
Essence Constellation and taken the first step to advancing your
Race.**

Choose your Racial Path now.

A list of options unfurled before him as time froze, but it was a short list.

Your bloodline grants you access to the following paths.

Path of Devouring.

Path of Blood.

Path of the Elements.

Path of Transformation.

Path of Stealth.

Each of them came with a burst of information that was limited, but
incredibly important.

The Path of Devouring focused on killing other forms of life and consuming it for energy, and at higher levels, non-living things as well. If he chose it, he would gain a Racial Ability to Devour Life.

The Path of Blood was about commanding forms of blood and life essence, whether for healing or destruction. For that, he would gain an ability for Blood Manipulation, which would grow into more complex things as he gained power.

The Path of Elements was similar to the one he had already started to walk, focusing on the elements that made up existence. Choosing it would add a racial ability for Elemental Manipulation. It was a more general ability than anything he had so far, its reach wider, but more diffuse.

The Path of Transformation focused on changing his appearance, strength, and body. At higher levels, it also allowed him to transform other things. It would give him an ability for Physical Transformation.

The Path of Stealth focused on concealment, infiltration, and deception. It would give him the ability to create illusions, hide in the shadows, and change his appearance.

Both the Path of Transformation and Stealth were tempting, since he would be able to change his appearance with either of them, and perhaps to hide his race and other information. For a moment, he considered them.

No matter how tempting that was, however, it was a short-term goal, and he would be able to accomplish the same thing on his own, as soon as his enchanting improved.

The various paths gave him a great deal of insight into the basic powers of Outsiders, at least of the ones who looked like him.

It felt like time was slow, but that didn't mean he had all the time in the world to deliberate on the choices, so he took the one that felt the most right to him.

Congratulations, Essence Bearer.

You have chosen *The Path of the Elements*.

As no Elder of your race is present, the World Core will assist you in configuring your soul essence to align with your Path.

With that, the power of the World Core poured into his body and wrapped around the essence constellation in his blood. A heavy, silver energy poured into the constellation, flowing through the strands.

Under the command of the World Core, the formation shifted, spinning like a nebula as it took on a shape similar to a natural rune. It was only a small change, like aligning the pattern to a particular magnetic pull, but the effect was immediate.

You have gained the *Racial Ability: Elemental Manipulation*.

For each new layer you add to your Essence Constellation, your ability will advance through a new tier.

He felt a sudden connection, a new awareness of the elemental energies all around him, and then he also felt his attributes rising.

Attribute Gain Quantified by Aster Fall Standard.

Strength increased by 4.

Constitution increased by 6.

Agility increased by 2.

Intelligence increased by 9.

Aura increased by 9.

Then the World Law's voice disappeared and time sped up again, as he saw the last flickering mote of essence from the Coldfangs disappear into his skin.

Racial Essence (First Layer): 1,151 / 2,500.

STR: 31

CON: 66 (68 with Belt of Gentle Climes)

AGI: 26

WIS: 47

INT: 139 (145 with Starfire Bracer)

AUR: 139 (145 with Starfire Bracer)

CHA: 30

All the aches and broken areas throughout his body flared back into his awareness as he saw the basilisk running toward him. His father was still on top of it and Krana and Lesat were chasing it from behind.

Its tongue lolled out of its mouth like an enormous whip of pink and grey that was stained with its own green blood. Its eyes were disks of furious, swirling essence as it headed for him in an uncoordinated charge, a bow wave of snow surging away from it.

Chapter Thirty-Six

BOUNTY HUNTER

His essence was nearly depleted, so Sam grabbed four auras from his storage and combusted them, taking himself back up to 92. He'd have grabbed more, but he wasn't sure how much his meridians could handle. Then he braced himself for the basilisk.

It arrived like an avalanche, pushing a tide of snow and rocks in front of it like a creature born from some frozen sea. The wave was nearly ten feet above the rest of the snow and only the top of the monster was visible behind it.

Before it could get any closer, a pulse of crystal flame pushed Sam to the side as he evaded. Racial advancement or not, he didn't plan to face the thing head on. A quick assessment pulled together all of his resources.

Sam's feet flickered as he ran on top of the snow, the elemental powder compressing beneath his feet on its own as it supported his weight. The flow of ice mana through the air all around him, as well as half a dozen other elements grabbed at his attention. The new Elemental Manipulation ability was bringing him more information than he'd had before.

Ice felt similar, like it had since he'd gained the Initiate of Ice trait, and he'd always been able to sense Fire well, but Earth and Stone around him had become more pronounced, as well as Wind, Water, and other types that he didn't have time to identify.

The elements had a liveliness and closeness to them that hadn't been before, as if he only had to reach out for them to respond. Fire and Ice were the most pronounced, but the others were there too.

His Essence Constellation had reached the first layer and was humming in his blood as his essence flowed along it, almost like another set of meridians. The pattern was unfamiliar, but it looked a lot like a natural rune that extended in three dimensions.

The basilisk spun to follow him, its enormous bulk turning as the wave of snow and stone crashed against a wall in the ruins, burying it more deeply. Icy powder flew in a giant curtain into the sky.

He didn't have any new idea for how to defeat the basilisk, so it was going to have to be pure force. He pulled another scroll from his belt pouch with one hand as he grabbed auras from his storage with the other. It took him about fifteen seconds to infuse the five auras into the Advanced Fire scroll.

When it was ready, he spun back around, a fiery sphere of tumbling blue, green, and red to yellow-streaked flames surging in his left hand. Around it, there was a layer of bubbling, dark shadow and frozen lightning that were barely containing the wrath within. At the heart of the spell, a *star* rune burned with brilliant white light.

With his new Elemental Manipulation, It felt like the elements were just a little easier to control than before, and it was easier to infuse the *star* rune into the center.

On the basilisk's back, his father hung on grimly with one hand as the Outsider flailed like a massive ship on the snow, one that was crashing into port. It slipped, its feet clawing for a grip beneath the snow as it floundered. Then its weight crashed down into the snow as it caught its balance and charged toward him.

A Starfire formed in his right hand as he threw aside his evasive tactics and headed straight for it. Its eyes spun with that sticky web of essence as it fixed its gaze on him, and his shield burned around him with an evanescent halo of flames. The *Stone* element in the essence was readily apparent to him, even as he pushed it aside. It was mixed with the basilisk's personal signature and there were a couple of other elements present, but it was primarily that.

The basilisk's jaws opened as it lunged for him, its fangs widening. The marks of the last explosion were apparent throughout its mouth, burned areas and broken fangs on every side. The Starfire and infused Fire spells were two shooting stars, one blue-white and one a strange amalgamation of twisting colors as they both headed for its mouth.

Its pink-grey tongue shot out toward them, but the monster's instincts were to capture and eat, not to avoid. Its jaws snapped closed around the spells and a moment later the layers around them shattered, igniting the runes at the center.

Muffled explosions tore through the air as the basilisk convulsed, its head slamming backward.

Sam threw himself to the side, pushing as fast as he could to get out of range. At the same time, Jeric released his grip, flying away from the basilisk in an arc before he slammed into a pile of snow forty feet away. The snow flowed around him, sinking to cushion his fall, but the impact was hard enough that he was buried almost eight feet deep.

The basilisk's body swelled like a snake that had swallowed too large of a meal and then its mouth opened in a roar, releasing a torrent of multi-colored flames that sprayed across the area.

The flames washed across the snow in an arc in front of the basilisk, melting it as a sizzling cloud of steam boiled into the air. The steam wasn't just from snow. A distinct odor of burning, coppery blood accompanied it.

The basilisk staggered, its wide-splayed claws spasming as its legs trembled. Its belly swelled wider as its neck pulsed and the monster gagged on its own destroyed organs, trying to breathe. The flames pouring from its mouth faded away to trickles, accompanied by the burnt stench of stone and something acrid.

When the clouds of steam cleared, the area in front of the basilisk was empty of snow. Instead, it was a torched black and grey expanse of ash resting on top of greenish paving stones.

The stones were precisely placed, their alignment still perfectly flat after all the years that had passed, with only a thin line visible to divide one stone from another. They stretched from one side of the open area to the other, part of a forgotten plaza or some open gallery.

The basilisk staggered, its claws sliding across the green stones without gaining any purchase, and then it slumped over, falling on its right side as its claws flailed feebly for purchase. It stretched out its neck as if it were trying to cough, and its chest swelled, but what poured out was a river of greenish blood mixed with black streaks and chunks of charred organs.

Jeric dug himself out of the pile of snow and started to run forward again, until Sam's voice rang out in an angry growl.

"Stop!" He wasn't planning to give it any time to recover, and he didn't want his father near it until it was dead. The shout halted Jeric as well as Krana and Lesat who were almost there.

The Outsider had been covered in a flowing layer of essence before that hardened its scales and acted as armor, but now that it was injured, that defense had disappeared.

Sam stepped forward as he poured his essence into creating a long, crystalline spear. Crystal flame surged with boiling anger and brilliant sapphire hues as he compressed it, forcing it together as he drew on his bracer to embed a *star* rune into the point.

His hands clenched on the haft, compressing it until it was blindingly bright. When it was ready, he stepped forward and timed it in between the basilisk's thrashing movement, aiming for one of its oversized grey-green eyes.

Then he hurled the spear with all of his strength.

The spearpoint blasted through the basilisk's eye with a sizzling *pop* and dove inwards, releasing a searing blast of crystal flame like a spike of meteoric fire as it burned through the creature's brain.

The scent of burnt copper and the acrid stench of acid-burned stone filled the air as the creature let out a final, dying groan and then slumped into the snow. A new wave of blood poured from its jaws.

Sam growled, his fangs bared, as a light pulse of hunger flashed through his essence constellation, like a memory of the void that had been there. He could sense the Stone element woven through the basilisk's scales as it separated from the more complex essence that had made up the monster.

As he watched, the basilisk's scales slowly turned white-grey, hardening into real stone as the essence that had filled it receded back somewhere into its corpse. The force of the World Law's attention weighed on the area, as if it were hanging there for the exact moment that the Outsider finally died.

The silence was expectant as they backed away, waiting to see if the thing was dead. The gore on top of the stones steamed, its heat dissipating as a layer of frost formed. It was gathering quickly and it drew Sam's attention to the flow of Ice mana through the area, which had started to increase.

There was a swirling pattern like rivers and flowing clouds on top of the stones in silvery-green lines, similar to the design on the pillars but thicker. As he watched, the moonlight struck the pattern and sank in, giving rise to a faint *chiming* sound. A moment later, another sound chimed in the air from a different region of the stone. With each chime, the Ice mana in the air intensified, as if it were being called by something.

The cold in the air deepened. A moment later, the clouds of steam froze, turning to dark crystalline flakes that drifted back down. Their color bleached under the force of the Ice mana, turning white before they touched the stones.

All around, more snowflakes began to drift down like a silent shroud. Within seconds, a thin layer of snow had formed on top of the revealed design. The chimes rang out twice more before the snow covered the visible stone. There was one last quiet chime as it continued to fall, and then the sound ceased.

In less than a minute, the revealed stones and the gore had all been buried in pristine white snow. A few moments later, the snow was three inches deep, covering nearly all of the gore, and it continued to fall steadily with deceptive speed.

The basilisk's corpse slowly turned whitish-grey from fangs to tail. Even the bone club at the end of its tail hardened, leaving just the spikes along its spine and the tip of its tail spur behind. Its remaining eye solidified to a dark greenish gem with a swirl of grey streaks.

When the changes stopped, the World Law's attention pressed down on the area, as if it were waiting, pushing Sam forward to gather the experience. When he touched the basilisk's corpse and found the silver thread of energy, it spoke, even as the layers of silvery light began to gather around him and the others.

The announcement was accompanied by the shimmering flow of experience chiming through his body.

Congratulations, Guardian. You have used your Class skills to eliminate an enemy of Aster Fall.

You gain 1,240,000 Class experience.

You have gained three Class Levels. You are now a Level 61 Battlefield Reclaimer.

You have gained three General Levels. You are now Level 61.

You gain +3 Intelligence, +3 Aura, and have nine free attribute points to assign.

Congratulations on reaching the Elite Tier.

You may choose one Class and one Subclass ability to upgrade by a Tier (to a maximum of Elite).

You may also choose one ability for your Class from the following list:
Transfer Aura
Shatter Aura
The notifications didn't stop there, even as he felt the experience settling into his body.

By eliminating an escaped prisoner from the Aster Fall World Seal, you have preserved the structure of the world.

You are *Acknowledged*.

Eliminate two more escaped prisoners or Flaws in order to remove the trait Defiant.

You have gained the Trait: *Bounty Hunter*.

[Bounty Hunter: *You gain an enhanced awareness of which creatures are natural to Aster Fall and which are not, as well as the ability to see through some illusions and forms of concealment. +5 Wisdom.*]

Elite Tier Reward Gained: You may choose one Skill or Ability to advance to Elite.

Make your choices now.

There were three choices hanging in his mind for ability upgrades, including the new ability and the decision of how to spend the attribute points. He made his selections quickly.

He put three points into Intelligence and Aura, which put them both at 145. For the last three, he added them to Wisdom. The Bounty Hunter trait had already pushed that attribute to 52, so now it grew to 55.

For the abilities upgrades, he chose what he had always chosen: Aura of Crystal Flames and Flame Strike to keep his attacks as strong as possible. Then he paused, reading the notification again as he considered the Elite Tier Reward.

There was something different about this reward, and it took him a moment to see it since he was so used to the standard upgrades, which allowed for an increase of one tier...but this one was different.

Elite Tier Reward Gained: You may choose one Skill or Ability to advance to Elite.

It was telling him he could choose *any* ability to take to Elite.

He froze for a moment as he considered the possibilities, his mind flying. If that were true...he could upgrade Reclaim Aura from Advanced to Elite instantly, or any of the others, even the new ones that he hadn't chosen yet, Transfer Aura or Shatter Aura, since he was pretty sure the World Law would allow that.

Reclaim Aura would let him gather more powerful energy from auras to use in crafting or battle, Intensify Aura would let him infuse more essence into auras that he stored, Imbue Aura would help with enchantments, Essence Shield would help with defense....

But...it seemed like a waste to spend it on Essence Shield or anything else that was already growing on its own, and he was doing fine with Reclaim Aura, even if he deeply wanted to improve it more.

The biggest advantage would be to apply the reward to one of the new abilities..., and after fighting the basilisk, he had an idea for what at least one of them did. The basilisk had used that Aura of Petrification to nearly destroy the adventurers and hinder the rest of them.

What if he had been able to *shatter* it?

He wasn't sure if that was how Shatter Aura worked, but he had to choose one of the abilities. His class was focused on auras, and if other Outsiders used auras in battle...being able to break them would be incredibly useful. It would also give him a unique role in battles against Outsiders and destroy one of their biggest advantages.

He looked over his other abilities with some regret, from Crystal Focus to Combust Aura, and even his skills like Analyze, Meditation, and Mana Transfer. Then he realized there was one new option that he was still forgetting about.

Elemental Manipulation.

He frowned as he studied it, examining the essence constellation that created it. Then he shook his head. That wasn't necessarily a good idea. The ability rose out of that constellation and he had no idea what would happen if he tried to force it to advance. There was a chance it could somehow advance the rune, but it could also end up crippling him or destroy what he'd already done.

More than that, the ability was already guaranteed to increase as he gathered more essence, each time he went up a layer. So, there was no need to push it now in a risky way. All he had to do was kill more Outsiders and it would improve naturally.

With that settled, he made his choice.

An enormous whirlwind of energy swept into him from the World Law, flowing through his body as it upgraded Aura of Crystal Flame and Flame Strike to the Elite tier. Then a section of it divided off, settling into his mind as a new, sapphire blue flame for *Shatter Aura*. At the same time, the full power of the ability settled into his body and meridians, creating new pathways.

As soon as it was established, a burst of information came to explain how to use it, but it was limited.

[*Shatter Aura: Destabilizes and destroys focused auras, reducing their components to natural energy. May be used to divide auras that have been gathered, to destroy objects enchanted with auras, and to break opposing auras in battle.*

Warning: *Do not attempt to use this ability to destabilize the natural auras of Aster Fall. Such an action constitutes a threat to the Seal.*]

The world wavered for a moment under the force of the energy, but his attributes were high enough to handle the influx and he didn't fall unconscious. When everything stabilized again, the World Law's voice rang out in his mind.

Guardian, you are Tasked to investigate the damage to the Seal in this area.

Rewards are variable.

Then it fell silent, leaving only the silence of the snow drifting through the ruins and the feeling of new power in Sam's muscles.

He looked around as he checked for the others around him, noting that his father, Krana, and Lesat were all absorbing some of the experience as well. Then his talons swept through the air as he called the essence from the basilisk's corpse.

It rose in a small storm of green-grey flecks that swirled out of the corpse and shot toward him, turning bright blue as they hit his body and sank in. The basilisk was worth almost three hundred points by itself.

Essence Constellation (First Layer): 1,432 / 2,500
Strength increased by 3.
Constitution increased by 4.
Agility increased by 1.
Intelligence increased by 5.
Aura increased by 5.

It felt like the gain was a bit less than it had been while he was still forming the First Layer, but it was still worth a lot. His talons curled into his hands as he clenched his fists and looked down at himself.

With all of the Strength and Constitution, his physique was improving. He was more muscular than before, but still lean and scholarly.

His attention turned to the basilisk as he searched for the aura in its corpse. It tasted of rock dust, age, and ashes, of stillness spreading beneath the stone and of life freezing as it slowly lost itself to time.

He failed to Identify it as it crumbled away, but he was fairly sure that it would be something like an Aura of Petrification.

As he was turning away, he looked for the Coldfang corpses, preparing to gather their auras and experience as well. The snow was continuing to fall, slowly burying everything in the area.

"What in the world…" Jeric muttered as he came up to join Sam. He was looking between the dead basilisk and the snow that had covered the stones below their feet. "This snow is unnatural."

His level caught Sam's eye as he analyzed him. His dad had jumped to Level 55 from the fight. He had probably also gained the Bounty Hunter trait. There was a trace of something deeper in his eyes than had been there before, as if he'd seen the trouble of the world more clearly.

"Krana! Lesat!" Jeric called over his shoulder as he caught sight of the other two and called them over. Then he turned to look for the adventurers. His expression turned grim when he caught sight of them.

"Help me gather the adventurers over here!"

CHAPTER THIRTY-SEVEN

ICE PILLAR

The adventurers were not in good shape. Cesten was standing on his own and it looked like he would recover shortly, but Selis, Arene, and Obel were a wreck. Many areas of their skin were ash grey, with areas that had hardened completely to stone, especially on their hands, forearms, and legs.

Obel had been doing better at first, but whatever artifact or other defense the wizard had used against the Aura of Petrification must have worn off.

"I don't think this is a curse," Arene gasped out, as she looked down at her hands, which she had trouble raising. Her voice was strained and her skin was flushed white and red, as if she had a fever. "I've tried to remove it, but it doesn't work. It's something else."

"It's stopped now that the basilisk is dead," Krana observed as she set to work on Arene, holding a healing scroll in one hand. Her eyes were shimmering with silver light as she examined the damage. "It is truly stone.... We may need to remove it and then encourage your body to regrow the damaged areas."

"You mean chop it off," Obel grunted as he tried to sit up, before giving up and falling back to his back. He was out of shape and it looked as if part of his belly had turned to stone. "Just do it."

Sam gave the wizard a glance, mentally upgrading his courage. He'd expected the wizard would be the least enduring, but it seemed he had hidden depths.

As for Selis, the Lykaris wasn't even able to speak. Half of her jaw had turned to stone and she could only mumble.

He shook his head as Crystal Focus ran through the damage and he considered the new Shatter Aura ability that he'd gained, but as far as he could tell, there was no longer any trace of the Aura of Petrification. It had done its damage and left, and now they had to deal with the aftermath.

"I'll gather the experience," he said as he passed a few more healing scrolls to Krana. "Maybe they can gain a level and add something to Constitution to help."

Collecting the experience and auras didn't take him too long. He could tell that the adventurers received a portion of it, from the silvery glow that surrounded them, but he didn't ask for details.

As for him, it was enough experience to push him to Level 62. He added the new points to Intelligence and Aura, as well as one to Charisma, since it was one of the traits that wasn't rising from gathering essence.

That and Wisdom were the two attributes not rising, and he wasn't sure why. Perhaps it wasn't in the nature of essence to be wise or charismatic? Or it might have something to do with his bloodline, which the World Law had mentioned when it offered him the paths.

Either way, he didn't want to leave weak areas in his attributes. He'd just seen what that sort of weakness did to the adventurers against the basilisk's aura, and Charisma was required for dealing with people.

He also gathered the materials from the basilisk that hadn't turned to stone, primarily the spike on its tail, its core, and the cores of all the Coldfangs. As for the basilisk's remaining eye, it was quickly shrinking as it hardened into some type of a gem, and he took that as well. If it continued at the same rate, within an hour it would be the size of his hand.

When he was finished with that and with gathering the auras, eight Auras of Frozen Blades had separated from the Coldfangs and rested in his hand.

Aura of Frozen Blades (Advanced)

The boost to his Wisdom had helped. His chance to gather a Basic aura had maximized at 85%, when he reached 45 Wisdom. Now, his Wisdom was 55, and he had a 75% chance to reclaim an Advanced aura.

He rubbed his chin as he did the math and sorted out the possibilities. If Advanced auras maxed at the same percentage, he would need another ten points in Wisdom to get there. Training Wisdom was good for his perspective on life, so there were other advantages to it as well.

When he was finished, he checked on the adventurers, but they were in the middle of a long recovery. Krana had helped Arene to heal, and now the priestess was pouring her efforts into regrowing the parts of her body that had been petrified.

He grimaced as he looked away from the scene, but there was nothing else to do to help. Arene could heal the others once she recovered. It looked like it would take a day or two to put them back together.

Instead of fussing with them, he headed for the building where the basilisk had been hiding, his curiosity rising. Halfway there, his father joined him.

"So, what do you think this was all about?" Jeric said gruffly, looking around with folded arms. "These ruins have something to do with Ice magic...and there has to have been some reason that monster was hiding here. What makes this area so important?"

Sam's attention moved to the stones that he could feel beneath the snow, where the enchantments were hidden now, as he turned the ideas over.

"Ice magic by the peak...ruins that seem to gather it, a connection to the moons...perhaps an elemental affinity pillar..." he was muttering to himself as he pulled ideas together. "A Grand Flaw and Outsiders everywhere...an escaped prisoner from some hole in the seal."

"Something about this area is important," Jeric agreed, listening to his son. "Maybe the Ice Sylph's story about this being a special place for Ice, and Lenei's idea about the seal being focused here, are true."

"There's definitely something going on with the enchantments and the moons," Sam agreed as they headed to the ruined wall that led into the building. "It's not clear what yet, or what the original purpose was, but Ice is important. There's no way that snow would have built up so quickly otherwise."

"Lenei needs us to scout," Jeric added, "but we shouldn't leave the adventurers alone here until they've recovered. We may have to wait for a day."

Sam frowned, his gaze turning up to the area above them, where the adventurers had planned to go for the pillar. The ruined temple up there was silent. Whatever had been there must have seen their fight, but they had either fled or were hiding. Perhaps they'd retreated to the main Flaw.

He didn't want to delay here, but leaving the adventurers alone at this point was the same as killing them, and that wasn't something he could accept.

"We may not be able to give Lenei clear directions," he agreed, his frown deepening, "but perhaps this basilisk will be enough evidence to pull the church to the ruins anyway. Let's see if there's anything inside and I'll contact her. It must have been here for some reason."

The front half of the building had been destroyed by the basilisk's exit, but as he got closer, it was clear that it was not the original work. The stones had only been stacked into place by a later hand, without the enchantments that were holding everything together.

Otherwise, they wouldn't have fallen so easily.

Inside, the tumbled stones gave way to swirled enchantments on the floor, similar to the ones outside that had summoned the snow, but here they were quietly humming. At the center of the space, the patterns flowed together into an ornate, circular sigil that was nearly ten feet across.

At the center, there was a crystal plinth that glowed with a steady silver-green light. There were strong currents of mana rising up from the enchantments on the floor and flowing into it. The mana filled the crystal pillar, which shone with light, and from there, it was somehow dispersed into the air, disappearing.

"What is that?" Jeric muttered from beside his son. "A nexus point for these enchantments?"

The word *nexus* resonated in Sam's mind and he started, looking around the room again.

"You think the adventurers were wrong about the elemental pillar being up above?" his father continued, staring ahead of them. "Maybe that thing's what they were looking for."

"Or maybe there's more than one?" Sam offered as he walked forward slowly, examining the pillar. All around it, he could sense the subtle flow of energy coming in from outside and concentrating, but it wasn't primarily Ice. It was something else, closer to pure mana.

"Interesting..." he muttered as he took in the rest of the room. It looked like this had once been a more complete building, perhaps a node of some type for the ruins when they had been new. Now, it was still doing that task, but it wasn't clear how effective it was.

"What were these ruins?" he wondered, his hand stretching out in front of him as he touched one of the flows of mana that was moving through the air. It tingled, like a frozen stream, but the cold invigorated him, changing to a strange sort of warmth that filled his body.

A moment later, he felt his mana rising, before he pulled his hand away and dispersed the mana back into the surroundings, where it rejoined the current. The Initiate of Ice trait was interacting with the flow of mana here, for some reason.

The flow of the elements through the mana around him also pulled at his attention, his new ability adding depth and clarity to what he could see. There was something here, if he could just figure it out....

A sharp cry from outside pulled his attention away as one of the adventurers was being healed. He frowned in their direction before he turned back again. *How did they expect to survive the ruins with their level of strength?*

If they hadn't encountered them, the adventurers would be dead by now. The first band of Coldfangs would have eliminated them. He grumbled to himself as he put the blame for the delay squarely on them. When it came down to it, the Flaw was more important than the lives of the adventurers, but he also couldn't bring himself to let them die.

A dilemma that defines the human condition.... The logical route was not always the correct one.

While the adventurers healed, perhaps he would have some time to study the enchantments. He also wanted to stock up on more healing scrolls and restore his protective ring.

"Arene is mostly healed," Krana said from the entrance, her voice resonating off the stones. She walked up beside Sam and looked toward the crystal plinth at the center of the room. "What by the Nine Smiths is that? It's invisible to my Sight."

"Really?" Sam sent a surprised glance at her and then turned back toward the pillar. "Some type of control node, I think. The basilisk must have been watching it. I doubt it was smart enough to use it."

"That implies it was put here as a guard," Krana replied as she studied the pillar. "It does look like a formation. I've never heard of a pillar like this in the ruins before."

"It's interacting with the Ice mana here, and with Initiate of Ice," Sam agreed as he examined it. It was located just at the center of the room. The stones around it were pristine, as if no dust had ever touched them, whereas the ones farther out had chips of stone and bits of rubble scattered on top.

"The enchantments here are more active than elsewhere," he said as he pointed out the new stones around the pillar. "Do you think this just appeared?"

"With the moons activating the ruins...perhaps," Krana frowned. "Researchers have been all over these ruins, but no one understands them. As for Initiate of Ice, the Ice Sylphs have a strange connection to these mountains, especially if their origin is true. Perhaps the trait is linked to the magic here...two sources from the same origin."

The pillar hummed with the flow of mana, drawing Sam's attention to it whenever he looked away. There were tiny crystalline flakes of ice drifting in the air around it, forming within the flow of energy, and it gave off a bright, blue-white light.

"I'll study it while we wait," he decided. At least this way, he wouldn't waste time while the adventurers recovered. He also needed to make some more scrolls and repair his shielding ring.

A few moments later, he had a message scroll in his hand as he recorded their find for Lenei and sent it off to her. Then he turned his attention to the pillar, sitting down beside it as he began to study the flows of energy.

Behind him, his father and Krana looked around the room and gave each other a wry look as they withdrew, heading back out to check on the adventurers.

***

The rest of that day and part of the next passed as Sam replaced the cracked core in his ring and meditated on the crystal pillar and the flow of Ice energy. The energy moved in curling strands, from ones as thin as a thread to ones as large as him.

The resonance of natural runes echoed through it at a higher level than he was able to understand, but meditating on the energy and being exposed to it was changing something in his concept of Ice.

He held the runes for Ice and Crystal in his mind as he studied, as well as Fire, sensing how they resonated here. He also practiced with Elemental

Manipulation, reaching out to mold the energy in the air around him, but he wasn't able to move the flows of Ice.

All he could do was manipulate the free Ice energy that was gathering around the area like a fog between the rivers that were the enchantment. Even that was useful as he formed one rune and then another, working to see which variation had the strongest influence.

He summoned crystal flame, weaving it through the Ice currents as he studied the crystallization effect and tried to trap the energy in his Crystal Field. After that, he tried to simulate the flow of Ice, changing the structure of the field and compressing it to match.

By the time the adventurers were healed, there was a thoughtful look in his eyes. He hadn't gained any notifications, but it felt as if something significant had changed in his understanding.

The adventurers came in to see the pillar as they recovered, but after touching it and trying some ceremony, they grumbled and left again. Whatever they were looking for, it apparently wasn't this one.

Sam ignored them, his attention on a flaming Ice rune that was changing shape between his hands. It was made of crystal flame and he was using it as a model to refine his understanding of how his magic could compress into a crystalline structure, comparing it to the Ice around him.

Eventually, he heard his father calling him and he stood up with a sigh, letting the rune fade away into the flow of natural energy. Then he headed out of the building to where everyone was gathered.

Cesten and the other adventurers were mostly healed now, although patches of their skin were still white or a newly regrown pink. There was an even more determined look in their eyes than before as they stood around the area, bundled up against the snow and cold.

Sam glanced down to his own clothing, which was his usual cloak over his shirt and breeches, and he gazed heavenward for a moment as he held back another curse about the adventurers' uselessness.

"We know it's not a good idea," Cesten was growling in response to something Jeric said, his hands raised angrily as he gestured in the air toward the ruins above, "but we can't go back now! We have to get up to that elemental pillar and see if it helps. At least that way this trip will be worth something!"

"You don't want to stay here for too long," Jeric said as he gave Cesten a grave look. "If the Outsiders wanted this area before, they'll probably come back for it. That pillar up above is the same."

"Help us get there and then we'll go," Arene spoke up, a pleading look in her eyes. "I know we're not strong enough to survive here with the Outsiders around. We never planned for them. Please.... This is the difference between life and death for us."

"We are only common adventurers," Selis said with a grimace, agreeing with Arene. "This is our chance to become something more, to break out of the frame that the world gave us. We have to seize it. Even if we die, at least we will have tried."

"No, we cannot ask you for anything more," Obel said weakly, shaking his head as he disagreed with Arene. His arms were completely white and pink, a mix of new skin and remaining spots of stone that hadn't been healed yet, and his face was still flushed. "You've done more for us than you needed to, and I recognize that. Please, don't feel pressured. We will survive on our own. If we fail, we fail. That is fate."

Sam walked up to the edge of the circle, looking around at the adventurers as a sigh built up. His father, Krana, and Lesat were standing across from the group, and he moved to join them.

"Lenei replied earlier," he added, looking around at all of them. "The Church is sending a single team in this direction, about half a dozen people. They'll be here in a day or so to take control of this area and study the pillar."

He wasn't entirely pleased with that, but since he couldn't stay, it was better to let the church have it than the Outsiders. He was also fairly sure by this point that the pillar wasn't a control node, but some subsidiary system of the ruins.

It was functioning, but it wasn't the central point. Letting the church take control of the area shouldn't cause much trouble, even if it would be difficult for him to come back here.

There was one advantage to the church showing up, which was that he could foist these adventurers off on them.

"We need to go up and see what's there anyway," he said, forcing himself to be polite as he looked up at the pillar. "So, you may as well come along. After that, you can return here and take shelter with the church forces, or let them escort you out.

"At any rate," he added, "we can't spend any more time here, so let's go see what that pillar is all about."

***

The trek up to the pillar was longer than it looked, since they had to find a pathway up to the next level first, which took them two hours out of their way. The snow drifts throughout the ruins were as deep as ever, and the adventurers tramped along on top of it with their snowshoes, sending strange glances at Sam's party.

"How are you walking on the snow like that?" Arene asked, when she couldn't hold back the question any longer.

"I'm an enchanter," Sam replied blandly, before he returned his attention to the area in front of them. "The enchantment to compress snow under footsteps isn't too complicated…it just takes a higher-level Ice core."

The answer was true, even if his response was an evasion. He didn't like lying, so evasiveness was the next best way to keep his secrets. He actually had created a design for something similar over the last day, using Crystal Field's compression and the compacting nature of Ice as a guide, but he hadn't tested it out.

"That must be mana-intensive," Arene muttered, but she turned around again when Sam didn't add anything else.

When they reached the ruined temple, the area was covered in new snow that obscured any obvious marks of enemies, but there were compacted areas beneath it that jumped out in his senses, places where claws and tails had compressed the snow.

A lot of them had been here, perhaps even more than had been below, but the traces had been wiped away by the mana flow of the ruins.

The ruin was a small circular building that did look something like a temple with a double-layered, curving roof and a spire-topped portico, but only the adventurers' map gave it that name.

The doorway was a gash of darkness that led inside, with a faint emerald green in the distance.

"We'll have to prepare inside," Cesten declared as he looked around the area. There was strained expectation in his voice. "We've brought the cores and mana crystals to offer, the formation pattern to lay it out, and the blood of Ice-element beasts. If it works like it's supposed to, the power of the ruins will increase our elemental affinities, improving our bodies and augmenting our spells."

"And then we might be able to hold our own against monsters at a similar level," Selis muttered, as orange flames flickered around her.

Sam shook his head as he listened to them. It sounded like a faint hope. Most of the time, power came from levels and the tier of your abilities, or the equipment you had. More powerful abilities were rare and harder to acquire.

The problem they had was what everyone with common classes and abilities faced. In his opinion, they'd be better off studying stronger skills, gaining better equipment, and working toward an improved class at their evolution, rather than placing their hopes on this.

This idea of boosting their elemental affinity.... While that could happen, and the Initiate of Ice trait was one example, he doubted it would work the way they thought.

Crystal Focus didn't reveal anything else besides the faint tracks of what had been here, so he said nothing as the adventurers ran awkwardly across the snow, their feet pressing down the snow just like the monsters had.

A frown flickered across his face as he looked at the snow drifting down, the tracks that they were leaving, and then the green gleam in the darkness of the doorway.

Before he could raise a hand in warning, Cesten ran across the entrance to the temple, his broad arms brushing across the stones of the doorway. From deep within, a brighter flare of light appeared as the mana flows shifted.

There was a loud *chime* as a pulse of Ice energy blasted upward from the stones hidden below the snow, and then suddenly everything disappeared. The temple, the snow, and the light were replaced by darkness that stretched into infinity.

Streamers of blue, green, and purple light cut through the dark, weaving swirling patterns like flowing clouds as Sam floated in the middle of nothingness. He couldn't sense anyone else within range of Crystal Focus.

Chapter Thirty-Eight
An Old Formation

The currents of multicolored energy in the void spun around Sam as he turned in place. It barely felt like he was moving and it was hard to get a grasp of up or down. The only marker here was the energy around him, strands of light that twisted through the dark.

Moonlight?

The thought flickered through his mind as the colors registered. They matched with the three moons: Silvas for the light green like a spring leaf, Caelus for the distant blue like the horizon, and Amaris for the dusky purple of passion and secrets.

The moons themselves weren't visible. There was only the light that curled in patterns similar to the enchantments in the ruins. The strands of light didn't feel like mana or essence...they were closer to pure aura.

It was as if he had entered the enchantment and these were the strands of moonlight coming from the sky, but there was nothing else. It also reminded him unpleasantly of the last time he'd been teleported to a void.

The light felt timeless at first, but as he watched, the curls of moonlight seemed to notice him and began to twist in his direction. They formed into cutting blades, broad expanses of shearing force as their presence sharpened. Then they spun through the darkness like ribbons turned to sawmills.

A trap.

They must have run into some sort of defensive formation in the ruins. That green light from inside the temple and the lack of monsters had made him uneasy, but he'd reacted too late to warn them.

Idiot adventurers.

He muttered to himself as his senses spun through the void, trying to find something to use to defend or to move out of the way. He obviously couldn't let the moonlight hit him. The ruins were far more powerful than he was and this trap was hardly normal. There was no telling what would happen.

He felt a surge of panic as he wondered if his father was in the same sort of place, and then he shoved it aside, forcing himself to remain focused. There was no guarantee that they'd all fallen into the trap.

His search turned up nothing useful. The only thing here was the moonlight itself. He could feel his essence, but he wasn't able to open his spatial bags. The twisting streams of light came closer as he took stock of the situation, cutting toward him with a sense of impending doom.

He had no other options, so he studied the moonlight as it approached, trying to get a feel for what it was. It was distant at first and hard to sense, but as it came closer, the intensity increased.

The green light was filled with an aura that reminded him of redfrost pines, the grasses of the Storm Plains, and the smell of fresh fields in bloom. The blue light was the cold of Winter's Peak, lightning sparks, wind and storm, flame, and explosive stone.

The purple was...wild chaos. Overwhelming emotions ripped through his senses. First, the explosive wrath of blind anger, soft love on a moonlit night, and then whiplash, manic laughter that rocked his mind.

He froze under the unexpected assault, convulsing as he pushed at the aura and tried to shove it away from him. Surprisingly, it responded, rushing away like a river parting. It only left the memory of its touch behind.

When his senses stabilized, the purple blade of moonlight loomed large in his vision, broader than he was tall.

He summoned up a pulse of crystal flame instinctively to evade, but the energy twisted from his control. Half of it dissolved into nothing that dissipated into the void.

Half.

The thought hit him in an instant as he tried again, reaching out with the part of the energy that was still there. The half that had disappeared was mana, but the aura was still there.

It had been a while since he'd used aura alone, but a formless pulse burst from his hand, turning into crystal flame as he pushed himself to the side.

The void rotated around him as he spun wildly, streamers of light flashing in his senses, until he managed to stabilize himself with another pulse of aura-based flame. The ribbon of purple moonlight that was closest to him spun away, slicing off through the void as he let out a breath that he wasn't sure was there.

It seemed like mana couldn't exist here, but aura alone did.

He let out another pulse of aura as he pushed himself to the side, moving away before a green blade cut through the space where he had been. A few minutes later, he had to do it again as the tail of that ribbon swept past.

His essence was down by about a quarter and there was a strange pressure in his meridians from the imbalance of too much mana compared to aura. With a flick of his hand, he released it, letting it twist away into the void until the pressure balanced.

He tried to activate the essence constellation, but as soon as its power touched the void around him, it was absorbed. Elemental Manipulation also failed, since there were no elements around him to reach.

The same pattern of evasion repeated again as he dodged one strand of moonlight after another.

He slowly lost track of time. The only marker was his diminishing essence, which continued to fall until he only had a couple of points left. The world around him was still filled with moonlight moving in endless spirals, cutting abstractly across the void.

He reached into his storage to combust an aura, but as soon as the Aura of Reclusive Tide appeared in his hand, it exploded outward, sending him hurtling away. The remains hung in the area like a watery fog before they faded away to nothing.

The void didn't seem to allow other auras besides the moonlight to exist in it.

He drifted there for a while as he watched the next strand of moonlight approach, his thoughts reflective. With a sigh, he pushed out the last of his essence and evaded it, waiting for the next one.

The pain of having drained all of his energy hit him, but it was meaningless here in the dark. His meridians were empty, as was his essence pool. There was a growing sense of dissolution all around, a relaxing nothingness as he felt himself fading into the void.

Last chance.... The thought came slowly as he felt the emptiness echoing like the gong of a solemn temple bell. Even at the last, he was unwilling to give up, and he tried to meditate again, to draw in energy from the void around him.

He'd tried before, but every time he did, it felt like his energy was draining out faster than anything he gained. Now that he had reached equilibrium with the universe around him, he felt the void more clearly than before.

The energy of the three moons crashed into his senses, startling him out of the daze that he'd fallen into. Each of them was a sharp spike of meaning, bringing a sense of life and the familiar feeling of Aster Fall that woke him up. These were the moons that had risen every night of his life, observing the world from on high.

He wasn't sure how long he'd been here, but a flash of memory came to him as he remembered something the World Law had said when he had learned *Shatter Aura*. It had warned him not to break the natural auras of Aster Fall.

The moons were part of the world and normally he shouldn't have tried to damage them, but what did that matter now? If he didn't do something, he was going to die here.

The only problem was that he didn't have any essence left.

He frowned as he studied the approaching moonlight and then looked to see how many auras were left in his storage. Perhaps he could use the explosion from them to propel himself away...and even grab some of the energy in them before they dissipated, if he tried to collect the aura and not the mana.

Or perhaps he could beat the void to the punch and *shatter* one...and then divide it up, pushing away the mana and keeping the aura for himself.

Before he tried that, he let himself just drift in the void, absorbing the feeling of the moons as they sank into his awareness. Now that his essence was empty, the void felt far more amenable to his existence, as if it no longer wished to kill him.

Time passed as he floated there, and it seemed as if the blades of moonlight drifted aimlessly now, no longer seeking him out. Perhaps if he allowed it, he could just float here forever... He gave himself a mental shake as he jerked back to awareness again.

He had too much to do to allow himself to dissolve into nothing. He wasn't going to let an ancient trap be the end of him. He needed to understand the mechanics of this place and escape.

He focused on the moonlight, letting it resonate with the emptiness in his body as he took the opportunity to study it. As he did, some barrier was passed and the moonlight surged into his meridians.

The auras and the raging emotions and elements of each of them filtered through him as the strands wove around the emptiness inside. Echoes of each moon engraved itself on his soul, cutting a path as it tried to make him a part of the void and left a swirling pattern behind.

Time stretched out in a blur of moonlight colors until they finished their work and moved on.

Sam let out a silent gasp as he choked for air and then took a breath of the nothingness all around. Looking inside, he could see ribbons of moonlight swirling around his essence constellation, like streams of astral light surrounding a nebula.

Nothing else seemed to happen, and so after he studied it for a while, he pushed it out of his mind and went over his plan.

When he was ready, he reached into his storage and pulled out another Aura of Reclusive Tide, pausing just before he pulled it through the dimension that separated it from the void. He sank into a state similar to meditation, reaching out to the aura around him. Right now, there was nothing there except for the moonlight, and that was far too complex for him to directly gather.

He yanked the aura out of the storage with as much speed as he could and tried to combust it before the void could reach it. As soon as it left the storage, however, it erupted, blasting his hand back as a pulse of energy exploded from the center and shattered it.

He pulled as hard as he could on the cloud that it had become, drawing the aura toward him. It was like trying to pull water through a sieve while a whirlpool pulled on it from the otherside, but specks of the energy flowed into his meridians, one after the other. Then it was gone as the void consumed everything that was left.

A slight smile curled his lips as he checked his energy reserves. He'd gained three points of aura.

Now that he was no longer out of energy, he felt the trap's attention fix on him again. The moonlight blades began to spin closer. As quickly as he could, he combusted another aura, and then several more. The blasts from each aura sent him spinning through the void, and he did his best to move away from the blades.

It took seven auras before he felt like he had enough to try *Shatter Aura*. 21 points.

He'd never used the ability before, but the World Law had given him some basic knowledge. The simplest method was to reach out with his own aura and drive it like a spike through whatever he wanted to break. Breaking one beam of moonlight might not be enough, or he might not be strong enough, but perhaps it would destabilize something.

He had to try.

The next strand of moonlight heading his way was blue, which was somehow fitting. Caelus was the elements, the one closest to his own magic. As it grew closer, he waited for it, ready to evade.

The blade cut closer to him and he pulsed out a tiny amount of aura, drifting off just to the side of where it was heading. It was as thin as a ribbon, translucent, and as dangerous as the scythe of a death god.

As the light swept past, he gathered his will and drove a spike of aura straight into the side of it. It was like plunging into a swirling tempest, the winds tearing him in every direction, but it was also fragile.

As soon as he touched it, it was also clear that this was not the real moon, but just some of its light. It was strong, but it was as brittle as glass.

KkkrrraaaCCcckkk.

A shattering sound echoed in his mind as the energy in the moonlight splintered like a fractured crystal. An explosion blasted outward from the blade as it turned into swirling winds and chaos, spiraling outward in a disk.

Sam grabbed at the energy, trying to pull it into himself, and this time Elemental Manipulation came to the fore, helping him to pull strands of the elements to him. A torrent of aura blasted his meridians and he absorbed a dozen points in an instant, and then more, until it felt like his body was straining under the force.

What he gained was only a fraction of the whole, and he couldn't stop the rest of the energy from spreading outward, which it did in an instant. The wave of aura blasted out through the void, hurling him backwards. He went tumbling uncontrollably, heading directly for a blade of green moonlight that bent in its trajectory to intercept him.

Another spike of aura formed in his hand. As he got closer, he pushed himself to the side with a small blast of aura and drove it into the edge of the ribbon.

This attempt was less successful. The spike tore through the edge of the aura like the edge of a leaf and then ricocheted away, catching nothing. He spun through the void in a tumble, eventually righting himself again with tiny pulses of aura.

There were at least a dozen strands of moonlight in sight and he frowned as he looked at them, looking for the best bet. After a moment, he found it.

There were three strands gathered near each other, one of each type, which seemed to hang in the center of everything. His aura was about half full and he pulsed toward them as soon as he found a path.

They grew gradually larger in his vision. Now that his attention was fixed on them, it was clear they weren't moving like others, but it was a long way there. As he got closer, he could see the three strands of moonlight were larger than the others around them.

He oriented himself to them, spinning around until they were vertical in his sight. Now, the void had a top and a bottom. He gave a grim smile, since there was no one to disagree. When he got close enough, he didn't hesitate. He reached out with a spike of aura and drove it into the closest blue strand.

The strand split apart like water, tougher than the last one, and he reached out to the edge of the gap he'd just made and drove another spike of aura into that, tearing at it. Then he pulled at the edges with Elemental Manipulation, pouring all of his energy into ripping apart the elements that made it up.

The strand slowly began to unravel, its substance tearing, and the void around him trembled as a shudder ran through it. With a whisper like a ghost escaping from a stone, the strand frayed, its edges pulling away from one another until it finally snapped.

An explosion of blue moonlight and chaotic elements exploded outward, engulfing him before he could move away as the strand fractured, changing into a disk. An instant later, a storm of cutting leaves and pulses of wild rage and love joined it as it became larger and larger.

Sam was dwarfed by the size of the erupting storm, swallowed by it as it expanded past him. A vibration like a mountain collapsing shook his bones as a thousand tiny leaves sliced through his skin and a torrent of raining emotions crushed his chest. At the same time, aura flooded his meridians, far more than he could contain.

He couldn't breathe or see, all he could do was try and pull in the aura to create a shield and endure. He was tossed left and right, up and down, until there was no way to keep his bearings.

And then the void shattered with a soundless explosion and the world around him changed.

He flew through the air in a tumble, spinning wildly as he pushed out his remaining aura into a shield. He struck something, his head and shoulders slamming into it first as he felt the shield absorbing most of the impact.

Snow compressed beneath him, stabilizing him as vertigo struck. When he came to, all he could see was white. His senses spun out around him as Crystal Focus became useful again.

He was half buried in the snow.

He pulled two auras from his storage and combusted them. Crystal flame poured out around him as he pulled himself out and forced his way to his feet. His body ached from a thousand strikes and cuts. Blood was running down his skin, filled with flickers of flame as it burned in the air.

The world came into view, but it wasn't the same spot he remembered. This was...

A tower of green stone stretched in front of him, one layer after another reaching high into the heavens. It was at least sixty feet high and fifteen wide, a monolith standing above the snow. It was engraved with a thousand patterns, each of them a shifting sigil that burned with silver-green light.

One of those sigils was dark now, directly in his line of sight.

Behind the pillar, there was a ruined hall that must have been a massive structure once, with walls even taller than the pillar and enormous arches that had once been a roof. Now, they were a stone skeleton, fragments grasping at the heavens. Through them, the stars were visible in the night sky.

The three moons hung there, visible through the gaps. Their positions marked out that it was just past evening.

Below him, the icy slopes of Sun's Rest spread out, their edges dark as moonlight played across the snow. Farther down, he could see the ruins extending in layer after layer, and past that, the city of Highfold at the edge of the valley. It was very small from here.

As he looked around again, it was obvious there was no more of the mountain above him. He was on a plateau of some type, at the very top of Sun's Rest.

An area that had once been dominated by this ruined hall and pillar.

CHAPTER THIRTY-NINE

THE TOP OF THE WORLD

The land spread out beneath Sam's view in dark, soaring mountains and snow-filled valleys. The Western Reaches stretched far off into the distance to the north and south, a line of white, night-edged peaks glowing with trails of mana. He was standing at the tip of a diadem, each peak a shining gem set into a band that crossed the world. Sun's Rest was the highest of them all.

The top of the world.

The thought flickered through his mind as he turned around and saw that he was alone. He touched the Amulet of Swirling Winds on his chest, searching through its connection for his father and the others, but there was no response. The amulet's charge was drained and it felt like something here was blocking it.

He ignored the wounds that covered him as he leapt toward the pillar and examined the rune that had gone dark.

The pillar's surface was smooth and cold beneath his hands, the stones unweathered by time. The sigils embedded in it were in a layer beneath the surface, but the part of the stone above them was translucent, making it look like they were engraved at different depths.

The dark rune was the focal point for the trap that had held him, but its energy had faded now. The World Law hadn't threatened him about shattering the auras inside at least.

Where were his father and the others?

He hadn't seen them in the trap, but they could've been in a different version of it or sent to another place completely. They might even still be on the slopes below. Perhaps the trap had targeted essence and he was the only one who had fallen in?

His senses poured toward the rune as he explored it, trying to access the formation that it was part of. He didn't think it would be successful, but as his essence touched it, the three strands of moonlight that had carved themselves into his essence constellation began to hum.

His aura flooded into the strands and then poured out of his hands in strands of twisting blue, green, and purple moonlight that flowed into the rune. His vision shifted suddenly as he connected to the formation.

Flickering images of other traps and locations throughout the ruins poured into his awareness, as well as a broken map of the area in three dimensions. The image faded in and out, as if it were having trouble maintaining its form, but he saw the slopes of Sun's Rest, as well as the two neighboring peaks.

The ruins spread across all of them, both above and below the ground, covering the area. The damaged areas were dark, and much of it was damaged, but the areas that were still functioning were lit up in the colors of entangled moonlight.

It was too much information to process all at once, even with his Intelligence, and his mind spun. He slumped down against the pillar in a daze as he lost control of his muscles, but his hands were still touching the stones.

The moonlight in his essence constellation grew brighter as it pulled more of his aura from him, taking only that and not his mana, and continued to pour into the pillar.

Auric Imprint Detected.

At that moment, the Guardian Star spoke, its voice ringing in his mind as it began to burn on his hand. The star floated up, a reflection of it shining in the space above his hand as it began to spin, its nine points flickering. Beams of multicolored light flared from it.

Analyzing....

Changes detected in Guardian's Aura.

Assessing threat....

The star continued to spin in place, the energy from it playing over the pillar in front of him and across his body. Its assessment weighed on him, and it felt like the star became heavier. Finally, the feeling disappeared and it spoke again.

Artifact detected.
Identified as "Moonlight Relic."
History: Early version of Seal Ward.
Purpose: Intended to repair Flaws in the Seal.
Age of Relic: 162,417 years.
Integrity of Relic: 32%.
Threat Level: Minimal.
Interface available.
Suggested Action: Access Moonlight Relic?
New capabilities will be added to the Guardian Star.

He wasn't sure what the star was asking, but it was clear that it wanted to do something with the ruins here, or perhaps with the pillar. His mind was in a daze from the information overload, but he got the impression that the Guardian Star and the ruins here were part of the same system.

The ruins were just a lot older and more broken.

He hesitated for a moment, as he tried to focus on the pillar again to search for his father, but the information was a massive spike of pain in his mind that sent him sprawling to the ground. He twitched there in a limp puddle, still bleeding from the thousand cuts the trap had left behind, but his hand was touching the pillar.

He had just enough focus to accept the Guardian Star's offer. He wasn't sure what it would do, but hopefully it would help. If his father was in a trap somewhere, maybe it could get him out.

As soon as he accepted, all of his aura poured out of him, flowing through the three strands of moonlight that were somehow inside his essence.

Interfacing with Moonlight Relic.
Activating Merger.

A wave of brilliant, rainbow light exploded out of the Guardian Star as it floated up from his hand. It shot through the sky until it stopped above the top of the pillar. It began to glow, its light increasing until it was far brighter than the moons.

The pillar shimmered in response, the sigils covering its surface lighting up. The entire area around Sam began to vibrate, a low *hum* filling the air as enchantments laid into the stones of this plateau activated in swirling, silver-green lines.

Energy flowed toward the pillar from the surroundings and upward, pouring into the star, which grew larger until it was half the size of the pillar. Several minutes passed as it continued to draw power. Then the nine points flared outward, brilliant light spreading from them to cover the pillar and the ruined hall.

The light was so intense it was almost liquid, bathing everything in radiance. His eyes snapped shut defensively, but he could still see what was happening through his eyelids.

The enchantments on the pillar brightened until they were nearly as intense as the star, and then a beam of three-colored moonlight shot upward from them, pouring into it. The star hummed in response, its size increasing as the three colors joined the radiance.

The strands of moonlight blended into the star, which turned white again except for the rainbow colors on each point. Then the light began to fade, as the pillar and the ruins all around dimmed, the enchantments quietening.

The Guardian Star shrank back down, shooting down from the top of the pillar to hover over Sam's hand. There was a new sense of liveliness to it, as if it had gained something important.

Access Acquired: Moonlight Relic.

Insufficient authority to claim ownership of the relic. Requires joint permission of Caelus, Silvas, and Amaris.

Access is limited to information and entry to some protected areas.

Damage to the relic is significant.

Stored power: 12%.

Auric Charge: 721,412 / 500,000,000.

The Guardian Star spun there, its points flashing as if it were pleased with itself.

A small chance exists to repair the relic. Guardian is advised to do so in order to support the stability of the Seal. It would protect the local region.

Study auric enchantments and initialize the self-repair mechanisms that have been broken by Outsider attack.

The best opportunity to charge the relic's energy arrives in 3.1 weeks and will return again in seven years.

Sam looked down at the small star that was once again just floating above his hand, his eyes wide. He'd known the ruins were old, but these were completely ancient. It also seemed like they were from a similar origin as the Guardian Star...some type of earlier attempt to protect Aster Fall?

He wasn't sure how the moons were connected or how he should get their permission to access the ruins, but he would worry about it later. The star had promised information.

"Search for my father," he told it, a frown appearing. Access to the ruins and a request to repair them was all well and good, but what he wanted was to know where everyone was.

Search initialized, the Guardian Star responded immediately. It was more active than it had ever been before. **Accessing Moonlight Relic and scanning the local area.**

Its points flickered, and the response came back.

Jeric Hastern has been located within the area of the relic, as well as an estimated 28 Outsiders, 132 monsters, 430 local beasts, 147 citizens of Aster Fall. Scanning is distorted in some areas due to damage to the relic.

Grand Flaw Detected.

Position: 34 miles west by southwest from your present location.

Five Subsidiary Flaws detected: 14 miles east by southeast, 17 miles southeast, 42 miles south by southeast, 24 miles west by southwest, and 54 miles west.

"Show me," Sam demanded, frowning at the star again. As soon as the command left his mouth, the star flickered and his vision changed.

He could see the ruins from above, as well as the swirling enchantments in a grand formation spreading through it. Most of those lines were dark, and others were flickering as if they were about to go out.

It was similar to the vision he'd had when he touched the pillar, but it was sorted now, organized by the Guardian Star, and no longer overwhelming. He felt like an eagle flying above the mountains, looking down at everything below.

Jeric Hastern's position is 37 miles south by southwest. He is approximately 7 miles from the Grand Flaw.

The view zoomed down the slopes of Sun's Rest and came to a stop on a ruined building near the edge of a cliff. It looked different from above, but the ruined temple's shape was clearly visible.

All around the temple, there was fresh snow slowly falling on signs of a fight. Corpses from large serpents, a wyvern, and two trolls were visible scattered around. The building itself was sealed by a glowing white ward, which looked like church magic.

The view swept down, piercing through the roof of the temple to reveal the interior. Inside, his father, Krana, and Lesat were seated around a small fire. They looked battered, but healthy. Across from them, the adventurers were in a worse state, with bandages and evidence of freshly-healed wounds.

At the rear of the temple, there was a small pillar of stone that was releasing an emerald green light. It was engraved with images of leaves and curling vines.

Wood Element Mana Gathering Pylon, the Guardian Star identified it as it pulled the information from the Moonlight Relic.

So much for an elemental affinity pillar, Sam muttered as he heard the name. Perhaps they were able to let that Wood mana flow through their bodies, but he had no idea what the effect would be.

"Can you allow my amulet to work here?" he asked, looking down at the Guardian Star. "Or will a message scroll reach them?"

You are currently at the control pillar of the Moonlight Relic. Communication from here to other locations is possible, but prevented by the ward around this plateau.

The Guardian Star was far more responsive now than it had ever been before. Apparently, it had gained something from the relic. It flickered on his hand as he felt a flow of energy shifting, and then it spoke again.

Communication is now enabled.

With its announcement, the Amulet of Swirling Winds came to life as the enchantment on it activated.

"Dad?" Sam's attention was fixed on the image the Guardian Star was showing him as his voice reached out through the amulet. His voice was tight. "Are you all right? How long has it been since we reached that temple?"

"Sam!" Jeric jumped up from where he was sitting as he shouted back through the amulet, his voice carrying a sense of deep relief. "Where are you?! It's been three days! The amulet wasn't working to locate you and even Krana's Far Sight was blocked. These ruins are dangerous. Are you safe?"

Sam let out a sigh of relief as he heard his father's voice. He looked down at himself, taking in the cuts that were covering his body. The bleeding had slowed and he wasn't going to die, but he needed to heal them at some point. He decided not to mention any of that to his father.

"I'm safe enough...I was teleported away by an old formation," he replied. "It was a trap, but not in good repair. When it broke, it left me at the top of the mountain. There's a control pillar here that I used to find you."

For now, he left out the rest of the details, including the true meaning of the pillar. He didn't know if the adventurers could overhear him, but he didn't plan to reveal such an enormous secret to anyone except his family.

"I'm so glad you're all right, son." Some of the tension eased out of his father's voice. "After you disappeared, we had some trouble here, but we took care of it. Now, we're bunkered down and waiting for church reinforcements. They should be here in a day or two. They were delayed by some other fights on the edge of the ruins.

"Wherever you are," his father continued, "if it's safe, you should stay there until we can meet up. There are too many Outsiders and monsters around here. Once the church arrives, we should have the forces we need to clear the area."

"It's not that simple," Sam replied, shaking his head, although his father couldn't see him. "I've scanned the area. There are five smaller Flaws and the one big one, as well as a couple of dozen Outsiders and hundreds of monsters and beasts.

"You're much too close to the main Flaw, and the Outsiders are going to be the strongest there. We need to break you out of that area and join together. I'll send you the details via message scroll...and to Lenei as well.

"We'll have to coordinate with the church to eliminate the Flaws one by one. Otherwise, the Outsiders will be able to travel from one Flaw to another and escape."

Jeric was silent for a moment as he took in what Sam was saying. His eyes seemed to see through the walls around him as he looked at the mountainside. Perhaps with his Earth Sense, that was true.

"Then we have three priorities," Jeric said as he looked down at the amulet. "Finding you, coordinating with the Church to destroy the Flaws, and eliminating the Outsiders here as well as the monsters under their control."

"Or humans," Sam added. "That Iceblood Guild could be bigger than just the three we met before. There are a lot of travelers exploring the ruins right now, and some of them might be working for the Outsiders."

"I suppose that could be." Jeric frowned. He clearly didn't like the idea. "We'll have to keep an eye out." His gaze turned outward again, toward the peak of the mountain.

"How long would it take to get to you?"

"A while," Sam replied as he looked over the path between him and his father. "There are a dozen layers to get through and I don't see a clear access point up to this plateau. Some of the connections between the layers are also completely destroyed. I'll have to explore to find the best path.

"More importantly, however, the main path leading up this way runs right past the Grand Flaw.... That's not something we want to cross until we're ready."

"Damn it," Jeric growled, his hands clenching as he thought about the obstacles between him and his son. "We'll work on it from both sides then. When the church gets here, maybe we'll have the forces we need to push through."

"I'll work on this side," Sam said as he expanded his view, looking over the ruins from above. The Guardian Star sensed his wishes and handled the change in perspective smoothly, as if it were reading his mind.

There were dozens of monsters surrounding his father's position and many that were near the peak as well. Some of them were scattered and easy targets, as long as he moved quickly.

"Try to keep fighting and level up from the monsters around there," he said at last, as he looked at the arrangement of the flaws. "I'll do the same from up here. We'll need to fight independently for a little while."

"Just for a day or two," Jeric replied, still growling. "At least we can keep in touch now. When you disappeared, I...." His hands flexed, his muscles bulging as he tried to restrain himself. "If anything happens to you, there won't be a ruin left for these monsters to live in."

"Then we'll make sure they understand their mistake," Sam agreed, his face tightening as anger rushed through his limbs. His hands were also curled into fists.

There were enough monsters all around the peak that he could probably gain several levels from them, if not more. Two days...or perhaps longer depending on how quickly he could make his way down. It might even be necessary to kill everything between him and his father.

Outside, dozens of monsters suddenly felt a sharp killing intent drifting down from the peak of Sun's Rest.

Chapter Forty

THE FIRST LAYER

The plateau was a circle roughly a mile across. Its edges ended in steep cliffs with no visible trail to the layer below, which was half a mile down in a nearly straight line. The only way Sam could imagine getting off the plateau and back on was teleportation or flying.

Had the builders been able to fly?

On top of that, the edge of the plateau was marked with a translucent silver-green barrier, one that stopped his hand when he touched it.

"How am I supposed to get down from here?" he muttered as he examined it, testing to see how dense it was. This had to be what kept monsters and everyone else away from the plateau, unless something else was going on.

This barrier is the control pillar's primary ward, the Guardian Star spoke up. **The central plateau holds the connections for enchantments throughout the Moonlight Relic and is off-limits to all but the controllers.**

"So how did it get damaged?" Sam asked, grumbling. "Outsiders made it up here?"

Evidence suggests so. The ward must have failed. Leaving the central plateau is simple. Some functions of the Moonlight Relic still exist. Touch the shield and envision where you wish to descend.

"What do you mean...can it teleport me?" Sam asked, as he considered how large the ruins were. The trap had brought him up here, so it clearly had some level of enchantment for that.

The Moonlight Relic was built as a spatial ward. It is heavily enchanted for spatial transfer, but the function is limited to areas of the ruins that are fully repaired and not currently near a Flaw.

"Can it send me to my father?" Sam asked, his eyebrows rising.

Negative. The area is damaged and too close to a Flaw. Transfer to the layer directly below the central plateau is the most efficient in terms of energy. It is the most intact. Other areas of the ruins may be possible once repairs are made. Nearly every section is damaged in some way.

Sam frowned as he looked through the barrier, examining the layer half a mile below. After a moment, he found a clear spot and fixed his attention on it.

Initializing Transfer. The Guardian Star's voice was authoritative. He felt energy flowing from it as it interacted with the relic, and then three strands of moonlight wrapped around him in a spiral and the world around him blurred.

There was a wash of blue, green, and purple that lasted for a blink of time, and then he was in a different place, standing on top of new snow as buildings rose up all around him. These buildings were mostly intact, far more than the tumbled stones that had been rebuilt for the others.

Whatever battle had destroyed the ruins, someone must have come along later and tried to rebuild it by putting the stones back, but without the enchantments, it hadn't worked. They must not have been the original builders.

What had happened to them?

To claim ownership of the relic, he needed the permission of Caelus, Silvas, and Amaris...but those were the moons. Perhaps the original builders had shared the same names?

He shook his head as he pushed the questions aside and looked around the area, examining this layer of the ruins. The building in front of him was two stories tall with a windswept style. There was a slightly arched roof with edges that curled upward rather than ending in a straight line.

The door was ten feet tall, much larger than normal for a human house, and there were tall, thin windows set around the outside of the building, which were covered over by a translucent crystal.

Curiosity got the better of him and he walked in, looking around the building. The first story was divided into one large open area with a large backroom and two smaller chambers, one of which was a washroom, if the basin in it was any indication.

The upper floor was divided into five smaller chambers, which might have once been bedrooms, and a larger gathering room at the back. Several of the windows were broken, letting in drifts of snow and a chill wind, but the remaining windows let in a lively green light that reminded him of a spring day.

The crystal the windows were made from had the same green tint. When he placed his hand on one, it drew mana from him and released a warm breeze that drove away some of the chill in the air. On a closer look, many of the areas of the home had enchantments laid into the stone, from the fireplace to the doors on the bedrooms.

"No wonder people come here to study enchantments," he said, shaking his head. "Even the houses are covered in them."

The first layer was reserved for high-ranking individuals, including the families of the controllers, the Guardian Star informed him. **Visitors were not allowed on this layer, as it is too close to the central plateau. Dignitaries were received on the second layer, which is larger and contains guest quarters. It is a quarter mile below this one. Each layer had its own defensive ward, but now only the one on the central plateau remains.**

Sam held back his surprise as he listened. It seemed the star had gained a lot of information from the relic when it accessed it, including this new sense of personality.

Had it seen all 162,000 years? If so, how could it not have formed some type of identity...and maybe it would actually be helpful now, unlike before when he'd had to force it to even scan the area around him.

Sam looked around the building with a thoughtful expression before he turned and left. The world must have been very different when this was new. What had it been like? And more than that...perhaps once they took care of the Outsiders, this could be a place to stay.

He had access to the formations here, even if it was limited, and he could set up a workshop to study and repair this place. Doing that would teach him plenty about the enchantments, which was why he'd originally come here.

He could make things for sale in Highfold and his family would have the convenience and protection of the wards. If he could repair some of the formations and get the teleportation working...they could come and go from here, and maybe even have defenses to keep out trouble.

But that's a thought for another day. First, he needed to deal with the threats and make sure that the Flaws were sealed.

"Are you able to find the closest monsters and Outsiders in this area?" he asked as he looked down at the star. "And can you send me back up to the plateau the same way?"

Transfer to the central plateau is possible from the inner edge of this layer. You will have to return here first and not be in combat. Teleporting during combat requires more energy and the relic will reject it. The Moonlight Relic is barely functioning and you do not have the authority to draw from its energy reserves. You are only able to access the operating enchantments.

On this layer, the closest monsters are two Level 65 arctic cave trolls half a mile to the east. Within a two-mile radius, there are 11 other monsters, 32 beasts, and 6 Outsiders. Levels range from 56 to 85. Some of the beasts have been attracted by the mana density here and taken up residence.

A map of the nearest enemies sprang into Sam's mind as the Guardian Star highlighted where they were. There was a mix of monsters, including arctic cave trolls, strange crystalline serpents that looked like moving ice sculptures, several ice wyverns, many scattered beasts, and two trios of Ice-bloods who were slowly moving through the ruins as if they were searching for something.

Sam studied the map as his eyes narrowed. The first layer was on a slope that circled the peak of Sun's Rest, creating a ring about a mile wide. The distance around it was close to seven miles. The monsters and the Outsiders were scattered around with plenty of room in between.

His fangs glinted behind a grim smile as he memorized their places and then ducked into the building behind him. A healing scroll appeared in his hand. The area around here was filled with challenges.

He just needed to make a few preparations and then the hunt would begin.

***

Light, powdery snow drifted through the air and settled onto Sam's shoulders as he leaned around a stone pillar, examining the trolls in front of him. They were bigger than the arctic cave trolls that had attacked the Ice Sylph village and he spent longer studying them than he usually did with monsters.

At the moment, they were fighting over the corpse of a large Cloud-Striped Snow Leopard they had killed, tearing at it and each other at the same time. They were hulking, white-skinned monstrosities with muscles that bulged into hideous contortions of veins and sinews.

Their jaws were wider and longer than the rest of their head, filled with fangs half a foot long, giving them a strange, triangular appearance, and they had long, drooping ears that nearly touched their shoulders.

Their arms dragged on the ground, ending in gnarled, oversized hands tipped with sharp claws. All over their skin, there was a sparse white and blue fur that acted as camouflage and perhaps defense.

He was confident in attacking them, but he was still hesitating as he considered what felt different about this battle. It took him a moment to realize what it was.

It had been a long time since he was on his own while fighting. Or perhaps he never really had been. His father had always been around, or at least nearby, for every battle since he unlocked his class, except for the fight with Lenei, and that time his mother had rushed out.

It was isolating, but at the same time he felt a strange sense of freedom. With no one around, he didn't need to hide his appearance or conceal the battle lust that sang out from his essence.

His blood echoed with a thunderous resonance as he looked toward the trolls, his expression changing as he let himself relax for the first time, sinking into the feeling.

Crystal flame spiraled across his body as his battle aura surged outward, his claws lengthening. A cloak of crystal flame swept back from his shoulders, its edges burning away in translucent streams.

Chunks of ice, flurries of snow, and blades of wind began to form in the air around him as Elemental Manipulation joined in, pulling on the elements.

The trolls were immensely strong for their size, but they didn't have time to see the blur of sapphire blue light that shot toward them until it was too late. Long, curving talons like crystal sabers tore through their skin, slashing across their necks and abdomens.

Then the blur was gone, leaving behind a glowing, blue-white sphere with a *star* rune burning at its heart that slowly fell to the ground between the two trolls.

One of them reached out to grab it with an angry roar that echoed around the area, but as it slammed into the sphere, the blue layers only collapsed inward toward the rune. The resulting explosion covered both trolls in an expanding wave of liquid starfire.

Their skin crisped, darkening in an instant as the blast washed over them, and they let out howls of pain and fury, which were cut short a moment later as a figure wrapped in crystal flames flew between them, slashing out again and again.

Sprays of white-green blood flew out behind each cut, burning away in crackling explosions as it touched the flames in the air. Chunks of stone, ice, and wind blades sliced around the slashing figure in arcs, slamming into the trolls and tearing at them.

Sam's fangs were bared and his face was hard as essence poured out of him into the aura, intensifying his strength. His essence stars burned with explosive force as his blood demanded vengeance and conquest.

His claws ripped through the troll's stomachs, sliced across their legs, severed their arms, and then finally slashed across their throats as their heads tumbled to the ground. The pieces burned with flame, searing away any regeneration that they might have.

A moment later, he stood over the corpses, glaring down at them as he felt his essence hit 25%. His breath came in short, sharp hisses as a growl rumbled from his lungs.

Despite that, he felt tension draining out of his body as if a cork had been pulled, ebbing away until he was calm and focused. Satisfaction tingled across his skin. He took a deep breath and let it out again. Then he scanned the area for other enemies before he let the battle aura fade away.

The next closest enemies are four local beasts, Diamondfang Ice Vipers, levels 56 to 59. They have established a lair inside one of the old buildings. There was no trace of judgment in the Guardian Star's voice for how he had killed the trolls. It was only suggestive, pointing him toward the next target.

**Once this area is clear, you should visit the closest supply point
to see what resources remain. It may be possible to repair some of
this section of the relic. The formation in that area is damaged, so I
cannot see inside.**

"Let me gather the experience from these," he replied as he took another
breath and reached down to touch the corpses. The shimmering chime of
experience rang in his mind as he pulled the threads of energy from the
corpses.

**Congratulations, Battlefield Reclaimer. You have used your Class
skills to slay your enemies.**

You gain 1,023,550 Class experience.

**You have gained two Class Levels. You are now a Level 64 Battle-
field Reclaimer.**

Total Class Experience: 9,868,490 / 10,240,000

You have gained two General Levels. You are now Level 64.

Total General Experience: 9,901,740 / 10,240,000

**You gain +2 Intelligence, +2 Aura, and have six free attribute
points to assign.**

The experience rushed through him in a surge of relaxing energy and
Sam let out another deep breath. It was more experience than he'd expected, even though these trolls had been Level 65. It looked like hunting alone
was effective.

He hesitated for a moment and then he put all six of the free points into
Wisdom, to help with collecting auras. The attribute rose to 61. Four more
and it should maximize his chance with advanced auras. As he finished, the
Guardian Star spoke up.

**Merging with the Moonlight Relic has given me access to its
observations of the World Core over the millenia. The World Core
continues to support your efforts and is assigning extra experience
for your battles near the Grand Flaw.**

**However, the experience transfer from high-level enemies is very
limited. You have gathered 5% of the experience from these trolls.
In a normal situation, you would receive a tenth of that. The rest is
diverted to the management of the Seal.**

Sam nodded as he collected the auras from both of the trolls. He already
had a few of the basic version, and the Auras of Enduring Stone (Advanced) swirled past his senses with the echo of oppressive, ancient weight.

The Diamondfang Ice Vipers are 0.6 miles to the northwest. The main supply point for the First Layer is 2.1 miles north of that, most of the way around the ring on the north side.

"Understood," Sam replied as he looked up from the trolls and scanned the area around him. He would have been covered in blood if not for his crystal flames. He located the vipers on the map and then looked for other enemies in the area, plotting out a path.

If he took time to rest between each fight, he wasn't sure how long it would take him to clear this layer, but if everything went well, perhaps he could finish it in a couple of days.

So far, there was no new word from the church forces, which meant his father was in the same location. Jeric had organized the adventurers and started to clear out monsters near the old temple, pulling them back in small groups. If it came down to it, they needed to make sure they could succeed on their own, rather than relying on the church.

When the path between the enemies was clear, he turned toward the vipers, his form blurring as he blended in with the snow and ice, slipping through the ruins.

Elemental Manipulation was helping him to use his Initiate of Ice trait. He was able to pull the snow around himself like a cloak, clearing his path and concealing himself from casual sight. He drifted across the snow like a frozen leaf, his footsteps barely leaving a mark.

***

The Diamondfang Ice Vipers were elegant and vicious, even in death. They were nearly two dozen feet of coiled muscle and triangular, wedge-shaped heads. Their scales were white and pale green, and their fangs were translucent, green crystal with hollow veins inside for venom.

He stood over them with his battle aura swirling as he looked down at their scattered corpses. He was covered in abrasions and slash marks from their strikes and where they had tried to coil around him. They'd been a much more dangerous fight than the trolls, mostly due to their speed.

The one that had coiled around him was lying in a dozen pieces all around, its white-green scales shattered. It was torn into chunks from where he'd savaged it with his claws.

Perhaps he should have used his bracer or more long-range skills, but...there was something deeply satisfying about facing his enemies with his bare hands and battle aura. He would have to be careful to judge his battles, so that he didn't get in over his head.

It was clear to him now that his transformation and essence both had given him a taste for blood and battle. It was something he was becoming more comfortable with, but not something he wanted to show his family.

The isolation was a chance to explore that side of things and to learn how to balance it. He bared his fangs in a savage grin and stretched his arms upward, feeling the smooth play of muscles beneath his skin as he let the feeling wash over him.

Guardian's mental state is stable, the Guardian Star advised, **but requires observation.**

Sam chuckled at it, pushing the statement aside as he pulled out a healing scroll and activated it, letting the white energy boil through his wounds. He knew that essence was more chaotic than either pure aura or mana, but he didn't feel like it was changing him.

No more than it already had.

When he was done, he bent down and collected the experience.

Congratulations, Battlefield Reclaimer. You have used your Class skills to slay your enemies.

You have gained 741,500 Class Experience. You are now a Level 65 Battlefield Reclaimer.

Total Class Experience: 10,609,990 / 11,250,000

You are now General Level 65.

Total General Experience: 10,642,740 / 11,250,000

You gain +1 Aura and +1 Intelligence and have three free attribute points to distribute.

The experience rushed through his blood as he assigned the three points to Wisdom. The Second Cliff at Level 66 was just ahead of him, but from the look of it, there was enough experience on this layer that he could move straight past it. He let out a deep breath and then turned to the task of harvesting the remains.

The vipers didn't have an aura to claim, but their venom almost felt like one. Their fangs dripped with a pale green liquid that hummed with the sense of creeping ice that froze the bones and stopped the heart. Even in death, their eyes held a cold, watchful presence that tracked everything and waited, biding their time until they struck.

He shook his head as he extracted the fangs and then spent a little while skinning them and storing the materials away.

When he was done, he incinerated the rest and looked up at the snow that was always falling here. It would cover over the signs of the battle soon. Something about the ruins seemed to keep it from building up past a certain level, creating an eternal circle of ice up here where the heavens were cold and clear.

When he was done, he looked at the map and then ghosted away through the snow, heading for the storeroom the Guardian Star had mentioned.

It was time to see what it would take to repair these ruins and what the original builders had left behind.

CHAPTER FORTY-ONE

MOONLIGHT STOREROOM

The sun rose slowly, turning the sky to a pale rose gold as Sam made his way to the location the Guardian Star had marked. Caelus hadn't risen on the eastern horizon, but there was a soft blue glimmer that presaged the moon's appearance.

All around, the peaks of the Western Reaches had begun to glow, soaking in the light as mana gathered around them and rippled in brilliant colors, building up into storms that would flow down the slopes.

The ruins of the first layer were far enough below the peak that the light hadn't reached them yet. Here, it was still shadowed. The area was more intact than the other layers and all through it ribbons of triple-colored moonlight twined from building to building, lighting up the dark for the inhabitants of the city to find their way.

Moonlight ran like a river across the streets, creating a web that outlined each building and lane. Blue, green, and purple streams decorated the sky, hanging over the open squares. The falling snowflakes merged with the enchantments, reflecting the light and giving everything a subtle glow.

The sight took Sam's breath away as he drifted between one building and the next, his steps light on the snow. He couldn't help but wonder what it must have looked like when it was new.

Perhaps one day, it could be again.

In that, it was a symbol for the world itself. He shook his head as he pushed the thought aside and focused on the location of the storeroom that was supposed to be in front of him.

On the way here, he'd avoided the monsters and beasts, which had delayed him a little, but it had been a good scouting expedition. He had a better awareness of what he was facing in clearing out this layer, and some of the battles would be intense.

"Are you certain this is the storeroom?" he muttered, his voice low as he directed his attention to the Guardian Star. "There's nothing here."

In front of him, there was only an open square, one of many on the first layer. It was illuminated by the ribbons of moonlight flowing above and the silver-green enchantments from the stones below. Even without his ability to see in the dark, this area would have been clearly visible.

The entrance to the storeroom is in the center of this plaza. To access it, you will need to move the snow aside. The builders chose not to use a spatial storage for this area, since it would be difficult to access if the relic were damaged. To open the entrance, find the keystone and infuse your aura into it.

You have an imprint from the Moonlight Relic, marking you as an official here. It will open for you.

"How did I end up with that anyway?" Sam asked as he thought back to the trap. The moonlight had cut itself into his soul, making its own way through his essence constellation.

You were marked as a Guardian. In the absence of a sentient controller, the relic has the self-awareness to appoint new individuals to help repair it. You were chosen to do so. If the relic had been in better condition, it would have been able to communicate with you directly.

"So I ended up as the town guard again? Or is it the town enchanter this time?" Sam let out a dark chuckle. "I suppose that fits. Are there others who have been appointed to repair the ruins?"

Negative. The Moonlight Relic recognized you due to the Guardian contract you bear. The signature of astral energy has to be close enough to that of its creators to meet its requirements. Great trust has been placed in you.

"Right," Sam said as he held back a sigh at the thought of more work to do. "At least it will be interesting. Now, how do I get into the storeroom?"

The keystone is approximately one hundred and forty feet in front of you. Walk forward and I will alert you when you are on top of it.

The star's directions were easy enough to follow. Before long, he reached the correct area and began to move the snow, using his connection to Ice to push it aside in waves as he dug through the drifts.

It was quick work, but the open square made him uneasy, especially with the moonlight above. It was pretty, but it also meant everything here was much too visible. He was concealing himself in a curtain of drifting snow, but that was suspicious if there was anything around that was smart enough to ask questions.

Whether it was luck or concealment, however, he made it down to the keystone without anything disturbing him. The last layer of snow drifted aside as he waved his hand, pulling it away with a wave of essence.

Below him, there was a humming enchantment that looked very similar to the rest of the ruins, swirling with the moons' colors, but it was in the form of an ornate circle instead of flowing lines. At the center, there was a diagram of three moons inlaid in the stone.

That is the keystone. Charge it with your aura. It may require a significant amount. You are substantially less powerful than the original controllers. They were near the peak for this world.

"So Level 399...or close to it," he mused as he did some quick calculations. At that level...how much aura would someone have? Assuming it was a core attribute...800...1,000? Did attributes change with an evolution?

He wasn't sure what attributes were like in the higher evolutions, since the information wasn't shared easily. The question was how much it was going to take to open a storeroom.

Classes had probably been different when the relic was new, so the same laws might not apply.

Right now, he had 155 base Aura, and 161 with his bracer. Hopefully, that would be enough.

He felt for the three strands of moonlight in his essence as he placed his hand on the formation, pushing the correct strand toward each moon as he let his aura flow into them.

The moons were blank, but it wasn't hard to figure out which was which. Caelus was at the center, slightly higher than the other two. Silvas was at the left, and Amaris was at the right. It was the same pattern as the Three Crowns for the festival.

Strands of blue, green, and purple moonlight poured out of his hand and into the moons as he felt his aura dropping. He automatically released the same amount of mana into his surroundings, but instead of wasting it, he pushed it into the snow all around him.

As he did, the snow was imprinted with his energy and began to feel more like it was a part of him, swirling more easily into a concealing storm. He was at the eye of the hurricane, where everything was calm, but around him the snow began to intensify, freezing into icy blades at the edges.

A hundred points of aura flowed into the keystone before he felt something shift. Below his hand, the outline of the moons was beginning to glow. When he pulled his hand away to check, there was the sliver of a crescent moon showing on each one.

Unfortunately, it was only at the outer edge.

Probably a thousand at least, he muttered under his breath as he considered how long it would take to charge it. He wasn't willing to combust more than a few auras, and he doubted that he could do more than ten at most, even with the upgrades from absorbing essence.

The only option was to meditate here and keep trying to fill the keystone, and that would take the better part of a day, if not more.

At that moment, however, the Guardian Star spoke up.

Initial activation successful. Requesting energy transfer from Moonlight Relic.

Transfer approved.

There was a low, resonant *hum* from the enchantments all around him that echoed through the empty square. It made his teeth ache as he felt energy surge upward from the stones at his feet.

A flow of silver-green energy poured up from the ruins, dividing into three strands of moonlight that poured into each moon, which began to grow brighter. The crescent moons expanded, filling in more of the three diagrams.

It was like watching a wave roll across the shore as the color swept across each moon, and he felt a distinct, vibrant aura from each of them. Caelus was distant and watchful, Silvas was warm with sharp spines, and Amaris was wild passion.

When each moon was completely filled, they were so bright that their light obscured the keystone. They floated upward, rising out of the stone as they spread out into a triangle around him.

It was a vertical design with Caelus above his head and Silvas and Amaris to the left and right at shoulder height. The space between them was about six feet across, enough for a couple of people to stand comfortably.

The hum of the enchantments changed to a higher pitch as the energy from the relic continued to pour in and the full moons flared above him. Three beams of moonlight shot downward to the stone at his feet.

The stone opened, flowing apart like water to reveal a staircase leading down. The moonlight shot down into the opening, bringing life to the walls as it lit the way. The moons rotated around him and then sank down, returning to the keystone, where they glimmered with continued energy.

A moment later, the stones around the formation surged upward, creating a triangular peak with an open doorway above the staircase. It was about ten feet tall, similar to the doorway of the house he'd seen.

The Guardian Star said nothing, but he could feel a sense of watchful expectation around him. He wasn't sure if it was coming from the star or the Moonlight Relic itself. He also wasn't sure how long he would be inside.

He sent a cautious look around him, examining the flurry of snow that was spinning here. Then he reached out to the mana he'd infused and pulled it back toward him, bringing the snow with it.

A moment later, a compacted ice wall surrounded the opening, with just a sliver of a gap near the top. On the outside, new snow was already falling.

Hopefully, that would be enough to conceal the entrance and make it look like a fallen pillar or building.

Without wasting any more time, he stepped forward, heading down the staircase.

The passageway was brightly lit from the moonlight running along the ceiling, walls, and floor. The stairs led down for about thirty feet through layers of greenish stone. In between the layers, there were strands of either energy or a strange, silver metal that ran through them like veins and glowed with power.

The fortifications of this storeroom are sufficient to protect it against almost every threat. It would require destroying the Moonlight Relic completely in order to break through.

After a few moments, the tunnel ended in a large, arched door with the three moons engraved on it, which was very similar to the keystone outside. Without being told, Sam automatically placed his hand in the center of the design and infused his aura.

This time, it only took a few points before the moons flashed, their colors lighting up. Then the door flowed away, the stone melting into the sides of the archway. The moons remained, shining at the center of a curtain of light that obscured the contents on the other side.

The light brushed over his skin with a familiar tingle as he stepped through.

The first impression of the other side was of a vast, dark space that reminded him of the trap he'd been in, but a moment later the darkness disappeared as moonlight shone down from the ceiling, revealing row after row of long, stone tables between towering shelves.

About half of the spots on the shelves were empty, but the rest were filled with silver crystals, ingots of strange metals, glowing spheres, and floating wisps of starlight and flames that drifted above the surface of the tables encased in protective formations.

The room was more than five hundred feet wide and the same deep, and the containers stretched back along the entire distance.

Analyzing...the Guardian Star spoke up, along with a quiet flow of energy from it that drifted across the chamber. A moment later, it announced its verdict. **There are sufficient materials here to repair the top two layers of the relic, and perhaps more, if you are efficient. That may be enough to allow it to initiate self-repair on the other layers.**

Sam's jaw dropped open as he looked at it all and he couldn't help but wonder what he could make if he had all of these materials to practice with....

Bear in mind that the Moonlight Relic will scan each item before allowing it to leave this chamber, the Guardian Star continued, dashing his hopes. **Only what is needed to repair the relic may be removed.**

Sam sighed. He was looking at the wealth of a forgotten past that dwarfed anything he'd ever known, but it seemed he couldn't call any of it his own. He wasn't greedy, but the sight was making his fingers itch.

Even if he could only use them for the relic, he didn't know where to begin. He'd have to learn. It was too important to the Seal and stability in this area.

He'd made a promise to protect his family and the world. Repairing these ruins would be a good start.

The real treasure is not these materials, the Guardian Star added quietly, as if it were trying to make him feel better. **Continue onwar d...straight ahead three hundred feet.**

Sam walked past the tables, his eyes brushing over everything he passed, which ended up with him turning in circles and having to retrace his steps more than once as he was distracted by some interesting item.

He tried to analyze some of the objects, but it failed every time, which wasn't a surprise. The Guardian Star could probably have told him what they were, but there were too many of them to ask about each one. Instead, he contented himself with sensing them through Crystal Focus and letting the impressions settle into his memory, so he would recognize them in the future.

The star's directions led him about two-thirds of the way through the storeroom to where another circular enchantment was marked on the floor. It had the same design of the three moons, glimmering faintly with light.

The area was separated from the tables around it, with about three dozen feet of clear space on every side. It was enough for a small crowd to gather, as if something was supposed to happen here.

Step into the center and stand above the three moons.

Sam followed the instructions absentmindedly, his attention traveling between the enchantment on the stones and the items on the nearest shelves. Once he was in the right position, he could feel a new flow of energy all around him, tugging at his awareness. The moons on the stone began to intensify, their light increasing.

Activating. The Guardian Star's word was quick and efficient.

The moonlight brightened, flowing upward around him in three colors that mixed with streams of silver-green energy. All around him, the floor began to flow, boiling upward like a hot spring as it changed shape.

At the center, where he was standing, an illusory mountain appeared, and then to the sides, two others formed as well. Rings of different colors sprang into existence around them, turning into pillars, walls, and tumbled stones that stretched across all three mountains, with each color signifying a layer of the ruins.

The illusion mixed with the flowing stone, giving life to a model of the ruins, including their position on the mountains. A moment later, the design expanded until it filled the empty space around him.

A silver and green stone pillar rose out of the floor in front of Sam, similar to the control pillar on the plateau above, but much smaller.

This is a model of the Moonlight Relic and a subsidiary control point. The original enchantments and design of the relic are contained inside, as well as a model of the current condition. It can assist with identifying critical areas. You will need it to effect repairs.

Now, place your palm on the pillar.

Sam turned around, his eyes widening as he examined the extent of the ruins. Here, there was no snow to obscure the view and he could see exactly how large they were. When he counted up the layers in different colors, it was clear that there were twelve of them.

Each layer once had a specific role, but at the moment, it is irrelevant. The Guardian Star spoke up to call his attention back to the present. **Place your hand on the pillar.**

Sam pulled his eyes away from the ruins and placed his hand on top of the stone. There were lines of runes and swirling strands of energy running through it. As soon as he touched it, that energy flared up, stabbing at his hand like a spear.

It was well contained, but he could feel enough power in it to obliterate a hundred feet in every direction.

The strands of moonlight in his essence surged outward on their own, wrapping around the energy and calming it before it could strike him, causing it to curve as it returned to the pillar. As soon as it did, the pillar came to life, warming up beneath his hand.

Imprinting.

The Guardian Star's voice was calm, but there was a weight hidden in it. The energy that had been routed back into the pillar flowed through a series of runes and swirling lines and then shot back toward Sam's hand, reaching out to the strands of moonlight there.

The auras of each strand intensified as they absorbed the new energy, becoming a little more vibrant, and flickering images passed through Sam's mind. Swirling runes and lines of power that matched those he'd seen in the ruins embedded themselves in his memory, layering themselves on each other in a massively complex pattern that hung there like a crystal diagram.

Then the real flood of information came, pouring into that design in a torrent of flickering signs and sigils that filled the pattern, so many of them compressed together that they turned from individual symbols into a river of liquid silver.

Then, it stopped, leaving Sam with a massive headache. The meridians throughout his body felt frazzled, as if they'd been scorched by the wave of power. In his mind, the diagram had taken the shape of a full moon, the information in it too complex to easily unravel.

Imprint complete.

The Guardian Star sounded satisfied with itself, as if it had accomplished something important.

You now bear the complete imprint of the Moonlight Relic, including a copy of its core enchantment, which is necessary to repair it. Every sigil here is part of that core, and without it you would not be able to access them.

Sam touched his forehead gingerly, feeling around the base of his horns. Despite the headache, he was surprisingly unharmed.

The relic may be broken, but it is easily capable of delivering an imprint without injuring you, the Guardian Star said, as if reading his mind. It sounded slightly miffed. **Only a low-tier enchantment would have that effect.**

Sam examined the construct in his mind for a moment and then turned his attention to the model of the ruins around him. Somehow, it felt more comfortable, as if it were familiar now.

He reached out and pulled a section of the illusion toward him, and it flew to the area just between his hands, growing larger. With another flick of his intent, it zoomed back out again and was replaced by a different section.

It didn't take him long to find the central plateau or the section where he was, but it was more intensive to find the area with his father. After a moment, the Guardian Star helped, lighting up a section of the ruins in his view.

He zoomed in on what had once been the tenth layer, the third up from the bottom. Here, nearly every enchantment was broken, each of them highlighted in a dull grey that showed them as disabled. The building with his father glowed with a slight green, evidence of the functioning mana pylon inside.

His hands flickered and the image zoomed out, overlaid with the diagram of what should have been there, showing him the connections between the mana-gathering pylon and the buildings around it.

The tenth layer was once the home of gardens and Wood-focused enchantments. Much of the local food supply was grown there.

Sam nodded, turning his attention away from that as his hands flickered again, pulling up another section of the ruins. This time, he was looking at the area that contained the Grand Flaw.

It was on the northern side of the seventh level, near what had once been a teleportation platform for shifting large quantities of goods. It was highlighted in the diagram's light in an angry red-yellow, the colors circling around a dark gap with triangular points at both ends.

Even in the moonlight of the diagram, it looked ugly.

"The enchantments here will take a while to learn," Sam said with his attention fixed on the flaw. "And right now, I need to make sure that this area is clear of dangers. I'll repair what I can, but eliminating the Outsiders here comes first."

Security and then repair, the Guardian Star agreed. **Repairs will be slow, given how much you need to learn. Several years at a minimum, even if the self-repair enchantments can be restored.**

There are still 11 monsters, 28 beasts, and 6 Outsiders on this layer.

The model in front of Sam spun until it was focused on just the first layer and then the Guardian Star zoomed it in, highlighting the locations of the enemies. With it all laid out in front of his eyes, it was a much more effective map than before. There was something about seeing it in front of him that made it more real.

He looked from one set of targets to the next, rolling his shoulders as he gave them a grim smile. He'd need a little bit to restore his essence, but once that was done...he'd return to his plan to eliminate every enemy on the first layer, and then he'd work his way down to the seventh.

"Then we should get started."

CHAPTER FORTY-TWO

HUNTING THE FIRST LAYER

The storeroom closed behind him with a resonant hum as the earth flowed back in, sealing over the entrance and restoring the unblemished appearance of the keystone. The three moons settled back into their positions and went dark.

The ice wall he'd created was still there, but his awareness swept out past it as he scanned the square, checking for visitors. There wasn't anything at first except for the snow and wind. He pushed out farther and just on the edge of his range, he saw the first one.

It was one of the crystalline serpents that the Guardian Star had pointed out to him, its body nearly thirty feet long with pale white, translucent scales that reflected the colors around it. It looked like a moving ice sculpture twisting its way around the buildings and over the fallen stones.

Hoarfrost Serpent. Level 67.

Behind it, there were two more at Level 65 and 68. A moment later, they moved beyond the range of Crystal Focus, gliding over the snow as pale blue tongues hissed out of their mouths. It looked like they were heading behind a building.

Scanning. The Guardian Star spoke up without his encouragement, flickering energy flying away from it. When they'd scanned the area from the storeroom, it had looked like some of the monsters were on the move. Now, that was confirmed.

Five monsters are within four hundred feet. The average level is 64. They appear to be moving into an ambush position on the opposite side of the square.

The star's voice held a warning. He could feel the sense of building threat all around him. He'd spent about two hours down in the storeroom, or perhaps a bit more, which had been a risk. It seemed they'd discovered his barrier while he'd been inside.

He was by himself and should be cautious, but what he felt the most was a desire to stretch his muscles and let his essence out.

Five prepared enemies near the same level as him might be a difficult fight, even with his bracer and auras, but a crackling fierceness flared through him at the idea. It was the desire to tear his enemies apart with his bare hands.

He didn't push it down. Instead, he drew on that feeling, letting it fill his muscles as he activated his battle aura. Crystal flame surged around him, spiraling as it extended his talons and formed into a rippling cloak.

"An ambush…" he growled as he considered what that meant. The desire for battle was surging through his blood, but his mind was clear. "Something must have set that up. So either one of these monsters is intelligent or there's another group behind them, like the Icebloods, who noticed something here."

Their awareness of what was happening in the ruins was better than he'd thought, but the arrival of new forces didn't change his mind. It was dangerous to run straight into an ambush, and that wasn't his plan. He'd fight the monsters, but he'd do it on his terms.

Since they were planning to ambush him, he'd come in from where they didn't expect it.

"Let them try. This way, I won't have to hunt them down later."

***

He left the ice wall up to conceal his movements as he pulled the swirling snow closer. He couldn't hide the ice wall from sight, but he could make sure that it drew attention.

He poured his essence out into the snow, binding more of it to his will. If anyone were looking, it would be blindingly obvious with the amount of essence in it. Hopefully, it would distract the serpents and whatever else might be watching.

At the same time, he used the fluctuations from the snow to conceal his activities as he thinned out a small section of the ice wall to create a tunnel. Once it was ready, he slipped out. He drew the snowstorm around him as he glided away, keeping the ice wall between him and the monsters.

Once he was out of the square, he darted behind a building and began moving in a large circle to the side. In the plaza, the snowstorm began to die down, but the snow continued to fall, as it always did here.

Four hundred feet ahead, thirty to your left. Three Hoar-frost Serpents are hiding around the corner and two Ebonstreak Hunters are on the roof of the abandoned workshop across the street.

The Guardian Star marked out the position of the monsters. They were out of range of Crystal Focus, which meant he couldn't get a good feel for their auras or strength, but it was useful to know their positions.

He sped between two buildings and scaled the side of a third as he approached the monsters, his talons gripping at the edges of loose stones. When he was on the roof, he flattened himself against the stones and peered over the edge to see what he was dealing with.

The Hoarfrost Serpents were on the edge of Crystal Focus, about eighty feet away from him, but the Ebonstreak Hunters were too distant. He had a moment to observe the forms of the giant ice snakes before he needed to move again.

They were much larger than the Diamondfang Ice Vipers and their scales radiated a chilling cold into the area around them, turning the snow a pale, fragile white that shattered into dust as their tails twitched. The wall next to them was coated in the same white frost. Perhaps that was where they got their name.

They were coiled up behind the wall in tight balls with their wedge-shaped heads protruding from the top and only the thin, translucent tips of their tail from the bottom. Their eyes were vertical, white slits with a sliver of blue at the center.

The serpents radiated Ice, but their hoarfrost wasn't a familiar or pleasant type. It was Ice that hated other elements and all forms of life, with nothing but the desire to destroy. Something about it was warped and unnatural, and deeply unpleasant.

The Bounty Hunter trait he'd gained from killing the basilisk let him know that the monsters were only half native to Aster Fall. They felt slightly out of place: not as much as an Outsider, but definitely not something that fully belonged.

He knew what his father would say, which was to avoid the fight unless he had no other choice, but the monsters were planning to ambush him.

That made it personal.

There was also the question of what was behind them or if they were acting alone. Whatever the reason they'd come here, it didn't bode well. He needed to clear as many of these monsters out of the first layer as possible before something worse appeared.

The worst thing of all would be if an entire army of them found him. If that happened, he would either have to abandon the first layer or try to retreat to the storeroom or central plateau.

What it boiled down to was a choice between being active and eliminating his enemies or being passive and running from them, hoping that they wouldn't find him. Unfortunately for the Hoarfrost Serpents, he wasn't in the mood to run.

The snow exploded beneath his feet as he jumped upward, racing across the roof. His battle aura flared around him as a Starfire formed in his left hand. A swirl of condensed crystal flame covered his right hand, flowing along his talons.

He leapt from that roof to another, turning to the side just enough to hurl the Starfire spell toward the serpents, and then he was moving again, pulling the snow around him in a curtain as he sprinted across the roof and leapt to another.

The explosion of the Starfire shook the surroundings, blasting upward in a fountain of sapphire crystal flame and burning astral light, but his view was blocked by the ruins as he leapt from one building to another, circling around.

It took only seconds for the blast to start to fade, leaving behind an echoing explosion that rolled through the ruins like thunder. If there was anything else nearby, it had just been alerted to a battle, but he ignored that as he leapt one more time off of the roof he was on, slamming into the ground with a resonant impact. He bent his knees and let the snow and his aura absorb the force.

He was directly behind where the Hoarfrost Serpents had been coiled up. The Starfire had scattered them, throwing them backwards, but it hadn't been targeted enough to do real damage.

Now, they surged forward to attack where the spell had been. White frost exploded around them, their thirty-foot-long bodies uncoiling in a flash as they searched for the enemy to the front.

A second Starfire shot between the serpents like a flickering, blue-white harbinger of destruction, its light reflecting from the snow. The spell flew ahead of the serpents and exploded right in front of them. A wave of brilliant flame lifted them from the ground, tossing them backward as they writhed, trying to coil into defensive balls.

He didn't give them the chance.

An Essence Shield wrapped around the area behind the serpents, slamming them back down toward the center of the blast and the flames. Then he was there, his talons lengthening as he bared his fangs in a growl and sprinted through the firestorm and slashed at the coils in front of him.

Pale white blood flew as scales shattered and he felt the sizzling bite of their hoarfrost lashing back at him. The head of one of the vipers flew away down the alley as he changed targets and raced toward another before it could coil up.

He cut long slashes down its scales, causing it to rear into the air with a high-pitched *hissss* as it curved its body and struck down at him. With a third of its body in the air, it was much taller than he was.

Its mouth shot toward him with two white fangs bared, each of them as long as his arm. Pale, dense scales lined the edges of its jaw and alabaster teeth ridges were visible inside its mouth.

Its head slammed into an Essence Shield that was angled to the left and Sam snarled as he darted underneath it, his aura brightening as he tore four long gashes through its scales.

Gouts of pale white blood poured out of the serpent in a torrent, exploding into acrid smoke as it collided with his aura, and then a massive weight slammed into his back, tearing him from the ground.

He was flung into the air, spiraling out of control as he flew toward the wall of a building. A surge of crystal flame blasted outward from him, pushing against the air currents, but it only redirected him slightly.

All he could do was harden his aura and gather an Essence Shield around him as he slammed into the stone. A blinding crackle of pain echoed through his bones like an enormous drum and the world flared with blue-white light. The Essence Shield shattered into shards.

His eyesight blurred, but Crystal Focus was active as he snarled. He evaded, pushing away from the wall with a surge of flames as he circled back toward the serpent that had hit him from behind.

At that moment, it was racing toward him, its head rearing back to bite. He gathered himself, crouching down slightly to launch himself toward it, but at the last moment, he caught sight of something else in Crystal Focus.

He threw himself to the side, rolling across the ground as he wrapped a shield around him. The area where he'd just been standing was consumed in a blast of ebony flames that ate away at the snow, corroding it rather than burning.

Another streak of the same fire shot toward him from a different angle, and he threw himself away again, gathering crystal flame beneath his feet as he stabilized himself.

Two dark forms were floating above the street, their wings outstretched. They were a weirdly twisted amalgamation of things, with faces like a bat, wings that ended in hooked claws, a thick ruff of dark fur around their necks, and a body that was a twisted, thin rail, as if it had never fully developed.

Ebonstreak Hunter, Level 64.
Ebonstreak Hunter, Level 62.

The two hunters wrapped their wings and dove, heading for him as two more balls of corrosive flames formed in their mouths.

At the same time, the last serpent was uncoiling toward him in another strike. This time, it was accompanied by a swirling white cloud of hoarfrost. The serpent opened its mouth, hissing, and a pale white frost bolt flared toward him. The tip of it was coated in a white glaze like the venom on its fangs.

Sam slammed his hand into the ground, using the rebound to redirect his fall as he pulled more crystal flame around him, gathering it around his feet. Then he leapt to the side, darting out of the path of the frost bolt as he summoned a wave of crystal flame arrows.

"Enough," he growled as he reached out to the snow all around him.

With a surge of will, he pulled at the snow and winds around the Ebonstreak Hunters at the same time as he released the crystal flame arrows. The arrows tore through the air with sizzling speed.

The hunters tried to evade, but the snow pressed tightly around them, trapping them in place. A moment later, their fragile bodies exploded as the storm of arrows blasted through them.

A surge of ecstatic conquest rushed through him, but the attack had delayed him. The Hoarfrost Serpent slammed into him from behind, its fangs slashing down toward his neck and chest.

Sam growled as the coils wrapped around him. The fangs slashed across him as his aura exploded. A curtain of crystal flame blasted outward, tearing through scales and pale organs as it sliced along the serpent's long body.

There was a moment frozen in time as the serpent struggled to drive its fangs deeper and Sam's attack cut through it at the same instant. Then the world began to move again, as the serpent fell apart in half a dozen chunks and the pressure around him dissipated.

He staggered as he dropped back to the ground and reached into his storage. He pulled out four basic auras and combusted them as he looked around the area.

The fight had been foolish, but there was a delighted satisfaction roaring through him that told him it had been worthwhile. It was like stretching a long unused muscle that had become cramped, and now it was humming with power.

He could feel a biting frost from the serpent's venom tearing at him, so he poured crystal flame toward it, meeting it with purifying flames. He pulled a healing scroll from his belt and activated it, feeling the different burn of the healing magic in his wounds.

He spent a few minutes collecting the experience and auras, as well as some of the scales and fangs, and then he ghosted away through the snow, searching for another target.

***

Hours passed as Sam hunted his way through the first layer. Some of the fights were quick ambushes and well-planned encounters of magic and manipulated elements. Others were savage blood contests where he tore apart his enemies with his talons and ripped their arms and heads from their bodies.

Crystal flame roared around him, burning away both their blood and his. One healing scroll after another crumbled to dust in his hands.

Surges of experience poured into his body, as well as a few new auras, and each time he felt a new level, he pushed it aside for later.

The fight with the serpents and Ebonstreak Hunters was not the most difficult, but it was the one that felt the most satisfying. There was something about facing a planned ambush and destroying it that brought out a burning delight that dwarfed the other fights.

Half a day later, nearly everything on the first layer was dead, except for the two trios of Icebloods and a few beasts. The Outsiders had sensed the danger and retreated, while the only beasts left were the three strongest: two Emerald Snow Moths at Level 80 and a giant Ice Centipede at Level 85 that had burrowed away into the packed snow at the edge of the layer.

11 monsters and 25 beasts had died at his hands, with an average level in the mid 60s. His gains were considerable, although the amount of required experience per level was surging into the millions.

As if to remind him, the World Law's voice resonated in his mind with the latest torrent of experience, as he stood above the corpses of two more Ebonstreak Hunters. These two had led him on a long chase before he caught them in an ice storm.

Somehow, the World Law had known he wasn't in the mood to listen to endless repetitions of experience, and now it summarized everything for him that he'd gained as his blood started to cool down.

Congratulations, Battlefield Reclaimer. You have used your Class skills to slay your enemies.

You gain 19,900,000 Class experience.

You have gained ten Class levels. You are now a Level 75 Battlefield Reclaimer.

Class Experience: 30,509,990 / 34,500,000

You have gained ten General Levels. You are now Level 75.

Total Experience: 30,542,740 / 34,500,000

You have gained +10 Intelligence, +10 Aura, and have 30 free attribute points to assign.

It was an enormous amount, but it was just barely enough experience to push him to Level 75, which required 30.5 million. Each level from 66 to 70 had required around 1.5 million, and then 71 had required almost two million.

Each level past 71 required another five hundred thousand more than the level before it, and Level 75 to 76 was four million flat. He shook his head as he looked at the numbers.

From the 11 monsters, he'd managed to gather five advanced auras, but he'd used up a dozen basic ones. There had been many more beasts here than monsters, unfortunately. He still had a sizable collection of basic auras, but he was down to just a few of each type and he wanted to save a good variety for enchantments.

As for the new ones, there were three Auras of Whispering Hoarfrost (Advanced) that came from a second set of Hoarfrost Serpents and now two Auras of Ebon Corrosion (Advanced) that came from the Ebonstreak Hunters in front of him.

He scanned the area for enemies as he finished harvesting resources and then he glided away on the snow, blending into the storm as he looked at his attributes. The levels had brought him up to 165 in both Intelligence and Aura.

After a moment, he assigned one point to Wisdom to bring it to 65, which would maximize his chances to reclaim Advanced auras, and then 10 points each to Intelligence and Aura, taking them both to 175.

He hesitated over the last nine points, but after a moment he assigned them to Charisma, raising it to 40. Along with Wisdom, it was a stat that didn't receive any bonuses as he gained new essence, and he had a suspicious feeling that it was more important than he knew.

He also remembered his father's advice from before, insisting that he'd need Charisma to get along with people. Eventually, he was going to figure out how to block Analyze and create a good illusion.

He continued moving through the snow, heading for a hideout that he'd spotted as he felt the energy of the attributes changing him, especially Charisma. His features itched slightly as they shifted again and for some reason he felt his mood improving, as he became a little calmer and more optimistic.

That startled him enough that he took a moment to examine the change. Somehow, Charisma was balancing his mood, making everything look a little brighter.

His thoughts were interrupted as the Guardian Star spoke up, drawing his attention away. The star had been extremely useful over the course of the day, scanning the area and tracking enemies for him. It was only so powerful within the ruins where it had access to the Moonlight Relic's awareness of everything happening, and it was better within the areas that were functioning, but it was incredibly valuable.

Enemies are approaching. It was silent for just an instant as it scanned the area and then it spoke up again. **More than twenty monsters are being herded in this direction by the two Iceblood groups, moving up from the second layer. They should arrive within the next hour.**

Analysis of the lower layers suggest increased activity among the Outsiders as well. Your actions here have been detected.

Sam pulled his attention away from Charisma as he let the Guardian Star show him where the approaching monsters were coming from. When he saw them, a burning delight spread through him as a dark smile lit up his face. He might be alone, but he'd never felt so free before.

"Then let's arrange a proper welcome for them."

CHAPTER FORTY-THREE

ICEBLOOD TRAP

He had an hour to prepare and the Outsiders shouldn't know he was aware of them. His thoughts burned like wildfire as he considered the best approach. He wanted something that would destroy them.

A few minutes later, he reached the hideout he was aiming for, a small ice cave he'd dug out beneath tumbled pillars, and he sank into meditation to recover his essence. He'd been worried about an army finding him, but with a bit of time, perhaps he could turn this into a bloodbath for the other side.

There are two issues to address, the Guardian Star announced, interrupting his thoughts. The sense of personality about it was even stronger than it had been that morning, when the star had started to refer to itself as "I," and now its voice held an overtone of seriousness.

"What is it?" Sam asked as most of his attention turned to enchantments he could use against the Icebloods. Perhaps he could magnify his elemental manipulation....

If he used the Aura of Frozen Blades to imbue a snowstorm, it would turn into a storm of cutting ice, or he could enhance an Ice scroll with auras and mix it with a Fire attack. Either one should cut down a few of the monsters.

Maybe he could do both? He just didn't have a lot of time to prepare enchantments.

Your actions today suggest a self-destructive desire for battle that is dangerous to your mission.

Analysis of your recent advancement indicates your Charisma is balancing the chaotic aspect of Essence in your spirit. You should invest in it more in order to keep a balanced mind.

Ideally, it should be at least one quarter of your Intelligence. That is 45 Charisma. Currently, you only have 40. It will also be valuable for persuading others to work with you. Repairing the Seal is not something to be done alone.

His first reaction was to ignore the star and go back to planning how to destroy the Outsiders, but he shook his head and focused on what it was saying. He'd just been thinking about how Charisma was important, and now the star's analysis supported it.

"Fine," he muttered, pulling his attention away from the Fire runes he could use with some difficulty. He was enjoying this battle, but he had the presence of mind to realize it was a little odd. "I'll add more later."

The advice made him wonder if the madness that was attributed to Outsiders was part of the essence system, as well as how they dealt with it. They had to have some way to increase their Charisma, or whatever attribute they used.

Having more Charisma would be valuable anyway, once he figured out how to block Analyze and could conceal himself in an illusion. He wanted to get into the city and see what it was like.

Unfortunately, that would have to wait until he figured out the right enchantments to get through the wards.

Second, the star said, drawing his attention back to it, **the Icebloods that are approaching have a strange layer of Essence around them, as well as talismans of some type. They appear to be executing a shamanic group spell to strengthen themselves and the monsters with them. The average level is 68, but it would be wiser to evaluate them higher.**

Even with your unique class and capabilities, facing this many monsters at once will be difficult.

I recommend that you work with the Moonlight Relic. You should retreat to the storeroom and study the enchanting patterns there. You may be able to activate one of the relic's old defenses.

Sam let out a low growl at the thought of retreating, his fangs flashing. The star's advice was similar to his father's, taking the safer course, but what if the enchantments didn't work or the Icebloods turned and led their monsters to attack his father next?

No, he needed something that would stop them here.

He pushed the anger aside and looked inward at the core enchantment the relic had given him. It was a shining silver moon hanging in his mind. So far, the enchantments inside it were too complex to unravel, but he did feel more connected to the ruins around him, as if everything were familiar.

Activating a part of the relic was a long shot, one with a timeline and variables he couldn't control. He would have to study the enchantment and then take who knew how long to repair whatever was broken.

He grimaced, shaking his head. The star's perspective was different than his. It was a good plan if he were by himself and didn't care about time.

Unfortunately, neither of those were true.

He needed to eliminate these monsters and then work his way down to the flaw. However, the idea of using the relic did give him an idea.

"The relic was built as a spatial seal, or something like that, right?"

Affirmative. It was built to stabilize dimensional space within the local region. At full power, it might cover a tenth of the planet. There should have been a network of similar relics, each of them working together to create a defensive system. However, it appears it was never completed.

There is some evidence that the Western Reaches were intended to be a formation to extend the relic's area of influence by tapping into the natural mana on the peaks, but that stage of the plan is missing from the relic's memory. It is likely that the battle which destroyed it took place first.

"So it would truly be the world's diadem..." Sam muttered to himself as he thought back to what he'd seen the night before, with the peaks of the Western Reaches stretching out like diamonds in a crown. Then he pulled his attention back to more immediate things.

"Are there any working enchantments that could help?"

The only enchantments in the ruins that might apply are some traps like the one which captured you, the basic energy distribution network that is part of the stones, and two layers of spatial defense, one of which is used to maintain the integrity of the stones here. The other supports spatial integrity for the relic's core systems, which exist half in this dimension and half in another.

It is a sad sight to compare it to what it once was.

Before he could ask, a map of the ruins sprang into his mind, highlighting the areas that were still functioning. There were no traps on the first layer, despite its better condition. The builders must have used a different defense here.

What did exist was a densely woven network of energy, as well as many buildings that had semi-functioning enchantments. As he looked over the map and at the route the Outsiders were taking to reach him, an idea began to turn around in his mind.

"Would the relic help, if I can get one of the enchantments working?"

Almost certainly. The Outsiders are a threat to it and their presence here goes against its primary purpose. However, it does not have the ability to act independently at the moment. The trap that captured you did so automatically when it detected your essence.

If you want the relic to assist, it might be able to power a larger enchantment or one of the defenses, but you would have to repair it, and that would take time. That is why it is more advisable for you to retreat and prepare.

"No, I'm not going to run and hide," Sam refused. His eyes burned with crystal flame as he put the pieces of a plan together. The core enchantment for the ruins flared in his mind as his awareness flowed into it. He didn't understand it at all, but there was one thing he'd seen before and could recognize.

The search sent a piercing stab of pain through his mind from the weight of information in the enchantment, but he pushed it aside as he kept looking. It hadn't been designed to harm him, but his Intelligence wasn't high enough to handle the level of complexity.

Fortunately, he didn't need to understand the full thing. He just needed that one specific part that had to be in here somewhere. It should be unmistakable at the first glance, especially to him.

The key rune to the trap that had been on the control pillar.

Night would come soon and moonlight would be everywhere throughout the ruins, woven into the enchantments. He remembered the cutting force of the strands in the trap when they headed for him. Thanks to the relic, that force was engraved into his soul.

He just needed to find the rune that would bring moonlight to life and then he could work with it, using the same concept as he did for the *star* rune on his bracer. It might not be exactly the same as the trap, and it would take some effort, but once night fell, he would have all the resources he needed.

His search through the core enchantment continued, pain spiking behind his eyes. After about half an hour, he looked up, his eyes gleaming with sapphire flame as a trail of blood ran down from the corners and streaked across his cheeks.

"Let's get back to the control pillar."

***

The core rune glowed in his memory as he laid his hands on the control pillar, looking at the dark sigil there. He'd paid a price to find the rune in the core enchantment. His mind felt like a mana storm had burned through it and his eyes were weeping blood.

Now, there was another step missing that he hadn't planned on. He needed to find the connection between it and moonlight. The aspect that bound them together.

The trap rune was extremely complex, a condensation of an entire enchantment somehow folded into a single sigil. He would have compared it to the three-dimensional pattern on his amulet, but that was laughable.

This rune didn't exist in three dimensions. It existed in at least six...and perhaps more. It was woven through aspects of time, aura, and other things that he couldn't grasp yet.

Without the core enchantment, it would have taken a lifetime to understand. Fortunately, the core enchantment and the control pillar were holding the rune stable, similar to his bracer, and he already had a connection to its concept.

His mind crackled as he pushed his awareness into the rune, searching for how the trap had functioned.

Below, the Outsiders were nearly to the first layer, which meant he didn't have much time to set things up. He might have to lead them on a chase around the layer. He could feel the Guardian Star's silent attention on what he was doing, but it couldn't help.

Above, the daylight was beginning to fade. At the edge of the horizon, he could see a blue shimmer that marked where Caelus would rise. He turned his attention away as he focused on the rune.

Time passed as the sky grew darker, and eventually the first ray of moonlight fell on the pillar as Caelus crested the horizon, illuminating Sam with his hands pressed against it.

As soon as it did, a rumble of rising power from the pillar flared through his meridians, touched the moonlight strands and core enchantment, and curved back like a moonlit lightning bolt.

The force of it made his hands shake as his nerves sizzled, but at the same instant, the moonlight flowed into the trap rune between his hands, flooding through it with the whisper of the night's arrival.

The rune was broken, but as the moonlight washed through, it came to life for a moment, illuminating the spirals of the enchantment and the flow of energy inside. It was only for an instant, but for Sam, who had been searching for that single connection with his entire spirit, it was enough.

The trap rune and one other rune for *moonlight* floated up from the enchantment in his mind and snapped into place. Sam staggered, his hands falling free from the pillar as the two runes merged into a single concept in his mind.

Then he fell to the ground, his body twitching from overloaded meridians and an exhausted mind.

It had been at least two hours since he'd started studying the pillar and the Outsiders must have flooded the first layer. Thoughts of them finding his father made him twitch as his hand tried to close, but the only thing beneath him was snow. Its cold warmth pressed against his skin like a balm.

Guardian, you must stand. Your task is not complete.

The Guardian Star's voice echoed in his mind like the chime of a gong drifting alone on the ocean, its sound sweeping out across the waves.... Sam groaned as he shoved the feeling away, his hand lifting to touch his head. It felt like he'd stuffed it full of rocks and then tried to break them by smashing it into a wall.

Guardian, you must stand. The star's insistent voice echoed in his mind again, rousing him before he could drift off.

The Outsiders are working their way through the first layer, laying a new ambush for you. They do not know who you are,

but they are aware that someone is hunting them there. They have already had too long to prepare.

"Urgh..." Sam muttered eloquently as he clenched his muscles and then relaxed them again, his talons digging into the snow. His body felt hot and swollen. The cold snow was relaxing, so he buried his hands in it more deeply, letting the feeling bring him to awareness.

The threat of the Icebloods crashed down on him as his mind cleared.

"Moving..." he muttered as he forced himself to his feet, staggering. His Constitution was working to heal his battered meridians, but it wasn't fast enough. He pulled out a healing scroll and activated it, letting the white heat flow through him. Healing scrolls weren't good at repairing meridians or the stress in his mind, but at least it might take the edge off.

"Let's go." He turned away, tilting to the side before he caught his balance, and then he pushed himself onward, heading for the barrier.

***

Without the teleportation system that had once existed, there was only a single staircase that provided access between the first layer and the second, and the Icebloods had established an ambush throughout the area surrounding it.

Monsters were stationed to guard the corners of buildings, main avenues, and open plazas, each of them within hearing distance of another. If a fight started, it would only take a moment before the entire group swarmed the area.

The Icebloods were hanging back near the staircase, keeping themselves at the center of their trap as they conducted some elaborate ritual.

He frowned as he examined the layout. He wasn't sure what it was, but he didn't like the look of it. They were setting up bone shards and talismans across the area, near each monster.

Whatever they were doing, he was going to have to interrupt it, and that meant pulling them away. There was no way he was going to walk right into their plans.

He was hidden in a building more than a mile from them, letting the headache fade and his meridians heal a little more. The trap rune was complete in his mind, like a single strand of the core enchantment that had come to life for him. He just needed to apply it. That required time and a way to catch all of his enemies.

He still didn't have a trap to use it in.

After a few moments of searching the map, he gave a brief nod and then darted out of the building, ghosting away across the snow to the spot he'd chosen.

On the way, he touched the Amulet of Swirling Winds on his chest, checking in on his father. Jeric had been busy, leading the others to eliminate the monsters and beasts near the temple. So far, they'd cleared everything within a mile of their base and a bit more than that in the direction away from the Grand Flaw.

No larger force had come to stop them yet, but Sam didn't doubt that something would appear eventually. Perhaps the Outsiders just wanted to deal with one problem at a time.

Lenei had also made contact. She'd convinced most of the church forces to gather at the ruins, now that there was evidence of a Grand Flaw, but it would take them a bit longer to arrive, since they had already started to disperse across the valley. They would also have to work their way through the ruins.

Once they arrived, Lenei would meet up with Jeric and the adventurers, and their forces would converge on the closest Flaws, working to seal them one by one as they approached the Grand Flaw.

Sam pushed those thoughts out of his mind as he arrived at his destination. He was near the outer edge of the ring and about a mile from the closest monster. The enchantments here were damaged, but the moonlight ribbons throughout the streets and plazas were still present.

He darted to the edge of the plaza, examining it for a long moment as he looked at the stones and the moonlight, imagining what it needed to be. Then he nodded and ducked into one of the tumbled-down houses nearby as he began to collect materials.

It took him about an hour, and he checked on the Outsiders' positions repeatedly to make sure they weren't moving, but eventually he finished the arrangement of what he wanted, setting the last piece of broken green crystal into place.

All around the plaza, he'd laid out shards of the green crystal from the windows, as well as chunks of stone and other objects from inside the homes that had once held heating or other enchantments.

All of the objects were laid out in the pattern of the trap rune, aligned with the swirling, silver-green lines of the relic's energy from the stones below. Around them, he'd frozen the snow into ice and carved the trap sigil into it, creating a fragile runic frame.

He needed something to hold the form of the trap, and these were the best materials he'd been able to find. In another place, it might not have worked, but nothing within the relic was a normal material. All of these items were highly attuned to the energy here and designed to accept input from an inhabitant of the city. Even the snow was infused with the Ice concept that created it.

If it didn't work, he'd created a secondary plan, which involved turning the center of the plaza into the biggest fireball he could, but he had some confidence in this approach.

Now, he just needed to set up the last part of the moonlight sigil and get the Outsiders here.

CHAPTER FORTY-FOUR

MOONLIGHT BLADES

Moonlight streamed down the walls of the buildings as Sam ghosted away from the plaza and the trap enchantment. In his hand, there was a chunk of glowing, green crystal with a *moon* rune engraved into the side. It was the final part he needed to activate his plan.

The question was if it would be enough.

Halfway there, he paused and examined one of the bone shards from the Iceblood Shaman that he'd collected at the Ice Sylph village, but the markings on it told him nothing about what they were up to. Whatever spells they'd used near the staircase, he wasn't sure what they would do.

He had the feeling that their true strength was in alchemy or these talismans, rather than straight forward battle. Perhaps that was why they stayed in the background. He was going to have to take his chances with that to get closer and lure them here.

He glanced down at the recharged Ring of Crystal Shield and his Amulet of Swirling Winds, plans flickering through his mind. There were twenty-three monsters and six Icebloods. It was a contest between whoever could get their enemy into a trap first.

He gripped the chunk of crystal in his hand as he ducked into a building and accessed the star's map. They were laid out in a half circle and strange bone spears with talismans looped around them marked out the points in a formation that connected them all. Without the map, he would have run right into it.

The monsters were a mix of Hoarfrost Serpents, Diamondfang Ice Vipers, Arctic Cave Trolls, and two Ice Wyverns. Near the Grand Flaw, there were more of the Icesoul Wraiths and other Outsiders, but the Icebloods had only chosen monsters for this group. Perhaps they were easier to control.

He spent a little while examining their pattern before he chose his target. He wanted to disrupt their formation and draw them out, and for that he planned to rely on the monsters' basic instincts for battle...and he knew exactly how to do it.

He'd had plenty of practice on the way to Highfold.

A wry grin flashed across his face as he thought of his sister and what she would make of this. Knowing her, she'd be right there trying to attack them and he'd have to hold her back.

He pulled a vial of wyvern blood from his dimensional pouch and studied it. Then, he sat down and retrieved his stylus and a few strips of wyvern leather. His hands flickered with crystal flame as he began to inscribe a series of runes related to illusions.

The runes were for *image, color,* and *sound,* as well as *monster, nature,* and *enhance.* He placed them into a six-pointed star formation, inscribing them onto the leather with the wyvern blood as a medium. Then he surrounded that with a binding pattern to intensify the nature of the base material.

Time blurred as he worked, but his previous efforts with illusions and the basic runes from the amulet ensured that he was adept with the concept. Making all of those toys for his sister had become something that might keep him alive now.

A little while later, he had half a dozen thin scrolls in his hands.

Scroll of Illusion: Ice Wyvern (Advanced, Special).

He'd sacrificed the last of his wyvern cores to infuse the scrolls with the right aura, but it was worth it. With that help, the materials from the ice wyverns had come together around the concept of 'wyvern' that was already present.

That was also why the scroll's quality had ended up as 'Special.' This illusion was closer to the Expert level. For a few minutes, these scrolls would bring to life an image of the wyverns he had fought before.

The effort resulted in around 12,000 experience, but Enchanting was at the First Cliff and it would take another 180,000 to push it to Level 34. Studying the core enchantment and the ruins would be a good source for that.

He darted back outside, pulling the snow close around him as he held a scroll in his hand. He moved to the point he'd chosen, just on the edge of the Iceblood formation, and scanned the map for the closest wyvern.

When he found it, he spent a few more minutes planning out his escape route and the path back to his trap, making sure that it was clear. Then he looked up into the night sky, tracking the position of Caelus as the moon rose toward its zenith. It was almost midnight now.

All through the ruins, strands of moonlight lanced between buildings and along the streets, illuminating the world in a triple aurora. The snow gleamed with the resonant Ice energy floating up from the stones below.

The wyvern was about four hundred feet from him, most of its body buried in a snow drift behind a fallen pillar. Only its head was visible as it kept watch on the area. He could just barely make out the spikes on its skull and a few green scales of its snout that were dusted with falling snow.

Without knowing that it was there, it would have been very difficult to spot.

He took up a position behind a broken wall that blocked the wyvern's view of him. The runes on the scroll shimmered in his hand, essence flowing from symbol to symbol as it activated. The lines turned bright green as the wyvern blood ignited, burning with a strange, rippling flame.

The runes burned brighter, their colors changing to shades of darker green and grey-white as their surfaces became pebbled and transformed into scales. Then the scroll dissolved into flickering motes as the scales continued to expand, surrounded by a swirling green mist.

Without hesitating any longer, he threw the spell out in front of him, letting it expand into a life-size ice wyvern.

As the illusory mist continued to spread, the monster towered into the air over him, its wings unfurling. The large, bat-like wings flapped at the air as the monster arched its neck, tilting its head back as its jaws opened to reveal rows of saber-like fangs.

RoooaaAAAArrrrr!

The wyvern's roar echoed out across the area, an exact copy of what it had been in life.

There was a moment of shocked silence as the sound echoed outward. In that pause, Sam sent the illusion racing out from behind the wall, right through the line of sight of the wyvern that was hiding.

Another scream roared out from its jaws, its wings mantling against the night sky. There was a subtle green glow of magic all around it, but otherwise it looked incredibly realistic, as if a living wyvern were chasing something across the area.

The wyvern had been told to wait there quietly in ambush, but it was still a monster. As soon as it saw the competitor racing through the area, its instincts to defend its territory and the command from the Icebloods to hunt prey in this area joined together. Another monster was chasing its prey!

It had no more patience! The prey had to be in front of it!

It would not lose out to another!

The wyvern exploded upward out of the snow, its scales vibrating as its muscles contracted like steel cables. Its head reared back and its wings snapped open, flaring outward to cover the stars.

RoooAAAAooORRR!

Its jaws opened and it lunged forward, letting out a roar that was even louder than the illusion's as it raced after it, its claws tearing at the snow in an explosion of flakes that flew in every direction.

Screams, roars, and explosive hisses echoed out in a cascade of fury as other monsters in the area saw what was happening and leapt up from where they were hiding. Now that one of them had moved, it was a beacon calling to all of them.

There was no hiding the disruption. The Icebloods had arranged everything so that the trap would spring shut in an instant, and now that worked against them as all of the serpents, vipers, trolls, and the other wyvern reacted. As far as they knew, the trap had been triggered.

Snow and small stones cascaded through the air as monsters surged toward Sam's location, their roars deafening the area. The Guardian Star helped him to track their position as he raced for his escape route, his attention fixed on the illusion.

He had to keep the fake wyvern ahead of the monsters.

Fortunately, it wasn't constrained by simple things like traction in the snow or fatigue. The illusion charged ahead of the wyvern and the approaching wave of monsters, sprinting down the road.

Sam struggled to keep pace with it, his attention split between the illusion and his own speed. He pulled the snow close around him in a concealing cloak, using the traction from Initiate of Ice to keep his footing as he raced along on the next street over.

After a moment, he threw caution to the wind as he realized he was falling behind. The illusion wouldn't be able to stay ahead of the real monsters if he didn't move faster.

Crystal flame surged around him as he poured essence into his evasion skill, using it to hurl himself forward like an arrow from a bow.

Even behind the buildings, his aura was a flaring beacon in the night. The monsters saw it in an instant. Some of them split off, heading for him.

His breath burned in his lungs as he pushed himself faster, his heart pounding. His essence-enhanced muscles pulled on his Constitution, drawing stamina and energy from his blood.

Roars echoed on every side, threatening explosions of sound and shrieks of anger.

He'd planned to use the other scrolls if the first one didn't get enough attention, but it wasn't necessary. The green crystal with the *moon* rune was clenched in his hand as he pushed himself harder, trying to reach his trap before the monsters did.

The only thing that let him get there first was his crystal flame and that the monsters hadn't been that close to start. Even with all of his speed, they gained ground with every second.

At the edge of the plaza, the illusion let out another scream as if it had seen its prey and then it sped forward to the center of the trap. A moment later, Sam blasted through the area himself, the cloak of dark blue flames around him burning like a teardrop against the snow.

Then he was past it, skidding to a halt as flame billowed out around him. He spun in place to look at the monsters, the rune shining in his hand. All around the plaza, streaks of moonlight surged from the corner of each building to the next.

His essence poured out of him and into the enchantment formation all around the area as his nerves pulled tight. His blood was thundering in his veins, but his mind was crystal clear.

He raised his hand with the runestone in it, pouring his essence into it as he reached out to the moonlight running through the streets.

The monsters poured into the plaza in a wave, chasing the prey that they knew was just ahead of them. The flare of his crystal flame and the roars of the wyvern drew them on, their impatience increasing.

The front ranks surged through the plaza, racing over the inscriptions and the chunks of crystal on the ground, but the others weren't there yet.

Sam shouted, reaching out with streaks of crystal flame as he slammed energy into three scrolls that he'd planted in the snow. Brilliant eruptions of aura-infused crystal flame erupted from beneath the snow, twisting upward into a shape that hardened into a half dome.

In an arc around the plaza in front of him, a giant, crystal blue Ice Shield infused with Auras of Enduring Stone and Frozen Blades flared into existence. The shield's geometric patterns were tinged with dark grey. Near the bottom were jagged blue arcs that reached out like a wall of thorns.

Roars and hisses tore across the plaza. An instant later, the front ranks of the monsters slammed into the shield, impaling themselves on the blades before they could halt their charge. Shrieks accompanied the splatter of green, white, and pale blue blood across the plaza.

Seconds later, the rest of the monsters surged into view in a tangle of writhing scales and claws. Diamond-patterned heads darted above the pack and then swept downward again like the fang-capped peaks of a rolling wave.

They heard the shrieks ahead of them, but in their rage the shrieks were the cries of their competitors reaching the prey. Their speed didn't slow at all as they rushed forward, slamming into each other as scales flew from the impact.

The Icebloods were nowhere to be seen, but there was no time to wait. Sam's hand rose as he poured more than a hundred points of essence into the *moon* crystal in his hand. At the same time, he reached down with a surge of crystal flame, activating the giant sigil in the plaza.

There was a sudden surge of mana in the area like a hurricane as mana slammed forward into the sigil. Energy in the area was pulled into the activation sequence and the tumult of sound followed it, leaving the plaza silent for a single instant.

A small green crystal flew upward from Sam's hand, opalescent as it tumbled in the air...until it struck a beam of blue moonlight. The rune brightened, shining like a green moon in the night as it suddenly swelled in size.

All around the plaza, a high-pitched resonance hummed like a wild flute playing on the night breeze. Then the moonlight descended.

Beams of bright blue, soft green, and dusky purple fluttered like silk scarves as they twisted through the air, separating from the buildings and the streets as they changed their paths. They twined around one another, forming cutting spirals across the sky.

The moonlight took on a crystalline gleam, a razor line so thin that it could cut the dark. Strands swept downward, flowing across the plaza with sweeping cuts in gigantic arcs from one side to the other.

The monsters in the plaza stood no chance. They were already pinned by the icy shield and the moonlight reached them in an instant. It was nothing that they'd ever imagined or planned for.

The only thoughts in the monsters' minds were of blood and prey. Some roared in pain as they struck the spikes. Rage resonated through them, but the moonlight was there before they could register its existence.

Arcs of blood swept across the plaza. At first, it was thin, a light splatter striking the snow. The monsters froze, their expressions halting, and sound disappeared. Some of them were caught mid roar and others were raising claws or tails to attack.

The moonlight swept by, reaching the far end of the plaza in an instant as it swirled back up into the sky, dissolving into smaller strands again as it flowed back toward the buildings.

In the snow below, the sigil twisted, burning in lines of triple-colored fire as it exploded from the strain of the mana it had drawn. A wall of multi-colored flames blasted upward, washing over the monsters in the center.

The heat sent Sam stumbling back, his hands and crystal flame forming a shield as the sigil twisted out of its lines, burning away the snow. The plaza turned to a superheated inferno in an instant.

Shards of green crystal and kitchen stones blasted outward, flying in every direction as the enchantments reacted to the overload. They tried to heat and cool the area in an instant, summon breezes, and create flames or boiling water.

Their reactions collided. The wind hit the boiling water and the flames, which then crashed into a cooling stone that tried to freeze them. The overstressed enchantments exploded, their sigils shattering from the strain.

Shards of stone and crystal ripped through the plaza in a second blast, not much smaller than the first. Sam's shield screamed as the forces tore at it.

He was thrown backwards, tumbling across the ground in a flail of limbs until he slammed into a wall with a bone-cracking thump. His head and neck whipped back and then forward again as his horns slammed into the stones of the plaza below him.

His head rang like a dull drum and his senses blurred as he lost track of what was going on. He was deafened. A moment later, a rumbling silence settled on the plaza as a haze of burnt stone, ash, and charred blood drifted through the air.

Everything tasted of flames and burnt crystal.

In that silence, there came a slow, soft *chime*. It was a dancing snowflake in the air, subtle until it was there, and it brought the touch of Ice.

It came again.

All around, a soft silver gleam began to shine up from the stones of the plaza that had been revealed by the explosion. The area was dark with charred flesh, rubble, streaks of burned limbs, and chunks of stone.

The silver light intensified as the chime came again.

Snowflakes began to drift down, forming in the air in response to the call like fairies summoned by a temple bell. They floated there, drifting idly in swirls as they began to fall.

The chime came again and the snowflakes were suddenly *more*, a soft blanket falling from the sky. In just a handful of instants, a light dusting formed across the plaza, settling on the debris.

Sam tried to push himself to his feet, but the world was spinning. His ears were filled with the sound of rumbling explosions and tinkling chimes. He put his hand beneath him to push up from the ground, but he only grabbed at the air and tumbled to the side again.

The sky spun above him as he looked up at the dark night, his eyes reflecting the moons. Drifts of snow fell downward, settling with a gentle caress as the chimes continued.

Two minutes later, the plaza was covered over by a blanket of snow, the evidence of the battle hidden like a secret of winter, and the chiming stopped. The silver light of the relic dimmed, fading to its standard glow.

Into the silence, six Iceblood Shamans slowly stepped forward into the plaza, their faces twisted as they raised their hands to the sky. Their palms dripped a pale blue blood onto bone talismans held in their grasp.

A swirl of essence swept up from them, sinking into the talismans, and then they threw them outward into the plaza. They shot out like bloody darts, heading for the monsters' tattered corpses.

Chapter Forty-Five

ICEBLOOD CURSES

The talismans struck the mangled corpses across the plaza, sizzling as the pale blood on them gleamed with an eerie, blue light. There had been twenty-three monsters, but there were five times that many chunks in the plaza now.

The bone shards ripped into the corpses and then kept going, tearing out the far side in a splatter of blood and viscera. When they emerged, they were slightly larger than before. They spun up into the air and then immediately shot toward another corpse chunk, doing the same thing again.

Like a nest of angry blue wasps, they burrowed through each chunk of flesh and erupted again, as their size continued to grow. Whatever the shamans were doing, it looked like it didn't matter that their forces had died.

Perhaps it had been their plan all along.

Guardian, stand and face the enemies of your world.

The star's cool words rang through Sam's mind, calming some of the spinning chaos that was his senses. His head felt like a wagon had run over it. He reached reflexively for his essence and the snow, pulling crystal flame and a flurry of ice around him.

His reaction was slow and the shamans had time to finish the ritual they were doing. The talismans ripped through the last of the corpses and flew back to their owners, three or four heading to each of them.

The bone shards had started out the size of a coin, but now they were giant disks, each the size of a knight's shield. They were pale blue and white, their surfaces covered in a swirling, dark script.

They rotated around the Icebloods like hunting hawks circling their masters and then they dove in, their shapes transforming. On the shaman to the front, the first talisman melted, transforming into bone armor that covered the Outsider from head to foot like a rippling carapace. The helm was some type of monster with wide mandibles. The Iceblood's eyes were dark pits beneath it.

The second disk transformed into a large bone shield like a ribcage, a spine extending down its back, and the third turned into a long spear taller than the Outsider with a wicked, sharp point. The black inscriptions on the talismans flickered with a red glow, lighting up with a stench of blood and decay.

Two of the Outsiders had a fourth talisman disk, which turned to a spiked wheel of bone that spun around each of them, the edges blurring with a savage red light.

Somehow, they'd turned the deaths of the monsters into their own power.

Sam managed to slam a healing scroll onto his chest as they were occupied with the talismans. He managed to roll to the side just as those two spiked wheels spun through the air, cutting through where he'd been lying an instant before.

Hsksakshsskksk.

The wheels hissed past with a sound like ghosts cursing the living, their spines tearing at the wind. The flames around him burned away at the energy with a sizzling eruption and then the snow was there, dulling the sound of the blades passing as it began to freeze them, and then the blades were gone.

Between the trap and the shield he'd thrown up, he was nearly out of essence. He threw himself into another awkward roll as he grabbed a handful of auras from his storage and combusted them all at once.

His essence surged back to 100, but the time it took to combust the auras let the bone wheels curve around as they headed for him again. At the same time, the six Icebloods weren't hesitating.

Their spears were raised in their hands as they began chanting, their voices harsh and crackling. Red and blue swirls of essence gathered around them, forming into spells that shot in Sam's direction.

There was a blast of impressions as the spells hit the edge of his aura, identifying the attacks as curses, poison, darkness, and more.

Sam growled with anger as he flung himself to the side again, the bone wheels shearing through the air over his head. A wash of crystal flame pushed him farther away, but he was too slow to avoid the mass of spells that struck all over the area.

As they reached him, a shimmering, blue crystal shield appeared as the Ring of Crystal Field activated. The curses landed against it, sizzling with corrosive energy as swirls of darkness bubbled up from the blue essence and venom etched its way across the surface, boiling with spite.

The shield eroded like a sandcastle in the tide, but it took the spells with it, their energy fizzling out in crystalline flickers. The barrier withstood the assault, but it was as thin as an eggshell by the time Sam got out of the way.

The bone wheels curved around toward him at the same time as the Icebloods attacked again. Two of them raised their spears, surrounding them in a pale blue energy as they hurled them in his direction.

Wrath boiled through his blood as his essence resonated through the constellation. His battle aura flared out around him as his talons lengthened and he threw himself to his feet, the cloak of translucent sapphire flame streaming out behind him.

He stared toward his enemies and the approaching attacks, his shoulders straight and face hard. Crystal flame and Ice energy surged around him in waves as he pulled on it with all his might.

He turned toward the bone wheels, which were the closest, all of his strength pouring into the flame around his talons and his speed as he slashed out at them. He met the spinning blades in a shearing wave of crystal flame that blasted out around him.

He ripped four cutting lines through the first blade, feeling a hint of dark resistance from the inscriptions before he burnt through them and his talons dug in. The bone wheel shattered into explosive fragments that flew outward, crashing against his shield as he spun.

Even with his speed, he wasn't quite fast enough to get the second blade. Its spiked edges tore at his left arm like a saw, grinding against the crystal aura that defended his skin. Then it broke through, tearing a long, ugly gash down his arm.

His aura fused back together a moment later, restoring the shield, as flames boiled up from his skin, purging the wound and sealing it. He pushed the injury aside, reaching out with a snarl as he grabbed at the bone wheel that had just struck him.

Before it could fly away, he slashed through it with both hands, shattering it into a dozen flying shards.

At the same time, a spear struck his left shoulder. Its speed dropped as it shattered his shield, but it still managed to stab him with a burst of sizzling venom that started to corrode his muscles. There was a dark cloud of a curse around the spear point as well, but it burned away as it encountered the flames that sprang out of his skin.

Before he consciously thought about it, he was moving again. He ripped the spear from his shoulder and broke it across his knee in a surge of anger. Then he charged at the shamans with the two halves gripped in his hands.

A wall of bones sprang up in front of him, spinning knobs of broken spines, femurs, and shattered finger bones like tiny arrows flying through the air. The bones struck the shield that was tight against his skin, knocking him to the left and right as he forced through it.

A spiral of crystal flame surged around him, scorching the bone spear in his hand black. He raised the spear halves as he leapt toward the shamans, the point and a jagged edge pointed straight at them.

The one in front brought his bone shield around, holding it in front of himself as he continued to chant, the spear in his free hand rising, but at that moment, Sam crashed down into him, the spear points leading the way.

Crystal flame surged as he stabbed the spear half into the Outsider's shield, knocking it to the side, and he spun around to the right. His foot lashed out, kicking the Iceblood's knee, and then the spear in his right hand came around, stabbing through the opening.

The broken spear tore through the Outsider's abdomen in a gout of blue blood and he ripped it free, stabbing again and again. His free hand came around, bringing the other half of the spear with it, and he roared as he raised them both into the air.

The Outsider had already collapsed to the ground as Sam drove the spear halves down, impaling it to the snow below. He left the spear there as he spun toward the other five, but his anger had made him delay.

One of the Icebloods in the back stepped forward, its spear ripping through the abdomen of its ally in front. The other shaman's mouth opened in a pained scream as it tried to jerk free and then froze up from the pain.

The attacker ripped the spear free, tossing it aside as he drove his hands into the wound, tearing out a stream of pale blue essence that pooled in his hands. It gathered that energy into a sphere and turned toward Sam, its fanged grin widening.

There wasn't a trace of remorse in its expression for killing its ally.

The other four Icebloods pulled away from that one, keeping themselves at a distance, but there was no surprise among them that he could make out. If anything, the twisted expression of the one to the right looked envious.

A sizzling cloud of pale blue smoke rose up from one of them and headed for Sam, along with a streak of acidic yellow lightning and a ghostly, clawed hand with yellowish-black nails that tore toward him.

The murderer stepped forward, twisting the essence between its hands like a skein of yarn as it transformed it into a miniature version of the other Iceblood, a tiny captured soul. It breathed a cloud of reddish energy on it and then threw it toward Sam.

A sense of heavy threat came with it, as well as a sense of twisted life and blood. It felt like the tiny soul was something that would warp whatever living thing it touched.

Sam darted to the side, an Essence Shield springing up between him and the oncoming attacks. The curses struck the shield with a resounding crackle, like acid eating into stone, and stuck to it as they began to burn. Essence drained out of him and into the shield as he kept it up.

Then the soul curse struck, the tiny red-tainted soul floating through his shield slowly, as if it were pushing through mud. He could feel the energy around it warping where it touched, like a hot iron against glass.

He locked a portion of essence into the shield, breaking the connection to him as he evaded again. The shield wouldn't last for long like that, but he didn't need it to. He sprinted toward the Iceblood who was controlling the soul, another shield springing into existence between him and the others.

He had to take out this one first. If he did, that strange curse should go with it.

His essence was tumbling again after absorbing all of the blows, and he drew on the elements around him for support as he slammed into the Outsider, tearing his talons across its abdomen as he dug into the ridges of the bone armor there.

The Outsider tried to bring its shield around to block, but it wasn't as fast as him. Its strength was in curses. Sam's talons sank into the bone and started to burn through at the same time as its shield slammed into his side.

He grunted as he braced his feet against the snow, his elbow hammering into the shield to block. He drove his talons deeper, tearing into the bone and ripping it aside. Then his talons sank into the skin below and he twisted them, ripping them free from the Outsider's side. A gout of pale blue blood boiled out, along with shards of tangled intestines.

The Outsider let out a cry like a strangled serpent, its voice choking off in its throat. The strength pushing the shield against him weakened. Sam's elbow slammed into the shield, knocking it aside as he tore his hands back the other way and then up, eviscerating the Outsider.

At the same time, he felt a boiling, acidic energy tear along his back, eroding the shield there as it splashed over his skin. A spear stabbed through the edge of his right thigh, making him stagger, and then another stabbed into his left side below his ribs and sank inches deep.

He spasmed, his talons grasping the prey...the Outsider...in front of him, and he let out a roar as he spun away from the strikes. But he didn't forget about his enemy.

As he jerked himself to the side, he tore his talons across its throat and grabbed onto its arm and leg, dragging it with him. His spin continued and he lifted the dying Outsider into the air and hurled it at the other four.

The shield he'd left in the air was already failing under the impact of the curses. Now, it shattered to crystalline fragments as the Outsider flew through it and slammed into the group on the other side.

The shamans staggered, collapsing backward as the body struck them, and in that pause Sam pulled another five auras from his storage, combusting them as he pushed fatigue out of his mind and moved back, a spiral of crystal flame surging up around him. Crystal flame sealed over the wounds in his skin, the flames hardening into a bandage.

Where he'd been standing a moment before, the red-hued soul curse collapsed into motes of curling light as the Outsider who'd created it died.

As the crystal flame condensed around him, he pulled the snow and loose stone in the area close. Using the elements took less essence than some of his other attacks, once he got them moving.

A whirlwind began to swirl around the area, the edges turning to icy blades as he stared across the space at the four remaining shamans. He poured out more essence, feeling a crackle of pain through his meridians and a resonant echo through his essence that reverberated with the elements around him.

Wind, Ice, Stone...those were the concepts here at the peak of Sun's Rest, and they whirled around him in a building storm. Moment by moment, more currents of Wind were pulled in by the expanding energy, intensifying the Ice blades and whipping the chunks of rock around him faster.

Loose rubble shook free from the plaza, floating up with a cloud of snow and shards of ice as it joined into the storm.

"*You...!*" One of the Outsiders stumbled as it looked at the storm and then at Sam, its sunken, white eyes widening. For the first time, it spoke in an intelligible way. The words weren't clear, but somehow its meaning was as the essence constellation in his blood echoed.

"*Elemental Lord!*" Another Outsider trembled with fear and fury as he looked at Sam, his actions halting. It wasn't clear which emotion was stronger in him as his face twisted, the mottled white streaks across his pale blue skin flushing paler.

"*How could...*" Another of the Outsiders muttered, looking between Sam and the whirlwind. His long, yellow-white hair normally reached his ankles, but now the knotted strands were flying behind his head, whipping in the swirling storm.

"*The Goddess of Shattered Skies has long been missing!*" A third Outsider roared in anger, his hands rising into the air as he prepared to leap at Sam. "*How could you have her power? She left no descendants! How do you have her lineage?!*"

Almost as quickly as they were surprised, the four pulled themselves together, their oversized hands rising as they prepared new curses. Streaks of bilious yellow curled around them like a plague fog, along with a crackling black lightning that began to spread along the spear that one of them still held.

Sam ignored them, his thoughts fixed on battle as he poured more essence into the whirlwind. He didn't care what they thought of his essence. They were invaders in his world.

He staggered slightly as he pulled more elements around him. The injuries he'd taken weren't light. He could feel seeping pain burning through his veins, warring with the crystal flame. Whatever curses they'd used, it would take him a little while to deal with them.

Time he didn't have.

The storm spun higher, forming a crystalline white and blue funnel around him that flickered with frozen flames. It was nearly fifty feet high now, a wall of tumbling ice and shards of stone, but his view of the Outsiders was perfectly clear.

"Die."

His response to their confusion was as simple as the blade of a scythe.

Most of his essence poured into the storm, balancing the elements there as he intensified it again, and then he attacked. The whirlwind swept out in front of him, crashing toward the four Icebloods like a massive, storm-tossed wave.

Their curses struck the whipping ice blades and shattered as the empowered elements tore them to pieces. The funnel spun over the four of them, catching them up in spinning blades that ripped away at their bone armor and forms.

Stones crushed their limbs, ice blades sliced into them with a shower of blue blood, and the hurricane force battered them into shapeless masses, slamming them into the ground and then into buildings as it blew them away.

Then the wind tore the pieces apart, howling with a high-pitched rage as it slammed into the other side of the plaza before it began to die down, as Sam staggered on his feet, but the only thing left of the Icebloods was scattered chunks across the stones.

There was only a word drifting in his ears, a final shout from one of the shamans before he'd been torn away by the storm:

"*False...!*"

The whirlwind faded away, but so did Sam, wobbling on his feet until he slumped over, falling to one knee as he caught himself on a hand.

The venom and curses from the shamans' attacks was like burning lead in his veins, chewing at him as he wobbled and fell over, his cheek against the cold snow. Everything felt heavy and hot.

The Guardian Star's voice was a distant, silver thread echoing in his mind, rousing him just enough that he fumbled a healing scroll out of his belt pouch, gripping it in a numb hand.

Then he drifted off against the snow.

CHAPTER FORTY-SIX

A PATH OF HIS OWN

The plaza was silent as snowflakes drifted down, covering the corpses that were scattered across it. Many of them landed on Sam, layering him in white. As the snow gathered, it flowed around his body, slowly lifting him up. Before long, it was a foot deep.

Sam lay on top of it, his body covered in streaks of blood, shards of bone, and mottled ash. The white light of a healing scroll still flickered over him, slowly sealing the major wounds closed.

"Urrgghh...." The sound was muttered as he coughed, half-conscious, and spat out a mouthful of dark blood. One of the strikes must have hit his lungs.

There was a stab of pain in his side from where a bone spear had got him, along with a dull, sizzling ache in his muscles. His veins felt hot and swollen. The incessant itching as he healed woke him up the rest of the way.

He fumbled a new healing scroll out of his belt pouch and activated it as he rolled onto his back, staring up at the night sky. A new surge of healing light poured through his body, along with an increasing ache that told him he'd used too much magical healing recently.

It would take a while to recover.

Time blurred as Caelus crossed the sky, heading for the western horizon. It felt like an hour, but based on the moon's position, it was at least three before he felt strong enough to stand up. There were only a few hours until sunrise.

Whatever curses the Icebloods had used, they'd done a number on him, but the ill effects had been burned away by his aura and the healing scrolls. He had to wonder if their magic was some part of the Path of Blood, with the way they'd drawn on the energy of the dead monsters, but based on their reaction to his elemental manipulation, perhaps that path was something else entirely.

Who exactly was the Demon of Shattered Skies? Or the other two? And why had the shamans referred to her as a goddess? He shook his head, pushing the thoughts aside.

Even if they had a culture with that demon at the top, the shamans hadn't hesitated to murder one another for gain. As far as he was concerned, they were all insane and that was the end of it. What he had to do now was clean up this area and then see where his father and the reinforcements were. It was past time to close the Flaw and clear out the ruins.

"Do you see the reinforcements in the ruins?" he asked, looking down at the Guardian Star. Perhaps it could find them with the help of the relic.

Affirmative. The star's voice was calm, with no indication that it was worried about his condition. Perhaps it lacked sympathy or maybe it just knew he would survive.

There are three forces approaching from the east and southeast that fit the description Lenei gave. Each group has twenty to thirty members with most of them between Levels 60 and 90. Each of them is led by an individual around Level 120.

"Hopefully, that'll be enough," Sam muttered. He was all for leaning on the church to carry out its mission, as long as they didn't cause him any trouble. "What do the forces at the Grand Flaw look like?"

The relic's awareness of specific details near the Flaw is distorted. That area is very badly damaged.

"So, we don't know how many are there," he concluded, "but it has to be more than what was here."

Your logic is sound.

Sam looked around the plaza, waiting for the healing scroll to finish its work as he located the corpses and chunks of monsters beneath the snow. As he did, he couldn't hold back a building frustration.

All the auras had dissipated!

He growled as he clenched his hands into the snow, but unfortunately, there was no getting them back. With a bit better planning, he wouldn't have passed out like that. His head was clear now that the battle had ended and he frowned as he remembered the star's advice about his Charisma.

Perhaps he did need to add more to that...but it had been satisfying to rip the Outsiders apart with his bare hands.

An echo of battle lust passed through his body, along with a sharp ache reminding him of what it had cost, both in terms of injuries and in materials. He muttered a curse and spat toward the corpses of the Outsiders as he pushed it out of his mind.

There were always more monsters in Aster Fall.

When the scroll finished its work, he pushed himself to his feet and then began to work his way unsteadily around the area, pulling strands of experience from every chunk he could find. He wasn't sure how the World Law determined which part of a corpse had experience and which didn't, but there was always one piece that had it.

Usually the one with the core in it.

He spent a while collecting those and ended up with 23 cores, along with the other most valuable materials, which made him feel a bit better. Elite-tier materials were useful for enchanting or selling, and this many at once was a significant gain.

The experience built up in a familiar silver aura and he felt the weight of the World Law's attention, but he ignored it as he turned toward the far side of the plaza where the Iceblood corpses had been hurled.

They were shattered figures, their gangly bodies torn apart by the fury of the storm. His talons lashed out toward them as he called to their essence, tearing it from the pieces that remained.

A storm of pale blue and red essence stars swarmed up like fireflies, flaring against the dark as they shot toward him. As they approached, their color turned to bright, sapphire blue and sank into his veins like a balm.

Everywhere the essence passed, the swelling that was in his blood and meridians faded, replaced by a cold joy and the energy of battle. His tendons and meridians writhed, expanding in an instant as they grew stronger, and his muscles became more defined.

From the six shamans, there were over eleven hundred essence stars.

Essence Constellation (First Layer): 2,571 / 2,500.

It was just enough to push him to the Second Layer. As the stars flooded through his blood, they filled all the remaining areas in the constellation there, marking out a shining, star-flecked rune in three dimensions.

The remaining stars swirled upward, layering themselves into new positions on top of it as they began to mark out the edges of another rune. Or perhaps it was an extension of the first.

Essence Constellation (Second Layer): 2,571 / 7,500.

New strength flooded through him as the stars aligned, and then he felt the energy of the first layer condense, surging through his veins. The world around him snapped into sharp relief, with new details of the elements flaring in his mind.

Your Racial Ability: Elemental Manipulation has reached the Advanced Tier.

The World Law's voice echoed in his mind, confirming the improvement. Then it continued, announcing the rest of what he'd just absorbed.

Attribute Gain Quantified by Aster Fall Standard.

Strength increased by 10.

Constitution increased by 12.

Agility increased by 3.

Intelligence increased by 14.

Aura increased by 14.

The surge of strength continued, boiling with a raging, hot desire for battle. For a moment, he felt his mind going blank, flowing away on that tide. Then, some sense of self pulled him back together.

At the same time, the Guardian Star's voice rang in his mind. It wasn't words, but rather a clear, chiming bell that brought him back to awareness.

Guardian, be aware of your Charisma. The effect of essence on your spirit is increasing.

Sam scrubbed his hand over his face as he shook himself, trying to settle his spirit as the changes continued. His horns grew a bit longer and thicker, his meridians became wider and more durable, and his skin and bones hardened under the effect of the new Constitution.

His overall build didn't change much, only becoming more refined, but it felt like he was gliding in the air as he moved.

At that moment, the World Law's next announcement chimed in his mind as a wave of experience flooded into him.

Congratulations, Guardian. You have used your Class skills to eliminate the enemies of Aster Fall.

You gain 15,700,000 Class experience.

You have gained three Class levels. You are now a Level 78 Battle-field Reclaimer.

Total Experience: 46,209,990 / 49,500,000

You have gained three General Levels. You are now Level 78.

Total Experience: 46,242,740 / 49,500,000

You gain +3 Intelligence, +3 Aura, and have nine free attribute points to assign.

The silvery, dancing bubbles of experience hit his blood in an entirely different way than the battle lust a moment before. These were astral music, their movements the echo of the celestial spheres.... His mind wandered, shaking under the force.

Flashes of the Nexus, his dreams, and the stars in the void beyond the skies fluttered through his mind, accompanied by the weight of the World Law's attention and the roiling tide.

Then it settled and he staggered, falling back on the snow as battle lust and joy warred in his veins, each of them trying to claim the territory. His mind spun with dizziness as he was battered between the two forces like a wandering spirit trapped between two giant worlds.

Then it passed as the energy became his own, but his mind was still spinning.

Without hesitating, he took all nine of the new attribute points and placed them all into Charisma, pushing it to 49. As the changes took place, he felt his features itching again. The strength of his personality soared, pushing its way up between the two forces.

Almost instantly, he felt his mind clearing. His perception of himself and his own desires sharpened as his sense of self became stronger. He gave it a moment to settle in, and then he glanced at his attributes, calculating what had just happened.

The gain from essence and the levels had pushed his Intelligence and Aura both to 192, which meant that for a moment his Charisma had been around 20% of his essence. With the increase to 49, it was just a hair above 25%.

He frowned. He hadn't liked the feeling of being battered between forces. The Guardian Star's assessment had been accurate. Even when he'd spent all of his free points on Charisma, it was still barely enough.

If he fought Outsiders constantly...it was possible for it to get out of control. Perhaps that was why Outsiders were so insane.

Maybe there were good-looking demons because they needed Charisma to try and keep their minds together...and the ugly ones were the most insane of all.

He muttered to himself as he made some plans to put more into Charisma as soon as possible. The attribute gains from essence were massively higher than his levels right now, especially as the experience requirement soared.

He was going to have to hunt a lot of monsters in the future until he balanced it out, and gave himself some buffer, since they didn't have essence.

Despite the problem, he was still pleased with his gains from the trap. On top of that, the first layer of the ruins was clear for now, which meant it was a fallback point if needed.

He accessed the Guardian Star's map, locating the church forces. From the look of it, there were adventurers and other groups scattered all across the ruins. Without the star to help, he would have been hard pressed to find those three teams. Only their size really made them stand out.

They were in the old twelfth layer, two below his father, as they approached from the direction of Highfold. If they were efficient, they would be able to join forces within a day, although they would have to cut around the southern slope of the mountain. Hopefully, Lenei was with them to make the meeting easy. Sam rubbed his chin as he studied the path down.

The Grand Flaw was on the seventh layer, but it was off to the south, nearly the same distance from him as his father. It was also blocking the only usable path between them, unless he jumped down from layer to layer, but there were several steep cliffs in the way.

The other flaws were scattered between the eleventh and sixth layers. He tapped his talons on his thigh as he examined them all. Three of them were on the side toward Highfold, but there were two that were on the western slopes of the mountain, including the most distant one.

They needed to close all of the lesser flaws and then push on to the Grand Flaw, which meant the easiest thing to do would be to divide their teams until they reached it. That hadn't been his initial plan, since he'd wanted to close the Flaws with the help of the reinforcements....but if he could take out the smaller flaws to the west by himself, and then meet the others at the Grand Flaw, it would save time.

If the church forces tried to get to those two, they would have to pass the Grand Flaw on the way. The only other route was for them to circle around the mountain to the north, which would take days, and time was valuable when they were trying to make sure the Outsiders didn't escape.

His father was probably asleep right now, but once the sun rose, he'd talk to him. With the right coordination, perhaps they could surround the Grand Flaw and reach it at the same time. It just meant that he'd have to take out those two on his own.

He looked up at Caelus, marking out the remaining time until dawn, and then his hand dropped to his belt pouch as he considered how much he could get done. If nothing else, he needed to replace the core in his ring and make a few more healing scrolls.

Before long, everything on the mountain was going to be embroiled in battle.

***

The sun rose on the first layer, highlighting the doorway of the house where Sam was working. His hands were flying as he inscribed another scroll. He'd replaced the shattered core in his ring and meditated to restore his essence. Now, he was working on his fourth healing scroll.

The trap and moonlight runes were bright in his mind, the first real connection he had to the core enchantment, but they were tiny flecks within the grand design. He could feel there were other moon runes in there too.

After this battle, hopefully he'd have time to study it, along with a safe place for his family to settle down. Siwaha was probably willing to let them stay with her, but he didn't feel like the Ice Sylph village was safe enough, even with her strength.

He wanted a place of his own.

A little while later, he put away the sixth healing scroll, which was the last he had time to make. The church forces had paused for part of the night and now were on the move again, heading to meet up with his father.

He touched the amulet on his chest, reaching out for the connection to his father, as he described his idea to split up the teams. He deliberately skipped over the battle he'd just gone through, as well as how injured he'd been.

He didn't want him to worry.

He also didn't say much about the ruins, especially not about the Moonlight Relic. That was a secret he would share with his family soon, but only with them. He'd make sure a privacy ward was as strong as possible and that nothing could be overheard.

News about someone understanding the ruins or an ancient relic coming to life was *not* something to let out into the world. He didn't want anyone coming to bother him in his new house.

"I don't like it, Sam," Jeric growled. It sounded like he was chewing on a stone as he considered what Sam was saying. "Let's just wait for the church forces and then we can meet up. Lenei should be here later today, and then we can figure out a plan of attack. Dividing up isn't smart."

"We need to get rid of all the flaws," Sam reminded him, "so the Outsiders can't escape through them. Otherwise, we'll just have trouble later."

"I'm sure the church can figure out a plan to deal with it all," Jeric said. Sam could hear him shaking his head. "You just sit tight and we'll come up there and find you. You haven't had any trouble yet, have you? It's been clear up there on the peak?"

"Ahh, no..." Sam hesitated. "No trouble at all. Just a few small monsters."

The silence from his father was loaded with meaning. As he pulled up the image of the temple he was in, he could see him frowning, his hand touching the amulet as he stared up toward the peak of the mountain. It looked like he was wrestling with saying something, but after a moment, he decided against it.

"Just make sure to stay safe," he said slowly, "and don't take unnecessary risks. Your mother and sister are depending on us to make it back. We're here to take care of business, not out to get killed."

Sam winced. His father's treatment of him had changed over the past half year and it wasn't the lecture it would have been before, but old memories die hard. Now, there was concern and a hope that he would be all right. There was frustration as well, because he couldn't be there to help him.

In some ways, that was even worse, but there was no way he was going
to tell his father about his plan to kill everything on the way down to the
sixth layer or that he was still planning to take out those two flaws.

If he didn't do that, not only would there be flaws for the Outsiders to
retreat through, there would be a wave of monsters from the west that
could pour down onto the Grand Flaw.

They had to clear their side and he had to clear his if they wanted a clean
battle at the end. Unfortunately, that wasn't going to be as safe as his father
would prefer.

"I'll be as safe as I can," he answered, before asking a few other questions
to get up to speed on current events.

When their conversation ended, he glanced up at the rising sun. It was a
bit past dawn now, and if he wanted to get down to the closest flaw at the
same time as the church forces got to theirs...that gave him a day, at most.

"How many enemies are between here and the flaw on the sixth layer?"
he asked the Guardian Star as he looked over the map, searching for the
best path. If he wanted to eliminate possible reinforcements too, he wasn't
going to be able to take the most direct one.

**There are 41 monsters, 112 beasts, and 53 citizens of Aster Fall
between here and the sixth layer. However, you should attack the
more distant flaw first. It is on the tenth layer, about thirty miles
farther from you.**

The map of the ruins sprang into Sam's awareness as the Guardian Star
highlighted two points. One was on the sixth layer and one was on the
tenth. The first was 24 miles southwest and the other was 54 miles to the
west.

It almost looked like the Outsiders had created the more distant one as a
fallback point, since it was directly opposite Highfold on the other side of
the mountain, but he wasn't sure how much control they had over where
the flaws appeared.

**If you close that one, it cuts off their retreat and gives you a direct
line to engage the next flaw before approaching the Grand Flaw.
Coming from that direction will also conceal that you were up here.**

Sam nodded as he looked at the map. The route was good. If he went
another way, it would involve more backtracking. His wounds were mostly healed, although the dull ache from too much healing magic was still
there.

His hand brushed across his amulet, weighing his father's words as he grimaced. He didn't like going against his wishes, but there were some things he had to do on his own.

He traced a line across the map, searching for the best route down. When he found it, he looked up, checking the position of the sun as he put it behind him.

"Let's get moving."

CHAPTER FORTY-SEVEN

A DISTANT FLAW

Crystal flame flared around him as he jumped, buffering his fall toward the third layer twenty feet below. Snow flew up in a welcoming billow around his shoulders as he landed.

He'd taken the staircase down from the first layer to the second since it had been too steep to jump, and then made his way around to the west. Now, he was facing the direction of the most distant flaw.

Flaw 5, as he'd decided to call it.

On the way back, he'd hit Flaw 4, and then meet up with the church and his father once they'd cleared out Flaws 1, 2, and 3.

He pulled the snow around him in a swirl as he sprinted forward through the layer, stretching his muscles. The Guardian Star's map was shining in his mind, highlighting the location of beasts and monsters.

Every time he got close to a reasonable fight, he moved toward it, eliminating them as quickly as possible. Then he harvested the key materials, auras, and experience. Most of the beasts and monsters were in the Level 40 to 60 range, which meant the experience was a steady trickle and the materials in his collection were increasing.

His confidence with Elemental Manipulation was also increasing, especially now that he'd used it in a life and death battle, but he needed more practice to really understand the depths of the ability. It was like a natural muscle. He might be able to reach out and grab a ball, but that didn't mean he knew how to play the game.

He practiced as he went, attacking the enemies that were closest to the path. It took him four hours to make his way across the second and third layer, passing through more than a dozen battles, and by the time he reached the cliff down to the fourth layer, he heard the World Law's announcement ringing in his mind.

Congratulations, Guardian.

You have gained a Level in your Class. You are now a Level 79 Battlefield Reclaimer.

Total Experience: 49,709,990 / 56,000,000

He ignored the rest of the notification, letting the World Law's voice wash over him. Then he took the three free points and assigned them all to Charisma, pushing it to 52.

He was going to have to put a few more points there before he was comfortable, since there were a lot more Outsiders ahead. He hadn't liked the feeling of being overwhelmed by essence.

The points in Intelligence and Aura brought them to 193, which was 199 with his bracer. A year ago, he'd have thought that was a lot, but at the rate he used essence, it didn't last that long.

More importantly, he was almost at the Expert tier. Hopefully, he could get there before he reached the Flaw, since it would be an immense help. At the rate he was going, it would take fifteen or more opponents around Level 50, since the World Law was still assigning him extra experience. Otherwise, it would have taken him ten times as many, or more in an area with limited experience.

If the town guards in Highfold were around Level 120, like the church officials who were leading the forces here, and if they had done most of their leveling the slower way...how many battles had they seen?

They definitely weren't people to underestimate.

He looked down at the cliff in front of him. Like the one above, it was an almost vertical slope, but it was nearly sixty feet down. It was also cracked in places, with ice packed between the cracks and spurs of stone jutting out. The builders of the relic had cut into the mountain to make these walls between each layer, and they must have once held real defenses, but now it was just the height.

He launched himself from the cliff, wind and flames swirling around him as he jumped from one protrusion to another, using his evasion skill and the help of the snow to keep his balance. A few seconds later, he skidded down onto the fourth layer.

He checked his map to make sure he was still on target, and then he dashed off again, disappearing into the snow.

***

The high mountain winds blew around him and made his cloak stretch out like a banner as he ran through snow-drenched, abandoned streets and across tumbled rooftops. The total distance to the flaw was 54 miles, and he'd crossed twelve of that, but he was just now approaching the sixth layer.

The lower layers were farther down the mountain and much broader, with room for tens of thousands of people to live, but except for the monsters and a rare traveler, they were abandoned, home to only the wind and snow.

On the Highfold side of the ruins, there would have been more adventurers, but here there were very few, which made it easy enough to avoid them. The size also meant there were a number of monsters living here. Without detouring much, he found quite a few.

He glanced down at the corpses of three Ebonstreak Hunters in front of a half-broken building. Their strange, thin forms were a sharp black against the snow. They'd been living in the building and something about their presence had made him single them out, heading for them instead of monsters that were slightly closer.

He still remembered how two of them had tried to ambush him.

He bent down, gathering the auras from them as the taste of boiling dark acid and corrosion hit his senses. A moment later, three Auras of Ebon Corrosion (Advanced) flowed into his storage. With his Wisdom at 65, he had the maximum 85% chance again, which let him get most of them.

He'd also figured out that he could intensify an Advanced aura up to 30 points of essence, which made them a much better source of energy than the Basic ones. On his infrequent breaks, he'd managed to charge up a few while meditating.

He looked up from the corpses to the early afternoon sun, tracking its position across the sky. He needed to get moving if he wanted to reach the flaw by evening. If he took longer than that, he wasn't sure he'd make it to the Grand Flaw on time.

He could practice more with Elemental Manipulation on the way.

***

He darted across the eighth layer, heading for the cliff, and then he leapt into the air. Snow, wind, and ice surrounded him, swirling upward to brace his fall, and for just a moment he floated there, looking down at the next layer sixty feet below

This time, instead of falling, he drifted downward, the wind condensing to provide some resistance beneath his feet as he pulled it hard around him. A moment later, he touched down on the snow, bending his knees slightly to absorb the last of the force. Then he was off again, sprinting through the tumbled ruins.

The slow fall was a part of Elemental Manipulation that focused on Wind, and he'd just figured out how to do it. He couldn't fly, but maybe one day he'd be able to do more. For now, it made it easier to jump between the layers.

The ruins on the lower layers were much more spread out. There were fewer buildings and more room for what must have been fields or parks, with a few pillars and tumbled walls that were widely spaced. The streets were also broader, capable of allowing four wagons to pass side by side, although now they were only straight, open expanses covered by snow.

He kept to the edges and off the main roads, following the Guardian Star's directions. He felt a pang of regret at the number of monsters he was passing, but he was short on time now.

It took him about an hour to reach the ninth layer and then two more hours to run across it and jump down to the tenth. Eventually he did, landing on the packed snow with a soft thud.

The broad shoulder of Sun's Rest stretched out before him, dropping away gradually toward the horizon where the peaks of more distant mountains could be seen, shimmering faintly purple and red in the sunset. The sun was dropping swiftly behind them, bathing the Western Reaches in dusky gold and peach hues.

The eastern view was blocked by the peak, but he knew Caelus would be rising.

It was a good time to seal a flaw. A hard determination flickered across his face.

***

The tenth layer was more than ten miles across and he moved carefully, following the star's directions. Now, he was looking over the top of a ruined pillar as snow dusted over his features, settling on his cloak as it hid him from view.

He was over half a mile away, which should be out of range of the Icebloods' sense for essence, but he wasn't sure. He'd have to get within a quarter mile to sense them, so it should be enough. For now, he was relying on the Guardian Star's scan to tell him what was there.

The flaw was inside a large ruined building, something that might have stored wagons or grain. It was a whispering sense at the edge of his mind, pulling him toward it with a promise of rage, destruction, victory, and battle.

It was...tempting.

He pushed the feeling aside, settling himself in his own sense of personality as he focused on his aura and breathing. Now that he was aware of the effect that essence and experience had on him, he planned to manage them like any other part of his personality.

If experience was champagne that bubbled with joy, then essence was a blood-drenched whiskey that punched you in the gut and said you could do anything. There might be a time to let those feelings out and really appreciate the glass he was holding, but right now, he needed a clear head.

Fifteen monsters are guarding the Flaw, as well as two Iceblood Shamans, three Iceblood Hunters, and an Iceblood Warrior. The star's words rang in his mind, identifying the opposition. **The average level is around 55.**

They are located approximately thirty feet inside that old warehouse, with guards on both sides of the entry, inside and out.

"That doesn't sound too bad," Sam whispered back, his voice more a thought than a reality. "I'll just have to hit them hard and fast."

It didn't sound like these Icebloods were the cream of the crop. Their levels were even lower than the ones he'd killed up above. If he unloaded his bracer and his best attacks, it should be enough to take out a lot of them.

Still, there was a word of caution in his mind that sounded like his father, reminding him that his injuries weren't fully healed and he didn't need to

take any risks. The ache from too much healing was still there and using
any more scrolls would make it worse.

He didn't feel like spending two weeks doubled over with phantom
cramps in every muscle. He had to be smart about this one and not just
charge in.

He rubbed his chin as he studied the guards, plans flickering through
his mind. There were half a dozen Coldfang Beheaders outside the
door, their long, wolfen bodies mostly hidden beneath the snow. Only
their more humanoid torsos were visible, their blade arms hanging
ready at their sides. From time to time, they turned and barked a word
to one another, but for the most part, they were silent.

Here and there, bone talismans were stabbed into the ground around
the area. Most of them were staves with strange inscriptions, but there
were a few long bones from monsters that made up odd, angled pyra-
mids. He wasn't sure what the enchantment was for, but he planned
to take it out as soon as possible.

He pulled a scroll from his belt pouch and then two of the advanced
auras as he slowly infused them into it. While he worked on that, he
kept his attention fixed on the building. A moment later, he held the
scroll in his right hand while a Starfire built up in his left. Then a swirl
of crystal flame condensed around him, building up into dozens of
brilliant arrows with white *star* runes on the tips.

He drew a deep breath and exploded out of hiding. His footsteps
thudded into the snow as he leapt over the fallen pillar, racing forward.
As he moved, the arrows surged around him in a wave and then split
off, nearly sixty of them heading for the bone talismans.

KrissSHHHhHHHHhh!

Explosive eruptions echoed down the line as the arrows slammed
into a shield that shimmered into existence. It was pale blue with
swirling red clouds like a frozen, blood-hued sky.

The Coldfang Beheaders lunged to their feet as they saw the explosion. They raced toward him, their claws digging into the snow and
throwing it in every direction. Their gazes weighed on the air like a
knife, as if they'd been waiting for prey to appear, and their blade arms
swept out wide.

The bone talismans shuddered under the impact, but the pale shield
held up. He didn't hesitate as he hurled both the Starfire and the infused

scroll at the barrier. As they left his hands, he was already darting to the side.

A rippling curtain of Fire infused with an Aura of Desolate Life and an Aura of Ebon Corrosion struck the barrier, roaring outward in a sheet of dark, tearing flames that chewed at the shield with a frightening hunger, licking upward like devouring tongues.

At the same time, slightly farther down, the Starfire erupted with a brilliant, blue-white explosion as the rune at the center blasted outward through the layers of crystal flame, delivering a reverberating, concussive force that shook the pale blue shield like a sheet. Bright flames licked along the edges, burning away the red clouds.

The bone talismans shuddered under the onslaught, and the shield thinned. It was already damaged by the crystal flame arrows and now the staves swayed in the wind like willow leaves as fine lines appeared across the bones. The inscriptions began to shatter, the dark, curling lines turning to dust.

The Coldfangs rushed toward him without hesitation. The dark flames and blue-white reflected from their icy blades, giving them a scintillating light in dusk.

Sam poured more essence out into his crystal flame spiral as he formed another Starfire in his left hand. He paid only half attention to the Coldfangs as the flight of arrows condensed around him. His eyes were on the building behind them.

At that moment, the ground around him shuddered as if an avalanche had struck it. Snow, rocks, pebbles, and chunks of frozen ice flew into the air, where they shivered for a moment before falling again.

The building exploded outward, the stones erupting like a volcano had just been born beneath it as they flew in every direction. Some slammed into snow banks and tumbled pillars. Others ripped through the air like spell shards, flying away faster than the eye could track.

Two stones collided with Sam's Essence Shield before he could react, but then he dived to the side and rolled behind a hill of loose rocks that was covered in snow. He darted back to the edge, trying to see what had just happened.

At the center of the explosion, there was an enormous, dark green mass that was slowly uncurling its bulk from the ruins of the building. It was so large that its limbs extended out past where the building had been, but it had somehow been buried beneath it.

Long, clawed legs covered in scales reached outward, tearing at the dirt that had once been a foundation as they grabbed for traction on the ground. Then a spike-crowned, wedge-shaped head reared above the rest of the body, stretching out a long, muscled neck. Behind it, two enormous wings unfurled, their breadth larger than three of the buildings that had been on top of it.

SkreeEEECCCkkkKKK!

Ice Wyvern Matriarch. Level 105.

A wave of twisted essence flowed around her, the remains of some formation or spell that was quickly dissipating into the air.

The wyvern matriarch's body shook as she stood, levering herself to her feet as her wings beat at the air. She was at least thirty feet tall and her wings stretched for almost a hundred.

A few dozen feet behind her, the flaw floated in the air, a rainbow gash through the dimensions that drew the eye like a single parchment curling into flame at the center of a library.

The matriarch's head bobbed as she searched the area, her nostrils flaring. The snow posed no barrier to whatever senses she had, and an instant later her head swiveled around to glare at him, her eyes like cut green crystals that pierced across the distance.

Then she lunged forward, uncurling like a bolt of green lightning. Her wings flared behind her, adding speed.

In the space behind her, six Icebloods stepped out from behind a pale blue shield, followed by a dozen monsters, but he didn't have time to study them.

Concealing formation detected. The relic here was damaged, allowing for an illusion. The Outsiders hid the wyvern within the fluctuations coming from the Flaw. As a monster of Aster Fall, the matriarch lacks sufficient essence to be easily detected.

Retreat is advised.

The matriarch is at the First Evolution. You will be at a significant disadvantage in trying to fight her.

The Guardian Star's calm voice echoed in his ears, but he ignored it, his attention fixed on the massive monster heading his way. His hands darted to his belt and his storage, pulling out another scroll and aura as he considered how to kill it.

He'd taken down the basilisk…but that had been with the help of his father and everyone else, and it hadn't been anywhere near as strong as this matriarch.

Crystal flame surged around him as he turned and sprinted away, pulling the wind and snow around him to add more speed. He left a streak of rippling flame in the air as he darted to the top of a broken pillar and launched himself off.

He landed a moment later on top of a building and put on more speed, his hands blurring as he poured the aura into the scroll. The Guardian Star tracked the movement of the wyvern, showing her closing the distance.

She was so large that every step she took was a gliding lunge equal to a dozen of his. She wasn't just a little faster than him. She was *much* faster, and she gained on him in an instant, even while she was still running on the ground.

If she took to the air, he had no idea how he would get away from her.

Without looking, he turned and hurled the scroll behind him, just as he felt the wyvern enter his Crystal Field. As the scroll started to explode, he spun in the air, launching himself backward.

The full two hundred charges blasted out of his bracer in an instant, heading toward the wyvern at the same time as the scroll exploded.

The matriarch's wings curved in front of her, surrounded by a shimmering, light green barrier like glacial venom. The scroll and the arrows exploded against that barrier as she continued to barrel forward, her thick legs clawing at the ground.

For a moment, the explosion deafened everything in the air. It was a roaring echo of a blast with hundreds of staccato bursts inside, a brilliant chain of power exploding in the night.

A moment later, the wyvern crashed through the barrage, her wings charred but intact. She lunged forward, her wings sweeping behind her as she leapt. Then she was airborne, her head swooped down toward him as her jaws widened.

Sam saw the widening jaws and a sense of calm came over him, his hands reaching out as his battle aura sprang into existence. He pushed all the other thoughts from his mind as his reality descended to a single, frozen moment. A rippling cloak of crystal flame spread like an aurora behind him as his talons turned to blades.

Two figures flew through the air above the snow, one a gigantic, green blur covered in spikes and the other small, surrounded by burning flames.

Chapter Forty-Eight
Natural Enemies

The elements roared in fury, spinning into a shield that shattered a moment later as the monster's jaws snapped down. Shards of hardened wind and ice flew around Sam, ringing off the tiny scales on the matriarch's head as his talons swept up to meet her, slashing toward her nostrils and eyes.

There was no time to dodge. Her mouth was almost as large as his entire body, with fangs as long as his arm. He tried to twist to the side with crystal flame flaring around him, but she was too close.

Her fangs crashed into his Essence Shield, long yellow spears stabbing into the crystal pattern, and for a moment they slowed. Then the shield shattered, splintering apart into frozen shards that dissolved into the air.

The jaws closed on him, biting into the Ring of Crystal Shield's barrier that sprang into existence like a blue sun in her mouth, and Sam's talons slashed across her face, leaving deep gouges in her scales.

The matriarch jerked her head, biting harder into the crystal shield, but the artifact held. She whipped her head back and forth and then flung him off to the side. Her wing came around, batting at him.

It hit with the force of an avalanche, a violent echo that rattled every bone in his body with a giant hammer blow as it threw him away.

He tumbled head over heels, pulling his aura in tighter as he poured essence into it. At the same time, he reached out to the wind around him. Instead of trying to slow his fall, this time he accelerated it, trying to push himself faster.

He was being knocked around like a child's toy, but his mind was clear. He needed distance...time to prepare. If he could get a couple of scrolls together....

Unfortunately, he wasn't going to get it.

The wyvern chased him, jumping into the air with a lunge as her wings beat down with a mighty gust, and then she was airborne, angling after him as her mouth opened again.

This time, there was a building roil of mist at the back of her throat that was quickly growing larger. Spinning trails of mana consolidated into a giant ball of green-tinged ice. All around it, there was a virulent glow of venom that hissed in the air.

Her mouth gaped wide as the venom ball shot out, heading for him even faster than she was. Even if he dodged it, he would set himself up to be bitten by her a moment later, so he took a different approach.

He hardened the shield around him and added a second, absorptive layer just as the attack arrived. The ball struck the shield with the force of a ballista, caving it inward in an instant.

Sam poured his essence into the shield, focusing on keeping it soft and pliable, as he pushed himself backward through the air.

Crystal flame, wind, and the wyvern's attack all combined to hurl him away.

Even as he flew through the air, the venom was corroding through the outer layer of his shield, so he shunted it to the side, deflecting the sphere at the same time as he lost the shield.

A new one sprang up, forming out of his aura, but his essence was dropping precipitously. As he looked back, the matriarch beat her wings and angled into a sharp vee, surging toward him again. There were white lines on her snout where his talons had struck, but he hadn't even broken through the scales. Her defenses were even denser than the first wyvern he'd fought, except the matriarch had truly come into her own

The same sense of calm was all around him, mixing with a desire for victory that pushed him forward. It sharpened his senses, but at the same time it brought with it an acceptance of reality.

The star had been right. He was outclassed in this battle, but there was nothing to be done now.

His hands spread out to the side as a Starfire took shape in each palm. The glowing white runes shone at the heart of cerulean blue spheres, like stars that had fallen from heaven and now burned within the ocean.

His hands crossed in front of his chest as he threw both spheres at her. They exploded across her head and chest, brightening into eruptions that shook even the massive matriarch. For a moment, she staggered in her flight, spiraling to the side as her wings swept around for stability.

But then she dived, her wings angled back as she dropped below the area of the explosions. Her wings beat as her head curved back up, her eyes fixed on him. There was a malicious light in them that said she was enjoying the chase. With a few wingstrokes, she regained her elevation, coming up even with him.

Absorbing the attack had gained him some distance, and the force of it hadn't dissipated yet. With the help of the wind, he was still hurtling through the air, but his attempts to go faster were failing.

The matriarch swept her wings back and surged after him, catching up easily. Her eyes were malicious, dark green lines as she tracked him. Then her tail swept around, smashing toward him in the air as the spike on the end hammered toward his chest.

Sam crossed his hands in front of himself, hardening his shield again, and took the strike directly. The bone spike crashed through the Essence Shield with a shattering explosion as he felt his essence drop like a rock, but he managed to twist to the side, pushing away from her with the air around him and a blast of evasive crystal flame.

At the same time, his talons slashed across her tail, leaving scored lines in the scales there. Unfortunately, that was the extent of the damage. He went flying through the air, tumbling wildly as he tried to right himself again, his senses fixed on the giant monster.

This time, the matriarch chose not to use another venom ball. She simply beat her wings harder as she gained elevation, angling up above him like a hawk as she kept her eyes on him. As she did, she moved slightly farther away, but in reality, the distance was an illusion.

In a second, she would dive, her speed accelerating as she angled down. He could already see how the trajectory would go. Her head would point toward him and her wings would sweep back as she sped down, her claws extended. The impact of a thirty-foot-tall wyvern matriarch would be like a building collapsing.

He reached out to the air around him, feeling the slipping streams as the wind sped past him. He was still flying horizontally across the mountainside, the wyvern's blow and his slow falling effect enough to keep him airborne.

His essence was down to a quarter. The initial attack and the matriarch shattering his shield had drained it. As the monster folded her wings and dived toward him, he reached out to the elements, feeling for anything that might help.

All around him, there was the whipping sense of the wind and the presence of Ice, but *there*, about a mile distant, he felt an incredibly concentrated presence of Ice that was denser than anything else around. He didn't know what it was, but he seized on it as an opportunity.

He pulled a slanted shield around him, covering it in a layer of slippery wind as the wyvern swept toward him. As best he could, he needed to be a bubble that blew with the wind. Whether or not he survived was down to perfect timing.

All around the wyvern, he could feel a wall of air that her massive bulk was pushing ahead of her as she approached. He focused his will on that layer, reaching out to catch the edge. Then, like a bubble bouncing off a sudden breeze, he used the force of it to hurl himself away.

The wyvern dove past him, her jaws reaching toward nothing, and Sam went flying through the air, surrounded by a layer of wind that carried him across the ground. As he bounced away, he called a new breeze to push him in the direction of the presence he'd sensed.

Tumbling through the sky, he pulled half a dozen auras out of his storage, combusting them one after the other to restore his essence. Six of the advanced auras burned away, returning him almost to full.

The wyvern screeched, her voice angry. There was a sound of mockery in it as she caught herself in the dive and swept upward again, heading for him as she gained altitude. She'd missed him once, but she didn't plan to a second time.

Sam grabbed at the wind around him, using it to keep himself upright and as light as possible. He was losing altitude quickly, but the wyvern's attack had thrown him up high and he was moving at an incredible rate. The presence that he'd felt was just ahead.

He reached out toward it, trying to figure out what it was. It was different from the wyvern, resonating with his Initiate of Ice trait.

The wyvern curved around, her eyes locked on him as she prepared to dive again. All around her, there was a glowing, virulent green aura that felt corrosive and dangerous. Whatever she was doing, it wasn't going to be as simple as the last dive.

She ducked her head, the viper-like wedge of it angled toward him as her wings swept back.

RooOOOOAAARRrrRRR!

At that moment, however, a streak of bright, blue-white frost blasted through the air, striking the wyvern's left wing. Ice crystals expanded all across the area, covering the wing. The impact sent her spinning around as she lost her balance.

An instant later, an enormous, white blur slammed into her with an explosive blast of wind and muscled bulk. It was even larger than she was, with four claws and legs extended as two gigantic, crystalline wings flared outward to brace in the air.

Those claws seized her by the wing and leg, preventing her from escaping as it smashed her into a dive toward the ground below. As they plummeted downward together, he saw what it was. The presence of Ice that he'd felt radiated from it like a frozen moon.

It was a massive, white-scaled drake.

Ice Drake. Level 130.

It was at least half again bigger than the wyvern, with a long, white body stretching backward. It was covered in scales that reflected the light and had translucent wings like a crystal sculpture that stretched for nearly a hundred and fifty feet. Despite its size, the drake's body was lean and angular, with four limbs compared to the wyvern's two.

The drake kept a tight hold on the wyvern as they headed for the ground, their speed increasing as they plummeted. His head shot down as he breathed ice across her wings and head, covering her in a thick coat.

When they were only a hundred feet above the stone mountainside, he released her. His tail came around with a resounding *THHWAAAACckK*, accelerating her fall.

Unable to free her wings from the ice or control her fall, the matriarch's green-scaled body struck the ground like a frozen meteorite, with a re-sounding *crack* of shattering tendons and wingbones that echoed across the area.

The drake circled once to regain his balance, his wings snapping out to the side, and then he followed her down, his mouth opening in a roar. A blast of frozen air condensed in front of him, forming into a massive ice crystal. The crystal shot ahead of him and slammed into her side, shattering her scales.

The drake didn't stop there. He followed the ice crystal down and slammed into her, forcing her into the ground, as his claws and tail swung around, slashing through her hide and hammering her deeper. His actions were quick and savage, as if there were old hatred in them.

His jaws opened wide to reveal long, translucent fangs like icicles. Green blood and scales exploded in a fountain as he tore at her neck, covering the land around the matriarch.

That was all Sam had time to see as his trajectory through the air dropped and he headed for the mountainside below. He grabbed at the winds around him to slow his fall and they hardened, providing some resistance.

His flight slowed and he began to drift down in an arc, but before he could land, an icy wind swept upward, swirling in a wave as it pulled him to the side. A sudden surprise flared through him, as well as a sense of panic.

Where had that come from?

His aura flared outward as he prepared to fight, but then Crystal Field brought back an image of what was around him and he halted, pulling his essence back in.

The presence that he'd felt had to be the ice drake, but this...this was a surprise. They had blended into the snow so easily that he hadn't even known they were there.

He pulled the wind and ice around himself, halting his fall as he drifted to the ground, and when he came to a stop, he was directly in front of six people, their lean, angular features setting off their crystal blue eyes.

The Ice Sylphs regarded him with severe expressions, their faces puzzled. A swirl of Ice came from them, testing his aura. The sense that radiated from them was similar to Siwaha's, but not as deep. Hers was a hundred layers of snow and different moods, like incense mixed with winter. Theirs was simpler and a little more jagged, auras that fit a hunter.

The one in the lead stepped forward, pushing a white cloak back around his head to fully reveal his face. His long hair was ice white, tumbling down his back, and there was a long bow slung over his shoulder.

"I am Siwasir," the sylph spoke slowly, his words betraying only a trace of irritation. There was also puzzlement. He looked somewhat like Siwaha, as if they were related, but Sam wasn't able to tell for sure.

"Elder Siwaha told us about you, Sam Hastern, but I did not expect to see you here. We have been hunting these Outsiders, but we were still studying their defenses when you attacked."

"Young and impetuous, despite your strength," another of the Ice Sylphs spoke up, her words flowing like the wind. "If you had spent longer watching before attacking, you would have seen that it was a trap."

"Still, your attack allows us to seize the opportunity," Siwasir added, nodding to Sam. "Elsanar smelled the wyvern matriarch here, which is one reason we waited. He is pleased that you lured her out and sprang their trap. It was good work to bring her to us."

The words crashed around Sam in a whirl of impressions as he stared at the Ice Sylphs, the reality of what had just happened settling in. Off in the distance, the titanic form of the ice drake was still tearing apart the wyvern's corpse.

A mile or more distant, the flaw gleamed in the air, and he could just make out the surge of monsters around it, which were even now headed their way, chasing the path the wyvern had taken.

"Your attack drew their attention and broke their shield," Siwasir added as he followed Sam's gaze. His hand reached up to touch the bow across his shoulders. "Now, we need to finish the work.

"Come! There will be time to speak later."

With that, Siwasir and the rest of the Ice Sylphs turned. Then they were moving, their forms rippling like a spreading frost in the air as they were suddenly more distant.

They were running so swiftly and smoothly that their motions could barely be called an effort. As they started to pull away, Sam pushed aside the questions on his mind and launched himself after them. Crystal flame and wind surrounded him as he raced to keep up.

As they ran, he glanced at the Ice Sylphs ahead of him, examining them. They looked like six siblings, all of them with very similar angular features, ice blue eyes, and white hair. They were wearing matching long, white cloaks and three of them had a bow slung over their shoulders.

Siwasir. Ice Sylph. Ice Spirit-Ranger. Level 112.
Ice Sylph. Sky Mage-Healer. Level 108.
Ice Sylph. Ranger-Ice Weaver. Level 114.
Ice Sylph. Ice Walker-Ranger. Level 104.
Ice Sylph. Healer-Ice Shaman. Level 121.
Ice Sylph. Ice Walker-Sky Mage. Level 106.

This had to be the warrior group that Siwaha had mentioned, the one that had been out hunting Outsiders in the ruins. The snow fluttered around them with a friendly curl and he could feel a sense of kinship with them. It was a comfortable, relaxing chill that calmed the nerves and cleared his mind.

He wasn't sure how they were here, but with their levels...the Outsiders had been kicking a hornet's nest to attack their village. It made a lot more sense now how the sylphs survived here in the mountains.

But the ice drake.... His breath caught as he looked back to where the enormous beast was still ripping the wyvern apart. How were they working with it? There was more going on here than he understood.

The monsters were racing in their direction at the same time as they headed toward the flaw, and it took only a minute to reach them.

The impact was a massacre. The Coldfangs that had tried to attack him were the first in front of them, and a ripple of white arrows with blue fletchings sprang through the air as they approached, accompanied by twisting blades of Ice and a sweeping wind that froze everything in its path.

Sam poured out a wave of crystal flame arrows and summoned a Starfire, throwing into the mix, but it was only one part of a much wilder battle.

Behind the Coldfangs, Icesoul Wraiths and a line of Hoarfrost Serpents and Diamondfang Ice Vipers rushed toward them, but the instant they struck at the Ice Sylphs' line, they were torn apart.

The six Icebloods tried to turn when they saw the disparity in the forces, retreating toward the flaw, but they hadn't prepared for this type of assault. With their trap sprung, they had no time to react. A wave of white arrows and spells struck them, ripping holes in their shields. Pale blue blood splattered across the ice.

Before long, the area was silent. The Ice Sylphs spread out across the area with their bows and spells ready, searching for anything that was still alive. After a moment, they returned, with Siwasir in the lead, and stopped in front of Sam.

"Thank you for the assistance, Sam Hastern," Siwasir said sternly, even as he bowed slightly, inclining his head to Sam. "Your attack was ill-considered, but without it, the battle would have been much harder." He sounded like an older brother or uncle lecturing him.

"But tell me, why have you come here? You are a long way from your family, and you are not strong enough to be here alone. The monsters in these mountains often reach the First Evolution, like the wyvern matriarch that pursued you."

"I was planning to destroy the flaw," Sam answered slowly, pulling his attention together as he looked at the dimensional tear behind Siwasir. "The church has sent reinforcements into the ruins, but they won't be able to close them in time without help. There are five subsidiary flaws, including this one, and then the Grand Flaw."

It took him a couple of minutes, but he explained his idea and the timing to eliminate all of the flaws. As he spoke, the Ice Sylphs' attention on him increased, their eyes widening.

"There are *four* other flaws?" The female Ice Sylph asked who was standing behind Siwasir, the Ranger-Ice Weaver. There was a blue tattoo that curled like a flower around her cheek. Her expression was shocked. "Then we have to get them as soon as possible."

"If you know their location, you must lead us there," one of the other Ice Sylphs agreed, switching to the new goal in an instant. "We knew there were flaws in the area, but not how many or where they were. We have been searching, but they are well hidden, and all we could do was follow the trail of the monsters and the tracks of the Outsiders.

"If Elsanar had not smelled the wyvern and thought something was suspicious here, we would not have found this area," Siwasir agreed as he gave Sam a considering look. "We'll destroy this one and then head there at once. If the humans are on the move as well, we will match their speed. We cannot allow the Outsiders to escape. They would only return again."

In the distance, the ice drake, Elsanar, flared his wings as he tilted his head back and roared at the heavens. Below him, the wyvern matriarch's corpse leaked green blood onto the snow.

The rest of the introductions took a few moments and then the Ice Sylphs turned their attention to the flaw. The rainbow dimensional tear was shimmering at the center of a devastated circle that was decorated with the remains of the building. Iceblood and monster corpses were scattered around.

Some of them were pinned through with white arrows that had blue fletchings and others were ripped to shreds by claws and ice magic. Chunks of ice and swirling frost marked the ground, its light blue color a hint different from the snow that was all around. He could sense the impression left behind, especially the ice that they'd used. It felt familiar to him, with a trace of welcome, like a neighbor he'd seen but hadn't met.

Without speaking, the Ice Sylphs darted around the area, collecting the experience and seizing everything useful from the Icebloods. The silver stream of experience began to bubble through the area, some of it coming to him.

There was also a surge of experience that flowed from the wyvern, although most of that went to the ice drake. By the time it was all collected, it was almost enough to push him to Level 80.

Total Class Experience: 54,709,990 / 56,000,000.

It wasn't the conclusion to the battle that he'd expected, but he was lucky to be alive. If the wyvern hadn't been here, he might have managed, but he wasn't the only one with traps and unexpected forces.

He'd been impatient. The wyvern had been more than he could handle, and it drove home some of the differences between him and the First Evolution. There had to be a higher mana or aura density in monsters after they evolved, which was why the wyvern's scales had been so hard to pierce.

The rainbow tear in the world slowly sealed over as the natural auras of Aster Fall flowed toward it, covering it in layer after layer of the elements and other, more abstract concepts. It was a flood of mountain wind, fluttering snow, quick-flourishing grasses that smelled of mint and jasmine, and a distant ocean breeze with a red-gold sun soaking into the sands.

With a final, ear-popping *snap* of air rushing in, the flaw disappeared, leaving nothing but the chill air of the mountain behind. Then the World Law spoke, its tone a little warmer than usual as it announced the results of the battle.

Congratulations, Guardian. You are *Acknowledged*.

Seal one more Flaw to remove the Trait: *Defiant*.

The Ice Sylphs looked around the area at the scattered corpses, making sure everything was still. Among the corpses, there were the translucent forms of Icesoul Wraith like blankets tossed to the earth, a couple of Arctic Cave Trolls, and the various serpents and Coldfangs.

Siwasir turned to Sam with an intense look. His head tilted toward him, a question on his lips.

"How quickly can you travel, Sam Hastern? I sense your Initiate of Ice...but that alone will not grant you the speed we need. We must move before the Outsiders learn of what happened here."

"I'll move as fast as I can," Sam promised, feeling a sense of challenge. Then he glanced around, looking at the dead monsters and Outsiders. "Just give me a moment to gather resources."

With that, as the Ice Sylphs looked on curiously, he turned toward the Icebloods and the other Outsiders as he tore the essence from their corpses with a slash of his talons. The glittering stars of essence rose up in an array of red and yellow stars from the Icebloods, the Icesoul Wraiths, and the Coldfang Beheaders. They surged toward him, turning blue as they struck his body.

Essence Constellation (Second Layer): 3,197 / 7,500.
Strength increased by 2.
Constitution increased by 3.
Agility increased by 1.
Intelligence increased by 4.
Aura increased by 4.

The average level of the monsters here hadn't been that high, but it was still around six hundred points.

After that, he darted around the area, pulling auras from every monster he could find. There were fifteen monsters and he ended up with a dozen advanced auras, including some Advanced Auras of Desolate Life from the Icesoul Wraiths, which tasted of ashen despair.

When he was finished, he stood above the Outsiders, looking down at them. He reached out, touching the corpse of one, and he felt it. It was the aura that he'd touched back at the Ice Sylph village, but that had burned away in his hand.

Aura of Blood Winter.

The taste of blood in the snow filled his senses as he pulled the auras from the corpses. It was a swirling, red taint as if a vein had been cut open on the ice. It was a natural aura of Aster Fall, something the Icebloods had stolen, so it wasn't evil, but the taste of it was...uncomfortable.

It felt like a mountain climber who had fallen into a crevasse, desperately reaching their hand up to the edge to pull themselves free as they sliced their palms open on the ice, only to fall back into the depths below. Five of the auras flowed into his storage as he pulled them free.

While he worked, the Ice Sylphs watched him curiously, but either Siwaha had told them about him or they felt no need to ask what he was doing.

As for the wyvern, everything about that corpse belonged to the ice drake that had saved him. As he turned to look, in the distance, Elsanar took to the air, his enormous, crystal wings beating as he began to circle above them. The sunset gleamed through his wings, sending a vivid rainbow of light that danced across the snow.

Sam turned, facing to the southwest and the direction of the next flaw. His face hardened as he gathered his energy around him and reached out to the wind and the snow, preparing himself to move. He looked around, making sure the Ice Sylphs were ready, but they were only waiting for him.

"Follow me," he said. Then he burst into a run, leaping across the snow with long, gliding steps as the Ice Sylphs flowed along behind him.

Chapter Forty-Nine

TRANSIT POINT

Sam sprinted across the tenth layer, his steps fluid. Behind him, the Ice Sylphs spread out in a wedge, their lean forms and white cloaks blending into the snow so well that they seemed to disappear between one moment and the next.

The snow curled around them in the same way it did for him, but it was much stronger. There was a constant flow of Ice humming in the air, resonating with their movements. If he hadn't been tuned into that same energy, it would have blurred his senses, hiding their presence.

They had no difficulty in keeping up with him. If anything, he was probably slowing them down. The only thing letting him hold the pace was his increased physical attributes from the essence he'd absorbed. He frowned, pushing more essence into his movement as he tried to propel himself faster.

As they ran, he reached out through his amulet to his father, checking on his position.

"Dad, I've found the Ice Sylph hunting party," he sent quickly, between breaths. "We've destroyed one flaw and are heading back for the other. Then we'll meet you at the Grand Flaw."

"You're not alone? Good!" Jeric's voice echoed in his mind, tinged with relief. "I was worried you'd run off and taken a risk all by yourself. Lenei and the church forces arrived about two hours ago. It was a bit hectic, but they destroyed a flaw on their way in already. We've sorted out the adventurers with them and we're all heading to the other two subsidiary flaws now. They're close enough together that we should be able to get them one after the other. Hold on a moment."

There was a pause and then Jeric's voice continued. "Lenei is here. I'm passing your message on to her, so she can tell the church. Since your information about the first flaw was good, they're inclined to trust the rest of it." There was a pause as he talked to Lenei and then he was back.

"She says the church wants you to stay out of it, since they don't want any distractions. We'll be at the next one in about two hours, since we have to backtrack south a bit to get to it. Then we can cut north toward yours and back around for the Grand Flaw. We may have to split our forces to do both."

"Dad, no," Sam insisted as he focused on a way to convince his father that would also work for the church. "The Ice Sylphs won't allow it. The six of them alone are at least as strong as the entire church force. This is their land, and even the church is only a guest here. We've already taken out one."

He glanced up at the sky as he checked on the position of the moons. It was early evening now and they'd been running for more than an hour.

"We'll be at the next flaw shortly and wipe it out. Then we'll move toward the Grand Flaw and keep an eye on it until you arrive. We have to make sure the Outsiders don't escape."

"Sam..." Jeric's voice was a hesitant rumble, one that became more resigned as he continued. "I'll tell the church about the Ice Sylphs, but don't take any extra chances, all right?"

Sam felt a flash of embarrassment as he considered his attack on the fifth flaw, but he pushed it aside. He might not have planned it that well, but it had still been necessary.

"I'll be fine," he promised. "Once this is done, we can settle in and have a real life here."

There were a few more words exchanged, and then Sam turned his attention back to running. When he looked over, he noticed that Siwasir had moved up to run beside him.

"Your father worries about you," Siwasir said simply. He'd overheard Sam's side of the discussion, enough that he'd made sense of it. The sylph was running so smoothly it was almost like he was standing next to him.

"You are at that age where some rebel against their parents' directions, but remember that he only wishes to keep you safe. All the same, a hunter must hunt, or he is not a hunter." Siwasir looked to the sky, where Elsanar was flying above them. The drake was nearly invisible, except for his wings that refracted the moonlight and sent an occasional gleam across the snow.

"Life is dangerous even if you stay at home, and then you will never grow," the sylph added. "That is also a form of death. Just be wiser in your actions and bear in mind that attributes do not change our basic nature. They only enhance what is already there. You will have to moderate your impulsiveness with careful thought." With that, Siwasir turned his attention back to the front.

Sam understood what he meant. He was saying that Wisdom might add to your perception, including of your own actions, but it didn't make you wise. You had to do that on your own. Instead of following up, however, he turned his attention to the ice drake. He didn't understand Elsanar's connection to the Ice Sylphs, and it had also felt like the drake had something personal against that wyvern.

When he asked, Siwasir looked to the sky to check on Elsanar's position before answering.

"The ice drakes are the lords of the mountains. They carry the lineage of an ancient ice dragon, and they have great hearts and keen minds. The wyverns, on the other hand, are monsters that corrupt the ice with their presence. They are a plague on the peaks." He sent a glance over his shoulder to Sam before he looked forward again.

"Do you know how quickly a wyvern grows and how much they eat? It takes a century for a drake to grow to adulthood, but for a wyvern, it is a tenth of that. They multiply like locusts, spreading everywhere, and as adolescents they hunt in swarms." Siwasir frowned, his lean face marked by hard lines.

"The drakes never have many hatchlings, and when they can, a wyvern swarm will hunt a clutch of young drakes, sometimes even the eggs before they hatch. They kill them to consume their mana and flesh. It causes the wyverns to grow even faster, and there are so many of them that the drakes cannot always stop them. Once a drake grows, they are stronger than a wyvern, but few make it to that age and their path is a struggle.

"Elsanar has lost several of his children to the wyverns and was hunted himself when he was younger. So, he hates them for good reason and would see the mountains purged of them."

Siwasir took a breath and let it out slowly, some of the tension easing from his face.

"He is here now because of the Outsiders. They have been helping the wyverns, protecting them and using them as guards, which will allow their presence to grow out of control if it's not stopped. That is a threat to all of the drakes."

When he finished, he was silent for a while as they ran along together. It was comfortable that way, with only the drifting snow passing across Sam's cheeks and the rhythmic cycle of his breath. There was something simple about the sylphs, or perhaps primal, that painted reality in stark, clear lines.

The other sylphs didn't speak, but they were a close and comfortable presence. It made him wonder what it would be like to hunt the mountains with them, running across the snow. Just by being near them, it felt like he was more a part of the snow and wind than he had ever been.

The rest of their run was in companionable silence as they passed through the tenth layer and the ones above it, zigzagging their way up the broken staircases and landslides that led to the sixth layer.

He did his best to lead them around any monsters in the way, and for the most part their path was clear. Twice an Ebonstreak Nighthunter glided above them, but each time one of the Rangers saw it before it could get close and a white arrow sent it tumbling to the snow.

Just as they entered the sixth layer, a message from his father arrived, letting him know that the church had arrived at the next flaw and was engaging the Outsiders there. The news made him jump, his aura sparking around him. He wished that he was there, watching his father's back.

But there was nothing he could do about that right now. He'd made his choice to go alone and now he had to see it through. At least Krana and Lesat were with him, as well as Lenei.

He pulled his attention back to the present, scanning the map as he adjusted their path toward the next flaw. The sixth layer had mostly been a housing district, and the streets were layered with abandoned shops and two-story homes.

In the night, everything was limned with moonlight. He led the sylphs through the streets as quickly as possible, bypassing all the monsters he could sense. The flaw was near the middle of the layer in an area that was curled around with narrow streets and tightly packed buildings surrounding a medium-sized plaza.

It looked as if it had once been a market center, probably filled with bakeries and shops for the people who lived nearby. As they approached, the Guardian Star's voice rang out in his mind and he halted, bringing the sylphs behind him to a stop.

Scans of this area indicate at least 20 citizens of Aster Fall are in the vicinity of the flaw. Several of them are badly injured. Distortions near the flaw may be concealing other Outsiders. There are at least four.

This area also has fewer beasts than average. There should be a reason. Be careful.

Sam frowned as he heard the report and a sudden memory of that brewer and his grandson back at the inn came to his mind. The Iceblood Guild had been trying to kidnap the boy, but until now, he hadn't seen any trace of prisoners or humans working for the Outsiders.

Was this where they were keeping them? If so, what were they doing with them?

Siwasir gave him a curious look as he hesitated, so he explained his thoughts.

"How can you sense them?" Siwasir asked, looking puzzled. "The ice here is quiet, and I cannot tell much of what is in the area, except for the traces of monsters." He glanced toward the sky, tracking the ice drake's position above. "Elsanar also cannot see a flaw or Outsiders here."

"I'll explain the story to you later," Sam replied as he held up his right hand, showing off the nine-pointed star on it. "This star is a magical construct, similar to an artifact, and it is very good at scanning for dimensional flaws. I was given it as well as a job to do."

He felt entirely comfortable explaining his story to the Ice Sylphs, who had already shown him great trust. He saw no issue with telling them the full story. If anyone were likely to believe him, it would be them.

It didn't take him too long to explain the major details, until the sylphs knew the story almost as well as his family. It was strange, since he'd just met them, but in a certain way he already felt like they were his blood relatives. There was an implicit trust when he felt their presence.

That had to be a side effect of Initiate of Ice, and there was a moment of doubt when he realized it, but at the same time, there was no harm in telling the story.

"I see," Siwasir said thoughtfully, his eyes narrow as he looked at the star. Then he turned to the sylphs behind him, giving them a nod as he accepted the information and turned the conversation back to the present.

"If they have seized captives, there must be a reason. We will be careful in our attacks to distinguish friend from foe."

"We're close now," Sam added, looking at the sylphs and then toward the area in front of him. "The flaw is inside that building in the plaza, on the right. It's just below ground on a lower level, which was probably used for storage once."

He pointed to one of the buildings that faced onto the plaza. The building had a narrow door to one side and a shop face that opened onto the square. It looked like there was an apartment above it for the shopkeeper.

The sylphs nodded and spread out, taking up positions as they scanned the area.

Sam looked over the map, making sure that the area was clear of monsters again, and then he was moving. A Starfire formed in his hand as he raced forward, and he sensed the sylphs moving all around him. Their formation was different this time. They were letting him take the lead.

Instead of a trap, it seemed like the Outsiders had chosen concealment as their main tactic to protect this flaw. If he hadn't known it was here, this would have looked like any other building.

As he approached the entrance, his battle aura flared around him, the cloak of flames stretching backward as his talons lengthened. He'd learned the last time not to rush in carelessly, but he had the Ice Sylphs with him now, which gave him confidence.

He hammered through the door with an explosive *crack* as he entered, throwing the tattered remains of it to the side. Then he was ducking as a warning screamed through his senses.

An Iceblood spear slammed through the area where his head had been and before he was fully conscious of it, he was spinning. His talons slashed up to the side, slicing through the bone spear shaft, and he surged inward.

Iceblood Hunter. Level 52.

The Outsider had been guarding the door, hidden in the shadows. He pulled his spear back as Sam rushed at him, but he only had time to bring it across his chest in a block. The broken shaft dangled loosely from his hands.

Flame and wind flickered around Sam as he darted forward, his talons slicing up and across before the Outsider could react. Pale blue blood splattered across the hallway, but at the same time, he heard a bell ringing from farther down.

The Hunter's corpse slammed into the wall, sliced into half a dozen chunks, and then Sam was running, heading down to the stairs as fast as he could. Entering the door had tripped some type of alarm spell, and now they needed to get to the flaw as quickly as possible.

Behind him, the Ice Sylphs flooded the hallway, bringing with them a chill breeze that coated the walls in ice. They were surrounded by sparkling auras of blue and white mana that made them seem like winter spirits.

They descended, slicing through another Iceblood Hunter and then a Warrior as they moved along a curving staircase and reached the basement. When they did, a large, open area spread out around them. It was lit by pale blue spheres of light that were attached to the walls, giving everything an unsettling cast. There was something corrosive about the light, as if it were darker than it should be.

The area was far larger than the building above had indicated. It stretched for more than two hundred feet to the front and the sides, extending under the plaza above. Perhaps it had once been a market area for when the weather was bad or a storage area for the merchants, but now its purpose had been turned to something else.

Long rows of dull, bone cages and shackles decorated the area, some of them filled with people and others with wild beasts. The bones that made up the bars were long and oddly shaped, with strange joints, as if they had been twisted into their present purpose. Dark, curling inscriptions covered them like thorns, giving them a threatening presence.

A sense of despair and the smell of recent death pervaded the area. Everything about the room stank. It was a combination of blood, pain, waste, and torture. Smaller bones from humans and other races decorated the floor, some of them still wet with gore.

Inside the cages, there were at least a dozen people and as many beasts. A handful of people and a few Outsiders were outside of them, moving around the area between some low tables that were scattered with packs of equipment, weapons, and other items that had clearly been taken from the captives.

At the far end of the area, the flaw glimmered in the air. Its rainbow colors rippled with a torrent of energy as flickering lights passed through it. Unlike most flaws, the edges of it burned with a ring of rotating flames, as if it were slowly searing its way through the world.

It was much larger than the other flaws he'd seen, big enough that a wagon could go through it.

All around it on the stone floor, there was a complex diagram laid out in bone talismans and curling inscriptions, marking out some sort of stabilizing enchantment that held it open. Some of the designs looked like hooks, as if they were pulling the flaw open, but he couldn't make out any more.

What was happening here was clear. For some reason, humans and beasts were being captured and either sacrificed or sent through the flaw to whatever was on the other side. It was some type of harvesting operation.

By the time he arrived in the room, the two Iceblood Shamans were already chanting as they prepared a curse. Three Iceblood Hunters and an Iceblood Warrior rushed toward the door, accompanied by an angry shout.

"You!" One of the human figures who was standing beside a table spun toward the door, shouting as he saw Sam. His eyes were wide, as if he recognized him. That didn't stop him from attacking, however. His hands waved through the air as a spell pattern began to form.

Human. Visionary-Arcane Healer. Level 42.

There was a moment of confusion as Sam stared at him, trying to place why he was familiar. Then the man's features and class registered. By that point, he was already a quarter of the way across the room. He twisted out of the path of a bone spear as he hurled the Starfire he was holding toward the flaw.

A Visionary.... The one who had been holding the horses when that Barbarian bothered them, in what felt like ages ago, back on the road to Highfold. The useless group that had driven the Flamecaller Devils toward them.

He was the one who'd whispered to that idiot, Jaser, not to attack Sam because he was an Outsider. Back then, he'd wondered how the man knew anything at all about Outsiders.

It seemed he'd just found the answer.

Behind Sam, the Ice Sylphs flowed out into the room, their movements like chiming crystal as spells and arrows flew from their hands. Unwilling to be left behind, Sam changed his target, charging toward the Visionary instead of the Iceblood Hunter that he'd been planning to kill.

KraaTTTToOOOOOMmm!

At that moment, the Starfire exploded in front of the flaw, releasing a wave of searing, white-blue flame across the inscription that surrounded it. An enormous wave of sound shattered the air in the enclosed cavern, loud enough to drown out everything else in the air.

A wave of compressed air followed it, blasting outward as it shattered everything within a few dozen feet of the flaw, including the two Iceblood Shamans who were trying to finish their curse and two humans who were standing near it, preparing to throw a package through.

In the wake of that explosion, a blur of crystal flame twisted through the air, and then Sam's talons wrapped around the Visionary's throat as he lifted him off the ground. Swirling bands of flame and wind wrapped around the man's body, pinning his arms to his side as his clothing began to char.

Sam held him there, staring into the traitor's eyes. He growled low in his throat as he considered how anyone could enslave their own people and sell them to Outsiders. Then he decided he didn't care, and a flicker of memory made him speak.

"You said I would use your skull as a wine cup if you angered me," he snarled. His words were barely intelligible. "You aren't worthy."

His talons flashed and the man's head went flying across the room toward the flaw. It tumbled in a wild arc before it landed with a dull thump. It rolled through the portal, accompanied by the weak hiss of the inscription on the ground.

Whatever was on the other side, the traitor was welcome to find out.

Blue-white crystal flame from the Starfire covered the formation now, chewing away at the inscription there as if the dark curls were charcoal. The outline of the flaw wavered as the magic holding it open began to fail.

All around, there was another volley of arrows and blasts of ice as the sylphs spread out, and then the room fell silent. There was only the movement of the sylphs as they confirmed the Outsiders were dead.

As he looked around, he could see that they had spared the remaining human traitors. Only three of them were still alive and they were bound in icy ropes, thrown to the side of the room like logs. Now, the cages were being thrown open by two of the sylphs as the rest began to gather the experience.

Their efficiency was incredible. Siwasir came up next to his side, joining him in looking at the flaw and the burning inscription around it.

"A transit point," he said slowly, his expression troubled as he pointed to the ring of flames around the flaw. "I hadn't expected to see one here. They are usually only seen in large wars, where resources flow through from the other side to support the Outsiders. The inscription they use tears at the Seal. The longer they exist, the more damage they do, even more than the other flaws."

"Where were they sending them?" Sam growled, his hands flexing as he took a deep breath. He could feel the dimensional ripples from the flaw now that he was this close to it, as well as something of the concealing formation that was all around it.

He studied the inscription, but the curls meant nothing to him. Whatever system they were using, it wasn't related to his form of enchanting.

"Flaws open from many different parts of the Outsiders' realm," Siwasir answered. "So, it is hard to say what they were doing, but it must have taken significant resources to open one this large."

Analysis of the flaw suggests the Icebloods were preparing for the transit of something larger, perhaps a war machine, the Guardian Star spoke up. **The citizens of Aster Fall and the beasts here would likely have been sacrificed on the other side to create a blood connection to this world. Some have probably already been sent over for that purpose.**

It is one way of stabilizing a flaw, and it is commonly used by Outsiders to prepare for a larger invasion.

At that moment, the final lines of the inscription burned away and the flaw rippled in the air, suddenly feeling more present than before. At the same time, the auras of Aster Fall rushed toward it, building up the pressure around it as they began to force it closed.

Sam growled as he compressed a Starfire between his hands. Before he thought about what he was doing, he threw it through the flaw to the other side.

Seconds later, the flaw snapped shut, disappearing from existence. The only thing left behind was the smell of charred stone and the whispering susurration of a desert wind cutting across the sand.

Chapter Fifty

HORNED HUNTER

"Why would people work for Outsiders?" Sam growled to himself again as he flexed his talons, his attention turning to the three traitors that were still alive. After they were tied up, they had been tossed to the side of the room against one wall.

Even after killing the Visionary, his anger was still running hot. If there had been more Outsiders here, he would have torn them to pieces. He looked toward the traitors, holding himself back from heading toward them.

They deserved to die, but there were people here who had more need for retribution than he did. All around, the Ice Sylphs were freeing the last of the prisoners. There were about a dozen of them altogether, with a mix of classes and levels.

Most were human, but there was one dwarf and a gnome, which was a race Sam hadn't encountered before. The basalt gnomes back in the Abyssinian Plains had only shared the name. His gaze moved around the room, settling on a handful of the prisoners as they were freed.

Forest Gnome. Tinkerer-Wizard. Level 32.
Mountain Dwarf. Brewer-Hall Guardian. Level 35.
Human. Painter-Weaver. Level 28.
Human. Warrior-Herbalist. Level 41.
Human. Enchanter-Diplomat. Level 43.

Those were the ones who stood out to him the most, and the ones who were the most spirited. The others had standard farming and artisan classes, along with a few Guards and Warriors. Their eyes were dim after their experience here.

The trapped beasts were left in their cages, since they couldn't be freed yet. The Ice Sylphs passed their hands over the bars, freezing the inscriptions and chilling the interior, and before long the beasts fell into a deep slumber, their fur dusted with snow.

There were about a dozen of them, mostly weaker beasts in the Level 30-40 range. They must have been brought up from the lower slopes.

"We'll release them once we're gone," Siwasir said as he saw Sam looking around. "It would not be right to rescue them only to kill them now. They can run free and find their own fate."

Sam nodded, turning his attention back to the prisoners. Rope marks and bruises decorated their bodies, but they were alive. The Icebloods must not have wanted to harm them too much before they were sacrificed.

Their expressions were grave as they were freed from their cages and looked to where the flaw had been. For some, it was a look of disbelief. For others, it was gratitude. The silence was broken a moment later, however, when one of the prisoners stared at Sam and shouted.

"Demon!"

The man who'd just been freed stared at him, his hands curling into fists. His clothes were tattered, but they had once been rich robes made from blue brocade. It was the Enchanter-Diplomat.

Sam reached up reflexively to his amulet, only to find that it was off. He wasn't wearing his hood either. He'd been thinking about destroying the flaw and not about rescuing prisoners who could see his face.

A sense of frustration filled him as he prepared to speak. How many times was this going to happen? Before he could say anything, however, Siwasir's voice rang out across the chamber as he came to his defense.

"He is not a demon from your legends."

The Ice Sylph looked around with a chilling light in his eyes, fixing his attention on the one who had shouted. Ice crackled angrily as it formed across the floor, turning into swirling lines like the patterns in the ruins.

He pointed at Sam, indicating the swirling light of the World Law and the aura of experience that was gathering around him. There was also a trail of moonlight in three colors that was rippling around his aura, an echo of his connection to the Moonlight Relic.

The energy highlighted his horns and cast his features into sharp relief, but instead of making him look evil, it made him look otherworldly.

"He is the Horned Hunter of the Moons," Siwasir declared, his voice grave, "your savior and a Guardian of the World Law who seeks out demons and destroys them. He is also a native of Aster Fall and a friend to the Ice Sylphs.

"If you oppose him, your invitation to this valley will be rescinded. You will no longer be allowed to dwell here or to study the ruins. Moreover, you will have insulted your benefactor. It is due to him that you are alive and free. Look!"

As Sam turned around, the silvery aura of experience continued to build up around him and the halo of light intensified. The voice of the World Law descended, echoing throughout the room. Unlike usual, this time the first words of the World Law were heard by everyone.

You are *Acknowledged* as a *Guardian of Law*.

Title Recorded: *Horned Hunter of the Moons*.

The energy of the experience settled onto his skin, shining like a brilliant sun that radiated throughout the room with a relaxing, confident gleam. At the same time, a new line appeared below his name with the title inscribed on it. It came with a note: *"Title granted by local authority."*

Then the World Law continued, so that only Sam could hear.

You have fulfilled the requirements to remove the Trait: *Defiant*.

Your Trait: *Defiant* is annulled and replaced with the Trait: *Guardian of Law*.

You regain +2 Charisma.

Authorities of Law will no longer dislike you on sight. Instead, you gain a small advantage to Charisma when speaking with them. Due to your shared goal, they will be more inclined to believe your words.

He felt his skin itching for a moment as his features shifted, correcting themselves. Some part of the World Law's energy also changed, removing a shadow that it had laid on him. He felt his spirit springing up with a new freedom, as if he were unconstrained.

On his status page, the trait for *Defiant* shifted, the name blurring as it was replaced by *"Guardian of Law."*

As a one-time reward for proving your dedication as a Guardian of Aster Fall, you may choose one Class Ability and one Subclass Ability to upgrade by a tier (to a maximum of Elite).

Future rewards are available if you continue to protect Aster Fall.

Make your choices now.

Time seemed to slow around Sam as the choices appeared in front of him. There were a lot of Class and Subclass abilities he needed to improve, but the opportunity in front of him wasn't one he could waste. He needed to choose skills that were otherwise very difficult to raise and that could enhance his ability in battle.

He frowned as he stared at his Subclass Abilities, which was where most of his combat ability came from. Essence Shield and Crystal Focus were both at Advanced, and Combust Aura was at Basic. Raising any of those would be useful.

For his Class Abilities, he had Reclaim Aura, Identify Aura, and Aura Storage at Advanced. Shatter Aura was at Elite already, which meant this reward wasn't useful for it, and Imbue, Intensify, and Assume Aura were all at Basic.

All of them were useful in some way, but he crossed off Assume immediately, as well as Identify and Aura Storage. Those could rise in their own time.

Assume was effective in battle, especially if he used it to imbue an aura into his spells or a scroll, but it was limited by the auras he had available. As for Identify and Aura Storage, those were linked to Reclaim.

As for what was left…Imbue was useful for enchanting and would help him make more powerful artifacts. He needed that to be higher if he really wanted to harness Advanced or higher auras. It was also a core part of his class, and who knew how many artifacts he would have to make to upgrade it on his own.

As for his subclass, Essence Shield would grant him better defensive abilities, and Crystal Focus would enhance his awareness for both battle and enchanting. Neither of those addressed his main problem, however, which was running out of essence in battle.

The short list he had left was Reclaim, Imbue, Intensify, and Combust. If he were able to reclaim higher-level auras, he would be able to get more essence from them and also use them in enchanting. If he upgraded Intensify, he could charge the auras he already had to hold more.

As for Combust, he wasn't sure what would happen if he upgraded it, but it should give him more efficiency or speed. Perhaps it would let him harness more of the energy in an aura.

Unfortunately, the first three of those were all from his Class, and he could only choose one of them, which meant his choice boiled down to Combust and one other.

In the end, he chose the one that was the hardest to improve on his own.

Reclaim Aura has been upgraded to Expert.
Combust Aura has been upgraded to Advanced.

The power of the World Law descended, swirling into an enormous whirlpool as it swept into his body and raced along his meridians. He could feel his connection to the world deepening, as if a veil were being pulled back, and a sharp awareness of the natural auras around him stabbed into his mind as Reclaim Aura improved.

Reclaim Aura was not a simple ability. In order for it to work, he needed to understand what he was dealing with. At the same time, Combust Aura was the opposite side of the coin. Where Reclaim caused an aura to condense to a point so it could be manipulated, Combust Aura destroyed that point, pulling it apart for energy.

His mind felt like it was about to split apart as the meaning of the two abilities shuddered through it. The sense of Ice, wind, the other elements, and even the life force of the people and beasts around him echoed wildly in his senses as his awareness improved.

Then it was done and the abilities settled into place.

Time restarted as the world began to move around him again, and the silver light gathered around him bathed the room in its glow before it faded away, leaving just the taste of winter pine in the air.

The man who had been reprimanded by Siwasir was staring at him, stunned silent as he saw the World Law's blessing radiating from the man he'd just called a "demon" in front of him. His expression was a study of confusion and shock, but it was difficult for him to argue with the light shining around Sam.

As a capstone to that, a moment later, the experience from the fight flowed toward Sam, accompanied by a bubbling river of joyful, drunken bubbles through his blood.

Congratulations, Guardian. You have used your Class skills to slay the enemies of Aster Fall.

You gain 450,000 experience.

Total Class Experience: 55,159,990 / 56,000,000

There had only been a handful of enemies here, so it wasn't enough to get him to Level 80, but he was close. The Charisma from removing Defiant raised that attribute to 54.

He wasn't sure what the title Siwasir had created was all about, but he could see it now listed beneath his name on his status page. He looked down at his hands, flexing his talons, and then he turned toward the man who had shouted.

The world felt thinner, somehow, as if it were no longer repressing him as much. It was partly due to his Charisma increasing and the force of his personality pushing against it, but most of it came from the new Guardian of Law trait.

For the first time, it felt like the World Law was on his side.

If he had an ability for his Charisma, he might have been able to harness it to persuade the crowd, but for now all he could do was speak naturally. Fortunately, Charisma helped to convey meaning, making it more likely that he would be understood. Siwasir's words had already set the man back on his heels, so all he needed to do was speak a few words to convince him.

"I'm not a demon," he told the man as his eyes glowed with bright, crystal blue flames. "I'm an Enchanter and this world is my home. These were my enemies as much as yours, and now you are free. The area directly around here is clear of Outsiders."

He ignored the man's confusion. If anything came of this, he would deal with it later. Right now, there was a Grand Flaw to close. He turned, waving his hand toward the pile of gear that was scattered across the tables.

"You should take your things and go. The ruins are not safe. Help the others here to leave as well. Highfold is on the other side of the mountain to the east. As for us, we are heading to destroy the Grand Flaw, which is the origin of all of this. The church is on their way as well. You do not want to be caught up in the battle."

The man gave Sam and the Ice Sylphs a confused look, his forehead wrinkling, but as he listened to Sam's words, he calmed down. Speaking intelligently had made Sam far more understandable.

"An Enchanter?" he asked with a frown. There was a tremble in his voice that marked his uneasiness, despite his attempt to hide it, but at the same time there was some strange interest there. He straightened his shoulders, taking on a more dignified appearance as he tried to assert his authority.

"Then you should know that I am Telen Borel, Expert Enchanter of the Ancestral Sun Enchanter's Guild," he declared imperiously, raising his chin into the air. His clothes were in rags, but his attitude made it irrelevant.

"I thank you for saving me and my team, and I know the other unfortunates here feel the same. These Outsiders and their monsters captured us three days ago and were certainly planning to kill us. The Highfold City Guard is not capable of doing their job! I request your assistance now in returning to the city. Once we are there, I will reward you well."

He paused as he studied Sam, a slight frown forming. There was a tingle of energy as Sam felt his Analyze. He was still hesitant, his gaze flinching away from Sam's face, but after all the Charisma that Sam had added recently, it wasn't because he was ugly.

"You say that you are an Enchanter," he added, "but surely it must be a profession for you at most? If you demonstrate your ability, I can grant you an apprenticeship with my guild. We are one of the foremost researchers of ancient ruins. Every apprenticeship is highly competitive!"

Telen was becoming more confident of himself by the moment now that he was free from his cage. He looked at Sam with a pompous curiosity, trying to decipher the puzzle in front of him. The idea of Sam being an Enchanter had got his attention.

Clearly, he'd lost his mind.

Sam's eyebrows rose, and then he turned to Siwasir as he decided to ignore him. Whatever the man had to offer, he doubted there was anything that could compare with the Moonlight Relic. Not to mention, he was acting like he was the one who had freed all of the people here.

"Let's go," Sam said to Siwasir as he turned away. "We can't delay. At the very least, we should try and gather some information before the rest of the forces arrive. We need to see what the Outsiders' defenses are like."

"Where are you going?" Telen demanded as he saw them start to withdraw. His head whipped around the room, taking in the three traitors who were still alive. His hands curled into tight, angry fists. "What am I supposed to do with these criminals?!"

Sam ignored him, as did the Ice Sylphs. He wasn't unsympathetic to the prisoners, but now that the Outsiders were dealt with, the major threat in the area was gone. They were all around Level 30 to 40, which meant they were reasonably capable of getting back to the town on their own.

"Your job isn't done yet!" Telen's voice became more strident as he saw them leaving. "You have to escort me back to Highfold. These mountains are dangerous!"

Sam shook his head, refusing to look back as he headed toward the corpses of the Icebloods. He bent over the first one, searching for the aura in it. With Reclaim upgraded to Expert, his speed at finding it was almost instantaneous.

The taste of frozen blood filled his mind, more piercing than ever before. The last time, it had been a hand grasping at an icy ledge. This time, it came with a sense of despair. It was a wolf's winter where the skies turned to blood and the land descended to chaos, where no bonds held one person to another.

It was part of Aster Fall, but it was a part that was wild and destructive, something that had to be reined in or destruction would follow.

A moment later, an **Aura of Blood Winter (Expert)** swirled free from the corpse and coalesced into a shining, brilliant sphere in his hand. It was brighter and a bit larger than the Advanced auras.

He pushed it into the storage in a hurry, unwilling to expose himself to it any longer. As soon as he did, he felt the storage dimension trembling. Just like the last time, the edges of the space began to warp under the intensity.

As he'd expected, as soon as the aura was inside, the storage shuddered as it began to expand. A responding force from somewhere else pushed back against it, stabilizing it.

Aura Storage has been upgraded to Expert.

Capacity has been increased to 1,200 auras.

The brief notification flashed in his mind and then disappeared. A moment later, the dimensional pocket was quiet again as the ripples in its structure vanished.

"What are we supposed to do with these traitors?" Telen shouted again, drawing Sam's attention back to the present.

"Kill them if you like," Sam said over his shoulder. "Or take them to the town to be judged. They're the ones who captured you. I think you can figure out an appropriate punishment."

He didn't care what happened to the traitors, and he doubted they would be walking out of the cavern now that the prisoners were free. He couldn't think of a more fitting judgment for them than to leave them at the mercy of the people they'd been about to sacrifice.

As for him, he wasn't in the mood to kill more humans. The Visionary had been enough.

He continued to ignore the Enchanter's protests as he collected the auras from the other Icebloods. The fellow was asking too much if he expected him to throw aside the Grand Flaw just to take him back to the city.

There were five corpses here, but he only managed to get three of the auras. It turned out there was a spike in difficulty in reclaiming Expert auras. At 65 Wisdom, he only had a 55% chance, instead of the 75% he'd expected. It meant he was going to need 95 Wisdom to maximize it, which was a lot to invest.

He could have tried to gather Advanced auras instead, but a sense of stubbornness made him try for Expert on all of them. It didn't take him long to finish, and a moment later he was heading for the entrance and the last two corpses there.

By a stroke of luck, he reclaimed both of the Auras of Blood Winter (Expert) from the Iceblood Hunter and Warrior by the stairs. Then he turned, swiping his talons through the air as he called to the essence in the Outsider corpses scattered through the area.

Dozens of brilliant stars rushed toward him, sinking into his blood as they joined the Second Layer formation. He was in a hurry, so he willed the World Law's notification to be more condensed. After a moment, it cooperated.

Essence Constellation (Second Layer): 3,861 / 7,500.

Attribute Gain: +2 Strength, +3 Constitution, +1 Agility, +4 Intelligence, +4 Aura.

He let out a deep breath as he tilted his head, his ears catching the sound of the captives moving about the storage room. Someone overturned a table with a jangle of metal striking the stones and a dull thud. There were angry shouts, as well as the thump of feet and the clash of steel.

The sounds intensified as he turned away, heading toward the plaza above, but neither he nor the Ice Sylphs looked back.

CHAPTER FIFTY-ONE

PREPARING AN OFFENSIVE

The Grand Flaw was on the seventh layer, a layer below and a little to the south. Sam's feet skimmed across the top of the snow, throwing up a light powder as he ran. Behind him, the Ice Sylphs followed easily.

The feeling of freedom flowed past his cheeks as he let out a deep breath. He felt different now that Defiant was removed, as if he'd finally gained access to the world. He hadn't let himself think about how much that trait had weighed on him.

His father's words were ringing in his ears. As soon as they'd left the fourth flaw, he'd checked in with him to share the news. His father's laugh was the sound of a man who'd never thought the day would come.

It made him grin as he ran, a feeling of exultation passing through him. The church teams hadn't reached their next flaw yet, but they would get there soon. When they did, his father should be free of the Defiant trait as well.

He glanced up at the position of the moons and then compared his father's position to the map of the ruins. It would be at least a few hours until they made it to the Grand Flaw. It would have to be enough.

Before the battle, he needed some insurance, just in case the Ice-bloods had something unexpected in reserve. Having the Ice Sylphs and Elsanar with him was a powerful force, but it wasn't a guarantee that they would win.

The Outsiders had been here for a year, and their traps and defenses were likely to be thick. Even with the forces they had gathered, he couldn't underestimate them. The trap with the wyvern matriarch proved that, as did the Icebloods' formation on the first layer.

The Outsiders' curses were dangerous, especially if they had time to prepare. He didn't want to run into something that an Iceblood Shaman had spent a year building.

That meant he needed to make two detours.

The only thing he had as a reserve was the Moonlight Relic and its core enchantment. The first detour was to take advantage of that. The second detour would be to get to Level 80 and the Epic tier. He was so close that he only needed to go out and kill a few monsters on his own, and he'd be there.

A short while later, he dropped down to a walk and looked around the area where the Guardian Star had led him. They were still on the seventh layer, several miles away from the Grand Flaw, but there were very few monsters here. The flaw was close enough that they could reach it quickly if needed, but far enough that they shouldn't fall into a trap unexpectedly.

"We're here," he called to the Ice Sylphs as they stopped near him. "I'll need a little while."

The sylphs looked around the area curiously, looking for the reason Sam had brought them to this place, but the area looked very similar to the rest of the ruins.

There were three ruined buildings surrounding a large, bowl-shaped central area. It was hard to see under the snow, but it had once been a lake.

In front of Sam, there was a tumbled pillar of stone at the center of the area. It radiated with the same silver light as the rest of the ruins, but there was a light blue glow seeping out from between the stones that created soft ripples in the air, especially at the very heart of the pillar where someone had stacked the fragments of the past.

A trail of liquid water ran out between the cracks in the stone, but before it could get far, it froze into a block of ice that covered half the pillar.

It will require two hours at a minimum to excavate the remains and test the basic function, the Guardian Star informed him. Its tone was doubtful, even though it was the one who had helped him locate the pillar in front of him. **The likelihood of success is slim. It would be more effective if you were able to repair it.**

"I don't need it to work perfectly," he replied quietly. "I just need it to be there in case there's something unexpected. Hopefully, it's not completely broken."

His eyes rested on the pillar in front of him as he reached out with Crystal Focus to feel beneath the ice. For the first time, he also drew deliberately on the energy of the core enchantment, holding it in his awareness.

This pillar had once been the Water Element Mana Gathering Pylon for the Moonlight Relic, and surrounded by a large, pure pool of water that poured out to the farms and houses on the lower levels. It wasn't the only water-gathering enchantment in the ruins, but it was the main one.

Integrity of the pylon is 13.9%, the Guardian Star reported quietly. **Be careful to account for damage to its enchantments as well as the increasing energy of the ruins.**

In four hours, when Caelus reaches its zenith, the alignment of the moons will be 34% complete. There will be a surge of energy at that time, which may affect the function of this section.

Sam glanced up at the position of Caelus before he nodded. He only planned to spend an hour here, which would be just enough time to dig it out. He would have to do the testing on the way.

He knelt down and began to shift the rocks that someone had stacked, working quickly but carefully. The mana gathering pylon was in pieces and he didn't want to damage it any further. Crystal flame and Elemental Manipulation combined to slowly shift the ice.

While he worked, three of the sylphs spread out into the night to scout the area. They disappeared so quickly it seemed like their forms turned to snowflakes and wind.

***

An hour later, the ice locking the last rock in place flowed out of the way, revealing what was at the heart of the pillar. It was a rod of sapphire blue crystal about the length of his arm, its surface heavily inscribed with swirling patterns.

There was a long crack along one side and two chunks were missing, giving it a tattered appearance, but the underlying force of the object was difficult to mistake. Even broken, there was a dense spiral of liquid water gathering around it, flowing from the center to each end. As it reached the end, it turned to mist, diffusing into the air like a rain cloud.

Sam focused on his connection to the core enchantment as he touched the enchantments on the stones directly around the rod, willing them to loosen. Then he wrapped his hand carefully around the rod, pulling it free from the heart of the pillar with a gentle tug.

This was the core of the water mana pylon, the centerpiece of the enchantments that had made it function. Once, the broken stones around it had been a much larger, inscribed pillar that was filled with enchantments to strengthen this object, infuse it with mana, and focus its Water element.

Now, the pillar was shattered and the core was damaged, but given the quality of the materials, even after all of these years, they hadn't completely failed. He didn't know what the rod was made from, but it was a key part of the relic.

Without the core enchantment and the imprint from the Relic, he wouldn't have been able to pull it free at all.

Pure Water Elemental Crystal, the Guardian Star reported. **Integrity: 61%.**

To repair it, you will need to place it in a solution of water-aligned elemental liquid and high-density mana, and then activate the relic's self-repair enchantments.

"I'll figure out a way to get one of the self-repair enchantments working after the flaw is closed," Sam replied as he looked down at the rod. "For now, I need it."

Make sure not to damage it further. There is no replacement for this item, even within the main storage room.

Without replying, Sam swiftly wrapped the crystal in a layer of hide. Then he tied it shut and slung it across his back. Almost instantly, the hide turned damp from the water released by the crystal, and he focused his attention on the elements as he diverted the water away from him.

He would have put it in a dimensional bag, but he was sure he didn't have anything of a high enough level to hold it.

He checked it again to make sure it was secure and then he turned to Siwasir, who was standing nearby watching the process. All around them, there was the beginning of a snowstorm. The wind whipped up a flurry of white crystals, driving it through the area in an intensifying billow that obscured everything beyond an arm's length.

The storm presented no difficulty to Sam or the Ice Sylphs. Instead, it was a harbinger of what was to come, as if Aster Fall were lending them its strength.

"I'll be back in an hour," he said, his face turning to lean, intense angles. "I'm going to find the three or four closest monsters and break through to Level 80. I'll return as soon as I can."

"Go and show your enemies who you are," Siwasir agreed. The Ice Sylph's expression showed no surprise. He only gave him a calm look as his long hair blew in the wind, his eyes intense. Snow screamed around him in a whirlwind. "Don't take unnecessary risks. I named you the Horned Hunter of the Moons for good reason. A hunter knows when to watch and when to strike."

Sam nodded. Then he turned, crystal flame and the wind pushing him forward as he disappeared into the storm.

***

As he ran through the snow, the map of the ruins sprang into his mind. The closest monsters were highlighted in brilliant colors, their presences overlaid on the ruins as the Guardian Star tracked their whereabouts.

There are six monsters within a half-mile radius: two Arctic Cave Trolls on the outskirts of this section and a pack of four Windscar Stalkers.

"What's a Windscar Stalker?" he muttered as he turned immediately in that direction, even though he'd never heard of that monster before. The Arctic Cave Trolls were a known enemy, but he wasn't sure two of them would be enough to get him to Level 80.

Instead of replying, an image of the monsters sprang into Sam's mind. He darted around the corner of a building and paused as he examined it, his attention focused. There were four strange monsters crouching down in the snow near a ruined wall.

Each of them looked something like a lean, white-furred weasel, but their heads were massively oversized for their bodies, resembling a crocodile more than a weasel. It gave them an ungainly appearance.

Their appearances are deceiving, the star reported. **They are capable of employing Wind-based attacks to accelerate their speed and they**

hunt with a pack mentality. Their favorite method is to use their large jaws to shred their prey so that it bleeds to death.

Sam frowned, but after a moment he was moving again in the direction of the Windscar Stalkers. The information wasn't that unsettling, but the things were definitely ugly.

"When did you learn about monsters?" he asked, puzzled. He still didn't know much about the star, and now that it had something of a personality, it was easier to communicate with it.

The Moonlight Relic has records of many monsters in its storage, some of which I was able to retrieve. Even without that, it is possible to scan the monsters and gather information directly. My purpose is to assist you. Analytical and scanning capabilities are part of that.

Its voice was matter of fact, without any particular emotional overtone. Even with its new habit of referring to itself as "I," it still wasn't exactly talkative, but it was definitely more self-aware than before.

Sam gave it a thoughtful look before he pushed the matter aside. He would study it when he had more time.

Despite the comment about the monsters' speed, he didn't hesitate. His eyes blazed as his battle aura poured out around him, accompanied by a pounding drumbeat in his blood that called him forward. Battle lust and a desire to tear his enemies apart made him stretch his talons as he snarled silently.

His reflection flickered from an ice-covered wall as he darted past. He was a dark, shifting form outlined in multi-hued light. With his horns and the increased attributes from absorbing essence, he was six and a half feet tall with a lean physique.

The sapphire glow of his crystal flame mixed with the wind and flows of Ice mana, swirling around him in an ever-building storm that was highlighted by the light of the three moons.

In the mix of shadows and light, he did look like a wild hunter.

He hurled himself toward the Windscar Stalkers, his pace increasing until he was a blur. He didn't bother with a Starfire. Instead, he channeled all of his strength into his aura to enhance his speed and strength.

The four monsters were around Level 50. They only had time to twist in place as he hit them. An eruption of flame and streaks of searing light exploded in their midst. Their oversized jaws snapped at him, their bodies twisting around like coils of rope.

Their fangs struck his aura, glancing off as their heads snapped around. Then his talons were there, slicing through the neck of the first one as he slid to the side and eviscerated another, tearing upward from below. The two monsters went flying away from him, their bodies severed.

He spun toward the other two, a pulse of flame accelerating his movement as they lunged at him. Killing the first two had made him pause in their midst just long enough that they saw the hunter who was attacking them, and their jaws snapped closed around his right arm and leg.

Sam twisted, his left hand slicing down through the neck of the first one as he tore through its body, slicing it into two pieces that flew away from him in a spray of blood. Then he kicked out, hurling the second one off of his leg.

It twisted as it flew through the air, its spine bending like a bow. Its legs flipped around below it and it crouched, ready to land. Before it could hit the ground, he was there, his right hand sweeping up.

A splatter of blood and white fur flew outward in a thin arc as he tore through its neck, and a moment later, its body crashed to the snow in a twisted pile.

Sam slid to a halt above it, his breath coming quick and even as he looked around for other threats, but the night was silent. There was nothing else nearby except for the wind whispering through the stones and celestial light stretching through the dark sky like ribbons.

Without any more hesitation, he searched through the monsters and pulled the threads of experience from them. This step was critically important and he couldn't delay. A moment later, the World Law's voice rang in his mind.

Congratulations, Guardian. You have used your Class skills to slay your enemies.

You gain 1,120,500 Class experience.

You have gained a Level in your Class. You are now a Level 80 Battlefield Reclaimer.

Class Experience: 56,280,490 / 63,500,000

You have gained a Level. You are now General Level 80.

Total Experience: 56,313,240 / 63,500,000

You gain +1 Intelligence, +1 Aura, and have three free attribute points to assign.

Congratulations on reaching the Epic Tier!

You gain the following ability for your Class: *Transfer Aura.*

You may now choose one Class Ability and one Subclass Ability to raise by a tier (to a maximum of Epic).

Sam didn't spend too long thinking about his choices. The points in Intelligence and Aura took both of those to 202, and without hesitating, he assigned the three free points to Charisma, taking it to 57.

There would be a lot of Outsiders to kill in the next battle and he wanted to make sure that the essence didn't overwhelm him.

As for the Epic-tier abilities, he considered for a moment whether to upgrade Shatter Aura, but in the end he went with Aura of Crystal Flame and Flame Strike again. Shatter Aura was already at Elite, and it would have to be enough to deal with anything that popped up. A strong offense had worked for him so far.

As he made his choices, he felt the energy of the world spinning around him in a vast whirlpool. It was much larger than it had been at the Elite tier and it extended through the ruins around him, stretching for nearly a hundred feet.

In that sweeping energy, there was the weight of the World Law, the intensity of auras, and something that felt like natural runes. Along with it, a voice he hadn't heard before rang out in his mind.

It was a woman's voice. She sounded young and old at the same time, as if she was tired, but her tone was determined. The words were accompanied by the ornate, archaic style that had accompanied every announcement about his class.

Congratulations on achieving the Epic tier. As you approach Level 100 and your First Evolution, remember this is only the beginning of your Path.

To have the best options present during your Evolution, you must raise all of your core Abilities to Epic before advancing. The deeper your understanding of the world, the more profoundly natural laws will resonate with you. Each achievement of your life forms the material for your future.

Once you are ready to Evolve, request the assistance of the World Core.

The voice faded away, replaced by the energy pouring through his body as his abilities surged upward. He could feel more clearly than ever before how the experience was rebuilding his body as it created new pathways.

Then it was gone, leaving only the changes and a shining sapphire flame in his mind for *Transfer Aura*.

He touched that flame as he focused on the ability, but as usual there was only the most basic of information in it. All he came away with was the impression that he was capable of moving auras around more easily now, transferring them from place to place without breaking them.

He wasn't sure if it would be helpful in the battle, but it might help him repair the relic later. Either way, he didn't have any more time to delay. He needed to get back to the Ice Sylphs and prepare the water pylon for the battle.

He only took long enough to search the four monsters for their auras. Three of them burned away to nothing as he identified them, but the fourth came away with a whisper, turning into a bright sphere in his hand.

It was a contained cyclone of energy, with winds twisting wildly through the interior. It came with the sense of sudden, cutting turns and winds whipping through stone tunnels at a breakneck speed.

Beyond that, there was a sense of contained fury, as if the wind wished for nothing more than to be free.

Aura of Twisting Wind (Expert).

He glanced up toward the moons as he ran, his eyes settling on Caelus as the moon rose toward the center of the sky.

CHAPTER FIFTY-TWO

THE GRAND FLAW

As soon as he was back to where Siwasir and the other Ice Sylphs were waiting, Sam held a brief planning session and checked on his father's location. Then he sat down with the Pure Water Elemental Crystal, placing it on his portable table as he got to work.

The voice he'd heard a few minutes before was still ringing in his mind, and he frowned in puzzlement as he began to study the crystal. It had been a woman's voice, rather than the World Law's, but he didn't know who it could be.

Did everyone hear a voice like that when they reached the Epic tier, or was it something the Guardian had done? The Astral Guardian was the only person he knew who could interfere with the World Law, and even he could only do it a little.

He shook his head as he continued examining the crystal, planning out the runes he would need. The water crystal was beyond his skills to create, but he could still use it as a focal point for an enchantment. Even damaged, it held the resonance of very high level Water runes.

It hadn't been the Guardian's voice, but perhaps there was more than one. It had sounded ancient, so maybe it was a former Guardian.

"Do you know who that voice was?" he asked, glancing down at the Guardian Star. The star was part of him, so if he had heard it, the star must have as well.

Negative, but it can only be a memory of the individual who designed your Class. Whenever a Class is created, its pattern is preserved within the World Core along with the memory of the creator. It is a message that was left for you.

"But my class is unique." Sam frowned as he looked down at the core. "At least in this generation. You mean there was another Battlefield Reclaimer at some point?"

Possibly, but a Class can also be created by another.

Sam frowned again. He had heard of his ancestors creating the Tower Magus subclass, but he didn't have any information on how it was done.

"Do you think there are more records in the World Core about my class?"

If there was a memory in the World Core, he wanted to get it. His class abilities didn't come with much information and the perspective of the creator would be invaluable.

Most likely. The Guardian Star's voice was emotionless. **However, accessing it is nearly impossible. If information was recorded for you, it will be delivered at the correct time. For now, the advice to train your abilities before Evolution is wise, in order to Evolve into a superior Class by meeting certain requirements.**

"What are the requirements then?" he couldn't help but ask. "And what are the possibilities?"

He didn't know a lot about Evolution, although he had heard that not everyone Evolved on the same path. A Warrior, for example, had at least a dozen common variants at the First Evolution, including some for military professions and others for being an adventurer or small-group fighter.

Sometimes, strange Classes were available that had never appeared before, or a Class could jump up in rarity. He didn't know the rules for that, but if it was just a matter of training his abilities up first, he would definitely do it.

More data is needed to predict the Evolution path for Battlefield Reclaimer.

"All right," he muttered as he continued marking out a runic circle around the water crystal. Once this Grand Flaw was dealt with, the path to the future was clear. He would make this mountain his base of operations, hunting around the area and eliminating threats while he focused on repairing it and improving his abilities.

The voice had told him to upgrade all of his core abilities. As far as he could tell, that meant all of his class and subclass abilities, at least the ones that could be upgraded. His Fire Affinity and Enhanced Senses were racial abilities, so he didn't think those counted.

It would be somewhat time-consuming to make sure all of his abilities were at Epic, but the Moonlight Relic's enchantments were based on aura, and surely studying that would help to get up his skills in Imbue, Intensify, Transfer, and the rest.

As for Reclaim Aura, he'd hunt more monsters and Outsiders and reclaim their auras. That would also let him get the battle abilities from his subclass to the maximum. Between hunting and enchanting, he'd be doing his job, growing stronger, and giving himself the best path forward for his Evolution.

Right now, however, he needed to focus on the Grand Flaw. As he continued to work, the design around the water crystal expanded, its swirling lines becoming filled with abstract symbols. Some of them were runes he had learned from enchanting, but most came from the ruins themselves.

The pattern was a rough approximation of the relic's energy transfer enchantment. He wasn't able to use the true version from the core enchantment yet, but he'd become very familiar with these lines that were everywhere here. With just a touch of insight from building the moonlight blade trap, he was able to recreate the most basic connections for them.

On top of that, the crystal had been part of the relic's enchantment for a very long time and was imbued with its purpose. He was only encouraging it to do what it had always done, like awakening a memory.

After a little while, he began to pull auras out of his storage, bringing them close to the crystal as he examined the reaction. He needed to find a few that were compatible.

***

"We're approaching the outskirts of the Grand Flaw now," Jeric's voice echoed across the amulet and rumbled in Sam's mind. "Are you safe?"

His voice was steady and deep. Whatever he'd experienced with the church forces at the other two flaws, it must have gone well.

"As safe as possible," Sam replied with a frown as he studied the area below. "Be careful of traps as you head forward."

He was observing the area around the Grand Flaw from nearly a mile away. It had taken them an hour to reach this point on the seventh layer, but it wouldn't take very long to close the rest of the distance. The Ice Sylphs were with him, preparing their weapons and spells for the assault.

Above, Elsanar was circling in the sky, so far away that he looked like a tiny speck against Caelus' blue disk. The Moon of the Heavens had nearly reached his zenith, marking out that there was barely half an hour left until midnight.

The Grand Flaw shimmered in his awareness as the Guardian Star projected a map of the area. The details were indistinct and he couldn't tell where the Outsiders were, but the flaw itself was easy to identify within the cluster of buildings.

This area was an old transportation hub and the flaw was inside a large building that had once served as a warehouse for shipping goods. Large expanses of open space surrounded it that had been staging areas for flying beasts, wagons, and even teleportation enchantments.

Now, the area was covered in snow. If he hadn't known the flaw was down there, it would have looked like any other abandoned section of the ruins. Knowing the Icebloods, however, it wouldn't be that easy.

There should be at least ten Outsiders here, along with twenty or more monsters, based on the relic's scan, the Guardian Star agreed, **but it is likely to be more. The fluctuations of the Grand Flaw are capable of concealing many additional presences.**

He frowned as he studied them, tracing the paths that he could see from the map and comparing it to reality to see if he could make out any changes. Instead of harmless open plains, the expanses of snow made him think of killing fields that could be hiding any number of curses or traps.

He wanted to be down there, cutting his way through the Outsiders as soon as possible, but he'd agreed to provide overwatch until the battle was underway, using his information on the flaw and the map of the ruins to help coordinate the arrival of the church forces.

He'd already helped to guide them in an arc, so they would come in from a flanking position rather than straight through the old staging areas.

Once the church engaged, he would add his strength from a distance. It wasn't as satisfying as tearing the Outsiders apart barehanded, but it would let him unleash his strength without revealing his appearance.

Lenei had never mentioned his appearance, and he had no intention of showing his face to the Church forces. Even the Guardian Star wasn't a guarantee that they would listen.

As far as he was concerned, it would be best if the church only heard of the 'demon' who was working with the Ice Sylphs as a distant rumor, something a hallucinating prisoner might have come up with. Let them think of Sam Hastern and the Horned Hunter of the Moons as two different people, and then forget about him.

And as an added benefit, staying at a distance would make his father worry less, even though there was still a stubborn streak telling him to be down there in the middle of it, cutting his way through the Icebloods and whatever they'd come up with.

He wanted to feel the impact as they disintegrated.... A frown distorted his features as he reined in the battle lust and let out a deep breath. With his Charisma, it wasn't difficult to restrain it, but it still seemed to slip out whenever he thought about fighting.

He reached back and checked on the water crystal across his back. The same hide was wrapped around it to protect it, but this time there was a large sheet of high-quality parchment rolled up beside it, one that he'd cut from the center of a wyvern wing and imbued with several different auras. He checked that as well, making sure that it was safe.

DRuUUmmmMMMmm.

A low, resonant rumble like the drumbeat of the earth marked the arrival of the church forces. The first sign was a long, white line that appeared above the snow with shining silver points, like an avalanche flowing in reverse that was crowned by stars. A moment later, the edge of the wave crested, breaking apart into orderly rows of cavalry atop stamping horses and armored war lizards with dark blue scales.

Behind them, infantry followed. Spears and helmets reflected the light of the moons and glowed with the brilliant white energy that the World Law had granted to the church. Blessed mana radiated from the Priests, Paladins, and other church warriors like a lake of righteousness.

The force was divided into three main sections, each of them about forty strong. Across those ranks, there were half a dozen Paladins, ten Priests, and more than a hundred Warriors and other classes who served the church.

They were distant, but after a moment he picked out his father from the ranks. He wasn't difficult to find. Jeric was riding beside Lenei at the head of one group, next to their commander.

Human. Paladin Commander-Bright Captain. Level 122.

It was a woman, a detail he could barely make out at this distance behind her armor, and her classes caught his attention. Her main class was also an Evolved Paladin and her subclass had to be some type of military or church class, one that was focused on commanding forces. He didn't focus on her for long, however, as his attention moved immediately to his father and Lenei.

Jeric Hastern. Earthen Marauder-Blessed Merchant of the Earth. Level 64.

Lenei. Paladin of Law-Spirit Healer. Level 66.

They had definitely gained a few levels from their hunting. His father had been 56 when they'd separated. It wasn't as many levels as he'd gained, but his father had been hunting with a group. Lenei had also picked up some levels. She had been 60 before.

Behind them, he caught sight of Krana and Lesat as well, mixed in with the church forces. They had both gained a few levels. Krana was at 65 and Lesat had reached 62. He was lined up with the church's infantry, and Krana was near their Priests.

The adventurer group was nowhere to be seen. They must have fled or been sent away once the church arrived.

With a wave of her arm, the commander led her forces forward, stopping a hundred yards away from the expanse of snow that led up to the buildings. The church forces were too numerous for subtlety, so they had chosen to not even attempt it.

Despite the battles they had just fought, they arrived in perfectly dressed battle lines, with every mount lined up shoulder to shoulder with the one next to it. Even though they had some injuries, their postures were upright and forceful. Their lances were a long row pointing toward the heavens.

"We're ready to support from above," Sam's voice echoed in his father's ears as he sent the message. *"As soon as you move, we'll attack. Be careful of traps in front of you."*

So far, there was no response from the Outsiders near the flaw. They were pretending not to be here, but it was unlikely that would last for long. Unless they were planning to retreat through the flaw, all they could do now was fight.

"Don't take any risks," his father's voice rumbled back. *"If you feel angry, step back. There's a better way. Fight with your mind clear."*

At the same time, Jeric passed the word on to the captain next to him, who nodded and turned to issue orders to her troops. The lines of mounts and foot soldiers shifted, taking on a new formation with the Paladins at the front. The Priests took up a supporting position behind them and blessings began to radiate outward as their magic flowed over the troops.

"A Grand Flaw is a scourge to the land," Siwasir said quietly from near Sam's shoulder. He looked over at the young man next to him, his gaze fixed on Sam's face. Calmness radiated from him. "The goddess granted us life in the midst of a war with Outsiders like these, but much worse. At our birth, we were shaped from her tears to fight them. As an Initiate of Ice, you are part of that heritage, Sam Hastern. Until the mountains crumble or Aster Fall stands on her own. Are you ready?"

His words evoked an echo from the land around them, a deep pulse of Ice and a powerful rumble from the snow. It called to Sam's spirit, bringing with it a desire for battle and a feeling of unshakable certainty, as if the land below his feet were rising up to support him.

"Until the mountains crumble or Aster Fall stands on her own," Sam replied, his voice echoing as he put that feeling into words. He was going to crush the Outsiders who had dared to invade his home. His aura intensified as crystal flame poured out of him, condensing into a battle spiral.

Below, the captain raised her hand and with a barked order, dropped it. The chanting of priests rose up across the field, accompanied by the drumbeats of troops hammering their weapons against their shields.

Spell formations flickered out around the field in spinning diagrams that surrounded the troops, sinking into their armor and weapons. As it did, the infantry stepped forward, raising their spears as the light surged around them.

The spears caught fire, outlined in that light, and at a shouted command, the ranks stepped forward as they hurled them into the air. All along the line, points of brilliant white light rose up as dozens of burning spears flew outward.

The barrage rose in a whistling arc and suddenly multiplied into twenty times as many, until there were at least a thousand spears in the air. Like a rain of judgment, they glowed brighter as they turned the zenith of their arc and hurtled down toward the field below.

Explosions tore apart the field of white snow as they landed, followed a moment later by a cascade of deep, booming echoes that rolled across the area.

For a moment, there was only a blinding light that obscured the field, but then a glowing blue shield became visible across the field, hugging tight to the ground. It was tattered in places where the spears had ripped through it, but it was still holding.

It was similar to the shield that had been around the fifth flaw, but there were cloudy red and yellow splotches swirling across this one.

With a rumble, the snowy plain shivered. Snow floated upward as an enormous current of mana became apparent. All through the area, the shield began to vibrate as that energy flowed into it and then it rose higher. The colors intensified as the gaps in it began to disappear.

"Paladins forward! Priests to support. Advance!" The Paladin Commander's voice echoed out across the area as she sent orders to her troops. All across the line, the Paladins at the head of the troops raced forward, their bodies turning into shining blurs of energy as they targeted the shield. Behind them, the chanting of the priests surged upward.

The land all around the troops was covered in a giant Ward of Law and now a deep, echoing *thrrummmm* of activated abilities and an enormous pulse of mana exploded upward, spiraling outward to form a row of flaming white hawks that soared through the sky.

Their size expanded until they were each thirty feet across and then they turned, folding their wings as they dived toward the barrier. They struck it with gigantic, echoing blasts of force that sent the cracks shivering outward as they expanded.

An instant later, the commander and the two other church captains blurred through the air ahead of their troops, slamming into the shield with explosive force. The glow of individual abilities outlined them, including a soaring force that ate away at the shield's edge. The shield shuddered as cracks sparked across its surface, but it continued to rise upward.

With those gaps, the Paladins could have broken through the shield, but they would have had to separate from the forces behind them. Instead, they stayed there, their abilities clashing with the shield as they raced across the snow, searching for the talismans that gave it life.

At that moment, the snowy plain shuddered. The buildings that had been on the surface swayed in the wind as they began to fall apart, and then they exploded, their walls blasting outward to reveal the inside.

Stones that had been stacked around the buildings went flying, blasting through everything within two hundred feet, but fortunately they fell short of the troops. In the dark spaces that were revealed, the looming forms of four enormous, dark beasts and a dozen small groups of Outsiders and monsters were revealed.

At the center of it all, a space suddenly sprang into existence between one instant and the next. A moment before, it had been nothing but empty snow that stretched between the buildings.

Now, the Grand Flaw shone there like a dark, burning sun.

It drew Sam's attention like an irresistible whirlpool. Just looking at it, it felt like he was falling forward, about to be swept away by it to another place. He only had to reach out and.... He pulled his attention away with a jerk, forcing himself to only look at it from the corner of his eye.

It was nothing at all like he'd expected. Instead of being a tear in the air, it resembled a roiling sphere. It was far larger than the transit point, stretching almost forty feet across from side to side. Seeing it, he started to realize why a Grand Flaw was something entirely different from a regular one.

There was a sense of space twisting in it, as if the laws of the world didn't apply. A ring of distorted flames swirled and curved back in on themselves before spiraling outward again. Ripples of colors passed across the surface, only to be swallowed and replaced a moment later by others.

There was a pause across the battlefield as everyone took in the Grand Flaw, and then a sweeping aura of blood-tinged snow swept outward as the surface of the flaw rippled. From inside, dark shapes appeared, slowly stretching as if they were being twisted apart.

A moment later, a horde of Outsiders flowed out from the interior, letting out roars as they raced onto the snow and joined the groups that were already in the area. Only a breath later, the number of enemies had more than tripled.

Eight Iceblood Shamans, four Iceblood Warriors, five Iceblood Hunters.... The impassive voice of the Guardian Star rang in Sam's mind, calculating the additions. It didn't take it long to finish, but the words sent shivers down his spine.

As well as twelve Greenscale Abyssal Serpents, eighteen Icesoul Wraiths, thirteen Diamondfang Ice Vipers, seven Coldfang Beheaders, three Ice Wyverns, and four Outsider war beasts at the First Evolution.

Ignoring the war beasts, the average level is 68. There are 74 enemies present.

The average level of the church forces is 62.

Comparative Force: 58% in favor of the Outsiders due to the advantage granted by the war beasts.

Just as he was about to ask what the war beasts were, the four enormous forms that had been hidden in the buildings raised their heads, shouldering aside the stones around them as they climbed to their feet. Each of them was taller than the building they had been in, even larger than the basilisk.

They were a strange amalgamation of features that gave off a sense of twisted, overwhelming strength. They were hugely muscled, with long tusks jutting from triangular, scaled heads like a lizard's, and they stood on scaled legs like tree trunks. Their bodies were armored in rows of tightly-placed overlapping scales in pale yellow and dark red, and below their jutting foreheads, six red eyes gleamed like dull embers. Sharp spikes covered their head, spine, and knees.

Outsider War Beast. Level 125.

The impression they gave was of overwhelming strength, as if anything that dared to stand in front of them would be trampled to nothing. Compared to their massive bulk, the forms of the three church commanders were tiny fireflies.

As he looked at them, a sense of just how bad the situation was filled his mind. He hadn't expected that they would have reinforcements waiting inside the flaw. Even with the church's preparations, the forces at the Grand Flaw were stronger. There was also no telling what traps or curses the Outsiders had prepared.

Down there, standing straight and serious as he raised his hammers into the air, his father stood side by side with Lenei at the head of the forces. He'd rushed forward with her to assault the shield.

Sam's attention locked onto him as the crystal flame around him surged upward in an enormous curtain.

CHAPTER FIFTY-THREE

THE FLOW OF TIME

A sense of overwhelming danger crashed down on Sam as he saw his father standing there. The Grand Flaw was much bigger than he'd expected, and with his dad's position at the front, whatever happened, he would be the first to face it.

The careful plan to attack from a distance flew out of his mind. There was no way he would let him face that alone. Before he even thought about it, he was running forward as fast as he could, leaping down the slope in front of him. A wave of crystal flame exploded outward in the air as he pushed himself faster.

Those war beasts had an advantage over regular fighters due to their size. It was the same as a Level 60 wyvern or basilisk against humans, but even more extreme. Level was only a rough guide when it came to giant monsters. Each of them was worth at least a few fighters, which meant the only way to deal with them was to gang up until their defenses crumbled.

Their only chance was if he and the Ice Sylphs joined in as soon as possible. Otherwise, he doubted many of them would be alive to return home.

He reached back to touch the water crystal on his back as he ran. Beside him, the Ice Sylphs ran as well, flowing like the wind as they drew back their bows and summoned sparkling currents of Ice. It was natural to attack, so they didn't think anything of his sudden charge.

He was halfway down the slope with a Starfire in either hand when his father's reminder rang in his mind. *"If you feel angry, step back. There's a better way. Fight with your mind clear."*

His steps caught, nearly making him stumble, but the snow firmed up beneath his feet and kept him upright as he continued to run.

Based on the plan, he was supposed to stop on the roof of a building just beyond the battlefield, taking up a position where he'd be in range for spells but not on the field. So far, they hadn't passed that point.

He growled as he changed his target, heading for it. Rushing onto the field would only distract his father at a crucial moment. As soon as his dad saw him, he would rush over to protect him. If he wanted to save his father, he had to do better than that.

There was still half a mile to the Grand Flaw, and the Starfires were burning in his hand. His mind cleared as he continued to run forward, and he began to think of how to best implement the plan he'd come up with. He hadn't expected there would be so many Outsiders, which meant he needed to make some changes.

So far, neither the church forces nor the Outsiders were moving on each other. The church was preparing another wave of distance attacks and the Outsiders were arranging themselves in front of the flaw, making it clear that they wanted to protect it.

That was enough to give him an idea. Force to force, the church was weaker than the Outsiders, but if the war beasts could be separated out and dealt with individually, and if any formations could be broken...the church would have the advantage on their side.

The problem was doing it.

He was nearly to the point where he was supposed to part ways with the Ice Sylphs, which meant he didn't have time to change the overall plan. All he could do was work on modifying it slightly.

"Try to single out the war beasts and take them down one by one!" he shouted to Siwasir, his voice carrying on the wind. "I'll work on disabling them!"

He infused the two Starfires with enough essence to cover the distance and then he sent them arcing into the air ahead of him. As they flew toward the Icebloods' shield like twin blue stars, he pulled the water crystal off his back and leapt onto the roof of the building.

If he wanted to help his father, he needed to hinder the Outsiders' movements and remove any formations they had. If he could do that, it would give the Ice Sylphs time to deal with the war beasts one by one and turn the battle to the church's favor.

The Ice Sylphs were still running, their bodies nearly invisible against the snow. In the next few moments, they would hit the edge of the snow field. The six of them were powerful, but they couldn't face an army by themselves. Before that happened, he needed to intervene.

As quickly as he could, he unwrapped the water crystal and laid out the parchment he'd made. Unfurled, it was nearly seven feet wide. At the same time, he sank his awareness into the core enchantment, sensing for the flow of energy through the ruins.

With quick motions, he adjusted the position of the parchment until it aligned with the ruin's energy lines.

This area had once been heavily inscribed with transfer patterns to support the teleportation and transfer of goods, both on the ground and in the buildings, and it was the work of an instant to make sure that the parchment was touching one.

As soon it was ready, he placed the crystal in the center and focused on the core enchantment. He'd created the enchantment that would bring everything together, but activating it was the most important part.

He placed one hand on the parchment's activation rune and one on the relic's energy line to the side. Then he sent a worried glance at his father and to where the Ice Sylphs were approaching the field before he closed his eyes. The core enchantment spun in his mind as he sank his consciousness into it.

Just as he began to focus, piercing shrieks rose into the air as three wyverns took flight from hiding places throughout the ruins. Their powerful legs propelled them from the roofs and their wings snapped open as they shot through the air, circling higher as they gained altitude.

He sent out a call to the Moonlight Relic, asking for its help. A moment later, it answered.

Energy Transfer Approved.

SnnNNaAAApppp!

There was a tingle of energy beneath his hand, followed by a sharp pull on his spirit like the world was turning in place. The transfer line began to hum. A silvery current of energy flowed upward from the ruins and flooded into the parchment's activation sequence.

Unexpectedly, and before he could see if the parchment was functioning, his perspective shifted as his spirit was pulled into the transfer line, swept away by the intensity of the energy.

The entire seventh layer appeared in his mind's eye as a great, silver web of energy like an ocean. Each line was a current pulling the waves in one direction or another, all of them swirling together into a vast network.

Looking at it, he was stunned into immobility by the sheer scale. A flood of information on the differing amounts of energy in each location, the damage to the transfer lines, the integrity of the enchantments, and....

There was too much for him to handle. He felt his attention splitting off, pulled in a thousand different directions that all demanded equal focus. The parchment beneath his unresponsive hand shuddered as the activation rune began to smoke from excess energy, its edges curling.

Then the Guardian Star was there, its indifferent voice flowing into his mind.

Moderating the energy transfer. Buffering Guardian's awareness of the core enchantment.

He felt the burden of managing all the lines of power fade, simplified down to a single task. It felt like he was a hawk flying above the seventh layer, soaring above the sea of energy. Wherever he turned his attention, the details suddenly jumped out to him.

A surge of gratitude for the star rushed through him, but he didn't have time to waste. In the confusion, his awareness had been tossed far away from the location of his body. He scanned over the ocean, searching for it.

Everything here looked different and it took him a moment to find it. It wasn't shattered ruins or fields of snow, but curling waves of power. To find his body, he had to use the mountain as the center point and overlay it with the map of the relic in his mind, searching for the place where he was supposed to be.

He just hoped he wasn't too late.

When he found it, he folded the wings of his spirit and dived. Rippling waves of energy and light passed over him. He wasn't sure how much time had passed, but as he approached his body, the Guardian Star began to feed him images of the battlefield, both what had just happened and what was still going on.

The shrieks of the wyverns tore across the battlefield as they launched themselves into the air, swiftly gaining altitude. Their lean, green-scaled bodies were like venomous blades cutting across the night sky. Each of them was close to Level 80 and their combined might was enough to cause even a First Evolution combatant to worry.

They beat their wings as they surged upward and began to circle, gliding over the battlefield as they searched for a target. The church forces saw them and the priests continued to chant, the words of their spells changing slightly. A gleaming white dome appeared above them, swirling with intricate runes on the interior. Strands of wispy light connected it to the Ward of Law that was all around their forces.

Green light surrounded the wyverns as corrosive energy built up around them and they swirled around each other, the three of them somehow twisting their energy together. Their mouths opened as one and three spheres of bubbling green venom flew outward, sizzling in the air as they shot down to crash against the shield.

The shield held, but as the spheres struck it they exploded outward, turning into a hissing rain that flowed across the surface and dripped down the sides. A vile green fog built up around the shield, covering it in a layer of mist that blanketed the area.

For now, the fighters under the shield were safe, but if any of them left the range of the shield, they would have to face that cloud of venom. The wyverns weren't able to kill them directly, but with that action they had limited their mobility and made it much more difficult for them to advance across the field.

If the shield broke, many of the weaker members would be poisoned. The pressure on the church forces had just increased, making it much harder for them to attack.

The wyverns swept through the air again, darting like lean, venomous fish through the skies as they curved around for another pass. If left to their own devices, they would be able to blanket the entire area in a cloud of venom.

At that moment, a thunderous roar burst across the heavens, echoing from one side of the field to another. A lean, white-scaled form with nearly invisible wings surged through the sky, his body angled for the wyverns. Behind him, Caelus was nearly at his zenith, the light of the blue moon refracting through the drake's translucent wings.

A bolt of sparkling ice led the way, freezing across the wings of one wyvern as Elsanar crashed into another, causing it to flip around in the air. His body was nearly twice as large as the wyvern's, and he grabbed his prey in his claws as his wings flared, stopping the rotation as he forced the wyvern down toward the field below.

He clamped his grip down on the monster as he roared again. His head rose as another bolt of ice tore through the sky to strike the third wyvern, covering its head and a portion of its wing in swiftly spreading ice.

The two wyverns that were coated in ice began to fall from the sky, their wings struggling to move. They had lost their advantage. As they tumbled through the air, Elsanar rode the third to the ground, his claws locked onto it.

Despite their height, it took only seconds for them to approach the snowy field. Just before they reached it, Elsanar's jaws snapped the wyvern's neck in a violent spray of green blood.

The dying wyvern crashed into the stones with an explosion of snow as the ice drake's wings flared again, lifting him in a curve as he glided across the ground. With mighty beats, he surged back into the air, each stroke carrying him higher as he curved around again.

As he came around again, the ice coating the other two wyverns continued to grow thicker and they were unable to maintain their altitude. They tried to stop their fall but failed, their wings too heavy to respond. They crashed into the ground, their bodies echoing with dull thuds.

It was impossible for them to survive for more than a few instants longer as Elsanar dived again, another bolt of ice forming.

A domineering roar echoed across the snow. From the first instant of his attack, the ice drake had demonstrated his superiority.

Without him, the church forces would have been cloaked in a continual rain of corrosive venom, their attention distracted by the bombardment that forced them onto their back foot when they needed to put their attention toward the Outsiders in front of them.

Flying monsters were difficult to deal with, especially if they were agile and had long-range attacks, but with Elsanar there, the pressure had evaporated. Across the field, the Paladins and captains standing at the edge of the shield let out a sigh of relief, turning their efforts back to the shield. Behind them, mana rose up from the ranks as a new wave of white hawks appeared, rising into the air before they crashed down against the shield.

The shield shuddered under the barrage and the gaps in it widened, but whatever the Outsiders had used to reinforce it, it wasn't breaking yet. The pale blue color was fading, but the yellow and red clouds inside were becoming brighter.

All along the inside arc of the shield, talismans shimmered into view. Each of them was a narrow, ugly spear formed from long bones. Skulls and smaller bones, including some fully intact hands, dangled from the points, which were large jawbones that had been sharpened at the end. On the inside curve, rows of sharpened teeth had been added. Some of them looked human.

At that moment, the Ice Sylphs arrived, striking the far side of the barrier like a wedge of hardened ice. All around them, flows of Ice mana formed into a crystalline barrier that was as sharp as an icicle.

Driven by the strength of six First Evolution sylphs, their spells drove into the barrier and tore through it like an arrow through a paper target. An instant later, they were through and heading across the snowy field with light steps.

Below their feet, bubbling dark red and yellow spots erupted upward, forming into bizarre shapes and phantasms, but the snow flowed around them, giving them sure footing as they continued on. Swiftly forming ice blocked the spells below their feet. They ignored the rest of the gathered forces and the curses erupting as they headed straight for one of the Outsider War Beasts.

Behind them, the shield rippled, the tears too big to seal over again. Instead of shattering, however, the blue color faded, the energy in it pouring into the red and yellow clouds. A moment later, the remains of the shield exploded outward in two waves.

The first wave was a sizzling, yellow cloud of corrosive gas. The second was a blood red haze.

The Paladins and Jeric were already at the edge of the barrier, and as the shield erupted, it blew straight past them. The yellow cloud clung at the edge of their personal shields, hissing as it tried to invade. Strange shadows leapt up from the red haze, like blood phantoms with long claws.

The curses rolled over them as they continued on to the forces behind. They mixed with the green fog from the wyverns as they collided with the church wards. A moment later, a brilliant white explosion ripped outward from the priests, but that was all Sam had time to see before he slammed back into his body and time resumed.

The field in front of him was a haze of curses, smoke, and enraged shouts. On one side, the church forces began to surge forward. There were holes in their lines where some fighters and mounts were lying on the ground, choking under the effect of the cursed gas. Priests were beside them, trying to heal them, but that drew attention away from the defensive wards.

The three captains and the Paladins shouted, orders pouring from their mouths as they rallied the capable troops to advance. The church line split instantly into two forces, one reserve that was watching over the wounded men and one that charged forward, joining ranks with their commanders as they headed across the field in three wedges.

On the opposite side, the Outsider War Beasts turned their reptilian heads to the sky and let out resounding roars. Icebloods, serpents, and wraiths swarmed up their sides, taking up a position on them as the great beasts tossed aside the stones in front of them and began to run, their claws slamming into the earth as they surged across the field. Their footsteps sounded like thunder echoing on the stones.

Before they could get far, the Ice Sylphs arrived, their strength slamming into the side of the nearest beast. Waves of Ice curled up around its feet, locking it into place as spears, arrows, and a rain of crystalline shards tore across it.

The attacks sliced through the Outsiders on its back and knocked it to the side, even as it clawed at the ground, but its defenses were strong enough that it didn't fall. Its scales shattered as meteoric bolts of ice tore at its body and blood began to gush down its sides, but it lifted its head and roared in anger. It wouldn't die easily.

To the side, in front of the charge of another war beast, Jeric continued to stand shoulder to shoulder with the Paladin Commander. Even across the distance, Sam could make out the familiar lines of his father's face.

The Paladin Commander might be able to go head to head with that war beast, or at least to survive a few blows, but if that monster hit his father.... Even with his enhanced Constitution, he probably wouldn't survive.

Despite that, his father had the same expression as when he looked at any difficult task, as if this wasn't much different than digging fence posts or taking in the harvest. It was straightforward bravery, an honest outpouring of who he was, even as his hands curled around his hammers. Despite everything that had happened, he was a simple man. He wasn't there for glory, but just to protect his family.

With that sight in front of him, Sam's awareness finally caught up with the flow of time. At the same time, an enormous torrent of silver energy surged into his enchantment from the Moonlight Relic. All across the parchment, thousands of flickering runes poured in, their energy combining to a single purpose.

The enchantment around the water crystal began to shine with a brilliant, multi-colored light as the auras ignited. The parchment began to crumble to dust, Sam looked upward, checking on the position of Caelus, the moon that guarded the elements.

With swift movements, he tilted the crystal to align with the angle of the moon, letting its blue light strike the crystal at the same time as the lines of the enchantment flared upward, wrapping around it in a layer of swirling, supercharged auras.

Energy gathered around the crystal like a bubbling spring as water in five different sparkling colors shot upward, each of them representing one of the auras that he'd infused into the enchantment.

Chapter Fifty-Four

FIVE AURAS

With the force of the relic's energy driving the enchantment, the Pure Water Elemental Crystal began to resonate. Despite its rarity, it only had one purpose, which was to create water, and that was the exact thing Sam was counting on. All around it, the aura enchantment he'd created hummed with power.

The water gushed out of the crystal in a bubbling stream. Each aura was like a lens refracting sunlight and the water began to change as it took on new properties. Five pillars of sparkling, multi-hued water formed beside the crystal.

The Ice Sylphs had stopped one war beast, but across the field, the other three thundered toward the church forces. They were only seconds away from striking the thin line of Paladins and his father. With their mass, they would crush them.

"*Stand behind me!*" The Paladin Commander's words echoed out across the field as she drew her sword. It was a long, two-handed blade with a thin, ruby line running across the surface, as if the metal had absorbed a line of blood.

The blade spun in her hands as phantom images of shattered swords appeared all around her. They were an echo of the battles she had fought and won, summoned up by the spiritual energy she was infusing into her weapon.

Unfortunately, there was nowhere for Jeric or Lenei to retreat to. The war beasts were approaching too quickly to flee, so all they could do was take up a position to the commander's side as they activated their own abilities.

Lenei's face was grim as she raised her shield and spear. Jeric's head turned to look toward Sam and he drew in a deep breath as his hammers spun. All around him, an echoing basso drumbeat of clashing stones reverberated in the air, until it felt as if everything in the area would be shaken apart.

The other two captains also shone with intense abilities as they flowed into a battle stance and prepared to face the beasts. Their postures reminded him of Lenei's attacks, but they were far more adept. Blades of shimmering white light and a sphere of crackling, white runes surrounded them.

The war beasts were nearly forty feet tall and almost as wide. They were also covered in a cloak of roaring monsters. The pressure that they brought with them was like a mountain collapsing. They covered the distance across the field in an instant as each step sent snow exploding upward, and they crashed into the Paladins' line like boulders striking a blade of grass.

The runic shields surrounding the Paladins bent like willow branches, streaming backward as they warped out of all recognition. A moment later, they shattered. The three captains sustaining them were at the First Evolution, but they still went flying, their faces pale as blood bubbled out of their mouths.

Jeric and Lenei had jumped, trying to dodge the impact, but the beasts were so large that dodging was impossible. They were both caught up in the edge of a shield as it shattered. Picked up by the force, they were flung across the field. They went spinning through the air wildly and slammed into the ground a hundred feet away, in front of the church lines.

It wasn't clear if they were alive or dead.

The monsters on the backs of the war beasts roared, their voices combining into a vicious tumult as they trumpeted their bloodlust to everything around. Their fangs were bared as they looked toward the church lines, ready to jump off and slaughter everything within reach.

The war beasts were slowed a little by the captains' blockade, but they weren't stopped. Even as the shields dissipated, they continued to charge, building new momentum as they headed for church forces.

Directly in their path, Jeric and Lenei lay buried in the snow. There was no movement. If the beasts reached them, they didn't stand a chance. They would crush them against the stones of the ruins.

At that moment, there was a shudder in the snow where Jeric had fallen, and then a hand appeared. It was shaky, but it was moving. He grasped at the snow as it slowly lifted him up. He climbed to his feet as he looked at the oncoming war beasts. His skin was pale, covered in streaks of blood and dust, and he only had one hammer in his hand, but he was standing.

Sam's attention locked on him. Fury and fear poured through his veins like liquid mercury, even as an icy cold logic kept him moving. His senses flowed out across the battlefield, riding along the lines of energy from the relic.

"*First Aura...Go!*"

He focused his essence along a transfer line that was between his father and the war beasts as he touched one of the aura pillars next to the crystal. The aura disappeared as it was transported along the relic's energy lines.

An instant later, a torrent of flowing water sprang upward from the stones below the snow, rising swiftly into a shining, translucent curtain that was as tall as the Outsider War Beasts. The light of the three moons reflected through it, sending a burst of rainbow light and a spray of ten thousand water droplets across the field.

Almost at the same moment, there was a soft *chime* in the air as swirls of silver energy flowed upward, blending into the water. With a sharp flicker that danced across the curtain, the water droplets instantly froze to ice, scattering across the field like frozen rain.

If Sam had been using his essence, he never would have been able to drive so much force. It was the relic's energy powering this enchantment. He'd just created the focus for it to follow.

The curtain flickered as its color changed from cerulean blue to a bright blue-white that was tinged with silver.

CraaAAAcckk!

There was a moment frozen in time as a massive crash of ice resonated across the area, as loud as a glacier rupturing. Every eye turned toward the wall of ice as cracks shivered across its surface like a shattered mirror.

Then a thousand swirling blades of frozen ice exploded outward, slicing through the air toward the war beasts. Each of them was fifteen feet across and half a dozen feet from front to back.

The beasts were covered in monsters and the ice blades sliced through them like swords through smoke. Every monster riding on the front of half of the war beasts was torn to pieces, chunks of their limbs and heads flying in all directions.

Then the blades struck the armored hide, tearing through them in a vengeance as scales and dark blood went flying. The beasts were so large that even the wall of blades looked normal in comparison, so they didn't die instantly, but as the blades shattered and disappeared, the beasts were left in a miserable state.

Their tusks were shattered to stumps, their bodies were lacerated from face to stomach, and their muscles were torn to ribbons. Their scales had been ripped apart, revealing the pale skin beneath, and blood poured out of them like a fountain.

The wall of blades had only extended for about half of their body length, so the monsters farther back had survived, but the war beasts' momentum had halted.

Stunned silence spread across the battlefield as the wall of ice shattered with another enormous *crack*, but it didn't last for long. The war beasts had nearly reached the church forces and the monsters outside the range of the blades were still healthy.

The church didn't know where the help had come from, but it took only a moment for the Paladin Commander to rally her forces. Her face was pale and she was holding her blade in a single hand, but her voice was calm.

"*Attack!*" Her command echoed out across the field as she directed the church forces toward the horde of monsters that was still alive. They also needed to finish off the wounded war beasts.

Jeric was instantly absorbed into the line of the church forces as they rushed forward, their weapons drawn.

Sam let out a slow breath of air as a flare of intense pain radiated through his meridians. He'd only served as a focus for the enchantment, but his essence was completely drained and it felt like his head was three sizes too small. He grabbed a handful of Advanced auras from his storage, combusting them one after the other as he took deep breaths.

The wall was based on the Aura of Frozen Blades from the Coldfang Beheaders. The water crystal had once summoned an entire lake of water for the inhabitants of the relic, which meant it was able to pull a massive amount of energy at once. He'd pulled it out of the pillar for that exact purpose.

When that much water hit the energy lines of the relic, which were attuned to elemental Ice...it only needed a little bit more focus to harness the collision into a deadly enchantment.

The downside was that he could only do it once for each aura he'd prepared and it still took all of his essence to focus it. One after another, he combusted the auras as he refilled his essence and searched for the next place to help.

Down below, his father was looking less pale now as he fought beside the church warriors. His hammer blurred in one hand as he held a shield in the other. All around him, the priests and church warriors were slaughtering the monsters, while the three captains focused their attacks on the war beasts.

To the far side, the Ice Sylphs were finishing off the fourth war beast that they had trapped, including the monsters that had been hanging onto it. It had taken them some time to break through the armored scales, but with six of them working together, they had managed.

"Humans! Know your place as slaves!" Across the field, a great roar went up as a large figure among the Iceblood Shamans rose to his feet.

Until now, he had been sitting at the back of the group, very close to the flaw. All around him, bone talismans were floating in the air. Unlike the other Iceblood Shamans, this one had spidery, red swirls running across his blue skin and he was nearly a foot taller.

Iceblood Shaman. Level 98.

That had to be their leader. He wasn't at the First Evolution, but he was close.

"You are ants on a broken world! Whatever force is helping you from the shadows, let's see if they can handle this!"

The shaman flung his arms to the side as he reached toward the Grand Flaw behind him. Somehow, his hands were coated in dark flames that mimicked the ring of fire around the sphere. The energy in the sphere turned fluid, expanding and contracting in waves as he pulled a boulder-sized mass from it.

"Do you know how so many portals appeared in this area?" he shouted as he raised the mass above his head. *"This portal is the culmination of my people's efforts over a hundred years! The power to control it is tied to my bloodline.*

"With another year to fully infuse myself with this world's essence and the blood of Aster Fall's inhabitants, I would have been able to Evolve perfectly. I would have been the first Iceblood in countless years to truly hold command over Blood and Ice!

"No one since our ancestor, the True God of Blood himself, has done such a thing!" The Iceblood was raging as he shaped the mass of energy between his hands. The words poured out of him in a violent torrent.

"I will crush you and drain your blood to complete the transformation!"

At that instant, a commanding roar shook the heavens as wide, translucent wings surged into view, scattering moonlight across the field. Elsanar's body was nearly invisible against the dark sky as he dived.

The ice drake had heard enough from this mouthy Outsider who dared to invade his territory!

His mouth opened as a glowing sphere of translucent white ice appeared in it. The edges of the sphere were white and the center was sapphire blue. Tendrils of Ice mana darted all around it like minnows in a stream.

It was far more powerful than the bolts of ice that he had used against the wyverns. Clearly, Elsanar had no wish to hear anything more from this Iceblood, and he wasn't hesitating to eliminate the threat.

As Elsanar approached the Iceblood, the sphere blasted out his jaws like a bolt of lightning in a clear night sky. It was even larger than the shaman himself and as it approached, its shadow fell over him, obscuring him from the light of the moons.

The shaman looked up at the descending meteor, his eyes narrowing. He had been planning to use the energy from the flaw against the church, but now he shifted his stance. His movements were swift as he raised the mass of darkness above his head. With quick words and gestures, he shaped it to a new purpose and threw it upward into the sky.

A spear shaped from spatial distortions and burning shadows flew upward, heading for the ice sphere. Force radiated from its edges as it tore through reality. It didn't seem as if it were flying so much as ripping apart the space in front of it.

When the spear struck the sphere, the ice exploded outward in a crackle of freezing force, turning into an ice storm with whipping winds that were strong enough to tear apart any monster under Level 100, but the spear pierced straight through the gathered energy like an arrow through a sheaf of wheat.

When it exited the other side, it had dimmed slightly, but the spatial distortions were still protecting it. It continued on its path like a bolt of black lightning as it headed straight for Elsanar. Although the drake was stronger than the shaman alone, the spear was formed from the Grand Flaw and borrowed its power.

The drake flared his wings, angling his dive to the side as he tried to avoid the spear, but he only managed to get partially out of the way. The spear tore through his right side in an explosion of white scales and left a gaping rent in his wing.

Drops of crystalline blood like liquid ice fell toward the ground. Elsanar's dive was interrupted as he spiraled out of control, and an angry roar echoed from him.

He might have been able to pull himself up from the dive and lessen the force of his landing, but he refused. Instead, his mouth opened as another ice sphere formed. It was slightly smaller than the other, but it was surrounded by burning white flames that were blazingly cold.

To form it so quickly, he hadn't just drawn on his mana. He'd infused part of his spirit into it. It made it stronger, but it also meant that there was no way he could spare the energy to protect himself from the crash.

The ice drake spat out the sphere as soon as it was formed. It blasted out of his mouth on the tail of his roar, growing in size as it shot toward the ground below. This time, he was so close to the ground that the shaman didn't have time to block the attack, but he had also been knocked away from his original path.

The ice sphere exploded among the gathered Outsiders and monsters a hundred feet away from the Grand Flaw, instantly covering the area in a frozen storm. The energy was so intense that everything inside turned to brittle ice in a moment.

When the force of the blast hit the ground, it rebounded upward, turning into a wave that ripped back through the area, shattering everything it had just touched. Monsters and Outsiders exploded to dust in an instant, their bodies disintegrating.

In the sky above, the drake tumbled out of control. He had given his all to attack the Outsiders, but now he didn't have time to moderate his fall. His one good wing flared as he tried to correct his path, but it was futile. He was sent into an uncontrolled spin as he headed for the ground.

If he hit the ground like that, the impact with the unforgiving stones of the ruins would be disastrous. If it didn't kill him directly, it would shatter bones throughout his body and leave him crippled.

Far across the field, Sam was already moving. He hadn't known Elsanar for long, but the drake had saved his life when they met. The impression he gave off was a pure strength of spirit and a commanding nobility that refused to accept any threat to his world.

"*Go!*"

A resonant chime from the relic rose up as an aura pillar disappeared from its place beside the water crystal. Sam had just regained his essence and now he poured it out again as he reached out to the ruins. The drake was falling swiftly, and it only took him an instant to find the area where he would land.

Of the five auras he'd infused, only two of them were at the Expert level. Now, he used one of them. The pillar that had just disappeared was a column of twisting, transparent force, as if it held a tornado inside.

It was the Aura of Twisting Wind from the Windscar Stalkers. It was also the only one of the set he'd prepared that might be able to help Elsanar.

As soon as the aura disappeared, it flared along the relic's lines and appeared half a mile away, directly below the drake. A wave of water a hundred feet wide surged upward from the stones, curving as it followed the silver lines. As it rose, it began to twist like a hurricane, spinning as it turned into a giant, rotating disk.

As Elsanar fell, the wave twisting around him in sparkling currents as it halted his fall. There was no way to avoid some impact, and the water struck him with the force of an avalanche, but it was constantly flowing. As soon as it absorbed the force, it shuttled it away again, spinning the drake into a roll.

Gradually, the impact of his fall was absorbed and the wave retreated toward the ground, leaving Elsanar lying on top of the snow.

Crystalline blood still covered his side and his broken wing was stretched outward at a jagged angle, unable to be retracted, but he was alive. He was also half a mile from the battle, out of range of the Outsiders' attacks.

Sam let out a gasp as he pulled his awareness back to his body and drew in a shuddering breath of air. Catching Elsanar hadn't used as much of his essence as the last attack, but it had still taken about three quarters. He grabbed auras out of his storage and started combusting them, ignoring their type and quantity.

The upgrade to Combust Aura was making him more efficient in harnessing the auras' energy, letting him combust more of them, but that was all. The Advanced ones were still giving him 30 essence. He hadn't had time to charge up more than a couple of Expert auras, but those were worth 40.

He was burning Advanced auras primarily, which meant it took him almost seven to refill his essence. With this handful, he had already combusted a dozen. He wasn't sure how many more he would be able to use.

Three aura pillars were left beside the water crystal as he turned his attention back to the battle. His expression was growing colder by the instant.

He didn't know what this Outsider Shaman was doing with the Grand Flaw, but he had to stop him.

CHAPTER FIFTY-FIVE

BLOOD WINTER

The shaman hadn't delayed after attacking Elsanar. He had already turned around to grasp at the flaw again and was slowly drawing out another mass of spatial energy. This time, as Sam kept a careful watch on the Grand Flaw, he saw the sphere decrease in size, contracting inward by a couple of feet.

It had been 40 feet across originally, but now it was down to 35. The flames swirling throughout it looked dimmer as well. All around the sphere, there was a building pressure from the world, forcing it inward.

Whatever the shaman was doing to create his spells, it was pulling energy from the flaw. The other flaws must have been created from this method as well. It made sense now how there had been so many of them.

It looked like the energy wasn't unlimited, but for the Grand Flaw to still be so large, it was clear that the shaman was building up its energy for something. From the little he knew of Grand Flaws, they were an enormous danger to the world. Even beyond the ability to create other flaws, there had to be something else behind them.

That didn't matter now, however. Whatever was behind the flaw, one thing was clear. This Outsider needed to die.

All across the battlefield, the church forces continued to advance, but they were slowed by the Outsiders and monsters that had still been alive on the war beasts. Dealing with the war beasts themselves, even when they were already half dead, was also a slow process that took up the full attention of the three captains.

The beasts were just too large. The ice blades had shredded their torsos and faces, but they hadn't penetrated deeply enough to destroy their major blood vessels or to puncture their organs. Even with their heads half-mangled, they were still thrashing, their massive claws and bodies crushing everything nearby.

The Ice Sylphs had just finished off the fourth war beast and now they turned their attention to the Outsiders around the flaw. Elsanar's attack had eliminated a swathe of the monsters, but many others were still alive.

A whirlwind of sparkling Ice flowed around them as they ran forward, heading toward the remains of the invading army. At the center of that field, the red-lined shaman stood, warping the mass of energy in his hands to some new purpose.

If Sam did nothing, they might be successful, but there was no guarantee. Over the past day, the sylphs had already started to feel like cousins to him.

The shaman's eyes were on the church forces as he molded the spatial energy. Waves of distortion rose up from it as the flames and rainbow darkness became something more sinister. It was some type of curse.

Given how easily that spear had cut through Elsanar, if the spell hit the church forces, it would be disastrous.

Sam glanced down at the three remaining pillars as he finished combusting the auras, returning his essence to full. He still had an Aura of Whispering Hoarfrost, an Aura of Ebon Corrosion, and an Aura of Blood Winter, which was the only other Expert aura. He needed something that would take out that shaman.

As he touched each of the pillars and felt the quality of the auras inside, his mind raced. He looked up, gazing into the heavens as calculations passed behind his eyes, and he finally nodded. When he looked down again, his aura had gone still. To anyone looking, it felt like his presence had suddenly blended into the world.

Even with the relic's energy lines transferring the auras for him, he needed to be closer if he wanted his plan to work. He had intended to stay off the battlefield, but he was going to have to change that. All he could do was to try and hide his appearance, so that no matter what people saw, they didn't put it together with Sam Hastern.

For that, he would have to rely on the Moonlight Relic. Without hesitating, he sent his intention to the Guardian Star and then pulled on the relic's energy that was all around him, layering it over himself like a curtain.

A swirl of silvery light rose up from the stones by his feet, flowing into the enchantment around the water crystal. Instantly, a spray of a thousand

water droplets rose up from the crystal. Under the influence of Elemental Manipulation, they flowed across his body, concealing his
features until they were only a blur.

At the same time, the aura of moonlight from the relic's imprint
poured out of his skin, flowing outward as it refracted through the
droplets. Like a rainbow born from a storm, the green, blue and purple
light shone outward, splintering into ten thousand rays.

The spray covered him like a cloak, hanging all around his body. At
the very top, his horns extended like two curving crescent moons.

He caught sight of his reflection from the ice below his feet, where
the spray from the water crystal had frozen on top of the snow. The
ice glistened like a mirror. When he saw the effect, he nodded. It was a
horned man surrounded by layers of moonlight and a storm.

For this battle, he would be the *Horned Hunter of the Moons.*

He would have to hope that the energy of the ruins and the water
elemental crystal would block Analyze. With the ruins active and the
water covering him...it might work. But now he needed to move.

He pulled half a dozen auras from his storage as he touched one
of the aura pillars that was floating around the water crystal and then
another, infusing half of his essence into each. Then as quickly as he
could, he combusted the auras he'd just grabbed, restoring his essence.

As he combusted three auras and started on the fourth, it felt like
his meridians were on fire. Boiling energy raced along his veins, searing
him as smoke began to rise from his skin.

The Second Layer of his Essence Constellation flared in his blood as a
web of energy stretched outward from it, spreading along his meridians
to buffer them, but there was still too much energy.

It seemed fifteen auras was his limit now, and he was already at
sixteen. He pushed the thought out of his mind as he combusted the
last two auras anyway and focused on the last pillar around the crystal,
pouring his essence into it.

While he focused on that, the other two pillars spread outward to
different parts of the field. It was nearly impossible for him to delay
their activation and a twisting pain wracked his spirit as he held them
in place, but they were waiting for his command to begin.

As soon as the final aura was charged, he sent it after them. As he felt it reach the correct position, he forced himself to his feet. With three auras active at once, it was far harder to hold them together than just one.

He cradled the water crystal in his hands as he leapt off the roof and sprinted toward the battlefield. It was the focus point of his illusion, but even if it hadn't been, it was too important to leave behind. The energy from the relic pulsed beneath his feet, hurling him onward. It felt like he was gliding across the stones.

It took him only a handful of seconds to reach the center of the battlefield, and by the time he was there, the shaman had already finished shaping its spell. A dark cloud stretched upward from its hands, flowing to either side like an undulating ribbon.

The dark flames of the flaw still burned inside the ribbon, which twisted in the air like a loose serpent, its edges coiling back and forth.

Behind him, the three captains were finishing off the war beasts as the church forces continued to advance across the field, but their defenses were nowhere near as strong as Elsanar's scales. If the energy from the Grand Flaw struck them, it would probably rip straight through.

To one side, the Ice Sylphs were cutting their way through the Outsiders as they worked their way to the shaman, but a series of talismans and curses hung in the air, delaying them.

He stuffed the water crystal into his belt as he stared across the field toward the Iceblood Shaman as his hands rose into the air.

"*Your opponent is me!*" His voice roared out across the field, the tone made deep and resonant as it echoed through the water around him. A trace of the Moonlight Relic's aura was there as well, infusing the words.

"*You asked who was helping from the shadows! Do you dare to ask that question again?! For harming the people of Aster Fall, the Horned Hunter of the Moons will be your death.*" His voice roared through the area. "*The moons guard the world and I guard these ruins! Did you believe you were the strongest thing here?!*"

The Outsider was pompous, so to get its attention, he did his best to be just as arrogant, but he didn't reveal the name of the Moonlight Relic or its secrets. He wanted the Outsider to be cautious, not curious. It wouldn't do to stir up its greed, and that went for the church as well.

As he finished speaking, his hands shone with rays of moonlight as he looked at the dark cloud in front of the shaman. It hadn't moved since he appeared and grabbed the shaman's attention. Without hesitating, he reached out to the first aura of the three auras.

"*You want to understand Ice?*" he shouted. "*Behold the meaning of Hoar-frost!*"

From the ground all around him, an enormous, curving curtain of water shot up toward the cloud. As it reached it, it exploded outward, turning to bright, white ice that froze into long crystals.

The crystals expanded in starburst chains like angular flowers blooming one after the other in the air. They pierced through the cloud in every direction, tearing it apart at the same time as they froze it, crushing it inside the crystals.

The bitter taste of winter's frozen ash spread through the area, carried along with the crystals. In nature, hoarfrost formed and destroyed itself between one moment and the next. It never lasted for long.

The Grand Flaw had spatial properties, but compared to the Moonlight Relic's energy, which had been designed in an ancient era to prevent spatial distortions, its strength was a strand of grass compared to a towering mountain.

Everywhere the ice spread, the spatial energy disappeared, sealed again as it returned to the dimensional barrier around Aster Fall.

"*Who are you to dare to interfere?!*" The Outsider Shaman roared in anger as it reached again toward the flaw, pulling out another, even larger mass of energy. The flaw shrank half a dozen feet in an instant. "*Without the power of Aster Fall, I will never Evolve! For that goal, ten million deaths is nothing!*"

Without hesitating, the shaman reached back and grabbed a second handful of energy, causing the flaw to shrink further as he added it to what he was already holding. He didn't bother to shape the spell for more than an instant. He slapped his hands together, crushing the energy into a ball that he hurled at Sam.

Sam's hand rose up again as another curtain of water roared upward from the stones at his feet. This water was as dark as ebony, so black that it looked like a hole in the night. With a gesture, he sent the wall of water roaring toward the shaman and the spell that it had just released.

The water echoed with a deep desolation and a feeling like it would corrode the world and everything it touched. When it struck the mass of energy, it swept it up in its momentum. For a moment, the sphere hung there, unchanging, and then the spatial distortion around it slowly began to separate, dissolving into the Aura of Ebon Corrosion.

The wall of water was much bigger than the shaman's spell this time. Even as it swept the energy up, it continued onward, crashing onto the Outsiders and monsters that were near the shaman.

Under the force of that wave, the forces closest to the shaman washed away like a sandcastle on the shore. Only the shaman himself survived, since he was standing directly next to the flaw.

The wave washed over him, but the spatial distortion around the flaw resisted its force, even as the burning sphere shrank beneath the onslaught. A moment later, the wave disintegrated into shadows, disappearing from the ruins.

Sam staggered as he felt his essence hit nearly nothing again, but he did his best to conceal it behind the curtain of water around him. Even though he'd charged the auras before, just directing the blows had taken nearly all of his energy.

The shaman looked around him, taking in the destruction of his closest forces with a building fury as he directed his attention at Sam. Behind him, the Grand Flaw fluctuated, its size a quarter of what it had originally been.

"It doesn't matter who you are!"

The shaman's voice was a bitter snarl as he grabbed for another mass of energy from the flaw. This time, the flaw shrank to barely five feet across, almost as small as a regular flaw. The flames surrounded it flickered with a pale light and nearly disappeared.

"I don't know how you summoned the energy for those strikes, but I can tell you are exhausted! Before, I would have allowed you to kneel and serve me, like others of this world have before, but now...die!"

The energy in his hands was more intense than anything that had come before. A sense of crackling disruption poured out from it, as if the edges of the world were breaking away. It was even stronger than the spear he'd used against Elsanar.

If Sam allowed it to land, there was no doubt that he would be torn apart by the force. His talons spasmed as he tried to control his temper, forcing himself to remain still.

He had one last aura to release, but controlling it would be nearly impossible. With the scorched status of his meridians, combusting any more auras would be futile. If it worked at all, it would only send him into convulsions. Despite that, his voice didn't hold a trace of fear as he spoke.

"*There's something you've forgotten.*" His words were as cold as winter as he slowly raised one hand and pointed at the sky. All around him, he could feel the flow of energy striking the ruins as the moons started to align. A distant chime echoed on the wind.

Above, with a slow movement, Caelus crossed the final, infinitesimal distance as midnight arrived. At that moment, as if a celestial chorus had been waiting for the command of its lead singer, three colors of moonlight surged through the heavens and fell onto the ruins below.

Like a cascading waterfall, the beams of light played across the ruins, sinking into the stones.

Another chime resonated across the stones, and then a third. The tune was a desolate accompaniment to the battle, a solitary bell in the night sounding above a frozen plain.

A sudden surge of energy rushed through the lines at Sam's feet, pouring upward into his body as it infused the moonlight aura. All around him, the projection of moonlight exploded outward, tripling in size.

It didn't refill his essence, but for that instant, there was a torrent of free energy to command and he turned it to his purpose.

"*Let me show you the meaning of a Blood Winter.*" His words echoed across the ruins, rebounding from the stones as he activated the last aura.

This time, it wasn't one curtain of water, but a dozen. They rose up from every silver line of the ruins near his location, a torrent of them pouring crystalline water into the air. He reached out all around him, guiding the energy with Elemental Manipulation and the Moonlight Relic's imprint.

CraaAAAAcckkK!

A shattering sound echoed outward as the water all around the ruins froze, turning translucent white. Along each crack, a line of red like blood spread outward, staining the edge of the ice.

At that moment, there were a dozen walls of towering white ice at the center of the battlefield, all of them surrounding the Iceblood shaman and the Grand Flaw.

"*What is this...?*" The shaman stared at the ice around him, his eyes widening as a flicker of fear appeared on his face. "*It feels like the ancients....*"

The walls of ice were dangerous enough, but something about the red streaks on them spoke to him on a primal level, resonating with the bloodline he had been trying to advance. It woke ancestral memories that he barely understood, ones that told him to be afraid.

At that moment, a voice whispered on the wind, shuffling between the walls of ice. On top of one wall of ice, the bent and aged figure of an ancient woman with long, white hair appeared. She was half transparent, but every line of her body cut the viewer to the bone, as if she were more real than anything else.

Her head turned slowly toward the Iceblood Shaman and Sam, her blank, white eyes passing over them until they settled on the flaw. A frown passed across her face, the expression barely a curve of her lips, but her disapproval was clear.

"*Beware of the winter, traveler. One side brings swift relief, and the other death.*"

At that moment, a legend that his mother used to tell him surfaced in Sam's mind, of the Boreal Dryad and Grandmother Winter. He didn't know what the apparition was or why it had appeared now, but something about it locked him in place. The look she'd given him was calm, but it felt as if the world were shaking.

A flicker of red appeared in the white of the apparition's eyes. Slowly, that expanded, like a drop of blood in a pool of clear water. The color extended until it flowed out of the corners of her eyes and blood red tears ran down her face.

Her mouth framed the words "*Blood Winter*" and then she was gone, as if she'd never been there. Instantly, a force shattered the ice walls as the red cracks expanded outward. Shards the size of buildings mixed with spears and icicles, all of them tinged red as they flew toward the Iceblood Shaman.

KRAAAAAAATTOOOOOM!

The explosion was so vast that it wiped away everything near where the shaman had been standing. Before it even reached him, his body froze to a pale white and then shattered from the force, turning to dust as the remains blasted outward on the wind, leaving only scoured earth behind.

It didn't stop there. The massive force slammed into the Grand Flaw, burying it in ice as it froze the flames around it, sealing the entire area into a block of frozen, white ice. Dimly, at the very center, there was a black gash that spun with rainbow colors, but it was only a speck compared to the ice around it.

In the wake of that explosion, silence fell across the battlefield.

Frozen ash drifted through the snow beneath the light of the three moons, slowly crumbly away to nothing.

EPILOGUE

The only thing left at the center of the battlefield was the sealed Grand Flaw, gleaming like a pinprick of dark flame in the ice. The shaman, the walls of ice, and nearly all of the Outsiders were gone, erased from existence.

Above, Caelus was just beginning to move out of alignment, and the power throughout the ruins began to fade. Without hesitating, Sam pulled on the remaining threads of energy and ran, disappearing off the battlefield in a blur of water and moonlight. The last vestige of power from the moons boosted his speed and snow flashed past beneath his feet.

Behind him, the church forces were just beginning to pull their attention away from the explosion, and before they could tell what was going on, he was gone, disappearing into the ruins like a fleeting shadow.

Behind him, he heard their shouts rising up as they targeted the remaining Outsiders and started to finish them off. His hand touched the amulet on his chest, searching for his father. When he found him, he activated it, whispering a reassurance to let him know that he was fine. At the same time, he pulled out a message scroll and sent it to Siwasir, telling him the same thing.

As he ran, he let the illusion fade from all around him. The water droplets faded away as the moonlight disappeared, returning his appearance to normal.

He could feel the silvery aura of experience building up around him as the church started to search the corpses, and before that happened, he needed to be hidden. The aura was too noticeable.

As for where he was heading...the peak of Sun's Rest loomed ahead of him as he ran across the seventh layer and then jumped up to the sixth. Wind and ice flowed around him, forming steps as he ran up the steep wall.

***

It took the better part of an hour for the church and Ice Sylphs to finish cleaning up the battlefield. As they worked, the Paladin Commander stood at the center of the area with her arms crossed.

Senra had a small frown as she watched the auras of Aster Fall seal over the Grand Flaw. Then, with a final *snap* of displaced air, the dark gash disappeared, leaving just the strange ice block that had surrounded it.

Her thoughts weren't on the flaw, since she had seen too many of those, but rather on the strange being that had come to their aid. The one who had been covered in moonlight and shadows, with two crescent moons on his head like horns.

He had arrived like a storm wind, suddenly present at the center of the battlefield, and then he was gone again just as quickly, after summoning up some other legend of the world to deal with the shaman.

The Horned Hunter of the Moons.

She could already hear her troops whispering the name, although she had no idea where it had come from.

Without him, their forces would have suffered a devastating blow. They'd underestimated the strength of this Grand Flaw. Even if they'd been able to eliminate the war beasts and deal with the shaman, it was unlikely that more than one in ten of them would have survived.

As for that spirit the Hunter had summoned...she'd only caught a glimpse of the old woman's bent back, but her white eyes were etched in her memory. Just thinking about them turning as red as blood sent chills down her spine.

This was not something for a little First Evolution like her to deal with. This was in the realm of World Spirits and the highest tier of magic. She would report the appearance to the church and let them deal with it.

Her eyes turned toward the Ice Sylphs nearby. They had gathered around the ice drake in the distance. From the look of it, they were healing his wounds, but he was so large that it would take quite a bit of mana before they succeeded.

She frowned again, but without hesitating any longer she signaled to three of her stronger Priests and headed over. The ice drake was a critical ally in the battle. The least they could do was to help heal him. At the same time, perhaps she could get some answers.

As they approached, it became clear exactly how enormous the drake was. He was as big as a fort, although most of it was his wings. She could sense her people's nervousness as they got closer. The drake's pure, crystalline eyes watched them come.

The Ice Sylphs and the drake radiated a sense of natural harmony, as if they were part of a different, more primal world, one that was very separate from her. There was something graceful about them. Despite her best efforts, it made her feel a bit out of place. It also reminded her that she was only a guest in these mountains.

One of the Ice Sylphs stepped forward, examining her and the Priests behind her. His movements were fluid, as if he were floating in the air.

"I am Siwasir. The ancient treaty has been upheld and the valley protected," he said formally, inclining his head. "Elsanar would appreciate your healing."

Without needing to be told twice, the Priests pushed aside their nervousness as they moved forward, joining the sylphs beside the drake. As they worked on healing him, Senra pushed aside her other thoughts and focused on the main question she had.

"Who was that...the being that came to our aid?" she asked, resting her hands on her hips.

"The Horned Hunter of the Moons?" A serious look passed across Siwasir's face and his eyes were grave. "A legend of the ruins. It is no surprise that you haven't heard of him before. Only my people keep those stories. It was surprising to see him here, but he must have sensed our need."

"A legend?" Senra frowned again, her fingers tightening on her hips. Something about that figure had made her uncomfortable, but she couldn't place it. At the same time, there had been an echo of the World Law around him, making it clear that he was part of the world. If it hadn't been for that, she would have a lot more doubts.

She had Analyze as an Epic-tier skill, but despite her best efforts to Analyze that figure when he appeared, all she'd gotten was a piercing headache, as if whatever he was, it was far beyond the level of her skill to understand.

"Who truly understands how ancient these ruins are," Siwasir raised one graceful hand and pointed up to where Caelus was still high in the sky. "With the alignment approaching, many old beings are stirred by the power of the moons. We can only be grateful that he came to our aid."

He seemed unbothered by the legend, as if it were only to be expected.

Senra gave him a doubtful look, but she could only shake her head helplessly as she thought about that being of moonlight and shadow.

"Well, whatever he was," she said slowly, "his legend is going to spread. Before long, people will come to the ruins to search for the Horned Hunter and to ask for his help."

"Legends move in their own time, which is very different from ours," Siwasir said quietly, his eyes fixed on the dark horizon, "but who can tell where the wind will blow. Perhaps they will find the aid they seek."

Senra shook her head and waited for the healers to finish. When they were done, she sent a last look at Siwasir before she returned to her troops, who were still cleaning up the battlefield.

***

An hour later, Sam sat beside the control pillar at the top of the ruins, his hands wrapped around the amulet as he finished speaking to his father and mother. He'd also sent additional messages to Siwasir and Lenei, letting them know that everything was fine.

The silver aura of experience and ringing notifications from the World Law were hanging on his mind and now that he finally had a moment to himself, it was time to deal with them. There had been more than a hundred people in the battle so he had no idea how the experience would be divided, but there had to be a lot of it.

The World Law's voice rang in his mind, accompanied by a flood of silver light that struck his bloodstream and turned into sparkling bubbles that rejoiced like the celestial spheres as they sank into his spirit.

Guardian, you have used your Class Abilities to eliminate the enemies of Aster Fall. You alone resolved more than half of the battle and it was your direct action that sealed the Grand Flaw.

You have completed the Task you were assigned to investigate this area and deal with the Outsider incursion. The threat from this invasion was far greater than the amount of experience available for it. As a result, you will be rewarded in additional ways.

From the battle, you gain 37,400,000 Class experience.

As an additional reward, you are granted experience for five levels.

You gain 34,319,510 Class experience.

You have gained nine Class Levels. You are now a Level 89 Battlefield Reclaimer.

Total Class Experience: 128,000,000 / 137,000,000

You have gained nine General Levels. You are now Level 89.

General Experience: 128,000,000 / 137,000,000

You gain +9 Intelligence, +9 Aura, and have 27 free attribute points to distribute.

In addition, you are granted an Epic Tier reward. You may choose any Class or Subclass Ability to raise to Epic.

For Sealing a Grand Flaw and killing the Outsider connected to it, your Soul Echo trait is increased by a tier. All attributes are increased by +4.

For killing three First Evolution Outsider War Beasts that significantly outleveled you, your Trait: Dauntless II is increased by three tiers. You gain +6 Constitution and +6 Charisma.

Guardian of Aster Fall, you honor our world with your effort. Make your Epic reward choice now.

With that, the World Law's voice fell silent. A whirlpool of energy began to gather, waiting for his decision.

After all of the combat choices he'd made recently, for this one, he chose something else. He was an Enchanter, and his ability to enchant with auras had been falling far behind his battle skills.

He chose to upgrade Imbue Aura.

There was no doubt he would need it for his own work and to repair the ruins.

The torrent of experience rushed through him, accompanied by three vast whirlwinds of power from the World Law that flowed into him as the traits and ability were upgraded.

The boost to Soul Echo raised his Wisdom to 69 and without hesitating, he assigned 21 of the free attribute points to it as well, boosting it to 90.

Then he put the remaining six points into Charisma. The increase to Soul Echo and Dauntless had just raised it by 10, and with this, it reached 73.

He felt the new attributes itching as his spirit strengthened and his features realigned. With the new Constitution as well, the damage he'd done to his meridians by combusting too many auras was swiftly healing.

It took a little while for the changes to settle in, and when they had, he turned toward the seventh layer, looking down at the area where the Flaw had been. With the help of the Guardian Star, he could see the troops leaving the battlefield as they headed back to their last camp.

He darted forward and touched the shield around the peak. A moment later, he was teleported down to the first layer. As soon as his feet touched the snow, he pulled a cloak of snow and wind around him, and then he was off, gliding over the distance.

Wind and crystal flame sped his steps as he headed back toward the battlefield. Since he'd had to leave so quickly, he hadn't been able to retrieve any of the auras, but there was still essence there.

It didn't take him long to arrive, and a moment later he was standing on top of the building where he'd activated the water crystal. Corpses were still piled across the area, left for the wind and ice to destroy. All around, the snow was drifting down, covering them over.

Before long, it was likely that the intensity of the elements here would cause the corpses to disintegrate, leaving behind nothing but the odd bone or trait as a sign of the battle that had taken place.

After a quick check around to make sure everyone was gone, his talons slashed through the air as he called to the essence that was slumbering in the corpses. A crackling wave of energy rose up from the bodies, forming into essence stars that flickered like spirits on top of the snow. With a commanding gesture, he pulled them toward himself.

Thousands of essence stars flew across the snow in an undulating wave, as if the stars in the night sky had descended to grace the mortal world.

As they approached him, their colors changed, turning sapphire blue, and they sank into his body.

A resonant song of life and destruction played through his mind as the stars flowed into his essence constellation, completing the rune that was the second layer. The remaining ones flowed upward, forming a third layer on top of it as they began to outline a new rune.

The voice of the World Law echoed in his mind, announcing the gains.

Congratulations, Essence Bearer, on reaching the Third Layer.

Your Racial Ability: Elemental Manipulation has been upgraded to Expert.

Essence Constellation (Third Layer): 7,934 / 15,000.

At the same time, the essence he'd just absorbed flowed into his attributes, boosting them.

You gain +11 Strength, +15 Constitution, +4 Agility, +22 Intelligence, and +22 Aura.

As his attributes changed, he couldn't help but glance at his status sheet.

STR: 63

CON: 113 (+2 with belt)

AGI: 40

WIS: 90

INT: 237 (+6 with bracer)

AUR: 237 (+6 with bracer)

CHA: 73

As the essence flowed through his body, there was a tug on his awareness that urged him to battle, whispering a promise of blood and destruction. It assured him there would be joy in tearing apart his enemies with his bare hands. It was a whispering susurration, a promise of the future in his ear.

With his enhanced Charisma, he shoved it back down, pushing it away as he cleared his mind. He would take the power that came with it, but that wasn't the future he wanted. As the desire for destruction crumbled away, he felt the explosive strength of the new attributes expanding his muscles and essence.

At the same time, all of the battles he'd fought over the past few days flooded his mind in an overwhelming tangle of life and death. All he'd wanted was to find peace with his family and to set up a small shop in the city, but fate had conspired against him. Everything he'd experienced and the battles he'd fought had built up to the point where he needed some way to express it.

Without planning on it, the moonlight aura he'd called up as the Horned Hunter exploded out of his body, blasting out from him in a wave of triple-colored light that reached into the heavens, shining across the ruins for miles around.

As the moonlight surged upward, he tilted his head back and let out a savage roar. It was a combination of fury at the world for its condition, a towering sense of conquest for slaying his enemies, and hope for a better future.

The roar combined with the moonlight and echoed down through the ruins, bouncing from wall to wall as it resonated between the lines of silver energy that glowed from every stone. Each time it encountered a moonlight strand that lit the streets, it redoubled, echoing more deeply as it passed from one part of the ruins to another.

As it traveled, the sound changed, blending with the desolate silver chime of the ruins as it passed up to the peak of the mountain. At the same time, the light of Silvas, Caelus, and Amaris shone across it, turning the sound into a liquid ripple of color. The roar mixed with the concentrated mana at the peak, gaining strength until it poured back down the slopes with the force of an avalanche.

Like an ocean tide, moonlight roared down the mountain and passed over the twelve layers of the ruins before it flooded the valley below. Wherever it passed, people heard the triple-layered song of the roar and turned their heads toward the mountain, their eyes rising to the peak and the three moons hanging in the sky.

In later years, each of them would swear that they saw the Horned Hunter of the Moons standing at the peak of Sun's Rest, his enormous body covered in shadows and moonlight as he tilted his head back to the sky and roared to the moons.

THANK YOU FOR READING!

~ The End ~

If you liked the story, I would love it if you left a review.

It means a lot more than you think.

See you for the next book!

You can follow my work on Patreon at https://www.patreon.com/riverfate. The early release chapters of the next book will be there as I write them.

If you would like a recap of the books or to reach out to me, you can follow the link below to the Guardian of Aster Fall Discord server.

https://discord.gg/HH2KZPxH5a

There is also a general channel for discussion of the latest books, frequently asked questions, and some art. We even have Aster Fall emojis. Thanks for reading!

Here are Some Social Media Groups Where You Might Find Me:

"LitRPG Releases": https://www.facebook.com/groups/LitRPGReleases

"LitRPG Books": https://www.facebook.com/groups/LitRPG.books

"GameLit Society": https://www.facebook.com/groups/LitRPGsociety

"Fantasy Nation": https://www.facebook.com/groups/TheFantasyNation

"Western Cultivation Stories (Xianxia and Wuxia, Etc)": https://www.facebook.com/groups/WesternWuxia/

"Cultivation Novels": https://www.facebook.com/groups/cultivationnovels/

"Fantasy Book Club": https://www.facebook.com/groups/9523731081
72759

Sam Hastern, Status Sheet

Sam Hastern
    General Level: 89
    Class Level: 89
    Class: Battlefield Reclaimer.

- Class Abilities: Reclaim Aura (Expert), Identify Aura (Advanced), Aura Storage (Expert), Imbue Aura (Epic), Intensify Aura (Basic), Assume Aura (Basic), Shatter Aura (Elite), Transfer Aura (Basic).

- Racial Class Ability: Aura of Crystal Flame (Epic)

    Subclass: The Scion of the Crystal Flame.

- Subclass Abilities: Crystal Focus (Advanced, 80ft radius), Flame Strike (Epic), Essence Shield (Advanced), Combust Aura (Advanced).

- Subclass Spells: Starfire, Spiral of Condensed Crystal Flame, Crystal Flame Arrow, Crystal Flame Sphere / Crystal Flame Fireball, Essence Blade, Crystal Wave, Crystal Field.

    Titles: Horned Hunter of the Moons.
    Professions:

- Enchanter, Level 42. (100% class contribution)

- Smith, Level 21. (100% class contribution)

- Essence Scribe, Level 31. (30% class contribution)

Soul Mark: A crystal blue eye with the merged aura-battle rune in place of the pupil.

Race: Outsider (Aster Fall)

Racial Abilities: Str/Con + 4, CHA -4, Enhanced Vision (Special), Enhanced Senses (Advanced), Fire Affinity (Special), Essence.

- Essence Constellation (Third Layer): 7,934 / 15,000.

- Racial Ability: Elemental Manipulation (Expert).

Health: 1,150

Essence: 243

(Regen is ~27.33% per hour. Base 14% at 10 Wis. +1% per 6 Wis.)

STR: 63

CON: 113 (115 with Belt of Gentle Climes)

AGI: 40

WIS: 90 (96 with staff)

INT: 237 (243 with Starflame Bracer)

AUR: 237 (243 with Starflame Bracer)

CHA: 73

0 free points.

Spells:

- Aura Bolt (Unranked)

Skills:

- Essence Control (Expert), Essence Refinement (Basic), Meditation (Basic), Analyze (Basic), Model Enchantment (Advanced), Mana Transfer (Basic).

Skill Tiers (20 levels to each):

- Basic (1-20), Advanced (21-40), Expert (41-60), Elite (61-80), Epic (81-100).

- Quality Grades: Crude, Common, Professional, Fine, and Superb.

Traits:

- The Guardian Star (Astral Contract).

- Guardian of Law: 6 Marks.

- Soul Echo II: +8 to all attributes.

- Dauntless V (+10 Con, +10 Cha).

- Craftsman: +2 Wisdom, +2 Constitution. (You will find it easier in the future to fall into a working trance and to endure long hours of labor. You will also find it easier to relate to other Craftsmen, gaining a natural Charisma bonus when speaking with them.)

- Mystical: +2 Intelligence, +2 Aura, +2 Wisdom. (You will find that it is easier to understand natural forces in the future.)

- Initiate of Ice: It makes it easier to live in Ice and snow, to walk through it, to bear the temperature, and to see natural Ice runes.

- Bounty Hunter: You gain an enhanced awareness of which creatures are natural to Aster Fall and which are not, as well as the ability to see through some illusions and forms of concealment. +5 Wisdom.

Contract Marks: The Guardian Star.

JERIC HASTERN, STATUS SHEET

Jeric Hastern

    General Level: 64

    Class Level: 64

    Class: Earthen Marauder (Rare):

- Class Abilities: Twin Hammers (Ambidextrous, Advanced), Enhanced Physique (Advanced), Earthen Shield (Advanced), Earth Vision (Subterranean), Earth Sense, Reverberating Blow (Basic).

    Subclass: The Blessed Trader of the Earth

- Subclass Abilities: Prospect Earth (Basic), Blessing of the Earth (Basic), Assess Item (Basic), Sacred Trade (Basic), Persuade (Advanced).

Soul Mark: Twin hammers crossed over each other, with a rune between the handles.

    Professions:

- Merchant, Level 7. (20% Class contribution)

- Prospector, Level 1.

- Miner, Level 4.

Race: Human

Health: 930

Stamina: 88

STR: 79 (83 with hammers)

CON: 89 (93 with two hammers)

AGI: 33

WIS: 20

INT: 20

AUR: 18

CHA: 46

0 free points.

Racial Abilities: None.

Spells: None.

Skills: Mana Control (Basic), Charge (Basic), Block (Basic), Kick (Basic).

Traits:

- Guardian of Law: 6 Marks.

- Soul Echo: +8 to all attributes.

- Earth Blessed: You will never be directly harmed by the Earth. This does not render you immune to spells, but lava, Earth mana, and other natural forces of Aster Fall will not damage you.

- Dauntless V: +10 Con, +10 Cha.

BOOKS BY DAVID NORTH

Guardian of Aster Fall (A LitRPG Progression Epic)
Amazon Series Link: Guardian of Aster Fall
Audible Series Link: Guardian of Aster Fall
Battlefield Reclaimer
Aster Fall
Moonlight Relic
Astral Threads
Path of Stars
Echoes of War
World Seal (Forthcoming 2024)
River of Fate (A Cultivation Progression Epic)
Amazon Series Link: River of Fate
Audible Series Link: River of Fate
The Jade Scripture
Sunset Knight
Emerald Alchemist (Forthcoming 2023)

Made in the USA
Columbia, SC
27 July 2024

2f5b0f2f-ab60-4e3a-b890-7667da2dd0b5R01